COMPLETE 1

Brighton Bad Boys

ISBN: 9798529921227

Hey there,

Glad you found us.

'Us' are me, Tilly Delane (not my real name), and The Brighton Bad Boys. I love these guys so hard, I really wish I could tell you who I really am but there are innocents to protect here.

So for now, I'm Tilly and proud - and here comes the warning:

There is a hefty dose of explicit sex in between these pages and while all of what happens between the couples is consensual and hot but nice, some of the overarching storylines and characters' back stories need a stronger constitution. So listen up:

The Brighton Bad Boys Trilogy is intended for mature readers over 18 years of age only. Additionally, if you have triggers, proceed with caution.

I also feel that there are a couple of things that need clarifying before you dig in.

Firstly, I made the deliberate choice to use US spelling for my American characters' POVs and UK spelling for my British characters' POVs. It's indulging an idiosyncrasy of mine. If I see US spelling, I automatically hear an American accent in my head. If I see UK spelling, I automatically hear a Brit. I hope you can get on board with that.

Secondly, The Brighton Bad Boys series is set in a slightly alternative version of my city, especially where the elements of corruption within the police force I allude to are concerned. I've lived in the real Brighton for most of my life and I have no intention of leaving any time soon, because it is possibly the most tolerant and liberal city in England, and that includes its police force. They're a good bunch. I'm glad I live here.

That's it.

Enjoy the trip!

TD

SILAS

Brighton Bad Boys I

Grace

By the time I get to the reception desk of the Palais Hotel in Brighton, it's nearly midnight and I'm drenched in two parts intercontinental grime steeped in travel sweat and one part torrential rain. Welcome to the south coast of England. What a cliché.

The blouse I'm wearing underneath my Marlene Dietrich style pantsuit, which looks on me nothing like it used to look on her, largely to do with the fact she was a blonde stick insect and I am what is kindly referred to as a 'buxom' bottle red, is sticking to my back and all I want is a shower. Or, even better, a bath. I'm jetlagged and tired from the two-hour bus journey, preceded by an eight-hour flight, preceded by an hour's cab journey from Friendship Heights to Dulles. Not to mention footsore from traipsing around London Heathrow for ages to find the exit to the coach station. So to say that I am not amused when the night receptionist looks at me apologetically is the understatement of the century.

"I'm truly sorry, Miss..." Her voice trails off because she has already forgotten my name. Inexcusable. If my mum was still the manager here, that'd be a black mark.

"Turner," I prompt.

"Miss Turner. There is no booking in your name. Did you say you booked through *Travelbritisles*? They went into administration last month, I'm afraid. Did you not see it on the news? None of their bookings were sent through to us, let alone actually paid for. I'm truly sorry but I just don't have a room for you. We're booked solid for the rest of the month."

To be fair, she does actually kind of look devastated on my behalf. Classic Brit. Very apologetic but totally unhelpful all the same. I know I'm cranky, but I can't help it. All I want is to get cleaned up and go to fucking sleep. Sure, I'm disappointed that I won't get to stay at the Palais, especially considering I worked my ass off all year to finance this trip and staying here was an integral part of the plan. Last time I came here I was eight. Mum (never Mom!) was still Mum and she'd loved showing me around her old stomping ground, as she called it. But, actually, right now, I don't really care where I sleep tonight. Anything with a roof over it will do.

"Don't you have, like, an overflow B&B or something you partner with?" I ask Gaynor, as her name tag informs me, with the sweetest smile I can muster.

It's how Mum used to deal with situations like this. She had a whole list of trusted inns she could ring in case people turned up at the Atlantis, back home, when it was full. And those inns would bend over backward to accommodate any custom she sent their way. Mutual back scratching 101. Having an in with the manager of the Atlantis could get them things for their guests a lowly innkeeper couldn't normally get hold of. Tickets to shows that were sold out, tables in restaurants that were booked solid for months, and so on.

But the concept is clearly lost on Gaynor. She looks at me with her big blue porcelain doll eyes and blinks a few times with her stupidly long fake lashes, clearly wishing I'd disappear in a puff of smoke around about now, so she didn't have to deal with me any longer.

"It's the Brighton Festival," she finally says, gently as if breaking the bad news to the family of a car crash victim. "I can guarantee you that there isn't a free bed in town. People rent out their *gardens* to campers during the festival, it's that bad."

"Great," I say, still not moving from my spot.

We have a bit of a silent stare out after that because she's not volunteering any solutions, and I am too exhausted to even contemplate my next move. While I make a mental note to ring my travel insurance to recoup the money on a room I evidently won't get to sleep in, I eye up the armchairs grouped around the two coffee tables that furnish the lounge. Two of them pushed together would probably make an okay sleep pod. I'm not overly tall at five feet five and a half. I could manage, in a sitty-uppy fashion. Gaynor watches me size up the furniture and panics visibly. She puts out a hand as if to stop me from doing something stupid and I smile inwardly.

Ten to one, she's just had a brainwave in my favor.

"Hang on," she practically begs. "I might have an idea. Wait here a moment, please."

She leaves her position behind the desk and disappears into the bowels of the hotel for a good ten minutes before she returns with a chamber maid. Though 'maid' is a euphemism in this case, if ever there was one. The woman is in her forties or fifties, hard to tell because it's obvious she's aged early. There is an ashen, tired look about her, reminiscent of the early days of Mum's chemo, though once upon a time this woman must have been quite stunning. The remnants of prettiness are still there in her bone structure and she could still be a looker, I decide, if her ash blonde hair was not cut in such a drab, short-and-practical fashion and had a color injection. And if maybe she wore a tiny bit of makeup, along with some pride. The utilitarian hairdo together with the gray maid's outfit, that is wearing her more than she is wearing it, make her look like the ward matron in a mental institution who is barely managing to stay on the right side of the bars. Yet, there is something steely and resolute beneath her stooped demeanor that makes me want to put one hand between her shoulder blades and another on her breastbone to straighten her out and tell her to stand tall like she was born to, the way Mum used to do to me. For a moment, I wonder if Gaynor has summoned her to help throw me out. But then the woman speaks, her voice seemingly projecting all the tiredness that *I* feel.

Weird sensation.

"Gaynor says you've come all the way from the States today, ducky?" she asks and the 'ducky' nearly breaks my heart. Nobody has spoken to me like this since Mum died. For a split second, I truly feel like the 25-year-old orphan that I am. I swallow hard but the woman, Sheena her tag informs me, alongside the info that she's actually head of housekeeping, which explains why she's still here at this late hour, doesn't really pause to let me answer anyway.

"You must be exhausted." She takes a breath, letting her eyes wander over me. I wonder what she sees, but before I can dwell on it, she carries on talking, cocking her head to the side a little. "Gaynor asked me if I can help you out because I rent my spare room to language students sometimes. I've got a Polish girl at the moment. Kalina. Ever so polite. Bit of a recluse. But if you want, you can come and stay with me tonight anyway. You can sleep in my son's room. He won't be home yet. He works nights. Doesn't get back till gone six in the morning. He can take the sofa. I'll charge you the going rate. Thirty a night, includes breakfast but it won't be cooked unless you cook it yourself. I was about to wrap up here and go home. Interested?"

She straightens her neck and I realize it's a kind of challenge. She thinks the entitled American in the expensive power pantsuit will refuse her offer. She has no way of knowing that the only reason I bought this outfit is because Mum would have expected me to look *nice* checking into the Palais.

What she also fails to realize is that at this point in time I'd be happy to sleep in a bathtub. So I answer without even thinking.

"Hell yeah, I'm interested."

SILAS

"Your turn in the shower," Gareth grins at me as he shrugs out of a dripping club-issue waterproof and hands it to me.

"Is it still hammering it down?" I ask as I slip my arms into the sleeves of the jacket and push my hands through the soggy knitted cuffs. Always a joy.

"Cats and dogs," Gareth informs me, while he scans the packed area around the top bar and the dance floor, running a hand over his damp skull. His buzz cut is so fresh he's practically a skinhead. Till yesterday, he had spiky dark hair with short back and sides. It was a good look for the ladies, but he's trying to show he's ready for the ring. Not that that's how it works. Or that there is technically a ring. Or octagon. Or any geometrical shape. He'll find out soon enough. "Shit for us. Good for business," he carries on by way of making inane conversation.

He's right. Normally during the festival, the club's pretty dead. People go to the shows and afterwards they either keep drinking in the venue they're in or they go sit on the beach. Regular clubbing goes out of the window. It's a hard month on the nightclubs that aren't part of the festival map. And TripleX is definitely not part of the festival map. It's barely part of the map. Despite the fact we're right on the seafront, you sort of need to know where the entrance is. And we like to keep it that way.

But on a night like this, the beach goers all suddenly stream through our doors. Like homing pigeons, they find the staircase that leads down to us as soon as the first torrent of rain comes down, and suddenly we have a whole load of clientele steaming up the place that we wouldn't normally have and don't particularly want back either. Fucking middle-class arseholes and university students. Gareth is new and doesn't get it yet. All he sees is people spending money on the bar. Which you'd think is good. And it is, provided they don't want to come back during fightnights. People get suspicious if they are let in freely one day but need a golden ticket the next. But on the other hand, the locals get suspicious if only the same select crowd is let in all the time. It's a fine balance because once the locals get suspicious, Diego, aka George Benson, can lubricate the cops' pockets all he likes. It'd be the beginning of the end.

Happened before. Not to Benson, yet, but to others. You gotta find that happy medium where nobody is suspicious of anything, the tax man is happy and there is no cause for the rumour mill to start churning. Constant battle. It's a small town. It calls itself a city but, really, everybody who is somebody knows fucking everybody who is nobody around here. I should know. I'm a rarity. Brighton born and bred. We're few and far between. Most folk who live here come to study at one of the universities and then get stuck, like flies on sugar paper. Never could work out where all the other Brightonians disappeared to. It's like once we got out of school, they dropped off the edge.

Everyone other than George. Diego. I need to stop calling him George in my head. It's gonna get me into trouble one day. It's difficult, though. I've known the guy since pre-school and, Spanish mother or not, he is blond for fuck's sake. How un-Diego can you be?

Maybe there is a different secret door for the other natives, up the street somewhere, and nobody bothered to let me in on the know. Would figure.

My crappy mood doesn't improve as I step out of the door and trot up the outside stairs to stand on the pavement by the railings and vet the punters as they attempt to come down. I flip up the hood on the waterproof a fraction too late and cold rainwater trickles down my neck, into my t-shirt and down between my shoulder blades. Fucking A.

I nod at Arlo, the other bouncer up here, who is checking out the legs on two barely legal girls as they clamber out of a cab to totter up to the door of The Cockatoo, the cocktail bar above TripleX. He makes out he's interested, but I'm pretty sure it's not the way his toast is buttered.

I watch the women, trying to gauge for a moment if they are hookers or just regular slappers and if they are of age. There is a guy on the door of the bar, but he's new and inexperienced and it's sometimes hard to tell around here. Especially since Diego rents a few of the apartments in the building above to ladies of pleasure. But these two are too young, and their dresses are way too short and cheap, to be escorts. I swear I can see the butt curve on the brunette peeking out from below the hem.

I make a sign at the guy on the bar door, Ben I think his name is, to check their ID, and he nods.

They giggle, nearly tripping over themselves, while they produce their driver's licences, and one runs her hand suggestively up Ben's arm.

Definitely regular slappers.

As they fall into The Cockatoo and out of sight, I meet Arlo's eye. He grins and comes over to me, before he goes down to the club to swap with whoever.

"Might tap that later," he tells me.

It's kind of sad that he thinks he needs to pretend to be straight to be accepted in this part of town, especially since a mile down the road you enter the biggest gay community in England, but I say nothing.

I say nothing, and he wouldn't really expect me to.

The guys all know I keep myself to myself.

I don't do hanging around after shutdown to pick up drunk girls from upstairs.

I don't do staff drinks.

I don't do socials.

I don't do going to the gym together.

I don't do friendship.

I don't do garden parties at the Benson Mansion on Woodland Drive.

I don't bet.

I work, I get paid.

I fight, I get paid.

End of involvement.

For a precious few minutes after Arlo leaves, I'm left alone out here. The weather has swept the street clean of people and there are barely any cars about, so I can hear the ocean above the sound of the now slowing rain. Listening to the waves crash against the groynes soothes me. I can see the lights of the pier in the far distance and the streetlamps and their halos on the opposite side of the road in front of the dark background that is the sea. This is the Brighton I love. The one in front of me. The one at my back? Not so much.

The peace doesn't last long as a set of traffic lights somewhere down the road changes and a line of cars starts approaching. I hear Mum's Ford Capri before I spot it behind some fat arse off-roader that's never so much as mounted a kerb. It makes me smile that I recognize the sound of the Capri's engine. She loves that bloody car. Had it for thirty years. Was a classic even then. Bought it when she was still modelling. It's a total money pit despite the fact she does most of the work on it herself. Her dad was a mechanic. Wish I'd met him. She knows her way around the basic combustion engine like nobody else I know. It's her metal baby. But it's more than that. When she plunged us into debt because of *him*, she was prepared to lose the house, asked me to sell whatever I had to sell, but she never once even contemplated selling the car.

My teeth clench and my jaw locks as I think of him. He's been sniffing around again lately. I haven't seen him, but I just know. I can feel it in my gut, in the prickle at the back of my neck. He's back in town. And I bet he's heard through the grapevine that we're doing alright. Time to come and fleece us again.

But not this time. I've got better since he left. Maybe not better than him on the whole. But harder and faster.

I watch the cars zoom by and for a split second my stomach bottoms out. There is a figure sitting in the passenger seat next to Mum, but they're on the far side of the road, so she or *he* is obscured by Mum. I can't make out who it is. It can't be Kalina because she's like clockwork. Bed at nine, up at six. Waves at me as I come in and she leaves, off to the language school or her unpaid job in a charity shop. So who the fuck is that in Mum's car? Fuck. I'm not exactly superstitious but I only just thought of *him*. And then this happens. Fuck.

It's only in the last moment as they pass me by that I see a glimpse of long red hair past Mum's profile and I relax. He's many things but a transvestite he is not. We're cool. I'm being paranoid. Probably just some colleague who Mum's giving a lift to. She's good like that. Heart as big as the fucking planet.

Grace

Sheena's house is actually two towns over, in a place called Shoreham. Not that you'd know it is a different place because the little towns along the coast melt seamlessly from one into the other.

After we leave the center of Brighton, we follow the coast road and the farther we drive the shabbier it gets. The area becomes less well lit, the houses smaller and dingier but still stupidly expensive, according to Sheena. She doesn't talk a heap, but she's asked me what I'm doing in Britain, so I told her about the Emma Turner memorial tour, and she's been telling me where we are at each point of the journey.

I can't really imagine these tiny matchbox houses costing the amount of money she quotes, but I guess that's the problem with finite space on an island. Mum always talked about how much she loved the amount of space she had in America and I'm starting to get the idea. Everything seems so crammed. Like a scaled down version of a real town. When I was eight, I didn't really notice. I guess because I was still little myself and also because we spent that vacation mostly doing the tourist attractions. The Pavillion, Sealife Centre, rides on the pier, daytrips to the surrounding area. Castles. Cathedrals. The Bluebell Railway. At the time, it was just endless fun, now I understand that she was trying to give me a piece of her roots. As if that were even possible.

Once we've passed a doll-size industrial harbor and a metal recycling plant on the side of the sea versus an estate of warehouses opposite, the scenery slowly improves again. There is a sailboat basin and a quaint little lighthouse and then more tiny houses but better kept. By the time we pull into a side street and drive into a pub's parking lot, the rain has completely stopped. Sheena switches the engine off and smiles over at me wanly.

"We're here."

"You live in a pub?"

That makes her chuckle.

"No, the landlady is a friend. I can park here overnight if I come home this late. My house is opposite."

She jerks her head vaguely in the direction where I guess her house is, though all I can see from my vantage point is the brick wall we're parked up against. She gets out of the car and I follow suit. It's some kind of cool low chassis classic. A Ford, I think. It has no central locking, so she manually opens the trunk that my suitcase barely fits in.

I lift it out and wait for her to put a big yellow steering wheel lock in place and then until she's finished locking all the doors manually. It seems like a pain in the ass to me, but every action is carried out with the utmost care and gentleness. It doesn't need much to figure out that this car is her pride and joy. It's funny because looking at her you'd think she doesn't care about anything that much. Shouldn't judge a book by its cover, I guess. When she's finally finished, she gestures for me to follow her.

We cross the road to a house with no frontage at all that opens straight onto the road. No front yard, no sidewalk, no nothing. She unlocks the red-painted wooden door, opens it and switches on the light in a tiny hallway, fitted with a threadbare blood-red carpet that also covers the staircase going up, which is situated to the left, about six feet in. Looking past the stairs to the end of the hallway, I catch a glimpse of a kitchen with black-and-white lino, like you find in a traditional diner. There are two shut pine doors to the right along the way. It's the kind of house my mum grew up in, I guess, what she used to describe as a 'two-up two-down'. A pleasant smell of citrus hangs in the air.

"That's it," Sheena smiles at me. "The bathroom is at the top of the landing. Your room is the first on the left upstairs. If you go on up, I'll find you some fresh linen to put on the bed and some towels. Silas is pretty tidy, so you should be fine going in there."

It is then that I realize I'm about to hijack some stranger's bedroom who doesn't even know I exist. I know zilch about this guy. I might be half delirious from being overly tired, but I still have a sense of invading somebody's privacy. So I don't make a move.

"Are you alright, love?" Sheena asks me, already halfway down the hallway and opening the cupboard under the stairs, which I guess contains her linens because she appears to be selecting a sheet while she talks quietly. I guess she's trying not to wake the Polish girl she was talking about. "Honestly, that boy is military grade pristine, you won't find any socks or grotty undies lying about, I promise. I also happen to know he hoovered before he went out, so it'll be fine."

"It's just..." I hesitate. "He doesn't even know there's gonna be somebody in his room, does he?"

"Well, no, not yet," she answers while she keeps piling pillow and duvet covers onto the sheet. "Doesn't have his phone on at work. But I'll send him a text, and I'll leave him a note. Don't worry, it's fine. We've done this before. The last one wasn't as pretty as you, though."

She looks over at me with a bit of a wicked light in her eyes, and for a moment I can really see the beauty she must have been once.

"If anything," she carries on, "he'll appreciate that you're not a sixty-year-old salesman who looks like Danny de Vito and that guy from Willow had a love child. Don't you fret now. Come on."

Having piled towels on top of the linen she is balancing expertly on her arm, she shuts the door to the cupboard with a well practiced nudge of her hip. She comes toward me, squeezes by me and starts climbing the stairs.

"Come on, I'll lead the way."

I lug my suitcase after her but stop halfway up when my eyes fall on a black-and-white framed photograph. I'm sure it's a Newton and the signature proves me right.

It's a headshot of a young woman looking over her shoulder. Not one of his overly provocative ones, more of a natural portrait, but still with the typical dramatic Newtonesque feeling of film noir going on. It looks like one of his headshots of famous people, but I can't place the face. Until Sheena stops at the landing and looks down at me.

"Flagging already? Only a few more steps," she says.

I can tell by her tone that she knows full well what I'm looking at and that I just clicked. She sighs.

"Yes. Me."

"In a Newton."

She carries on.

"Yes, in a Newton."

I keep following.

"Wow. Must be worth a bomb."

She laughs without mirth in it.

"I wish. No such luck. You can buy me for $29.99 from eBay. I ain't no Marilyn."

Her tone tells me the subject is closed, no matter how curious I might be. We make the rest of the way in silence and she leads me into the first bedroom on the left.

As soon as I step through the door, I can smell him. Her son.

Silas, I remind myself.

The room smells of a person, a *male*, in the best possible way and it floors me.

It's wood smoke and soap and leather and lemongrass, and pure man. And something else, something I can't put my finger on, something salty.

A warm feeling of arousal hits my belly like hot soup on a winter's day. That mixture of coming home and that first spoonful of heat hitting your insides and warming up your core, sending happy ripples down into your nether regions.

I look around wide-eyed and see that Sheena wasn't lying. Whoever lives here is a neat freak. The queen bed is made as if drawn with a ruler. There is a wooden wardrobe with wrought iron fittings, a black desk housing a computer with two monitors and an office chair. The walls are off white, the carpet blue.

On a pine bookshelf sit paperbacks, neatly arranged by author. Alphabetically, of course. Iain Banks, Julian Barnes, Alex Garland, Kazuo Ishiguro, Irvine Welsh. All titles that my local bookshop would stock in the Contemporary British section, regardless of the fact most of them are so old they should really be classics already. Not a single author I've read but every single one I've heard of. Mostly because they've been made into movies. I'm not big on gritty. I like reading to escape, not to carry on thinking about what a shit deal life is and how much it hurts to be human.

A lone succulent plant, of the kind that looks like a fleshy artichoke falling open, sits on the windowsill. Its leaves are shiny, and I'd bet my bottom dollar they get wiped daily with a damp cloth to clean them of dust.

There really is no clutter.

On the wall opposite the bed hangs a single large grayscale art print. It's a nude, a young man lying on his front, asleep on a bed, sheet crumpled between his legs. His hair is long enough to obscure the visible side of his face so that only the edge of a full, almost effeminate bottom lip peeks out from between the strands. The line of his jaw hints at a strong bone structure and at teeth set in anger. He doesn't look relaxed, more like he's on the verge of waking up, coiled to snatch the artist from their perch, flip them over and pin them to the bed.

I clench at the idea and a shiver runs through me. A good shiver.

His body is lithe but muscular with beautiful shoulders and arms and, hands down, the best buttocks I've ever seen. As soon as my eyes fall on them, I have an almost overwhelming urge to dig my nails into those glutes.

Another whirl of arousal hits me in the gut. I'm getting slick. What is it with this room? I feel my cheeks starting to burn.

Still, I can't help but step closer, and I realize that the print is not a print at all. It's a genuine pencil drawing, which explains why it seems so alive. I can barely suppress the impulse to run my fingertips over the glass, to somehow touch this man.

I shake myself out of my trance and avert my eyes before I embarrass myself further.

While I've stared at the drawing, Sheena has started changing the sheets on the bed for me. I stop idling and step up to help her, grabbing the duvet and taking the cover off it. The action releases another dose of that male scent into my nostrils, and I can barely refrain from sticking my nose right into the cover and taking a big lungful.

The jetlag must be making my senses hypersensitive or something. This is getting silly.

Sheena looks at me surprised.

"That's kind, ducky, but I got this. All part of the service," she says, smiling encouragingly at the towels she's put on the chair. "You grab yourself a shower while I do this. You look a bit flushed. I bet you can't wait to get cleaned up."

About an hour ago she would have been right. But by now I just want to sink into that bed. It feels like I've been awake forever. I slept a little on the plane, but the woman next to me kept waking me up to go to the bathroom every half hour.

It would be rude to stink up the fresh linen with my travel sweat, though. So I open my suitcase and root around for my wash bag, a long t-shirt and some yoga pants, grab a towel and make my way to the bathroom.

SILAS

We shut shop at 5am sharp, and I'm on my bike by half past.

That's the pedal version.

I used to have a motorbike, a CBR600, but that got sold in the first round of debt he left us with. Before we found out the true extent of the shit show he left us with. It stung, but I'll have another one, one day. Wouldn't be ideal to come to work on anyway. There are plenty of cunts who think it's fun kicking over the motorbikes parked up at the seafront. Arlo rides and he's on fairing number two in as many months. Not worth it.

Right now, this second, I'm actually quite content pedalling through the grey mist of morning. It's not exactly a beautiful dawn, but there is something about the air that isn't all bad. It's not too cold either and I look forward to my dip in the sea.

When I get to the lighthouse, I can see that there are two dog walkers already out on the beach. Whatever. They can like it or fuck off. It's not actually illegal to be nude in public in the UK. As long as you're not doing it deliberately to upset anyone. I don't know them, I couldn't give a toss about them, so it would be hard for them to prove my impending nakedness was aimed in their direction. I just want to get out of my clothes and into the water.

I get off the bike, push it onto the pebbles as close to the water edge as makes sense and drop it, then strip and lay my clothes onto the bike frame, so they don't touch the wet stones. I scan around for the dogs because I'm about to run into the surf and I don't want one of them chasing me, biting my dick off. Not that I use it much but I'm kind of attached to it.

The off-the-lead collie in the far distance is focused on the ball launcher in the dog walker's hand. The brown pit bull type closer at hand is on a lead and is out here pretty much every morning. The guy handling the pittie catches my eye and doesn't bat an eyelid at my state of undress. He raises his hand in greeting and I salute back.

Then I turn towards the sea and run.

The trick is not to stop, not to think till you're fully submerged. And then the best sensation in the world hits you. The ice-cold water numbs all of you, plunges your body into oblivion, so it feels like only your soul is left swimming.

All the pain goes away.

I hold still in this kind of suspended state of being as long as I can but then, without fail, there is that primeval moment when my survival instinct kicks in and I start crawling. Faster and faster, until my body begins heating up and I feel like I'm burning, like a fireball meteor slicing through the ocean.

Grace

I wake up from muffled voices below. Somebody, a female, not Sheena, is saying 'Good morning' and there is a male voice but it's so low I can't hear what it says. Not a lot, though. There are soft steps on the stairs, the sound of the bathroom lock and then the low rumble of the shower being turned on.

I have no idea what time it is, but I can see the gray of morning through a gap in the curtains. They're weird, those curtains. Total contrast to the rest of the room. Tie-dyed with a hippie moon/sun face in gold printed over both sides that joins where they meet. *So* not in line with the rest of the *decor* at all. That was the last thought that I had before I drifted off.

I could check my cell for the time, but it's all the way over on the desk. I didn't have a charger that fits the British sockets, so I switched the computer on and plugged it into the USB port. Need to find a British charger. Need to ring my travel insurance to see if I can recoup my money from *Travelbritisles*. Need to sort somewhere else to stay...need to...

I fall asleep again.

Next time I wake, the sun is high up in the sky and the rays are creeping into the room around the curtains, like golden tentacles come to snatch me from sleep. I get out of bed and check my cell. It's past midday. I listen out but the house is quiet.

There is a piece of paper that's been pushed under my door. When I spot it, my heart stops for a moment and I well up a bit. Stupid emotions. It's the kind of thing Mum used to do. I never knew another kid whose mum would leave notes under their door. The others all had mothers who'd just barge in, tell them whatever they had to tell them and barge out again. Mine was very much of the conviction that you didn't wake sleeping lions or sleeping children. Even if the child happened to be in her twenties already.

I miss her.

The pain steals my breath for a moment. I swallow it down and go to pick up the note.

I read it while I walk to the bathroom.

Ducky,

It occurs to me that I never even told Sheena my name. She knows what I'm in Brighton for, but she has no idea who I am.

Hope you slept well. I thought it best to let you rest. You looked exhausted. Had to go back to work but help yourself to anything you can find in the kitchen. (Then wash up!) I've rung around a few hotels in Shoreham but they are all booked solid until the festival is over. Also got in touch with the language school people but they are struggling to find host families for their students themselves, so nothing there. You'll probably find it's the same story in a 10 mile radius of Brighton for the rest of the month. Not sure what your plans are but I've left Silas a message telling him he might be kipping on the sofa again tomorrow to give you more time to sort yourself out. He won't mind. No obligation on your part but I wanted you to know you're not out on the street. Make yourself at home. I left a key to the front door on the kitchen table, so you can let yourself in and out of the house. Just be mindful of Silas. He's asleep in the front room. He'll be up by around 3pm. Kalina normally comes home at 6pm and I'll be back at 9pm. Different shift today.

Sheena

I read the note a few more times while I go pee, wash and brush my teeth. I savor the flavor of the words, over and over. I think about the woman who wrote them as I examine my face in the mirror and squeeze a zit that's threatening to break out on my chin. Happy traveling complexion. I look like shit. I run Sheena's offer of another night through my head as I push into my skin until all the impurity is out, and I see that satisfying little blob of blood appear. Kindness pours from between her lines. Haven't had that in a while. I blot at the blemish with a piece of toilet paper. I'm being treated like a child in all the best ways, but I don't quite know how I feel about that.

Part of me wants to grab my stuff and run.

I've just got used to nobody giving a shit about me, with the exceptions of Vince, my manager at the Atlantis, and Cindy, pretty much my only friend left over from high school. I don't think I can handle a stranger being nice, making me feel part of the planet.

Another part would like to stay another day and take the breather Sheena is offering me.

I think back to the moment when she examined me last night in the hotel lobby. I'm starting to wonder if what she saw was not an arrogant American in a power suit at all but a frightened young woman who had lost her only real family and who had no idea where to go from here. The woman who is staring back at me right now.

I look at my messy hair and groan. I couldn't find my brush last night, it's buried somewhere in the depth of my suitcase, so I washed my hair without brushing it first and then slept on it. Big mistake. I'll need to buy some detangler somewhere later.

By the time I'm finished in the bathroom, I still haven't made up my mind about staying another night or what the fuck else to do.

I decide it might be worthwhile asking this Silas character if he *actually* doesn't mind me occupying his room. See what his reaction is, then make a plan. With that in mind, I pick up my stuff and Sheena's note, open the bathroom door — and walk straight into him.

SILAS

To say I was pissed off by the note I found taped to the staircase when I got in would be the understatement of the century. My mother and her fucking notes.

Granted, I don't have my mobile on at work and forgot to switch it on after, but still. Bloody unilateral decisions, bloody fucking notes.

Not that it would have made any difference. Either way there'd be a fucking body in my room. In my bed. 'Cause Mum would have ignored me anyway. As she does.

I've told her time and time again that we can do without. We don't need the extra money now that I'm working for George — Diego. Fuck, I *really* need to get out of that habit. Mum doesn't know about the fightnights and I have no intention of telling her until I have enough dough stashed away to pay off the loan she took out against the house to pay *his* fucking debts off. Fucking cunt. But I'm making good enough money just from bouncing anyway, so that between us we can keep up with the repayments and the bills and shit until I come clean. So we don't need any more ad hoc guests.

The students are one thing. Kalina is nice enough. So was the last one. They're no trouble. Don't mind them. Do mind having to sleep on the shitty sofa bed in the living room. The mattress is paper thin, you can feel every spring in the shitty mechanism underneath it. I don't even bother anymore. I just put the sleeping bag on the floor. Call me a pussy but sleeping on the floor isn't my ideal scenario after a long night at the club. So to find *another* note just now, pushed under the living room door, telling me she's offered the guest my room for *another* night really qualifies as the fucking highlight of my year. And it's only May.

I march up the stairs, crumpling up said note, and make a beeline for the bathroom to take a leak. My eyes are still down on the ball of paper in my hand when the bathroom door opens and a warm wave of soft, curvy woman crashes into me.

She steps back immediately and before I look away from my hand, I see that she, too, is holding one of my mother's infamous notes. Only hers isn't scrunched up. It's being held reverently by elegant fingers that end in unvarnished nails and that are presently smoothing out the crease made into the sheet by our collision. I've never seen hands as expressive as this. The way they are holding that piece of paper tells me more than I ever thought was possible to gather from a split-second image.

"Sorry," she says softly in an American accent. "I wasn't looking."

I look up from our hands and into her face, and we stare at each other for what seems like an eternity.

Her complexion is blotchy, she has circles under her amazing green eyes and an angry red spot that I swear she's just squeezed on the side of her chin. Her long red hair is bed-tousled and full of rats' nests.

She is absolutely the most fucking beautiful woman I have ever seen.

Grace

I recognize him immediately, though he is bigger, much more built than the young man in the drawing. It's the corner of his mouth that gives it away. And those teeth set in anger. That jawline.

It goes with Slavic cheekbones, a Slavic nose that's been bashed in a few times for good measure, medium brown, almost copper-colored, eyes and dark blond hair, shorter than in the picture.

He looks a lot like his mother in a weird way. And an awful lot like trouble.

He is wearing bleached-out denims but is naked from the low riding waist up, and I can see some dark, angry bruises across his abdomen. His very sculpted abdomen. I've never had any dealings with fighters, but it seems obvious what they are. Fight marks.

And just like I wanted to stroke the glass over the drawing, I feel my hands itching to reach out and touch those purple smears. Touch *him*. His scent is undiluted now that he's standing right in front of me and it's not just a lingering memory in a room. It's a full onslaught of deliciousness on my nostrils, and it's doing funny things to me.

My insides have gone mushy. My pussy contracts once, hard, around nothing, giving me a jolt all the way up to my tits. That's never happened to me before from just looking at a guy.

I mean, *really*?

My breathing has sped up and I try to suppress it, try to get a grip. This is stupid. I've never had a reaction like this to a man before. I feel like an animal. At the mercy of my pheromones. It makes me feel almost ashamed but then, in the periphery of my vision, I see the movement in his pants.

His dick is twitching. He's reacting to me the same way I'm reacting to him, and that gives me a rush like nothing I've ever experienced before.

I'm twenty-five, I lost my virginity at sixteen in a pretty unspectacular but not terrible fashion to a guy who was nice enough but not exactly the love of my life. I've had a few boyfriends since. Though not a lot in the last five years.

After Mum was first diagnosed, the supply kinda dried up. It's amazing how unattractive you become to the male of the species once you're caring for the terminally ill. But the ones I did have before that? Not a single one of them ever made me feel as heady as this.

By just standing there.

Doing nothing.

SILAS

Shit. Fuck. Bollocks.

I've never had a reaction like this to a woman before.

I want. My dick wants. My *soul* wants.

This is the last thing I need. I don't know what to do with this. I don't do vulnerable. And lust makes you vulnerable. There is a reason there are so many films in which the man gets stabbed by the woman during his last thrust, literally. In those moments, from just before you come until your dick finishes jerking, you are meat. Weak.

I can't be weak. It needs trust and I don't have any. I find it hard to let go. Really, really hard.

I'm twenty-five and I've had exactly two girlfriends. Niamh, my first, I had known most of my life before we got together. She's been a friend since primary school. I trusted her with my life. Until *him*. And all the bollocks that went with that. She lives in London now. Has done alright for herself. Runs a funeral home with her soon-to-be husband for her soon-to-be husband's father. I meet her for coffee sometimes when she comes down to visit her parents. We're alright. In a blanking-that-shit-out kinda way. Met her man once, too. Nice guy. Reserved but solid and you can see in the way they look at each other that they are happy. That they fit. I'm glad she's happy. I'm glad she got what she needed. I'm glad she's found someone who can give her all the stuff I couldn't. Excitement. Orgasms. The flat. The mortgage. Kids one day.

After Niamh, there was nothing for a long, long time. Then came Cerys. Approached me at the beach two years ago as I came out of the sea and asked me if I fancied doing some nude modelling. She was an art student at Brighton Uni. Had come out to Shoreham that day to sketch the lighthouse. Cerys had her own issues, though. Big issues. Sex between us was the most painful thing. Two people humping without either ever getting to the finish line. Frustration city. Outside of that, we had nothing in common. Picking a place to hang out? Two hours. Deciding on a takeaway? Three hours. Picking a film? Five. The whole thing didn't last long. No idea what happened to her afterwards. Completely lost touch.

From Niamh, I have a scar on the back of my left hand from when she ran me over with ice skates outside the Pavilion when we were twelve and a fuck load of trust issues. Though technically they are *his* fault.

From Cerys, I have a nude drawing of me on my bedroom wall. About sums it up.

And now I'm staring at this gorgeous woman and there is a voice inside my head wondering what she will leave behind.

Fuck.

Grace

We keep staring at one another and someone soon has got to break this deadlock.

Speak, woman, speak.

"You're the guy in the picture," I blurt out, wondering where the traditional 'Hi, I'm Grace, nice to meet you' I had planned on got to.

But it lifts the spell. He looks away, and I realize he's embarrassed before he even utters his first ever words to me.

"It was a present," he mumbles.

He has this really low voice. Not deep, just low. The kind of voice that demands everything around him to be quiet so he can be heard. It's a sort of reverse psychology authority thing that sits in direct contrast with what is happening to him right now.

He's blushing. Not fully but there is a faint stripe of red that starts slowly appearing along his jawline as he looks past my shoulder into the bathroom. It's ridiculously cute on somebody like him. Like when a mountain lion rubs its head against a tree trunk and starts purring. I want to giggle so hard it gives me hiccups. He looks at me again and the urge to giggle stops dead in my throat. So do the hiccups.

"You're the woman in my bed," he says.

Yes, I think, *I am the woman in your bed.*

The heat is back on full force and I can see in his eyes that he is as shocked about what just came out of his mouth as I was about what came out of mine a minute ago. There are definitely some filters missing here. Maybe that's what true attraction is all about. Convention and politeness go out of the window. All that human bullshit we plaster all over everything. Instead, we just say what we're actually thinking. Let the hormones do the talking.

We're back to the staring game and the longer it goes on the more charged the air becomes between us.

My pulse is racing, my insides clench and unclench in rhythmical intervals and my skin feels too tight for me. A furtive glance down tells me his cock isn't just twitching anymore, he's got a raging hard-on now, bulging out his jeans. And I've got the wet pussy to match.

I wonder if he can smell me. *I* can smell me.

He's caught my eyes wandering and his breath hitches. He glowers at me, and I know if he pushed me backwards, planted me up against the sink, pulled my pants down, bent me over and shoved into me from behind right now, I'd happily let him.

And that's so not my scene.

I'm not into sex with strangers, rough and ready, spanking and having my hair fisted and being fucked until it hurts. I'm pretty vanilla.

I have my kinks, I think. In my fantasies, I have a thing for doing it outside, not that I've ever had the chance to try.

But, really, I like kissing for hours. Making out on the couch until bedtime. A cock in my mouth to explore without hurry, to savor not to milk as quickly as possible.

A guy's mouth between my legs when every lick of the tongue is complete in itself, not a chase to orgasm.

And when he enters me, I want it to be with *love*.

Not *en vogue*, I know, but there it is.

Put the race on me and I clam up. Demand I come for you and I want to vomit.

I like normal guys with normal physiques whose chests are comfortable to lie on and not like a slab of stone. Who snuggle up when they are done.

Not this.

This beast-man type.

SILAS

Fuck me. I don't even need to look at her nipples to know they are hard as diamonds.

It's all in her face. She's horny as hell. I can smell it on her.

I know I could just take her, here and now. She'd love it. A hard ride, bent over, hands on the edge of the sink, me fisting her hair and spanking her arse.

If I was that man.

But I'm not.

There is enough violence in my life. The last place I want more of it is with a woman. If anything, I would just want to hold her. Spoon against her, cup her breast, stroke the pad of my thumb over one of those pebbled peaks and kiss her neck until she shivers and moans. Until she turns her face to kiss me, so I can leisurely tongue fuck her mouth.

Shit. Where the fuck did that just come from?

This has got to stop. We've been standing here a good five minutes now. Her on the bathroom tiles, me on the landing. I frown at that. She's got bare feet and the floor in the bathroom is always fucking freezing. I don't want her getting a chill. I want her to be...what the fuck? Enough!

"I need a piss," I inform her gruffly and it finally dispels the magic.

I step to the side, so she can come out onto the landing and she leaves promptly, walking back to my room without looking over her shoulder. I should take a leaf out of her book and not stare after her, but I do. I already know her front is soft and squishy with big, heavy boobs, thanks to our collision. Now I see her butt and I'm doubly fucked. Round like a peach and just the right kind of jiggly. I might find it hard to get intimate with a woman these days, but it doesn't mean I don't know what I like to look at.

And, man, I like what I see.

Grace

It takes me ages to compose myself after the Mexican stand-off on the bathroom threshold.

I get dressed and try to brush my hair, but I just end up braiding it loosely down my back with a promise to take care of it later. I take the sheets off the bed, fold them and put them in a neat pile on the desk. Then I pack my suitcase and lug it down the stairs.

No way am I staying another night now. I've made up my mind. It's not exactly part of the plan, but I'm going to London. There must be a cheap hotel somewhere that has room. Stay there for a couple of nights, regroup. Think what Mum would have wanted me to do. After all, this trip is all about her.

As I make my way down, the smell of fried bacon hits my nostrils and I realize I'm starved. The last thing I ate was half of one of those meals on the plane, which consisted of tough chicken with rice in a tarragon sauce that still repeats on me each time I think about it and a small lump of rock-hard bread roll that competed in carat with the small rectangle of frozen butter I tried to spread on it. There was a 'cheesecake' for dessert, but it had a dubious gelatinous quality, so I didn't even try it. That was about twenty hours ago. And that bacon smells good. But there is only one person in the house who could be frying it and he's the last person I want to see.

That said, there is still the matter of settling up. I can't just leave the house without paying for my stay. So once I'm at the bottom of the stairs, I dig out my money and count out the amount Sheena wanted for the room. I stand there, staring at the cash in my hand for quite a while, not sure what to do with it. I need to leave it somewhere. And write her a thank you note.

Means I need to ask for some paper and a pen. I sigh deeply, bracing myself. Off to the kitchen I go.

I leave my suitcase by the front door and make my way toward the bacon wafts. The closer I get the more my stomach starts to rumble. I'm not just starved, I'm ravenous. As soon as I'm out of here I'll find myself a café or something. But first things first.

He's standing by the stove, his torso thankfully covered up in a gray t-shirt now — tight, of course — and is idly turning bacon rashers in a pan. I notice that there are two plates on the countertop with two pieces of white bread laid out on each, carrying slices of tomato and lettuce leaves. There is a selection of sauces on the side. Ketchup, mustard, mayo and something called HP.

I stand in the door for a minute and watch him, while his eyes remain trained on the frying pan. I know he knows I'm here and is deliberately ignoring me. But it's not rude. It's...*shy*, it suddenly dawns on me. He's finding this about as difficult as I am. I want to laugh out loud at that. I watch him gather himself before he turns to me and attempts a smile. Looks good on him. He's got really nice lips, fuller at the bottom than the top and very, very kissable. Shit. Here we go again. I close my eyes for a second, squishing the lids together hard, then open them again and smile back.

"Hi," I say. "I'm Grace. Grace Turner."

"Silas."

"I know."

"Are you a vegetarian?"

"No."

"Good. Want a BLT?"

I can't help but beam at him.

- 23 -

"Hell yeah!"

SILAS

That smile.

I'm sure mountains have been moved and countries been renamed for smiles like hers. She's got these amazing lips that turn up a little at the corners, cat-like, and when her face lights up it's like the sun comes out. Romantic tosh, I know, but true all the same.

I beckon her forward and gesture at the condiments on the worktop.

"Choose your weapons."

She stuffs a wad of fivers she's been holding in her hand into the back pocket of her jeans and comes over to stand next to me. She looks at the different options and selects the mayo jar. As she unscrews it, her elbow brushes lightly against my arm and I can feel it all the way down to my toes. Here we go again. Ridiculous.

I clench my teeth hard to suppress what's going on and wait for her to finish putting mayo on her bread before I transfer the bacon slices onto their nest of lettuce and tomato. I do the same with mine and reach for the HP.

"What is that?" she asks.

I notice she is waiting politely for me to finish putting my sandwich together before she starts on hers, despite the fact I can hear her stomach rumbling. I like that. She has manners.

"Brown sauce," I reply. "I thought your mum was British. How come you don't know what brown sauce is?"

She freezes and looks at me shocked. I wish I'd kept my mouth shut.

"How do you know that?"

"Let's sit down."

I cock my head towards the breakfast table, take my plate and carry on talking while she follows me over and we sit down opposite one another.

"Mum rang about ten minutes ago," I explain. "Told me to be nice to you. Said you're on a pilgrimage for your dead mother who was originally from around here. That's how I know."

"Right," she says and looks down at her sandwich. "Actually, she was from Surrey, but she used to run the hotel your mum works for. Before I was born."

I can see that all of a sudden she's struggling with the idea of eating. My fault for being so blunt.

"Eat," I tell her.

And, after a while, she does.

Grace

I need to start chewing slowly because the fact that Silas knows why I'm here took my saliva away.

That's personal.

I wasn't expecting him to know anything about me.

I'd told Sheena the basics when she asked me what I was doing in Brighton. I didn't tell her about the list or that Mum had been the manager of the Palais once upon a time, but I did tell her that I was on a kind of memorial tour for my British mother.

I don't know why I find it uncomfortable that Silas knows why I'm here, only that it feels too close.

As I chew, my hunger comes back and I enjoy the sandwich. The man knows how to fry bacon just the right kind of crispy. I look up at him and find his eyes on me.

He's got his sandwich suspended in front of his mouth, untouched. He's clearly been waiting for me to start and now he finally takes a bite.

We eat in silence, just looking at each other, and something weird happens. The air between us changes. It's full of electricity again, but it's more...gentle, I guess.

I look around the kitchen. It's crammed, clean, neat and in desperate need of updating. The units are dark wood effect, old and a bit shabby, the stove is gas and cheaply made with bits of the white enamel chipped out along the edges. The table we are sitting at is white brushed and pushed up against the wall below a window with five matching chairs around it. There is a vase with yellow and orange tulips on the windowsill.

Next to Silas is a door to the backyard and just as we finish our sandwiches, I hear the sound of a cat pushing through a cat flap, followed by a loud meow. I turn to see a black and white feline pad into the kitchen. Silas pushes his plate away and his chair back, so the cat can jump onto his lap.

"Hey, girlie," he greets her as she treads around on his thighs and pushes her head into his hand, purring loudly.

He concentrates on making her purr louder and louder with tickles and strokes for a bit until she gently bites at his fingers, and then he looks up at me.

"This is Luna. Do you like cats?"

Do I like cats? Good question. I have no idea. If you grow up in a hotel, you don't get to keep animals. The Atlantis had a fish tank in the lobby. That's the closest I ever got to having pets.

I shrug.

He gives me a confused look.

"What's that supposed to mean?" he asks.

"Means I don't know. I never had much dealings with them."

"Fair enough. Well, this is Luna and if you hang around long enough, you might meet her brother..."

"Sol?" I interrupt.

He looks surprised.

"How did you know that?"

"Lucky guess," I hedge, but then I tell him. "Your curtains. You have a thing for the sun and the moon."

He freezes and frowns before he pushes Luna off his lap and starts tidying the plates away into a dishwasher.

"So," I say to his back and take the money out of my back pocket. "Thank you for breakfast, lunch, whatever. It was delicious. Now, do you have a piece of paper and a pen, so I can write your mum a note? And where's the best place to stash her cash, so she'll find it?"

He shuts the dishwasher, turns around, leans against the counter and crosses his arms in front of his chest. It does interesting things to his biceps that I really am trying not to notice. I've never in my life been interested in a man's biceps before. I decide it'd be a lot easier to maintain that stance if his t-shirt wasn't so tight. He frowns at me.

"You're not leaving."

"What?"

"Mum says you're staying. So you're staying."

"It's fine. I've already decided. I'm gonna go to London instead, figure something out."

"You're not listening. You're staying." He sighs. "If my mum's got a bee in her bonnet about you staying, you stay. It's as simple as that."

I raise my eyebrows 'cause it sounds like they've decided I'm moving in.

"How long for?" I ask.

He shrugs.

"How long were you booked at the hotel for?"

"Four weeks."

"*Four weeks?*"

It's the first time I've heard him raise his voice a little and I realize it's powerful, he just disguises it well.

"Who's got the money to stay at the Palais for *four weeks*?" he adds. "You minted or something?"

"No, I worked my ass off for a year and saved up every penny. And I booked through a discount site." I pause to pull a face. "That's gone belly up."

"Hmm," he grunts and scowls at me. "I can't sleep on the living room floor for four weeks. That's ridiculous."

"You slept on the *floor*?"

He pinches the bridge of his nose.

"The sofabed's a nightmare. It kills your back," he mutters.

"That settles it." I stand up and leave the money on the table. "I'm off to London. Tell your mum thanks and that I really appreciated the rescue."

"She'll have my fucking hide," he mumbles, rubbing his face with the hand that was just pinching the skin between his eyebrows, and straightens up. "I got an idea."

I don't want her to go. It's as simple as that.

I don't need or want the complication of her in the house. But I don't want her to go. And it's not even about the insane attraction I feel to this woman. The loss of that I could deal with. I'd welcome it. I *really* don't need a distraction like that. In my fucking home.

No, it's about what happened when we sat there eating together.

For those few minutes, I was at *peace*. While in the company of another human being. For the first time in, I don't know, maybe ever.

There is something about her presence that is soothing. Like the ocean. And I'm not prepared to let that walk out of the door just yet. There is also the fact that Mum was very clear. When I started moaning at her about the American in my room, she cut me down in flames. Told me in no uncertain terms that this was a young woman who was lost, and she needed a temporary home and we happened to be it. I'm not sure why she's so adamant, but when she gets like this, there is no arguing. So I didn't bother.

"Go on, then," Grace says impatiently, and I realise that I said I had an idea but then stayed quiet for a whole minute.

"I never get in till around six or seven in the morning," I start. "And I don't normally go to sleep till eight or nine, then get up at three. We could share. If you get up and are out by nine, I get in there, and then you can have the room back by, say four at the very latest."

Now that it's out of my mouth, it sounds utterly idiotic. But she doesn't seem to think so at all. On the contrary, her face lights up.

"Really? You'd do that? You wouldn't mind?"

I shake my head.

"No, it'd be cool. No skin off my nose. If it keeps everyone happy, I'm happy."

There is a moment when I can see her thinking it over, making her decision, and then she does something I wouldn't have expected in a million years.

She comes over and fucking hugs me.

Grace

I don't really think about it, it's an impulse.

As soon as it sinks in what he's said, I feel so relieved I want to cry. I didn't really want to leave this house and go to London. It's weird, but attraction to him aside, I feel like I've come home for the first time since Mum passed.

It happened while we were eating those stupid sandwiches. Just sitting there. Relaxed. With the sunshine falling through the window onto the silly tulips on the windowsill and the cat jumping onto his lap. I can't explain it.

And my instinct is to wrap my arms around the man who has just made that happen, who has just decided he'll let me stay here. And breathe. For the first time in months.

So I cross the kitchen and I do. It's not even a real hug, because it's all on his outside, my arms wrapped around his still crossed ones, my face turned so his mouth is roughly by the top of my ear, and he gets a nose full of my hair. It's like embracing a stone statue. It should be kinda awkward, but it doesn't last long enough for the embarrassment to really kick in. I just say 'thank you' while I squeeze him and then let go without looking at him.

I turn away to go back to the table and grab the key that Sheena left on it for me.

"In that case, enjoy your room. I'm out," I say, without making eye contact again.

Then I leave to explore the town, his scent in my nostrils.

I've finally figured out what that salty tang is.

Beneath soap and wood smoke and man, he smells of the ocean.

SILAS

It's fightnight and I'm headlining, but I'm not feeling it tonight.

Not that I ever really wanted to punch people for a living in the first place, but I have enough anger in me to at least not give a shit if I do. Or did. Things have changed in the last few days. And not necessarily for the better.

It's her, that calming influence she has. She's messing with my mojo. Though I barely see her.

We've fallen into a rhythm that seems to suit both of us perfectly well. She's got this list of stuff she has to do while she's in England. Not sure what it is about or what's on it, but I know it contained having High Tea at the Grand among other things. I know about that one because she took Mum along. Nice of her. Mum hardly ever gets out. Bit of an irony that they went to another hotel, I guess, but still, I think they had fun. They came back laughing at any rate. Mum looked ten years younger.

Grace also went shopping with Kalina at some point, though I'm not sure that's on the list. They seem to be getting on alright. Good for Kalina. She's been with us four months now and she was finding it hard to make friends, I think. She's the only Polish girl on her course, and the charity shop where she volunteers is run by a bunch of old biddies. Like they all are. She's only eighteen, so a lot younger than Grace, but Grace doesn't seem to mind.

Not that I really know.

We only ever see each other in passing. Literally.

Grace usually sits on the landing when I come out of my morning shower with all the stuff she needs for the day by her side. We sail past one another, and I go into my room to slip in between sheets that are still warm and smell of her. I can never decide if that's heaven or hell. My dick has very clear ideas about it, but I've started silencing him in the shower beforehand since I can hardly do it in the bed she's going to sleep in that night. Somehow, we gave up changing the linen between our shifts on day two. I had all intention of putting the sleeping bag on top of the bed, but when she saw me with it outside the room, she just took it off me and hung it over the banister.

"Just get in the damn bed, I don't have cooties," she said.

It made me laugh.

Then I did as I was told.

And found out that just the scent of this woman makes me rock hard.

So that first morning, I snuck back into the bathroom as soon as I heard her leave the house and jerked off like a teenager. I'm usually alright coming on my own, provided the door is locked, the windows are shut and there's nobody else in the room. But coming on my own with her scent in my nostrils and the image of those cat-like lips saying 'good morning, sleep well' to me was doubly easy. Thinking about it now makes my dick twitch again and I groan inwardly.

Fucking terrible timing, mate. Having her around is gonna kill me. Or make me blind. Whichever comes first.

In my bid to get her out of my head, I catch Arlo's eye.

He's sitting in his chair, kneading his hands. He's my opponent tonight and since TripleX was built as a nightclub, not a fight venue, there are no dressing rooms. We all just sit in the office together waiting for our turn until the last two fighters are left. We are the last two tonight.

There is no pretence here. We don't do all that growling at each other beforehand or any of that shit. We're all here for the same reason: we have money issues and we don't care enough not to get hurt. It's a job. An illegal one, which means it pays more than fucking minimum wage, but a job nevertheless. We're colleagues. So when Arlo and I hear the crescendo outside the door as the previous fight comes to an end, we nod at each other amicably.

May the best man win. I hope I don't kill you.

We don't say it. We don't need to.

I think about Grace again and what I will cook for her tomorrow. That's the other thing we do, we eat supper together if she's back from her outings already when I come in from the gym. Just like the first day, we don't talk much. Often, we just sit there in silence, but I've found a couple of things out about her by now. We're the same age, born days apart. Her at the end of March, me at the beginning of April. She bartends in the hotel in DC where her mum used to be the manager until she got cancer.

There is a knock on the door, signalling that it's time Arlo and I took our sorry arses out onto the dance floor.

As I step out into the roaring crowd, I watch Gareth prop up the loser of the last bout and take him to the exit, along with his minder. They're gonna be shoved in a car and taken back to wherever. He's some outsider, not part of the club. He's got blood streaming out of his nose, his left eye is rapidly swelling shut and he's barely walking. But he's alive. At this point anyway.

The winner is a guy called Goran, who's technically part of the club although he doesn't bounce here anymore. Used to. Does security for the old Benson now. Whatever that means. I honestly don't want to know. The shit old man Benson is into makes me wanna puke. Dog fights. Cock fights. And all the other shit the history books will tell you stopped happening after the Victorian opium houses were shut. Did it fuck. If you ever want to bang a corpse, old man Benson is the guy to ask.

I watch Goran shake some hands in the audience, being congratulated. He looks totally fine and goes to sit somewhere with the punters. Diego slaps him on the back as he goes past to stand on the dance floor and announce Arlo and me.

I push any lingering thoughts of Grace and home out of my head. They have no place here.

Welcome to hell.

Grace

I've been here a few days now and it feels like forever. In a good way. Shoreham is tiny, so I already know it like the back of my hand. There are shops and restaurants, cafés, pubs and even an arts center where they put on shows and concerts, but it's all within a one-mile radius. It's like a pocket-size town but with all the trimmings. Already half the population knows me by sight and nods a greeting when they see me. I like it. It's also really pretty and a bit wacky. It's got an estuary where the river Adur goes into the sea and there are houseboats, big ones, moored on the other side of the estuary. Some just look like suburban little bungalows with flowers in window boxes, but others have been turned into some weird fantasy thing, like they're from a psychedelic children's TV show or something. It's cool.

Every morning after Silas comes home, I leave the house and make sure that I'm out until his up-time. It works. I get the feeling he likes having the house to himself when he's asleep. Some evenings he's already gone again when I get back, but on the others he has been there to make me dinner.

Each time he didn't ask me if I wanted any food.

Just made enough for two and put a bowl in front of me, telling me to eat. Exactly like that first morning. When we're both in the house, I sit in the kitchen and read until he's gone, so I'm just there anyway and I get to watch him cook. Sexy as sin, even when he's just chopping carrots, dressed in jogging bottoms and a ratty old t-shirt. Sadly, I haven't managed to catch another glimpse of him half naked since that first day despite the fact I sit on the landing every morning waiting for him to come out of the shower.

The thing is, it's not just about the way he looks and smells and about the fact I fantasize about him every night. It's the oddest thing between us. When we're in the kitchen together and he's silently making one of his thick soups, because that seems to be his diet staple, it feels like I've known him forever. Like that's what we are meant to do for the rest of our lives. Sit in a kitchen, make soup, *be*.

When he leaves again, it always feels like I'm being pushed out of reality and back into some side story that shouldn't be my life. Hard to explain.

Aside from obsessing about my hostess' son, I've also started ticking items off on Mum's list. Two, so far. I went and had tea at the Grand, and I made friends with someone I wouldn't normally make friends with.

Kalina is really nice. Her English is quite limited, but we do girly stuff together like paint our nails or do makeovers and that doesn't need much talking. She's really artistic, so way better at all that stuff than I am. It's like having the little sister I never had but one that is much more talented at being a girl. Which is totally ironic because she's the one with the pixie cut and the combat boots, a tiny fierce tomboy with huge brown eyes, and I'm the one with the waist-long hair and the lacy tops.

I like a bit of frill. Not too much, I'm pretty much a jeans girl when I'm not working, and a black-skirt-white-shirt one when I am because that's hotel bar uniform, but that doesn't mean I don't like a pretty dress and nice shoes sometimes.

Kalina goes to a language school three times a week and works in a thrift shop another three. You can hardly get into her room because she's hoarding all sorts of shit in there that she's bought to take back to Poland. I think she's got an eye for good vintage stuff. Not sure if she'll keep it or sell it when she goes home but she'll need a truck to go back if she carries on like this. She's staying another two months.

I wish I was.

When I went to the Grand, I took Sheena with me. I wanted to thank her properly for putting me up, but also because I would have felt weird doing High Tea on my own. Halfway through tea, she leaned over and told me I was starting to sound more British by the day. Made me feel really happy, closer to Mum. I've felt more contented since I got here than I've felt in a long time.

So I'm not sure what is different tonight.

I'm tossing and turning in bed and sleep just won't come. I've had some trouble with jetlag before, but the fresh sea air around here seems to help with that, so I know this is not that.

It's nearly midnight, I heard Sheena come home about twenty minutes ago, and I should be long out for the count. Actually, to say I heard her is entirely wrong 'cause as always I'm plugged into my I-pod. Tonight, Billie Holiday gets the privilege of singing me to sleep. I like the old jazz singers. They make me feel safe. There is a piano in the bar at the Atlantis and when I was little, my mum would often take me down there in my stroller on jazz evenings to let the syrupy atmosphere lull me to sleep. No, what I really mean is that I felt the door open and shut when Sheena came in, the small shudder that the action sends through the house.

In another bid for sleep, I roll from one side onto the other and stick my nose deep into the pillow to take a lungful of Silas' scent. It's a bit of a naughty pleasure and I congratulate myself, not for the first time, on convincing him to use the same bedding as me instead of crawling into that horrible sleeping bag every night.

It's been both heaven and hell snuggling into his scent each evening. It's funny how something can be both calming and arousing at the same time.

I tentatively stroke my hand down my belly and slip my fingers into my panties. I'm wet, I've been perpetually wet since I got here, and I start stroking my clit leisurely.

Normally it doesn't take me long to get myself off. Practice makes perfect. And due to a lack of proper boyfriends in the last five years, I've had a *lot* of practice. But tonight, I just can't get there. I can't settle on a fantasy. My mind keeps wandering. I can't even say where. I remain restless.

I'm not into psychic mumbo jumbo, but it feels like there is another presence in the house, and it's not exactly benign.

The thought makes me take my hand out of my panties and sit bolt upright in bed.

Now that I've thought it, I can't help being paranoid. I take my ear buds out and strain my ears. Sure enough, there are noises downstairs

- 34 -

that are not normally there at this hour. Sheena tends to come in and go to sleep. She has the other room downstairs, the one that isn't the living room, closest to the kitchen, and she tends to brush her teeth down there and fall into bed. Fuck knows where and when she goes to pee. But tonight, there are definitely voices downstairs. A female, Sheena, I hope, and a male.

Not Silas. Too rumbly for that. Like rolls of thunder in the distance.

I listen for a while as the exchange gets more heated. I know it is, despite the fact it's not getting louder. But there is something about the rhythm that changes, that tells me it's getting more intense, turning into an argument.

Finally, I hear a chair scraping back on the lino and an internal door being opened with a loud creak. I realize it must be the kitchen door and that alone tells me something strange is going on. I've not seen the kitchen door in this house shut even once since Sheena rescued me from my fate as a homeless tourist.

"Fucking don't then!"

The man's voice travels through the house — loud, angry and dark. His timbre makes the walls shake.

It's followed by a thud and I have no idea how I know, because there has never been any violence in my life, but I'm certain it's the sound of somebody having their head rammed against a wall.

A second later, the front door is slammed shut.

I'm out of bed and out on the landing in a second. There, I bump into Kalina who's already out of her room. Her arms are poled on the banister, and she is tentatively looking over the edge to see if she can see anything from there. She looks over her shoulder at me when I join her. She is properly sheet rumpled, her short hair standing in all directions. Her dark eyes are squinting under the light. She must have been fast asleep. Enviable. We stare at each other for a second and she shrugs helplessly, which tells me she hasn't got a fucking clue what's going on either.

In a silent exchange, we agree to go down and check on Sheena, but just as we are about to leave the landing, Sheena comes halfway up the stairs and looks up at us. She has a fake smile plastered across her face, but I can see her hands shaking.

"Sorry about that, girls. All good. Go back to bed."

She turns back downstairs without any further explanation, and that is that.

Kalina and I frown at each other and then go back to our bedrooms.

I lie awake forever after that, listening out for every small sound.

Who the fuck was that?

SILAS

I won, but I'm broken.

I really wasn't on form and Arlo has been getting steadily better. When he first came, he was supposed to be just fodder. Diego even had a bet on that Arlo would bottle out of the first fight. But the guy is as desperate for cash as the rest of us, and he's tougher than he looks. Plus, he's been training night and day since. It pays off.

I need to be more vigilant. I can't afford to lose top spot. Not yet. I only need five more wins at twenty grand a piece and then we're in the clear. And then all we have to do is keep it that way. Keep *him* out of our lives and we're good. The thought of him automatically makes me pedal harder and it fucking hurts.

I'm so bruised, Diego even offered me a cab home, but I refused. Don't show weakness. Arlo, that sneaky fucker, managed to land one on my jaw, which has already turned a nice shade of bright red. Give it a couple of days and that'll be a proper bruise. That never happens. Not on my face. They go for my face and they are toast. That's how I won in the end. He should have kept away from my head and he might have had me. But you go anywhere above my neck and I go fucking ballistic. They had to take him to A&E. I feel a pang of guilt at that but not for long.

We all know what we let ourselves in for.

It'll be a headache for Diego, though, 'cause the coppers will want to know what happened. Here comes the cock-and-bull story about weekenders from London looking for a fight. Average height, average weight, average everything. But Diego has got this, I'm not worried. I'm more worried about the bollocking I'll get from Mum when she sees my face. She'll think it happened bouncing and she won't like it.

I'm careful not to walk around with my shirt off in the house anymore these days. The morning I bumped into Grace was a slip up. I don't think Mum would buy it any longer if she saw the rest of the marks on my body. She doesn't like me working for a Benson, even though she loved George when we were younger. She just hates old man Benson and his cronies, the head crony in particular. They're not movie-style mafia or anything, but they've been part of old Brighton for a few generations. And old Brighton is not gentry. It's the whores that serve the gentry.

I finally get to the lighthouse, so I dump my bike and strip off.

Looking down at myself, I can tell I'll have a black-and-blue mosaic across my abdomen by tomorrow evening.

Compared to what I'll look like off the back of tonight, I looked like I'd only been in a mild little scrap that day Grace caught me with my shirt off. I still can't believe I let her catch a glimpse. What a moron. But I hadn't expected her to be in the bathroom that first morning. And she never said anything. I need to be more careful. Can't have her telling Mum what she saw.

I look around. The beach is deserted this morning, and I breathe a sigh of relief. I've had enough of people for one night. For a moment, as I push through the pain to run naked into the sea, I wonder if I have internal bleeding. If maybe, today, I won't come back from the sea.

Half an hour later I know there is no such luck.

Grace

"Grace?"

I'm still mostly asleep when I hear his voice. I can't quite rouse myself. After that strange incident last night, I lay awake until dawn. It scared me. My mum used to say the more terrified I was the deeper I'd sleep, but not last night.

What I witnessed is so far removed from everything I've ever known that it might as well be on TV. I might have a bit of a sailor's mouth on me but, really, I'm just a well brought up girl from a nice part of Washington, D.C. My peers were the children of civil servants, museum curators and government officials. Sure, we had metal detectors on the gates of my high school, but they never went off. And, sure, we get the occasional drunk in the Atlantis' bar causing a bit of a scene, but it's a five-star hotel, even the drunks are five-star assholes.

At some point in the night, I went to the bathroom and I was crapping myself just having to cross the landing. Luckily, the cats, both of them, managed to sneak in and onto my bed, and it was only then that I finally found enough peace to fall asleep.

Sol is the negative image of his sister, more black than white, and they cuddled up like yin and yang at the foot end of the bed, warming my feet. They are there now, slowly getting up, stretching, purring and meowing a greeting at Silas.

Silas.

He's in the room.

I wake up fully.

He's standing in the doorway, looking at me.

SILAS

Fuck me, she is beautiful.

She wasn't there sitting on the landing, waiting like normal, when I came out of the shower. So I assumed she'd got up early and gone out already. Didn't occur to me that she hadn't got up at all yet and that she'd still be in my bed. She looks so peaceful, my dark mood lifts instantly. I almost regret having called her name to wake her, but I really, really need my mattress to sleep on today. I can't take these bruises onto the floor, they'll go necrotic.

I watch her struggle to consciousness and my dick springs to attention. I didn't take care of him just now because I wasn't in the mood. Pain, *real* pain, isn't sexy. It fucking hurts. But all it takes is for her to open those emerald eyes and for that pussycat mouth to curl up at the corner and he's all game down there. It helps that the duvet has ridden down to her waist, she's wearing only a ribbed white man's vest, *kryptonite*, and I can see *a lot* of her cleavage. As her eyes flutter open, she can't help but notice what's happening to me, I'm wearing jogging bottoms for Christ's sake, and her tongue darts out to lick her lips as she tries hard to look everywhere but there. It's not a conscious action and that makes it five times as sexy.

"Hey," she mutters, finally settling on my eyes in her search for an anchor in the room. "Are you back early?"

Before I can answer, she frowns and starts rooting around in the bed for something that turns out to be her I-pod. She looks at it and starts swearing.

"Shit, Silas, I'm so sorry." The moment she utters my name, it's like a bolt through the heart, and, yeah, down to my dick. "I totally overslept."

As she sits up, the cats that were curled up by her feet when I came in and have started rousing jump off the bed. They pad over to me and rub up against my legs. I bend down to stroke their heads, hiding my hard-on, willing him to go down. Sol takes a swipe at me and draws blood from the back of my hand. That helps. I straighten up.

"Whoa," Grace mutters, putting a flat palm on the mattress to steady herself. "Gimme a minute. I feel a bit woozy."

"Heavy night?"

She gently shakes her head.

"No. I rarely drink. Just couldn't sleep. Didn't fall asleep until, I don't know, about an hour ago?"

My turn to swear.

"Shit, Grace, I'm sorry. I'll go and sleep in Mum's bed when she goes, or something. You get some more rest."

"Your mum's going to work?" she asks, and there is a strange quality to the question.

"Yeah, 'course," I answer.

"I guess Kalina is already out?"

"Probably."

There is a weird moment when she looks at me very, very intensely, and I can tell something big is about to shift in my universe.

"There was a man in the house last night," she says slowly, and I freeze.

A chill creeps down my spine.

"I think," she carries on, then pauses as if she is searching her brain for the truth in her words, "I don't know exactly, but I think he shoved your mum into the wall."

"Fuck," I say and look at her as my brain goes into overdrive.

I was right, he's back. And Mum let him into the fucking *house*. She never fucking learns. I knew it. All those texts she was suddenly getting. All those 'I've got to take this' calls then disappearing into her bedroom. Still, what Grace says shocks me. He's never been violent at home. But that doesn't mean he wouldn't be now. It's been a long time. I wouldn't put it past him. I wouldn't put *anything* past him if he's desperate enough.

Grace is watching me closely. It's clear to her that I know who he is but that's not the question she asks.

"Is he dangerous?"

"Not in the way you might think."

I see the fear in her eyes and also the exhaustion of a sleepless night. I wonder what she sees in mine, because again something happens to the quality of the air in the room. Another shift. Between her and me this time.

She draws up her legs and curls into a ball, lays her cheek sideways onto her knees and just looks at me questioningly. She is making herself small and suddenly I know where she is going with this. I might have only had two girlfriends but I ain't stupid. And we've been dancing around each other for days now. Like a fight in which neither opponent throws the first punch. Now it's there, in her eyes. The first punch. And I'm acutely aware that if I duck from it, it's gonna cut her like fuck. So I don't duck. I just lay down the rules.

"Move over," I say. "No touching."

She smiles.

"No touching," she agrees and scoots towards the wall to give me more space.

By my feet, Luna has started gnawing on my big toe in a desperate bid to make me go feed her, while Sol is already halfway down the stairs, meowing loudly.

"I'll be back in a second," I say to Grace. "Just feeding these guys."

I turn away and go down to the kitchen, gathering my thoughts.

This is a stupid, stupid idea.

But I can't back out now.

More to the point, I don't *want* to.

Fuck knows, I need this as much as she does.

Shelter. Companionship. Peace.

By the time I get back to my room, she is fast asleep again, face turned to the wall.

Or so I think.

I wonder for a moment if I should just leave her to it and go crawl into Mum's bed after all, but then she lifts the duvet behind her.

"Get in," she demands.

I swallow hard at the sight of her arse. She's wearing just normal white cotton knickers, nothing special but, man, they may as well be the finest lace lingerie the way they show off those perfect ripe cheeks. Her vest top has ridden up a bit and reveals a strip of skin along the small of her back. She has dimples there, left and right of her spine, and I feel the overwhelming urge to kiss them.

Then maybe a little lower.

Now I really, really wish I'd jerked off in the shower.

Grace

I know he's looking at my ass, and I know he likes what he sees. I know because he just made this really low sound in his throat. Something between a growl and a moan and it goes straight to my core. I bet he doesn't even know he made that sound.

I wonder if I've made him hard again. I hope so. I want him to suffer as much as I do if he insists on this stupid no touching rule. Who is he kidding? We're on a roller coaster and he knows it.

I feel empowered by the effect I have on this man in a way I never thought possible. I used to sneer at women who would get off on how they could drive a man crazy. My friend Cindy used to brag about how she could orgasm by giving her boyfriend a blowjob. Used to think it was just hyperbole. Now I'm not so sure.

He's still hesitating, and I flap the duvet I'm holding up behind me a little.

"Come on, I'm getting cold," I say, and my voice sounds unintentionally husky.

I sense him move across the room, and then the mattress dips behind me. He hasn't shed either his sweatpants or his tee and I'm disappointed. Even if we're not touching, I was hoping for the warmth of his skin next to mine.

He lies on his back and crosses his arms behind his head.

It's amazing how much you can tell is going on around you without even looking. I never noticed that before. He's making me notice a lot of things I've never noticed before.

Like the fact that if you are aroused enough, the ribbed cotton of your tank top really rubs over your nipples each time you take a breath. I desperately, desperately want him to spoon me, put a hand on my tit and stroke that nipple just a little. I think that's all it would take. It would be enough. I'd go off like a rocket. The thought makes me huff out a suppressed sigh.

"Grace!" he hisses warningly, and I clench at the sound of his voice. "Go to sleep."

"Why?"

"Because we're not doing this."

"Why not?"

I never thought I'd ever be this forward, but in a strange way, his restraint makes it easy. I feel him gingerly turn onto his side. He groans, but this time the sound doesn't spell lust. It spells pain. I think of those bruises he had the day I met him and the red mark I saw on his cheek earlier.

"Are you alright?" I ask.

"I'm fine," he answers. "Go to sleep."

I nearly die from electric shock as he gently pulls my hair away from my neck and plants a kiss just below my ear. A shudder runs through my whole body, from that one brief touch.

"I thought you said no touching," I murmur.

"Make no mistake," he says softly. "I want you."

And then he goes and does one better.

He licks up behind my ear in one long, slick stroke of the tongue. My pussy contracts sharply and I jerk.

"More," I moan, loudly.

"No," he whispers in my ear. "Not today. Go to sleep, Grace."

I want to protest, but I can hear in his tone that the verdict is final.

I try to control my breathing and, eventually, it works.

I sound like I'm asleep.

ꞮLAS

I can't believe I just fucking did that.

Me, Silas O'Brien, the guy who dated his first girlfriend for weeks before the first chaste kiss. What the fuck is happening here?

But she smelled so good I just had to taste her. Fruity. Niamh always smelled flowery, of lily of the valley. Cerys was an incense girl through and through. Neither did anything for me. Grace? She smells of vanilla and berries, marshmallows and woman. Tangy and sweet. She smells *right*. I just wanted to see if she'd taste the same.

And I love that spot just behind a woman's ear.

The skin is so delicate there, the scent of the person so pure. While I stare at the patch of skin I just licked, suppressing the desire to taste her again, taste all of her, I watch her control her breathing and, after a while, she drifts off.

I wish I could. But that moan still sits in my eardrum, like an itch. That moan! The unashamed request for more. I shiver at the memory and my hard-on twitches, sending contractions up my spine.

She's like every fantasy come true. I keep staring at the side of her neck, rising and falling with her breaths, until I can't lie on this side any longer. It hurts too much.

Arlo really pounded my front at some point last night. Got me in a tie up and just went to town. I'm pissed off something chronic about that. With myself. He should never ever have got close enough to get me in a clinch in the first place. I was sloppy. If he was any better, he could have had me on the floor. Lucky for me, he is still nowhere good enough.

I roll onto my back and Grace whimpers in her sleep. She shuffles backwards until her arse rests against my hips. As if we were already lovers, as if we *had been* lovers for a long, long time. It would be so easy to roll over again, pull her pants down and explore her just a little. Run my hand down her crack, upwards, through her slit, finger her from behind until she bucks in my hand and then let my dick follow.

I know she wouldn't protest. I bet she's slick as fuck already.

But she's too good for that.

Too good for the shit show that is my life.

The thought is a sobering one. But not sobering enough for my cock. If I ever want to get to sleep, I need to get him off. It's risky, I know, but I'm too tired to get up again and I can make myself come without a sound. And without ejaculating. A neat trick I learned from sharing a room. From before I needed to be on my own with the door and windows locked.

Curiosity grips me. I wonder if I can get there with her next to me or if I'll clam up.

I turn on my other side, away from her, and slip my hand under the elastic of my jogging bottoms. I'm commando in there and I grip the shaft of my dick. I let the pad of my thumb run over the slit. It's slick with precum and I spread it around the head, pretending it's her, me entering her.

Then I squeeze myself even harder and pump my fist rapidly a few times. I'm already at the cusp when I hear her.

She is moaning in her sleep. A good moan.

The sound makes me go over the edge before I can grip the base of my dick to make the spunk go inwards and I spill all over my hand.

And it feels good.

Healthy.

Normal.

While I come down from the high, I hear her breath hitching and she starts shuddering next to me. The good kind of shuddering.

She is having an orgasm in her sleep.

Grace

I sleep all through the day and when I wake up, I'm alone in bed.

As the memory of the night, *morning*, hits me, I feel mildly ashamed of myself. I'd never done that. Got myself off while someone was sleeping next to me. I've never done that masturbating-while-being-watched thing either. Not the kind of show the kind of guys I've been with were into. Now I wonder what it would feel like, not just getting off lying next to him, but to have him watch. The idea at least feels interesting, very interesting. But before I can explore the thought a bit further, maybe in the shower, I need a pee and food.

I'm starving. I realize I haven't eaten since last night and that was almost a whole day ago. It's a repetitive theme since I got here. I forget to eat unless Silas feeds me. I get up, slip into my yoga pants, make a pit stop in the bathroom and then pad quietly down the stairs. There are voices coming from the kitchen. Sheena and Silas. It must be very late, or she's come home from work early.

"I tell you she is wrong," I hear her say.

She sounds exasperated. Like somebody who is telling the truth but isn't being believed. Silas says something, but it's too quiet for me to understand.

"She can't have seen it because it didn't happen," Sheena says, raising her voice, her tone annoyed now. "I did crack my head against the wall, but that was entirely my fault."

I stop dead in my tracks a few steps before I reach the bottom of the stairs. I don't think this is a conversation I want to walk in on. I hear Silas laugh at her words. A sarcastic, joyless sound that makes me realize I have never heard him laugh. Neither like this, nor genuinely.

"No, really, hear me out," Sheena carries on.

She's gone from annoyed to pleading.

"He stormed out when I told him that he couldn't move back in right now. You know, in a huff, like he does. I grabbed his shirt because I didn't want him to leave. I haven't seen him in so long and he looked, you know, *remorseful*. So I thought...anyway, he ripped loose and I fell back against the wall. He didn't lay a finger on me, Silas, I promise."

Silas says something that, again, I can't hear, but it feels like it's the end of the conversation. In any case, I decide to carry on walking. They must have heard the toilet flush, so they shouldn't be that surprised if I appear in the kitchen.

When a minute later I do, Silas is standing by the kettle, in the process of brewing tea. It's odd because to my knowledge he avoids caffeine. He's a bit of a health and fitness freak. No caffeine, no sugar, gym every day. I frown at that thought because my gaze falls onto the clock on the wall and normally that's exactly where he'd be at this time. Four until six, training. Home for dinner. Out for work. Back sometime between six and seven in the morning.

He turns and smiles at me standing in the doorway and indicates one of the two mugs of tea he's been making.

"Earl Grey?" he asks while he takes the other one and puts it in front of Sheena. "Here you go, Mum."

"No, it's okay. You have your tea, I'll make my own," I say.

He looks at the mug, confused, then at me.

"This *is* for you. I don't drink tea."

He picks it up and holds it out for me.

I smile and come towards him to receive my gift.

SILAS

Grace comes towards me and takes the mug off me, smiling.

I have started living for that smile. It's the best feeling if I can make it happen somehow.

"Thank you," she says, and briefly, gently lays her hand on my abdomen in gratitude.

I try desperately not to but I still flinch in pain when she touches me. I wasn't half wrong with my prediction. Under my t-shirt there is an artwork of purple bruises crisscrossing my body and even the lightest pressure hurts like hell. My heart stops when I realise she's noticed. For a moment, her gaze flicks to her hand on my body, and then, as she withdraws it, her eyes find mine. I plead with her silently not to mention anything in front of Mum and somehow, thank fuck, she gets it. She nods ever so slightly then leaves me to take her tea over to the table and sit down opposite Mum.

"Hi, Sheena," she says with a big smile. "How come you're home?"

"Hi, sleepyhead," Mum answers, smiling back. "Half day today. I get one of those every so often."

Mum blows on her tea and examines Grace thoroughly. I'm not sure if it's because of what I told her Grace said about what happened or if it's because she can put two and two together and knows we slept in the same bed, *at the same time.* Either way, she doesn't seem to hold it against her because she puts out her hand and strokes once over Grace's cheek with the back of her fingers. Oddly intimate, I think. I've never seen her do anything like that to Kalina. Or any of the other students for that matter.

"How are you, ducky? I haven't really seen you since you took me to the Grand. How's your stay?"

Grace blows at her tea and looks at Mum over the rim of her mug.

"I'm good, thank you. Enjoying myself."

"How's your list coming along?" Mum asks with a smile.

"Haven't ticked anything else off yet, but if the weather is nice, I'm aiming for Bramber Castle tomorrow. I just haven't figured out how to get there. There doesn't seem to be any public transport?"

"Ah," Mum coos. "You're right, there isn't any. Silas," she says to me with a smirk, "why don't you take Grace in my car?"

She couldn't be more obvious if she tried, and I just laugh at her amiably.

"Go have a bath, Mum," I tell her, and she gets up from the chair.

"That's me told," she says to Grace, collects her mug and leaves the kitchen.

Grace

We wait until Sheena has shut the bathroom door noisily and we can hear her running the bath above our heads. Only then do we look at each other. All the light-heartedness Sheena brought to the table evaporates in an instant.

Silas is still standing by the kettle and I haven't forgotten the flinch I felt when I touched his abs.

It wasn't a good flinch. It wasn't a 'get off, you're too close' flinch either.

It was a flinch of pain.

I get up slowly from the chair, maintaining eye contact as I approach as if he were a wild animal. Not that I know anything about approaching wild animals. The wildest thing we have in DC are eastern gray squirrels. But it feels like that. Like I can't look away or he'll bolt. When I stand in front of him, I can sense his impulse to retreat, but he has nowhere to go, the counter is at his back.

I grab the hem of his t-shirt and start carefully pulling it up.

"Grace," he hisses as his hands shoot down to hold mine still and stop me in my tracks.

"Show me," I say quietly. "Or I'll tell."

He throws his head back, shuts his eyes, takes his hands off mine and lets me continue. I lift the shirt as gently as I can, and what I reveal makes me gasp.

His torso is one big bruise, there is barely any normal colored skin between the purple smears. It's worrisome but there is also something oddly fascinating about it at the same time. I've never seen anything like it.

While my left hand still holds up the fabric, I can't help but touch the fingers of my right to the marks. Lightly, so as not to hurt him. He shivers as I run them down, past his navel, and then swipe sideways across his v-cut. I'm lost in my exploration when suddenly he snatches my hand up, holding it firmly in his, bunching up my fingers.

It's only now that I see his knuckles are also discolored. I look up and see that he's opened his eyes and is looking down at me, his copper-brown irises burning with intensity. I can barely look at them, and it's when I avoid them for a second that I spot another dark patch of hemorrhage. The red mark I saw the night before has turned into a purple smudge along his jaw. He hasn't shaved, clever man, so it's well hidden amid tawny stubble. But it's there alright. I want to reach up and touch that mark also, but he's holding on to my hand.

"Does it hurt when I touch you?" I ask, and he almost imperceptibly shakes his head before he lightly presses his lips to my fingertips as he keeps holding my gaze, fast this time.

I'm not allowed to skip out and it gives me a sudden rush like no other.

His eyes are hungry, devouring mine, but in a different way from before. The longer he looks the quicker the current of electricity that courses through my veins pulsates.

My heart starts pounding in my chest so wildly, I wonder why I can't hear it on the outside.

This is different from before.

Before this, smelling him, watching him, lying next to him went straight to my sex.

This is deeper, more, *everywhere*.

Right now, every nerve ending in my body is on high alert.

I'm *alive*. So alive I can barely handle it.

I need to say something to take some of the heat off or I think I'll die.

"What happened?" I ask and get another barely there shake of the head.

Then his other hand comes up and wraps itself gently around the back of my head. His fingers are warm. He cradles me there while his thumb on my cheek takes leisurely swipes across the skin just in front of my ear.

It's the kind of stuff you see in movies but that never happens in real life. Not in my life anyway. My past boyfriends might all have been nice guys. Held my hand, kissed for hours, waited for me to climax before them. Or at least until they thought I'd climaxed. But not one of them ever touched me like this. With reverence. As if I were truly something special. I find myself quivering at the thought, and a smile touches his lips. His gorgeous, kissable lips.

He leans down and touches his forehead to mine. I can feel his breath fanning my face, and I realize he is shaking just as much as I am. Then he does something so sexy, my knees want to buckle. He runs his nose slowly up and then down along the side of mine. There is something so animalistic yet so loving about it that I can't help but reach up to him and lay my hands on the side of his throat, his pulse. I want to pin him to me, never to stop what he's doing right now.

But he does.

He stops.

To slant his head and ghost his lips over mine.

"This is a terrible idea," he mumbles against them, and I can feel how part of him is willing himself to retract.

But I can also sense the other part, the one that is making us both shiver deliciously with the nearness of the other, with the knowledge of what is about to happen. Because there is no way on earth I'm letting him out of this now. I don't know what his deal is, but right now I don't give a damn. I *need* him to carry on or I'll spontaneously combust. So I let my hands slip around to the back of his neck and he knows he's lost.

He kisses me again. And again. Just as softly as before. Until we increase the pressure, simultaneously, no pushing one way or the other. And then, suddenly our mouths are open, our tongues playfully testing each other out. Again, there are no bosses here. Just play.

Until he takes the lead.

And then his tongue is everywhere, fucking my mouth, all slick and big, sometimes leisurely, sometimes hard, while one of his hands is still on my neck, steadying me, massaging the base of my skull and the other is on my shoulder, his thumb sweeping over the side of my throat.

I half come up for air and moan deeply, but he barely lets me breathe before a new onslaught. My insides turn to mush, my pussy keeps clenching around nothing each time his tongue dips in and out of my mouth. Instinctively, I press up against him, my body wanting to feel his erection between us.

He winces as my stomach pushes into his abs. Shit. I forgot.

I shuffle away again, and he breaks the kiss, only to whisper against my mouth.

"Careful," he mumbles.

I want to say sorry, but his tongue is wrapped around mine again in an instant.

I want him so much it hurts.

Everywhere.

I can feel a climax building. I've never come this close to an orgasm just from kissing. I didn't even think that was possible. I just need a *little* more.

As if he'd heard me, the hand that was at the base of my throat starts to travel down, his little finger flicking beneath the neckline of my vest, touching just the top of my breast.

I let out a groan and it spurns him on.

His tongue goes even wilder, fucking into my throat, deeper than before, more urgent, and then his whole hand cusps my breast. His fingers in my neck hold me still as he flicks the pad of his thumb back and forth over my stiff nipple.

Again and again.

Until I break apart.

I feel like the fucking king of the castle.

I just made her come.

With a kiss.

She is still shuddering, and I draw back to watch her, reluctantly sliding my hand out of her vest and off her boob. Her face is flushed and there is an almost embarrassed smile on it as she opens her eyes and looks around my mum's kitchen in wonder. Her gaze travels back to me as she bites her bottom lip.

"Hmm," she murmurs.

I lean forward and whisper in her ear.

"You are amazing."

Because she is.

It makes her smile up at me properly when I lean back again, and then her eyes wander to my hard-as-iron dick between us. I had the decency to sling some briefs on this morning, along with a fresh pair of jogging bottoms, so he's constrained against my body, but the head has snuck up behind the elastic and I can tell the exact moment she realises it's peeking out. Her eyes are downcast, fixed on it, and she licks her lips.

She reaches out but I catch her hand before she can get close and gently bend it away.

"No. Not now. Not here," I state hoarsely.

She frowns at that but accepts my words.

"When?" she asks simply, her green eyes tearing away from my indecent exposure and boring into mine.

I pull my jogging bottoms higher to hide him away while I think about my answer. It's a good question. I don't know. I'm not sure I can handle this. She is like purgatory and I'm not sure I'm ready for ascension.

And there is more stuff going on I don't want her mixed up with. At least not till I know what it is.

"I've got to go to work," is all I say.

She cocks her head at that and squints at me doubtfully.

"You never leave this early."

She's right, I don't.

But then I don't normally get phone calls from Diego in the middle of the day either.

Grace

After he leaves the house, I'm lost.

There was this awkward moment when he came back to the kitchen after he'd changed, just before he went out of the door, and we looked at each other, both thinking we should hug and kiss goodbye. Like a couple. But we didn't. Because we're not. We're...heaven knows what we are. A holiday fling, I guess. All I know is I want more of it.

And that I don't like whatever he does that gets him battered like that.

I ponder on that while I wait for inspiration to hit me as to what I should do with the rest of the day. Sleeping in until the afternoon has completely thrown me out of sync again and I get the idea that my body thinks we're back on DC time. Great.

It takes me a while to admit to myself that my fidgetiness has nothing to do with my inner clock. I miss him already and I'm scared.

I'm scared that whatever he does is gonna get him killed.

SILAS

"Come in."

Diego beckons to me as Goran ushers me into the office at the Benson Mansion. Apart from one children's birthday party when we were eight, complete with bouncy castle, popcorn, candy floss and ice cream vendor, for which us plebs were ushered straight past the side of the house and into the garden, I have never been here.

The Bensons had just moved in then, and I guess they wanted to show the rest of the old neighbourhood how far they'd gone up in the world. To be fair, they never took George out of school to put him in private education or any bullshit like that, even after the big move.

Still don't know what made them go from old-time relatively small fry to big fish in the Brighton pond. Don't wanna know either.

Suffice to say that one year they were just running some gambling rigs, a bit of illegal fighting here and there, but nothing to write home about, and the next they were suddenly major players.

The rumour mill always churns on about how their ascension happened to coincide with a certain fire in town, which eliminated all hope of a certain structure ever being restored, making certain powerful people *very* happy. But I don't buy it.

It's more likely to do with Grandma Benson.

Grandma Benson was a character, not in *old* Brighton but in *ancient* Brighton, and seriously minted. I never met her because she didn't really mingle with her son, George senior, much, but I know my old school friend, who is currently looking at me from behind a desk, inherited the TripleX building from her. That's serious property.

Unlike this.

They call this place the Mansion, but it's one of these things that start as a joke and then become the norm. Really, it's just a detached five-bedroom mock Tudor family home with a decent sized garden, an indoor pool under something that looks like a dome-shaped greenhouse and a triple garage. Would still cost a cool two mill or so if they ever put it on the market. It's the thing with this town. Property is fucking stupid money. Once upon a time, Woodland Drive was where the slightly richer people had their family homes. Now it's full of internet celebrities and gazillionaires who make their money doing things no honest working person will ever understand.

The heretofore slightly richer people now live in Mum's old terraced house up muesli mountain.

And we live in Shoreham.

"Snake," Diego greets me by my fight name once I've crossed the threshold and indicates the empty chair across from him. "Take a seat."

I didn't pick my name, he did, but I guess it suits my fight style and physique well enough. I can feel Goran's eyes on my back, checking me out as I pass him, sizing me up for our forthcoming match. Since he won the penultimate bout last night, we'll be up against each other next, headlining. Diego runs the nights like a league and right now we're numbers one and two. The season finishes in ten weeks, five more rounds. And then I'm out. For good.

I know Goran's itching to cut that short and take me out.

He's about twice the size of me and thinks it'll be a walk in the park. We'll see. I've studied him. He's lumbery and overprotective of his right knee. I don't think he's aware of it. I'm guessing it's an old injury that doesn't even trouble him anymore, but the important thing is, his guardedness makes him unbalanced. I'm as sure as you can ever be that I've got this. Provided I heal okay in the next couple of weeks, until we're on. Fucking Arlo.

I take the chair that's offered and lean back, looking around. It's just a home office like any other. The desk is dark wood, massive, old and covered in green felt. There is a smaller, modern one, hosting a laptop, pushed against its side to form an L-shape. The carpet is dark grey with a swirly beige pattern, the walls off-white. Dotted around are some nondescript amateur watercolours of the seaside, a few of those old prints with dogs playing snooker and some pages from *The Illustrated London News* from the late 19th century. One showing a bare-knuckle boxing duo, others showing cock and dog fights. Subtle.

It's all very pretend bourgeoisie. Not that any of the Bensons would know what that means or how to spell it. Diego was always bottom set in English. He can't read or write to save his life. Not many people know that.

Right now, though, here, he's definitely top set. His back is to a French window that looks out onto the garden. There is a massive cherry tree behind him. It's in bloom, pretty.

An irrational thought flickers through my mind. Is this the last pretty thing I'm ever going to see?

It's stupid because the Bensons are crooks but not killers. That's why they get on with the police so well.

But — I've never been summoned like this before and my gut, what Arlo left of it, tells me that it can't be a good thing. Another irrational thought follows hot on the heels of the first one.

I don't want the last pretty thing I see to be a cherry tree. I want it to be a pretty American with long red hair, green eyes and a cat pout.

I let my gaze wander away from the tree and look at Diego. He's still smiling, showing his full set of perfectly corrected teeth. Makes him look like a fucking movie star. Brad Pitt's little brother. Only blonder.

He nods to Goran, and Goran shuts the door. From the outside.

We're alone.

Diego's smile falters. He looks serious but not pissed off. One of the advantages of having known your boss from when you were both in nappies is that I can read him like an open book. We're okay. But we have a situation.

"We have a situation," he says. "You went a bit heavy on Arlo. So the pigs aren't happy."

Shit.

Shit. Shit. Shit.

I feel sick.

"Is he dead?" I ask levelly, my heart pounding in my chest.

I haven't killed a man yet and I'd like to keep it that way.

"Nah," Diego answers, grinning. "He might need a hearing aid, but he'll live. Just got some overzealous piglet not happy with the usual write off. So I'd like you to lie low for a bit. Take a holiday or something."

He must be having a laugh. I can't afford to take a fucking holiday. That's the problem with a secured loan versus the nice normal mortgage no bank would give us because we weren't earning enough. You miss your repayment, they take your fucking house.

"Geo–" I catch myself. "Diego, I can't afford to take a holiday, man. I need the money. I don't have to fight but let me at least carry on doing the door, please. Or stick me on some other security detail. I've worked for Santos-Benson security before. Julian likes me. You must have gigs going away from the club," I plead.

He frowns at me the way a mother frowns at her children when they aren't listening.

"Stand up," he says.

I have no idea where he's going with this, but I do as I'm asked.

"Take your jacket off."

I take my jacket off.

"Lift your shirt."

What the fuck?

I lift my shirt.

He stands, leans over the desk and studies my bruises. What's with all the interest in my injuries today? First Grace, now George. He nods sharply at what he sees.

"That's why you're taking a few weeks off," he states unequivocally and sits back down again. "Sit," he demands a second later, and I do. "I can't afford for your mum to find your sorry arse dead in bed one morning. She'd have my hide."

He grins again and I can't help but smile back. Mum always had a reputation among my school friends for being something fierce, basically because any time a teacher would be unfair to us, she'd come in and rip them a new one. Back when. Before *he* broke her.

"So do us a favour," he adds, "and go sit on the beach for a month."

I take a big breath, but he fends me off with a gesture.

"On the house. Full pay."

Too good to be true.

"For what?" I ask, and his grin goes wide like a crocodile's at the dentist.

"I'm glad you asked," he responds. "I'm scheduling you for a fight. Outside the league. Something a bit different," he pauses, cracking his knuckles, and a cold shudder runs down my spine.

I don't like this.

I don't like this one bit.

"Who am I fighting?"

His smile contracts until only a knowing smirk is left.

"Oh, you'll like it, Silas," he whispers, and I notice he's dropped the 'Snake'. "You'll like it a whole lot. And it's gonna make us all a boatload of cash. He isn't new to the game. Just come down from London. We'll build it up while you're gone, and then we'll stage a proper clash of the titans."

He gets up and puts out a hand.

"Just stay away from the club in the meantime. Stay west of town for a bit. Deal?"

It's not like I really have a choice, and he knows it.

I shake his hand, and I am pretty sure I've just sold my soul to the Devil for a golden fiddle.

Grace

When the front door opens, Sheena, Kalina and I are sitting in the kitchen playing Texas Hold'em.

With Monopoly money.

Sheena has a massive thing about not playing for real cash. Suits me 'cause I suck royally at this. I may be the only American at the table, but I've never played poker before. Kalina and Sheena had to explain the rules to me. I'm not sure I'll ever do it again. Way too stressful. They are both absolute fiends at this and it's a bit like being the little clown fish who is watching two sharks circle one another, deciding who gets to eat the little clown fish. But I'm really enjoying their company. Kalina is sitting cross-legged on the chair at the head end of the table, one eyebrow permanently hitched and giving nothing away.

She had some social afternoon drinks thing with her course today and she's wearing a shimmering top and jean shorts with a white frilly hem. No idea where they went but she smells like candy floss and has come home with a partial face painting, a glittering butterfly on her temple. She looks like a fairy princess instead of her normal 'I wish I was a boy' outfit.

I'm sitting with my back to the door and Sheena opposite me. I'm seeing a side to her that's really making me laugh. Inwardly, of course. Poker face and all that jazz. She's adorable, though. She's wearing a white terry cotton bathrobe that's got the Palais logo stitched on a totally pointless breast pocket and her short hair is still hidden under a towel turban, despite the fact she came out of the bath two hours ago and cooked us all soggy pasta with pesto in the meantime. And she's pulling the most pokery poker face imaginable. The thing is, it seems to work.

She's taking us to the cleaners.

It's a good distraction. To a point.

I'm still out of sorts with what happened earlier. In this kitchen. I look around furtively, as if there was anything to see. As if the tiles on the wall are somehow screaming, 'Grace had an orgasm in here! Just over there, by the kettle! Just from a kiss and a little bit of nipple action!' The thought alone drives another bolt of pleasure through me, but this one is mixed with a whole lotta fear and insecurity.

It's the strangest thing because when he's around I don't even think about how insane our attraction to one another is. It just is. But as soon as he's not there, I start questioning my every reaction to this man. You'd think it would be every woman's dream to find a guy who can just make her come like that. But, actually? It's scary as hell. Especially if you know barely anything about him, really.

That's not how that's supposed to go, according to my mother.

According to my mother, you go on a few civilized dates, you get to know each other, see if you have anything in common, check out if your politics, beliefs and outlook in life match and if they do, you take it from there. If he then rocks your boat in bed, bonus. You don't just go *'you smell so good, I want to eat you whole'* and fuck any getting to know each other slowly tropes.

That said, my mother met an American history professor with a penchant for the British Georgian era while he was staying at the Palais, fell into bed with him, got pregnant, followed him to America, realized said historian had no real ambition and no zest for anything that wasn't already dead and buried, split, got the manager's job at the Atlantis, raised me on her own and to my knowledge never had another love affair until she died. I don't even know if she ever had sex again. Sad thought.

Thinking about it like that, I see where she was coming from. Still, I'm not her, there is very little chance of me getting knocked up because I have an implant and I'm only here for another three weeks. So I'll just keep going with the *'you smell good approach'* for now.

And, boy, does he.

I catch his scent now as he enters the kitchen.

He stands a couple of feet behind me and goose bumps break out on my neck.

Good ones.

The best kind.

Sheena looks up from the cards in her hand and the mask of indifference she's been wearing turns into a frown.

"What are you doing home early?"

He doesn't answer immediately, and I look around to catch a glimpse of him. He's standing there like a little boy who's been naughty and who doesn't know which lie to tell. It's a bizarre look on somebody like him.

"I've taken some time off," he finally says. "A month to be precise."

"What?" Sheena puts her cards down and glares at him.

He holds up a hand reassuringly.

"It's fine, Mum. I got it covered. We'll still be able to make payments."

Her frown deepens and for a moment they hold such intense eye contact with one another it's uncomfortable to be around, but then they break away from the encounter and the vibe in the kitchen returns to normal. Sheena picks up her cards again, but there is no way I can concentrate now. Not with him in the room.

"I'm sorry, ladies," I say with a big smile, putting down my hand. "I'm fried," I blatantly lie. "I need to catch some sleep."

I get up from my chair, turn and come face to face with Silas.

Just the look in his eyes makes me tingle from the roots of my hair to the tip of my toes. I can see him searching my face, and then he smiles, just a little. Just one corner of his delectable mouth turning up.

"I'll be up in a minute," he says, and my heart fucking stops.

He's basically just proclaimed to all and sundry, to *his mother*, that we'll be sleeping together.

Not that he's even asked.

Or I ever said yes.

SILAS

It's a bold move, entirely unlike me.

I was raised by Mum to believe in what she calls courting. Taking it slow, being friends first, all that crap. Which isn't really crap. I know that. It's what Niamh and I were built on. She was supposed to be my one. Until *he* fucked it all up for us. But this thing with Grace? It's completely different. It's like she's in my blood. I've known the woman a week and I can't imagine her not being here, her scent not lingering in the air. Torturing me, *healing* me.

And the thing is, I decided something after I left the Bensons' today. If there is even the remote possibility that I'm gonna get killed in a month's time, I want to spend that month with *her*. Have more of what happened in the kitchen this afternoon. Have whatever she is willing to let me have. And she seems to be okay with that idea 'cause I can hear her going up the stairs and opening the door to my, *our*, room.

At the table, Kalina and Mum have put their cards down. Kalina unfolds her crossed legs and moves around to sit in Grace's chair.

"Heads up?" Mum asks, and they nod at each other before Mum starts reshuffling the pack.

She throws me a quick look, somewhere between curiosity and a warning. But she doesn't say anything. It's so surreal for me to behave this forward with a girl, I think even Sheena O'Brien is lost for words.

I turn around and follow Grace up the stairs, my heart racing faster with every step I'm getting nearer to her. It's taken pretty much all my courage, declaring us just now like that, but I really did have a bit of an epiphany when I left the Benson Mansion.

I saw the old man come back, parking up his 4x4 on the driveway. I guess he'd been out in the country, shooting pheasants or something, since the car was proper dirty and he had all the gear. Flat cap, tweet jacket, rifle, the lot. The gentrification clobber is funny as hell to me because I remember him in the cheap suits he used to wear, sporting knock-off Rolex watches.

He got out of the car just as I got on my bike and he looked at me in a way that left no doubt that he knew why I was there.

So I'm pretty sure I know what they're up to. I've seen it before, once or twice.

They don't do it often but occasionally they go for a big rig. They're gonna build up this other guy, and then they are going to tell one of us to lose, depending on the odds. But if that's me, I already know I won't stay down. Not 'cause I'm stupid or because of honour or any shit like that, but because when that red mist descends, I will fight till I'm done. Always. I wouldn't be able to pull the plug. Even if I wanted to. It's as simple and as fucked up as that. 'Cause I'm a fucking psycho.

I stop in my tracks.

What the fuck am I doing?

I can't drag her down with me.

I turn around and bolt out of the house.

Grace

I can *feel* the exact moment he changes his mind.

I listen to him ascend the stairs, and then suddenly he stops in his tracks and the next thing I hear is the front door falling shut.

I'm stunned. And stung. It fucking hurts. Like nothing's ever hurt before. Full frontal rejection. I should be used to it. But normally it comes when I mention the cancer patient at home.

Mentioned. Past tense. I need to remember that.

It doesn't come after we've already slept in the same bed.

After he's given me an orgasm.

After it's been decided we're gonna do it again.

It comes from some guy called Brad or Chad or Tatum who looked like potential until he realized I might have some other obligations aside from baking him apple pie, fucking him senseless and bearing his children. Not from...*Silas*.

That thought alone is absurd.

How can I presume to know this man already, how can he be so ingrained in my soul after what?

A week.

A week of nothing.

Not that last night was nothing.

Not that this afternoon in the kitchen was nothing.

Not that the way he looked at me about five minutes ago was nothing.

I'm so frustrated I want to scream.

Instead, I start sobbing.

Until there is a gentle knock on the door.

I wipe the tears from my face.

"Come in," I say, my voice hopeful, despite the fact I haven't heard the front door open again since he left and I can't feel his presence in the house.

It's Sheena.

Luna follows hot on her heels, immediately overtakes her, jumps on the bed next to me and starts rubbing up against me, purring. I pat her head, avoiding Sheena's eye contact.

When I get home, I'm gonna go to a shelter and get myself a cat. It's a flight of fancy, of course. 'Cause in reality, I'll have to room with some randoms and pets are usually a no-no. Reality sucks. But it was a nice thought.

The mattress next to me dips and I finally face my hostess. She's taken the towel turban off and her hair is spiked up in all directions, making her look like a hedgehog. She puts her hand on my arm, just above the wrist, and gives it a gentle squeeze.

"Don't give up on him, ducky," she says. "He's a troubled soul, my Silas. But a *good* one. He'll come around. I've never seen him like this with a girl before. Not even with Niamh. Hang on in there."

"Who's Niamh?"

"She was his first and only serious girlfriend."

"Ah," I say, my heart dropping about two stories. Here we go, an ex he never got over. What d'ya know.

She shakes her head.

"Don't even think it, ducky. That was ages ago. When they were teens. Ended just before his twentieth birthday. She's in London now, getting married soon and he's had at least one other bite at the cherry since. Besides, it didn't end well. Though they're still on speaking terms. But, trust me, there is nothing left there."

"What do you mean, it didn't end well?"

She takes a deep breath as if she is about to tell me a long, heart wrenching story but then she shrugs.

"Truth be told, I'm not sure. All I know is they were fine one day then not the next. Maybe a bit tepid but fine. You know, lukewarm as opposed to the burning hot between you and him."

I squirm. It's weird hearing his mother say it. But she just shrugs again and raises her eyebrows.

"I'm not blind, ducky. And you two are *scorching*."

Her voice is so matter of fact, there is no real room for embarrassment. It's still weird, though. The idea that what happens between this guy and me is palpable even to others. Even to his *mum*.

"The thing is. He's not been okay ever since. But with you? He can't seem to handle it, but for the first time in a long time, I think there may be hope for that boy. He needs this. And I don't really know you, Grace, but I think you might need this, too," she carries on and grins, making her instantly look twenty years younger, before she gets up, stands in front of me and lays her hands on my shoulders, imploringly. "So do us a favour, ducky. Don't give up on him."

I don't tell her that I don't think I could, even if I wanted to.

Silas

I sit at the beach in the darkness, listening to the waves for a very long time, before my thoughts start kicking into gear.

When I got here, I was just numb. Numb with the realisation that for the first time in a very long time, I want something, *someone*, for myself but I can't have it, can't have her.

It's been over five years since *that* night. Since *he* fucked off out of our lives and left us with this mountain of debt. Not counting the Cerys fiasco, all I've done since then is work, train, fight, repeat. It's taken four seasons to build up my rep as Snake and get to the top of the league. Not that I really care about the status. But I was so close to just finishing on a high note, wiping the slate clean and being done with it. A few more fights and I could have started on becoming the kind of man a woman like Grace deserves.

I could have left TripleX, doing something normal for a living. Fuck knows what, but that's not the point.

But with this new deal on the table, there is no chance of that.

It's one thing being an illegal fighter, it's quite another being part of a rig where no doubt powerful people will be conned out of a sizable chunk of their ill-gotten gains. The more I think about Diego's proposal, the fishier I think this set up is. The maths just doesn't add up. There is something he isn't telling me.

And then it hits me.

It's so glaringly obvious it should have come with its own personal neon sign.

One month isn't long enough to build someone else up to make it worth a rig.

You need titans to put on a clash of the titans, and a titan needs breeding for at least a couple of seasons.

What the fuck is Diego up to?

Who the fuck am I fighting?

Grace

After Sheena leaves, I lie wide awake until the small hours.

I go pee three times, creep downstairs to get a glass of water, try reading, try listening to music, play around on my cell, but nothing keeps me occupied for long, or gets me to sleep.

Not surprising, considering I'd been asleep all day.

Not surprising, considering I keep listening out for the front door key entering the lock.

I wonder where he went. Did he change his mind about taking a holiday and went back to work? I know he's security in a nightclub. I wonder what kind of club it is. I haven't really explored the nightlife in Brighton yet. Not on my radar. I'm not big on going out dancing. It's not that I don't like to dance, I do, but working in a bar means that on my nights off I like the quiet. My own company and a book, now that I'm not coming home to caring for Mum any longer. Sad for a young woman in her mid-twenties, really. Maybe I should go out one night while I'm here. I wonder if Kalina knows where to go. Maybe we could go together.

I'm thinking about it when I finally hear the sound I've been hanging on for.

The key turns in the lock downstairs and my heart starts racing as soon as I hear it. A quick glance at my cell tells me it's one in the morning, so he didn't go back to work. I feel relief at that.

It's not really presumptuous to think that his bruises are connected to what he does for a living and I don't think he's fit to go back. Those were serious injuries. It dawns on me that that is what the 'holiday' is about. It's sick leave. He just couldn't tell his mother.

I listen out for his movements, waiting, hoping he'll come up, but he doesn't. I get up as quietly as I can, because if there is one thing I've learned staying here it's that British houses are extremely badly soundproofed. I step softly over to the door and open it a little. The hallway is plunged into darkness, but some light shines up from the kitchen. I hear the faucet running downstairs, and then it's turned off. He kills the light in the kitchen, the flick of the switch loud in the quiet, traveling all the way up to my ears. After that, I feel more than hear his movement through the house. His steps are light, barefooted.

I open the door farther and half push my body through the gap, still listening intently. My breathing seems like a steam train in the quiet and I hold my breath. His footsteps move along the hallway and then stop. I'm convinced he's got one foot on the bottom step and I can feel myself clench in anticipation.

But then I hear him turn and move away, followed a few seconds later by the soft click of the living room door being shut. Tears of frustration pool in my eyes, but I'll be damned if I let myself be written off like that.

I go back to my, *our*, room, switch on the light and open the wardrobe of which Silas so gallantly cleared half for me when we came to our arrangement.

I don't own any sexy lingerie, there has been zero need for it in my life so far, but I do have a nice cream silk blouse that hangs long enough to cover my ass when it's not tucked into a skirt or pants. I take off my yoga pants, panties and camisole and slip on the blouse. I love silk, *real* silk, the way it's cool and warm at the same time, the way it caresses your body like a summer breeze. There is nothing like it. I spent an entire month's tips on this blouse.

For a moment, I think about running a brush through my hair, but it seems too contrived. *Hey, look at me, just casually strolling by in my sexy silk wear with my freshly combed tresses.* The blouse on its own will have to do. There is no mirror in this room and actually that's cool by me. I already know when it comes to him, to *us*, it doesn't matter how I look or what I wear. He'd have me in my rattiest old gym shirt. The silk is purely for me, for my confidence. It's armor in case he turns me down again.

I shut my eyes for a moment, swallow hard and then I leave the room.

I switch the TV on with the sound so low I can barely hear it, sit down on the sofa and wait for the paracetamol to kick in. I'm in fucking agony. I slide down a little and lean my head against the back rest, so I'm not as creased at the midriff.

It's funny, the curve of pain. For the first few hours, the adrenaline completely kills it, then it starts hurting and then a day and half or so later it starts *really* hurting. I'm at the *really* hurting stage. I barely made it home from the beach just now. I have to concede, whatever else he is up to, George has done me a favour laying me off.

The pain killers will do fuck all, I know that already. Ibuprofen would be more effective but, like aspirin, it thins the blood, tends to make the bruising worse. And I stay away from all things opiate based. Codeine, morphine and all that shit. Dulls the head, slows your reflexes. Not for me, thanks.

I know I'm just distracting myself from not thinking about her.

Upstairs. In my bed.

I need to apologise to her. I shouldn't have done that. Told her I'd be up, in front of my *mother*, and then just leave her hanging. She must think I'm a complete dick. Fuck.

I squish my eyes shut in annoyance at myself. As I open them, I catch a movement at the edge of my vision. The door handle is being pushed down gently. My heart stops. I know it's her. Mum is fast asleep, she sleeps like a stone these days. Besides, she'd just barge in like a normal person, and Kalina doesn't ever come in here.

I let my head roll to the side and watch Grace step into the room then gently shut the door again, her back to me, not looking. She looks like one of those airbrushed fucking fantasy drawings, doused in the blue-grey light coming from the telly.

She's wearing a shimmery, light-coloured blouse that reflects the sheen from the screen, making her glow almost eerily. The hem falls past her butt to mid-thigh, not revealing anything but the most innocuous part of her legs. Yet the fabric skims over her curves in all the right places in all the right ways.

Her long red hair is wild, falling down her front and obscuring her nipples under the silk, but I just know they are stiff as fuck underneath. My dick wakes up at that thought — and the sight of her.

This woman.

She turns to lean against the wall and looks at me. One knee locked, the other hitched up and the leg resting on the ball of her foot — that stance all prostitutes know the world over. Only on her it isn't cheap, it's fucking mind-blowing. I can't help but stare. Then she smiles at me and bites her bottom lip.

I'm fucking toast.

Grace

Hell, yeah, the Julia Roberts routine is working for him.

He's hard, his cock straining visibly against his jeans zipper.

I did that, by just standing here.

The thought gives me a glut of pleasure, and I shiver as I can feel myself turn to syrup.

We do that thing again, where we just stare at one another and the heat in the room goes up with every second that passes. I already know he's not gonna bolt on me again and it would be so easy to put on a show for him. I'm not wearing any underwear. He doesn't know that yet. I could slowly unbutton my blouse, let one hand go to my breast, the other between my legs. Pleasure myself while he watches.

Another jolt, another rush of liquid.

What would it be like? I've never masturbated in front of somebody before. Would I even be able to make myself come? Or would I feel too under the spotlight, under too much pressure? I've been thinking about it all afternoon, how he achieved with a kiss what no other has been able to achieve with full on intercourse and I've come to the conclusion it's 'cause *he wasn't even trying*.

I watch the hunger in his eyes, watch how his hand comes over his hard-on and pushes down hard. I'm not even sure it's a conscious gesture until he moans under the pressure.

I can feel moisture run past my slit.

I've never been this wet before.

I've got to see, find out for myself.

Without any show, I hitch up my blouse, expose my sex and cup myself. The motion pushes my lips slightly apart and my juice oozes out, as if I'd squeezed open a ripe fruit. I let go, shocked at my own arousal, smooth my blouse down again and try to collect myself. I breathe, trying to still the pulse in my clit.

This wasn't the plan. At least not like this. First, we need to talk. A little.

SILAS

That was without the shadow of a doubt the sexiest thing I have ever seen. Her cupping herself. Her syrup dripping through her fingers, glistening between them in the flicker of the TV. The shock on her face. Fuck me. I want her to carry on. I want to watch her. Really, I want her to do a whole load of things, and then I want to do a whole load of things *to* her.

This is so not me.

Not anymore.

Never really was.

Only with her, it seems to be.

Not that that helps because realistically I can't do shit right now. I'm in excruciating pain. I wouldn't be able to move the way I would want to move. Wouldn't be able to give her what I want to give her. Not by a long shot. So I wait for what she does next, in the hope she'll carry on fingering her pussy, but she doesn't. Instead, she speaks.

"You didn't come up," she says.

Sounding normal. How the fuck is she managing to sound this normal? I'm getting the impression this is a woman who you could go down on while she's behind the bar and none of the punters on the other side would be any the wiser when she comes in your mouth. My dick goes even harder at the image. I had no idea that was my scene.

"No," I grunt out in answer.

Like a caveman.

"Why not?"

There are so many answers to that question and I can't think of a single one of them right now. All I can think is that I want to watch her come. I want to see her face as she loses all control. And then I want to feel that mouth that she's licking right now wrapped around my dick. Watch me slide in and out of those pussycat lips.

That thought snaps me out of the trance that's got us in its grip, and

I go very, very still inside. I look for the frozen bit inside myself, the dark matter I never want to unpack. And, yeah, it's still there, alright. But that doesn't change the fact her lips would look amazing around my cock. It takes me by surprise that I can allow that image, but I embrace it, warily.

I realise she is still waiting for an answer. I try to find the truth, all the truths, for her in one word.

"Conscience," I finally reply.

She smiles at that.

"Fuck conscience," she says.

And starts coming towards me.

Grace

"Pretty sure that's the attitude that got the world all fucked up," he quips, and I'm impressed that he's found his capacity to string a sentence together.

A second ago it seemed like he'd gone all singular words on me. Which, granted, with Silas is still more than his usual silence. But there was also a weird withdrawnness I hadn't witnessed before. Like he'd completely disappeared into his own head. So I wonder where this sudden soliloquy has sprung from. But as I get closer, I see the vein pulsing in his neck and the twitch on his upper lip, and suddenly I have a pretty good idea.

He's nervous.

He's turned on but he's also a little insecure, *vulnerable*, and that gives me the confidence to carry on doing what I'm doing.

I come to a halt in front of him and stand between his legs. We look at each other without touching for a beat until, suddenly, quick as a snake, his hands come up, under my shirt and grip my hips, firmly.

An entirely new sensation blooms in me. I feel *held*. Not just in place but in time and space. I have barely processed the sensation when his thumbs start doing that swiping thing, so near my sex yet so far away. He's gonna drive me crazy.

I lean forward, my long hair falling between us. I've got to kiss him. Now. My mouth finds his and I press my lips to him, tenderly. He shudders then draws back a bit to speak.

"Careful, I'm still in agony, Grace. I can't really move."

I nod in understanding and kiss him again before I let my mouth trail around to find his ear. I suck his earlobe between my teeth and play with it a little before I let the tip of my tongue run around the shell of his ear. I have no idea if he'll like this, I know I would. I think. Again, not something anyone has ever done to me.

He bucks on the couch and I smile to myself. I guess he likes it.

The buck comes with a moan that's part pleasure, part pain from the involuntary movement. But he never lets go of my hips. It's then that I know that no matter what, he'd never ever let me fall. The realization is almost too big to bear. Part of me wants to run. But still he's holding me fast.

"Touch yourself," he says hoarsely.

It's not a command, it's a request.

"I want to watch you."

I can feel in his hands on my hips that he is shaking with desire. I'd bet my bottom dollar that this is new territory for him as much as it is for me. I straighten up and unbutton my blouse. I don't let it fall to the floor, I leave it open at the front. I'd feel too exposed entirely nude, I need the idea that I could cover myself if someone came in. Suddenly I feel self-conscious again but somehow, he knows.

He looks up at me then kisses both my hands that are hanging by my sides in turn before he leans forward and plants a kiss on my sex. Nowhere near the squishy bits, just softly on the silk fluff covering my mound, a fraction above my slit. The way my body reacts, though, you'd think he'd stuck his tongue all the way up inside me.

He looks up at me again and slowly I bring my right hand in front of me and slip a finger between my lips. I'm dripping. Literally. No need to dip into my hole and gather the moisture to spread around my clit. It's there already, smothering it. I'm almost *too* slick, I can't get the friction I need.

And I can't watch him watch me, it's too intense, so I shut my eyes and miss the cue that tells me one of his hands is about to slip around and spread my lips apart.

So he can see, I realize.

It does something else as well, though. Holding me open like that spreads tension across the skin, pushes my clit against my finger and suddenly the friction I need is there. I add a second finger and I rub over my clit in nice tight circles, feeling the tension build deep in my belly.

If I were alone, I'd be flying already, but something about knowing that he's there, holds me back, *frustrates* me. I can't get there knowing these could be his fingers, knowing he could *help* me here. I open my eyes and look down at him. His gaze is fixated on my fingers. It's hot, the way he watches me. But it's still not enough.

"Silas," I call to him hoarsely, and he looks up. "Please."

Silas

"Please," she says, and I know exactly what it is she needs.

I've never been so sure of anything in my life.

I cross two fingers and slide them into her slowly. For a moment, she forgets to circle her clit and I catch her finger with my thumb, like we're playing thumb war, and kick start it again. She clenches around me when I do, and I feel another stream of her syrup slick her up. Jesus. I've never known a woman could get so *wet*. I'm slowly circling my crossed fingers inside her, pushing the rest of my hand against wherever it finds skin.

She's panting and gyrating on my hand while her fingers flick ever more quickly over her clit. Her juices cover our hands and I'm torn between wanting to watch her come like this and wanting to taste her.

She makes the decision for me when her free hand suddenly cradles the back of my head and gathers me forward. I lean in, ignoring the sharp pang of pain that that elicits from my bruises, and with one long lick over her fingers and clit, I push her over the edge.

Grace

I see stars. For real.

His tongue hits my clit and my fingers at the same time and his digits inside me gyrate harder, hitting just the right spot.

I explode and the orgasm punches holes all through my body. There are fireworks behind my eyes. My pussy contracts so hard, so rapidly, it's painful. And when I come down, I'm a bit lost but for that one steadying hand that throughout all of this Silas kept on my hip. It's grounding me.

So is the smile he gives me as he slowly slides his fingers out of me. They trail up to my abdomen where he writes something invisible across my tummy in the ink of my juices. It's erotic in a playful way I didn't think he'd have in him and I look down in wonder.

"What's that?" I ask, still breathless.

He grins at my belly button, pulls me towards him and kisses me where he's just drawn the letters.

"Not telling," he says.

There is something so sweet about it, it somehow doesn't go with the raging hard-on that's still straining against his jeans. Or with any of him, really.

He sees me looking and a serious expression spreads over his face. He starts buttoning my shirt up from below, reaching up as far as he can. Then he pats the space on the couch next to him.

"Sit down," he says.

I narrow my eyes at him and look pointedly at the bulge in his jeans.

"What about you?"

He takes my hand and tugs at it, using the other to guide me into a sitting position next to him.

"He'll shut up in a minute. Just sit with me for a bit. He'll get his turn. But first let's do this."

He twists toward me and I can see in his face that the movement hurts him, but he dismisses the pain as if it weren't important. Then he reaches up into the hair at the nape of my neck and pulls me in for a kiss. He leisurely plays with my mouth for a few minutes, caressing me with his tongue, chasing mine, and then he draws back and smiles.

"Who are you, Grace Turner?" he asks gently, sprawling his other hand over the swell of my left breast, roughly where my heart should be. "Tell me your secrets."

And I do.

SILAS

We sit in the living room until the small hours and alternate between kissing and her telling me about her life.

She's snuggled into my side, the one that hurts a little less than the other, and she remains mindful of my injuries, keeping herself light against me.

My dick goes hard and then partially calms down again a few times during the night. She's taken to rubbing the bulge when we kiss, staying on the outside of my jeans, and I won't let it go further. Not yet. It takes all my willpower, but no matter what, I'm scared enough to stay in control. And she seems to get that without me having to spell it out for her.

Not that she's not pushing the boundaries every so often.

There is a moment, while I'm not watching 'cause I'm too busy concentrating on sucking on her neck without leaving hickeys, when she's massaging my dick through the denim, and then her fingers curl around the waistband and she touches the top of his head. I nearly come there and then. It's like she's turned back time for me. Turned me back into that teenage boy, so full of lust and devoid of darkness.

She's amazing.

When we're not caressing each other, she talks or sometimes both. She tells me about growing up in DC, about her mum, about her dad who remarried and who's got a new family she never sees despite the fact they only live two blocks away. About not going to university because her mum got sick and about not having a clue what she wants to do with her life. She doesn't talk about feeling lost, but she doesn't need to. I get it anyway. I feel the same.

Granted, I still have a mum.

But Mum knows so little about the real me, the me I've become, it's almost as if we were strangers. At some point during that whole lark of picking up *his* — I force myself to think his name for the first time in ages — *Rowan's,* debts, we stopped being mother and son and became business partners.

Business partners without a business.

I don't really want to go down that rabbit hole right now, so I concentrate on the beautiful woman sitting next to me. While Grace talks, she goes from being super animated one minute to stroking my face, she seems to have a thing for that, the next.

And it's those caresses that really get under my skin.

Being touched with that much love and care. As if I somehow matter to her already.

There are a few times when I feel the impulse to bolt from her again, but I remind myself that there is no need.

We're safe, we're on a time scale.

She'll be gone in three weeks.

And I'll likely be dead in four.

Grace

I wake up to the sound of somebody jingling car keys next to my ear.

I try to pry my eyes open, but they're not playing ball. It was *very* late. Or very early, depending on your point of view.

Silas and I sat in the living room all night talking, cuddling, making out a little more. Like kids. It was nice. Correction, it was *great*.

Admittedly, I used up most of the oxygen in the room, but even though he only said marginally more than usual, I found out his deepest, darkest secret. Around five in the morning the no-sugar eating plan goes out of the window and he'll make you candied bread if you ask nicely. Way too much candied bread, so he has to have a whole load as well. And he pulls the most adorable face if you let him have sugar. I get the feeling that before the muscle and the fighting, he was just this really normal, sweet kid. The kind I would have made eyes at in high school. Though I have to admit I'm starting to appreciate the muscle as well.

Since I couldn't touch most of him for fear of hurting him and he wouldn't let me get down to business, I played a lot with his arms last night, running my hands up and down those curves. It's funny how that word is always used for women's bits but, actually, it's men who have curvature, really. Hard, smoothly skinned, perfect curves. Women have jiggly lumps. I giggle into the pillow at my own thoughts and he nudges me.

"You're laughing, which means you are awake, Grace Turner."

I love the way he says my full name. No idea why. I love it even more that he lowers his mouth to hover by my ear now and starts whispering into it.

"Come on, beautiful, it's afternoon, the sun is shining, the car is washed, probably, and I've packed a picnic."

I turn my face toward him, open my eyes and lay a hand on his cheek. I swipe my thumb through the tawny stubble. It's longer and softer than it was yesterday and just the right kind of rough. His eyes are trained on mine and my heart begins pounding again already.

"Kiss me first," I demand.

And he does.

Gently at first and then thoroughly.

SILAS

I have no idea why Bramber Castle of all places but apparently, it's on the list.

It's not even a castle. It's the remnants of a wall on a motte in forested land and a tiny chapel with a graveyard that has about twenty headstones in it, at most. Around the bottom of the motte there is a dry moat, a dark and dingy circle of soggy leaves that you can walk around in, if you fancy getting your boots muddy.

"It really is completely unspectacular, Grace," I tell her again.

I've been warning her for the entire drive here not to have any expectations, with graphic descriptions of how there is *fuck all there* to see and she appears to be in stitches. I didn't think I was being particularly funny, but it makes me happy to be able to make her laugh. She has a nice laugh, all deep and husky, like it should belong to a woman twice her age who smokes three packs a day and drowns a bottle of Scotch each night.

"I have no idea what I said that's so hilarious," I say as we go around the roundabout and take a sharp left up the steep stone chip path that leads to the ruin.

The Capri bottoms out on the ascent, slipping and sliding on the shitty road surface and throwing up stones at the paintwork. I groan inwardly. Mum will kill me if there is any damage to her baby.

"It's not *what* you're saying," Grace informs me. "It's *how* you're saying it."

"And how am I saying it?"

"With a *lot* of words."

She composes herself as we pull into the car park, for want of a better word. It's basically a slightly bigger gravel patch with room for about five cars. Four if they are Land Rovers. Three if one is a bus. Today, there is only us.

"What's that supposed to mean?"

I park up and she looks at me sideways with an indulging smile. The kind you get from a teacher who really likes you but who you're driving nuts.

"That you've said more in the last ten minutes than you've said since I've met you. I like the strong but not so silent version of Silas."

"You had me down as the strong and silent type?" I ask, gobsmacked.

"Well, yeah."

She makes a 'duh' face at me then gets out of the car.

By the time I've secured the Capri to Mum's specs, Grace has already wandered off towards the little chapel and is looking at the graves.

I sidle up to her.

"In school, I got more detentions for talking in class than for fighting, I'll have you know."

She grins and I know it's the 'I'll have you know' that got her. She loves those English phrases the way I love it when she says shit like 'cooties'. It tickles her. But she doesn't rib me for it. Instead, she wanders over to the next gravestone.

"So what happened?" she asks when I follow her.

Rowan, I think unbidden. *Rowan happened.*

And for the fraction of a second, I even contemplate telling her about him. Maybe not all of it but at least some of it. The more palatable parts. The debts. But she's already found another grave and looks intently at the weathered inscription.

"Hah!" she exclaims, pointing. "There I am!"

I look at the gravestone and sure enough, one of the names on it is *Grace*.

I frown.

"Is that some kind of game you play? Finding Graces in graveyards?"

"No, dummy," she says, laughing and slapping me playfully on the arm. "Although I like it. I might do that from now on. Sounds like a hobby. I need a hobby now Mum's dead. No, she," she adds, pointing at the name on the stone, "I believe, is the reason I'm called Grace."

She takes my hand, entwines her fingers with mine and drags me away from the chapel and up the motte, towards the lone wall that is the 'castle'. All the while she carries on talking, as if we did this all the time. Walking around landmarks, holding hands.

"According to my mum, she and my father came here for a picnic the day after they made me. Or at least the day after they first fucked. I don't know how often they did it before he went back to the States. Whatever. The important thing is, after he returned to America and she found out she was pregnant, she came back here to think about what she was gonna do. Like have me or not, ya know. And at some point in all of that she found my name on a tombstone."

She lets go of my hand, cocks her head, pulls a face and points at it with both index fingers.

"Ta-da."

Grace

He smiles at that. Properly. Eyes, mouth, cheekbones and everything.

It's friggin' amazing to look at. This serious, serious guy with all his muscle and bruises and fucking brooding *darkness*, who's given me barely as much as a tilted-up corner of his mouth so far to show amusement, is in a full-facial smile attack.

I stare at him in wonder before he comes around to stand in front of me, reaches out and clasps my shoulders just by my clavicle. Clasps them in his strong, busted-up, steadying hands and starts doing that sweeping thing with his thumb, brushing the base of my throat with each swipe. And then his face goes serious, still smiley but earnest at the same time.

"I'm glad she did," he says, and when he sees the mystified expression on my face, clarifies, "have you."

And with that he completely undoes me.

Tears well up in my eyes and I can feel the need to cry the way you feel the need to pull out a splinter. The first drop spills over and starts running down my cheek, and then he does the most amazing thing.

He doesn't wipe it away, he doesn't tell me not to cry, he doesn't say something about how he didn't mean to do that. No, he pulls me close and wraps me in his arms and lets me sob into his chest until I'm full on ugly crying, shaking all over. The harder I cry, the more I push up against him, practically trying to clamber into him and my belly makes contact with his. He winces, but when I try to draw back and apologize for my clumsiness, he holds me even tighter, pressed against those bruises we both know lie beneath his shirt.

Silas

I let her cry for as long as she needs to, which isn't that long. After a while, she unhuddles a little and looks up at me with a tentative smile.

"I need a tissue."

She sniffles.

"There are some in the car," I reply, but she doesn't make any moves to step out of my embrace.

I like it. The making her feel safe thing. Safe enough to come in front of me, safe enough to laugh, safe enough to cry. It makes me feel like I can still do something positive in this life. On occasion. The image of her coming on my hand last night floats through my brain. God, she was spectacular. My dick stirs, inappropriate wanker that he is, and I know she can feel it.

She steps back a little, letting one hand slide down my back until it reaches my buttock and lets it rest on there. Well, almost. Her fingers are actually gently kneading and probing. Like I wouldn't notice. But she is so surreptitious about it, it's horny as hell. Jesus, I can't keep up with her. A minute ago, she was still in grief mode.

She brings her other hand around the front and indicates my general abdominal area.

"How long until you're healed, you think?" she asks, the trace of a wicked smile playing around her lips.

"Couple of weeks," I answer truthfully, and her face falls a little.

I bark a laugh, cup her jaw in one hand and tilt her head up.

"I can wait," I say to her, searching her eyes, silently trying to transmit the words I should really say but can't, not without an explanation that I'm not ready to give just yet.

I need to wait. I'm not ready. Yet. But whatever you do, don't stop trying.

Then I shove those thoughts out of my mind and just kiss her. Those lips. They are divine. I know it's romanticised crap, but it isn't. Not with her. I could kiss her all day. And then some. She never seems to wear lipstick or any of that shit, so you're guaranteed to get the taste of pure Grace. Today, it's pure Grace with a seasoning of saltiness from her tears. I lick at her lips and she opens her mouth, her tongue eager to meet mine. We stand there for a few minutes, tongue fucking again until we're both breathing erratically. We part for air and she stares into my eyes for a moment. I can practically see her brain cells ticking over. And then she speaks.

"Show me the woods," she says in a low purr, and before I can respond she's suddenly tugging me along again, down towards the moat.

Grace

I'd spotted the entrance to the moat as soon as we got here. Not that it's hard to find. You park up and level to your right is the chapel, the motte is in front of you and the dirt bank that leads into the dried-up moat is on your left.

I practically pull Silas along behind me, back down the motte, and then we slide down the bank together. He huffs a few times in pain but doesn't complain. Like he ever would. I couldn't imagine doing anything but being laid up in bed if I had those injuries of his. And here he is, driving me around, taking me to Bramber, holding me tight and now horsing around in the mud with me.

And it's super muddy when we hit the bottom. Squelching. It's also immediately dark around us, in that beautiful, inimitable gray-green light of the woods that I love so much.

The smell of wet earth and of last fall's decaying leaves that cover the ground below our feet mixed with the fresh spring scent of the blossoming trees on the mound above our heads hits my nostrils. Their root systems grow down over the bank and into the trench of the moat, and you have to be careful not to trip over the hidden ones that snake along the ground like fingers, so we have to step carefully as we begin making our way around, hand in hand, until I find the thing I'm looking for.

SILAS

It's a different world down here. Quiet and dark and earthy.

It speaks to a part of me that hasn't been awake in a long time. The one she's been prodding and poking and bringing back to life ever since she turned up. The one she is trying to rustle awake a bit more now, if my gut instinct is right.

I see her eye up each and every single one of the occasional trees that have rooted down here, in the middle of the moat. They're all much younger than the ones above us, slender and often growing a bit askew, leaning this way or that. I know the moment she finds the one she deems right, her eyes lighting up with mischief.

The tree is tilted heavily, easy to lean against. She tries to pull me around to back me up against it, and I know in a flash what it is she wants to do. No chance. No matter how much I would love to see my dick in her mouth, I stand my ground and she frowns at me.

I shake my head and spin her around to turn the tables on her.

Grace

He backs me up against the tree in three quick paces, braces a hand on the trunk above my head, cradles my jaw in the other, the way he does, and then starts kissing me again with fervor, taking up where we left off above. It's dominant and sexy and yet I want to howl with frustration. This wasn't what I had in mind. I wanted to taste him, seduce him, give him back some of what he has already given me.

In the last two days, this man has given me two earth-shattering orgasms *and I haven't even seen his cock yet.*

I had plans for that. They involved my lips, my tongue, a little bit of teeth and hopefully a whole load of come to swallow. I want to see him lose it the way he makes me lose it.

While I'm half seething about his diversion tactics and half being driven wild by his kisses, his hand leaves my jaw, trails down my neck, slips under my neckline and into my bra. He cups my breast and squeezes, hard, giving me a jolt all the way to my clit. How the fuck does he do that? He keeps kneading my tit rhythmically, scissoring my nipple between his index and middle finger every so often. I see sparks every time those pincers clamp down on me and I have to shut my eyes, leaning more heavily against the trunk in my back. I moan into his mouth. He withdraws to let his lips trail around my jawline, up to my ear.

"You are so fucking hot," he growls and pinches my nipple again at the same time. Then his tongue licks, all flat and soft, along the shell of my ear and I forget all about him holding out on me. I forget my own fucking name.

Another moan escapes me, louder this time.

"Again, louder," he whispers as he relaxes and shuts those fingers around my nipple then circles my ear with his tongue again.

I actually buck at that — while I give him exactly the noise he's after. What did I say about demand not being sexy? Boy, was I wrong. I hear him choke at my response and draw back. I open my eyes. He's looking at me, shaking with lust. His face is flushed, he's panting. I've never seen anything sexier.

"I want to touch you," I implore hoarsely. "Please."

A flicker of pain lights up in his eyes then dies again. He nods sharply.

"My way," he says, and then he takes the hand that was steadying him against the tree trunk down from above my head, runs it lightly down my arm and takes the back of my hand in his palm, lacing his fingers through mine.

He brings our hands to his bulge and pushes them down hard. This much I was allowed to do before, so I already know he's big. Not huge, not stupidly hung, not intimidating, but *big*.

He's wearing Levis today and once he gives me a little room to maneuver, I can slip my fingers through the gaps between the buttons of his fly. When I do, I hit the opening in the boxer shorts just right and a second later I've got the silky skin of his shaft under my fingertips. He shivers under my touch, groaning, and it gives me a rush like no other.

He's still got his palm over my hand, but he's forgotten to be bossy about it, so I start unbuttoning his fly, one-handed, my instinct telling me that if I bring the other hand into it, he'll clam up again. Instead, I use that one to reach into the stubble on his cheek, stroking his face reassuringly while I, *we*, liberate his cock from its prison.

I glance down as soon as it springs free. It looks gorgeous, all smooth and thick with a nice, gentle curve. I don't get to look for long because as soon as he's exposed, his head falls forward, the cheek I'm not caressing leaning against mine, the beard bristles scratching me lightly each time he moves.

We're really close up against each other now, cheek to cheek, his hand still on my tit and my, *our*, hands on his cock. There is barely room between us for what we do next, but it makes it so much more intense.

We start pumping him, slowly at first, and I'm learning with every move just how much pressure he likes. His grip on my hand gets firmer, his breathing in my ear louder, and I can feel those early drops of come running down onto our entwined fingers. And then, suddenly, without warning, he really starts fucking into our hands. A steady but fast rhythm that makes my insides clench like crazy because I know he would drive me insane with it if he was inside me. The idea is making me moan in tune with him and I grip onto his jaw, trying to steady him, me, both.

And then he falls forward, silent, violent shudders racking his body.

His cock pulsates, like a heart beating in my palm, and a ream of semen spills over our hands.

SILAS

I'd forgotten how good it is to feel somebody else's hands on me.

For the touch not to be solely your own. I'd forgotten how light you feel when you come down to earth after the explosion. I'd forgotten how much I craved *intimacy*.

This woman. She has no idea.

I take one hand out of her bra and with the other one let go of hers. I wipe my spunk off on the tree, button up, and then I gather her into my arms. I'm still shaking, and I still can't find any words, so I nuzzle her neck and I hope that speaks for itself.

She laughs lightly while she takes a leaf out of my book and wipes her hand on the bark behind her before she accepts my embrace.

"Picnic?" she whispers into my ear as she hugs me back softly. "Somebody mentioned food."

Grace

The next ten days are probably the favorite of my entire adult life. We basically go and live in each other's pocket.

By day, Silas keeps helping me with working through my list, never once questioning the significance of the items on it, no matter how mundane. Sometimes I tell him what they are about, like I did with the tombstone at Bramber, sometimes I don't. Sometimes he doesn't realize that what we're doing is even on the list. Like when we go to Devil's Dyke and buy a soft ice cream with a 99 Flake stuck in it from an ice cream truck. He probably thinks Devil's Dyke was the point when, actually, we could have had the ice cream truck soft ice cream with the 99 Flake stuck in it wherever.

The list is not really about places. It's about details. Favorite stories I used to get Mum to tell me. Mostly, it's just a stupid exercise in trying to stay on her trail. I read a thing once, a quote by someone, about how we don't let go of grief because often grief is the last thing that connects us to that person. What a load of horseshit. Show me the person who said that, and I show you someone who is incapable of forming relationships. Because if you had a bond with the dead person in the first place, you don't fucking need the grief to cling on to. You have memories. And they are never the ones that come with a hash tag. But sometimes you can write their essence into a list.

Those are the days. At night, Silas and I carry on exploring one another though nothing happens beyond getting each other off with our hands and mouths. I say that, but I'm still not allowed to go down on him, while he will put his mouth on me all the friggin' time. Everywhere. The man's tongue is God's gift to women. Or at least to *this* woman. He can play me like a fucking instrument and I'm rapidly learning that, yes, the multiple orgasm thing is actually a thing.

But no matter what, there is still this barrier on his side that I can't break through. A darkness that descends upon him each time I accidentally trip those invisible don't-touch-me-there wires. It's frustrating and more than once I want to ask him what his deal is, but I always chicken out at the last minute. I'm not scared of the answer, but I get the feeling if I press him, he'll never open up. So I just wait, hoping that he'll get there before I have to go home, back to a Silas-less life. The thought of having to go back home at the end of my stay makes me almost unbearably sad, so I concentrate on remaining grateful for small victories. Like the first time he lets me jerk him off without holding my hand. Or the way he let me bite his ass when I had my hands on him about an hour ago.

It's early afternoon. We came home from today's outing to an artisan market, where I managed to buy a hand-knitted black beret from a little old lady who ogled Silas in the most comical way, shortly after lunch because it had started raining cats and dogs.

As soon as we got back, we ran upstairs, shelled out of our soaked clothes and started making out. I can't call it anything else. We're like two teenagers finding our way around our bodies. His bruises have started to fade a little now, slowly turning from purple to eerie green, and if I do it lightly enough, I can touch his abs now. But I still like exploring his back best. He's got the most amazing shoulder line and back muscles. They don't ripple when he moves, they fucking *flow*. But he still can't lie on his front, so he was propped up on his side, me behind him, when I began slithering down on the bed, to bring my face level with those glutes I've had my eye on since I first saw them in the drawing. I wrapped my arm around his hipbone, took his already rock-hard cock in my fist and started pumping him leisurely. Once he started squirming in my hand, I gently clamped my teeth into the hard muscles of his butt. Then I licked over the bite. Bite, pump, lick. Over and over — and each time he bucked into my hand, I thought I was going to die with pleasure. And that was *before* he took care of me.

I luxuriate in the memory while I lounge in bed a little longer and bemoan the fact that he's left me here by myself. I wish he'd stayed after he'd wrung the last orgasm from me. But he's decided it's time he picked up his gym routine again, so he doesn't lose his next fight.

Because, of course, there *are* fights. Bouncing, my ass. And the next one is a big one. It happens after I'm gone. That much I know. It's all I'm allowed to know.

'Cause it's illegal.

Figured that one out all by my little lonesome self. To his credit, he didn't deny it when I asked him straight. Just nodded and then shut me up with a kiss.

SILAS

The rest of TripleX train in Fight or Flight in Brighton. I don't. Aside from the fucking stupid name, it's full of arseholes, most of whom I know. And I'm not exactly welcome there either. It's owned by old man Benson's best mate, Cecil O'Brien. Yeah, the surname thing is no coincidence. He was Mum's husband before the guy who fathered me came onto the scene. She never changed back to her maiden name, so I got Cecil's surname despite the fact my father was a Hayes, apparently. Fucked off when I was still in nappies. Made room for the next cunt, who I also barely remember, and then the next cunt and his fucking brood.

My teeth clench when I think about them, *him,* but no, not going there today. Cecil never stopped having a big hard-on for Mum. When they got together, she'd just lost a baby, having come home pregnant at the height of her modelling career, and was everything a man could want in a woman. Sassy, beautiful, successful in her own right. Brighton's very own Linda Evangelista. And I think that's what he still sees when he looks at her now.

But it's also why he hates my guts. I'm the living, breathing reminder that Mum fucked around on him. To be fair, she did it *once.* He, by all accounts, did it constantly. If I were actually Cecil's kid, I'd have eleven half brothers and sisters. No shit. Five of them from one woman, two of them from another and the rest came out of miscellaneous vaginas over the years. I don't get guys like that. If I have a woman, I have a woman. *One.* But if I look around me, I seem to be the odd one out. Everybody fucks around on everyone all the fucking time around here. Small town England. We don't show a nipple on TV before 9pm, but we fuck our best mate's girlfriend then swap her back for our own. And nobody bats an eyelid. Not my style. If I had a woman, I'd want to be with her, make memories, grow old together, have a life.

If I had Grace.

I push the thought out of my mind as I open the door to the Shoreham Gym and Martial Arts Academy, normal fucking name for a normal fucking place, where one can do some cross training and then beat the shit out of a sand sack. Of course, they run classes, too, and I even take the occasional one. They're all really nice guys here and David, the bloke who runs the place, will buddy you up with a training bro outside of class if you ask, but needless to say, there aren't any sparring partners for what I do. Not that I need any more training in being an arsehole, I've had that all my fucking life.

I nod at the characters that are already in the room, the same faces I see here normally. Four to six is a good slot. The classes don't start till later in the evening, so it's mostly council workers and office bods trying to stay healthy, couple of beef burgers but it's not really the right gym for them. David doesn't tolerate even a whiff of steroids in his shop. It's why I like the guy. Nobody asks me where I've been for the last ten days, though I can see in some of the looks I'm getting that my absence has been noted. A couple of them know what I do for a living, the legit part anyway, and if I don't show up for a while, they just assume I got busted up bouncing.

I start my warm up routine and soon realise that a week and a half of the good life with Grace has already taken its toll. Not much of a toll but enough to take my edge off. I can't afford that. My bruises are still hurting some but nothing like they did in the beginning, despite what I keep leading Grace to believe, and I power through my cardio and weights before I get to punching the sacks. I practice some kicks and punches before I suddenly feel like I'm being watched. I look around and sure enough, Arlo is standing by the door, looking at me, his right hand is in a splint and the left side of his face is mashed up. The hue of the discolouration tells me, that's still courtesy of me. I frown at him and return to pummelling the sack in front of me. No idea what that fucker wants. Though it's clear he's come out here to see me. The guys know I train here. Wonder how he knew I'd be back today, though. Not really like I've been sticking to my schedule lately. I keep throwing my punches until I can feel him breathing down my neck. I stop and look at him standing next to me.

"Arlo," I acknowledge his presence and nod at the splint. "Boxer's break?" I ask unnecessarily.

"Yup." He touches the splint with his other hand.

"Yeah, I'm not surprised, man. You hit with all four knuckles. Did nobody ever teach you only to land the top two?"

He looks at me wide-eyed. Fucking amateur.

"Like that." I throw a slow-mo punch at the bag, illustrating.

"Right," he says.

"How's the ear?"

"I might need surgery."

"Sorry to hear that." There is no harm in being polite. He grins at my unintended pun, so I know we're good. "Why are you here?"

"Just checking on how the Snake is doing. They say you got laid off for a month."

He's scoping me out. Interesting. Well, two can play that game.

"Sure did."

My choice of phrase makes me smirk. Such a Yank thing to say. Grace is rubbing off on me.

"Rumour has it there is gonna be a big one," Arlo fishes. "Off the record."

I bark a laugh. Like anything else is *on* the record. I see in his confused expression that he doesn't get it, though, and I can't be bothered to explain it. So I nod an affirmation and remain silent. Sometimes not saying anything makes people tell you more than they intended. 'Cause they have this burning need to fill the silence. Arlo is one of those people.

"They say it's not gonna be at the club." I prick up my ears. This is news to me. Diego gave me a date, 6th June, but there was no mention of a venue change. I'd assumed we'd be in the club, like normal. I'm inclined to proactively pick Arlo's brains a bit now but it turns out, I don't need to. "They say it's gonna be at the Mansion." This makes me look up and cock my head. Arlo grins. He can tell I'm surprised. "Apparently, you're gonna be the entertainment at the old man's 60th. And it's gonna be *brutal*."

He's been sent here to scare me. What a joke.

Then my brain backs up a little.

At the Mansion?

Who the fuck does Diego think he is? Leonardo de fucking Caprio?

I punch the bag but stop myself from showing just how fucked off I am because if Arlo knows this much, he might have some more useful info and I don't want him to think his mission is accomplished. Just yet.

"Anyone know who I'm fighting?" I ask casually.

"Shit. You don't know?"

"Nope," I answer, realising from his tone that he has no clue either.

"Damn. That's why I came here. I hoped you'd tell us. See, Diego won't let us mere mortals make-book on this. Won't tell us shit. But the guys and I thought we could do our own little pool, ya know. Only we don't know who you're up against."

I look at him and shrug.

"I haven't got the faintest, mate, sorry. Some upstart from London, far as I know."

I return to throwing punches at my friend, the sandbag.

"Aren't you curious? They say they've put him up at the Bensons' in the meantime and that he's a fucking beast."

I nod, still throwing punches.

"Who are *they*?"

"The guys."

"So let me get this right, nobody knows who the fucker is I'm supposed to be fighting but still you all know where he's sleeping and that he's massive?"

I raise my eyebrows at him pointedly then return to my routine and don't look at him again.

Finally, he leaves.

Looks like tomorrow Diego and I need to have a chat.

Grace

After spending a week and a half constantly in Silas' company, I feel totally bereft without him within forty minutes of being alone.

Pathetic, really, but fact.

But since he's started talking more, it's become apparent that he's not just eye candy with a mildly dangerous vibe. He's bright as hell and funny as fuck. His observations of people, places and the world in general are hilariously acute and his delivery friggin' genius. You just gotta catch 'em when they come out.

He has me in stitches at least once a day, and it feels good to laugh. Really good.

I hadn't realized how little I've laughed since Mum's been gone. I wonder what she would have made of him. She used to hate me swearing, although her favorite comedians were always the filthiest mouthed. Thinking about us watching late night comedy together gives me one of those little paper cuts to the heart that always happen when I think about her. It'll sting all day, especially when I least expect it.

I give myself a kick up the ass and decide to go have a shower then search up the shows playing at the Theatre Royal for the rest of this month, in the vain hope I can get *any* tickets for *anything*. This whole festival thing has thrown that plan sideways as well. There are a few things on my list that are just not gonna happen. Staying at the Palais, watching something at the Theatre Royal from the front row. I was stupid, really. I didn't organize anything other than the ill-fated hotel room before I came. I had this idea I could just waltz in and do. Stupid but lucky, I think, as my eyes fall on the drawing opposite the bed. Very, very lucky.

That man.

I will miss him like crazy.

I finally swing my legs out of bed, root around on the floor for my panties and tee and slip both on. I heard Kalina come in a little while ago, so I'm not gonna cross the landing in my birthday suit. Just as I'm about to grab my towel from the radiator by the desk, there is a tentative knock on the door, and I can hear Kalina call my name.

"Come in," I say, and Kalina opens the door, sticking her head around the frame as if to check if the coast is clear.

"You alone?" she asks.

"Yep. Come in."

She steps half in and stops, one foot in the room.

"You got time?"

I nod.

"What's up?" I reply and indicate the desk chair for her to sit on, while I go back to the foot end of the unmade bed and sit my ass down opposite.

She swivels the chair around to face the room and folds herself onto

- 89 -

it, cross-legged. She looks around a little before she answers my question with a shrug, and I realize she's never been in here.

"I'm bored," she says in that totally factual Polish way of hers. "I don't see you."

I feel a pang of guilt. First, I made a friend, and then I dropped her like a hot potato as soon as Silas was free to play with all day.

"I'm sorry," I say. "I'm a shitty friend."

"Pah," she utters, which I believe is Polish for 'ain't no biggie'. Then she smiles, nice and easy, and makes a 'forget it' gesture. "So what are you doing now?"

"Right now?"

She nods.

"I was going to have a shower."

I omit my plan to search for theater tickets. It can wait. Especially seeing that Kalina's face lights up.

"Can I do your hair after?"

I smile.

"Of course, you can."

SILAS

When I get back from training, laughter from the kitchen greets me, the best sound in the world. I make a detour to see what's happening before I get under the shower.

Grace is sitting at the table and Kalina is standing behind her, braiding Grace's hair, though 'braiding' is the understatement of the century. It's a fucking work of art what she is doing to my girl.

My girl.

My brain stutters at the thought.

Eventually, I'll need to rein this shit in.

She's not my girl.

We're having some fucked-up fun until she goes back to America. We half talked about it. Half. I didn't tell her how difficult the sex stuff

- 90 -

is for me or why, but she seems to get it and she heard me when I said I find it difficult to let go with people, so let's just fool around a bit. She has no idea how far out of my comfort zone she's already pushed me, or how eternally grateful I'll be to her for what she's doing, and I'd like to keep it that way. Maybe it's just what I needed. A fling where none of it really matters, to heal my wounds. But I don't want her to remember me as a fucking rescue mission. So, yeah, I need to rein this *my girl* shit in. As I think it, she looks at me with the biggest, happiest smile on her face and the fact she looks at me like that makes me warm all over. Fuck.

"I'll be in the shower," I choke out and turn away, but Grace calls me back.

"Silas?"

"Yes, milady?"

I pivot back, comedy style, to look back at them and it doesn't fail to make them giggle a bit more.

"Kalina and I were thinking, could we maybe do something together. The three of us? Tomorrow?"

I freeze for a second as they both look at me expectantly and am about to say no, 'cause I got a meeting to go to, even if Diego doesn't know it yet. But then a plan presents itself, fully formed, in my head. It'll be fucking perfect, actually. I smile at them.

"Absolutely. Either of you ever been to the dogs?"

"What?" they ask in unison.

"Greyhound racing," I explain, and both of them shake their heads.

"Good. In that case we go to the track. But we'll do it in style. I'll book a table in the restaurant. You two can get dolled up." I say, grinning. "I'll even wear a suit."

Grace

I watch his back as he walks away to go up and shower and regret that I can't just hop in with him. Not that I'd mind having a second go under the water, but I couldn't destroy Kalina's creation already. She is putting the finishing touches of hair glitter on, and then I'm allowed to go have a look in the mirror.

The only one available is an old full-length stand up one with a baroque style gilded frame around it, which is part of the treasure Kalina hoards in her room. So we go up and squeeze ourselves into her Aladdin's cave.

When I see my reflection, I am once again amazed by what this girl can do. I look like I should be playing Titania in *Midsummer Night's Dream* or something. There are intricate braids piled in loops on top of my head, mixed with loose hair strands and decorated with leaves made of fabric, pearls and glitter. I look stunning even though I'm still just wearing a tee and my yoga pants.

"Wow," I say. "That's amazing."

I look at her reflection next to me and at her short hair.

"How did you learn to do this?" I ask.

She smiles.

"All my life I have hair to here."

She indicates her teeny-tiny butt.

I didn't expect that. She carries herself like she's always been a short-hair girl. I'm impressed. I don't know a lot of girls who'd chop off long tresses like that. For a moment, I wonder if she did it for charity, a cancer wig or something, and it makes me swallow. Then I just ask.

"What made you cut it off?"

A gloomy expression washes over her face, something between regret and defiance, but then she grins.

"Emancipation."

Whoa.

"Did it work?"

She shrugs and I'm left with the distinct feeling she doesn't want to talk about it, and that's okay by me. So I change the subject.

"Will you do it again? Tomorrow? For dinner?"

Her face lights up and she claps her hands.

"I love to. What we wear?"

I shrug and she looks at me with a reproachful scowl.

"Silas is wearing suit, so we wear dresses, right?"

"Right," I agree and sigh.

I don't know her that well but one look around and I know where this little Andy Warhol of second-hand shopping is going with this.

"We better go shopping tomorrow then," she decides and claps her hands excitedly.

ILA

I don't see much of Grace the next day because she and Kalina have gone out shopping for dresses. They are both seriously excited about the prospect of a posh meal out, so I've tried my best to make it clear to them that the restaurant at the dogs is not exactly the Ritz. It's the dogs.

Kalina nods at that and I have a funny feeling this girl knows exactly the kind of venue I'm talking about. She even asks to see my suit before they set out, gives it a good old glance over, compliments me on the dark blue fabric and then drags Grace into town.

I spend the day feeling pretty much lost without her and get restless when they're still not back before I go to the gym.

So I go early and cut the routine short.

By the time I get back, Grace and Kalina have barricaded themselves in Kalina's room. When I knock on the door, they tell me to go away. I feel a bit like a groom who's not allowed to see his bride.

The thought makes my heart trip and my conscience rear up. I feel bad about using them, but it's the perfect opportunity to glean information from Diego without being obvious. Much better than marching into TripleX and demanding an explanation.

The thing about Diego is, he is a total creature of habit, so I know for sure he'll be at the Coral, the greyhound stadium, tonight. Like every fucking Thursday.

He has his own table and normally a couple of floozies by his side plus whoever he has decided is his best mate that week. Sometimes old man Benson is there, too, but it's more of a Diego thing.

I'm already standing in the hallway of our crummy little house, fully dressed in my suit and a white shirt, open at the collar because I won't wear a fucking tie, not even for this performance, when I see Grace and Kalina come down the stairs in their evening wear. They both look absolutely stunning in completely different ways. Grace's hair is made up like the day before and her makeup is all green and earth colours, with eyeliner that really brings out her cat features. Still no lipstick, though, and it makes me smile. And instantly want to kiss her.

She is wearing a rust-coloured, slinky, slightly shimmery dress that hugs every single curve on her beautiful body and ends asymmetrically mid-thigh on one side and at the ankle on the other. She has an ivory-coloured stole thrown over her bare shoulders. On her feet are simple sandals with ankle straps that match the stole. I'm glad she isn't wearing high heels. She isn't a heels woman, and I wouldn't want her to feel uncomfortable.

Kalina, on the other hand, is wearing what must be six-inch black patent leather stilettos under a much shorter, strapless green sequin dress with black sequin trimmings that looks like it must have once cost a bomb. In total contrast to Grace, her makeup is very dramatic, all old movie style with dark red lips and smoky eyes, and she has gelled her hair down into a kind of very short Charleston do. A black velvet choker encircles her neck. She looks *different*.

It takes me a minute to realise what it is but then it dawns on me. She isn't tottering on our threadbare red carpet in those heels, she is walking in them like a pro, like she's been wearing heels all her life. Like she's been wearing these kinds of clothes all her life. Like she is a completely different person.

Gone is the pixie in dungarees, replaced by a girl, *woman* I correct myself, because she sure as hell looks like one right now, who in tonight's little production appears like the only one who won't be in over her head. And that's without knowing the script. Or even that there is one. She sees me look and laughs.

"Do well?" she asks playfully.

"Hell yeah."

I grin up at them just as my phone dings to tell me the taxi is outside.

"Let's go, ladies."

Grace

Silas in jogging bottoms and a tight tee is good, Silas in jeans with no tee is great, Silas in a suit with a white shirt open at the collar is smokin' hot as they say in the South. I am almost paralyzed with instant lust the minute my eyes fall on him, standing by the door and taking in Kalina's artwork as we come down the stairs.

Because that's what we are, serious works of art.

If I ever get married, I want this girl for my stylist. She even manages to make clothes shopping not a cringefest. She has this amazing eye for what will fit you and look good on you. So I'm glad Silas answers 'hell, yeah' when she asks him if she did well. I might have had to strangle him if he'd said anything else. After jumping him first. He really looks unbearably handsome in that suit.

And then there is the fact that I'm getting more and more impatient with just fooling around like we do.

I want this man's cock inside of me.

In my mouth, in my pussy, maybe even my ass — I don't know if I'd like it, but with him, I'd be happy to try. The point is, I'm *so* past just feeling him in my hands. I huff out a sound of frustration when I pass him by as he holds the door open for Kalina and me on the way to the taxi. He grabs my wrist and stops me in my tracks.

"You okay?" he asks, searching my face.

"Just dying with desire over here," I quip and want to carry on walking, but he spins me back around and crashes his lips to mine.

He wraps his arms around me and kisses me deeply for a moment then draws back and whispers against my lips.

"I missed you today."

"Me, too," I murmur back.

"You look gorgeous," he mumbles and kisses me again, his hand finding my naked leg on the side where my dress is cut high.

He slides it around to the inside of my thigh, hitches it higher and finds my panties. He presses a thumb against the fabric covering my crotch.

"You're soaked," he states the friggin' obvious.

I'm painfully aware that we are standing in the open doorway and Kalina is looking right back at us, a hand already on the handle of the taxi's passenger door. She can't see what he's doing because the short side of my dress is facing the house and he's embraced me in a way that shields me from her view, but she still feels *very* close to us on this street with no sidewalk.

"Silas," I pant.

He pushes his tongue into my mouth one last time and simultaneously withdraws the thumb, only to slip it around the edge of my panties and give my clit one, quick, hard stroke. The bastard.

When he withdraws, I snatch his hand up and, looking deep into his eyes, I stick his thumb into my mouth, suck my juice off it and play around the pad with my tongue. I can see the desire blooming in him and I let go with a smile.

"Let's go" I say, and leave him adjusting the hard-on in his suit pants while I get into the cab.

SILAS

I timed it so Diego and his entourage would already be at the Coral when we get there. It's important that we have the entrance and we do. It's easy since it's not exactly packed. It never is, because the food really is cheap and cheerful and the drinks selection basic to say the least.

Diego pays the kitchen to have his favourite champagne on ice and lets them bring in local lobster, especially for him and his table. Beats me why he keeps coming here if not for the spit and sawdust trip down memory lane. There is nobody to lord over either. All the old guys who knew the Bensons from way back are long dead and gone. Whatever, not *my* fucked-up psyche. My fucked-up psyche has other things to worry about.

The waiter shows us to our table, and I nod a greeting at Diego in passing, a beautiful woman hanging from each of my arms.

I didn't engineer that.

Grace hooked herself under as soon as we got out of the cab and after some silent exchange between the two of them, Kalina did the same on my other side. Perfect scenario but seriously weird. I really am not that guy. But it totally serves its purpose.

I can see Diego's interest being piqued immediately when we saunter in. He's sitting with two of his regular girls, waitresses from The Cockatoo who all vie for pole position on his dick all the time, because each and every single one of them wants to land him. But Diego is not stupid. He won't fall for any of them. He'll fuck 'em happily, though.

Interestingly, the chair normally reserved for this week's best friend is empty. I have to admit, there is something comical about us, little George Benson and little Silas O'Brien, each with two overdressed women hanging from our arms, eyeing each other up. I can see in the smirk around the corner of his mouth that he's thinking the same and for that brief moment in time we're friends again. It's over in a blink, and Grace, Kalina and I proceed to our table.

Before we are even seated, Grace and Kalina start cooing over the dogs already racing on the track below. Neither of them has ever been to a greyhound race, so everything is interesting and exciting to them.

To me the whole thing's just a bit sad.

When I was younger, we had an off the track greyhound, Condor. He was the most timid thing ever and I always wondered what, or who, made him that way.

The waiter has barely taken our drinks order and is explaining to the girls how the betting works, when another waiter appears by his side.

"Excuse me," he butts in, "but the Benson table is asking if your party would care to join them?"

I twist my body to look behind me at Diego. I deliberately placed myself with my back to him, so that he wouldn't think I'm here for him. Which, of course, I am. He knows it. I know it. But there are rules.

He's talking into his mobile while he makes eye contact with me and beckons us over jovially. I turn to Kalina and Grace.

"You okay with that?"

Grace narrows her eyes at me.

"Who is he?"

"My boss."

As I answer, it suddenly dawns on me that I am about to drag her into my world. The last eleven days hanging around with her, letting her decide what we're doing, just *being*, have been such bliss and so far removed from my 'normal', I conveniently let myself forget that she doesn't have a clue about my real life. Sure, she's figured out what I do, but there is a massive difference between knowing in theory and suddenly being introduced to arseholes like Diego.

"At the club or the *other* boss?" she asks dryly with a surreptitious side glance at Kalina, who is still engrossed in watching the track.

Or so we think. Until Kalina turns her head to me and pins me in a dare-stare.

"Both," she says.

What the fuck?

"How do you know?" I ask her, and she shrugs as if it weren't a big deal.

"Your mum and I talk," she says casually.

Hang on, *what?*

Mum knows about the fightnights?

I stare at Kalina, or rather Kalina's profile because she's turned back to the track despite the fact there aren't any dogs on it at the moment. And suddenly I feel so stupid, it hurts. *Of course* my mother knows. She is Sheena O'Brien. She might be hiding in housekeeping at the Palais, but even if she ended up cleaning the toilets on the pier, she'd still be old Brighton.

She'd still be Sheena fucking O'Brien.

I'm officially a total moron.

Before I can dwell on it any further, Grace makes a move and gets up.

"Right, let's go."

"Are you sure?" I ask, looking up at her.

"It's why we're here, isn't it?" she answers wryly.

She ain't daft, my woman.

Grace

I don't show it but I'm absolutely seething.

He could have told me.

It was obvious from the moment we walked in that we were here because of the guy who is right now being introduced to me as 'Diego'. He looks about as much as a 'Diego' as ... but apparently that's what we are supposed to call him.

I was surprised to learn that he is Silas' boss and the organizer of the fightnights. He looks about the same age as us. And the way they are together, I would bet my bottom dollar they've known each other since kindergarten. It's just something about them. Like they aren't really the people they are but playing parts in a make-believe game. Although I know it's all deadly real. The bruises on Silas are all I need to remember that this ain't no game.

Introductions are being made while we are still standing.

The two women Diego has with him are called Brooke and Kim. They are both pretty brunettes with nice smiles but neither appears to be the sharpest tool in the shed. Diego bids us to sit down. Silas hesitates for a moment. He nods at the empty space opposite Diego.

"Who's your invisible friend?"

Diego smiles, and it's an odd smile. It tells me Silas has just somehow insulted him, but I don't get how. There is so much fucking history between these two, it's palpable.

"It appears, you are," Diego answers, and it makes Silas smirk.

I've never seen this side of him. He feels different all of a sudden. Not like the guy who will cuddle Luna on his lap, not like the guy who will snuggle up against me at night, not like the guy who packs picnics and buys me soft ice creams with 99 Flakes in them. He feels...*dangerous* to know.

It's hot.

And scary as fuck.

I look at Kalina, but she seems fully in her element, eyeing up our host. She kinda pushes Brooke — or Kim, I've already forgotten which is which — along into the next seat with one small raise of her eyebrows and sits herself down next to Diego. I happily go sit on the other side of the other brunette because it means I get to be next to Silas who is taking the empty chair of unknown significance.

Once we've all got our asses parked somewhere, Diego asks if we want champagne and lobster. Kalina answers for all of us when she says yes, as if it were her god-given right to have champagne and lobster, and how silly of him to ask. I look at this eighteen-year-old and have the sudden epiphany that she could wipe the floor with me where street smarts and dealing with shady types is concerned. What the fuck happened to the innocent girl in the dungarees?

Diego smiles at her indulgently.

"Kalina?" he asks. "Is that a Russian name?"

She snorts derisively.

"Polish," she answers, in a way that settles matters way beyond what nationality she is.

Diego nods respectfully.

And, honestly, I don't even want to know.

SILAS

I look at Grace and feel like a complete arsehole.

I can tell she feels majorly uncomfortable at Diego's table. She looks so pretty, and she so doesn't belong here. She belongs in some cool American jazz bar with some billionaire boyfriend whose dealings are a hundred percent legit and who whisks her away in his private magic jet carpet to Paris for the weekend. Or some shit like that.

Instead, she's sitting in the Coral, with two Brighton lowlifes, a couple of dumb bimbos and a Polish gold digger. Betting on dogs.

Way to go, Silas.

And yet she looks at me with those eyes.

Hungry.

Like she wants me.

All of me.

Grace

As the evening progresses, I find myself loosening up a bit.

The champagne helps, I have to admit. But so does the knowledge that Silas isn't drinking. It makes me feel safe to know that at least one of us has their shit together. When Diego tried to fill his flute, Silas put a hand over it and told him he was in training. Diego smiled at that but didn't comment. Something about that frustrated Silas, but I don't know what it was. There is so much subtext between these two it's unnerving.

"Excuse me, I need the bathroom," I say after we've trashed the lobster and I stand up.

I'm a little shaky on my legs. I've only had two glasses, but they've gone straight to my head. I look at Silas.

"Would you show me where they are, please?"

"Sure," he answers and gets up. Smiling, he takes my elbow and guides me away from the table. "I'm sorry," he says, as soon as we are out of earshot, moving his hand to the small of my back.

"What for?"

"Dragging you into this," he states factually as we step out into the corridor behind the restaurant.

We near the restrooms and stop by the one that has the ladies sign on the door. I turn to look him in the eye, swaying a tiny bit. His hands come up and he steadies me by laying them firmly on either side of my neck, his fingers cradling the base of my skull. It's instantly grounding. God, I love his hands, I love the way he holds me.

"You okay?" he asks.

"I'm fine," I say and give him my best kitten smile. "Better if you give me a kiss before I go in."

His eyes light up and he backs me up against the wall next to the door, putting a leg right between mine. And then he kisses me, one hand sliding up from my neck to tangle gently in my hair as his tongue and mine ravish one another once more. Any lingering trace of anger at having been dumped in this situation dissipates as we kiss and when he withdraws, my heart is pumping fast and my sex is dripping.

This man.

SILAS

I apologise to Grace for messing up her hair. Then I let her go into the ladies' room and find the gents. I have to wait a minute for my dick to go down before I can even think of going for a piss, so I stand by the sink and let cold water run over my hands. I'm looking at the stream flowing over my wrists, cooling my pulse, when I hear the voice behind me, like thunder rumbling in the distance.

"Well, hello, little brother."

My head jerks up and I meet his dark eyes in the mirror. I hold their gaze as I give him the customary reply.

"I'm not your brother."

He laughs at that.

"Maybe not but it turns me on to think you are."

"You sick bastard."

I want to turn around and punch him there and then, but I don't. Because I know that's what he's after. And I'm not giving him the satisfaction.

"I watched you come in," he says, stepping up to my side.

If I turned sideways, I could look at him directly, but instead I keep staring at him in the reflection.

"With your two chicks," he carries on. "They're hot. You always did have good taste. And there was me, thinking all this time you didn't like a threesome. I guess it just wasn't the right combo."

Then he laughs that filthy laugh of his and my blood runs cold. The impulse to fucking murder him is strong, but I think of Grace and manage to keep it together.

"Fuck off," I tell his reflection, and he grins. Then he leans over and whispers in my ear, so close I can feel his hot breath fanning over me.

"See you on the sixth, little bro."

I watch his bulk retreat through the door.

And then I zone out.

Grace

It takes me a while to fix my hair back in place, so when I come out of the bathroom, I expect Silas to be long finished and waiting outside for me but he's not. I give him a few minutes until it becomes evident he's not gonna reappear. I go back to the table, fully assuming he'll be there. But he's not.

I sit down, confused, and want to get up again immediately, but Diego reaches across the table and holds down my arm against the white linen cloth without so much as looking at me. His palm on my naked skin gives me the creeps and I wriggle but he's strong. He is also fully engrossed in a conversation with Kalina, completely ignoring his two escorts, who look bored out of their brains. Only when there is a break in the flow between Kalina and him does he turn to me, his hand still forcing me to stay in place.

"Stay seated," he demands, looking at me through storm-gray eyes as if there were no other person at the table. "Silas came here to find answers."

A loaded smile spreads across his face.

"He's busy finding those answers."

When he sees the horrified expression on my face, he starts patting my arm instead of holding it down any longer. Doesn't make it any less creepy.

"Don't worry, he'll be back," he says and as if on cue, he turns around to jut his chin out at Silas who's just entering the restaurant again. "Look there he is."

He's right. And he's not.

Because the man who's coming towards our table may look like Silas, but he's pure fury.

SILAS

I make a beeline for Diego and pick him up out of his chair by the collar. He's built, he goes to the gym to maintain his image, he even used to fight a bit back when we were way younger, but he is no fighter. Never has been. He can still hold his own in a brawl, but he doesn't stand a chance against someone like me. Too slow. Too afraid to get hurt. And that's exactly the fear I see in his eyes right now as I get in his face.

"What the fuck, George? *Rowan?* Really? Why? You lied. You said it was some bloke from London."

In the corner of my eye, I can see the waiters get all huffy and I'm sure I'll have about ten seconds before security will get here, so I let go of Diego again and watch him stumble back against his chair. I got to hand it to the fucker, though, he doesn't flinch, just grins at me and then signals to the two bouncer guys who, lo and behold, turn up right then, not to bother. They don't exactly leave but neither do they come any closer, just remain hovering to see how this pans out. I'd do the same.

Diego sits himself back down and looks up at me with a neutral mask on his face.

"*Technically*, he did come from London. I knew you wouldn't shake on it if you knew who it was, but it's the old man's sixtieth and I'm expected to do something special for him." He shrugs. "Just so happened that your brother—"

"Stepbrother," I interrupt him.

"Stepbrother, then, don't see what difference it makes."

You have no idea.

"Besides, far as I know, your mother officially adopted him when that fucker of a dad ran off, did she not? That's why she's paying off his debts, isn't it? Must be galling. Well, you should be grateful 'cause it could be a whole load worse if it wasn't for me. He came down, asking me for a loan to pay back some cunts he borrowed off in London. I thought it'd be nice for Pops to finally get the chance to watch the clash he and Cecil always fancied laying on. The Snake against the Python. Went to Cecil with the idea and he fucking loved it. Prepared to put the prize money up at a hundred thou. Of course, Cecil's backing your *step*brother. Dad, I bet, will be backing you."

He studies my face, gauging my reaction, but I remain blank.

"Not sure yet who I'll put my money on."

I take a step back.

"What if I don't fight?"

He gives me a condescending look.

"Don't be stupid, Silas. That'd be your mum's loan on the house repaid, right? In *one* evening. No more fucking around at TripleX. Of course you'll fight."

He grins knowingly, while I sit there stunned about how well he still knows me, how much he still knows *about* me, how much he can calculate my calculations. Especially when he delivers the kicker.

"And you will love every fucking second of it. Cause you *hate* him."

Can't argue if a man is right.

Grace

We don't stay after Silas and Diego have their exchange.

Silas bungs a wad of cash onto the table and says, "For the lobster," then indicates to Kalina and me that we're going. We'd figured as much, so we're out of our chairs as quickly as our dresses will allow.

Diego takes Kalina's hand and kisses it as she politely says goodbye to him. He doesn't dare do the same with me when I glare at him but still tells me that it was nice to meet me. You gotta love the British and their manners.

On the way back home in the taxi, Silas sits next to me in silence, while Kalina is riding shotgun, chatting to the driver. His English is about as broken as hers, so I don't know how much they are actually communicating but at least they are trying. Unlike some other people back here I could mention.

I turn to look at Silas' stoic profile. Gone completely is the chatty, funny, bright guy of the last few days. He has been replaced again by the man I first met outside the bathroom door. Sullen, broody, tense. That coiledness is back, the feeling that if I touch him unexpectedly, he'll strike me first and ask questions later. Like a snake. I've not seen him fight, but I have a pretty good idea where his fight name comes from now. Still, I want some answers. He fucking well owes me that much. Just to be on the safe side, though, I scoot over a bit more to my side of the backbench before I talk to him.

"Who the fuck is George?" I ask.

He briefly looks at me, confused, and then barks a laugh. Apparently out of all the questions I could have asked I've gone for the most amusing.

"Diego," he answers, looking away again. "His real name is George."

"Right," I say.

I have a million other questions.

Like *what's the deal with the stepbrother you never mentioned and all that hatred pouring out of you*?

And, *is that the guy that came to the house?*

And, *this fight, is it to the death?*

Because, honestly, at this point I wouldn't put it past these people. They look like cute British movie gangsters on the outside, all bark and no bite. But I saw the bloodlust in Diego's eyes when he said, *because you hate him*. These guys ain't pretend. They're the real deal. Who the fuck else would pay a hundred grand to see a couple of guys beat each other to a pulp as party entertainment?

So, yeah, I have questions. But I don't know how to talk to this stony version of Silas.

It hits me like a sucker punch that I still barely know this guy.

SILAS

I watched you come in. They're hot.

He saw her.

He fucking saw Grace.

He's not worthy to be on the same planet with her, let alone lay eyes on her.

I watched you come in. They're hot.

The words keep going round and round in my head.

I watched you come in. They're hot.

He's going to want to put his hands on her.

He'll know exactly which one of them is mine.

I need to keep her safe.

Grace is asking you a question, my brain informs me, she wants to know who George is. What? Oh, right. I laugh because it's such an unimportant detail.

"Diego," I answer and look away again.

I can barely look at her without guilt choking me. How could I be so stupid and put her in harm's way like that? I should have kept her miles away from everything to do with the Bensons.

"His real name is George," I carry on explaining. "George Benson."

I need to keep her safe, *close.* I need to keep her close. I need to keep her *mine.*

I force myself to look at her and realise there is a whole seat width between us in space. She is looking at me with questions and worry in her eyes and it's the concern that gets me.

I reach out for her hand and my heart trips when she takes it.

Grace

Something happens, I don't know what, and suddenly, just like that, he's back in the room, taxi, whatever. He reaches out across the gulf between us and takes my hand in his.

Electricity shoots up my arm, giving me tingles all over.

This man. I'm doomed.

He gently tugs, to bring me to his side, and I close the gap. His other arm comes up to cradle my cheek, his fingers sprawled, the way he does, and he leans over to give me the gentlest of kisses.

"I'm sorry for tonight, Grace."

There is a whole load I want to say to him, but I'm too happy to have my Silas back to spoil the mood. Especially when he starts stroking down my throat, running his hand down to the swell of my breast, only to slip the tips of his fingers under the neckline. I shiver and feel my nipples stiffen against the fabric. He looks down at them.

"You're not wearing a bra," he mumbles, and then he ducks his head down and bites that hard pebble through my dress. My butt lifts off the seat and I suppress the loud moan that wants to escape me.

In the front, Kalina and the driver are still talking, about K-pop, of all things, but I'm not sure they are entirely oblivious to what is going on behind them. The thing is, it doesn't put a damper on it for me. It just makes it hotter. Silas' face comes up to mine again and he starts kissing me fervently. I notice an urgency in him that wasn't there before. He's still holding back, but I can feel a need that's new. While his tongue tangles with mine, his hand dives under the dress fully and he cups my breast, kneading it and flicking my nipple just the way he knows I like. Blindly, my hand wanders over to his crotch and finds his cock, straining against the suit pants. I rub him hard through the slightly scratchy material, feeling around his shape as best I can. He groans quietly into my mouth and the sound sends a jolt of pure pleasure to my core.

I'm vaguely aware that the taxi has come to a stop, and then I hear Kalina and the driver clear their throats. Silas and I split apart and see their faces turned to us in the gap between the driver's seat and the passenger side. Kalina is pulling a 'get a room' face and the driver is grinning from ear to ear.

I feel myself blush, which is something I haven't done since high school. Silas remains unfazed and pays the driver while Kalina and I get out. Kalina fishes in her clutch for a house key.

"You two," she whispers, and then she makes an *ooh la la* kind of gesture, grinning broadly.

I don't think I've seen anyone flick their fingers like this in real life, ever. It's cute. I want to thank her for taking me shopping and doing my hair and everything today, but as soon as she lets us into the house, she skips up the stairs at record speed, leaving me behind to wait for Silas.

"Have fun," is the last thing I hear her say before she shuts her door upstairs.

A second later, strong arms wind around my waist from behind and hands land possessively on my belly. He pulls me back, pushing his hard cock up against my ass, and then he nuzzles through my hair until he finds the side of my neck. His lips latch onto the delicate skin he finds there and he sucks gently. Still standing in the open doorway, I start grinding against him. He growls though his tongue never stops drawing circles within the suction.

"Silas," I pant.

I can't help myself, I take one of his hands in mine and slide it up my body until it finds my right breast. He starts massaging it through my dress, synchronizing his movement with the heavy circles his other hand is rubbing over my abdomen. It feels absolutely amazing, this pressure going through me. Like he's found a pleasure spot I hadn't even known existed, deep down in the belly of the beast. My entire sex is humming with desire for him now and I know a finger fuck will just not be enough, not tonight.

I want all of him.

I want him to fill me up and feel him shudder as he shoots his come inside me.

I reach around to clasp my hands to his hips and gyrate my buttocks harder against his cock, practically making him dry hump me from behind. He groans, pulling me even tighter against him. He stops sucking my neck and I can hear him breathe heavily as he runs his mouth up to my ear, only to say the words I'm dying to hear.

"Tonight you're mine. Completely."

Silas

I finally shut the front door behind us, and then I gently push her up the stairs, cradling her hips in my hands. Her ripe arse sways before me and I can smell her through the thin fabric of her dress. I can't wait to sink myself into her. Rage and lust have somehow fused within me into a burning need to possess this woman, tonight.

I'm done hiding.

I'm done locking doors.

He will never have this one.

This one is *mine*.

We arrive outside our bedroom and she turns around to face me. She slides her arms around my neck, cradles the back of my head in her hands and looks deep into my eyes. She is trying to simmer us down a bit, but my heart is beating so fast it's scary and my dick is so hard it's painful. I can't hold back now, and she can see it in my eyes.

"No condom," she says, decisively.

And I stop breathing.

I don't ask her if she's sure, I just kiss her again and gently push her back, all the way through the door until the back of her legs hit the bed.

Grace

He doesn't quarrel and the thought of having him bare gives me a new high of anticipation as he backs me through the door, kicks it shut without letting go, and then I find myself with the back of my legs up against the bed.

I'm not stupid, I've thought about it.

One of the perks of fooling around for a bit without fully doing the deed is we've had conversations. Many. About everything. He knows I have an implant, not that I've really needed it in the last few years, and that in any case I've never done it without a condom. None of the boys — and yes, they were boys compared to him, here, now — I'd been with were innocent enough for me to take the risk. And none of them stuck around long enough to take the test.

I know Silas did take one, after Niamh, and says he always used condoms with the only other woman he was with after her. I believe him. A flash of jealousy goes through me when I think of Niamh and that I'm giving him one of my firsts that he can't give in return any longer.

I would have wanted that, for *me*.

It's an oddly possessive feeling that I've never had before about anyone.

I'd think about it more, but he's got me up against the bed, kissing me hard, while my arms are still wrapped around his neck, holding on for sheer balance, and his hand is going under the short side of my dress and starts pulling at my panties. All thought process goes South. When my panties are halfway down, trapping me, his palm travels up on the inside of my thigh and he cups my whole sex in his hand. He begins massaging it in undulating circles, the way he was massaging my belly earlier. Hidden away in my slick, slick folds, my clit goes nuts from the diffused pressure. Drop after drop of my creamy syrup finds its way onto his hand through the closed slit, and he keeps rubbing it all over my mound, slicking me up from the outside. I don't know if I want to scream with ecstasy or frustration. He hitches up the rest of my dress with his other hand and starts kneading my ass, one finger resting in my crack, lying at the entrance to my anus. Just lying there, doing nothing, driving me wild, making me moan loudly.

He stops kissing me to push his body up against me further, so that we're cheek to cheek and he can move the hand on my ass down and around between my legs. As he moves, the woolly material of his suit jacket cuff scratches over my butt cheeks. He opens my slit from behind, and I can feel myself spilling onto his hand. His breath hitches next to my ear.

"You're so, wet, Grace, always so wet," he mumbles then licks the soft skin behind my ear as his hand with all my juices on it travels back up my ass.

I love how he calls me by my name. Not babe, not doll, always Grace.

He leaves a trail of wetness when his fingers travel up my crack, and then one of them pushes in a little. Playful. Testing. I jerk forward with pleasure, mewling. We haven't done this before. *I've* never done this before, never let anyone even close to that part of me. The idea always seemed too lewd but God, it's *good*. He plays around the rim a bit more and sparks fly through me, different from anything I've ever known.

I'm close to coming and he hasn't even touched my pussy yet, not directly.

"You like?" he asks hoarsely into my ear, and all I can do is nod and make a strangled noise of pleasure.

"Good," he says then lets go of all of me abruptly to take a step back.

Through my lust-addled haze, I watch him shrug out of his jacket, undo his belt and push his trousers and briefs down, just far enough to let his cock spring free. I reach out for it, but he catches my hands midair.

"No. Turn around. Put your hands on the bed."

He smiles and lets go of me. I do what he asks. I hear him unbutton his shirt cuffs and rolling up his sleeves before he lifts the hem of my dress again and bunches it up around my waist. My legs are still restrained by my half down panties, but he doesn't make any move to take them off.

Instead, he just spreads my legs as far as they will allow, until the fabric digs almost painfully into the side of my thighs, and then he positions himself at my entrance. I'm so bound like this, I can't spread my pussy for him, so he reaches around and holds the lips apart. He slowly starts sliding into my hole, holding his cock in the other hand, guiding himself in. He doesn't ram into me in one stroke but moves in tantalizing increments, back and forth, a quarter of an inch at a time. I contract around him with every new move he makes, and his cock responds with little shudders. When he's about half in, he leans over my back, works his arm under my dress and up, so his hand reaches my left breast, and he cradles it in a firm grip. He angles himself above me, so his other hand can slide around my ass and his thumb finds my anus. He caresses it teasingly, just like before, as he presses his other arm down across my abdomen, holding me tight. Then, suddenly, he pushes the rest of his length all the way inside me, hard this time.

And then he starts fucking me.

There is no fooling around any longer.

He possesses me.

From inside.

Slowly but forcefully at the same time, barely pulling out of me before he rams back in.

Filling me up completely the entire time.

Never withdrawing.

It's relentless.

He fucks me with one hand on my tit, an arm across my belly, his cock all the way inside me and his free hand wandering back and forth between pushing his thumb into my ass and his fingers playing with my clit. Until it stays at my back.

"Rub yourself," he tells me with a hoarse voice, and I do.

I circle my clit feverishly, while his thumb fucks my ass and his cock fills me completely, undulating in a steady rhythm.

And then I come.

I come so hard I find out why the French call it 'the little death'.

SILAS

I'm balls-deep inside of her when she starts milking me and already barely hanging on. So I let my orgasm claim me and we come together. Blissful oblivion engulfs me as I fill her up, shuddering violently.

Our legs buckle in unison and we collapse onto the bed, a tangle of humans, clothes and juices.

I can't believe that just happened.

I've managed to get there without the doors shut.

I've felt a woman come on my dick.

I want to both laugh and cry. I'm still inside her after I shift a little to the side in order not to crush her, and I carry on holding her tight from behind.

I never want to let go.

I look at her pretty hair, the fabric leaves adorning it, crushed like autumn foliage, and smile.

"Wow," she mumbles into the mattress then turns her head awkwardly over her shoulder to kiss me, a fleeting brush of the lips. "That was something."

I swallow hard and suddenly I feel sick.

This is not how it should have been.

Not with Grace.

She deserves so much more than a filthy rage fuck with the clothes still on. She is so much better than this. She should have had the old me, not this fucked-up, distorted version.

The irony doesn't escape me that the girl who wanted it lewd and dirty got the sappy vanilla guy and this beautiful, gentle woman got the depraved arsehole. I start to pull out of her, but she reaches behind me to land a hand on my butt and holds me to her.

"Not yet." she mutters. "Stay."

So I stay.

Grace

Eventually, we grow sticky, cold and uncomfortable and we decide to go have a bath together.

I sit between Silas' legs in the steaming tub, facing away from him, and he carefully takes the braids and decorations out of my hair, leaving them on the edge of the tub. When he's taken the last braid out, he sweeps my hair to the side and kisses my neck. Then he slings his amazing arms around me and gathers me in them as he lies back. I sink against his chest, letting my hands run up and down his beautiful forearms and turn my head to look up at his face. Even from this weird angle, I can see there is a myriad of emotions playing on it. It's almost too intimate to bear. I quickly give up trying to decipher each and every one of them.

"Tell me something," I say. My voice comes out hushed.

"Like what?" He smiles down at me.

"Tell me a half-truth you tell people then tell me the true truth."

He frowns.

"What's that supposed to mean?"

"You know," I say, reaching up into the short beard that's growing over his face by now to run my fingers through it. "Something you tell them that's true, but you are, like, omitting a whole loada shit in between."

"You like the beard?" he asks me instead.

I snake my arm up around his neck and pull him in for a quick kiss and savor the way it feels against my skin.

"I like you either way," I say when I release him.

He looks into my eyes for a long time after that and my heart suddenly starts beating like crazy again. It's then that I realize the difference between this man and all the rest. We can go from cozy and chilled to hot and the chills in two seconds just by looking at each other.

He smirks, sharing my thoughts. His cock stirs against my back. He comes in for another kiss, but I put a finger up to his lips, holding him off.

"Half truth and true truth first," I demand.

He draws back and then kisses the inside of my palm.

"Give me an example," he hedges.

"Like when I used to tell people I couldn't come dancing 'cause Mum was sick, when the whole truth was, I didn't want to come dancing because I didn't know if that would be the night she'd die."

He thinks for a moment then nods pensively.

"I'm gonna miss you when you're gone," he says slowly.

I frown at that. Not quite sure if he is stalling again or if this is his answer.

"So what's the whole truth?" I ask, settling on the latter option.

He pins me in that copper-brown gaze of his again, and a whoosh of electricity goes through me, like a wave.

"I'm going to miss *us* when you're gone."

SILAS

It's later that night, after we've dried ourselves and are all cuddled up like two cats, under the duvet in the dark, that I find the balls to apologise to her.

"Sorry," I mumble against her forehead as I run my hand in long strokes down her back.

Her skin is super smooth, and I can't get enough of the feel of her. I love holding her like this, lying on our sides, facing each other. There is something innocent and sweet about it that doesn't often happen in my world.

She chuckles.

"What for?"

"It shouldn't have been like this," I say, still talking to her hairline.

She wriggles away a little, and I know she's looking up, as if she could scrutinize me in the dark.

"What shouldn't have been like what?" she asks, and I can hear in her voice that I have genuinely completely lost her.

"Our first time."

I breathe out, giving myself a pause before I force out the rest.

"It should have been gentle and loving, not so..."

I try to find a better word, but I can't, so I stick with the truth.

"Angry," I finish.

And she laughs. She fucking well laughs. Then she pushes me onto my back and clambers half on top of me, sideways across my chest. Her long hair falls around me and tickles my skin.

"That was an angry fuck in Silas' world?" she teases.

I swallow hard. She has no idea. I pumped her *full* of my hatred and frustration.

But before I can say any more, she runs her nose along mine and says softly, "If that was angry, what is gentle Silas like?"

It's a challenge.

And I show her.

Grace

When I wake up the next morning, he's not next to me, but I can still feel him all over my body.

His gentle hands.

His nose running down mine.

His kisses like butterflies landing on my skin until my every nerve cell is awake.

Touching me deliberately, carefully, everywhere but *there*.

Then finally, finally entering me, followed by an eternity of slowly sliding in and out of me as he towers above me, arms poled either side of my head.

Stroking me from the inside.

Loving me.

And still I came for him. Not hard but *soft*. An orgasm like stars dotted across a night sky. So unlike any other it made me cry a little.

The tears want to come back even now and I'm almost glad he isn't here. I need to gather myself, *find* myself, before I can face him again. Because it'll be just me who'll be getting on that plane in a few days. And who knows what'll happen to him after that? The thought is hardly bearable.

SILAS

I had to leave her and go for a swim. It hurt too much. I couldn't keep looking at this gorgeous, funny, smart woman in my bed, my saviour who's slowly but surely lifting the curse without so much as trying and know that she will be gone from my life in just over a week. I want her to stay, want to go with her, want to keep her. I don't think I've ever felt like this about anything or anybody. Not even Niamh. Not even *before*.

I take a deep breath and dive under the waves.

Grace

The next week goes so quickly it may as well be a dream. The closer we get to my departure date the tighter we hold on to each other at night, the more desperate we fuck, the less we sleep.

We spend every second of every day together. We finish my list as much as possible, even go to see a random show at the Theatre Royal that neither of us pays too much attention to. Another day, he takes me to Oxted, the little village in Surrey, where my grandparents were from and where Mum grew up. I never got to meet either of them and they were cremated, so there isn't a grave to visit, but we have a picnic in the churchyard of the little church adjacent to my mum's primary school, which still exists, anyway.

I've learned that Silas is big on picnics. He loves putting random stuff together from whatever he can find in the fridge and then feeding me titbits and letting me guess what I'm eating. It's a game I'd happily play until the day I die. One thing I never do get to do is stay at the Palais, although Sheena keeps an eye out for any cancellations for me. Some things are maybe just not meant to be.

But we don't only do what I came for. More than once, Silas makes up our agenda. A cathedral here, a day in the forest that's home to Winnie-the-Pooh there, a day on the beach in between. And finally I get to find out why he smells of ocean all the time. I even get to come to the gym with him to watch him train every day.

Watching Silas train is a sight to behold. He's fast. Incredibly fast. And *beautiful*. But it doesn't change that what he is preparing for is nothing like what happens in the gym. I'm scared for him and more than once I think about changing my flight, but when I mention it, the look in his eyes says it all. He doesn't want me here when it goes down. *'I don't want you to see the real me. I want you far, far away, safe'* he says. I want to call it melodramatic bullshit, want to ask him who the fuck he thinks I'm sleeping with if not the real him and tell him I can handle it — that I can handle anything after watching my mum die — but I don't.

I get it.

More than he realizes.

For no other reason than that I get *him*.

I'd be a distraction, a weakness. I'd be a reminder on the sidelines that actually the fighter is *not* all he is. And he can't afford that. This isn't just your standard, ordinary, highly illegal bare knuckle fight the winner of which stands to get a small fortune. I got that memo. I'm not stupid. It's a showdown between stepbrothers that's been long in the making. How long and why, I have no idea. But I have a gut feeling it's tied to his darkness, his inhibitions. The whole thing has the scent of something primeval and base and somehow *sexual*. And, yes, of course, I wonder. I wonder in directions I really don't want to think in and that makes me sick to the core, so I don't ask but I keep my lips away from his dick.

And love him all the harder with everything else I got.

Silas

I wish I could stop time. We have one last full day left and then, tomorrow morning, I'm taking her to Heathrow. She'll get on her plane, go back to America and hopefully forget about me. In time.

I'm not stupid.

I know she's fallen for me as hard as I have fallen for her.

It's there in her laugh when we're out and about, there in her every touch, there in the way she clings to me when she comes apart in my arms, in the way she caresses me at night after she thinks I've fallen asleep. I've never been loved like that and I know I never will again, but that doesn't mean I can let her stay. She's asked, has offered to change her flight. But I don't want her to.

I don't want her to watch me kill.

I don't want her to watch me die.

And no matter what security measures the Bensons put in place, between Rowan and me there can't be another outcome.

One of us is leaving old man Benson's party next week in a body bag. Or a rolled-up carpet. Whatever.

And I want somebody in the world to remember the person who is lying here right now, holding a beautiful woman in his arms, about to wake her with kisses all over and promises of a picnic breakfast in the garden.

I want somebody to remember *me*.

Grace

There is nothing quite like being half asleep still and having a sexy, muscled man with incredibly silky skin and a beard, just the right side of not scratchy any longer, kissing himself all the way down your body. Until he lands on your sex, gently parts your legs, insinuates himself between them and pulls you fully into consciousness with one long lick of a flat, soft tongue from your perineum all the way to the top of your mound. So that you buck awake seeking more of his mouth on you and, of course, he obliges, lapping at you leisurely and with so much adoration that for a long time you don't know whether to have an orgasm or die from feeling loved.

Until he makes the decision for you, suddenly seriously turning up the heat by suckling your clit in earnest, bringing you just to the brink, letting you hover there until you already start clenching around nothing, only to slither up your body, swift like a snake, and fill you up with his cock in one fast, sure stroke. So you come around him, the first time that morning, just as he enters, each of your spasms drawing him in deeper.

That's how Silas wakes me on my last day. A sweaty half an hour and another orgasm later, we are hugging, nose to nose, sticking together and laughing.

"Morning," he says, kissing the tip of my nose.

"Morning," I respond.

"So, what do you want to do today?" he asks.

He's careful not to say it but the *on your last day* hangs heavily between us, although he kind of goes and addresses the elephant in the room easily enough with the next part.

"I've been told to have you back here by seven tonight. Mum wants to cook you a goodbye dinner, God help us."

He brushes his lips against mine.

"But Kalina is making some Polish dessert, so we won't starve," he reassures me.

"I'm kind of looking forward to tasting your mum's food after all I've heard about it," I say, grinning at him.

Apparently Kalina and I got lucky the day Sheena made us pasta and pesto because allegedly her inability to cook a decent meal is legendary. According to Silas, I'm yet to find out.

"I'm not gonna have food poisoning on the plane, am I?"

"Nah, there won't be an organism left alive on whatever she makes. Her speciality is charcoaling things."

"Yum."

"So, what do you want to do today?"

He hugs me a little tighter. I think about it for a moment while I nuzzle his chest.

"I want a normal day. With you. Here. In Shoreham. Have a shower.

Go to the beach, watch you swim. Take a walk along the houseboats. Spend my last English currency in thrift shops. Go have lunch in a café. Then a bit more of this."

I kiss him, with a little tongue, to illustrate what 'this' is.

"And a bath. And then maybe we could help your mum with dinner? 'Cause as much as I'm looking forward to experiencing one of the famed Sheena O'Brien kitchen fiascos, I think I'd rather not regret my last meal here."

He looks into my eyes for a long time after that, not saying a word. Then he smirks.

"Let it not be said that my woman doesn't like having a plan."

There is a moment when he says 'my woman' where we both know that in a parallel universe that's exactly what I am. And there we live in the same country, have normal jobs and are very, very happy. But not in this one. He kisses the tip of my nose again.

"Let's get this show on the road."

$SILAS$

I try not to think about her leaving because each time I do, there is a caveman inside of me who wants to chain her up in our non-existent basement and never let her go. The thought that by this time tomorrow she'll be *gone* pulls all my insides into one tight ball of pain. So I do my best to stay in the moment.

We do pretty much everything on her list and by the time we get to the little café I've chosen for lunch, we have a whole charity shop bag full of nonsense that she'll be taking home to the States.

"I have no idea where I'm going to put all this stuff," she laughs, looking at the bulging bag next to the chair she flops into. "I don't even have a flat to go to."

I remain standing because this is a go and order at the counter kind of place and frown down at her. We've talked a lot in the last three weeks about all sorts of stuff, but we never once discussed the future. 'Cause we knew we didn't have one, I suppose. But it never occurred to me that she didn't have a place to go back to.

"What do you mean?" I ask while she peruses the menu.

She shrugs absentmindedly without taking her eye off the blackboard hanging above the counter.

"We were living in the manager's quarters at the Atlantis until Mum got too sick to work, and then we had this shitty little apartment together, but after she died, I gave it up. I didn't want to be there anymore. It was never our home just the place we waited for her to die. So the last year, I've been rooming with people. But I gave up my last room before I came here. It seemed silly to pay rent on a room when I'm not there. And I really hated my roommates."

She stops talking to study the board properly and smiles at me.

"Can I get a latte and a slice of goat cheese and caramelized onion quiche, please?"

I smile back at her.

"Sure. What are you going to do?"

She shrugs.

"Don't worry, I'll find something."

I don't like it, I don't like it one bit. But there is nothing I can do about it. The only thing I can do is get her a latte and a goat cheese quiche. So I head to the counter.

Grace

I watch Silas go and order our food, and then he half turns to me and holds up a hand, signaling he'll be right back. He disappears down a short corridor by the side of the counter, towards the singular restroom. I watch his back, the grace with which he moves, and I'm so absorbed in what I see, I miss the person approach who suddenly sits down in the chair next to me. I turn, a 'sorry but that seat is taken' on my lips, and freeze.

The guy who is looking at me with an insolent smile instantly gives me the creeps. It's not that he's ugly. On the contrary, he's actually extremely good-looking, handsome even, in a dark sort of way.

He's tall, built, filling out the white tee and cargo pants he is wearing to bursting point with muscle. His eyes are a deep chocolate brown, big but with a vaguely Asian slant. His short, unruly but dead straight hair also speaks of some heritage from far, far away and he has that extremely chiseled look many women swoon over. Not my thing. I always think those guys look too much like cartoon heroes. Not that this guy would wear a cape of righteousness, if the menacing vibe I'm picking up here is anything to go by.

Even though it's not really possible, I instantly know who this is. Maybe I caught his scent that night he came to the house, or maybe it's because he's blatantly transmitting it, but there is no doubt in my mind that this is Silas' nemesis.

Rowan.

We just stare at each other for a long time in the most unwanted intimate way. I want to push my chair back, away from him, but I suppress the impulse. Because something tells me that's exactly what he wants.

"Hey, pretty woman," he finally says in a deep timbre, and I can't help but laugh at him.

And I mean *at* him. It's the cheapest line ever. Yeah, Julia Roberts and I might both use the same color number for our hair but that's pretty much where the similarities end. I ain't no Vivian and he sure as hell ain't no Edward Lewis. My Edward Lewis is leaner and meaner than him — and just coming back from the restroom, wiping his wet hands on his jeans.

"You stalking us, you perverted fuck?" Silas growls down at him as soon he arrives at the table.

He appears deceptively calm, but I can see behind his stoic mask that he'd have no problem putting his hands around this guy's neck and squeeze until he's dead. That's a revelation I'm not sure how to deal with. And I don't get the time because the next thing I know, Rowan's hand comes up to my face and he starts running an index finger along my jawline.

"You told her how much you like to share yet?"

I flinch back from his touch.

Out of the corner of my eye, I can see Silas making a move towards Rowan. It doesn't take a genius to work out what's about to go down and that at the end of it there won't be much left of this bijou little café. But before anything else can actually happen, I get out of my chair, hustle myself into the space between them, push Silas back with my ass, and slap Rowan full force in the face.

"You might like to share, but I don't," I spit down at him. "Now fuck off and leave us alone."

Rowan looks at me surprised then laughs.

"Oh, I like her. She's got spunk."

He gets up and looks over my shoulder at Silas.

"See you on the sixth, little bro."

I can feel Silas wanting to go after him, but I reach behind me, grab his arms and wrap them around me, holding him to me as fast as I can. I can feel the tension in his body, the coiledness of his muscles and though it's highly inappropriate, it's also *hot*.

We watch Rowan retreat through the door and Silas relaxes against me. I smile to myself because he could have been angry at me for stepping in but he's not. No, he gathers me up against him even tighter, kisses my neck and whispers in my ear.

"I love you, Grace Turner."

SILAS

I tell her I love her and catch myself by surprise.

The thing is, it's true.

I might only have known her a month, not even that, but when she is around, life is not a chore. It's light, a gift. Even with everything hanging over me, having her with me makes the moment worth living.

She spins around in my arms and looks at me wide-eyed, but before she can say anything, the waitress, who's missed all of the shenanigans, appears with our food and drinks and a smile. Like the polite people we are, we sit down and let ourselves be served.

Until the tender moment is gone and what remains is the burning question in her eyes, the one that reads *what the fuck was he talking about?* Because she isn't stupid, my Grace. She heard what Rowan said and she knows he wasn't just teasing. The thought makes me feel sick and I put my half-eaten sandwich down.

I take the hand she slapped him with in mine, turn it up and stroke her reddened palm.

"Does it hurt?" I ask her, and she giggles around the mouthful of quiche she is chewing.

She swallows.

"A little," she answers truthfully. "I've never slapped somebody before. It stings."

I kiss her palm and it's then that I make the decision.

She deserves the truth about me.

"I will tell you," I promise. "But not here."

Grace

In the middle of Shoreham, there is a church with a little cemetery and that's where he takes me. Seems to be almost a regular thing with us, cemeteries. I'm half tempted to play my new 'Grace' spotting game, but the air he gives off is too heavy to allow for any delay in proceedings.

I feel like if I procrastinate with tombstone gazing first, he might not tell me what he's come here to tell me. So I let him lead me over to a massive tree and we sit in the shade, opposite one another, legs crossed. He picks up a small stick and starts peeling the bark off it with nervous fingers while he talks.

"That was Rowan," he begins, and I nod.

"I figured."

He frowns at me.

We've never spoken about his family much, and I can see in his eyes that he's confused as to how much I know already, so I go on to explain.

"The guy you're fighting next week. Your stepbrother. You talked about it with Diego at the greyhound track."

"Right. Yes."

I've thrown him off track.

"I pay attention," I say with a wry smile. "Bartenders' affliction. He's also the guy who your mum claims didn't push her head into the wall."

He narrows his eyes at me, and I shrug.

"I may also eavesdrop on occasion. Also bartenders' affliction. But that's as much as I know. Tell me about Rowan."

He takes a deep breath and rotates the skinned wood stick in his hand.

"Mum's never been great at picking blokes. Understatement of the century that. She used to be a model when she was younger, and she was *in demand*."

"She must have been, otherwise she'd hardly have worked with Newton."

He smiles at that.

"Yeah, she was pretty high up there but the problem with modelling is, it attracts arseholes and Mum really does pick 'em. So when she was at the height of her career, some arsehole in the industry got her knocked up. We're not overly religious or anything, like not at all in my case, but Mum was raised Catholic and the idea of an abortion went completely against her grain."

"I'm glad about that," I joke, but he shakes his head.

"Thanks, but no, that particular baby wasn't me. Anyway, when she found out she was pregnant, she took a break from modelling, came back home to Brighton and promptly hooked up with another cunt. This cunt couldn't stand her sassy mouth. So one night, he beat her. Badly. She had a miscarriage."

My hand flies to my mouth.

"Fuck."

"Fuck, indeed. But it gets better. Enter Cecil O'Brien, a guy who had the hots for Mum since fucking pre-school. She was his childhood crush all grown up into this internationally successful model, he was an MMA champion. Match made in fucking heaven. He takes care of the cunt for Mum and eventually Cecil and her get married. That's why we are still O'Briens even though Cecil isn't my father."

"What?" I ask, my head swimming.

What a back story. I feel positively boring in comparison.

"Yeah. Cecil was a nicer type of arsehole but an arsehole, nonetheless. Was. Past tense. Now…never mind. Either way, he wasn't the most faithful of people. Kept shagging other women left, right and centre. So eventually Mum got her own back with the next cunt. My father. He didn't stick around, and I don't think she wanted him to either. He was supposed to be just a revenge fuck. Only it went hideously wrong and she got knocked up again. With me. Cecil was even gonna take her back *if* she had an abortion. But full circle back to

Catholic upbringing and I was born. Needless to say, Cecil hated my guts. Still does."

A bunch of puzzle pieces are falling into place for me right now. There was a Cecil mentioned in connection with Diego setting up next week's fight, and I'm certain it's the same one. It's not exactly a common name. But that's not what we came here to talk about, so I prompt him a little.

"Rowan?"

Silas takes another big breath.

"Yeah. He came with cunt number...I've lost count. A guy called James. Came after we had already been priced out of Brighton and relocated to Shoreham. Actually, he wasn't really a cunt. Just an opportunist. He was just some random builder bloke who did some work on the house for us, made eyes at Mum and then moved in, complete with his whole fucking brood. He was basically looking for a new mother for his kids. His wife had died a year or so previously in a freak accident. He had a daughter called Sammy, she was quite sweet, and a little boy called Adam. They were fine. And then he had Rowan. Twelve, same age as me. Though he always made a big fucking deal out of being six months older than me. He wasn't James' son. James had kind of inherited him from his dead wife. Fuck knows who his father was. But anyway, Rowan moved into my room with me and when Mum kicked James out after a couple of years, that's where Rowan stayed. Well, not in my room, he moved out into the one Kalina is in now, but the point is, he stayed with us. James didn't want him, so Mum decided to keep him. Like a fucking pet."

"Well, I get why you didn't like him. Must be tough having somebody dumped in your space like that."

He looks up at me for the first time since he's started talking about Rowan and his eyes bore into me with an intensity that makes me shiver. I can tell he's making a decision there and then about how far I'm allowed in. Then he shakes his head.

"No, Grace, I fucking *loved* him."

It's the first time I've ever said it out loud.

I did.

I loved that fucker like an actual brother. I would have died for him. No question. I know how I just sounded to Grace but, actually, Rowan moving in and then staying when Mum kicked James to the kerb was the best thing that ever happened to me.

Before Rowan, I'd been fucking lonely most of the time. Mum was always at work. No matter which cunt was sharing her bed, she always, always maintained her independence. It's what killed it with James. He wanted her to stop working and take more care of his kids. She told him to fuck off. She liked Sammy and Adam well enough but she ain't the mummy type.

Never has been. I was at nursery all day from the moment I hit six months. She's good with teens, though. Once you can let yourself in and out of the house with your own key, she's a top mum. Before? Not so much.

So before Rowan, I'd been pretty lonely, and it was like having a ready-made brother. We got on like a house on fire. Even in the two years we actually shared my room. Both loved the same kind of stuff, both got into MMA at the same time. Best sparring partner in the world. Thick as thieves we were.

Till Niamh.

I realise that I've disappeared into my own head when Grace takes the stick away from me that I've been twirling in my hand and pokes me with it to regain my attention.

"We were like actual brothers," I carry on. "I remember the day Mum officially adopted him, which took forever because of all the legal shit, but I was so chuffed. Fucking made. We were already into competition fighting then, both of us. But strictly legit MMA fights, nothing like the shite that goes down at TripleX. Or so I thought. Turns out, Rowan was already knee-deep involved with the Bensons back when we were still at school."

Grace frowns at that.

"How did you not notice?"

"Niamh," I answer. "We'd all been friends for a long time, but then Niamh and I got together and you know how it is, first love and all that. I kind of lost track of where Rowan was most nights."

Despite everything that fucker has done to me, I still feel a twinge of guilt at that. Maybe if I hadn't been so fucking wrapped up in Niamh and trying to make her happy, he wouldn't have fallen off the tracks. And maybe if he hadn't fallen off the tracks, he wouldn't have felt the need to annihilate me, *us*.

I've thought about that night a hundred million times backwards, forwards and sideways. Till it became an obsession I had to break, and at the end of the day I still think he did what he did because he was *hurt*. Because I'd taken my eye off him and he'd got into trouble, and he wanted to punish us for not noticing how far he'd slipped. But no matter what, there are things there are no excuse for.

It's a Friday night, the house is empty apart from the two of us and things have just got serious. We're both naked, lying on our sides, kissing. I'm stroking Niamh's breasts the way she says she likes, and I tweak her left nipple. She moans but I'm not sure if it's a real moan. I feel the pressure building again and not in a good way. We've been together nearly three years, have been having full on sex for the last two, but still I have never been able to make her come. Not with my hands, or tongue, or dick. And I've tried. Boy, have I tried. It's a dark cloud that continuously hangs over our relationship. For a long time, she pretended, and I was naive enough to buy her climaxes. Then one day, she confessed. Since then, I've done everything she's asked me to do, exactly how she's asked me to do it, did it every which way she wanted to do it, played every role she wanted me to play and some of it was downright filthy. But nothing. She senses me getting tense and reaches down to wrap her hand around my dick. I'm hard for her whatever. I'm nineteen and I get hard if a chick licks her lips, so no matter what the difficulty between us, having Niamh naked in my arms will make me hard like a rock. She takes her lips off mine.

"Relax," she says.

She pushes me onto my back and starts sliding down, kissing a path down my body and then latches onto my dick. She loves giving head, loves being in control. She gets off on the power trip, she says. And it's true, nothing gets her wetter than knowing she has me at the flick of her tongue. And she is so fucking good at this. I've never been with another woman, so I have no comparison, but I don't need to. I can't imagine another woman's mouth on me like this. She is the one. She sucks me just right, going long and hard, soft and slow, licking around the head, teasing me with the edge of her teeth and even gently suckling on my balls in a way that drives me nuts. Soon I'm at the point of no return, that moment when the house could be on fire but you can't stop, you have to climax first no matter what, though you're not quite there. I've been watching her but now my head falls back and my eyes close. I vaguely register the door opening and a movement in the room. My eyes flutter open and I see Rowan standing behind her. His jeans are undone, and he is holding her by the hips. He grins at me as he enters her from behind, shoving his full length into her in one swift stroke. It pushes her mouth further onto my cock and she moans around it. A real moan. Rowan pumps into her rough and fast, while Niamh's sucking on me gets erratic and desperate. But I'm too far gone already. I spill into her and while she lets my come drip from her lips, I watch in a mixture of post-orgasmic bliss and total horror how Rowan grabs around her waist, his hand disappearing to what I'm sure is her clit as he pounds her like a rag doll. And within seconds, she starts trembling all over, coming with a choked whimper, my softening dick still in her mouth. A real orgasm.

It's funny how in actual fact it doesn't take more than a few sentences to tell the story, here under a tree in the middle of the cemetery. I had to shut my eyes, though, to go through with it and now I open them and look at Grace. I'm not sure what I was expecting to find, but it sure as hell wasn't a deep frown line between her brows, telling me she doesn't think I've finished. Shock, maybe. Horror. Disgust even. But not an 'and then what?' frown.

"Okay," she says slowly. "Not what I was expecting, and I get now why this—"

She points at my crotch.

"Doesn't want to go in here."

She points at her mouth.

"Though I'd still like to try to convince him otherwise. But here's the real question, how come you *hate* Rowan, but you still meet up with Niamh for tea?"

Grace

He looks at me in that completely blank way people have when they're not comprehending a single syllable of what you've said.

"Why would I be mad at Niamh?" he asks, and I get the feeling we need to back up a bit. I clearly heard a different story from the one he's been telling me.

"Right, okay. Tell me what happened next. I mean immediately after. Did you guys talk about it?"

"What?? No. What happened immediately after is that Rowan took his dick out of my girlfriend, and then he disappeared out of the house before I could get mine out of her mouth. Literally. That was the last I saw of him until we went to the dogs. He came back the next day, while I was out, to pack a bag. And then he was gone. That's when we found out he'd been running up debts left, right and centre with bookmakers.

And that he had been fighting for the Bensons as payback. Still left us with the lion's share, though."

"Okay. Forget Rowan for a minute. What about Niamh? Did you talk to her?"

He looks at me with regret then shakes his head.

"I couldn't be with her after that. It was just too much. I knew it wasn't her fault, but still...We just kind of split there and then. Didn't even need saying. We looked at each other and we knew we were done. Never mentioned it."

"Are you sure?"

"About?"

"That it wasn't her fault?"

He gets pissy at that and in a way it's a relief because up to now he's been too fucking stoic about the whole thing. Robotic.

"What do you mean? Did you listen to a single word I said?"

I know I'm on thin ice when I respond, but I also figure I'll be gone tomorrow and maybe, just maybe, I can serve that purpose for him. The one who brings the truth. Who mentions the fucking obvious.

"Every single one. And what I hear is the story of a woman who's got fucked-up sexual stuff going on, so she goes and sets up some fucked-up two brother fantasy to service her fucked-up sexual kinks. And burns two people in the process."

He looks at me wide-eyed, and I realize that he really thought that she was an innocent in all of this. God, men can be such idiots.

"Trust me," I add wryly. "A woman doesn't orgasm when she is raped. Especially not one that has problems climaxing. I would bet my bottom dollar that she set this up."

He doesn't say anything for a long time after that, just stares at me, almost angrily. Eventually, I get to my feet and dust myself off.

"Enough of this. I don't want to spend the rest of my time with you talking about your fucked-up ex and your fucked-up stepbrother."

I lean down to bring my face to his and give him a good view of my cleavage.

"I want to spend it as *us*."

He smiles at that and I know we're good.

I know it's a fucking cliché, but I feel lighter after I tell Grace about what happened with Rowan, Niamh and me. I find her evaluation of it hard to stomach but nevertheless I feel better. She threw me a bit with her nonchalance but, actually, I liked the way she reacted to me telling her my deepest, darkest secret. Neutral. Logical. Astute. Grace.

I also get that she doesn't want to carry on talking about it, so after our little heart-to-heart under the tree in the cemetery, I push the past out of my mind. Practice has made perfect and I actually manage to give her my full presence in the present after we leave to make our way home to supervise Mum's cooking. By the time we get to the house, it's clear we are bloody well needed.

Mum's decided she is making lasagne, one of the few things she thinks she can cook and has already managed to burn the mince in the frying pan. It really is a gift. I take over as soon as we get in, ordering her to make some cocktails for Kalina, Grace and herself while I do the food. Sheena O'Brien is great at cocktails. Or so I've been told. I don't drink. Grace doesn't really either, the only time I've seen her drink was at the track when Diego plied the women with champagne, but tonight she gratefully accepts the Gimlet Mum puts in front of her.

Kalina, who comes down as soon as she hears Grace and me return, is game, too. So while I stay at the hob, making the bolognese and then the béchamel sauce for the lasagne, I listen to the women talk and laugh and get tipsy. It's nice. Especially when Grace comes over and helps me cut the onion, garlic, red pepper and carrot that Mum forgot to fry with the meat.

There is a weird sense of family in the air that I'm not used to, like an American fucking sitcom or something. One that is utterly unfamiliar but that I really, really like. There is even a cake. On the windowsill, there is a cake with a hole in the middle cooling down, which I assume Kalina has made since there is no way on earth you'd find my mother ever doing any cakey-bakey. Those cake bakes at school? I was the kid who brought in the multi-pack from Tesco. I smile at Kalina across the kitchen and jerk my chin in direction of the cake.

"Did you make that?"

She nods.

"Is Kolasz."

"Okay."

She grins.

"Is wedding cake, really, but who wants to eat cake only once a lifetime?"

It takes me a second to get my head around her syntax but then I laugh. The girl is fucking genius if you pay attention. Grace looks over at her with the kind of affection that says she figured that one out a long time ago. She leaves her carrot chopping station and goes over to hug Kalina.

"I'll miss you," she says.

Grace can't see it, but I can. Kalina shuts her eyes tight for a moment and she looks like she's about to cry, but then she laughs instead as she withdraws from the embrace.

"No need. Wait until you taste Kolasz. You will take me with you in hand luggage."

Grace steps back a bit and scrutinizes her playfully.

"Yep, you'll fit in the overhead locker just fine. You can come."

Then she turns to me with a big, cheeky smile.

"Sorry, Silas, it's a dog crate in the hold for you."

Our eyes meet across the kitchen and there is so much longing between us it's a miracle the kitchen doesn't spontaneously combust.

How am I ever going to live without her?

Grace

If the occasion wasn't so sad, it'd be a grand kitchen party. We have the radio on some bizarre music station, called *SAM FM,* that plays hits from the last fifty years with no apparent rhyme or reason peppered with the occasional cryptic pre-recorded one liner and while Silas prepares the food, Sheena slowly but surely gets us rat-assed on Gimlets.

I've heard of them. I've been tending bar at the Atlantis since I was old enough to tend bar, and they sit firmly on our classic cocktail menu, somewhere between the Manhattan and the Cosmopolitan, but I can't remember anyone ever ordering one.

They're delicious. Finally, I have the answer to the question what purpose lime cordial serves.

The tipsier we get the more amused Silas seems and the more Kalina starts nagging Sheena to let her give her a makeover while the lasagna is in the oven. Three Gimlets later, Sheena finally gives in and lets Kalina get her makeup case. Though 'case' is an understatement. It's more of a trunk. On wheels. I want to help, but Kalina shoos me off, so I offer my services to Silas instead.

We're told not to look as soon as Kalina finishes examining Sheena's profile by cradling her jaw and turning her this way and that under the kitchen light. It's quite impressive how this slip of a girl at only eighteen can hold her liquor. She's definitely still more sober than I am. She opens her box of tricks and begins working her magic on Sheena, and we turn our backs to them and start preparing the salad, hip to hip. Silas does pretty much the lot while I hack at the bell peppers. He looks over, tuts in my ear, places himself behind me and shows me how to wield the knife professionally, hand over hand, in a reenactment of every cheesy pool playing movie scene. But with knives. And vegetables. I can feel his hard-on against my butt and grind into him a little. I hear him subdue a groan and giggle a little. Which means I'm on my way to pretty sloshed. I never giggle.

"You know, children, I may have my eyes shut but I can hear perfectly well," Sheena says, amusement tinting her voice.

"Shshsh, no moving, Sheena," Kalina reprimands her. "Let children play."

It's funny, but it is exactly how I feel. Like a naughty child. I make us put the knife down, toss the pepper pieces into the salad and sling an arm backwards around Silas' neck. Then I turn my head, so I can kiss him. He responds hungrily. With a lot of tongue. Relief washes over me, and it is only now that I realize our earlier heart to heart had me all tensed up, wondering if it would taint the sexual ease between us somehow. It really, really hasn't. When he withdraws, we look into each other's eyes and the heat between us is as palpable as ever.

"How long until the lasagna is done?" I mouth.

"Half an hour," he whispers back.

We turn towards the door.

"We'll be back in a bit," Silas informs Kalina and his mum in an admiringly neutral tone. "Salad is done. We'll be back before the lasagne is done but if not, it needs to come out in thirty."

Then he pulls me out of the kitchen by my hand, and I grin at Kalina as we pass.

She tsks back at me with mock disapproval, but the gleam in her eyes tells another story.

Pretty sure she won't let the lasagna burn, no matter how long we take.

As soon as we leave the kitchen, Kalina turns the radio up to full volume and starts singing along.

SILAS

I pull her up the stairs to our room. *Our* room. I swallow. This time tomorrow it will be just my room again.

My life.

My fights.

The thought nearly kills my mood but then we're at the top of the landing and Grace twirls around to face me and pulls me in for another kiss. She is slightly tipsy and sloppy with her tongue and I love it. She backs into the room, pulling me with her by fisting my t-shirt and we land sideways on the bed. I catch my fall, so I don't crush her and search her eyes.

She isn't so drunk that they are glassy and sparkle at me with all the desire I've come to know from her. It's the biggest high, this hunger in her eyes. For *me*.

"God, you turn me on so much," I whisper before I lean down to suckle the patch just above her clavicle.

She loves this. She loves having her skin sucked and my mouth wandering along her neck to behind her ear, never letting up, like a sucker fish. The harder the better. I always have to be careful not to leave hickeys behind but today I don't care. I want to mark her as mine.

I want the guy sitting next to her on the plane tomorrow to see at first glimpse that she is fucking *taken*. Even if technically she is not.

I know it's juvenile. I know leaving hickeys is fucking base as shit and makes me a chav, but I don't give a shit. I suck hard, and she yelps then moans in pleasure, bucking under me.

There are sounds coming out of this woman I haven't heard before and she is fucking *loud*. But, again, I don't care. My name is in there somewhere and I've never heard her scream my name before.

We've always been quietish, mindful of Kalina and Mum. But the music is turned up so high downstairs, there is little chance they can hear us. And even if. It's too good to stop. Grace's guttural sounds as she moans and groans and calls my name and 'yes' and 'more' and 'harder' gets me so riled up I think I'm going to come in my jeans just from the friction she causes by rutting against me. And, fuck me, is she rutting. I need something to hold on to and my hand goes to the hem of her shirt, rucks it up and finds her bare tit. I let up from suckling just below her ear to comment.

"No bra again."

Her hand goes onto the back of mine and pushes it down harder around her fullness, while she arches her neck up against my lips.

"Don't stop."

Like I was going to.

I latch back on, and she slings her legs around my hips, gyrating against me.

I know I'm gonna come if she doesn't stop.

"Grace," I hiss.

"Shut up and suck," she demands.

I do as I'm told, and her hips get more and more demanding. She is shamelessly dry humping me now, and I can feel her climbing higher and higher, her breathing coming in short, desperate pants until she starts shuddering in my arms as her orgasm rolls over her.

I take my mouth off her and watch her face as she comes, eyes shut, cheeks rosy, biting her lip.

She opens her eyes and looks into mine, her face serious for a second before her mouth curls up at the corner.

She flips me over onto the bed and laughs.

"You so let me do that. No way could I actually shift your butt like that," she says.

"You have me at a disadvantage, milady," I tell her, and she wriggles around on my hard-on a little. I groan.

"So I do," she grins, sliding her hand under my t-shirt.

It travels over my abs, up to my chest, and then slowly down again to get to the button at the top of my jeans zip. She touches the head of my cock as she undoes it and a shudder ripples through me. Her eyes are on my fly and she licks her lips. I clench inside. It's not a bad clench but still, I grab her wrists.

"Grace," I say with a warning tone.

She looks at me, determination in her eyes.

"Look at me, Silas. One lick. That's all I'm asking."

I take my hands off her and dig my fingers into the duvet beneath us, by my hips.

I nod, sharply.

"One."

"One," she confirms.

I lift my hips to help her slide my jeans and briefs down and shut my eyes.

"No," she says and leans over to grab a pillow then pushes it under my head and shoulders, her shirt tails all the while softly brushing over my hard-on. "Watch!"

So I do.

I watch as she settles back down on my thighs and runs one fingertip along the length of my shaft.

I watch as she lifts herself off me and shuffles around, so she is between my legs.

I watch as she gently cradles my balls in her palm.

I watch as she licks her lips.

I watch as she runs her tongue in one, long sloppy stroke all the way from my balls up to the tip and swirls it around the head, my cock all the while twitching, trying to find her mouth. A mind of his own.

"You taste so good," she murmurs, looking up at me. "Stop?" she asks.

My hands finally let go of the duvet and I sit up, slip one hand into her hair and cradle her while I run one finger of the other hand along her lips. That beautiful cat-like mouth.

I shake my head in answer to her question and she smiles.

And then she wraps a hand around my shaft to feed my cock into her mouth, and I can't get enough of watching her. She is glorious as she sucks and swirls her tongue around me while her hand pumps me leisurely, fingers sliding patterns through her saliva.

And then, suddenly, she runs her thumb gently along my banjo string while sucking at the top then slides her whole mouth down my length and I'm done for.

My body tightens and I claw her head, grunting her name, as I spill into her. I fall back but I can feel her swallow and it's an amazing feeling.

A first.

Niamh wasn't a swallower. She'd take the come, but politely spit it out. I catch myself and banish the thought. It has no place here. It has no place between the beautiful woman climbing on top of me right now with a grin rivalling the Cheshire cat's on her face and me. Ever. I look at her and I see both pride and concern in her eyes as she strokes my face.

"Okay?" she asks.

I pull her down for a kiss, tasting myself on her, and roll us onto our sides.

"Yeah," I say, stroking her face right back.

Such a small word but I'm pretty sure she knows all the words it represents.

'Cause she is Grace.

And she gets me.

I can see it in her eyes.

Grace

We lie for a little while just gazing into each other's eyes and stroking each other's face.

Over the last month, I've kinda got used to looking at his body, got used to the abs, the tight butt, the sculpted arms and the shit-hot back muscles, but I don't think I would ever get used to how utterly handsome he is.

In that dangerous, had my nose broken a few times but that just highlights how fucking fantastic my cheekbones and my mouth are kind of way. But even if that handsomeness got lost, I would never tire of looking into his eyes. He's got these amazing, very defined dark circles around the irises, like you normally only get from colored contacts, and from there the copper-brown color goes in concentric circles from very light to darker and darker, and in between the circles are shot through with rays of yellow-green flecks. Hazel, I guess, is the official term for them. But it isn't really their eccentric coloring that has me captivated. It's the expression behind them, the total adoration and love with which they view me. As if I were something fucking special.

As if to prove me right, he smiles and breaks the silence.

"I want to give you something. A token, something of mine, so you won't forget us."

I want to say something about how there wasn't a chance in hell I'd ever forget him, but he puts a finger against my lips.

"Wait here a sec."

He leaves me on the bed while he goes to the wardrobe and rummages around a bit. He emerges with an old, rusty biscuit tin in his hands, opens it, shuffles some stuff around in it and then takes something very small out. He puts the tin back and returns to me, looking at the object sitting in his palm with a wistful smile. He sits back down at the edge of the bed and gestures for me to join him. I sit up and shuffle over until I'm next to him.

"I wish I'd thought about it earlier because then I could have got a chain for it, but I only just had the brainwave," he says, somewhat sadly.

Then he turns up my palm and drops something into it.

It's a wrought silver pendant, a beautiful art nouveau 'G'.

"Wow, Silas," I look up at him, stunned. "It's absolutely gorgeous. Where did it come from?"

As we both stare back at the treasure in my hand, I'm secretly praying his answer is not gonna be 'my gran' or something like that because then there'd be no way I could accept it.

"I found it," he replies to my great relief. "James moved in with a metal detector and before we got into MMA, Rowan and I spent endless hours on the beach, metal detecting."

He looks away with a mildly embarrassed smile.

"We were twelve, we thought it was cool. That," he nods at the pendant. "Was the first actual thing I ever found. Mum even put a picture of it on lamp posts and social media because it looked like something someone would be searching for, but nobody ever claimed it. I took it to a jeweller once and they reckoned it was genuine nineteen-hundreds. So I like to fantasise it came from a shipwreck. You like it?"

I wrap my arms around him in a tight hug, the pendant carefully cradled in my hand, and clamber onto his lap. I hold him tight, tears pooling in my eyes.

"Lasagne is ready!" Sheena shouts from downstairs, and I reluctantly let go.

He lays his hands on my face, when I lean back, and wipes my tears away with his thumbs then gives me a gentle kiss.

"I take that as a yes. Let's go eat."

SILAS

When we return to the kitchen, I am instantly reminded of what an absolute beauty my mother is even as a middle-aged woman.

Kalina has gone all out in the makeup department, in a starkly edgy way, which suits Mum down to the ground, and has even managed to do something with the godawful frumpy haircut Sheena O'Brien has been cultivating for a few years now, simply by slicking it back with some product. The whole effect is that of a 1980s faux noir pop video. Mum's bone structure lends itself to stark lighting and dramatic makeup, and it makes me both happy and sad to see her like this. Happy because it reminds me of the person beneath all the crap that fate has slung at her over the years. Sad because ever since Rowan landed us with all that debt, she's kind of completely given up on all of life, bar trying to keep us afloat. It pisses me off and it reiterates the point why I need to win this fight. Maybe once she doesn't need to fear losing the house any longer, she'll return to the living.

While I take the lasagne out of the oven, Kalina clears the table of her paraphernalia and Grace asks her if she has any hair braiding string in her beauty case. She does and Grace fashions herself a necklace out of three different autumn colours for the 'G'. Mum doesn't say anything, but I can see her watching Grace with a faint smirk playing on her lips. She catches my eye and nods approvingly.

We sit down and eat and drink, though Grace switches from Gimlets to water, proclaiming she doesn't want to be hung over on the plane. I like that. A lot. Because I cannot make love to a woman who's off her face. And that's what I want to do before she goes.

We've fooled around, we've fucked, we've shagged, we've made love.

And before she goes, I want to love her once more, gentle and slow.

So that that's what she remembers.

What it feels like to be loved.

That, I can give to her.

Grace

It's only when I'm on the plane that I allow myself to feel sad. Silas took me to the airport in Sheena's car and all the while we kinda pretended it was just another one of our outings, laughing and joking and listening to *SAM FM* on the radio, playing recognize the tune before the lyrics start.

Once at Heathrow, he insisted on going the whole hog by parking up, taking my luggage to the check in for me and seeing me all the way to security. There, he held me for a long time, rubbing circles on my back and nuzzling into the side of my neck. I took a last lungful of Silas' scent, and then he kissed me, one long languid kiss, and sent me on my way with a hoarsely whispered *goodbye*.

We both turned away and I didn't look back. I couldn't. During the endless hours waiting on the other side before my gate was announced, I tried not to think about what I was leaving behind, but the irony didn't escape me that on my way to England nobody had been there to see me off, nobody was being left behind. Now, on the way home, I was leaving behind the one man who'd ever made me feel *loved*.

I shut my eyes, lean my head against the backrest of my aisle seat and think of him above me, last night and then again this morning, slowly sliding in and out of me, like he was savoring every stroke, every moment inside me. My insides clench at the thought with both lust and sadness.

He is going to be a hard act to follow.

I smile to myself. I'm pretty sure that was his intention and though it should annoy me, it doesn't. Not even remotely.

He's raised the bar. To top notch. And I'll be eternally grateful for that.

Still smiling, still with my eyes closed, I reach up to rub the pendant dangling around my neck between my fingers.

"Wow, that's one hell of a smile," says an unfamiliar male voice, traveling over from across the aisle.

I open my eyes and let my head flop to the side to look at the stranger. He's a good-looking guy in a business suit, not surprising since I spent all my air miles accumulated over five years to fly business plus on this trip in honor of Mum. He's a bit older than me and would give Chris Pine a run for his money in the blue eyes, chiseled chin department. He probably works out, don't they all, and he might even be sophisticatedly funny. He probably gives good mouth, too. He has those kinds of lips. But he does absolutely nothing for me.

"Thanks," I answer. "I was just thinking about the last orgasm my boyfriend gave me this morning."

To say he looks taken aback is an understatement. I can sense the woman who is sitting in the window seat in my row chuckle quietly, as she keeps staring studiously at her tablet. There is nobody between us and I didn't exactly lower my voice. She heard.

"Hooo-kayyee," the guy replies, nodding. "I'll let you get on with that."

"Thanks," I say, let my head loll back to its original position and shut my eyes again.

My boyfriend, I think.

And then I let the tears roll.

It's not like the guy next to me is gonna ask what they're about.

Walking away from Grace outside security at Heathrow was the hardest thing I've ever done. I went to collect the Capri from the car park in a daze, drove out of the airport and onto the motorway, feeling like someone had sucked out my soul.

- 141 -

I've been stuck on the M25 for almost two hours now. The motorway is choc-a-block and I haven't made it very far. I can still watch the planes take off and land above my head as we crawl along, feeling a stab in my chest with each one I watch leave, wondering if that's the one that is taking her away from me. We didn't address it, but we both know full well we're never gonna have the funds to see each other again.

She is completely skint with not even a home to go back to, and even if I win next week, the prize money plus all the cash I've hoarded from winning so far will be swallowed up entirely by our loan repayment. Rowan really knew how to rack up the numbers being a loser. Mum can start breathing again, I can stop fighting and do something normal. But at no point will there be money to finance a transatlantic relationship. That's for movie stars, rock gods and gazillionaires. Not for the likes of us.

So after all is said and done, I didn't see the point in asking Grace for her contact details. We spent so much time together, I've never needed her number while she was here and that's probably a good thing. It would just sit there on my phone, taunting me. I'm sure Kalina has it and I could probably find Grace on the net or through the Atlantis. But what's the point in prolonging our pain by 'keeping in touch'?

Absurd sentiment, 'keeping in touch', if you never get to hold them again, never get to *actually* touch them again, never get to sit in a kitchen together eating breakfast with cats meowing at your feet again.

What's the fucking point?

Grace

I cry myself to sleep on the plane, not waking up until we get to Dulles. As a bonus, I miss all the delicious airplane food that way. Only drawback is, I'm absolutely parched when I wake up, but it's too late for the flight attendants to bring me any water because we are already mid-descent.

By the time we touch down, I'm half delirious with dehydration and it makes me panicky about not having a fucking clue what to do next. I haven't got enough money left to stay even one night at the only place in DC I feel at home, so I guess some grimy hostel it'll be.

I really should have organized something while I was still in England, but I didn't want to. I didn't want to think about going home, about the loneliness awaiting me. I take out the phone I haven't looked at in weeks and see that there are two messages from Cindy. One asks if today is the day I'm back. The other asks to ring her as soon as I land. She's the only person other than Vince, the bar manager at the Atlantis, who knows, or cares, that I've been away, but it still surprises me that she remembers exactly when I'm due back. It makes me feel slightly less desolate. It's kind of nice to know that there is at least one person back home who would have noticed if I'd disappeared on my trip to England. So as I wait for my luggage a bit later, newly purchased water bottle in hand, I call her. It's early afternoon in DC and I wonder if she would be at work. You can never tell with Cindy because she works as an office temp, but she picks up the phone on the second ring.

"Gracie!"

She is the only person in the world who calls me Gracie but because she comes complete with this whole Dolly Parton type persona, including hair and figure to match, she is allowed to. It also helps that she is pretty much the only friend from high school who never deserted me throughout all the trials and tribulations of Mum's illness. Basically, Cinderella Dawson, yeah, no shit, that's her name, is a total sweetheart. So she gets to call me Gracie as much as she likes. But not without a little teasing.

"Cinderella!"

She laughs.

"You are the only person in the world other than my mama who gets to call me that, you know."

"Hey, you are the only person in the world, and that includes my dead mama, who gets to call me Gracie."

She laughs.

"I've missed you. What are you doin'?"

"At the moment? Waiting for my luggage."

"Right. Where are you staying? You gave up your room, didn't ya? You'll be holing up in the Atlantis for a bit?"

I snort.

"I wish. I ain't got no money for that, honey. I'll be finding myself a nicely unhygienic hostel for a couple of nights and hope I can find someone in desperate need of a roomie somewhere by the weekend. It's that or ringing my dad."

"Fuck that," Cindy says decisively. "Come stay with us. There are, like, four billion rooms in this house. You'll love it."

A lump forms in my throat.

"Who is us?"

"Ah, yeah, you missed that. You remember the job interview for PA I went for as a bit of a joke?"

"Yep."

"Well, I got the job. And it comes with its own friggin' apartment. It's, like, mostly the basement under the main house plus half the first floor. It's friggin' huge." There is a pause, long enough for me to watch my suitcase go around the belt and disappear into the belly of the airport again because I just don't know what to say. Cindy is being a lifesaver, but at the same time I suddenly feel distinctly like a stray that people keep taking in.

"Gracie?" Cindy asks into the silence and suddenly her tone changes from bubbly-excited to serious, dropping the traces of fake Southern and going straight into pure DC. "Honestly? I could do with the company. It's a great job but there isn't a ton to do. I can't go out, though, because I still need to be here on standby all the time. And there isn't really any other staff. He's quite the recluse. He basically sits up there being clever on the computer and I'm down here being less clever on the computer. So I barely see anyone. I'm bored out of my mind. Come on, stay with me, find your feet, tell me stories of England."

I still hesitate, and she sighs.

"You can pay me rent if you want to."

I smile. She knows me so well.

"Okay. Give me the address."

SILAS

She's been gone twenty-four hours when I finally manage to pick myself up and kick my arse to the gym.

When I got home from the airport yesterday, I just curled up with Luna and Sol on the bed that still smelled of her, stared at that stupid arse curtain of mine, and shut down. Stayed catatonic until Kalina came home and brought me some Kolasc on a plate, which I ate only to be polite and that turned to dust in my mouth. She was followed by Mum who came up later and gave me a hug. A fucking hug. From my mother. And it's not even Christmas, New Year or my birthday. I escaped the house after that to go for a swim, but I couldn't face the gym. Bright lights. Other people. All that shit.

But today I'm here, working through my programme, even asking around for a sparring partner, but nobody wants to take me on. Bunch of pussies. I'm about to go back and kick the shit out of the sand sack when the door opens, and Diego's blond mop appears in the doorway. He looks around, taking in the Shoreham Gym and Martial Arts Academy, and I can see in his expression that he thinks it's a decent enough place but a tad small. Arrogant git.

We make eye contact across the floor, and I cross my arms in front of my chest, standing my ground. If he wants to talk to me, he can come over to where I am standing. This isn't the club. Here, he is not my boss.

He grins at me in understanding, shucks himself out of the thin tan leather coat he is wearing over the dress pants and waistcoat of one of his infamous beige three-piece suits, and hangs it on a hanger by the entrance. Then he takes off his poncy Italian leather shoes and stashes them in the outdoor shoe rack like a good boy. He pads over to me on socks. They are black with some sort of pattern. As he comes closer, I see that they have pictures of the Roadrunner all over the left one and of Wile E. Coyote all over the right one.

I can't help but feel amused. Roadrunner was Diego's nickname in the ring when we were youngsters. Because he would tap out and run off. I like that underneath the guy with the stupid wannabe mafia rebrand there is still good old George who is big enough to own his rep as a bit of a coward, albeit on his socks.

He nods at me when he arrives in front of me.

"Silas."

"That's my name."

"Good to see you, man. How's the bruising coming along?"

"Gone," I say and lift my vest to show him.

"Good," he says, examining my abdomen closely. "So you're ready to face your bro-"

He catches himself.

"Rowan next week?"

I shrug.

"That's the plan."

There is another thoughtful silence on his part, and I'm starting to wonder what the point of him showing up here is. So I ask.

"Why are you here, George?"

He doesn't even give me a look for using the name he hates so much, and that gives me pause more than anything else. When he finally looks up, I see something I can't quite identify in his eyes. Then it hits me.

It's *concern*.

Well, shit.

"I don't know," he answers slowly. "It's all got a bit out of hand, this thing. Your brother, sorry, *Rowan* is training like a man possessed. And he looks good, man. He's a beast. But what concerns me more is Cecil. I tell you old O'Brien is out for blood. Yours, to be precise. He must really fucking hate your guts. I overheard him offer Rowan 50k on top of the prize money if he knocks you out proper."

He pauses and looks over my shoulder into the distance to gather his thoughts, while I reel at the fact that a fucker like O'Brien can just lay fifty grand on the table as if it were Monopoly money, while my mum works herself to the bone for peanuts. But what else is new. Apparently a lot, as I find out when George starts talking again.

"And Cecil has, like, completely taken over the whole show. I mean, I was never gonna keep it a surprise or anything. Half the fun was always gonna be the lead up. You know, Dad and him sitting in the pub for weeks on end beforehand, yaddering about it, egging each other on with their wagers, all that crap. But I didn't anticipate Cecil completely taking control. I was just gonna put up a ring in the garden, straw bales or something, nothing fancy. Fight on grass, like the good old days. After dinner. But now he's got Dad to have the pool pumped out and mats put down in there. The *pool*, Silas."

"The easier to wash down the blood," I say sarcastically, and he looks at me, nodding gravely. "Well, great. Thanks for giving me the heads up," I add and turn away.

His hand lands on my shoulder, and I look back at him.

"I have a bad feeling about this, Silas. I don't want anyone to die on my watch. *In our fucking house.* I need you to win this. So nobody gets killed."

I glare at him.

"Who says *I'm* not gonna lay *him* out permanently."

He frowns.

"'Cause you're a fighter, man, best we have, but you ain't a killer. And that's a good thing."

I nod and start walking away. I hate to admit it but I'm kind of touched by his faith in me.

"Anything I can do, man, just let me know," he calls after me.

I start shaking my head with my back still to him but then I have an idea. He's the Roadrunner, but he's better than nothing. I turn back fully and flash him a grin.

"I could do with a sparring partner. None of these pussies here wanna take me on."

His eyes go wide for a second.

"You're shitting me, right?"

I just keep smiling until he sighs.

"Fuck me. Great. Got any spare kit?"

Of course I do.

Grace

Four days after moving into Cindy's, I'm already doing my third shift behind the bar of the Atlantis since coming back, and I realize that I've kinda just slid back into my old life as if it were a slipper.

Only now I'm rooming with a friend I like rather than some idiots I hate. Cindy didn't lie. Her apartment is massive, the spare room I'm in about twice the size of Silas' bedroom, and the guy she works for pretty much a hermit. But a nice one. Cindy introduced us first thing and asked if it was okay for me to stay. He said it was her apartment and if it made her happy to have somebody there, she was welcome to let me move in with her permanently. Then he told her she shouldn't let anyone take advantage, though, and should definitely charge me rent and keep the money.

I've never met anyone like him. He's a good-looking guy despite being an ubergeek and he clearly has a shit ton of money, so he is probably on all those 'most eligible bachelor' lists. Ergo he should have a load of women and general entourage hanging around all the time, but as far as we know he hasn't had a single visitor since he hired Cindy three weeks ago.

I'm not surprised. He's so cripplingly shy he couldn't even look me in the eye for longer than a second when he shook my hand. When he talks to Cindy, he's mostly talking to his shoes, too. Unless he's giving her advice, like making me pay rent, or showing her how to do something on the computer. Then he's quite authoritative. But the rest of time? Heaven help. It would be cute if he was younger but in a man in his early thirties it's kinda heart-wrenching to watch.

His name is Leon, but he is about as far removed from a lion as you can imagine. More like a really sweet black-haired, blue-eyed, skinny kitten. If it wasn't for the fact that this is her first ever proper non-temp job and I wasn't cramping her style, I know Cindy would be all over that. She likes the long and lanky vampire type. She's always looking for the Nick Cave to her Dolly Parton.

Me? I'm not looking for anyone or anything anymore.

Before I set off for England, I had this grand idea that in that month I would finally figure out what I want to do with my life. Mum didn't leave me any money, but she left me brains. I just don't know where and how to apply them. But rather than clarity, England has brought me a hurting heart and the feeling that I'm living the wrong life.

I miss Silas so much I feel it as physical pain sometimes.

On that thought, I stop wiping the bar down and look around the empty room. It's lunchtime, there is one couple in the far corner, drinking wine, and that's the whole extent of my customer base so far. It's a good thing the Atlantis pays me an actual wage and I don't have to survive just on tips. With a deep sigh, I turn away and I start busying myself with cutting lemons and limes for later on in the evening.

I don't really think about how stupid an idea that is until I hold the knife in my hand and the memory starts flooding my entire body. Memories have been doing that a lot lately. Mostly at night when I can't sleep but also often in the daytime during mundane tasks. It's like you can take the girl out of the boy's life but you can't take the boy out of her soul. Or something like that. This time it's Silas showing me how to chop bell peppers, hand over hand, his hard cock pressing against my ass, his breath in my neck, his scent engulfing me.

Five nights ago.

An ocean away.

"Hey Grace, you okay?" Vince asks me. "You're crying."

He's standing by my elbow and handing me a napkin. I take the napkin and dab at the tears I hadn't noticed were running down my cheek until he mentioned them.

"I'm okay. Just tired. Still struggling with jetlag, you know."

"Hmm."

He studies my profile.

Vincent Scerri is in his late forties and he's been the bar manager at the Atlantis since I was a little girl. He was one of the few Atlantis employees who used to come to the apartment after Mum got too sick to carry on working and check in on her. He squeezed my hand at the funeral when I needed someone to squeeze my hand since my father hadn't come, worried it might upset his wife.

Vince is about as much family as I have in the world, other than Cindy, though funeral handholding aside we've never been touchy-feely or heart-to-hearty. Which makes it even more disconcerting when he leans in and sniffs the air around me.

"I smell bullshit," he says.

It's shocking because I don't think I've ever heard him cuss or use a word like that. He's way too softly spoken and polite. So I turn and look at him wide-eyed.

"Vince!" I scold him.

He takes a step back and examines me, unrepentant.

"You're not jetlagged," he states dryly as he shrugs. "I've got four sisters and three daughters. I know tears. Those aren't tired tears, they're love tears, missy. You're in love. Makes me wonder who the lucky fella is and why it is a crying matter."

He holds up his fingers in a 'wait a minute' gesture then pours a couple of glasses of Pinot Gris, shoves one at me and points to the table nearest the bar.

"Let's sit," he demands.

I follow him, sipping my wine on the go. We never drink on the job and I feel naughty.

"You're not gonna fire me for drinking, right?" I joke while I plonk my butt in a chair opposite him.

He raises his glass.

"Talk, bellissima."

So I do.

I've told Cindy a little about Silas, of course, but I tried my best to make it sound light-hearted, a fun holiday hook up. Under Vince's serious stare I feel like Mum's kinda listening in, so I'm honest. All the way honest, including telling him about the underground fights and Silas' entanglement with Brighton's bad boys. I can see Vince's face grow more and more serious as he listens to my story. When I finish, he nods gravely.

"Well, I can't say your mom would have approved," he says slowly, and I think, *yeah no shit, Sherlock,* but before I can retort, he softens the blow. "But this Silas character must be pretty damn special if he has you all tied up in knots like that because you, Grace Turner, are one smart cookie and far from easily impressed."

Vince calling me a smart cookie makes me smile properly.

"Yeah, right," I say dismissively to mask how pleased I am with his compliment.

"You say he is a good man?" he asks, and I nod. "You say he made you happy?"

I nod again.

"So what's a little illegal fighting on the side?"

"Vince!" I exclaim, my eyebrows shooting up, shocked for the second time tonight.

He grins.

"Hey, I'm Italian."

That makes me laugh out loud. Vince is like the nicest, gentlest guy I know and there is no way he has any connection to anything mafia. Besides, we're in Washington, D.C., we don't have organized crime here, we have politicians for that. And I happen to know that the Scerris have been in DC for five generations. They are a family of shoemakers, making made-to-measure luxury shoes. Both of Vince's brothers still maintain the family business. They are as quiet as he is. He lets me finish laughing, and then his eyes turn soft.

"Seriously, Grace, you like this guy?"

"Yeah, I do, did, whatever. Where are you going with this?"

"I'm not going anywhere," he answers cryptically. "But you sure should."

"What do you mean?"

I frown at him, and he points at the door.

"Get outta here, Grace. You should have never come back in the first place. Go max out your credit cards and get yourself another flight."

He repeatedly jabs his finger in the air in the direction of the exit, sternly, as if I were a recalcitrant child.

"Go back to England, go back to your man."

I stare at him aghast.

"I can't just go back there. I can't leave here."

"Why on earth not? You got dual citizenship, have you not?"

"Well, yeah, it was important to Mum that–"

He sighs as he cuts me short.

"Yes, *I know*, belissima, it was important to her that you'd keep the connection to her roots. You seem to forget, your mom and I were friends. If you'd been christened, like I wanted you to be, I would have been your godfather."

"Really? An Italian godfather? Now that would have been cool."

I grin at him, feeling the wine warming my cheeks.

"We're digressing. You're missing my point, Grace. So I will spell it out for you. What exactly is keeping you in DC?"

"Mum," I answer angrily. "Don't you get it? Mum is here."

He reaches across the table and takes my hands.

"Your mom's gone, Grace," he says gently but firmly. "She's in a hole in the ground in Oak Hill Cemetery. She doesn't need you anymore. Here or anywhere."

I try to pull my hands out of his grasp, but he won't let go.

"She would want you to follow your heart," he carries on. "She'd dance with joy if she knew you've fallen in love with an Englishman."

He takes a breath and squeezes my hands.

"I will tend her grave, Grace. I will put fresh flowers on every week, just like I've done this last month, and I will make sure the world still sees that she was loved."

Tears spill from my eyes again, and he finally releases my hands, so I can wipe at them. I sniffle and shrug at him dejectedly.

"It doesn't matter," I tell him. "I haven't got any money to get back on a plane any time soon."

He cocks his head.

"Sounds to me like you need to get on one much more pronto than 'any time soon', belissima. When is this fight?"

"Tomorrow. But I mean it. I can't. I'm all maxed out already."

He reaches across and pats my cheek.

"Hmm. Then let me see what Uncle Vincent can do for you."

SILAS

"Man, you really have the hots for me, don't you?" George taunts me as he has me in the second triangle hold this session. "You really do love it between my legs."

With my free hand, I tickle him below the ribs, and I can feel him holding in the chuckles as I practice my escape. Soon as I'm out and up, we call it a day. We've been going for over an hour, through all the takedowns and chokeholds under the sun, though George can't do a flying scissor for toffee, so we left it out.

At the end of the day, it makes no difference anyway. There is a reason Rowan is called Python. He's a master at chokes and George is nowhere near his calibre. I'm more of a kick 'em and punch 'em in the right places as soon as you can kinda guy. I found out early that the best bet is to not let them get up close and personal in the first place but lay them out from afar. Wait and strike. Hard and fast. Knock out, don't choke out. Most of my fights are over in seconds because I try to avoid all that rolling around on the floor bullshit as much as possible.

If I wanna roll around, I wanna do it with a woman.

Grace.

Fuck, I miss her.

But the fact of the matter is that in a street fight among real fighters, nine out of ten times a choke still wins. And I haven't fought anyone like Rowan in years, so I've been practicing.

George goes to pick up his towel and dries his sweaty face, still laughing, and I go and pick up my water bottle. He's been good as gold, turning up to spar with me every day since he came to check on me. I thought he was just gonna stay that first session but no, he's taken it upon himself to make sure I don't lose on Saturday.

Part of me thinks he's got money riding on it though he swears he doesn't. Either way, it's actually been really cool having him around. It's like we're having an illicit affair, where I get to call him by his real name and he gets to horse around with me like the good old days when we were both still living in Brighton, going to the same school, eating microwave popcorn on my mum's living room floor, watching Tarantino films, feeling like right little bruisers 'cause they were all 18s. George is not remotely good enough a fighter for his services to really help me, but if nothing else it takes my mind off Grace for a couple of hours a day.

"How are you feeling?" George asks me.

I give him a small smile. He deserves it.

"You're gonna invite me for a cuppa before I have to go and be Diego again?" he adds by-the-by and that really makes me smile.

Firstly, because I love the self-deprecating part of this guy. I hadn't seen it in so long I thought it was gone. Turns out it was just hiding beneath the surface. He can still take the piss out of himself with the best of them. And secondly, because I have the sneaking suspicion that coming over to mine for a coffee after our training sessions is a huge part of the attraction for him.

About as huge as the hard-on he has for a certain young Polish girl I live with and though he won't touch her 'cause he reckons she's too young for him, it doesn't stop him from going all googly-eyed over her in my mum's kitchen each time he comes over.

It's hilarious to watch.

Diego, night-club owner, organiser of the biggest illegal fight club league on the south coast, Prince Regent to a much wider operation nobody in their right mind wants to know the details about, turning into little George Benson with a crush on a girl so bad he'll happily hang in our crummy little house.

"Sure," I say. "Let's hit the showers first, though. Wouldn't wanna overwhelm Kalina with your manly smell, now, would ya?"

His face turns serious, and then he comes over to me and grasps my shoulders.

"I miss you, man," he says and lets go, turning away.

I swallow hard.

I know what he means.

Somehow the world was a lot better when we were just kids and the shit that went down was our parents' shit that went down and not ours.

Grace

"Are you sure you want to do this, honey?" Cindy is sitting cross-legged on the bed in my room, watching me frantically fold the clothes that I just dragged from the dryer.

"Ouch," I swear as I accidentally touch the scorching hot zipper on a pair of jeans.

That'll teach me not to wait out the cool cycle. But I don't have time. My flight leaves in five hours and I've still got to get my shit together and get to the airport.

"Yes, Cinderella, I am abso-fucking-lutely sure about this," I say, not really stopping to look at her, while I keep piling stuff into my suitcase.

Back into my suitcase. I only unpacked it not even twenty-four hours ago. Until last night, I lived out of it, not wanting to subscribe to the reality of being back in the States. Well, I'm fucking well unsubscribing again now.

Cindy makes a squealing noise.

"I knew it," she claims. "Holiday fling, my ass. You *looove* him."

I look up at her, raising my eyebrows.

"You're such a child, Cinderella Dawson!"

She smiles at me broadly.

"Yes, I am," she admits proudly then makes a sweeping gesture around the room. "But a child with a huge apartment, medical insurance, pension plan and a scorching hot boss."

In that exact moment the noise of a throat clearing comes from the door and — it couldn't be more sitcom perfect — Leon is standing there. Cindy goes wide-eyed but to her credit she doesn't blush.

"I'm sorry to interrupt," Leon says to the wall behind her as if he hadn't heard what she just said. "I've been trying to call you, but you haven't answered, so I came to see if everything is alright down here."

"I'm sorry." Cindy scrambles to the edge of the bed and gets up. "I left my cell in the living room. My bad. It's just that Grace is leaving us again and I wanted to spend her last hour with her."

Leon frowns at that and looks at me directly.

"You are leaving again?" he asks me sharply, and I'm surprised at his tone.

So is he I guess, since he immediately looks at his shoes again as soon as I meet his gaze.

"I am," I answer gently because I get that he is just upset at me on Cindy's behalf. "I'm going back to England."

"That's a shame," he mumbles. "I was hoping you'd keep Cindy company for longer."

He sighs.

"I'll call for my driver. What time do you need to leave here?"

"Six, but you don't need to do that. I can get an Uber."

He looks up and frowns directly at me.

"No," he says decisively. "My driver will take you."

Then he turns and leaves.

He's a strange, strange man.

But I kinda like him.

SILAS

The night before the fight, I sleep abysmally.

When I finally give up rather than wake up, I know with total clarity that I've been bullshitting myself. I convinced myself that it was better if Grace was long gone by the time this came around, but now I wish she was here, by my side, getting me through the next hours.

The day leading up to a fight is always a bit bollocks. It's a bit like when you're scheduled to go away somewhere but you're not leaving till the evening. Your bags are packed, you're primed to go and you can't really get stuck in much else because you know you'll be leaving soon and need to be ready.

Not that I've gone many places in my life. I'd like to, though.

If I win tonight and we can wipe the slate clean, I'll find a new job and I'll start saving up to maybe go and see a little of the world one day.

Today's day-before-the-evening will be even longer than normal since my weeks with Grace have completely thrown me out of sync. Whereas before I'd get up at three in the afternoon, I now wake at nine every morning. It's been bliss not working in the club. I hadn't realised how much I love being up and about during daylight hours. But today it just means that there'll be even more time in which I don't know what to do with myself.

I swing my legs out of bed to start my pre-fight routine of light snacks every couple of hours and waiting around. You don't want a full stomach but neither do you want to be starved by the time the ref goes 'and fight'. I briefly wonder who Diego will have 'refereeing' tonight or if there'll be anyone at all down there in the pool with us. The job is paying lip service at best when it's at the club. Wonder if they'll even bother tonight. I push the thought aside as I go to open the bedroom door. No point pondering. I'll find out soon enough.

I step out onto the landing and hear Kalina laughing downstairs, followed by my mum's voice and it stops me dead in my tracks. Why the fuck is Mum home? She should be on an eight to eight, which would have been perfect in terms of her missing out on the car that is supposed to come fetch me at seven to take me to the Bensons. It can only mean that she has taken the day off.

Shit. Fuck. Bollocks. Awkward.

I go to take a piss then proceed down to investigate.

I find Mum and Kalina sitting in the kitchen drinking tea. Mum looks up at me when I appear in the door frame and shakes her head disapprovingly.

"You look terrible, Silas. Go back to bed. You need your rest if you want to hand Rowan his arse tonight," she says evenly and makes a shooing motion. "Go, sleep. I wake you at midday with some apple and banana porridge."

I stare at her, flabbergasted.

She knows.

Of course she fucking knows.

Sheena O'Brien never just knows the half of it, she always knows the fucking whole of it.

"Is that why you're home?" I ask her.

She raises her eyebrows in mock pity.

"What do *you* think?"

"You're not planning on being there tonight, are you?"

She laughs mirthlessly at that.

"And on what planet do you reckon I'd have an invitation?"

The one where Cecil wants to see you suffer, I think. But I keep that thought to myself. I'd rather not give her any ideas.

"So why are you not at work?" I reiterate the question.

"The better to look after you today. Now go back to sleep."

She points at the door, but I hesitate. Might as well tell her in case something happens to me tonight. I look at Kalina and I feel bad for not trusting her, but I'm not taking any risks. Not with that amount of money.

"Come upstairs with me for a sec," I tell Mum.

She frowns but follows me upstairs when I turn around and go back to my room.

As soon as we're inside, I tell her to shut the door, and then I kneel in front of my bed. I look back at her over my shoulder.

"I need you to come over here. I want to show you something."

She comes over and lowers herself to her knees next to me.

"What is this?" she asks.

"You'll see," I tell her. "Slide your hand along until you find the patch in the carpet. Like, feel around for a ridge where I cut into it with a Stanley knife."

She frowns but starts rummaging around.

"I think I got it," she says after a few moments.

"Great. Lift out the patch. Then feel around for a loose section of floorboard."

She does and I can hear her tip the floorboard up.

"Can you feel it?"

"Yes," she answers.

"Great, put it all back together and remember it's there," I say and stand up.

She does as directed then scrambles back to her feet. Then she goes toe to toe with me with her hands on her hips, cocking her head and looking at me questioningly.

"I've been saving up my prize money over the last couple of years. There is a hundred grand under there," I tell her, matter-of-fact.

She gasps and takes a small step back, throwing her hands up.

"You what? Why? Silas, what on earth?"

I shrug.

"I was gonna give you the whole lot once there was enough to pay off the loan, but I don't know what's gonna happen tonight, so I thought I'd better tell you where it is."

"Why in heaven's name didn't you tell me earlier?"

"'Cause you would have stopped me."

She rolls her eyes.

"Too right, I would," she says, sinking down on the bed, and shakes her head, exasperated yet with a smirk. "But do you have any idea how difficult it is to whitewash a hundred grand?" she asks. "Would have been much easier to do it in small increments!"

"What?"

She pats the space next to her, and I sit down. She takes my hand in hers and strokes the back of it with her other hand, just like she used to when I was little and she was explaining the world to me.

"For someone who works for the Bensons, you've learned astonishingly little. You didn't think I could just roll into the bank with a suitcase full of cash and tell them here you go, have your money back, did you? That money needs to come from somewhere, Silas. And 'my son earned it with illegal fighting' is not an answer the bank, or the tax man, will accept. I need to somehow make it legit."

I stare at her sideways, feeling about four years old. I so often forget who my mum once was that each time a reminder like this comes along it slaps me in the face like a wet fish.

"Shit, Mum. I didn't think of that."

"Clearly," she grins. "But I appreciate the sentiment."

"So how are we gonna do this?"

She pats my hand and winks at me.

"Let that be my concern. I still have connections. That money down there will be white as bleached linen in a couple of months' time. It'll cost about fifteen percent, but I say it's worth it. Smaller increments would have meant I could have done it much, much cheaper. But you live, you learn. So how much more are you bringing home tonight?"

I smile at her, appreciating her confidence in me.

"The rest," I say and see her face fall.

"Another hundred K?" she asks, going white as a sheet.

I nod. She clasps my hand.

"Don't, Silas. Back out. That's too much. One of you is going to get killed. They don't lay on that kind of brass unless they want blood. Please."

I've never in my life heard my mum plead. It's part of why she drove the men in her life so nuts. She wouldn't back down, wouldn't cower, wouldn't plead. She is pleading now, but I know I can't back out. I need to finish this. Not for the money. But for me. And for Rowan. For our story to finally fucking *end*. She sees it in my face before I can answer.

"You can't," she says soberly, tears in her eyes.

I shake my head. She nods. And I know she understands. She never knew what happened between Rowan and me, just that it was bad, but still she gets it. On some primeval level, mother to son.

"Okay," she says at the end of a sigh and gets up. "Go back to sleep. I'll bring you that porridge in a couple of hours."

She is almost at the door when she turns back for a moment.

"And Silas? I love you."

Then she leaves and I crawl back into bed.

And bizarrely, I actually manage to fall asleep again.

Grace

The journey back to England is literally and figuratively the longest of my life. Literally, because at such short notice Vince couldn't get a direct flight for me, so I had to fly Aer Lingus and have a stopover in Dublin for five hours, turning an eight-hour flight into something that lasts approximately two centuries. As a bonus, though, the Irish flight attendants are extremely funny, clowning around in the aisle the entire way from Dulles to Dublin, and have me in hysterics, even if I only understand half of what they are saying sometimes.

Figuratively, because worry that I won't make it in time before the fight to kiss Silas and tell him I love him trumps my fear of flying and prevents me from sleeping even a wink during the thirteen-hour journey.

When all is said and done, Heathrow spits me out onto the curb by the bus station on June 6 at 1700 hours. Which is too fucking late in the day.

Frustration claws itself through my delirious overtiredness and I want to cry, but then I have one of those rare moments you get long after somebody dies when you hear the deceased's voice so clearly in your ear, it feels like they are standing next to you.

"In for the penny, in for the pound," Mum says in that beautiful, well brought up British accent of hers that she never lost. "Get a cab, Grace. Another couple of hundred pounds won't make a difference."

Who am I to argue with my dead mother?

Silas

I don't know the bloke who picks me up. He's one of old man Benson's crew and he doesn't talk to me beyond confirming he's got the right man on board. He takes me over to the house and passes me on to Goran who greets me outside, waiting for me on the drive. Goran takes me around the back to the garden and shows me the pool house, explaining in the fewest words possible that that's where the fight is going to happen. I can tell he's still miffed 'cause he never got to go up against me. Tosser.

He studies my face when he switches the lights on in the main pool room, gauging my reaction. I have to admit, if I hadn't been forewarned it would have shocked me to see the pool pumped out and the floor tiles covered in mats. I note that the sides are not cladded in anything, so if you get your head rammed against those or, better yet, the aluminium ladder leading down into the basin, you're probably fucked. Nice.

Around the top of the pool, Benson has had benches put up. I look up at the lighting rig above and realise there are cameras there. Actual fucking cameras. What the fuck? I let my eyes search the pit below, and then I see more of them. Tiny black eyes fixed to sides of the pool. Goran follows my gaze and barks a laugh.

"Yeah, man. They're live streaming this one. There is some serious dosh shifting owners tonight."

I nod sharply.

"So where do I wait?"

He beckons me to follow him out and leads me across the lawn to a summer house. He opens the door and switches the light on. Once inside, it transpires it is more of a guest cabin than a garden hut.

There is a sofa, which I assume folds out into a bed, a dresser, a corner with a hotplate, microwave and kettle, a toilet and shower. On the coffee table are a selection of protein bars, chocolate, isotonic drinks and bottled water. I dump my bag on the sofa before I look at the brands. I keep my poker face on but inside I'm smiling. George would make a fantastic girlfriend or manager. He knows my preferences.

I look at how the furniture is arranged, and I'm pretty sure the fact that there is enough floor space to warm up is also due to George doing some shifting. I hope I survive the night to thank him.

"Where is Rowan?" I ask Goran, but he doesn't answer me.

"You have about an hour," he informs me instead. "Somebody will come and get you when they're ready for you. Don't leave here."

On that note, he turns away and leaves me to it.

Grace

By the time my cab pulls up outside Sheena's house, it's nearly eight o'clock and I know I'm too late. I realized a while back that I wasn't gonna make it. The traffic on the motorway was insane and we were at crawling pace for ages, so I've long given up hope but even so, my heart seems to open wide when I see the familiar red door and a sense of belonging washes over me.

I'm home.

I hand the driver my card and he swipes it through the card machine before getting out and unloading my luggage from his trunk. As he shoves the bags at me, I mumble an apology about not having any cash for a tip and he shrugs then gets back into the car and is gone. I knock on the door and wait. After a couple of minutes, the door opens and Kalina is standing in front of me, her eyes wide with concern at first, before she squeals a welcome.

"Sheeena! Sheeeena! It's Grace. Grace is back!" she shouts into the house then opens the door fully.

I drag my stuff across the threshold and watch Sheena come toward me from the kitchen. I've never seen her like this. Kalina has clearly been doing her makeup again and she looks as stunning as previously, but it doesn't disguise the fact her brow is furrowed with worry or that beneath the foundation her face is ashen.

"Grace," she says quietly and opens her arms.

I stumble toward her and sink into her hug. We cling together for a few seconds, two women drowning with concern for the same man, and it is then that I know she knows what's going down tonight. I pull back a little and we look at each other.

"You know?" she asks, and I nod.

Suddenly I feel her back straighten under my hands, until I let them fall away.

"Right," she says resolutely. "We're going. We're gonna stop this fight before it gets out of hand. I'm not letting them tear up my boys, no way. Let's go."

She allows me enough time to go for a pee and wash my hands, while she and Kalina get their shoes on.

As we squeeze into the Capri minutes later, I'm woefully aware that

I've been on the road for nearly a whole day now and I absolutely stink. I'm also insanely grateful for these two women who when I mention it, point out that we have bigger issues than a bit of body odor right now. After that, we all fall quiet.

It's a tense half hour ride to the long, winding suburban road that Sheena tells us is called Woodland Drive, where the Bensons live. The houses I guess are posh and big by British standards, though no bigger than your average family house in Bethesda. But apparently this is where the rich Brightonians live.

"That's the one," Sheena says as we pass a house that has a gazillion cars on the drive.

More line the road all the way up the next slope. You can tell there is a party going on by the sheer amount of vehicles clustered around here. Sheena parks up as soon as she finally finds a space half a mile away, and we clamber out of the Capri.

She doesn't bother with the normal locking up ritual before we hurry back toward the Bensons' house.

SILAS

I've been on my own, warming up and waiting, for about an hour and a half when the floodlights over the garden come on. I stop stretching and watch through the window as the guests are led over to the pool house. There is about forty of them, at a guess, all dressed in evening wear. The men wear dinner suits, the women long dresses and jewellery.

Old man Benson himself and Cecil head the procession. George, Arlo and Goran are at the back, herding any stragglers. Most of the crowd is made up of old man Benson's, Cecil's and Mum's generation, interspersed with some select younger ones who seem infinitely more excited than the old guys. Strictly no under twenty-ones. Of course.

There are a couple of faces among the older lot that I recognize from fightnights but other than that the audience is made up of a completely different calibre of cunts, friends of George senior and Cecil, I guess, rather than regular punters. I'm starting to get the necessity for the cameras now. Gotta make money if money's to be made is the old git's motto. Should probably have it translated into Latin and put in a fake family crest. I look around for Oleandra Benson, George's mum. She's nowhere to be seen, but I'm not surprised. The woman who gave my friend his gangsta name lives her life at the bottom of a brandy bottle and has probably passed out somewhere already. It's one fucked-up family.

As the throng of people slowly filters into the pool house and disappears from view, I see George stop and jut his chin out in my direction and say something to Arlo. Arlo peels off to come towards the summer house. Next, George tilts his head in the direction of the main house and says something to Goran. Goran starts retracing their steps. I guess that's where Rowan is then. George stays where he is and looks over to where I am. He sees my face at the window and lifts his hand in greeting. I appreciate why he is not coming over to talk to me at this point. It wouldn't be good if he was seen favouring one of us. I salute back and watch him turn to hurry after the rest of the crowd. Arlo opens the door to the summer house and smiles at me.

"Ready, Snake?" he asks.

I can see he is pleased as punch that he's been asked to assist here tonight. I haven't seen a single one of the other club fighters here. I wonder if they have been given access to the live stream or if that's just for the guys with the serious betting money.

Irrelevant.

It's fight time.

I nod back at Arlo and grab my water, towel and mouth guard off the table. The guard is the only piece of protective equipment none of us at TripleX is too proud to wear. We'll all happily run the risk of losing eyes, hearing, kidney and brain function but forking out for new teeth every five seconds is too fucking expensive. Me? I also wear a cup. Some of the others don't. Stupid. I hardly know Rowan these days, but my money is on him wearing protection, too. He loves his dick too much to let anything happen to it.

"Let's go," I say to Arlo and push past him out of the door.

In the corner of my eye, I see Goran and Rowan approach from the other end of the garden, but I don't turn to look. Arlo and I arrive at the entrance to the pool house first and he leads me past the benches and the people to the aluminium ladder.

You can tell these are not the same kind of people who come down for fightnights. There is no roar, more of an awed hush. It's exaggerated by the fact the lighting rig is pointed at the pool, plunging the benches in semi-darkness. It's clever because it means the cameras won't accidentally pick up any faces.

In the pool pit, some big, stocky guy with a bald head, long beard and wrap-around sunglasses who I've never seen before waits for me. He points at a corner to indicate which one is mine.

Over the PA I hear someone whose voice I don't recognize announce my arrival in the ring. The voice is bigging me up. 'Undefeated TripleX champion blah blah'. I don't really hear it because my eyes, my ears, my sense of smell, my entire fucking being is focused on the guy climbing down the ladder now.

Rowan looks good.

Last time I saw him without clothes on was before the Niamh fiasco. Before either of us had bulked out. He'd already stopped seriously training for a while by then, spending most of his time losing money, drinking and not sleeping enough. Pretty sure he didn't say no to the occasional line of coke then either. And it showed.

Now is a different ball game.

I already knew from our run-ins at the greyhound stadium and in the café that he's fucking big now, but the bloke coming down into the pool is not just huge, he's in prime condition. There isn't an ounce of superfluous fat on his body, not a hint of bloatedness or sleep deprivation. His movements are fluid, his muscles bulging.

Rowan has always been a couple of inches taller and a stone or so heavier than me, but now he's a fucking *monster*.

If this was legit, we'd not even be in the same fight. I'm a weight class below him.

Last time I saw him naked he didn't have any tattoos yet, either.

But he's gone the whole cheesy hog with a python winding itself around his torso and over his shoulder, where its head emerges across his shoulders, among a huge back piece of jungle flowers and skulls. It pisses me off, because inking that kind of artwork costs a boatload of money.

Money he should have been sending back to Mum to pay his fucking debts off.

I watch him dump his shit in the opposite corner of the pool and put his mouth guard in before he turns around and makes eye contact with me across the diagonal of the pool. In the background, the announcer's voice is bigging him up now but again I don't really hear it. My gaze is fixed on my brother's dark brown, almost black eyes.

Yes, *my brother*.

There is something in his expression that snaps me out of the red mist I've been seeing him through since that fateful day and I suddenly realise it's him. It's Rowan.

My Rowan.

My thick-as-thieves stepbrother.

Metal detecting. Watching movies. Playing Grand Theft Auto. Doing homework. Sparring. Cooking together so we didn't have to endure Mum's food. I try to push these thoughts aside. They have no place here. But I can't. There is a glint in his eyes I know all too well. And that I loved once upon a time. Mischief. But not aimed at me, aimed to draw me in.

What the fuck?

The ref, though calling him that will be a euphemism here, there'll be no refereeing worth shit, beckons us to the middle of the pool. Never once breaking eye contact, we proceed to meet either side of him. He gets straight to the point at a whisper, low enough for the cameras not to pick up the sound.

"Right, there are only two rules. Number one, I stop the fight, you stop. There are some fine ladies and gents here, they don't want to see too much gore. You got it?"

He makes a pause for us to fill it with our affirmatives, though Rowan mutters something that sounds like, 'you're wrong, that's all they want'.

"Number two," the ref continues, ignoring him. "One of you taps out, you respect the tap out. You don't tap out, you do so at your own risk. Are we clear?"

We both mumble a 'yes' and split away to take our stances. The ref points at me.

"Are you ready?" he shouts, and I nod.

He points at Rowan.

"Are you ready?"

Rowan nods.

The guy slices his hand through the air like a guillotine.

"Let's fight!"

And then he gets the fuck out of the way.

Grace

Half a mile can be endless if you are trying to get somewhere fast.

It feels like forever before Sheena, Kalina and I get to the Bensons' house and weave our way around the vehicles in the drive to get to the front door. Before I can ask how Sheena plans on getting in there, she's already rung the bell. We wait but nothing happens. She tries the bell again.

"What now?" I ask her, after it becomes apparent that nobody is coming.

"We go around the back," she answers, already moving around the house to where there is a high gate to the garden.

It's locked with a code pad and guaranteed to have CCTV pointing at it, but Sheena clearly doesn't give a fuck.

"Gimme a leg up, will you?" she asks me.

I do, and for the first time in my friggin' life the three wasted years of being a cheerleading base in middle school finally come in handy. After I throw her up, I realize how seriously fit for her age Sheena is, when she manages to pull herself onto the top of the gate and swings a leg over to sit astride it. She turns toward us, holding herself up on poled arms as she slings the other leg over. Then she slowly disappears from sight as she lowers herself down on the other side. The last thing we see are her hands curled around the top edge of the gate and a second later there is a thud as she lands on the ground.

"Shit," she exclaims. "There is a code pad on this side, too. I can't let you in, girls. I gotta go. I can see them. They're all in the pool. It's started already."

Her muffled voice floats over to us, getting progressively fainter as she obviously moves away. Kalina and I are left behind, looking at each other dumbstruck. There is no way on earth this tiny girl will be able to get me up there.

"You lift me," Kalina says decisively after a few seconds. "I try let you in house."

I like the way she's thinking.

Silas

We've been circling each other for a little while now, checking each other out. Testing, looking for weak spots, chinks in the armour.

I can't see any.

Rowan is a mountain.

He's managed to land a trio of punches on me, but I mostly ducked out. I've given back a couple of leg kicks, an uppercut and decent kick to his right kidney when I was sure he was focused elsewhere and wouldn't have time to grab me. That's my one advantage. I'm much, much faster than him. But though the kicks were hard, I'm not sure he even felt them. He's rock solid. And he hasn't touched me yet. But that's Rowan's M.O. all over. Tire the opponent out, go for the choke.

I'm getting bored now.

Time to go in.

Grace

The minutes between Kalina disappearing on the other side of the gate and me going back to the front of the house and waiting in the hope that she'll somehow get in and manage to let me inside rank right up there with the longest in my life.

The sense of gratitude when she opens the door and grins at me, while chewing on a piece of cheese, is indescribable.

"Come." She waves me inside. "Nobody here. All in the garden."

I hurry after her as she leads the way through the hallway into an open plan living-dining area, where the remnants of the dessert and cheese courses are still laid out on tables. She grabs a couple of French Fancies from a platter of sweets as we pass, not even breaking her stride.

We step through open patio doors, out onto a deserted terrace, and that's when I see the indoor pool in the distance. The enclosure is dome shaped and fully transparent. It's filled with people, sitting on benches. The doors are open and the hum of excited voices travels over to us. As we get nearer, I can see Sheena, near the entrance, standing frozen to the spot next to a bench. The tense line of her shoulders tells me that we are too late.

She's watching the fight.

I run faster, my heart pumping with adrenaline.

Nobody bats an eyelid when I come through the doors, stopping dead in my tracks next to Sheena, or when Kalina follows a few seconds behind.

Everybody is transfixed by David and Goliath in the pool pit.

I look down and bile of fear rises in my throat.

SILAS

He got me.

It was inevitable, really.

Anyone who's ever watched Jerome Le Banner versus Nokveed Devy could have told them that.

I could have told them that.

Although that's probably a bad example 'cause there were no choke outs in that fight.

There is gonna be one here.

I know it, Rowan knows it.

I'm just not quite ready to give up yet.

Still looking for wriggle room.

Not done.

But he's got me locked down tight in a figure four, and I can feel the fucking oxygen deprivation already.

And I can feel the rest of it, too.

His body against my back, encasing me.

His breath by my ear.

His scent engulfing me.

He smells like Rowan.

Of course, he does.

And as I start to fade, absurdly, that gives me comfort.

But then suddenly, the fear kicks in.

He'll kill me.

It's not fucking worth it.

I have shit to live for.

I found a girl.

The girl.

I let her go.

But I can get her back.

Somehow.

But not if I don't tap out.

"Don't!" Rowan's voice is like thunder in the distance in my ear. "Do. Not. Tap. Out. Trust me," he whispers.

And then he tightens his hold even more.

Blackness.

Grace

I scream when I see Silas go limp. It's way louder than the rest of the noise made by the gathering, but I don't care if people are looking at me or not.

All I can focus on is Silas.

And Rowan, letting go of him, laying him back gently onto the mat. He strokes his head and waits.

Seconds tick by.

I feel Sheena, grabbing my hand and giving it a squeeze. There is something reassuring about it.

"He'll come out of it," she says confidently.

I wish I could be so sure.

There is still no movement.

I watch on as Rowan looks up to make eye contact with some old balding guy sitting in prime position on a bench opposite from where we're standing. Next to him sits a man who I'm guessing must be Diego's father.

The fact Diego is by his side kind of gives it away. He looks pale.

The balding guy nods once, sharply, at Rowan, and then an ugly grin spreads over his face. I can feel Sheena coil with anger beside me, but I get distracted by Silas moving his head.

The sense of relief I feel is second to none.

Rowan leans down to him, talks to him quietly, gently extracts Silas' mouth guard and then cradles him while he barks at the ref to get his arse in gear and get some water. The ref, who never even bothered counting Silas out, wakes from his trance and springs to action, following Rowan's orders.

Sheena suddenly vacates the spot by my side and marches over to where the Bensons are. They notice her as soon as she starts moving and the ugly grin on the baldy man's face falls. When he gets up from the bench to greet her, he is actually blanching. She says something to him.

And then she slaps him. Hard. Not once, but twice.

Right slap, left slap.

Like something from an old movie.

Only in the old movie he'd grab Sheena's wrist before the second slap and then brutally kiss her or some rapey shit like that. In real life, she lands both of them squarely, then backs away, calling him a depraved cunt, loud enough for everyone to hear.

I'm guessing that's Cecil O'Brien then.

Kalina nudges me, and I glance at her.

She swallows a bit of French Fancy then looks expectantly at me, her eyes indicating Silas in the pool as Rowan is giving him water.

"Go!" she says.

Coming around after a choke out is never a joy. You always have a mild headache and feel a bit out of it. But not in a fun way, more in a fucking disorientated kind of way. Like, I wouldn't advise driving for half a day or so after.

What it doesn't normally come with is hallucinations but, apparently, tonight it does.

As Rowan cradles me and plies me with water, I watch a redhead with a phenomenally lush arse stuffed into a pair of faded jeans descent down the ladder into the basin. The shade of her hair is the exact shade Grace uses and she's wearing a cream silk blouse just like the one Grace utilises as lingerie and Grace's favourite make of boot. From behind she looks just like her and when she turns around, I realise I'm either still out and dreaming or, more likely, I'm awake and tripping from the lack of oxygen. Or maybe I'm dead.

The woman moves towards me and I prepare myself for the moment she metamorphoses into whoever she *actually* is.

But it doesn't happen.

Grace remains Grace.

"Silas," is all she says as she kneels down by my side and reaches out to touch me.

"Grace?" I ask.

She nods.

"I came back."

And then she's in my arms.

Blood, sweat, tears and all, soaking her fine silk blouse.

And I'm fucked if I'll ever let her go again.

Grace

He holds me tight all through the night.

As if he's afraid I'll be gone again if he lets go.

As if.

But I totally get it.

As I drift in and out of sleep, each time I wake I touch him all over to make sure he's alright, he's breathing, he's alive. Right now he's spooning me, and I wriggle around in his arms, turning to face him. I study his face in the diffused light of the early morning that sneaks in around the curtains. His cheek is a bit swollen, but I've seen him look worse. Way worse.

I'm glad it's over, though.

For good.

When we got back last night — Kalina and Sheena in the Capri, Silas and I in Diego's car — Sheena put her foot down as soon as we got home and she'd put the kettle on.

She told him straight she'd rather lose the house than for him to carry on fighting. Not that she thinks she will actually lose it. Apparently, Silas has got a stash of cash already and Sheena reckons she'll be alright covering the rest in the years before she retires. I didn't say anything at the time because Sheena was on a roll, but if we stay here for a while, then I can contribute, too. There must be bar work in a place like Brighton. Or something. We'll figure it out.

Silas' eyes flutter open under my scrutiny and he smiles.

"Hey, beautiful lady. You're still here."

"Yep. Not going anywhere."

"Good," he says and kisses me.

Languidly.

Igniting the fire in my belly like only he can, leisurely tongue fucking me.

Jesus H Christ, I live for this man's kisses.

It takes him all of half a minute before I'm sopping wet. Admittedly, it helps that I can feel his hard-on press against my belly. He cups my ass cheeks and pulls me closer against him, pushing a knee between my legs to part them. A second later, I'm riding his thigh and he's rolling it against my bare lower lips. My clit, buried between them, goes nuts. She's missed him about as much as I have. I moan into his mouth. He pulls back a little and watches my face as his thigh keeps undulating.

"I love how flushed you get," he says hoarsely and lifts a finger to stroke it over my burning cheeks. "Here."

He lets the tip wander down the side of my neck and across the top of my breast.

"And here. So fucking pretty."

He cups my left boob, palms it and lowers his mouth to suck on my nipple. Hard. A bolt of lightning goes through my body and I buck.

"Good?" he asks, grinning against my flesh.

I pull him back in.

"More," I demand.

And he gives me more. He sucks and licks, kneading the other nipple between his thumb and index finger until I'm close to coming already. I have no idea how he does this.

Then he retracts, and flips onto his back, taking me with him. I rearrange my limbs so I'm straddling him fully, my clit resting on his shaft. He grabs my hips and holds me while I start sliding my clit up and down his length, coating him in my juices.

"Grace, you're killing me," he moans. "I'm gonna come like this if you don't stop."

"Uh-uh," I mutter.

Then I lift myself off him to reach between us and position him at my entrance. I slide down a fraction of an inch, just enough to hold him there with my pussy and look into his eyes. It's a challenge, a stand-off to see who gives in first, but he doesn't break. So I clench, suckering him in just a little more, resisting the temptation to slide down his whole length and ride him. Hard. I need hard right now. I want to be taken, want to surrender, want to get fucked so deeply I can feel it behind my eyeballs.

He groans, loudly. But he resists.

I clench again, drawing him in another fraction of an inch.

And then it happens. I can see in his eyes the exact moment he loses his shit.

He bucks up into me, ramming his full length inside, and then he fucks into me from below in long and hard strokes, holding my hips and lifting me up and down in rhythm with him, taking all control away from me. And I love it.

His hands direct me and tilt me back, and then suddenly the angle is just right. He hits the spot and I start contracting, but I keep hovering on the edge. Then one of his hands leaves my hip, trails around and finds my clit. He flicks his thumb over it. Once, twice, and then I explode.

As the orgasm punches through me, I can feel him jerk up, his cock twitching hard inside me, shooting his come. It hits my cervix like a jet stream, a new sensation that draws out my climax and brings a depth I've never felt before.

As I come down slowly from my high, I collapse on top of my shaking man.

His arms immediately wrap around me and after he's collected himself, he peppers the top of my head with kisses.

"You're amazing," he mumbles into my hair before he falls back again.

I prop myself up and look at him.

"I need to tell you something," I say, and I feel how he tenses beneath me, expecting some bad piece of news.

I stroke his brow to soothe his fear.

"I love you."

A smile lights up his face as he slaps me playfully.

"You little cow, I thought you were gonna say something like 'I've gotta go back to the States'."

Suddenly he frowns.

"Do you? How long are you here for?"

I smile back at him.

"For as long as I want."

His eyes go round.

"Really? Like, for real? Don't you need a visa or something? If you need us to get married, we'll get married, you know."

I grin.

"Good to know. But, no, courtesy of Mum I already have dual citizenship. I can stay, I can work, I'm good."

His face falls a little at that and I realize how that sounded. I punch him lightly in the chest.

"Don't feel rejected. You may still do the whole getting down on one knee business after an appropriate period of courting. But I draw the line at getting married after *one* month."

He laughs, flipping us back over, so he's on top.

"And that, Grace Turner, is why you are the woman for me," he says.

And then we kiss some more and eventually we fuck some more.

Until the doorbell, followed by a voice like rolling thunder greeting Sheena on the doorstep and the subsequent smell of fried bacon wafting through the house, lures us out from between the sheets and down into the kitchen.

ROWAN

I hang around in the pub car park for a while, long enough to watch the postman push some letters through the door and the cute little Polish pixie that Diego won't shut up about leave, before I muster the courage to approach.

There is something utterly terrifying about knocking on a house that was once your home but where you're not really welcome any longer, so my heart rate goes through the fucking roof as soon as I actually ring Sheena's doorbell.

She opens not even a minute later, dressed in a terry cotton bathrobe, pinched from the Palais, and sipping tea from a mug. I already knew she'd taken the day off. I swung by the hotel first. She looks me up and down wordlessly then turns back into the hallway, beckoning me in with a wave of the hand.

My pulse quietens a little as I follow her into the kitchen. At least I'm in. Step one.

"You want a cuppa? Kettle's just boiled," she asks me, not really waiting for an answer, or even making eye contact, before she gets a mug from the mug tree, puts a tea bag in and drowns it in hot water. I watch in silence as she dips the bag in and out for a bit and puts milk and sugar in, deciding for me that I'm having both and in what quantities. She shoves the mug at me.

"Take it. Sit down."

I do as I'm told and take a seat at the table, dumping the small sports bag I've been carrying on it. I wait patiently while she gets a packet of bacon out of the fridge and peels apart twelve rashers before placing all of them on the grill rack then goes to wash her hands.

While she is busy, Sol comes through the cat flap and starts meowing by my feet, rubbing up against my legs. I bend down and give him scratches around the neck and the ears until he suddenly, without warning, claws into my hand, drawing a pin prick of blood. He's been unpredictable like that from day one when Silas and I went to pick up our kittens.

We were fourteen. James had just dumped me on Sheena. Condor, their old greyhound, had not long been put to sleep. And Sheena thought a pair of furballs might cheer us up. They did.

I straighten back up just as Sheena finishes the bacon operation and finally comes over to sit opposite me. She looks at the bag on the table then back at me, taking a sip of her tea.

"I take it, that's my money in there," she states dryly, looking at me over the rim of her mug.

I nod, relieved that she's guessed why I'm here, taking a whole load of awkward out of the situation for me. I always liked that about her. Sheena O'Brien is nothing if not straight to the point.

"It's not all of it," I confess. "I still owe you. But it's a hundred and thirty-five thousand. And I'll start paying back the rest as soon as I can," I promise her.

"A hundred and thirty-five?" she asks, her eyes going into slits. "I thought last night's prize money was a hundred. Where'd the other thirty-five come from? You didn't borrow it, did you?"

I swallow hard.

"Silas didn't tell you? I thought that was why you slapped O'Brien last night."

"I slapped Cecil 'cause he's a cunt who should never have been part of making my sons fight each other. I would have slapped Benson, too, given half a chance, but I missed my window of opportunity there," she responds.

I barely get a chance to feel my heart clench at the fact she still considers me her son before she carries on.

"What did Silas not tell me?"

"O'Brien offered me another fifty grand on top if I won."

"I thought that was only for killing me," Silas' voice joins our conversation.

I turn around to see him standing in the door frame.

"That's the problem with vague wording," I answer. "He said to lay you out cold. I laid you out cold. Just not as permanently as he would have liked."

"And he paid out?" Silas asks incredulously.

I nod, a small smirk forming on my lips. It was an *interesting* discussion about semantics, to say the least.

"Yup. The whole fifty K."

"Well, to that arsehole, fifty grand is petty cash," Sheena says with a sigh and grabs the bag to open it and look at the notes.

Behind Silas, the pretty American redhead appears, slinging her arm around his midriff.

Grace, I remind myself. *Her name is Grace.*

She looks bed tousled and thoroughly fucked, and I feel the same twinge of jealousy I felt last night in the pool when she came and whisked Silas away from me. But it isn't the same feeling I had about him and Niamh. It's not about having a girl steal my best friend, my *brother*. It's about possibly, one day, having what they have. One day, when I'm maybe worth it.

Grace starts sniffing the air.

"Does that bacon need turning? Smells, erm, *crispy*."

Sheena gets up like a shot and Silas, Grace and I look at each other, all suppressing grins. Grace has clearly already encountered Sheena's legendary culinary skills. While Sheena turns the bacon, Silas and Grace come further into the room. Grace goes over to the kitchen counter and starts helping Sheena with cutting up bread and tomatoes for a round of BLTs. Silas comes and sits down next to me.

"So what's happened to the other fifteen?" he asks, nodding at the bag.

I swallow hard for the second time since getting here.

"I need it."

He bristles but to his credit he keeps his voice even.

"What for?"

I look down at my busted hands.

"Rehab," I say under my breath, then repeat the last part, louder, turning to look him in the eye while I say it. "I'm going into rehab. There is a residential clinic on the Isle of Purbeck, near Swanage, and they don't just take junkies and alcoholics, they take gamblers. Well, at least they said they'd take *me*. But it's intensive and expensive, it costs ten grand for four weeks."

Silas holds my gaze and I see a myriad of emotions go through those hazel eyes of his. God, I've missed him. Still miss him. Because it will never be the same. The only real friend I ever had and I fucked it up royally. We never talked about what happened with Niamh, and it still embarrasses the fuck out of me even thinking about it. She got to me, got under my skin, made me believe he was in on it. Why the fuck didn't I check with him? Because I was thinking with my dick. That's why. Because I'm a kinky fuck and because the idea appealed to me so much it never occurred to me that it might not appeal to him.

"Whose idea was it?" he asks, reading my mind the way only Silas can.

"Niamh's," I answer truthfully and though he flinches, I see in his eyes that he believes me.

He breaks eye contact, nodding absently. Then he looks at me again.

"If you need more time at that clinic, let me know. We'll pay for it," he says. "Just don't take *too* long. And don't worry about the rest of the loan. It's covered. Just don't get into any more debt, will ya?"

I frown but before I can ask, Sheena and Grace turn up at the table with a round of BLTs. As they put them down, I see the pendant dangling from Grace's neck. It makes me smile. I remember the day Silas found that. He was fucking made up. I'm glad he's finally found a rightful owner for it.

I hope he gets to keep her.

He's a good bloke, Silas O'Brien, and he deserves all the happiness in the world.

∞

ROWAN

Brighton Bad Boys II

ROWAN

I like the open countryside. It makes me feel less in everybody's face.

At six foot three inches tall and packing 240 pounds of pure muscle, I always feel like King Kong in New York when I wade through Brighton or London or Manchester. Wherever there is human civilisation, really.

But out here, walking across the wide-open heathland on the Isle of Purbeck in Dorset, where there aren't any other people or buildings for miles, I feel like I'm not in the way, or about to accidentally break something, or someone.

I bet the others are going to have a field day with that.

I can see it now.

Me, standing up in the inevitable circle.

Hi, my name is Rowan, I'm twenty-five, and I'm an addict.

Clap, clap.

I also suffer from a bull-in-china-shop complex, a severe case of in-the-way paranoia, and anxiety around fucking shit up.

Hums.

All of these originated with the death of my birth mother when I was eleven in what has widely been described as a freak accident.

Silence.

After Mum's premature demise, I tagged along with her then husband, not my biological father, and my toddler half siblings into my stepdad's next relationship. When he and his next woman split up, he took off with his own babies and left me behind in the care of my stepmum, who eventually adopted me.

Shocked mutterings.

All was well for a few years, until I fucked up my hitherto brilliant relationship with my stepbrother, Silas, by fucking his girlfriend while she still had his dick in her mouth.

Gasps.

Aside from being a kinky arsehole, I had also racked up a couple of hundred thou in gambling debts behind their backs at that point, so I did the only thing a worthless piece of shit like me can do. I scarpered. And left them to pick up the pieces.

Clearings of throats.

I went to hell, beyond, and came back.

Impatient noises.

Now I'm here.

Thanks for listening.

I'm gonna sit down now.

I might save the juicier revelations for a rainy day though. Won't give 'em the scandalous parts right at the beginning. Won't give 'em the self aware, articulate version of me so readily.

Will give 'em the brute ex-MMA-and-illegal-fight-club-fighter, who doesn't have two brain cells to rub together, first. See what they do with that.

Those counsellors will need to fucking well earn my trust to justify their extortionate rehab fees.

'Cause that's where I'm headed.

I am walking across this breathtakingly beautiful nature reserve through the sweltering late June heat with a backpack full of all my earthly belongings, in order to get to a remote rehab centre, imaginatively called The Village.

It's situated in what was until a few years ago a ghost village of typical Purbeck limestone houses with thatched roofs, dating back hundreds of years.

There is a whole load of history behind the why and how it became deserted, which they wax lyrical about in the online brochure that you can download from the website of Halosan, the American chain of clinics that owns it. They bought it up a few years ago and turned it into a gated community for addicts in recovery. When I flicked through the pdf on my phone, it came across like a fucking movie set.

At first, I didn't really consider it an option. Too squeaky. But while I rang around a bunch of other rehab places, I found out something sobering, no pun intended.

Barely any of them even consider gamblers, and then only if there is a co-morbidity (yup, King Kong here knows words and shit) with some nice, solid substance abuse they can get their teeth into. I guess it's because there is something tangible to do when you detox a junkie or dry out an alcoholic. There are drugs you can give them to ease the transition.

Would have been easier to find a place if I was still into the chemical enhancement of life. But I dropped that shit all by myself when I got to the third ring of hell. To survive there, you've got to have your wits about you. I only have the betting left now.

But us pure gamblers are tricky bastards from the medical point of view. There is nothing to *apply* during the chrysalis stage. No pills to push. Which turns out just hunky dory for me. But makes it hard to find a residential place.

Most help with gambling addiction comes as weekly therapy sessions along with separate meetings with a financial advisor.

But I need a clean break.

I need head space, away from everyone and everything. I need concentration to silence that little voice that constantly calls to me. To find a fight, a race, a match and let the fever take over.

Because for me, it's not about the money or the adrenaline rush you get from winning. For me, it's all about the action. Being part of it. A substitute for being in it myself. Despite the fact I miss being in it as much as I miss a hole in the head. Fucked up much?

On their admission form, they've got me down as a gambler, but I'm not.

I don't do casinos or online poker or any of that crap.

I put bets on action. On people. On dogs. Every once in a blue moon, if there is nothing else, on horses. If it's people, it's the fighting kind. If it's dogs, it's exclusively the racing kind. If it's horses, it's the *flat*-racing kind.

I have feelings about that shit. Strong ones. The last time I beat someone within an inch of their lives without getting paid for it was when one of the sick bastards at the Benson Mansion thought he was doing me a favour and took me to some dilapidated farm, where another one of the staple Brighton arseholes was training up fight dogs.

Brighton is home, but sometimes I really wish I could start over somewhere new. I tried, for years. But it turned out no matter where I go, there are Benson types that will find me and sucker me in.

The Bensons are old school Brighton underworld and the bane of my life.

Old man Benson is a cunt of the highest order. He's probably well into those dogfights. Not that I want to know. His son, George, aka Diego, because he's a poncy prick who wanted a proper gangster name, runs the Brighton fightnights. The human ones. George junior and I haven't always seen eye to eye, but he wouldn't stand for the kind of sadistic shit his father is into, that much is certain.

And he's currently in my favour. Very fucking much.

Diego played a huge part in pulling off the stunt that got me out of debt to my family and brought a truce to Silas and me.

Silas and Diego go all the way back to fucking pre-school. Always made me jealous 'cause they already had bags of history when I first arrived at Sheena's house. Sheena is Silas' mum and the woman who was stupid enough to adopt me. Sheena's always had a soft spot for Diego, too, so I guess he really is okay, deep down.

Old man Benson and his cronies are vile though. Really, really sick.

I think Diego got a bit of a final eye-opener in that respect when he organised the fight between Silas and me that ultimately led to our reunion. Or maybe Diego knew already but it needed his oldest friend's life being gambled with for him to snap. Who knows.

I still can't quite believe we actually went up against each other. I can't believe I agreed to fight my brother. That I willingly put Silas' life on the line.

And most of all, I can't believe that after all of that we are *good*. That Silas still loves me. At least a little. That Sheena, Silas and Grace, his girlfriend, let me stay with them until there was space for me at The Village. Silas even offered to drive me here in Sheena's car today, but I declined.

This is my journey. Either into disaster or the sunset. We'll see.

There is no rail service on Purbeck, so I had to get off the train at Poole. The Village offers a driver service, at extra cost, of course, or you can get a cab from Poole station, but I didn't fancy either. I bought a map at the Tourist Information, got on the bus to Studland and started hiking from there.

Good choice, other than that I forgot to refill my water bottle and now I'm parched. It's way too hot for June even with the permanent breeze from the ocean in the air. I stop, drop my backpack, sit on it, wipe my brow and consult the map. If I'm not mistaken, *The Village* is only about a quarter of a mile ahead now, so I decide to polish off my last water before hoisting my backpack back on and marching onwards.

Raven

It's 3pm and I'm pissed.

That's American pissed, not British pissed, and the fact that my brain offers that explanation up to *myself* tells me I've really been on this godforsaken island too long. And by that I mean the whole of the UK, not just the peninsula of Purbeck.

And to think how excited I was when Halosan offered me the chance to go to Europe for a year to set up one of our two new complexes and train the local nurses.

Look at me being the company bot, using the pronoun *our* in there.

But it's not far from the truth. Halosan has pretty much owned me since I was nineteen. They put me through five years of die hard, rock 'n roll, you-are-now-a-fully-fledged-RN-specialising-in-recovery nursing training and in return, I got tied in. As per post-graduation contract, they still own me for another six months. Then I've done my time for them.

Not that it's been a hardship. The pay is great, the benefits exemplary and because you live in at the centers, you don't have rent to pay. The only snag was a no-pregnancy clause, but that has posed no problem for me. I'm twenty-eight now and I have no intention of having a baby this side of thirty. If ever. I got life to live first.

I went into the Halosan program straight after high school, courtesy of John, my foster dad, who knew I'd always wanted to become a nurse. So he searched high and low for the best program for me. He's good like that.

He and his wife Elena run a group home for twenty kids and no matter what any of them want to be, he'll always find the best route for them to get into whatever that choice is. So John found me the Halosan offer and I've been with the company ever since. It's been great, but I want to see some shit before I commit to anything else, especially a baby.

As if getting into the Halosan training program in the first place wasn't fortuitous enough, toward the end of my contract, Halosan also offered me the lifetime opportunity to go to either Lake Como, not far from Milan in Italy (*yes, sir, thank you, sir*), or Purbeck in Dorset in the UK (*excuse me, sir, where, sir?*).

I got Purbeck.

It's beautiful but it's also nowhere near Milan, or any other big city. Getting to London from here takes half a day. Not because of distance but because the British transportation system might as well still depend on stagecoaches. They'd probably get you there faster. So I've only been to London a few times and haven't really gone anywhere else other than Poole and Swanage, the nearest small towns, ever since I arrived here ten months ago.

But that's okay. I get four weeks off at the end of my stay to explore at least a little of the rest, and of Europe. Not long now.

This is my last intake of guests and my trainees are all up to standard. They're good, actually. Especially Christine, who will take over from me as head of nursing once I'm gone. She comes from somewhere 'up North', talks in a funny accent, has a super wry sense of humor and absolutely loves it here.

Me? I can't wait for my Purbeck year to be over now. It's been a ball, but I'm done with the vista now. I want to be somewhere else. Not bothered where exactly but I'm bored with this.

Which is probably why I'm so extra crabby right now about Mr. Rowan Hadlow, Fuller or O'Brien. The guy with the three different last names who didn't turn up for registration by noon, like all the other good little lambs. Instead, he called to say he was 'walking' and wouldn't get here before late afternoon. Walking from fucking where?

So he's missing the induction talk that is in full swing in the main hall of the therapy center, which used to be the village church. And so am I. Because I'm out here at reception, where the entrance to the church used to be, waiting for the fucker. Just my luck that the one candidate who can't keep to a simple timetable happens to be staying in *my* house. Awesome.

The big door to the main hall opens and Elias slips out. Elias is one of the younger nurses here, at twenty-three, and he's got a bit of a mouth on him, which needs watching. He's half Irish, half English with an accent that changes depending on which part of his heritage he wants to ham up. Today is Irish Elias.

"Hey, Ray," he mock whispers as he sees me, while he shuts the heavy door quietly.

I hate being called Ray. It's not my name. It's either Raven, or if you are my foster parent or someone official, you may call me Ravenna but it's never ever Ray.

"Not my name, sunshine," I volley back, and he grins.

"Awh, you still got a face on ya. Still waiting on three-name-man?"

"Keep it zipped, Elias," I reprimand him and watch him roll his eyes as he walks over to the restrooms.

I'm angry at him because he shouldn't be saying stuff like that in public. But if I'm honest, I'm even more annoyed at myself for being unprofessional earlier and making an indiscreet comment about the fact this guest, 'idiot' I think was the word I chose at the time, comes with medical records in three different last names. Shouldn't have slipped out. Did. Bad.

Firstly, because it's confidential information that Elias has no clearance for, only the counselors, Christine and I. Secondly, because it's judgmental.

And I know from my own experience that an individual can come with different last names for different parts of their life due to no fault of their own. Before ending in the system, I'd been a Lavetti, a Miller and a Grady.

My graduation papers are in the name of Vanhofd. I asked for that one. It's John and Elena's last name. Their group home was the only time in my life I felt safe, so when I turned eighteen, I asked them how they'd feel if I legally changed my name to theirs. They were over the moon. I think if they weren't dependent on the money they got for all of us foster kids, they would have adopted us anyway. Every single child that ever passed through their hands. They're that kind of people.

I know people assume growing up in the system is always a bad ride, but for me it was the best thing that ever happened to me. I wish it had got me sooner.

Fuck me, I'm in an antsy, reminiscent frame of mind today.

It's something about this guy, who fucking better arrive soon if he doesn't want to encounter my full wrath on day one. He's not even here yet and already messing with my mojo.

I watch the clock and a full five minutes later, Elias reappears from the restroom.

"Did you fall in?" I ask snarkily, and he laughs.

"Gotta relieve the boredom somehow," he answers good-naturedly, with an obscene gesture and a smirk.

For a moment, I wonder if he actually did go and jerk off, but I doubt it. He's all mouth that one. Probably just played around on his cell, checking on some sports news.

Elias is a huge boxing and MMA fan and there is some big fight on tonight he keeps yakking on about. Which brings me back to Mr. Noshowyet. According to his records, he's a twenty-five-year-old ex-fighter who's got a gambling issue. No drugs, no alcohol. At least not according to his admission form. I got doubts. But if it's true, it makes him both interesting and a loose cannon as far as I'm concerned. I'm good with alcoholics and junkies. You keep them fed, you don't feed their narcissistic egos and leave the rest to the counselors.

Gamers and gamblers can be tricky.

I have an interesting bunch this time. Aside from Mr. Getyourfuckingassherepronto, I have an eighteen-year-old called Tristan with a gaming problem, an alcoholic businessman in his late forties called Simon, and a repeat customer called Charlie who, *nomen est omen*, has a cocaine issue.

Charlie is twenty-two, the guitarist in a soon-to-be-famous rock band, and here for the second time already. He was in my first ever group on Purbeck and it's kind of sad that he's back for my last, but I prefer that to him giving up on rehab altogether. Sometimes people need a few tries before it really clicks and they can flick that switch in their brain for good. It's a good thing Charlie's parents are not short of a bob or two, as Elias would say. They can afford to keep sending him back on a regular roster if they need to. I like Charlie, I hope he makes it, but I also know from experience that the younger they are the higher the chance they'll relapse. It's the idea of immortality, of none of it counting yet, that keeps them hooked more than the actual substance.

And coke is always a bastard anyway. Because it can short circuit the healthiest person any time. It can kill you the first time or the thousandth time. And there is sweet f.a. you can do for the victim when it fries them. No matter if you are a doctor, a nurse or the fucking Antichrist.

I know. I really, really know. When I was twelve, I watched the Antichrist try and fail to revive my mother.

In a way it's a shame that the professional boundaries tell us not to divulge personal information to the guests. I could probably scare Charlie into becoming the first ever totally sober rock star with my stories. But that's not what I'm here for. I'm here for…the bell.

I stare at the face of the asshole I've been waiting for on the CCTV screen. He's a good-looking bastard. Kind of chiseled, I guess, although the scruffy beard softens the angles. He's got big, dark eyes, an interesting arch in his thick black eyebrows and short, equally dark, unruly hair.

"Hello, I'm Rowan O'Brien," a voice like rolling thunder in the distance filters through the intercom.

That settles the name question, I think, while trying hard to ignore the goose bumps erupting all over my body.

What a voice.

"Good of you to join us, Mr. O'Brien," I answer snippily as I press the buzzer on the entrance gate. "Follow the main path to the reception of the therapy center in the old church, please."

I watch him disappear from view and my heart starts pounding, knowing he's entered the complex and is on the approach.

What the fuck is that all about?

ROWAN

Some bodiless female voice with an American accent tells me to follow the main path. It's a good thing I've spent the past two weeks in the company of Grace, which has desensitised me somewhat to the Yankee drawl. Not that Grace is too bad. She's from Washington, D.C. and speaks almost like a normal person. But before being put through the Grace cycle, I would probably have turned on my heels if an American had greeted me here. I love American music and I'd really like to see some of their scenery one day. But that whole fake 'have a nice day' crap and, worse, the non-fake 'we're better than thou' attitude really gets on my tits. Post spending time around Grace though, I step through the gate without a second thought.

It falls shut behind me with a soft click, and I can't help but to turn back and check that the large metal 'press to exit' plate actually works. I push it down and try opening the gate from the inside.

Yup, they weren't lying. You can leave any time.

I turn to follow the directions the woman on the intercom gave, running a hand through my sweaty hair. I'm suddenly intensely aware that I'm soaked through and probably stink to high heavens. I've always been great at giving bad first impressions and it looks like today I'm seriously on form. Oh well, whatever. They're getting paid a ransom to put up with my shit, so let's start how we mean to carry on.

Three quarters up the path, I spot a water fountain and I stop to drink. I drop my stuff and don't bother filling my bottle first or cupping my hands. I drink straight from the spout. I take gulp after gulp after gulp until I finally feel like my thirst is quenched.

"When you've finished fellating that spigot, follow me, please, Mr. O'Brien," a clipped female voice says from a few feet away.

It's that bloody Yank again.

"I don't know how you give blow jobs, lady, but your mouth is supposed to *touch* the object you're fellating," I respond even before I've straightened up and looked at her. "Which mine wasn't," I add once I've reached my full height.

Then I *see* her.

And when I say see, I don't mean her black locks piled into a haphazard ponytail, her olive complexion or the black nurses tunic over skin-tight jeans showing off a pair of good pins that end in DMs. I don't even mean her wide set indigo blue eyes that sit in total contrast to the rest of her colouring.

I mean *her*.

What lies behind those eyes.

There is a sense of recognition I've never had before.

Those eyes have seen shit. Too much. Too early. Those eyes can hold you in your deepest, darkest hours because they've been through it. They've been *you*.

Me.

They've been *me*.

What the fuck?

The adrenaline of fear spreads through my body like wildfire as my heart starts pumping, pushing blood through my veins at twice the normal speed and suddenly everything comes into hyper sharp focus. But still, all I really see is her.

We're in an invisible ring, staring at each other, each unwilling to back down, each choosing fight over flight. My fear morphs into competitiveness and I feel a small smirk curling up the right side of my mouth.

Bring it on, woman.

Raven

I came out to meet the guy because he took longer than is normal. I thought he might have gotten lost. Though that's pretty hard when going in a straight line down what was once the only road in the village. But it's a rehab clinic. Folk are kinda lost by definition when they get here. So I came to see what was taking him so long and found him going down on the water fountain.

I mean, seriously, the way he hulked over it, half his face under the stream, his tongue lapping at the water, was obscene, *feral*. So my smart mouth decided to make a comment. A wholly *unprofessional* comment, and now I'm standing here mesmerized like Mowgli meeting Kaa.

'Cause he's staring me down like a pro.

I can't look away from his eyes. They are huge, a deep, warm brown, and they tell me stories too close for comfort. This is a guy who gets it. Life. The ugliness. The bits where other people play three monkeys. He sees them.

He sees me.

And I see him.

A shiver runs through me, dries out my mouth and throat and drives me to the edge of nausea.

But I won't budge.

I learned early and the hard way that they only get nastier if you turn and run. Better to stay and stand your ground, step into their space. No matter how much fucking bigger they are.

So I do.

I take a couple more steps toward him and watch as the smirk he was wearing transforms into a big smile that slowly spreads across his face, until it reaches his eyes and parts his lips, baring his teeth. It occurs to me then that he is *extremely* good looking, especially for a Brit. No offense to my current host nation but it doesn't exactly produce a whole lotta good looking people with decent orthodontic work. It's actually quite refreshing how few of the natives I've encountered have had their teeth straightened or bleached, which makes the near perfect set of naturally pearly whites his smile reveals so much more appealing.

"Good afternoon," I introduce myself before I fall deeper into the observation that Rowan O'Brien is not just gigantic in stature but also gigantically hot. "I'm Ravenna," I add, pointing at my ID tag before I offer my hand for him to shake. "But most people call me Raven. I'm your host."

His smile condenses again until it's just a faint play around his lips as he steps forward to take my hand in his.

"Rowan," he says, just as our palms collide in front of us and then adds something else that I don't hear through the rush in my ears.

Because as soon as my skin meets his, I know that we are in deep, deep trouble.

And I mean *we*.

I can see in the dilation of his pupils that the physical reaction goes both ways.

And if I had any doubts left, they are extinguished when he suddenly loosens his grip and runs his fingers lightly over the inside of my wrist, mid-shake. It's a deeply intimate gesture that sends a bolt of arousal all the way to my core.

He watches me as he does it, grins and lets go. Then he turns to grab his stuff off the ground, shoulders his backpack and looks expectantly at me. As if nothing had happened.

"Where to?" he asks, and I can't even find enough saliva in my mouth to answer him.

I just turn and gesture for him to follow me.

ROWAN

I'm rock hard.

There are no two ways about it. Our palms touched and boom, all the blood went south. I haven't had an instant erection like this since I was a teenager. Admittedly, it doesn't take a whole lot to get me going, but it normally takes at least *something*. And by that I mean a little more than just a handshake.

But apparently not with this one.

My dick is kept only half in check by the confines of my faded black cargo trousers. Never have I been so glad to be wearing the three-quarter length, light army jacket that I'm wearing today. Buttoned up despite the heat, so it doesn't get tangled in the backpack straps when hiking, it hides a multitude of thoughts of sin.

Thoughts I'm trying desperately not to carry on thinking as I follow her up the path to one of the grey stone houses on the left. I count twelve of them, eight on the left, four on the right. The remaining green space, on the edge of which I found the water fountain, lies in front of the old church. There are low level signs everywhere, pointing out the obvious, such as the therapy centre, and providing arrows towards the not so obvious, like the pool and gym.

"Oh yeah," I say to the back of Raven's head. "I remember I read there was a newly built pool, gym and sauna. Are they open?"

She glances at me over her shoulder, frowning. I think she might frown quite a lot. She has the early stages of two permanent frown lines forming between her eyebrows but on her even those look fucking sexy as hell. They give her face character, hint that she can take charge if need be.

I like that. I like my women strong and dirty. I like the idea of taking somebody so in control and making them lose it. For fuck's sake, I need to get a grip here. This is not a shagging holiday on the Costa del fuck that I've never even been to. This is *therapy*.

"Sure," she answers my question with that typically American undertone of 'why wouldn't they be'.

She clearly hasn't stayed in England long enough to know that facilities are not exactly guaranteed to work here. Then again, I need to remind myself that this is a private clinic, not some health service funded backroom in a community centre.

We reach the first house in line, in front of the church, and Raven, she is definitely a Raven and not a Ravenna, opens the unlocked front door to usher me in.

"Welcome to your home for the next four weeks," she says as I pass her by and step into a dingy hallway.

It's always the same with these thatched roof country cottages — look pretty on the outside, are dark and gloomy even on a glorious day like today on the inside.

It takes my eyes a moment to adjust. By the time they do, Raven has disappeared into a room that lies beyond the staircase with a brief instruction to take my shoes off and put them on a rack by the door. I hear a tap run while I do as I'm told, and just as I put my walking boots in the designated space, she reappears, drinking water from a tall glass in big gulps. She looks at me while she brings one leg up to rest on her other thigh and starts blindly undoing the lace on that boot, all the while still taking sips of her water. Once she's put the foot back on the ground and has toed off her boot, she puts the glass down on a side table and repeats the process on the other side.

A dancer in DMs.

I fucking love it and my dick still does, too. He loves it so much, I can only half take in what Raven is saying once she starts giving me the house rules speech.

"So, the shoe rack is a hard and fast rule. You can walk around the downstairs with boots on but not up the stairs, please. We have cleaners, but if everyone walks around in their shoes, the carpet doesn't stay clean for five seconds. I like a clean house."

The way she emphasises that last bit is odd. There is a story behind it. But not an OCD one.

I suddenly get a flash of the child version of the beautiful woman in front of me, barefoot in a nightie that's two sizes too small, her hair grimy. A black-haired, blue-eyed ghost child living in squalor.

I shake it off. My mum always used to say that my vivid imagination would either make me a lot of money one day or end me in trouble. It hasn't. Yet.

"There is a hook there for your jacket, too," she cuts through my musings, but I shake my head.

"It's okay. I'll keep it on for now," I say then give her a smirk. "And don't sweat, I'm fully house-trained. I even pee sitting down."

She doesn't bat an eyelid. Hard crowd.

"So how does this work?" I ask, making a sweeping gesture to encompass the house at large.

She frowns.

Like I thought, she frowns a lot.

"Did you not read the brochure?"

I scratch the back of my head with a sheepish grin.

"I skimmed over it," I admit and watch her take a deep breath, no doubt in prep for another speech, but I cut her short. "Look, I might as well tell you now 'cause I can already tell it's gonna get on your tits, but

I'm the one who will ask you all the questions you already answered in a speech, or in your email, or your brochure, or your sign post, or whatever, as and when I need to know the answers. I ain't terribly good at retaining information until I actually *need* it. One too many blows to the head."

I wait for a scowl but actually what I get is her first proper smile.

She's a fucking stunner.

"Well, in that case I guess it does not matter that you're missing the tour and the induction in the hall. Come on," she says, turning to put a foot on the bottom step. "Let me show you your room and tell you what you're here for."

There is a gently ribbing edge to it and it makes me itch to hear her in full on taking the piss out of someone mode. I bet she's hilarious in an edgy, push-all-your-buttons way. But she turns professional again as we walk up and she explains the concept of The Village to me.

"The houses on this side of the road all have four rooms for clients and one staff head of house, your host. In your case, me. All heads of house are qualified nurses–"

"Why?" I interrupt her.

"Because our substance abusers are often under prescribed medication to help them with their withdrawal or to address the underlying mental health issues that led them into addiction in the first place. And because Halosan's clinics are always as remote as this. The company wants to make sure there is first class medical assistance if needed. I'm the senior nurse here, Christine who is head of house at number 12 is my deputy. The houses on the other side of the road do not have client rooms. Number five is the premises manager's and his wife's, Alan and Barbara Allsorts. You won't see them a whole lot, other than Alan doubles up as our personal trainer and gym super. He's ex-SAS, so don't be surprised if he creeps up on you. Seven, nine and eleven are occupied by our counselors. Seven is the Denyers, they are a couple and facilitate the group sessions. They also head the program here. Not much to say about them. Nine is Dr. Lewin, she's a CBT specialist in addiction counselling and eleven is Dr. Rothman, he's person-centered. I'll warn you now, those two do not get on. You've been allocated Lewin as your one-to-one therapist."

We've reached the landing. There are three rooms here.

"All client rooms on this floor have en suites," she says as she turns the corner to go up the next flight of stairs. "But because you didn't come this morning for check in, you got unlucky and have the attic room next to me. Which means we have to share a bathroom. And I tell you now, it gets stuffy up there in this heat."

I stop for a second halfway up this flight of stairs and look down at the rooms on the first floor, trying to suppress the rush I get from the idea that the two of us are going to share a floor.

"Who else is in the house?" I ask, and she stops to look where I'm looking and sighs.

"If you'd checked in earlier, you'd have met them. Room 1 is Tristan, he's only eighteen and he has an online gaming problem, so when I give you the Wi-Fi password, I'd appreciate it if you kept it to yourself. He's on a strict no electronics diet for the first couple of weeks. Room 2 is Simon, he's an alcoholic. Room 3 is Charlie. He's got a pretty serious coke habit and he's been here before. You'll meet them in a while. Come on."

She beckons me upwards, and I follow her to what is an attic conversion. She wasn't joking. The air is so hot and thick up here, you could cut it with a knife. There are two bedrooms next to one another and a small toilet and shower bathroom. Everything above my head is slanted and I have to make sure I don't knock my head. When we get to the door to my room, Raven puts a hand on the door handle, opens it and then turns to look at me, frowning.

"Be careful you don't knock your head."

She hesitates and shakes her head.

"You know, this is dumb. I'll ask Tristan to switch rooms with you. That way I can keep an eye on him, and you don't have to hunch over all the time. How tall are you?"

"Six three," I answer and stop her in her tracks when her body language indicates she is going to drag me back downstairs and make me swap. "And no. I'm fine up here. If this Tristan kid is all settled in, I don't want to mess with that."

What I really want to say is, 'No, I like the idea of you sleeping next door to me while I jerk off to images of fucking you so hard you are screaming my name to kingdom come'.

Because, let's face it, that is exactly what is going to happen.

She shrugs in response, but I see her lips quiver before she carries on talking. She finds the idea of me next door either just as arousing, or she's a little scared. Either suits me. Both would be preferable.

"If you're sure, then settle in," she says evenly, nodding at the functionally furnished, predominantly cream-coloured room and I step past her, dropping my backpack onto the bed. "I'll meet you downstairs once you've unpacked," she carries on. "The others should be back from the induction in about ten minutes and then y'all cook together."

"What?" I look at her aghast.

"You cook. It's part of the program. Doing normal everyday tasks together. We draw the line at cleaning, though. Like I said, we have cleaners. They're trustworthy, but if you have any valuables, I'd use the safe in the closet. Anything else I can help you with, just ask."

She looks up into my eyes and I can see she knows it's the wrong thing to say as soon as the words have passed her lips, and she sees my grin.

I can't help it.

I step into her space and lean down to whisper in her ear.

"Plenty."

I breathe against her earlobe and watch as the soft flesh behind it ripples with goose bumps.

I straighten up to immediately back off and give her my biggest smile.

Then I watch as she turns on her heels and leaves the room, flustered.

Oh yeah, it's gonna be fun playing with that one.

Raven

The guy is an ass.

An incredibly attractive ass but an ass nonetheless.

What a jerk.

I've read the phrase 'she bristled' a thousand times in my life in a thousand different novels, but I've never felt like that exact word.

It's a privileged word. Reserved for princesses and pretty, precious girlies. Not for the likes of me.

But right now, this fucking minute, I'm *bristling*.

How fucking dare he breathe on me like that?

How fucking dare my clit *respond* to him breathing on me like that. And, oh boy, respond she did.

I stomp almost all the way back down to the kitchen before I realize I've forgotten to give him the Wi-Fi password. Or to deliver the how-to-set-the-code-on-the-room-safe instructions. Or the how-to-leave-the-bathroom-after-you're-done monologue. In short, any of the basic information I'm supposed to impart when showing a client to their room.

It riles me that he has that effect on me and I'll be damned if I let it go. So I turn around and traipse back up until I'm back at his still wide-open door. I take a step in and lift my hand to the wood for a courtesy knock but freeze the action midair when my gaze falls on his back and I realize what it is he's doing.

He's discarded his jacket on the bed and is standing by the open dormer window, leaning forward, his arm resting over his head on the lintel above the window. He's still wearing his cargo pants, but by the way they hang low on his hips now, I can tell he's unbuttoned them at the front.

His top half is covered only by a tight black tank top, so his arms and most of his shoulders are on show. The guy is pure hulking muscle. There is ink visible on his shoulder blades, but his arms are tat free and I can see his right biceps ripple as he moves his hand slowly back and forth.

The hand that is hidden from my view.

The hand that without a doubt is currently stroking his cock to satisfaction.

I want to retreat. I really do.

But fascination roots me to the spot.

He's so surprisingly gentle with himself.

I don't need to have the full visual to see that.

The heavy scent of him, sweaty and salty and with a tinge of lemongrass, hangs in the air.

A wave of arousal washes through me.

I'm getting slick and the hum in my clitoris that started with him breathing on me is getting heavier.

Shit.

I need to leave.

I'm watching a Halosan client masturbate.

Instant dismissal.

Instant debt of nursing school fees. Clause three in the contract. If for any reason the candidate is dismissed before the five-year tie-in, the school fees are to be repaid to the company in full.

But I just can't find the strength to back away. I'm bound, somehow part of this, even though he does not know I'm here.

He's speeding up now, making noises low in his throat. Animalistic grunts that go straight to my core. I helplessly clench my thighs and ass a few times to relief some of the pressure building up inside me, but it only makes it worse.

And then he comes with a loud groan, shaking violently, making my heart beat as fast and erratically as if the orgasm had been mine.

I need to get out of here before he sees me, I manage to think, as he puts his dick away immediately after his climax, buttoning up his fly.

I'm about to make my escape when he speaks, his back still to me.

"Nice view."

He turns and looks at me while he wipes the come off his hand onto his vest, all casual like, as if it weren't even happening. As if he were merely drying sweaty palms.

"I'll need a shower before I come help with the cooking."

ROWAN

She doesn't miss a beat before she replies, all casual.

"No problem. You have a good hour before we congregate. Do me, and yourself, a favor and rinse the shower tray when you're finished and run the squeegee over the glass. Towels are in the closet. And if you shave, rinse the sink properly. If you got valuables to lock away, you can set your own code for the safe. Instructions are in the guest manual. If you feel sick at any point and need medical assistance, there is an emergency button on the nightstand, but to be honest, it just goes next door, to me, so you might as well just holler. Wi-Fi code is Halo3579 with a capital H. Like I said, do not give it to Tristan under any circumstances or let him have access to your phone or computer or whatever you've brought with you. Part of your rehab is to look out for each other," she rattles off.

She comes across as completely unflustered, but I'm not buying it.

I'm sure she's seen it all, being a nurse, and has probably had her fair share of people trying to touch her up or get her to touch them up. And she's probably always quite blasé about it, but I'm also damn sure she doesn't normally stop and stare.

Or is turned on.

And I know she is turned on.

I could feel it, when she was standing there, could feel the other person in the room, could feel her becoming part of it.

And now I can *see* it, too.

In her flushed cheeks, in her slightly shaking hands, in the way she's obliviously still pressing her thighs together.

But there is no way in hell she's ever going to acknowledge it. So I play ignorant. Won't mention a thing. Even if I can see her nipples poking through the bra she's presumably wearing, all the way into the heavy fabric of her tunic. I take a leisurely look at them, making sure she sees what I'm looking at, then I pull my spunk smeared vest over my head and fling it on the bed.

"Right," she says and clears her throat before she turns away. "I'll be downstairs. Join us when you're ready and settled in."

I watch her scurry off and curse the fact I'm hard. Again.

Shower, here I come.

It's gonna be a long four weeks.

Raven

It's gonna be a long four weeks with this guy next door to me.

I already got his number. He likes to provoke. And I'm a sucker for a provocateur. I like to resist. I like the fact that I get *the choice* to resist. And I like the tension. Not sure I like that much of it, though. I might just break.

It's been a long time since I got to fuck someone. Over a year. It's tricky working for Halosan. You are not allowed to fraternize with the clients, obviously, but relationships between staff are also discouraged, unless you are already married to one another, like the Denyers. Dating people at work is not exactly forbidden but the bosses don't like it. And if the bosses don't like one thing you do, they quickly find other stuff they don't like about your conduct. And before you know it, you're out on your ass with a ginormous student debt and a bad reference.

So I've always been good and played away from the clinics. Hooked up with a local wherever I was. There's nothing easier to find in the world than a repetitive one-night stand with the same person. The last one of those, Jason, was over a year ago, when I was posted to our clinic in the Rockies.

Jason was a chef in the nearest town, ran his own restaurant. No time for a girlfriend. Always so exhausted, he never once challenged my need to be on top. Perfect match for mutual itch scratching. He had ink, too. Lots of it. I recently saw a meme that made me think of him. *A tattoo sleeve used to mean you were a biker who'd kill. Now it means you're a chef who makes a lovely pork belly with balsamic drizzle.* Tagged him. He didn't react. Which illustrates why he was perfect. Absolutely no sense of humor. No chance of falling for him.

Funny that, because Rowan up there has humor by the bucket load in his eyes and only the one tat as far as I could see, but there is an edge to him that tells me he might just kill. For the right cause. Or the right person.

It's a fucking huge thing his tat. As soon as he took the tank off, I saw what it was. A python, winding itself around his torso and over his shoulder, where the head emerges in a canvass of jungle flowers and skulls. It's all one single image that comes alive when he moves in a way that a whole lot of patchwork ink never can.

I stop as I reach the kitchen and rub my hands over my face trying to rub the image away, refocus on my job.

I hear the front door open and the subdued voices of my other three guests as they step over the threshold and take their boots off like good little lambs. I go and switch the kettle on. Something I learned in my time here: when in the UK and people come in, you switch the kettle on — even if it's a hundred degrees outside.

ROWAN

I take my time showering, unpacking and then sending a message to Silas, letting him know I arrived alright.

It feels funny doing that after all the years we didn't have contact, but I promised him I would.

I hold my breath until he pings a message back. It's a thumbs up. Nothing more, nothing less. But it means the world to me. That bloke will never know just how much I love him. It's good to have him back in my life, no matter how wary he is of me.

I sit on the bed for a while longer, reading the guest manual, stalling. I could hear voices downstairs when I came out of the bathroom, so I know my other 'housemates' are back, and I can smell the acrid stench of barbecue coals being lit outside wafting in through the window. Somebody is using a liberal helping of methylated spirit to get it going.

Having jerked off a second time in the shower means I feel spent and less on edge now. Tired.

I could do with a snooze, but according to the timetable at the front of the Halosan guest manual, dinner prep starts at 5.30pm and everybody is expected to pitch in. Not quite sure what there is to prep for a barbecue, but I guess I'll find out. Once I move my arse downstairs. I'm still not moving. Because of *her*. Now that the lust has been serviced, at least for a while, I'm kind of scared of her. Not sure why.

My phone pings again and it's another message from Silas.

May the force be with you.

It makes me smile.

And gives me the boost to push myself off the bed and go meet the others.

Showtime.

Raven

Food prep is already in full swing when Rowan finally graces us with his presence. I quickly introduce him to Tristan, Charlie and Simon then hand him a knife, so he can chop salad bits, like everyone else.

That's our contribution tonight.

Behind the houses, the once individual gardens have been opened up to become a communal space with a long patio running the entire length of all eight cottages. In the summer, the individual houses cook for themselves during the week and eat either indoors or at their own patio table. Saturdays is communal barbecue night. On Sundays, it's a two-mile hike to the next pub for a carvery lunch, then fend for yourself in the evenings.

The pub is tricky for our alcoholics, but it's all part of the Halosan concept. Dr. Alma Halstroem, the founder of Halosan, strongly believed that part of rehab is being exposed to normal everyday activities. She had this idea that a rehab clinic is not just a place to sober up. In actual fact, we only take people after they've detoxed in a hospital setting already. No, Halosan clinics are educational facilities where people concentrate on retraining their mindset for the real world, venturing into the real world included.

Still don't much like taking alcoholics to the pub, but at least I understand the theory behind it.

To be frank, I don't much like the Sunday carvery at The Windchimes, period. It's pretty much everything that gives British food a bad rep around the world, on a plate with soggy gravy. It's a shame because I know that not all English cooking is terrible, but at The Windchimes it definitely is.

I usually like the hike, though. It's a great way of getting to know the guests, walking and talking.

But that's tomorrow. First, we have to get through the awkwardness that is the first barbecue on arrival day.

I watch as my house finishes putting the salad together.

Rowan chops cucumber, peppers and beetroot like a pro, fully absorbed in his task. He's not in any way trying to dominate the room, but he still takes up a whole load of space with his sheer size.

Charlie is shaking the vinaigrette, talking up a storm about how he met the Foo Fighters at a festival last month and can die happy now.

Tristan is zoned out, painstakingly disemboweling tomatoes at such slow speed that Simon, who was draining olives and corn, steps in and takes over.

I shouldn't really allow Simon to do that, but since we want to eat this side of midnight, I let it go.

Once we're done, we join the growing numbers outside.

Forty people sounds like a lot, but in reality, it's a pretty small number of faces to be milling around, and it's easy to keep track of one person in that crowd. And I'm keeping track, whether I want to or not.

I can't help it.

I watch Rowan all evening, always hyper aware of where he is, how far or near in relation to me, who he's talking to, what he's doing.

And he surprises me.

He appears much easier to be around than I would have thought. He has a knack for wry comments that make people laugh and they instantly like him for it. In particular, Charlie and Elias seem to be drawn to him like moths to a flame. Charlie looks less like a rock star in Rowan's presence than a young buck deep in the throes of hero worship, and normally cocky Elias is all demure and hanging on every word dripping from Rowan's lips. What the fuck is that all about?

But to my surprise, Rowan doesn't exactly bathe in their adoration. He seems uncomfortable with it, as his main focus appears to be on trying to prise Tristan out of his shell.

The boy is so far out of his comfort zone, away from his console and among real people, it's painful to watch. He sits in one chair all evening, hardly touches his food and keeps looking at his hands, his longish fair hair falling forward into his eyes, sewing machine leg going into overdrive. The first time Rowan talks to him, he almost jolts out of his chair with shock. I'm watching them from afar as Rowan patiently keeps trying to engage Tristan in a conversation, when Elias suddenly appears by my side.

"If you weren't so pretty, lass, I'd have the right hump with ye," he says, and I roll my eyes.

He's really laying on the Irish thick tonight and I have a funny feeling it's to do with the rather pretty ballerina in his house who's come here because of an addiction to heavy duty prescription pain meds, following a back operation. Elias has no misgivings about openly flirting with guests. He's been warned off by the Denyers twice already, but he just doesn't give a fuck.

And unlike me, he's a free agent. Halosan doesn't own him the way it owns me. If he gets fired, he gets fired. But he doesn't end up with instant debt. Lucky him.

"What are you talking about?" I ask and watch his eyebrows wiggle.

"Ye don't know, do ye?"

"Know what?"

I can barely suppress my irritation. Elias annoys the fuck out of me ninety percent of the time. Good for him that he's charming, helpful and funny the other ten. It also helps that he is easy on the eye, in that brown wild locks, blue eyes, Irish kind of way and that he's a damn fine nurse.

Back in April, we would have lost a guy to a heart attack if it hadn't been for Elias' lightning fast reactions and tenacious dedication to keeping the guy alive until the air ambulance arrived. Typical, in The Village we have not one but two hospital grade defibs, but where were we when it happened? Out on a hike. So Elias kept the guy alive with good old-fashioned CPR. We took turns but, really, he did most of it.

He slings an arm around my shoulder and gently steers me, so I've got a clear line of sight on Rowan.

"Not only did ye get the rock star, lass, you got yourself a fuckin' legend in yer house."

He nods in the direction of Rowan who thankfully remains oblivious to us as he is still trying to extract words out of our gamer.

"That there, Ray, my sweet, is none other than The Python."

The *Python*?

What the ever-loving fuck?

The guy is nicknamed for his tattoo?

I honestly want to crack up laughing. But then a small voice inside me tells me that that's not so different from having *my* name kind of tattooed all over *my* back and that I should probably shut the fuck up. Pot, kettle and all that jazz.

"Enlighten me," I manage to say evenly instead. "Who is The Python? Is it like The Rock?" I mock.

Elias chuckles.

"No, nothing like The Rock. Dwayne Johnson is a pussy compared to this guy. We're talking bona fide, illegal fight club, gauge-your-eyes-out, squeeze-the-last-breath-from-ya, leave-ya-for-dead champion."

I laugh.

"What a load of baloney, Elias. I'm not that gullible."

His face turns serious and his accent slips into meticulous British English, which is the first clue he's being serious.

"Straight up, Ravenna. I'm not joking you."

As soon as he calls me Ravenna, I know for certain he's not fucking with me. I think of my notion earlier that Rowan looks like a guy who would kill. For the right cause, the right person. Maybe I wasn't that far off. But maybe it's more about the right *price*. I blanch at the thought.

"Hey, you're going a bit pale there, Ray," Elias comments, giving my upper arm a bit of a rub. "Don't worry, lass, as far as I know he hasn't actually offed anyone. Though, truth be told, I wouldn't be surprised. The guy is ruthless. His choke outs are legendary."

I frown at him.

"How do you know about him?"

He takes his arm off me and shrugs.

"Bloke's gotta eat and illegal fight clubs need patcher-uppers. It's well paid work."

"*You?*" I ask in disbelief. "*You* patched *him* up?"

"Not him, no," Elias answers in that typical tone people have when they suddenly distance themselves from something they claim they've been involved in. "Others. Didn't do it for very long. But everyone who's had anything to do with that scene knows of The Python. Like I said, the guy's a legend."

And with that, he leaves me standing, staring at, apparently, a legend.

And the legend?

He is staring right back at me, his dark eyes devouring me inch by inch.

ROWAN

God, she's sexy.

I want to eat her whole. And her hole.

I've been watching her all night, the way she moves around, always alert, *seeing* everything.

And all the depraved bastard that I am can think about is how she might taste.

I bet she likes long, sloppy laps of the tongue. She looks like the kind of woman who has a really sensitive clit, where you've got to be careful when you go in for the suckle not to do it too hard. Something about the way she pushes her legs together when she's aroused tells me she is protective of her little pearl.

I wonder if she's bare, has a landing strip or is *au naturelle*.

If she's sensitive, she probably has a bit of bush. I like a bit of fur. Bare girls are fine, but they gotta have the mound for it. If the mound hasn't got the right curve, it makes them look like a prepubescent girl and that's a major turn off for me.

This one is all woman. Not because of the tits and the arse, though both are plenty fine, especially the latter, but because of the way she holds herself. She's confidence porn.

Shame that she's just found out who and what I am. There is no point wondering what that Irish medic just told her. He's not exactly discreet. Just my luck that I'd bump into someone who knows who I am in the middle of nowhere in fucking Dorset. Really? Really, really? Apparently so. By the look she's giving me now, she's just been told exactly who the *Python* is and that he eats babies for breakfast. Great. Which is why it's doubly surprising that she starts walking towards me.

Oh yeah, I wasn't wrong, this one meets whatever scares her head on.

Fucking beautiful.

I'm hard as a rock again.

Raven

I meet his gaze and seconds later, my feet start moving toward him of their own accord.

There is no point in trying to hide. He'll be in my house, on my floor, for the next four weeks, so I'll put an end to it before it even starts. Silence the tiny voice in the back of my head that tells me I like it.

I've never been looked at like this and it's making me all sorts of wet.

Sure thing, I've had men *leer* at me before. But he's not leering. He's…smoldering.

I can't really say what the difference is. The stare is the same. Maybe it's to do with the thoughts behind the stare. He isn't mentally undressing me then spitting me up to stick his dick in me.

In his mind, I'm already buck naked and he's doing things to me that are all about me. About what I want. Really want. Even if it's more than I can handle. The idea really turns me on, and I feel another glut of moisture slide down my insides and pool between my legs.

I try to ignore it and keep approaching.

"Hi, boys," I say when I arrive at the table where Rowan and Tristan are sitting.

It comes out breathy, like Marilyn Monroe taking the microphone when she entertained the troops. I want to slap myself. Tristan looks up at me, wide-eyed, mumbles something, pushes out of his chair and bolts.

"You scared it away!" Rowan mocks. "It was almost ready to eat out of my hand."

I smile. I can't help it. It's his delivery. In that rumbly, thunderous bass. It's pitch perfect.

"Sorry," I say. "I was just trying to check in with you guys."

"Making sure I'm not corrupting the young Padawan," he states with a smile around the eyes but an edge to his voice.

I shake my head.

"No, not at all."

We stare at each other again in silence until he pats the chair next to him.

"Sit."

I do but on the chair opposite him, with the table between us. It's safer that way. He crosses his arms on the tabletop and leans forward, holding my gaze hostage.

"I don't know what that Irish dick just told you, but I'm not gonna kill the kid, okay? I don't kill innocents. Relax."

He holds my eyes for some time after that, and the conflict I see behind his stare makes my insides turn to mush. There is so much more to this guy than meets the eye. And the weird thing is, I *do* relax. He smiles, earnestly, knowingly, and gives me a small nod. Then that smile turns into one of his arrogant fucking grins.

"So, tell me, Raven. What's the Halosan stance on dalliances between guests and staff? Is it like a teacher fucking his pupil?"

I love how he slips in a word like 'dalliance'. I mean, who does that? More to the point, what *guy* does that? Without sounding camp? Rowan Hadlow-Fuller-O'Brien, that's who.

After a furtive glance around to make doubly sure nobody is in earshot, I lean in, mimicking his posture.

"It's very much like a teacher fucking her pupil," I whisper across.

My casual change of the gender of the personal pronoun does not go unnoticed. It lights up a fire in his eyes that has my heart racing. Shit. Not good. I was supposed to be cutting him down. What am I doing flirting with him? Better lay it out, loud and clear, with no room for misinterpretation.

"Worse because certain staff had their training paid for by the company and if they get fired, they have to repay their student fees in full. That'll be eighty thousand bucks in my case. Not happening."

There, I've said it. End of story.

He nods then looks away over my shoulder into the distance, thinking.

"What about sleeping with other staff? That allowed?"

I shake my head, wondering why I am even letting him carry on pursuing the subject.

"What about the locals?"

I raise my eyebrows, not that he can see it because he is still examining the scenery behind me.

"Yeah, outsiders are allowed," I answer. "As long as I don't bring them to The Village."

"You found anyone around here then?" he asks casually, still not looking at me.

"No," I say.

He makes eye contact with me again. And, boy, can I feel that contact. I can feel it all the way from where it hits my eyeballs down to my toes in one liquid rush.

"You're nice and pent-up then," he states, and I swallow hard.

I'm about to respond with something like 'you gotta stop talking to me like this' when he abruptly gets up. There is no denying the erection that is straining against his pants. It's unashamedly in my line of sight.

What is it with this guy? Is he always up and ready to go?

The thought, like just about every thought I'm having about him, makes my insides clench.

"Excuse me, I've gotta hit the sack," he says, tips his head at me, and grabs his and Tristan's finished-with plates to stack them. "I'll take these. Is there a dishwasher?"

"Yes. It's..."

"I'll find it," he interjects then looks around. "Anything else you want me to bring inside?"

"No. It's okay. We'll handle the rest," I respond, almost on autopilot.

I feel weirdly dismissed and as soon as he leaves, there is a void in the space around me that I can't explain.

Part of me hopes he'll come back out.

But he doesn't.

I don't see him again for the rest of the night.

ROWAN

It's the longest night I've ever had. Trumps even the night before I had to go and nearly kill Silas. And that was fucking long.

But that one was all psychological. This one is mostly physical.

It's stuffy and hot under the roof, so I'm lying naked on the bed with the dormer window open and the door ajar to create the semblance of a draft. It means I can hear every little sound she makes as she comes up the stairs later, goes in and out of the bathroom and into her room. She is trying to be quiet, but my senses are so heightened to her presence I can hear her breathe as she crosses the landing.

My mind keeps wondering what she is or isn't wearing. Whether she has opened her window, too.

If the draft is caressing her skin the way it caresses mine.

If her nipples are pebbling.

If she's hot and sweaty at the nape of her neck.

If she would like someone to lick off the sweat and then blow over the skin to cool her down.

If she's got her hand between her legs.

But I also wonder other things about her as I keep playing idly with my dick, not really masturbating but just keeping us in that limbo between arousal and ecstasy. I can do this for hours. I love it. If you pitch it right, there is a weird sort of serenity about it. It's a state that's helped me through a lot of shit. I think it might be what tantric sex is all about, not that I am prick enough to call it that. But to stay like this, I can't just think about her tits and arse and cunt and licking and fucking her.

I have to think about other stuff, too.

Like where she comes from. If she has family. What that weird vision was of her as an urchin. Why she feels so oddly familiar. As if we were two of a kind.

Something deep inside me kind of knows the answers already, but they aren't sexy, so I go back to tits and arse and cunt and licking and tweaking and sucking and fucking.

It's a weird undulation of thoughts and images that I keep going until the small hours, when I hear her crying out in lust in her sleep before I finally fall asleep, with my dick still in my hand, hard and unspent, and a smile on my lips.

Raven

I wake up early as always, despite the precious few hours of sleep I've had, with a fully formed question on my mind. Is it possible for someone to weave an atmosphere across an entire floor from behind a closed door?

It's a silly question really, because I know the answer already.

Sure thing, it is. My mother, not Elena but my real mother, when she was still alive, could infuse an entire house with her anger, her despair, her narcissism.

Scrap that, she could project it over an entire neighborhood. So you couldn't escape her mood even when you'd finally gotten to school five blocks away. But I think the difference is that my mom never projected anything positive or nice. That's not to say she didn't have her good moments. She did. But they were exactly that, *moments*. They never lasted long enough to dye the air happy, the way her black moods painted everything gray.

What Rowan did last night was the same but different. Somehow, he managed to make arousal hang in the thick air under this roof like it was a tenacious but delicious smell, taunting me all night.

I finally fell asleep at about one, exhausted from keeping my desire at bay, from refusing to get myself off to images of fucking this guy.

Only to go and dream of a shadowy figure with a python for a cock pounding me senseless, until I screamed out my orgasm in my sleep.

I know I did. I woke myself up with the sound of it then immediately went back to sleep, trying to chase the dream while vaguely registering the soggy mess I'd made of the sheets.

I'm still liquid between my legs and down to my ass cheeks as I open my eyes to the day, but I no longer feel possessed. The early morning air brings a fresh breeze through my open window. I take a big breath before I swing my legs out of bed and make my way to the shower.

I like to be up and having my coffee in the kitchen a good half hour before anybody else in the house rises. It's the only time in the day that I truly get quality alone time. One of the drawbacks of the job. And I need my alone time.

Before I was moved into care, my own company was all I ever really had, sporadic stage entries and exits of my mother and her 'boyfriends' notwithstanding. And although I soaked up the presence of other people, the safety in numbers, like a dried-up sponge once I got to Elena and John's, it still took me years to truly acclimatize to the hustle and bustle of a group home. Once I'd gotten used to it, I was old enough to move to the dorm at nursing school. Same again. Then came the various Halosan settings. Same again. So you could say I'm well seasoned in rooming with lots of other people by now, but no matter where and with whom I'm living, I need that half hour to an hour in the morning by myself, being just me.

So when I go downstairs and enter the kitchen after my shower, wearing my Sunday best, makeup and all — it's the only day a week I'm out of my tunic in my own chosen skin and I always make the most of it — and find Rowan in the process of pushing down the coffee grind in the big cafetière, I'm not exactly ecstatic at the sight of him.

Actually, that's a lie.

The sight of him is magnificent, barefoot and in low slung extremely faded jeans and wearing nothing but his tattoo and muscle on the top half.

It's his *presence* I resent.

But even that resentment I can't keep up for long when he offers me coffee.

"Do you want some?" he asks, still looking at the cafetière rather than me.

"Yes, thank you," I reply, and he looks up.

I watch his eyes go wide as he takes me in and a small, appreciative smile forms around his lips. But he doesn't say anything. He doesn't need to. It's all there in his eyes. He likes it. He likes me in my own clothes and for that I almost completely forgive him for stealing today's alone time from me.

She is a fucking wet dream, standing there in fishnets and a short, black, cherry-patterned fifties dress with a halter neck, with her tits falling out.

Her makeup, too, is all retro pin up with lipstick the same shade as the cherries. Her hair is styled in a quiff with a bright red bandana holding the rest of her locks back from her face.

And when she turns to shut the kitchen door, I glimpse the edges of ink on her back.

Big ink. All black. Something with feathers.

I hadn't pegged her as rockabilly punk at all, but now that she is standing in front of me in her civilian garb, I kind of instantly forget what nursey Raven looks like, because *this* is the woman she is underneath all the time. It's glaringly obvious in her every move that she feels happy in this skin. Whether in her uniform, or naked and barefaced, this is still the woman she is, always. No wonder I'm so drawn to her.

"Milk and sugar?" I ask her as I pour milk into the bottom of my mug.

"Yes to milk, no to sugar," she answers, and I move on to the next mug with the milk bottle.

I top up both mugs with coffee and hand her one. And yeah, cliché over fucking cliché, I feel a fucking zing all the way to my toes when our fingers brush in the process.

"Thank you," she says, and for a few moments, we just look at each other over the rims of our respective mugs.

I blow on my coffee, take a sip and cock my head.

"You look like you should be in Civet," I say all casual and watch her face explode in a wide smile.

Bingo. Knew it.

"You know *Civet*?"

She is genuinely surprised and so she should be. Civet weren't that well known in the UK. I kinda like them because they were almost as good as The Distillers but hotter to look at. Aurally, I have a thing for female punk bands. Visually, I prefer a pin up. What can I say, I'm a bloke. So they were the perfect storm in my eyes.

"I like Punk when it's good and people can play their instruments," I say.

"Huh," she utters and sips her coffee.

I've thrown her. She didn't expect that. Wonder what she did expect. So I ask.

"What kind of music did you have me pegged for?"

She shrugs and spills some of her coffee over her hand. She licks it off before she answers, and I barely hear what she says — too busy processing the image of her tongue darting out from between those cherry red lips and caressing the side of her hand.

"I dunno."

She looks up at me from under her heavy eyelashes.

"Aren't you guys supposed to be into rap and hip-hop and..."

She cuts herself off.

"And shit?" I finish the question for her because I'm not bound by remaining professional here, and grin. "And who exactly are 'you guys'?"

"Fighters," she answers.

I nod slowly.

"Maybe. But I haven't sustained quite enough head injuries for that yet."

And that's when I hear her properly laugh for the first time.

Raven

He's so dead pan it's hard not to laugh, or not to like him. He waits until I'm finished and before he speaks again.

"To be fair, I like good rap and hip hop. And, yeah, you're right, there is a lot of it played on the fight circuit. There isn't really a genre I don't like. But it's not something I'd buy."

I nod, put my coffee down on the counter and start opening cupboards to get stuff onto a tray for breakfast in the adjacent room. It isn't really my job to lay the table, the whole house is supposed to pitch in and do everything together, but to be honest this whole Scouts' team philosophy Halstroem had going is trite when it's forced. Rowan and I are here in the kitchen first, and since I won't be getting my alone time anyway now, we might as well start the day.

Another thing I like about Rowan is that I don't have to tell him what to do.

A lot of guests stand around at first as if they'd never opened a cupboard or put a breakfast together in their lives, but he just gets on with it. While we cart stuff from the kitchen next door, we carry on talking about music and the conversation is just easy. It's good because we have similar tastes but not the same, so there is a lot of 'oh you gotta try them'.

By the time we set the table, I feel like I've spent the last half hour with a really good old friend, rather than this hulking hot mess that I met less than twenty-four hours ago.

I even stop seeing that he remains half naked the entire time.

It's only when we hear the footsteps of the others coming alive above us and he looks down at himself that I wake up again to the sexy giant of a man in front of me.

He clears his throat.

"I'd better go and get a shirt on," he says soberly with not a hint of teasing. "Wouldn't want them to get the wrong end of the stick."

I swallow hard as he moves past me to go in search of clothes.

I can handle having an easy conversation, not so sure I can handle protectiveness.

ROWAN

The walk is great.

The scenery is just as stunning as it was yesterday, and I get to watch Raven's fine pegs as she walks ahead of me the entire two miles, in her DMs and fishnets with her dress swishing around her knees, while she is talking to Simon, the alcoholic.

He is an odd fish in our little five fish pond because he is so much older than the rest of us. I spoke to him a little last night and his problems are kind of a lifetime ahead of mine, or Tristan's, or Charlie's.

His wife of nearly thirty years threw him out five months ago because she'd had enough of him drinking and his anger issues. From the way he tells it, he wasn't that bad. But my gut feeling is, he went for her a few times. It's funny because speaking to him sober as he is now, he doesn't come across as the majorly aggro type. On the contrary, he seems affable, funny, likable, intelligent, if suffering from a severe case of verbal diarrhoea. Still, there is an underlying edge to him.

I've known guys like him. He's pretty much like a lot of the aged fighters who hang around gyms and come to fights, drinking and betting. In their heads, they are still on form and in control and top dog, when in real life, they are just swaying drunks with popping veins and bloodshot eyeballs who lose a lot of money and treat their women, if they have one, like shite.

Not that Simon's a fighter, he's a suit, but same difference.

He talks about his family a lot. Showed me pictures of two gorgeous teenage girls in his wallet. His daughters. Apparently, his wife throwing him out just made her a bitch, but his older daughter telling him she was scared of him and didn't want contact as long as he was still drinking sent him into rehab. The power of children. Good on her. But it begs the question what does a man have to do to make his child scared of him?

It makes me wary of him and I keep a close eye on his interaction with Raven. I also doubt he's gonna make it in the long run. That old adage of you want to do it for yourself springs to mind. I know *I* do. Betting nearly cost me everything I love, and most of all, it turned me into a complete cunt and a slave for a while. I got out of slavery and I don't wanna be a cunt for the rest of my life.

Somebody falls in step with me and I turn my head to see the young blonde ballerina from the Irish nurse's - Elijah? Eli? Elias? something like that - house sidle up to me.

"Hey," she says.

"Hey," I reply.

We walk for a bit without saying anything else. It's weird how just somebody else's presence can alter your thought patterns. With her arrival in my periphery, I suddenly stop contemplating the people around me and see the view again. The stunning blue of the sky, the width of the heathland.

"Beautiful around here, isn't it?" the blonde says in a plummy voice, and I nod. "What's your name? You weren't at the induction and I didn't get a chance to talk to you last night at the barbecue."

She's friendly, not at all shy but also not brazen or condescending. I like her. In a display cabinet kinda way. Her world and mine are galaxies apart, I'm sure.

"Rowan," I say. "I arrived late."

She giggles.

"Yeah, I know. Everybody knows. Ravenna was mightily put out about that. I'm Ann-Marie. Pleased to meet you."

Mightily put out. Pleased to meet you.

Yup. Galaxies. But, hey, no harm in a bit of friendly banter between aliens.

"How do you find your house, Ann-Marie?"

She hesitates before she answers, and I glance over at her in the pause to see her cheeks blush.

"It's good," she says then hurriedly changes the subject. "Is it allowed to ask why you're here?"

"You're allowed to ask anything you like, Ann-Marie. Doesn't mean you'll get an answer, but you will on this one. It's kind of the point of us being here, isn't it? 'Fessing up. I have a betting issue."

"Oh," she exclaims. "How unique."

I'm not sure if I want to piss myself laughing or howl in despair at the gulf between us. So I do neither.

"What about you?"

"Fentanyl addiction."

And just like that my view of her changes in an instant. She's a hardcore junkie, fighting a hardcore fight. Hats off.

"Whoa. That's hardcore shit. How did you end up taking that crap?"

"Back operation."

"Fuck," I say.

Good luck, girlie, I think.

Raven

We have a deal with The Windchimes, so the table is normally laid for us either in the function room or under a wooden shelter in their beer garden if it's a nice day. Today we're outside and you can see the people at the other tables, mostly tourists, eye us up with curiosity.

I don't blame them. Our cohorts rarely make sense to the outside observer. I think most of the time people decide we are on some kind of corporate retreat. I've been asked a few times in the past, and when that happens, I answer neutrally, 'We're from The Village.' Eight out of ten people just accept that answer. Number nine will ask 'which village', in which case I give the name of the village that The Village used to have, and leave them frowning. And then there is number ten, a local who knows what that means, looks around for her handbag and drags it onto her lap before she urges the husband that it's time to leave. Today is clearly the turn of the tenth one in the shape of a middle-aged woman in a flowery dress who grabs my wrist as I pass her table on my way to the bar to give them our collective drinks order.

"Excuse me, young lady, I couldn't help wondering who you people are," she says in a tone that suggests she's already worked it out and disapproves.

I look silently back and forth between her hand on my wrist and her face until she drops it. Then I answer.

"We're from The Village," I inform her and watch as she grabs her handbag from the floor and lifts it onto her lap.

So predictable.

I'm about to move off without further comment when the woman's eyes grow big at somebody behind me. I already know by the happy shiver running through my body who it is before that thunder growl voice rolls over my shoulder.

"That's right, lady," he says. "You keep hold of your valuables. The junkies are about."

The woman gasps and kind of shrinks away in her seat. I turn to tell Rowan off, but when I meet the twinkle in his eye, I can't help but smirk back at him.

"Come on," he says to me, ignoring the old witch now. "I came to see if you need some help. And to ask you something."

We move off together and he holds the door open for me when we enter the back corridor of the pub. I roll my eyes at him and he shrugs.

"Can't help it. It's how Sheena brought us up."

"Who's Sheena?"

"My second mum."

That's right. I read that in his file. His mother died when he was eleven. Doesn't say how. At first, he stayed with his stepdad and half siblings, and then he was fostered by non-family and adopted by that same woman a few years later. She's down as Mrs S O'Brien on his forms as his next of kin. I guess I now know what the S stands for.

"You always do what your mom tells you to do?" I ask teasingly as I throw him a look over my shoulder, and nearly choke on my tongue at the expression on his face.

It's fleeting, but it's pure sorrow.

Shit. What did I say?

I automatically start hurrying toward the bar as we enter the main pub area as if I could run away from what I just saw in his eyes. Before I can get anywhere, though, his large hand clasps around my shoulder. The dress I'm wearing is strapless and I left the shawl I used to keep the sun off on my chair, so his palm makes direct contact with my skin.

Oh my fucking god.

It's the first time he's touched me since our handshake yesterday, and I can feel it in every fucking cell in my body. I half expect the shape of his fingers to be branded into my skin when he lifts it. Not that he does. His hand stays there while I spin around to face him.

We look at each other for what seems like forever, just staring.

I'm vaguely aware of his thumb swiping back and forth over my clavicle, almost like he can't help it. Truth be told, I'm not even sure he's aware of it.

I am.

I am more aware of that thumb than of anything else in the universe.

He clears his throat.

"Why the rush?" he asks.

"Erm."

I don't know what to say. I can't think. At least not beyond totally inappropriate stuff like, *for fuck's sake move that hand lower, cup my tit, move the pad of that thumb over my nipple, tug on it, let me take you to the restroom, let me back into a stall, climb on your lap and fuck your brains out.*

I can see in his eyes that he can read my thoughts perfectly well, and it's confirmed when he finally releases my shoulder, only to use the same hand to adjust his junk.

"I was gonna ask you a question," he says evenly, still fucking rearranging his hard-on. "I couldn't help but notice that everybody ordered soft drinks. What's with that? Are we all expected to stay sober, even if alcohol is not our problem? I kinda fancy a beer, you know. I haven't had a pint in weeks. Not since before I started training for my last big fight. I'd quite like a lager after that walk to be honest."

I shake my head apologetically.

"Again, that was covered in that induction talk you missed. In support of our recovering alcoholics we all agree not to drink during the Sunday carvery."

He frowns.

"That's dumb. I mean that's the whole point of this, isn't it? Going out into the world and not falling into temptation. Besides, I'd bet my arse that Simon wasn't a pub boozer anyway. He's got stay at home, get pissed over the course of the evening then get narky with the wife and kids written all over him. His problem will be passing the alcohol aisle in Sainsbury's, not sitting in the pub not drinking. I bet he fucking excels at not drinking in public."

I narrow my eyes at him because, although he's probably right where Simon is concerned, I don't like the way he looks down his nose at a fellow man in recovery.

And there are also a few more alcoholics in the other houses, some of whom might well be pub boozers, as he calls it. I'm about to say something but Rowan isn't finished.

"So is nobody allowed to bet on Ascot either?" he asks somewhat petulantly.

"What?"

"Well, if I'm not allowed to drink, then nobody should be doing any gambling on account of me. And no *Candycrush* on account of Tristan, and no sticking your hand in the medical cupboard on account of Ann-Marie, no food bingeing on account of any bulimics, no..."

"I get your point," I interrupt him.

"Oh shit," he says, his face suddenly turning crestfallen from his previous slightly ribbing expression, and he cups his crotch protectively for a moment. "There aren't any sex addicts among us, are there?"

I hate the fact he makes me laugh.

"No, not this time."

A wolfish grin spreads across his way-too-fucking-handsome face and his eyes light up.

"Well, thank fuck for that then."

"Rowan, I told you, I-"

"Ha! Gotcha," he interjects then leans forward, over my left shoulder, until his mouth is level with my ear and whispers, "You've thought about it, haven't you? You've thought about everything you *didn't* see yesterday."

He blows lightly across the shell of my ear, and I nearly turn into a puddle.

My hand darts forward on its own accord because I need to hold on to something, need something to steady me. That something turns out to be the edge of his left pec, so that my palm is spread over his sternum, which means I can feel his heart through his skin-tight white tee.

It's beating. Fast. Erratically.

"I told you, I can't," I mumble, and he makes a hissing sound.

"Who says I'm talking about you," he says teasingly and straightens up. "Halosan can't tell the guests not to shack up, can they now? Ann-Marie is cute. Bit ribby but I bet she makes up for it in bendiness. And posh birds fuck well, all that 'plum in mouth' translates."

It's like the proverbial bucket of cold water. I retrieve my rebellious hand and let my spine snap straight, glaring up at him.

"You really are a-"

He puts a hand across my mouth and grins mischievously.

"Now, now, Ravenna. Was that something unprofessional you were about to say there?"

He winks and takes his hand away, only to drag the pad of his thumb across my lips.

I hate myself for the way it makes me shiver. That fucking thumb, I should bite it the fuck off.

But then he smiles, a genuine smile reaching all the way up to his hungry, hungry eyes.

"Don't you worry, there is no competition here," he whispers and brings his thumb to his mouth and kisses it where my lipstick has stained it red. "None," he reiterates and turns away toward the bar. "Right. I'm gonna get me a beer."

ROWAN

I regret that beer for the next thirty hours solid.

Not because I wake up the following day with a hangover. I don't. A pint of lager, and I only had the one, doesn't even make a dent in it for me, even though I rarely drink. There is just too much of me to soak it up.

Not even because of the scathing looks I got from my, what did Raven call them again? *Fellow men and women in recovery.* No. That was kinda the point. Like it always is with me.

And not even because it overshadows my entire first day in rehab proper, being the subject *du jour* in both my first group session and my first one-to-one with my allocated therapist. In the group session, they practically annihilated me under the not so careful guidance of the Denyers, Judy and Ed, a middle-aged couple with his-and-hers short grey hair, his-and-hers thick framed glasses and his-and-hers M&S wardrobes. It was hilarious. I really struggled to keep a straight face. But I did it.

And the Oscar goes to Rowan O'Brien for looking contrite.

The counsellor chick who does my one-to-one slot, Dr Lewin, loved it, though. I could practically see her salivating over this *case*. Idiot. But at least an easy-on-the-eye idiot, in a mid-forties but still wears the boho wardrobe she cultivated in her twenties and her ash blonde hair in a French plait with artful wisps framing her face kinda way. She is all about the knitwear, Sheena would say. She seems okay though. We'll see how useful she'll prove. Seems a bit obsessed with my thought processes. Didn't quite get it when I tried to explain to her that ninety-nine percent of the time the *lack* of thought process is my problem.

No, the reason I still regret that pint a day later is because Raven stopped engaging with me the minute I took my glass back to the table in the pub garden. No matter how many jokes I cracked about the atrocious food, no matter how much I tried to bait her, she completely shut me out. She ignored me during the carvery, during the walk home, during the evening that followed, even during the fucking *night*. It's fucking impossible really, but I just *know* she consciously made herself *not* think about me next door somehow. As if I were just any other guest.

And I don't like it.

I don't want to be just any other guest. I get that she can't go there with me without putting her job on the line and incurring a mountain of debt, but I still want to be *somebody* for her. Not a lover, if that's too costly, but also not just another face that happens to pass through here. I may only have known this woman for all of two days, but I know I want to be the Rowan to her Raven, even if that makes zero sense.

So after the first day of therapy is done, I do a few rounds in the gym, which to my surprise even boasts a punch bag corner, swim a hundred lengths in the pool, and then I go and do what I do best.

Eat humble pie.

I have a fucking black belt in eating humbles.

I find her in the communal garden, sitting at the table outside our house, reading. Not an e-reader, an actual book. I've not heard of the author, but the way the name of the writer is printed bigger than the title and the font is frill-less, I can only assume it's a thriller or a police procedural. Fits her. I bet she inhales reruns of CSI the way others snort coke.

I'm pretty sure she's noticed my presence standing in the backdoor, but she isn't going to make it easy for me and doesn't let on. I clear my throat.

"Raven? Can I talk to you for a minute?"

She slowly lifts her eyes from the page and looks over to me, disdain marring her features. I hate that she looks at me like this.

"Can it wait? I'm on my break. I have an hour before we start dinner prep. Come back then?" she suggests coldly.

Fuck this.

I approach and sit down opposite her, already talking before my arse hits the chair.

"No. It fucking well can't wait. But I'll be quick, okay? I came to say sorry for yesterday. I was out of order. I shouldn't have done it. I won't do it again."

"Yeah, right," she shrugs it off as if I'd lied to her a million times before and that pisses me right the fuck off.

"Oi, if I say I won't do it again, I won't do it again, alright?"

She flinches at my 'oi' but composes herself quickly and levels her eyes with mine.

"You're an addict, Rowan. Do you know how often I've heard an addict say they won't do it again?"

"In this line of work?" I ask dryly. "I suspect a lot."

I can see the tiniest smirk form around her beautiful mouth and the relief I feel is ridiculously out of proportion to what is happening. I want to dwell on this relief, but I know we are nowhere near there yet.

"Look," I forge on, "I was an arse. I *am* an arse. It's kind of why I'm here, if that makes sense. I act on impulse. Do first, think later. I'm trying to change that. So I can't promise that I won't piss you off again, or break the rules, but I can promise you that I won't bring another pint to the table."

She nods slowly, then seeks my eyes and something has changed. High and mighty Raven has left the building and the woman I have a hard-on for is back in her place. Not just a turn of phrase, her gaze meets mine and my dick springs to attention. Stupid dick.

"You made me look bad," she says neutrally but very quietly.

Outside the other houses, more people are starting to spill out onto the terrace and lawn, and I guess she doesn't want anyone to hear her swear. And swear she does.

"I'm mostly pissed because it reflects badly on me if you break the rules. I'm responsible for this house. I'm *head* nurse of the entire program here. If you behave like shit, it means I have a discipline problem on my patch and that makes it harder to stay on top of people like Elias. He's a good nurse, but he's also a wild card with fuck all respect for anyone. This is my last intake of clients here before I go back to the States. I want it to go smoothly. I want to go back to HQ and be able to report that Purbeck is up and running and handed over to the locals without a hitch. And I really want it to be a success for Charlie. I don't want him to come back here a third time. Those are my goals. Don't keep pissing on my goals and we can be friends. Keep pissing on my goals and I swap you out for one of Christine's guests. I have the power to do that. Now leave and let me read my fucking book. I want to find out if the girl's still alive before we start cooking."

Raven

I look away from his amused eyes and at the page in front of me. I hear him push his chair back and get up then watch him over the edge of my book as soon as he turns and walks back into the house.

I breathe out heavily as he takes with him the faint scent of chlorine that let me know his wet hair was damp from a swim, not the shower.

For a moment, my brain conjures up the image of Rowan in jammers, water running down his powerful torso in rivulets, the sheen making the python glimmer under the poolside lights as if it actually had scales, and I want to punch myself for being so stupid.

Silly bitch that I am, I just let him back in.

Should've kept him out. I had found the key out of the torture chamber that is lusting after one of my guests, *this* guest, only to turn around mid-escape and run straight back in.

I'm a total idiot.

After that revelation, there is no way I can concentrate on my novel again, so I just sit there, my eyes going over the words without taking them in, while my mind is still with the man I assume has gone upstairs to shower the chlorine off.

It's another sexy image that bores itself into my mind, and what started off as a mind poster of him in the pool soon turns into a series of random thoughts of naked Rowan. A collage of desires, interspersed with flashbacks to him leaning at the window, jerking off to the view of the village.

He was right with what he said yesterday in the pub. So, so right. I've thought about everything I didn't see. I *keep* thinking about everything I didn't see. I wonder what shape he is. Curved or straight. Thick or thin. Whether his size matches the rest of him. I wonder if he's circumcised or not.

I've never had an uncut cock. Seen plenty of them but I've never *had* one. My generation was the last in the States for which it was pretty much a given that boys were cut. Does it make a difference? Does it *feel* different? Does the extra skin make a difference?

I've washed all sorts in my life as a nurse, long, short, thick, thin, some flaccid, some semis and some fully erect and, yeah, it desensitizes you to the thing. So I don't have that cock fetish so many women seem to have. At least I never did. Until now. Until I *couldn't* see. The image of Rowan by the window comes back to me and my insides clench, hard.

I shut my eyes for a second, feeling at odds with my lust against the background noise of more guests coming out of the houses to mill in the garden.

I startle when I hear somebody plop down in the chair next to me.

I open my eyes and to my relief find I'm looking sideways up at Christine. It's always looking *up* where Christine is concerned. Standing or seated, she is the tallest, broadest woman I have ever met, and not pretty by any standards. Not even a little. Not at all.

Her features are almost rough and her straight brown hair is cut in an asymmetrical short bob that screams lesbian. Yet she has more lovers, of the male variety, down in Swanage than the town's spectacular sandy beach has sunsets over a summer. I think it's all in her eyes. She has what the phrase 'baby blues' was coined for. And they always sparkle with wit and sarcasm. The tits probably help, too. She has phenomenal tits on an otherwise unspectacular body.

"Soooo," she says, half turning to watch the gathering crowd behind us. "Have you given any more thought to trading your fighter boy?"

I'd mentioned to her in passing earlier that if Rowan keeps being a pain in the ass, I might swap her a guest.

"He ain't no boy," I reply in my best pretend Southern drawl because I know how much she loves it when I respond in what she perceives as the only American accent worth its salt.

We regularly gloss over the fact that I was born forty plus states over from the Deep South.

She barks a laugh.

"Trust me, pet, they are *all* boys in *my* bed."

I have no doubt. The weird thing is the way she says it makes me sit up. I don't like her thinking about Rowan that way. I particularly don't like her thinking *I* might be thinking about him that way. But the way she suddenly shoots me a glance sideways, I know I already fucked that up by accidentally swallowing a rod just now. I'm officially screwed.

"Chillax, pet, I ain't shagging clients. Not daft. I look forward to stepping into your shoes in a few weeks. Hate to see you leave, but like the idea of your salary. But you? You need to get laid or summat. You're more pent-up than a herd of sheep at market. You're oozing sexual tension all over the place. So, you want to trade?"

I play along just to keep up the illusion, but I can tell by the way she's asking that she knows I'm not really going to give him up.

"What ya got?"

She grins.

"I see your fighter," she starts.

"Gambler," I interrupt.

"I see your *hellraiser*," she retorts, grinning because she for one loved the fact that he brought a beer to the table yesterday. "And raise you either of my two smackheads, or an anorexic, or a Prince Valium. Your pick, I'm not fussed."

"Sounds as much fun as my lot. Hmmm."

I pretend I'm thinking on it.

"No, thanks. I'll pass."

Then I suddenly realize what she said.

"Hold on, why do you have two smackheads in one house?" I ask, surprised.

That shouldn't happen if it can be avoided. We try to keep the heroin junkies separate from one another. They have an annoying habit of talking each other out of rehab. And I'm in charge of the allocations and I know that wasn't on my plan. I frown.

"Huh?" Christine utters, looking at me with a deep v between the eyebrows that matches mine. "I assumed the Denyers ran it past you first. They swapped my alky out for Gillian's junkie."

I take a sweeping look around the garden. Other than Elias, who I happen to know is in the gym right now, like he is everyday around this time, all other nurse-hosts are out and about. Aside from Christine and me, Gillian, Oz, Eileen, Iris and Matty, short for Matilda, are all out here.

They are a good crew. I headed the recruitment process for each of them. Shortlisted their applications, ran the interviews, though the Denyers and Lewin sat on the panel, of course. Rothman joined the clinic later.

This is *my* team. We are responsible for the guests night and day as is fucking obvious by the fact that the therapists don't join us for the barbecues or the pub or any other communal activities. To keep their professional distance. They do the therapy shit, I run the daily show.

So to say I'm pissed that the Denyers think they can just supersede my allocation decisions without consulting me is an understatement. I'm fucking fuming. I'm also really annoyed at myself for not noticing the change right away.

Because I've been too fucking preoccupied with fantasizing about Rowan Hadlow-Fuller-O'Brien's penis.

"Right," I say, scraping my chair back and standing up.

Christine puts her hand on my arm when she sees me zero in on Gillian.

"Be kind, Raven," Christine says gently. "Don't give her a hard time. She's only little. She probably thought Ed and Judy had spoken to you first, too. Same as me."

I look at Christine and note how ridiculous it is that despite the fact I am standing and she remains sitting, I am still not exactly looking down at her. Down*er* maybe but not down. She is *that* tall. And she is right, too. Not Gillian's fault. She should have come and spoken to me about it, though. They both should have. I nod at Christine then make my way over to the girl in question.

Gillian is one of the youngest of us. This is her first job after qualifying and I had my doubts about her because of her age, but something in her application form resonated with me. She wrote in it that she became a nurse because she saw her father die of alcoholism. I invited her for an interview, and she impressed all of us with her quiet thoughtfulness.

As I cross the lawn now, focusing on the slender young woman with thin, straight blonde hair in a perpetual low ponytail, I wonder why the Denyers thought it was a good idea to double up on the alcoholics quota in her house. Odd thing to do, given Gillian's background. We all struggle most with the ones that cut closest to the bone. Personally, I try to avoid coke whores in my house at all cost, not that many of them ever make it into rehab. And though he is no whore, there is a reason I'm so fixed on wanting Charlie to succeed.

"Hi, guys," I address the group of Matty, Oz and Gillian when I get to them, and they all murmur a hello. "Gillan?" I say with a smile. "Can I have a word?"

She looks at me wide-eyed. I've never singled her out before.

"Sure," she responds quietly.

I jerk my head in the direction of my house and we start walking.

"Everything okay?" she asks.

"Yeah, everything is fine. I just got a question."

I lead her into the house through the backdoor and realize that Rowan, Simon, Charlie and Tristan are all in the kitchen and have started cooking without me. Apparently under Rowan's guidance, who is standing at the stove, frying onions and garlic. I notice that there seems to be no bad blood between Simon and Rowan any longer. Good. I like a peaceful house. All four nod at us as I lead Gillian through and into the dining room before I shut the door.

We sit down at the dinner table and Gillian looks up at me expectantly. I get straight to the point.

"Did Ed and Judy swap guests around between you and Christine?"

Her eyebrows shoot up.

"Yes. I thought you knew."

I shake my head.

"No, I didn't. Do me a favor, when something like that happens, come and talk to me. Or, once I'm gone, talk to Christine. Nurses take their instructions from me, from whoever is head of nursing around here. The Denyers might run the therapy program but they do not run the guesthouses. That's the head nurse's job. Just remember that next time."

"I'm sorry, Raven," she mumbles.

"It's okay, not your fault. Tell me, did they say why?"

She shakes her head. I study her for a moment.

"And how do you feel about having two alcoholics in your house?"

I know I'm prying, but that's also part of my remit. Making sure my team can deal. It's a tough job. We might not be on the frontline in ER or in pediatric oncology here, but this job is draining in another way. You never get to go home and switch off. You're dealing with mental health twenty-four seven. Even at Christmas. They get one month off in August when the whole facility shuts for maintenance and that's it. To my surprise, Gillian gives me a massive smile.

"It's great, actually. They are both so amazingly positive about being sober and turning their lives around. It's cool."

Her expression turns wistfully sad for a moment.

"I wish..." she starts but doesn't finish the sentence.

And that right there is why we try to avoid dealing with the ones closest to home.

"You wish your dad had been the same," I supply, and she nods.

I get up, and when she follows suit, I open my arms and draw her into a hug. I squeeze her briefly then let go.

"I get it, sweetie. Tell me if it gets too hard for you. You're doing a great job here."

She smiles at my praise and takes the cue when I open the door for her.

I accompany her into the kitchen and watch her leave through the back door with not one but two questions in my mind.

Firstly, what the fuck are the Denyers playing at?

Secondly, since when were drunks in early rehab ever positive about being sober and not whiny motherfuckers whose world revolves solely around their pain?

Weird.

But then the smell of curry and cilantro reaches my nostrils, and I turn to my guests who are still chopping and chatting. Actually, it's mostly Simon having a long monologue about how he used to cook for his family all the time because his wife wasn't the best chef and giving Rowan lots of helpful advice on how to cook the curry. I tune out to most of it but can't help noticing that all the while he's sitting on his ass at the breakfast counter, looking at his soft drink. As if he could magic some alcohol molecules into it, if only he stared at it hard enough. At one point, after receiving helpful tip number twenty or thirty, Rowan steps away from the pot on the stove and points the wooden spoon he was using to stir at Simon.

"Hey," he says amicably. "If you're that good a chef, knock yourself out. I don't have to be alpha around the hob, you know. I'll happily sit back and eat *your* food."

I shoot him a warning look, but Simon is so absorbed in himself he doesn't hear the jibe, he just responds to the friendly tone.

"No, that's alright. I'm sure you got this. Smells good."

I can't help but grin at Rowan. He's good. He's real good. He holds my gaze a little longer than necessary and my heart slides all the way from my chest into the soles of my feet in one swift whoosh.

Here we go again.

ROWAN

Simon is a bellend.

I already knew that, but it becomes ever more apparent during dinner, which we have inside to escape a heavy summer shower, and the impression lasts all the way through washing up. He is all inferiority complex drowned in self obsession and masked with bragging.

He manipulates the entire conversation all evening, bringing every single topic under the sun back to him, throwing his age around and just talking, talking, talking. I don't blame his wife for leaving him. If he's like this sober, what on earth was he like drunk?

To be fair, it doesn't really bother me because the kind of conversation I want to have with Raven isn't meant for other people's ears anyway, and I'll happily blank him out while I keep sneaking glances at the pretty lady at the head of the table.

But I feel sorry for Charlie and Tristan. They seem bored out of their skulls, yet they are both too polite to excuse themselves. Coming to think of it, it's probably good for Charlie with his coke-inflated, born-with-a-silver-spoon-in-his-mouth rock star ego to not get a word in edgeways.

Okay, so I don't feel sorry for Charlie, but I really do feel sorry for Tristan. He appears utterly lost in all of this. We're in the middle of an elaborate story of how Simon once played snooker with Ronnie O'Sullivan when an idea hits me.

I excuse myself from the table where we are still sitting, after-dinner cups of tea and coffee at the ready, and go to the sitting room where I spotted a bookcase with board games and battered novels the other day. I look through and, bingo, there it is. I pull the little case out and carry it back to the dining room.

"Right, you two," I address Charlie and Tristan, rudely cutting through Simon's airtime. "Either of you know how to play backgammon?"

Tristan shakes his head in a fashion that tells me he doesn't even know what backgammon is. Charlie nods.

"Yeah. I used to play with my sister when we went on holidays."

I slide the case over to where he's sitting.

"Brilliant. Take it, teach Tristan. Come back to me in a couple of weeks when either of you thinks he's any good. I'll play you. Now scarper. Go next door, put the TV or music on, play. Train me a champion. Vamoose."

Their gratefulness is almost comical. They can't get out of the dining room quick enough, now that a grown-up has told them what to do.

Simon glares at me because I pissed all over his tale by sending away half his audience. Tough shit. I meet his eyes, and he backs down really fucking quickly. He's not so demented as not to recognize that he's outclassed, outsized and outweighed, despite the fact he probably boxed with Chris Eubank once or some shit like that. He takes a last gulp of his coffee and gets up.

"Right. I'm going to have a bath," he says and turns to Raven. "Good night."

I get a sharp nod and then he leaves.

Fucking finally.

Raven

"Thank fuck for that," Rowan says under his breath as soon as Simon is out of the kitchen.

When Rowan says anything under his breath, it's like a tiger purring. That voice. He should do voice-overs. I'd buy anything he'd try to sell me.

I watch as he sits back down. I'm still at the head end of the table and he chooses the chair to my right. I immediately feel the air change. The two of us alone in a space. It makes me both giddy and afraid, sharpening my senses into fight or flight. And it makes me wet. So very, very wet. So the impulse is to stand up, flee, get away.

"Stay," Rowan growls, even before my body language could possibly have told him that I was about to stand.

He just knows. This perfect stranger, this *addict*, can already read me better than any other person I've ever met.

"No, I can't," he states factually, as if he just saw directly into my friggin' mind. "I'm just good at cold reading people. It's important shit in my line of work."

"What? In gambling?"

"Betting. Yes. It is, to a point. But no. I meant kicking the shit out of people."

Now it's my turn to read him. And I do. He hasn't been this outright about what he does and he's gauging if I condemn him. I don't. I watch him exhale and realize he was holding his breath. It's the first time I get a hint that he doesn't just want to get between my legs. It's important to him what I think of him.

Sweet. And so misguided.

"Don't do that," he says into my thought process.

"Do what?" I ask.

"Make it cheap and nasty."

"Make what cheap and nasty?" I plead ignorance, but he just looks at me.

With hammed up disappointment. And mirth. So much fucking mirth it makes his dark eyes glow from within.

I can't help but grind my ass into my chair. And suddenly I realize that this is going to happen no matter what.

Not because he'll hound me until I give in but because *I want him*.

I sigh.

He leans back in his chair and laces his hands behind his neck to cradle his head as he looks up at the ceiling.

"So, we were saying..."

He pauses, clearly with the intent to taunt me a little, but if he thinks I'm wondering what comes next, he's more stupid than I thought. I know exactly which conversation we are picking up here, even if it was two days ago.

"You're not allowed to shag the guests, you're not allowed to hook up with the other employees, but you are okay to fuck the locals, correct?"

He doesn't look down to see me nod, just carries on his stream of consciousness.

"But I've been thinking, purely hypothetically, of course."

He looks down with a devilish grin at the wall opposite him, still not making eye contact.

"How would your bosses react if one of their employees was, let's call it *violated*, by a guest? Would they back said employee up if she pressed charges or would they try and brush it under the carpet to preserve the company's reputation? Maybe even buy the employee's silence off? What do you think?"

His expression has changed to dead serious by the time his eyes land back on me. My heart starts racing, because I know full well he's propositioning me.

"Raven?" Rowen prompts after almost a minute's silence. "What do you think?"

I watch his eyebrow tick and I know he is nervous. It's a fucking bold move. I swallow hard.

"They'd want it buried," I say with quiet confidence, while a weird cocktail of sweet opportunity and bad taste roils my stomach.

He smiles warmly.

"Good," he says and gets up. "I'm going to bed. See you in the morning, beautiful."

I stare at him, my heart still pounding in my chest. What the fuck have I just agreed to? Did I just give consent to be raped? What if...I don't get to finish the thought because he's almost at the door when he turns back, returns to the table, leans down on his elbows and pins me with a serious gaze.

"You know, ever since the *metoo* campaign, I've been in a quandary. Don't get me wrong, no means no, stop means stop. Always. But if you have the hots for a woman and she for you and say you happen to be sleeping in the room next to her and one night you creep in and start stroking her and licking her pussy while she's asleep and when she wakes up she doesn't say no, she doesn't say yes, she just lies there and enjoys what's happening, is that consensual? Or is that rape? I don't mean in the eyes of the law, or in the eyes of her bosses. I mean between that woman and that man."

He stops to give me another one of his smiles while I stare at him, my mouth dry as a desert.

I keep staring into his eyes like the proverbial deer in headlights as a yard sale of emotions, feelings, lust and hurt starts warring inside of me, really seriously flipping my stomach now.

Too close yet so, so different.

My brain floods with random memories, good and bad, until I settle on a clip of Dr. Meyer, my mentor, the bushy eye-browed, kind and ever so wise old man who coached me through nursing school. I hear his voice as he says 'fight, flight, freeze or please and you were trying to please, my dear, for survival'.

And I realize that right now I'm freezing.

When I don't want to.

When I don't need to.

Because for some unfathomable reason, I trust this man in front of me.

This gambler.

This fucking thug and possible killer.

And the minute that realization hits me, some weird shit happens inside of me, as two divergent parts of my being that have been apart forever and a day come back together, and my belly suddenly settles.

"Answers on a postcard," Rowan says softly, as if he knows what he's just done.

Then he straightens up again and leaves the room.

This time for real.

I lay off her after that for almost a whole week.

Total cunt that I am, I obviously overshot the mark there. I was going for a bit of alpha dirty talk. Most women love it.

It's that stupid voice of mine. I kind of hate it. I mean after ten years, I've grown into it, literally, but I'm still not a fan. It gives people preconceptions. But it certainly helps with getting laid and with Raven, I thought maybe, while we're at it, we could negotiate a cover story, possibly even a safe word, to protect her just in case we were found out, but instead I hit a fucking nerve a mile wide.

I saw it in her eyes.

The look.

The look Silas had after that shit with Niamh happened.

The *raped* look.

Raven has history. I'd bet my last penny on it, if I were still betting.

Shit. Fuck. Bollocks.

Not that it makes me want her any less.

On the contrary, some weird part of me that I don't even recognize wants her even more now. Wants to put her back together, wants...*redemption*.

And that makes me loathe myself even more.

I will not use her to heal my soul. She deserves better than that. Any woman does, but Raven in particular because she's fucking awesome.

As I simmer down on the sexual bullshit for the following week and try to simply be around her each day without putting my fucking foot in it again, I realise more and more just how amazing this woman is.

There is an individual rhythm to rehab for everyone in the house and somehow she manages to be the metronome for each of us, regardless of the fact that we're all so wildly different. She watches over us with a quiet competence that makes me feel safe for the first time in my life since my mum, my real mum, died.

Do I have mummy issues? Definitely. It kind of comes with the territory of being solely responsible for your mother's death.

But it's not a maternal kind of safe I'm getting from Raven. It's not protection from the big, bad world that her presence cocoons me in.

It's simply knowing that there is another adult in the room who may not be flawless but who knows what they're doing, what they're about, how to handle themselves and who is looking out for me.

There is reassurance in that.

Reassurance that not everybody you meet is a fucking child out to get all the toys, that there are still people who take a measured approach, people who *care*.

That's what Raven is, measured but caring. Especially when she's facilitating our little group's widely different stances on life around the dinner table. You'd think that after a day of mindfulness, anger management therapy, group therapy, individual therapy, physical therapy aka time in the gym or pool and recreational therapy aka gardening or hiking or knitting or whittling or pottering or fuckknowswhat, we'd be too powered out to be at each others' throats in the evenings.

But these are dark times, and both Simon and Charlie have a habit of getting political.

The weird thing is, they're the exact opposite of how I would have pigeonholed them if I'd given it a thought.

Despite belonging to a passive-aggressive, alcoholic, self-obsessed businessman, Simon's heart is in the right place and somewhere beneath the damaged personality there hides a good guy who wants a fair and equal society and all that lark. I could weep at his naivety.

Charlie, despite the rock star credentials, is unashamedly right wing. Though it shouldn't really have surprised me. He's a public schoolboy from an aristocratic background with fantasies of becoming one of the mega-rich through the power of music. And for him, it's guaranteed. At what point Charlie hasn't cottoned on to the fact that his bass player is still stacking shelves in a supermarket whenever they're not on tour, not because he thinks it's cool but because they haven't made it yet, and may never, but because the bassist still needs to eat and isn't from a moneyed background is beyond me. Especially since Charlie told me so himself.

Princes and paupers.

Rulers and gladiators.

I could contribute shit to their discussions that would blow their fucking minds.

But I don't.

While Raven negotiates the debates between Charlie and Simon and even Tristan, who is a political newt, with an unbiased grace that is awe-inspiring, I keep mostly shtum and eat my food.

At least until Thursday's debate rolls around, which ends abruptly when Simon gets a phone call and leaves the dinner table.

It is then that Charlie turns to me.

"What about you, Rowan? You got an opinion on anything?"

I look up from my summer pudding and zero in on him until he's fighting hard not to cower in his seat.

"Many," I growl. "They're just not palatable for public consumption."

I'm still eyeballing him when out of the corner of my eye, I see Raven suspend a spoonful of dessert in front of her mouth and shoot me an amused glance. She lowers her laden utensil back into the bowl and leans forward on the table, not quite into my space but almost.

"I don't know. But ain't that for the public to decide?" she asks.

My eyes immediately snap from Charlie's to hers, but my annoyance dissipates as soon as I see the impish light flickering in her eyes. She's got a fucking point and she knows it.

"Maybe," I concede as I get lost in the dark blue of her irises.

It really is an astonishing colour. But not as astonishing as the woman herself. We hold eye contact and the longer it goes on, the harder my heart starts pounding in my chest.

It's a new sensation. I've never felt this before.

Frankly, until I met her, I thought it was a load of bullshit, that when people talked about their heart skipping a beat because they're in love what they meant was that they could feel the fear of rejection.

I know all about the increased heartbeat of anxiety and fear.

Of course I do, I'm a fighter. Anyone who tells you a fighter doesn't know fear hasn't got the faintest. It's a fucking prerequisite for the job. No fear, no adrenaline. No adrenaline, no fight reflexes.

But *this* is not fear. Or anxiety. Not even lust, though I can't deny the fact that her challenging me like this has just woken up my dick.

No, it's a different beat entirely. And as I keep staring at her, I realise it's different because it's not mine at all, it's *ours*.

"Backgammon?" I hear Tristan ask Charlie in the background, followed by the sound of both of them excusing themselves and scramming from the dining room.

They think two of the grown-ups are having a fight.

They couldn't be more wrong.

Raven

My heart is in my throat as we keep staring at each other.

Something just changed, something deep and profound.

After a week of him keeping his distance and decidedly *not* visiting me in my room despite me holding my breath each night, we're back in the game. Only this time, it's a whole new level.

I want him to kiss me. Here and now, consequences be damned.

The thought jolts me.

I'm not a kisser. It's not my thing. Never has been. Saliva exchange with another person does not hold any attraction for me. I do it, sure, to please whoever allows me access to his penis at the time. Because it's expected, part of the script. But it always makes me feel slightly nauseous. Maybe because my first kiss, tongue and all, was forced on me by one of my mom's *friends*. I was eight.

Maybe because it's just not hygienic.

But right now, I couldn't care less. I want Rowan's mouth on mine, want his tongue down my throat. I want it with a ferocity that sets my entire being alight and scares me in equal measures.

Who the fuck is this person that's taken over my body? This is not me. So, so, so not me.

So I dodge.

"Care to elaborate then?" I ask in a whisper, still not able to break the spell.

Something changes in his gaze then, the warmth is supplanted by a darkness not many would be able to bear. But I'm Ravenna Vanhofd. I can deal. Especially if it detracts from this sudden desire to feel his lips on mine.

"You think you can handle it?"

"What?" I grin. "An opinion? Yeah, I can handle an opinion."

"It's not an opinion," he says darkly.

"What then?"

"Fact as opposed to fiction."

"I'm intrigued."

It is then that he breaks eye contact and makes a sweeping gesture around the empty table.

"This," he says with a snort. "That thing those guys have been doing, night after night, it's bullshit. They're discussing shit as if there was such a thing as a democracy. As if it fucking mattered whether you're left, right, centre, far this or far the other. It's an illusion. The only thing that matters is if you're above or below. And, gorgeous, we here are *all* below."

"Democracy is dead, huh?" I ask with only a slightly needling undertone.

It's kind of cute having this growly voiced mountain of a man spout teenage crap.

His smile is scathing.

"It never existed. And if it did then only for about a second. Believe me, Raven. The shit I've seen and *done* when I was fighting in London beggars belief. That wasn't the shit you see when you type bare knuckle street fighting into the internet. Not even if you type it into the dark net. That stuff, the people who came to see me get my head kicked in, they have their own fucking web. They're not even on the same satellites. Ask your Irish buddy one day. Though he won't give you an answer. 'Cause if he does, he's dead. Within the hour. Even out here. Trust me, democracy is nothing but the modern day version of Christianity. The Sheriffs of Nottingham are well and truly alive."

"Huh?"

I frown deeply, because he's genuinely lost me now.

"It's the illusion of self direction and having a morsel of power that keeps people in line. The way that the threat of heaven and hell used to keep the great unwashed in line back in the Middle Ages."

I digest this for a minute. The content *and* the realization that Rowan O'Brien isn't just muscle and brawn and sex on legs but brains as well. Then I smile and I can tell it throws him sideways.

"It's still progress," I point out.

"How is that progress?"

I shrug.

"I'd say if we've moved on from being kept in line by being threatened with eternal punishment by an invisible higher power to being kept in line by being given the illusion of self responsibility that's definitely developmental progress. At least on our part."

He cocks his head at that, and his eyes go from dark back to warm, a genuine smile playing around his lips.

"I've never met anyone like you before," he says, and my heart, which chilled out a bit at some point during the last couple of minutes, skips a beat again.

But before I can answer, Simon bursts back into the dining room, swearing.

"That fucking cow!"

He slams down in his chair and starts shoveling the rest of his half-eaten dessert into his mouth.

"She's taking the kids away over the weekend! To my mother's *gîte* in France. Without me. They're going to see *my* mother. Without me. How fucking dare she? While I'm stuck here, in this shithole."

Chewing shuts him up for a couple of seconds, allowing Rowan to frown at him.

"Surely it's good that they get to see their grandmother?" he states with an unmistakably threatening question mark at the end.

Simon starts eyeballing him with bloodshot eyes. They often are. Side effect of being a choleric. He needs to watch that. I take his blood pressure every day and it tells me he really should try to practice some more mindfulness. One heart attack during my tenure here is plenty.

"What the fuck do *you* know?" he barks.

Simon's spittle, red-tinged from the fruits in the summer pudding, lands on Rowan's white tee. Rowan looks down at it, looks up and rises from his chair. Simon blanches. He's not too far absorbed in his little pity party to realize that he's bitten off more than he can chew if he goes up against Rowan.

I'm about to get to my feet and step in when Rowan holds out a reassuring hand in my direction, without taking his eyes off Simon. Rowan leans forward, placing his lower arms on the table as he gets right up into Simon's face, studying him intently for a minute.

"I don't know shit about being a father," he growls. "Hey, I don't even know shit about *having* a father. But I had two mothers, both awesome people, awesome women. *Women* are amazing, so much better than us dickheads with dicks could ever be. So I don't need to know anything about your situation to know that you are a cunt if you begrudge your girls a good relationship with their grandmother. And I don't need to know anything about your situation to know you are an even bigger cunt if you're not over the moon that your ex is clearly trying to maintain that relationship despite you fucking up your marriage 'cause you couldn't keep your head out of the bottle."

"Ha! That's what the bitches want you to think. But that's just them ganging up on me, painting me the devil."

Rowan just keeps looking at him, shaking his head.

"Did you really just call your mother, the mother of your children and your own daughters, bitches?" he asks evenly, then straightens up to look in my direction. "Right. I'm clearing up. Let's leave this fuckwit to wallow in his self-obsessed moan fest."

No matter how much I want to whoop at that after having listened to Simon's monologues for the last week solid, I can't have a guest talking to another guest like that.

"Rowan," I say warningly, but he waves me off.

"Sorry, Raven, but sometimes you've just got to call a spade a spade."

And with that, he calmly stacks some of the empty dessert bowls and carries them toward the kitchen.

I watch his retreating back and realize that I'm falling.

Hard.

ROWAN

"So, Rowan, tell me, how are you today? How do you feel now that you've got your first week in rehab under your belt?"

Dr Lewin looks at me with the mask of expectant neutrality I've come to expect from her by now. She is a funny bunny, this woman. Beneath all that softness of the knitwear and locks of hair escaping her plait, there is a steely, impenetrable distance. Out of all the therapists here, she is the only one who insists on being called Dr Lewin rather than by her first name. The other guy, Rothman, is happy for people to call him Frank. The Denyers are Ed and Judy. But not Lewin. I realise that I don't even know what her first name *is*. So I ask.

"What's your first name?"

And this is the first time all week her mask breaks. Not massively, but there is a faint smirk around her mouth.

"It's Caitlyn but you may carry on calling me Dr Lewin. Welcome to therapy, Rowan."

I cock my head at her.

"Are you taking the piss, doc?"

She shakes her head.

"Dr Lewin, please. And no, not at all. This is your third session this week and we've gone through the motions of talking about your betting. How it started, what your triggers are, how you can avoid them next time, but you may as well have been filling out a questionnaire in a self-help book. With the exception of the first session, when we spoke about your *faux pas* at the pub, you have given nothing of yourself. You haven't actually been present in this room. You just became present. So welcome to therapy, Rowan. What's changed?"

"What?" I laugh. "All of that just because I asked you your *name*?"

She shrugs then nods.

"Bit self obsessed, isn't it?" I ask, grinning but holding up a hand. "Just kidding. I don't know. I don't know what's changed."

It's a lie, of course.

I know exactly what's changed. What's changed is that I think I might be falling in love for the first time in my freaking life and I haven't got a clue how to deal with that and that's clearly bringing my guard down, so I make silly mistakes like asking people what they're called.

Dr Lewin's current squint tells me she isn't buying my pledge of ignorance in the slightest. But I'm hardly gonna tell her that I have a hard-on as big as Big Ben for one of the nurses here. I'm not stupid. I know Lewin is bound by confidentiality, but I also know it would alert her to a situation I don't want her alerted to. For Raven's sake.

Me? I couldn't give a shit if the whole fucking world knew how desperate I am for that woman. I'd like nothing more than to claim her as mine, though I'm pretty sure she would take exception to being claimed as anyone's property, and good on her, but I can't cost her her job and plunge her into debt. Even if plunging people into debt is my speciality. Ask Sheena and Silas. They nearly lost their house because of me. How fucked up is that?

So Lewin and I sit in silence.

Because apparently, that's what therapists do. They leave you steeped in silence until you carry on talking. It wasn't how I imagined this at all but it kind of works. It means that I can sit here and ponder the Raven situation to my heart's content, while the good doctor thinks we're breaking open my issues or some shit like that. But then Lewin suddenly breaks protocol.

"Rowan?" she asks gently. "You checking out on me again so soon?"

Well, fuck me, she has a sense of humour.

I frown at her.

"Is that even allowed? You asking me like that? I thought you had to sit there and wait for me to carry on."

She laughs at that, actually laughs, and shakes her head.

"No. That's Rothman's approach. They lead, he jogs along beside them, trying to keep up. I'm a cognitive behaviour therapist, I don't have to go by my client's pace, though it often pays to. I'm allowed to ask as many questions as I damn well like."

And she swears. I'm starting to like her. And for that, I want to give her something. I might not be able to give her an honest answer to the question what's changed, but I can give her a bit more than I've been giving her so far.

"I'm tired of pretending I'm someone I'm not."

"So, tell me, who is it you are and who is it you're not?"

I bark a sarcastic laugh at that.

"Starting small, are we?"

She shrugs and then we sit in silence again. For about forty minutes. While I evaluate my life. All of it. Life before mum's death. Mum's death. Being dragged along with my stepfather. Landing on Sheena's doorstep. Finding a brother in Silas. Betraying my brother. Running. Straight into hell. Clawing my way out. Getting here. Raven. The fact I still didn't make my move last night, despite the fact she was ripe for the taking. Because I'm just not worthy. And because I don't want to break her more than she already is. Finally, I clear my throat.

"I'm not a monster."

I take a deep breath then exhale slowly.

"But I'm a total liability."

Dr Lewin smiles at me warmly.

"Well done. Hour's over. I'll see you on Monday."

Raven

I'm just parking up outside the house after my shopping trip to Swanage when I see Rowan come out of the church building and my heart stops. Not in the way that it seems to do that every time I see him but in the way it used to when one of my foster siblings got bullied at school and came home with a tear-streaked face.

And we often came home with tear-streaked faces.

Not that Rowan is crying.

But he looks broken.

Utterly defeated.

And I know exactly who's done that to him. I know all my guests' therapy schedules by heart, but even if I didn't, I could take a damn good guess.

Lewin does that to people. Deconstructs them before putting them back together again. I don't like it, but it's effective. I give her that. And it's never really bothered me that much before. But, hell, does it bother me now. All my protective instincts are on high alert and I want to go and kick her fucking ass for making Rowan look so dejected.

I carry on watching him through the windshield of the company SUV that I took into town and stay put until he's turned to the back of the building, my guess is to go to the gym. I've learned this much about him in the last week. Where my foster mom Elena stress baked and I stress clean, Rowan stress punches the living daylights out of a sandbag.

I know, not because I've seen it but because I asked Alan if he knew what was going on after Rowan came in a couple of times after the gym this week, emptied all our ice cube trays into a mixing bowl and stuck his hands in it for as long as it took for all the ice to dissolve. But you never see a mark on them the next day.

Today his anger is in a different league, though. I can see it in the way he's carrying himself, his stride, the air around him. It's a good thing I went shopping. I'm so fed up with the lack of ice for my drinks in this stinking heat, I bought him five of his very own two kilo party bags of cubes. That should last him a while.

I wait until he's completely out of sight then begin unloading the groceries. Most of our stuff gets delivered once a week, but Elena taught me to pick my own veg out, so I like going to the farmer's market on Fridays.

I make a couple of trips back and forth, store everything away and then go and drive the car to the main parking lot. I pick up the last of the bits and pieces I've accumulated between here and town until there is only the small paper sleeve that's sitting on the dashboard left.

With a rush of nerves, I grab it. It took me ages picking the right card, searching my soul, wondering what the hell I thought I was doing, nearly chickening out a thousand times. But if I had any doubts left, I don't now. Not after I just saw him, all vulnerable and beat like that but still coming up fighting.

Now, I just have to write it and wait.

ROWAN

I'm shaking with fatigue when I finally finish beating the shit out of my friend, the punch bag. I didn't stop, not even to take on any water. Now sweat is running down my back and into the waistband of my boxers and I'm on the cusp of serious dehydration.

I realise I've accumulated quite the audience when I turn around to go to the water cooler. I didn't have a bottle with me, I didn't even stop to go to the house and get my kit when I came here after my session with Lewin. I just headed straight for the gym, stripped down to my shorts and did what I do best. The idiots staring at me are damn lucky I didn't go commando today.

The thought makes me smile and it's the first sign I'm back amongst the living. I die when my humour dies. I'm not dead yet.

I only make it a few steps before Alan Allsorts, heaven help him if that's his real name, the ex SAS soldier who doubles up as the premises manager and gym supervisor around The Village, is in my face, holding out a bottle of water at me. I take it and nod at him gratefully while I take a sip.

"Go on, people, get back to your own routines. Give the lad some space," Alan barks over his shoulder at the group still standing in a half crescent around the mat.

The martial arts corner is situated in the far end of the gym behind a partition and it doesn't take long before my fellow men and women in rehab vacate the vicinity and give Alan and me the illusion we're alone.

He's a big bloke, Alan, almost my height and width and he hasn't let civilian life get to his waistline yet, despite being somewhere in his fifties, at a rough guess. He's got a buzz cut and a silver beard with a waxed, twirl-end moustache, which makes him look like something out of a comic book. But the warning Raven gave me on my first day about Alan sneaking up on you wasn't a joke. The whole man isn't a joke and when he fixes me with a serious stare, I swallow hard.

"You alright, son?" he asks evenly.

I nod through more sips of water. He cocks his head to examine my knuckles and I think I can see approval in his eyes. I'm sure he was expecting blood, but that's for amateurs.

"Not a speck on you. You're a pro," he echoes my thoughts. "Now listen, that was a good show, but that's enough. Third time's the charm. Don't do it again. If you are using the bags in here, you're using gloves from now on."

He holds up a hand before I can protest.

"Not because I'm anal, though my wife will be the first to tell you that I very much am, but because sooner or later one of these muppets is going to try and copy you. And then somebody is going to break their hand and I'll get sued for liability. I don't fancy that. Do we have an accord?"

It's the strangest feeling, but I know there is only one way to answer this man, though on the other two occasions I've encountered him, materialising from out of nowhere, I've just called him Alan. But not this time.

"Yes, sir," I answer and there isn't an ounce of piss-take in it.

He commands respect, and truth be told it feels good to give it. I can see him smile even through his beard and moustache combo.

"Good."

He turns around and starts walking away but stops after a couple of paces.

"Lewin?" he asks into the air in front of him.

"Yup."

He nods.

"Figures. Now, next time she gets to you, knock on my house. I have my own bags out back. You're welcome to use *those* any time."

"Thank you, sir."

"You're welcome, lad. Now, go hit the shower, before you start stinking up the place."

He walks away and I take a look down my sweaty torso.

There are showers in here, of course, and spare towels on shelves by the entrance to the pool, no need to bring them from your room, but I don't want to stand under the spray next to the people who just watched me fight my demons. In my underpants.

I want privacy, my own space. My own bathroom. *Raven's* bathroom. I want her shit surrounding me, her expensive, colourful, bunny friendly soap and shampoo bars all lined up neatly in empty scallop shells. Her girlie paraphernalia that are spread out all over the side of the tub.

So I pick up my tee and jeans from the floor, where I dropped them earlier, climb back into them, make my way through the gym, past people watching me from under their lashes and falling eerily quiet as soon as I get into earshot. I grab my boots from the rack by the entrance and walk out barefoot.

Raven

It's my reading hour, but the last thing on my mind is sitting outside with my book. The murderer is on girl number three, but frankly I couldn't give a shit if she lives or dies.

After putting the groceries away, I spent an eternity agonizing about what to write. And when I finally decided on the right bunch of sentences, it took me another ice age to make up my mind whether I was actually going to go through with it. Then there was the next eon, picking out the right place to leave it for him. That one seemed like such a final act. Like once I've opened this door, there is no shutting it. The point of no return.

But now it's done, which leaves me feeling jittery while I putter around the kitchen, pulling pots out of the cupboard and setting to work scrubbing their undersides. I should probably get out of my own clothes, which I wore for town, and back into my tunic for this, or at least wear an apron, because I'm ruining one of my favorite polka dot mini dresses right now, but I can't stop.

If I stop and get back into my uniform, I have to think about the fact that I am a twenty-eight-year-old woman with a career on the line, not a crushing, *obsessing*, teenager.

And I don't want to.

I like the fucking feeling.

I get it now. I never had this when I was the right age. I used to rib my foster sisters relentlessly if they were fangirling over some pimply-ass guy at school. Now look at me.

I've just put pot three on the draining board when I hear the front door open and my heart goes into overdrive. I don't know how it knows it's him, but I have no doubt it's right.

Expecting him to come in here first to treat his hands, I go to open the freezer and pull out one of the ice cube bags. I had to do some serious reshuffling to make them all fit, so in the process of pulling it out I pull half the contents of the shelf with it. They land on the floor with a racket and I swear under my breath as I kneel to pick things up again.

Seconds later, I catch the scent of fresh male sweat through the tendrils of cold in my nostrils. I look up just as Rowan arrives by my side. He doesn't say a word as he crouches opposite me and starts helping.

I get to my feet to put the first bits back in the freezer and when I turn back, holding out my hands to receive more items from him, his mouth is smiling, but his eyes are hungry. Too fucking hungry. The fire in them makes my pulse pound in my clit.

His gaze snaps to my shaking hands and then suddenly I'm on the floor with him, sitting on his lap.

He is so lightening quick, I only realize when I'm already straddled on him what he's done. He's sat back, grabbed me by the wrists and pulled me on top of him, so I've landed with my knees either side of his hips and my crotch firmly resting against his cock. Which is hard.

Of course.

Before my brain catches up fully and I can withdraw, he reaches under my dress, splays his left hand across my bottom and brings me up harder against the rod in his jeans. At the same time, his right hand goes up to my cheek, cradling me. But it is more than a cradle. The fingers of his enormous hand reach far into my hair and entangle themselves.

It's a tether.

I can't pull away without hurting myself, but that's okay, I'm still on top, I can deal.

He doesn't try to kiss me, just looks into my eyes and starts rocking beneath me, rubbing himself against me, his left hand kneading my buttocks through my fishnets and panties, holding me in place. Between the hand in my hair and the bear grip on my ass, I'm trapped. The realization hits me like a bullet. For a moment, I freak, despite the warmth in my belly that unfolds as he keeps rocking against my clit, sending shivers through my pussy that are teasing out the first, lazy clenches of an orgasm.

An orgasm that never takes hold because suddenly he stops.

Through the haze of his own lust he *sees*.

And he stops.

His grips become gentle and I'm left with the knowledge that I can pull away now. His eyes, burning with desire a second ago, go soft and he clenches the hand that was on my cheek and runs his knuckles down my cheekbone.

"I'm sorry," he whispers. "I couldn't resist. You make me so fucking hard, Raven. But that's no excuse."

He sighs as he takes me by the hips and lifts me off his lap, far enough for me to get some traction without fumbling around. The next thing, I'm standing in the kitchen again, he's back on his haunches, and we're picking freezer stuff off the floor.

As if nothing's happened.

I tell myself that this is a good thing because Simon, Tristan and Charlie should be back any minute from their afternoon activities. Shit. I hadn't even thought about them when I was down on the floor, happily letting Rowan rut against me. Annoyingly, the thought gives me another unholy thrill.

Rowan hands me the last item from the floor, one of the ice cube bags.

"I bought those for you," I say, my voice surprisingly even, considering my clit's still throbbing, my pussy is swollen and drenched in anticipation of an orgasm that never happened, and my heart is still pounding in my chest.

He smiles at that. A big, little-boy smile that transforms his whole face.

"Thank you," he says then gets up to get a bowl from the cupboard.

He rips open the bag, empties half of it into the bowl and shoves it into the freezer. His arm brushes my nipples as he reaches past me. A small gasp escapes me, and he smirks. I look down and see his cock twitch against the crotch of his jeans. And I can't help it. I splay my hand against his rock-hard abs, feeling every ridge beneath the fabric of his tee. I hitch it up a little and let my thumb sneak below the waistband.

I allow myself one short swipe against the slit on the head, creamy with precum, while my entire body vibrates with desire. He shudders at my touch and I can feel another glut of my own juice drip down my pussy and soak my panties. I grin up at him.

"Two can play that game," I tell him hoarsely as I take my hand back again.

Just then we hear the front door open and Rowan retreats quickly, snatching the ice bowl off the counter. He cradles it in his arm and makes his getaway.

"I'm gonna take this upstairs, ice my hands, have a shower, get out of your hair," he mumbles.

I quite liked you in my hair, I think but I don't say it.

There was something there. In the tether. Something new and healing, even if it scared the fuck out of me. And I want more. I have a funny feeling, between us we could glue some of my parts together again. And maybe even some of his.

He's already turned his back on me and is walking out of the kitchen when I call after him.

"Rowan? Check your post."

ROWAN

As soon as I enter the hallway and spot Tristan, Charlie and Simon all clustered around the bottom of the stairs, I transfer the ice bowl from cradling it in my arm to holding it awkwardly with both of my hurting hands, in front of my boner. For probably the first time in my life, I feel conscious of the state my dick is in. I never had a problem with it before. Not even as a teenager.

Silas was always the one who'd grab that cushion to hide his erection or who'd sit that bit longer at his desk in school. He was self-conscious, shy. Me? I never gave two shits about who knew that I was ready to fuck wherever, whenever. There's nothing shameful in being aroused in my book.

But these arseholes don't need to get any ideas about Raven and me, so I clench my teeth because, fuck me, do my hands hurt right now, and carry the bowl like an imbecile would.

"Hey," Charlie greets me as I try to squeeze past them.

"Hey," I say back.

He nods at the bowl.

"I heard about that. You went to town on that bag, they say."

"Did a bit," I concede quietly.

"You're a fucking Neanderthal," Simon mutters at the floor as he undoes his shoelaces.

I stop in my tracks.

"Ye what?" I ask.

He remains bent at the waist but looks up, eyes bloodshot with anger that has clearly fuck all to do with me because I haven't seen this arsehole since breakfast.

"You heard," he says, eyeballing me from below.

Interesting factoid about me, I don't get off on anger and this scenario brings my hard-on down quicker than a cold shower. I turn to the stairs, put the bowl down on a step and slowly pivot back to face him. I can see him swallow as he straightens up to watch me approach, until we're toe to toe. I look down at him.

"You got a problem, mate?"

"Yeah, you. You think you're so fucking special, but you're nothing but an arrogant arsehole with too much muscle."

I smile. And watch him get uneasy.

"And how do you figure that one?" I ask him evenly, friendly even.

"Says on our itinerary that houses are supposed to do something together on a Friday afternoon. So where the fuck were you when we just went for our hike?"

"Let me get this straight, you're bitching at me because I didn't come along to your knitting circle?"

This earns me a snigger from both Charlie and Tristan who are watching this exchange with mouths agape. Simon, however, is far from amused. His face is turning crimson, his fists are balling up by his doughy, middle-aged side and his eyes are popping out of their sockets. If it wasn't so sad, it would be comical because, for fuck's sake, the bloke's gotta strain his neck to look up at me while he's letting his anger get away with him. I take a step back to make it easier on him then cock my head.

"Look, mate, I appreciate that you are a complete wanker with a drink problem and an anger management problem and a life that's gone down the shitter and I feel sorry for you. I really do," I say, and pause to let him digest the first bit before I go on. "But me going with you on a bit of a walk ain't gonna change any of that shit. And taking your crap out on somebody who is twice your height, twice your weight and half your age is never a good idea. Not even if that hypothetical bloke is just a regular bloke."

I lean forward and get so close in his face, our foreheads practically touch.

"And believe you me, I'm not a regular bloke. So fuck off and leave me alone, you pathetic failure of a human being."

He gasps and I straighten up to turn back to my original mission of going upstairs to finally ice my fucking hands. I flinch when I see Raven standing in the kitchen doorway, eyebrows raised. Fuck. Wonder how much she heard of that. We make eye contact and she shrugs imperceptibly. Okay, good, we're good. She's not mad.

"Didn't I say play nice, boys?" she asks sharply.

Ok, she's a little mad.

"He called me a Neanderthal," I say indignantly and hearing myself almost makes me want to burst out laughing.

I sound like a little kid.

"Not interested in who started what," she answers resolutely.

Heaven help any children this woman might have one day. The thought gives me a weird tug in my belly. I shelve it for examination later.

"Simon, a word please," Raven carries on. "Rowan, go do your thing. Tristan and Charlie, once you've washed your hands, come back and start dinner prep, please. Rowan, you're excused from cooking tonight. Take care of your hands, have a shower, come down when you're ready."

She doesn't wait to see if any of us follow her commands, just turns towards the dining room and expects Simon to follow.

This woman.

My dick's twitching again.

Better get out of here and do what nursey says.

Raven

"Let me cut straight to the chase," Simon says before I've even shut the door to the dining room, or his butt hits the chair. "I'm going to change houses. I don't think this one is the right environment for my recovery process."

How fucking dare he pretend that he has asked me for this little conference and not vice versa?

But I don't say a word while I release the door handle, turn toward him and cross the room to plant myself on the chair opposite his, which is awkward because the dominating ass has placed himself at the head end of the table.

I silently hold his gaze and raise an eyebrow instead. Inside, I'm seething but you wouldn't know. I've mastered the art of not showing my emotions to perfection. I learned early that survival of the most unaffected looking is a thing.

The eyebrow, in combination with the stern expression on my face, does the trick and the next bit that comes out of his mouth sounds a lot less certain.

"I mean, Dr Rothman has already green-lighted it. He just needs to run it by the bosses," Simon continues, almost apologetically. "He said it would be no problem swapping me with one of the guests in that blonde's house. Gillian?"

I cock my head at that and try my hardest to keep my face neutral while my cogs are churning. Something is off. Miles off.

I don't know what Rothman's game is here. When I went to question the Denyers as to why they'd seen fit to mess with the guest allocations in Gillian's and Christine's houses, they'd been highly apologetic and assured me it had all been one big misunderstanding. That request, too, had originally come from Rothman, and they'd assumed Rothman had already cleared it with me prior to talking to them.

I didn't know if to believe them at the time. It felt a lot like between the three of them they were trying to squirrel away one of the head nurse's responsibilities around here, making use of this period when my foot is already half out of the door and Christine's isn't in the door yet. For what reason, I have no idea. Room allocation is a headache.

I didn't challenge Rothman at the time because Frank Rothman and I don't exactly get along. The guy is a ginormous slimeball with a wishy-washy way of talking and the kind of leery, roving eye that makes me want to hurl. He thinks it's okay because he's a mid-thirties, full-head-of-sandy-blond-hair, blue-eyed, classically good-looking slimeball, but for me that makes no difference. He gives me the creeps. He reminds me of at least two of Mom's 'boyfriends'. One of whom I'd rather not think about. Ever.

I realize that I'm still sitting in silence and that Simon has started fidgeting in his seat, not with impatience to get away but with anxiety. Such is the patented nurse Raven stare. I let my lips curl up in a snarling smile.

"Let me get something very, very straight," I say slowly. "Frank Rothman has no jurisdiction over who sleeps under which roof around here. That's my job and without my say, that's not going to happen, are we clear?"

I see the veins in Simon's neck pop, but before he bursts, I hold my hands up in a pacifying gesture.

"Now, I hear loud and clear that you and Rowan don't get along. But even so, you are under no circumstances moving into Gillian's house. For reasons I can't divulge, and that Rothman is not privy to. Suffice to say, it is not going to happen. I *can* look into swapping you in elsewhere if you insist, but, frankly, we are a whole week into the program, and I think it would be too disruptive for the other person. I will discuss it with Rothman, though, if you wish."

He gasps for air like a fish out of water.

"What other person?" he asks when he finally finds his breath.

And that right there is the problem.

"The person you would be swapping with," I say gently.

Something I learned in my career: if an adult acts like a three-year-old, explain the world to them like you would a three-year-old.

He looks at me wide-eyed as comprehension takes hold. And suddenly he turns all British.

"Well, I wouldn't want to inconvenience anyone," he mutters, and I give him a big smile.

Atta boy.

"That's great, Simon. I knew you'd understand. I'm sure you and Rowan can learn to get along if you both try a bit harder. We are all adults here after all," I push.

And, bingo, he starts nodding like one of those toys on a car dash.

"Quite right. Of course. I'm sure we'll rub along just fine. I'd still appreciate it if you could at least discuss a swap with Rothman."

We nod curtly at each other and get up.

Meeting over.

Now, what the fuck am I gonna do about Rothman?

ROWAN

When I come back from icing my hands and taking a shower, the atmosphere in the house has changed completely. Tristan, Charlie and Simon are in the kitchen, cooking chilli con carne and it's — quiet. Now, there is a first.

"Anything I can do to help?" I ask while standing in the doorway and kneading *Melrose* into my hands.

Melrose is the best stuff ever. It's a thick lanolin stick that smells intensely of lemon grass. It always reminds me of Silas and Sheena. Their house always smells a little of it because Sheena uses it for her housekeeping hands and Silas, well, for the same reason I use it. It keeps the calluses on your hands supple. Little known fact, bare knuckle fighters like to keep their hands moisturised. There is nothing more damaging to your punch than cracked skin. Looks good in the movies, fucking pain in the arse in real life.

"The boys and I got this," Simon answers pleasantly enough. "But you could lay the table."

"Can do," I say. "Where is Raven?"

"Gone to speak to Christine," Charlie answers, while he measures out rice in a mug.

"Who's Christine?" I ask because, honestly, I still haven't got a clue who is who around here outside of the people I've actually had dealings with so far.

"Her deputy," Charlie answers. "The Northern one with the tits."

I nod and start collecting crockery from the cupboards.

"In or out?"

"Out," all three answer, and I start going about my business.

Ten minutes later, I am just finishing up laying the patio table when Simon appears outdoors and sits down at the place I'm just putting a knife and fork out for. He looks up at me as if I were his waiter.

"We need to talk," he says gravely.

"Stand up then," I immediately shoot back.

I can't help it. The guy is such a fucking arsehole.

He sighs, audibly, and looks around, over to the tables outside the other houses where people are busy with their own dinner preps. It's a gaze that makes no sense, halfway between trying to rally up support and making sure nobody is actually listening. It hits me that this guy is ultra paranoid.

"Why don't you just sit down?" he asks, and I have to concede that if I don't, I'll actually be just as much of a git.

I pull out the chair next to him, swivel it around, so I'm looking at his profile, and sit.

"What can I do you for?" I grin.

"Can you be serious for a second?" he asks, while he shuffles his chair, so we are facing each other.

"I don't know, can I?"

I shrug but then give him an opening anyway.

"I'll give it my best shot. Go on."

He leans in a bit, and suddenly we're really close.

"Look, I don't think you get it," he says and holds up a hand to silence me immediately as I take a gasp of air. "No, seriously, hear me out. You, Tristan, Charlie, you're all young. You have your lives ahead of you. I know it's a cliché, but it's also fucking true. You can still make of your time here whatever you want to make of it. Anything. Anything at all. Me? I've placed my bets. My bet was pretty conventional, but it was a good one. It was a beautiful woman, who may not be so beautiful any longer, but who was *mine*. I was going to grow old with her. My bet was two daughters who are turning out to be amazing human beings. My bet was a house, a dog and some nice stuff. We're not rich, but we are comfortable. And I worked for it. Really fucking hard. And I've lost it. All of it. Because I'm an addict. This here–"

He stops speaking for a moment to make a sweeping gesture.

"This is my last chance to maybe — maybe — get it all back. So I *need* it to work. Do you understand? And you and your anarcho bullshit is pissing all over my chances of success. So, please, can I have some support here? Can you just get with the program, *please*?"

I contemplate him silently for a good half a minute, letting him think I'm considering it, mulling it over, before I lean in. We're so close now, if we were that way inclined, people would think we're about to kiss.

"No," I say definitively.

And this time it's my turn to hold up the silencing hand while *he* gasps.

"Now, you hear *me* out. My world does not revolve around *you* and *your* addiction. *My* world revolves around *me* and *my* addiction. And maybe I need this anarcho bullshit, as you call it, to break out of mine. You ever thought of that? Maybe it's part of my process. But it shouldn't bother you 'cause it's got fuck all to do with you. What I do or don't do has no impact on *your* recovery, man. It's yours. And maybe I'm even good for you, you know. Because your problem, Simon, isn't the alcohol. Your problem is that you are a control freak. You want to dominate every situation you're in. You're so scared of the world, you're incapable of just peacefully coexisting with it. So you either try to control it or blot it out, I guess. Honestly, you could probably learn a lot from my anarcho bullshit. But for now, you just need to learn to live with it, mate. One week down, three to go."

On that note, I stand up and go back to the kitchen to get some trivets for the table. I don't look back, but I know I leave behind a broken man.

It feels like it always feels, no matter if it's achieved with fists or mind bullets.

It feels shit.

I can't sleep.

There are a million and one things running through my mind and I just can't find peace. It would probably help if I was lying down, not standing by the dormer window, looking out at the myriad of stars dotting the night sky over Purbeck, but I tried that. It didn't work. I tossed and turned.

Lying on the right shoulder: wondering where the fuck Rothman is and what he thinks he's doing.

After I spoke to Christine to warn her about the therapists trying to muscle in on our territory, I marched over to Rothman's house. But he wasn't in. Instead, Lewin next door heard me knock — I didn't exactly hold back on the knuckle power — and stuck her head out of her window.

She informed me that Rothman had gone to London for the weekend. That's another anomaly. Although the therapists sign off Friday night and don't sign back on until Monday morning, it's highly irregular for one of them to just leave and not let the nursing staff, the *head nurse*, know they're gone.

Lying on my back: wondering about the dynamics in my house.

My bunch were super quiet tonight. Admittedly, I tried to avoid eye contact with Rowan, because I felt like everyone in the room would just look at us and *know* about us dry humping on the kitchen floor, so that didn't make for a rousing atmosphere.

But I wasn't the only quiet one. They were all subdued.

Simon hardly said a word all evening, looking like he was on the verge of tears half the time.

Charlie wandered off as soon as he had shoveled the last forkful of food into his mouth, over to Elias' crowd. He and Elias have some kind of comp going on around who's gonna tap the ballerina in Elias' house. It'd better be Charlie, because otherwise my last act here will be to fire Elias' sorry ass. Don't care anymore how good a nurse he is. I'm running out of patience with him.

When Charlie left, Tristan looked so dejected that Rowan took pity on him and asked if he wanted to play backgammon after doing the dishes. And that's what they did. I watched them for a while. There is something really sweet about how Rowan treats the kid in our house.

But I confess, I was staring mostly at Rowan's hands as they shifted counters. Wondering what, other than tangling in my hair and kneading my ass, they could do to me.

Lying on my left: asking myself if Rowan saw my card.

It would have been hard not to. I left it on his bed. But when he came down after his shower before dinner, he didn't give any indication that he'd read what I'd written. Or maybe he had, but he didn't understand what it meant? Not everyone is as detail obsessed as me.

Answers on a postcard.

Those were his words. So I answered on a postcard. A one liner.

Between them, they'd have an accord.

Maybe it doesn't make sense to him, though.

Maybe he's forgotten he said that.

Maybe he's never watched *Pirates of the Caribbean.*

Unlikely but possible.

It's my favorite movie of all time. I will never be sure if it's my favorite because Elizabeth Swann was such an eye-opener for me, or because it was the last film I ever watched before my already shitty life turned to hell.

I was eleven when it was released. My mother had split from her last meal ticket and was trying to get her shit together. For a change. My mother getting her shit together meant scrubbing up and finding someone who could buy her better drugs.

Tom.

Thomas Edison Carter. Yep. You got it. Named after the light bulb guy. One of the Rothman-types. But not slimy. At first.

Tom was loaded. Dealt in real estate. Not billionaire loaded, but suddenly there was a nice apartment, food in the cupboard and clean, new clothes. My mother got out of bed, made breakfast and sent me off to school. A *good* school. Until then, my education had come mostly from science shows on TV and the library.

Tom didn't really live with us, but he'd come around every evening then be gone in the morning. Never left as much as a toothbrush behind. Not that I really noticed at the time.

I was too happy to be out of the bedbug infested pit we'd stayed in for the previous eighteen months with Roger the Dodger. Roger was the cheapest pimp my mother ever had. Turned her from coke onto meth. Ignored me. Totally. Like an unwanted pet. It's a miracle he didn't encourage my mother to put a bowl on the floor to feed me from. But then, there wasn't much food during that time to put in such a bowl.

Tom was like a Disney prince come to save us.

He would give me pocket money. Pocket money. It was a completely alien concept to me. And he'd *see* me. Said hello and goodbye. Smiled at me. Even championed my causes, like convincing my mother to let me go to the movies when *Pirates* came out, with Michael, who lived down the hall, and Michael's mom. It was a PG-13 and I really didn't look my age, let alone older.

Michael was a little older than me and in special ed. Not so special he needed somebody with him all the time, just special enough to be shunned and taunted by the other kids in the building. That made two of us. Thankfully, most of it went straight over his head and he'd stayed the friendly, happy soul that he was. I wasn't so lucky. Blessed are the stupid as they say.

His mom was over the moon when I started hanging out with Michael. She wasn't the sharpest tool in the shed either, but they were really nice folk. Milk and cookies nice. Of all the people I met before I ended up with Elena and John, Michael and his mom are the only ones whose fate I sometimes wonder about.

So for a while it all looked good. Deep down, I knew it wasn't going to last. Those periods in my life never did. But Tom was different from the others. Nice. Solid. I allowed myself hope. Little did I know he completely controlled Mom's substances. Little did I know the deal my mother and he had going involved *me*.

It was at that point in my spiraling thoughts while tossing and turning that I got out of bed, put my airpods in, stuck on John Mayall and wandered over to the window to stare at the stars.

I spent most of my life trying not to think about Tom. I haven't blocked any of it out and I have spoken to people about it and all that, but it's a ticket to nowhere. Ironic though it sounds, considering I work in a profession surrounded by therapists, I don't really believe talking helps all that much.

What has happened has happened, and the best you can do is to keep collecting up all your pieces each time you move on and try not to drop too many along the way.

I was lucky in a way because I'd already started masturbating and getting myself off most nights, long before Tom ever laid his hands on me. So I knew sex had the potential to be a nice thing before he got a chance to completely ruin it for me.

I can still come quite easily. As long as I treat the man as nothing but a human dildo.

My breathing stops there. Because suddenly it dawns on me that this is the real reason I can't sleep. Because for some unfathomable reason, the man next door is already more than a human dildo to me.

And because, technically, he's not next door.

He's standing right behind me.

ROWAN

I watch her for a long while as she stares out of the window before I slip into the room fully and approach her from behind.

She's wearing a long, white cotton tee with the sleeves cut off that just about covers her butt, and I can clearly see the tension in her shoulders and in the stance of her naked legs.

This is not the woman who wrote me a postcard quoting *Pirates of the Caribbean* to say we're on.

This is not a woman waiting for her clandestine lover with a wet, aching pussy.

It's not even the practically minded nurse having second thoughts about laying her career on the line for a good pounding.

This is a girl in pain, fighting her demons.

I fully expect her to turn around any moment and send me back on my merry way, but she doesn't. With every step towards her, my heartbeat quickens and pumps electricity through my body.

This is a new thing. A her thing.

Normally when I'm turned on, I feel my pulse in my balls, radiating down from the femoral artery. With her, I feel it fucking everywhere. As if each of my cells had its own little power station. And each step I take closer without being rejected fires those stations more.

It is only when I am close enough for my breath to fan across the top of her head that I see she's wearing airpods and suddenly my body simmers down a notch. I don't want to startle her.

So I stop moving and just stand there for a moment. I wait, letting the air between us mingle and mix, heat up and start humming.

Until I'm right back where I started and my body is vibrating like a leaf in an earthquake.

She steps back, a millimetre, into our space.

It's then I know I have her.

Raven

He isn't doing a thing.

He just stands there.

Heat radiates off him in a way that tells me he is stark naked. The realization makes my insides clench. Once. Hard.

He's come both vulnerable and prepared. I'm in awe.

He smells of lemongrass beneath the musk that is pure man, a combination that will forever be Rowan to me now, no matter how short-lived this may be, or how long I live.

The air between us starts humming. My nipples tighten against the fabric of my sleep shirt and that dull pressure in my belly starts that says I *need*. My breath starts coming quicker and my pussy swells and coats up, moisture dripping down and pooling behind the seam.

So far so normal.

Other than my heartbeat. My heart rate is so high I think I'm going to have a coronary. This is new. It's a Rowan thing.

Of course, my pulse *always* quickens in anticipation of fucking a guy. It's a necessity. I can explain it medically to anyone who cares to listen. But this is different. This is beyond my blood supply rearranging itself in my body to support impending sexual activity.

It's sublime.

And fucking scary as all hell.

So where I'd normally turn around, take my guy and ride him hard until we're both sated, I stay dead still and try to just fucking breathe. And then, when I'm finally on top of my breathing, I shuffle back just a tiny, tiny bit. Imperceptible. But not to him.

Oh no, not to him.

ROWAN

It's all the invitation I need.

She is mine now.

Slowly, I lift my left hand, gather her hair in a ponytail and gently wrap it around my fist.

A shudder goes through her.

I blow on her neck and in the light of the moon, I watch goose bumps erupt on her skin. For a second, I wonder if I should take the airpods out of her ears. It's killing me that I don't know what she is listening to, that she can't hear what she's doing to my breathing.

But I decide against it. If she wants them out, she is free to take them out. I suspect she won't.

Then I stop thinking, and do.

She trembles when my lips find her neck and I give her a long lick across before I land on the side, just below her jugular and nip her. Hard enough to sting, soft enough not to be an arsehole. She whimpers and my rock-hard dick trembles in the air between us, the tip brushing over the tee covering up her butt.

My knees go a bit soft and I have to bend down and lean my forehead against her shoulder for a moment to gather my wits. I had a plan. I was going to go long and slow and draw it out all night, but I don't think I can.

I need to come. *She* needs to come. This has been brewing since the moment we first looked at each other and it needs release.

I want to be inside her so bad.

Inside *her*, not inside a plastic wrapper that's inside her, but *her*.

With the last shred of decency I possess, I remind myself that that is not an option, that that needs discussions and preparations we don't have the time for just now.

Then I go to work best I can under the circumstances.

Raven

He's done it again, the hair tethering thing.

I don't even think he realizes it, but it *does* something to me. Something I don't have words for. It makes me feel weirdly safe. When it really, really shouldn't.

It makes me feel safe and cared for and grounded and anchors me in the present. I can't escape into flights of fancy, have to stay here, in this reality.

And in this reality, I want him inside me so, so bad. Him. Rowan *The Python* Hadlow-Fuller-O'Brien. Completely. Naked. Bare. I know I'm safe. I know I'm clean. But is he?

So no. Not today. This much rationality I still cling to despite all my instincts screaming at me to fuck it, and be fucked. But again, for no sane reason, I trust him. He wouldn't just plow into me bare without my consent. Whatever he's up to, I'll be protected.

I whimper when he nips my jugular. He's both so gentle and so fucking feral at the same time. I've never known anyone like him. Or maybe I did, and they never had a chance to show it.

As if he knows that I'm thinking of other people, he takes his forehead off my shoulder where he was resting it for a moment, and nips me again, a bit harder this time. The pain brings me back to the here and now.

I can feel him grunt against my skin before his mouth wanders back to the center of my neck in open-mouthed kisses that drive me nuts. Then his teeth find the neckline of my tee and clamp down on the fabric. His free hand comes up, his fingers pinch the fabric and with his teeth and his hand, he tears apart the back of my shirt, all the way down.

A thrill goes through me like I've never known before.

When he's finished ripping the cotton apart, he tugs the remnants of the garment over my right shoulder then helps the rest of the fabric fall free from my left side. He takes a sharp breath, sharp enough so I can *feel* the air being sucked in by him, and stands back for a moment.

I know what he's looking at.

He won't be able to see much in this light, but it still feels like he's taking in my raven one feather at a time. It's a big piece, not quite as big as his, but it covers the whole of my back. A raven landing in a storm, her wings cloaking around her body, the claws spilling over onto my right butt cheek.

He skims two fingers over it, growling his appreciation and not once faltering when he hits the bumps in the road, the scar tissue beneath.

And there are many, many bumps. When he's finished with his exploration, he suddenly slings his arm around my front. He holds me to him, brushing against my tits as he does, the hairs on his arm teasing my nipples, seeking as much skin contact as possible and nestling his enormous erection against my spine.

I'm completely naked, standing back to front of a naked beast under the light of the moon.

I'm at his mercy.

And John Mayall is still singing the Blues.

Time for John to take a break.

ᚱOWAN

I don't think she knows it, but when I press every inch of skin possible against her, she emits a low growl. It is the sexiest sound I've ever heard.

And suddenly I want her to hear me, too.

I want to whisper in her ear how fucking hot she is, how tiny her body feels compared to mine, how much I love her round thighs and her bubble butt and the swell of her belly, a real woman's, not trained away and made flat to look like a man's.

I want her to hear how much I plan to worship her tits, plenty big on her, yet perfectly sized to sit whole in my hands.

And as if she can hear my thoughts, she reaches up and one by one takes the airpods out of her ears. For a moment, I hear the faint echo of an unmistakable blues guitar and a smile tugs on my lips as she carefully lops them onto the carpet, to land by the skirting board. She's got taste, this woman, that's a cert.

"John Mayall, huh?" I whisper into her ear and gently bite down on the now accessible right lobe.

She whimpers in answer then slings her arm backwards to reach up around my neck, arching her back and pushing those tits out like ripe fruit. I straighten up to look over her head at them. She's so small compared to me, she barely makes the height to furl her hand around my neck.

She's on tip toes when she looks at me over her shoulder, drawing my gaze away from her tits and to her face, and our eyes finally meet in the dark room.

My heart stands still for a moment at the desire I see there. It's almost unbearable. I've been with more women than I care to remember. Some good, some bad, none ugly, but I've never felt like I do in this moment.

Like that person belongs to me. Mine. Completely.

It's so overwhelming I want to run. All the way back to the ugliness I came here from. To the fights and the blood and the gore and the broken, debauched people of the life I made.

But then her tongue darts out of her mouth, wetting her lips and all thought leaves me again. I still hold her hair wrapped in my hand and I pull up a little, so she has to stretch a bit more, until her legs start trembling with the effort to hold her up. For a moment, I bask in her helplessness.

But I'm a killer, not an arsehole, so I bend my knees a little, giving her taut body some slack. Then I let my hand travel down her belly until I find the apex of her thighs. I slip my flat palm in between and cup her mound. It hurts my battered hand a little, but it's a good hurt. It reminds me who I am.

She trembles when I lift her up.

Raven

I'm not a pixie size woman, I'm five four and I weigh one-hundred and forty pounds, but he cradles my pussy and lifts me up as if that's nothing.

He slides me up until his cock is nestled firmly against my butt. Then he bends us both forward, so it slips right between my cheeks, sitting long and hard all the way along my cleft before he brings us upright again. He presses my body against his and I can feel the ridge of him against my butthole as my ass cheeks take his dick in a tight grip.

"I love your butt," he rumbles, and I feel my juice drip through my slit, into his palm.

His thumb caresses the soft hair on my mound in gentle, sweeping motions, infuriatingly far away from my clit.

I wonder what he makes of my bush. I only ever shave a little around the back but nothing ever around the front. I like that I have hair there, that I am a *woman*, not a girl. I don't want to be anywhere near a guy who needs a clean-shaven pussy to come. Call it a hang-up. And, again, like with the pain he dished out earlier to bring me back to the room, it is as if he knows exactly what it is I need. That I need verification, to know we're on the same page.

"Soft," he growls in my ear. "So fucking silky. I knew it. I had you down as a fur girl. I love that you're a fur girl. So fucking sexy."

I whimper at his words. Nobody has ever spoken to me like that. He tugs my hair to bend my head back more. His dark eyes glimmer in the moonlight as he looks into mine. And for a moment, we're just suspended in this absurd pose, drowning in each other's gaze, while my feet dangle in the air, like a fish on a hook.

He smiles before he leans in and ghosts his mouth over mine, gently, just a hot breeze fanning over them. He holds his lips there, barely touching mine, and I can feel him grin just before he crooks his middle finger and slices through the seam of my pussy until it finds my hole. I jolt up as another surge of liquid lust seeps through me. I make a noise I barely recognize when he just plays around the rim a bit instead of inserting it where I need it.

"You want more?" he growls against my lips.

"Uh-huh," I manage to breathe.

"Say it, Raven. Say you want me to finger fuck you. Tell me you want me to make you come."

"I do."

He grins wider against my mouth as he dips in a little deeper. But not fucking deep enough. Nowhere near.

"You do *what*, Raven?"

"I want you to make me come," I answer hoarsely then bite his lip.

It's like a rag to a bull. With a growl that vibrates through his entire body, he takes my mouth, opening me up and entwining his tongue with mine while he plunges his finger into my pussy and starts massaging my insides.

He's fucking *massaging* me, and I can already feel the orgasm build.

It scares the living daylights out of me that he can get me this high so quickly, and I automatically flee the scene in my head and start thinking about the wallpaper in my room at the cheap motel where the cockroaches came out of the drain each time you showered.

"Oh no, you don't," he hisses, and I realize that he's stopped ravaging my mouth. "You stay with me, Raven. I'm gonna make you come. And you're gonna like it. You're going to like that you are helpless in my arms. You're going to like that while I finger fuck you, I'm gonna rub my dick all over your arse and I'm gonna spurt all over your back. You're gonna fucking well *love* it, you hear me?"

He lets go of my hair and slings his free arm around my torso until his hand finds my right tit. He cups it then pinches my nipple. Hard enough to draw me back to the present, skilled enough to give me another bolt of lust.

"No more going away in that pretty little head of yours. You stay here, with *me*."

And then he is *everywhere* again. His tongue is in my mouth, his finger is stroking my walls and the heel of the same hand is undulating over my clit. His other hand is kneading my tit in the same slow, infuriating rhythm as he holds me even tighter than before, moving me up and down to massage his dick in my cleft, like a rag doll used as a fuck toy, and making my butthole spark with pleasures unknown.

He's not even inside me and I'm being more fully possessed than I knew possible.

And he's right. I fucking love it. I want all of him, everywhere. I want him to grow two dicks and five hands and three tongues and fill me up *everywhere*.

I want him to fucking obliterate me.

His movements are getting more and more desperate, jerkier, *gruntier,* quicker. And the more he loses his shit, the higher I climb.

His grip on me gets so hard I can barely breathe, his motions coming faster and faster.

And then he stops, and I feel the judder of his orgasm against my backside, his load hitting my spine.

But what undoes me, really, is that he never falters.

We're not done when he's done.

All through his release, he keeps up his onslaught until I finally give up, and give in.

The orgasm explodes in my head, my heart and my pussy, so fiercely I have tears streaming down my face when I come down.

She's limp in my arms, and there is a part of me that's worried I've broken her.

I don't mean figuratively, I mean literally.

I was holding her so tight, maybe I cracked a rib or two.

"Raven?" I ask her in a whisper as I gently set her back on her feet, and relief washes over me when she chokes out a response.

It's just a noise but it's not a dying noise, so I guess her ribs haven't gone piercing her lungs or some shit like that.

"Are you alright?" I ask while I gently swivel her around by the shoulder to face me.

But she doesn't look at me. Her eyes are scrunched up and there are tears streaming down her face.

Fuck. Fuck. Fuck.

I thought she was enjoying this. I'm sure she came. Hard. But maybe not?

Maybe...oh, I don't know. All I know is that my heart fucking breaks at the pain on her face. Those cute frown lines are crater deep right now and I know I put that expression there. It stings. It fucking cuts me to the bone.

This isn't *'we have an accord'*.

Nowhere fucking near.

Fuck. Fuck. Double fuck.

I wanna say something. I have no idea what, but I take a big breath anyway. See what comes out. But before I can, she holds up a hand, her flat palm turned towards my chest in the universal but polite 'fuck off and leave me alone' gesture.

"I'm fine," she says in a steely, quiet voice that tells me nurse Raven is back in the room and opens her eyes. "You need to go now. I don't snuggle."

I'm being dismissed and that pisses me right the fuck off.

I've clearly broken it already, so I might as well break it some more, right?

"Yeah, well, tough titties, neither do I," I reply. "But I do fucking well clean up after my shit."

I pick her up in the same breath to sling her over my shoulder, making full use of the fact she can't protest without raising the whole fucking house. She doesn't struggle as I walk backward till my legs hit the back of the bed. I sit down before I slip her off me to slide her sideways onto the bed.

"Don't roll on your back, you're covered in spunk," I inform her, matter of fact. "Stay while I get something to clean you up. In fact, don't fucking move a muscle, or next time I'll get *serious*. You hear me?"

She nods, not moving, not looking at me.

I turn my back to her and start walking away. I'm already at the door when I hear her hiss.

"There ain't gonna be a next time, asshole."

And there she is.

Relief is fast becoming a familiar emotion.

I grin to myself.

Whatever you say, honey.

I got this.

Raven

I don't move. Not because he ordered me not to but because I can't. I'm frozen.

Too close.

Too fast.

Too fucking much.

I try not to think about it and concentrate on the here and now. I try to listen out for his footsteps, but I don't hear a thing. He sure moves quietly for such a giant. He doesn't even switch the light on in the bathroom.

Eventually, all I get is the sound of the running water and then the faucet is turned off again and half a minute later he is back by my side, the mattress dipping under his weight as he sits down behind me. He gently cups my shoulder and rolls me fully onto my front. The next thing I feel is the dampened half of a hand towel being swiped deftly over my back. He wipes me clean then uses the dry half of the towel to rub me dry.

He is neither gentle nor rough but efficient, almost professional, in his movements, like a good nurse would be. And that calms me to no end.

He stays well clear of my pussy, too, despite the fact she could probably use a good scrub and all. I'm so soaked it's insane. I'm making a mess on the sheets. When he's finished, he gently puts the towel on the bed next to me.

"Here. I said I'd clean up *my* mess. You wanna clean yourself, go ahead."

He gets off the bed, and suddenly I don't want him to leave.

"Don't look," I whisper as I roll back onto my side, open my legs and start cleaning myself up.

"Not looking," he says as he walks away, not to the door but back to the window. "But be careful. That's my guys on that towel. I was the best swimmer at my school aside from Silas."

"Who's Silas?" I ask as I mop myself up, giving myself involuntary sparks as I rub over my still sensitive clit.

I'm not worried about immaculate conception, I'm on the pill, but this is good. We're chatting. He's being flippant. This I can handle. Chatting is good. Flippant is good. If he's flippant, I can ignore that he just turned my world upside down, or the fact that he's bending down to pick something up off the floor by the baseboard and that he shows me a full flash of his absolutely glorious ass in the moonlight that slants in through the window.

"My brother," he answers. "Kinda the reason I'm here. You'll meet him on halfway day. I hope."

Halfway day is exactly what it sounds like. Halfway through rehab, we invite the families, or other nearest and dearest, of our guests, so they get a chance to start making amends. It's the only part of the classic 12-step-program Halosan embraces. It's a taster of things to come for the rehabees but at a point when they are still cushioned by us here. There's always a small number of guests that don't make it past halfway day, but I'd bet my ass Rowan ain't one of them.

"Can I turn around yet?" Rowan asks, and it's only then I realize how safe I really am with this guy.

He does what he just did to me, but if I ask him not to look while I clean up, he doesn't look, he doesn't argue.

I fling the towel on the floor next to the bed.

"Yes."

I can't see the expression on his face when he turns back to me, backlit as he is, but I just know he's carefully schooled it into a neutral expression.

He comes over and holds out something in his hand. I recognize my airpods and it makes me smile. In his own fucking way, Rowan Hadlow-Fuller-O'Brien is a British gentleman.

"I know you said no snuggling and I respect that, but can I stay at least for a little bit?" he asks.

ROWAN

My heart is beating in my throat.

She looks back and forth between the airpods in my open palm and me, and I swear I can see her swallow.

"No snuggle," she says as she snatches one of the airpods out of my hand.

Just one.

My already overworked heart skips a beat.

"No snuggle," I confirm.

"Just two people listening to music, right?"

"Just two people listening to music."

I sit down on the bed next to her. Carefully, so she doesn't spook.

"I get to choose," she declares.

She turns onto her back and props herself up on her elbows. I try hard to ignore what that does to her tits in the dim light because I can feel my dick stirring again and that would be so not good right now. Fucking bad idea. But all he sees is that we are still naked, he could go again, and her tits look fucking delicious. So I will him down.

"You get to choose," I assure her while I stick an airpod into my ear.

"And you're not allowed to laugh at my choice," she adds.

I cock my head and frown at her.

"Why would I laugh at your choice?"

She shrugs and shuffles up on the bed to get her iPod from the nightstand.

- 274 -

"'Cause it's not badass."

"Who says I only do badass?" I respond and hold out my hand in a silent demand for her pod.

"My choice, remember," she says.

"Yeah, yeah," I respond. "Change of plan. I pick the first one and then you can have all the others."

She possessively furls her hand around the little rectangle, but I just keep holding out my hand and eventually she gives up and slides it into my palm.

"One, O'Brien. Just one."

I smile as I scroll through her music, realising quickly she doesn't have what I'm looking for. Wi-Fi is my friend, and I Spotify it instead. The whole thing takes a little while, but she lets me get on with it while she fumbles her airpod into her ear and waits.

I hit play and make myself comfortable on the bed, propping myself up against the headboard and waiting for the first soft guitar chords to hit.

She recognizes it. Of course she does. Not many English-speaking souls on the planet who haven't heard Simon & Garfunkel's 'The Sound of Silence'.

"Really?" she asks just before their voices start up in that perfect harmony of theirs. "This? Why?"

I reach out to cup her cheek in my hand and swipe a thumb over her lips. It's a gamble. A fucking huge one. But I figure I have fuck all to lose here.

"'Cause it's both my favourite and my least favourite song in the whole world and I want you to know not everything about me is badass either."

I leave it there. Despite every fibre of my being wanting to pull her up onto my chest and making her curl up to me, I respect her rule and let my hand drop again.

For the first minute of the song, she just keeps staring at me. Then she crawls up the bed and settles in next to me, flush, shoulder to shoulder, arm to arm, leg to leg.

I close my eyes and let the music take me away until the song finishes, and I hear her pick up the pod and press play again.

Same song.

Same arrangement of limbs.

But this time, she slips her hand into mine and keeps it there, our fingers entwined.

Raven

I wake up the next morning, alone and with the faint smell of lemongrass in my nostrils he left behind on my sheets. And I'm chill. Completely.

It's the strangest sensation.

I keep my eyes shut, nestle deeper into the mattress and remember him leaving sometime around dawn, throwing a sheet over me and giving me a kiss on the temple. And I remember wanting to reach out to keep him with me. Just there, by my side, not snuggling but holding hands, sharing the soft underbelly of our musical tastes.

I've never let anything like this happen before.

Men are for fucking.

We meet, we get off, I go home. I don't spend time.

Rowan got one of the last firsts I had to give.

And I don't regret it.

But it can't happen again. There is too much at stake.

Time to get up and kick some addict ass.

ROWAN

I might be an ogre, but I'm not daft, and I know she is going to feel weird about the whole intimacy thing when she wakes up.

Not the getting off together. I'm certain she's fine with that, despite the tears, but about what came after. I get the distinct feeling she doesn't do being *close*.

I do. I fucking crave it. Not with the people I'm shagging normally because that just muddies the waters, but I *like* being close to people. I was close to my mum until I killed her. I was close to my half brother and sister until their father decided I was dead weight. I was close to Silas before I fucked it up.

I think of Silas and his brand-new American redhead as I slip into the gym early in the morning, strip and slice into the water of the empty pool.

Water and Silas always go together in my head. The guy is the meanest swimmer I know. Fucking fast in a pool, absolutely fearless in the ocean. In those years when we weren't talking, if I was a free man, I'd sometimes go for a dip somewhere just to feel near him. I love him so fucking much, so I'm not lying when I say I'm happy for him. But I also feel a sharp sting of envy when I think of him with Grace, for there is no way that *I* will get to keep *my* American princess.

I won't allow it.

I might only have had two hours of sleep, but my mind is clear.

I watched over her for the longest time before I finally managed to drag myself away, knowing that there wouldn't, *couldn't,* be a repeat.

I destroy everything I touch, and she's already broken as fuck.

And I refuse to become the final nail in her coffin.

Raven

Rowan makes it so I never have to have *the talk* with him.

I don't see him for the whole of Saturday. Rumor has it he's hanging out with Alan Allsorts, but we meet in the kitchen for barbecue prep that evening. I take one look into his eyes, and he tells me wordlessly that he knows exactly where I'm at.

We have an accord.

And for the next couple of days, he simmers right down on the heat. He still looks at me and I still look at him. I remain hyper aware of his proximity whenever he is near, and each evening in bed I hold my breath, but he doesn't come closer than is appropriate for a client-nurse relationship again.

We still talk, about music, about books, about the world going to the dogs and about life in general, and he's still easy company, but we're being adults about the whole thing.

Boundaries restored.

And not before time, because I have bigger fish to fry than pursuing an impossible relationship.

Rothman is back, and it's time Frank and I had a little chat.

It's late Monday evening, long past dinner and well into social time, when I find myself outside Rothman's house, about to knock on his door. I stand on the doorstep and hesitate for a moment. The guy really, truly skeeves me out and I fancy going in there like a hole in the head, but it's gotta be done.

Just as I finally lift the cast iron door knocker, a door opens at the other end of the row of houses on this side of the road, and somebody spills out amid a cloud of male laughter. I don't need to look across to know who the person hitting the doorstep is, but I do anyway.

Rowan catches my eye and his laughter simmers down into a warm smile, followed by an inquisitive frown. He turns away again to say his last goodbye to Alan before the door shuts then makes a beeline for me.

My heart starts racing as he comes closer. Stupid thing.

"What are you doing here?" he asks, and it's not in a casual tone.

It's also none of his business, but there is a protective edge to his voice I can't ignore.

"I need to talk shop with Rothman," I answer truthfully, and let go of the knocker for a moment to sling my right arm around my chest and rub my hand over the biceps of my arm.

Rowan's eyes narrow at the stance. He doesn't ask questions, but he gets it.

"Hmm. Need some muscle to loiter outside?"

It's silly how relieved I am at his words. Why the fuck would I need a security guard just to talk to some nerdy psychotherapist about keeping to his remit around here? But that doesn't change the fact that I instantly relax and stop rubbing myself when Rowan makes the offer. And I've been around too long to deny string-free help when it's up for grabs.

"I don't think I need it," I answer with a half-hearted laugh and see him suppress a flinch of rejection. "But I'd sure as shit *like* it."

"Good," he says, clearly relieved, and breathes out heavily. "I don't trust that guy. He's a slimeball."

That earns him a proper grin from me.

"The brute's acute," I quip, and he softly punches my shoulder.

He hasn't touched me since he left my bed two mornings ago, so this is the exact moment I find out that my sex ed books in high school were wrong. Way, way wrong. The shoulder, too, is a highly erogenous zone. Shit.

"The brute's got an IQ higher than most of these doctors put together," he answers with a grin then gets serious. "Although maybe not higher than Lewin's. She's *good*."

I nod. I can see in his eyes that after taking him apart on Friday she must have gone to work putting him back together again in his session today.

"She is. She's tough, she puts people through the wringer, but she's solid."

He nods and I can see in the movement in his throat that he wants to talk to me about it, but he shakes it off.

"How long do you need before I knock and come looking for you?" he asks instead.

I shrug.

"Dunno. Ten, fifteen minutes? Shouldn't take long."

He nods then juts his chin out at Rothman's door.

"Go on. I'll be by the water fountain."

He takes a breath and grins down at me.

"I haven't fellated any water in a while."

Then he walks away, and this time when I grab the knocker, I actually use it.

A few moments later, the window above my head opens. Rothman sticks his head out. He watches Rowan's retreating back before he notices me.

"Oh, Ravenna, I didn't see you there. What a surprise," he yells down. "Do come in, the door is open."

I enter the dim light in Rothman's hallway, and immediately his voice rings down from the landing above.

"I'll be there in a minute or two. Feel free to go to my therapy room. Make yourself at home."

As soon as he says it, I startle at a sudden realization.

I've never been in here since the therapists moved in.

I know fuck all about Frank Rothman, other than that he gives me the creeps based on a vague visual similarity to my childhood rapist.

All the houses' layouts are identical, though, so I know where to go.

In the counselors' houses the lounge is the therapy room.

I move forward into the hallway, but then curiosity leads me the long way around, through the kitchen, where I grab myself a glass of water, and dining room.

Something strikes me as I take the standard issue glassware while I nosy around. Nothing's been changed anywhere in number 11 since the contractors finished remodeling the old abandoned village that once stood here in The Village.

I saw all the houses before anyone moved in and all interiors are the same, but the Allsorts, the Denyers and even Lewin have turned theirs into individual homes. They haven't completely redecorated them but added a picture here, different curtains there, changed the lamp shades. That sorta thing.

Rothman's, at least on this floor, still looks *exactly* how it did when the official Halosan reps cut the ribbon on the therapy center. Weird.

I let myself further into the therapy room, a bland set up of a writing desk in one corner and a pair of identical armchairs facing one another by a net curtain obscured window. I stop to study the only alteration he's made to the room. Framed copies of his PhD, MSc and membership of professional bodies certificates hang in a neat line up above a gas fireplace. All they tell me is he studied in London, graduated five years ago and his middle name is Josiah.

I spin around when I hear Frank Josiah Rothman's feet coming down the stairs, so when he appears in the door frame, I'm facing him.

He looks less slick than I've ever seen him before. His hair is mussed, his face slightly flushed and he's in the last throes of fastening his belt buckle. It doesn't take a genius to work out what I interrupted. It also doesn't take a genius to work out that he doesn't have anyone up there. And the look he gives me makes me absolutely sure he only just got to the finish line. With me already in the house. I want to hurl, but all I give him is my curtest matron-of-the-ward nod and raise my glass.

"I helped myself to some water in your kitchen. I hope that's okay."

"Of course," he answers and indicates the chairs. "Take a seat. To what do I owe this pleasure?"

"My apologies for coming over this late in the evening," I say, while I move across and lower myself onto the edge of the seat. "I was hoping to catch you at the weekend, but you weren't here."

"No problem," he answers smoothly.

He takes his position opposite me and studies my coiled-to-leave-at-any-moment stance. Like a good little therapist, he mirrors my body position and looks at me expectantly. Suddenly it occurs to me that this was a huge mistake. I'm confronting him on his own turf.

Goosebumps crawl across my flesh when my eyes land on his hands. I wonder for a moment if he's left-handed or right-handed. I try to push the thought away before it tests my gag reflex. Instead, I think of Rowan, waiting outside, watching my back. The image calms me and it's then that I can smell the soap on Rothman's hands and relax a little. At least he had the decency to wash his hands.

I clear my throat and fix Rothman in a mildly disapproving stare that works a treat on hospital patients stepping out of line on a ward.

"Frank," I start, and give him a small, dishonest smile. "I am afraid this is not a social call. I'm giving you the chance to explain yourself before I contact head office about your conduct."

He sits bolt upright at that. Good. I have his attention. I don't let him speak before I continue.

"It appears that you have been reorganizing room allocations without clearing this with me first."

I let it hang there and watch him relax a little. He thinks this is not a big deal. He's wrong. I wonder how he's going to play this. The answer is, badly. Because the idiot draws the superiority card.

"Well, I think we can both agree that although assigning guests to houses may be on your job description, Ravenna, as a therapist I am best placed to alter decisions if I deem them counterproductive to my clients' progress."

"Wrong. There is good reason the placements of the guests fall under the head nurse's remit. Do you have the Halosan house allocations supervisor qualification?"

He laughs and I can see in his eyes that he thinks I'm being sarcastic, that I made it up. I frown because he should be aware that I'm not. But this is the first time I'm dealing with outside providers, as HQ call them, so maybe he is genuinely oblivious.

In the States, all Halosan staff have been through our in-house training and know why who is responsible for what. These international centers are different. I am the only one here who is *fully* Halosan trained. I hate how that actually gives me a sense of pride. How pathetic is that? But I park this little inner discourse for examination another day as I pick up the conversation where we left off.

"I am not joking, Frank," I tell him. "I went through months of training pertinent to successfully allocating guests to nurses and houses. You don't just look at your individual client, you look at the *group*, you look at the group in relation to the background of your host nurse, personal and professional. You factor in type of addiction, medical background, known trauma, known triggers, known–"

I cut myself off there and change tack, smiling into his stunned face.

"Tell you what, pass me a piece of paper and a pencil."

I watch him go to his desk, where he takes a stack of A4 sheets out of his printer and starts rummaging around for a pencil until he finally finds one in his leather satchel on the floor. He comes back to bring me both and then I go to work.

For the next ten minutes, I dazzle him with what I inwardly decide to call my wedding planner act. I don't use real guests or our real nurses for my examples, but by the end of my demonstration I've produced a sprawling spider diagram, illustrating exactly what goes into the process. Until I'm sure he gets the picture of how truly complex house dynamics are.

"As I pointed out earlier," I say, signaling that I'm done by sticking the pencil behind my ear, "months of training. And experience, Frank. I have done this for some time. That is why I have much higher clearance than you, or Lewin, or even the Denyers regarding our staffs' personal backgrounds. Because it's on a need to know basis. And I am the only one who needs to know. For this." I stab my index finger at the piece of paper. "Now can we agree that there won't be any more reshuffling without clearing it with me first?"

He's still frowning at the paper on my knees, but he nods slowly.

"So what happens when you leave?"

"Christine takes my place."

"But she does not have your training," he points out.

I don't know why he's drawing this out. He's like a dog with a bone and it's getting on my nerves now. We should be done here. I want to get out of here. Nothing's changed in the last fifteen minutes. The guy is a creep and I've made my point. But I won't let my annoyance show on my face. I want him to get this into his thick skull, so Christine doesn't have any problems with him when I go home.

"Christine's had a year's worth of evening tutorial from me alongside online training sessions with HQ. She was essentially linked into the training by Skype. So, yes, she does have my training."

"Shit," I hear him mutter under his breath while my face is turned to the floor as I lower the paper onto the carpet.

It's an odd reaction, but I let it go. It really is time to leave before my cavalry breaks up the party. I've been here too long, and I can fucking well *feel* Rowan approaching Rothman's front door.

"Are we good here?" I ask.

He leans in and puts a hand on my knee.

"We're good," he says with what I'm sure he thinks is a charming smile, but I can barely hear him through the noise in my ears.

Bile rises in my throat.

But then there is a knock on the front door, loud enough to cut through my panic attack.

I never loved anyone as much as I love Rowan in that moment.

ROWAN

I get antsy after about fifteen minutes. After another five, I walk up to Rothman's house and knock. Loudly.

It doesn't take long before Rothman answers the door with Raven standing right behind him. It is hard to tell in the gloom of the hallway, but she appears pale. Before Rothman can say anything, I speak.

"Excuse me for interrupting," I say, smiling politely. "But we have a bit of an emergency at the house. If you're finished here, Raven, could we have you back, please?"

She slips around Rothman, and despite the green hue on her face that becomes apparent in the orange glow of the late sunset, she manages to play along without missing a beat.

"Don't tell me it's the Wi-Fi again," she says, holding my gaze.

My heart starts pounding with the proud realisation that she is anchoring herself in my eyes. At the same time, anger vibrates through my body. What has Rothman done to make her need anchoring in the first place? As if she can hear my thoughts, she surreptitiously shakes her head, signalling, 'let it go and let's get outta here'.

"However did you know?" I mockingly respond to the Wi-Fi question to keep up the farce.

We are already a couple of steps away from number 11 when she looks back over her shoulder at Rothman.

"I'm glad we had a chat, Frank. It's good to be on the same page," she says to him evenly then walks away without sparing him another glance.

And in that moment, I realise that this woman is a professional through and through. I haven't got the faintest what their confab was about, but I know it made her feel majorly uncomfortable. Yet she comes out with the upper hand, and smoothly so. I march silently beside her, feeling like a fucking child in comparison.

I sense that she doesn't want to talk right now, that she needs time to get back her bearings, so I think about the choices I made instead. About the world I chose, about *the people*, about the fights, the gambling, the debauched men that never grow up and their dumb bitches, who think the bigger the crime the higher the status. And who wash up battered, bruised or fucked to death because they believed the trashy romance novels that told them bad guys are sexy.

They're not. They're arseholes.

Like me.

I think of my mum and how disappointed she would have been in me. She was a professional. Like Raven. Not a nurse, but a teacher. Someone who society depends on.

We touched on the subject of Mum in my session with Lewin today. Lewin knows the facts and I really appreciate that she is the first person ever not to say that it wasn't my fault. She just acknowledged in a really neutral tone that objectively, yes, it was.

Something happened inside of me when she said that. Some knot pinged open that I've been carrying since that day.

Raven and I arrive at our house just as my thoughts meander to Adam and Sammy, my half brother and sister, who I haven't seen since their dad decided to take off with his own brood but leave me behind with Sheena and Silas. That was eleven years ago. Adam and Sammy are teenagers now. I wonder if I'd even recognize them if I passed them in the street these days.

I'm dragged from my ruminations when Raven clears her throat, her hand on the doorknob. I look over at her profile. Her pallor has returned to normal.

"Thank you for rescuing me," she says quietly.

I bark a quick laugh.

"You don't need rescuing, lady. You're tough as nails."

She shakes her head, and it's then that I see she is actually still shaking slightly.

What the fuck did Rothman do?

I know better than to ask, though.

"What are you doing with the rest of your evening?" I enquire instead.

"What? Once the Wi-Fi is sorted out?"

She chuckles, and the sound warms my soul. I pull my mobile from my pocket and look at it.

"Oh, my bad. It appears to have magically reset itself."

She looks over at me with a smile that lights up my soul.

"Well, waddayaknow."

"Sooo, back to my question..."

She shrugs and turns the doorknob. I'm not ready to split from her for the night, though. Sex may be off the menu, but I still want to be around her.

"You wanna spend some time?" I ask, and it earns me a raised eyebrow. "Not like that. I heard you. Even though, technically, you didn't say anything. No, I mean, in the garden, in plain view. Just hang for a bit."

"Okay," she answers as she pushes open the door. "See if those boys have relinquished the backgammon set yet. I'll whoop your ass."

I snicker at that.

"Not a chance, lady. Not a friggin' chance."

Raven

It so happens we have to win the board off Tristan and Charlie first in a winner stays on match. Rowan lets me take that one, and I know he's studying my every move as I play Charlie while we sit outside at the terrace table in the ever-dimming evening light.

Tristan also stays to watch, and when it gets almost too dark to see, he goes and gets matches from the kitchen to light the candle in the hurricane lamp on the table. It makes my heart soar that our shy little kid is starting to do stuff like this. Taking the initiative, taking part.

He's still awkward as hell, but at least he's not frightened away by everything and everyone anymore, not even when Elias and Ann-Marie, the ballerina, come over and sit with us after everyone else has gone inside their houses.

I only half listen to the banter going around the table, mostly between Rowan and Elias, while I concentrate on wiping the floor with Charlie. It takes a while, but in the end, he sits defeated. When we're finished, he looks at me in disbelief.

"You're a fiend," he says and mimes taking his hat off to me. "Where did you learn to play like that?"

"Foster kid," I let slip out without thinking.

I hear a sharp intake of breath from Elias but nothing from Rowan or any of the others. I shrug as I smile into the round of faces illuminated by the gently flickering light on the table.

"Group homes, guys," I explain. "BG is one of the few board games you can play even when half the counters are missing. You just use quarters and dimes instead. You ain't seen nothing yet. You should see my drafts skills."

I laugh to lighten the mood then nod at Rowan.

"You're on."

He swaps seats with Charlie and we set up the game. We've barely begun when a new presence comes out through the backdoor and marches over. Simon rocks up at the table and, as per usual, doesn't take anybody else into account when he interrupts my move in a demanding tone.

"So here you all are," he says irritably. "I was expecting you to come knocking on my door, Raven. I assumed you'd let me know when I can swap."

"You can't," I answer dryly, moving my counters along the board.

Suddenly he's bent down and his hot breath is in my profile.

"What?"

"Back off," Rowan growls at him, and Simon subconsciously shuffles back a bit.

Enough, so I can turn my face to look at him without almost having to kiss the spittle off his chin.

"I spoke to Rothman and we cleared up a few misunderstandings. Like, that he doesn't interfere in my job and I don't interfere in his. As I said before, Simon, house allocation is my responsibility. And I say, you are staying here. Too late in the day to change it. Now can I get back to my game, please?"

He straightens up with a sharp intake of breath, and I half expect him to stomp away like a toddler but, to his credit, he doesn't. He stays a few moments longer and watches Rowan and me play before he quietly withdraws back into the house. Probably to write a letter of complaint to HQ or some shit like that.

Let him. I have faith in my bosses. They'll treat it as what it is: part of his healing process. He needs to let go of his control freakishness. Not that that is an official term. But he still hasn't got a grasp on the fact that here he is not the big controller. He's just an addict in treatment with a bunch of other addicts.

But he still puts my teeth on edge, and I breathe a silent sigh of relief once he's gone.

I watch Rowan's fingers move counters along the board.

Fingers that only two nights ago were plunged deep inside me.

The thought catches me off guard and I feel heat pooling in my belly. I look away from his hands. And straight into his eyes.

A small smile plays around his lips.

The ass knows exactly what I am thinking.

He hands me the dice and the subtle touch of his skin sends me into a tailspin of desire.

"Your turn," he says.

ROWAN

The house settles into a new routine over the next few days.

I stick to my resolution and keep out of Raven's room, though it gets harder with every moment I spend in her company. And I spend a lot of time in her company.

That's our silent trade off. No more sexual gratification but we get to be...friends. For real.

We spend every minute that isn't taken up by therapy for me or work for her together. Always in view of other people, often with the rest of our house. And by default, it glues all of us together more. I learn stuff about Charlie and Tristan and Simon that I wouldn't have if it hadn't been for the pull this woman has on me.

Simon gradually mellows the fuck out somewhat, and once he does, he's actually okay to be around. I learn that he really, truly loves his wife and kids. As he gets more and more nervous towards halfway day and seeing them, he stops talking about them as if they were commodities and more like they are actual people. There might be hope for that cunt yet.

Charlie, it turns out, was *terrible* at school and has a massive chip on his shoulder because of it. He doesn't think his parents are gonna show up at the weekend and he pretends he's not sorry about it.

Tristan is the son of a single mum who never let him out of her sight before this. As I listen to him talk about their weirdly symbiotic relationship, I secretly think it's no wonder he wound up addicted to online gaming. She wouldn't allow anything outdoorsy. No parks, no bicycles, no swimming.

He still can't swim.

He had the obligatory swimming term in primary school but never managed to get past doggy paddling. So I offer to teach him. It's a fucking life skill. We live on an island.

He refuses at first but when Raven promises she'll come along, too, he reluctantly changes his mind. He says he's embarrassed in front of the other guests, so I use my in with Alan Allsorts to secure a private evening slot for Tristan's lessons.

The gym and pool shut at 9pm every night, but after some negotiation, Alan agrees that we can use it afterwards for an hour. He's greatly reassured once he hears that Raven will be there to provide medical assistance if need be, but he still makes me promise to stay by Tristan's side every step of the way and makes me swear that I know my rescue hold before he is satisfied enough to give me the key to the gym. By the time he finally slips it into my hand, I feel like this is a proper badge of honour.

"I'll put a *Private Lesson in Progress* sign on the door for you when I leave," Alan says and looks at Raven, Tristan and me as we stand by the side of the pool on Thursday night, after he's given us the last instructions about how to turn the lights off and the alarm on. "Just in case people see the lights on and think they can walk in. I doubt it, though. Hardly anyone comes after dinner. It's usually just Elias. But he's been and gone tonight. Sometimes you get the odd guest but not out of this lot. Just post the key through my letterbox when you're done. Have a good evening."

We bid him the same and then he's off, the door closing softly behind him.

Tristan looks at the water, terrified.

"I'm not sure this was such a good idea," he stammers.

"Don't be silly," Raven says and starts stripping herself out of her jeans.

She's clearly got her swim stuff on under her clothes already, because I doubt she'd strip off in front of Tristan otherwise. I haven't seen her in anything but her tunic since this Sunday's lunch in the pub, when she rocked one of her dresses again, and I realise I relish the prospect of ogling her in some skimpy bikini more than is good for my sanity. But when she pulls the tunic over her head, what she reveals is far from skimpy.

It's so much sexier than that.

It's a full cover all, and then some fifties retro style, polka dot number with a fucking skirt. She looks like Jane Russell and Elizabeth Taylor had a love child who made off with Marilyn's wardrobe. Tristan and I swallow in sync and I can't even blame the kid.

"Right," I say, clearing my throat, and look at Tristan. "Let's get changed and showered before we go in, right? Cold is good. Makes you freeze less in the pool."

Raven unashamedly grins at us.

"You go, guys. I showered before I changed, I'm hopping straight in," she informs us with a wink.

A fucking wink!

I'm so gonna murder her later. When nobody is looking.

She turns her delectable butt towards us, making my cock remember how much he enjoyed being trapped between those buttocks. Then she dives straight into the pool and starts swimming. Not daintily, like those women who try not to get their hair wet, but properly, her head bobbing up and down as she slices through the water. She's a strong swimmer and heaven help me if I don't find that even more of a turn on. I'm rock hard in my jeans and somehow I need to cool it, so I can give the kid a lesson in how not to drown.

While I watch Raven, Tristan turns towards the changing rooms and after another moment, I follow him. I take a few minutes behind closed doors to think of some stuff I'd really rather not revisit, and it does the trick. By the time I come out, my dick is behaving. For now.

While I brought my black Speedo trunks with me to Purbeck — they're part of my standard kit — Raven had to take Tristan shopping in Swanage for his. I guess the selection in his size, S for scrawny, wasn't great because I can't imagine he would have willingly picked the orange and black tiger stripe loose-cut swim shorts he is wearing when he comes out of the cubicle. They are hideous. But I don't need to add to his nerves by pointing that out. He is visibly shaking, and that's before our stint under the cold shower.

When we approach the poolside, the terror on his face is undeniable, and I'm starting to wonder if this was really such a great idea. But then Raven's face pops out of the water with a big, fat smile on it and I immediately change my mind. This was a great idea. Though maybe not for Tristan.

She looks up at him and beckons him to the far side of the pool, which for some unfathomable reason was built to be the shallow end.

"Hey, Tony Tiger," she greets him with a purr. "Come to the other side. You can stand there. It's only about five feet deep."

Tristan relaxes at that and starts walking around. Raven crawls across to meet us and when Tristan sits on the side of the pool to let his legs dangle into the water, she holds out a hand for him. He takes it and a surge of idiotic jealousy runs through me as he slides off his butt. Part of me screams it wants to be the kid who's lured into the water by this sexy-as-sin polka dot siren.

As if she can hear my thoughts, she smiles over her shoulder at me while Tristan gets his body acclimatised to the temperature in the pool and blows me a kiss behind his back.

First a wink and now a kiss.

The water seems to bring out a side of her that I'm seriously loving, and I hop in before my dick starts loving it a bit too much again, too. He just about succumbed to the ice-cold pre-pool shower and to the bunch of really unappetising thoughts I ran through my head, but he'd be only too happy to put away childish things and get back in the game. In actual fact, he already half is.

I groan inwardly when I remind myself that that's not what we're here for.

Then I put on my coach face and get to work.

Raven

I love, love, love swimming. As soon as I hit the water, I feel free in a way that I don't get to feel anywhere else.

It is the single only thing I share with my mom. Before the drugs took their toll, she was an ardent swimmer. Wherever we went, she would always scout out the nearest free public pool even before she'd scout out the cheapest takeout places.

She taught me when I was so little that I can't remember ever not being able to swim. When I think of that, I wonder if she might even have liked me as a baby and as a toddler. My mistake, I believe, was that I grew into a small person.

And as soon as that small person grew big enough to escape her narcissistic web from time to time, I would disappear down to the local pool for hours. And nobody ever questioned the pale, way-too-young girl with the scuffs and bruises alone in the water.

My heart breaks for her when I think of how invisible she was.

But she's not invisible now.

Right now, she is a grown-ass woman in a dead sexy polka dot swimsuit who's got to teach a kid to swim and, maybe, just for shits and giggles, drive the other instructor a little bit crazy with desire.

I'm playing with fire and I know it, but I can't help it.

Almost six days of perfect restraint.

Of bedroom doors that stayed shut and of being just *friends*.

And I fucking well can't take it anymore.

Seeing him practically naked, in his skin-tight trunks that leave nothing to the imagination, doesn't fucking help either. I'm mesmerized by all that big but supple muscle and by the python writhing around his torso with every move he makes, the jungle on his back.

And he catches me looking.

And he looks back.

It leaves me in a strange heat, a compulsion to flirt with him that paints every bit of professionalism I've put between us over the last week a lie.

I want this man.

I've wanted him from the moment I first looked into his eyes.

Half having him hasn't quenched my thirst. The threat of losing my job and ending with massive debt hasn't quenched my thirst.

Getting to know him has made it worse.

My heart starts beating erratically at the thought. It's another fucking blurred line. I don't do getting to know my fuck buddies. Ever.

But he's slowly but surely getting under my skin. I blame the close living quarters. Though I could choose not to spend as much time with him, of course. But us hanging out together has been good for the whole house and, really, who am I kidding? I gravitate towards him each free minute we have like a moth to the flame.

"Earth to Raven," Rowan waves a hand in front of my face. "You ready to roll?"

I blush, I fucking well blush, because I didn't hear a word of what he's been saying.

So far, he's had Tristan show him what he can already do in the water. There was a pitiful doggy paddle to start off with. Then Rowan made Tristan kick water while holding on to the side, and after that he made him float on his back. Presently, the kid is figuring out how to stay afloat on his front with the help of a swim noodle while learning how to move his arms for breaststroke.

He's weirdly uncoordinated and the nurse in me wonders whether the overdevelopment of fine motor skills for gaming has somehow been to the detriment of his gross motor skills. It sure as shit looks like it.

I look away from assessing Tristan's present position and up at Rowan. Our eyes meet across the spluttering Tristan between us. There is the ever-present humor in Rowan's dark brown gaze but also something else. Something I haven't seen before and that makes me stand up taller and pay attention.

Determination.

Focus.

For the first time since I've met him, I can see a glimpse of the fighter.

And fuck me if that isn't sexy as hell.

ROWAN

I love this sassy water vixen version of her.

I love the lust in her eyes, and I love that her nipples are poking holes through the fabric of her swimming costume.

But we're here to do a job.

It gives me a warm surge when I see her recognize that, and she springs to action. For the next hour, we put aside the red-hot tension between us and work on Tristan.

By the end of the session, the kid's knackered out, but he's made some progress. He can now do the breaststroke, with a woggle, across the breadth of the pool, which is not bad for a first lesson.

I call it a day when my gaze falls on the clock on the wall and it tells me it's way past the time Alan allocated us. Above us, the natural light that falls onto the water through the glass ceiling has faded to black, leaving only the poolside lights and a couple of harsh overhead neon strips to illuminate the building. Tristan stands up in the water and I clap him on the back, gently so as not to break his scrawny spine.

"That was quite a leap, mate. Well done. Same again tomorrow?"

He blows out an exhausted breath but nods.

"Yeah."

Raven, who's gone off to swim to the other end of the pool, climbs out and shouts across to us.

"Stay where you are, guys. You need to see this."

She goes to the light panel by the door and switches everything off, bar the faint strips of emergency lighting at the bottom of the basin.

"Raven? What the fuck?" Tristan exclaims in shock.

It's the first time I've heard him swear, but the only answer he gets is a giggle from her in the distance. Then she jumps back into the water and crawls back to us.

"Sorry, but we gotta see this," she says cryptically when she arrives by our sides then lets herself flop onto her back to float. "Oh, hell yeah. I've only seen this in the winter when it gets dark early, never in the summer and never with the lights off. Come on, guys, get on your backs."

It doesn't occur to either of us not to follow her instructions. And we are rewarded handsomely.

Above us, a gazillion stars are visible through the skylight.

We stay silently on our backs, slowly drifting until everything's gone quiet and all the ripples in the water have smoothed out.

"Wow," Tristan whispers after a while, and it makes me smile.

"You said it, mate," I whisper back.

And it's then I feel the small hand of the woman floating next to me slip itself into mine.

She squeezes it gently and I feel like a giant.

In all the best ways.

Raven

The three of us remain quiet as we pad along the grass on naked feet, boots in hand.

The nightfall has cooled down the temperature a little, but it's still warm and it's nice to feel the gentle breeze in my damp hair. I look over my shoulder at Tristan behind me, and Rowan behind him, and feel a strange sensation. Of belonging, camaraderie, invincibility. And then it hits me like a freight train. *Friendship.* For the first time in my fucking life, I feel that thing that all the other teens felt when they were out and about, horsing around with their *friends.*

Michael was like a pet puppy.

The others at the group home were my fellow sufferers who'd finally landed on their feet.

My cohorts in nursing school were my study peers.

Christine, Elias et al are colleagues.

But this?

This is friendship. Inappropriate but true.

Unbidden tears shoot into my eyes when I realize that I had to get to twenty-eight before catching a glimpse of what other people take for granted.

I wipe them away with the back of my hand as we arrive at the house and slip in quietly.

Soft acoustic guitar chords greet us from the living room. When we stick our heads around, we see Charlie sitting on the sofa, cross-legged and so blissed out by his own music, he doesn't even acknowledge our arrival.

Tristan slips past me into the room to sit by Charlie's feet and starts watching him raptly with chlorine red eyes. He looks tired but happy.

I remain in the door with Rowan behind me as he radiates heat that crawls up my spine. It crawls up and then down my back, sprawls around my rib cage like a hug and reaches inside of me with invisible tendrils, all the way into my core. My pulse speeds up as I allow his presence to infiltrate me. He is so close I can smell him. He smells of pool and lemongrass and man.

Heat blooms between my legs. He's not even touching me and my pussy starts clenching at the thought of him and at the memory of the orgasm he gave me too many nights ago. The memory I've been reliving every day since, with my fingers on my clit and dipping in and out of myself, but never quite reaching. Never quite feeling what he made me feel, any climax I bring on myself being a mere shadow of what he teased out of me.

I shiver at the thought and suddenly I hear his voice rumble in my ear, so hushed it could be a figment of my imagination.

"Yeah, I can't forget either. You want more, don't you, Raven? When all is said and done, you still want me to fuck you till kingdom come."

It is so fucking corny and it should turn me right off, but it doesn't. Not even close.

I feel a glut of my juices slipping down my insides, my insides clenching. I swallow hard at the realization that there is just no fighting this.

I *need* this man.

Fuck knows why or why him.

But it doesn't stop me from freezing at the fact that we're still looking into the living room, and though Rowan is mostly hidden in the shadows of the dark hallway behind me, Tristan and Charlie could still hear. Or sense. I feel like it's impossible they wouldn't feel what's going on, considering the pure energy vibrating between Rowen and me. But Rowan disagrees.

"Look at them, they're completely oblivious," he murmurs then takes my hand off the door handle that I'm still clutching.

He bends my arm back to press my palm against his erection. My fingers instinctively curl around his length as much as the confines of his denims allow and a low hiss escapes him. He pushes my hand up and down over his thick shape.

"He's been standing for you all week, Raven."

His words turn my knees to jelly, and I want to double over to contain the liquid lust dripping from my core. I'm wetter than I've ever been. So wet, I fear it'll be *audible* when I move.

Then he serves the final blow.

"I can smell you, lady. All the way up here. Through your clothes. I can smell your honey. You're wet for me. And I can't wait to taste you. Now say goodnight to them."

He releases my hand and falls into chorus with me when I brightly say goodnight into the living room, loud enough to be heard over the guitar playing. Tristan waves, and even Charlie stops looking down at his instrument and gives us a nod.

We retreat into the hallway and up the stairs. Rowan walks behind me and I can feel his eyes on my butt. We cross the first landing and I note that there is no light strip under Simon's door, indicating he's gone to sleep already.

As soon as we get to our floor, Rowan grabs me by the shoulders from behind and steers me through the door to my room. His grip goes firm, a silent command to stay put when he releases me briefly to shut and lock the door. He switches the lights on but dims them to a soft level. Then his big hands land on my hips and he pushes me along to the bed.

My legs hit the bed, and he slides his hands around and under my tunic until his fingers find the button atop the zipper of my jeans. He pops it and slips a hand inside to shield my mound while he pulls the zipper down with the other one.

In all my heat, my heart stills for a moment with the knowledge that he's observant enough to remember I'm pantyless. We left our swimming gear behind in the pool to dry and he must have noticed that I hadn't brought anything for afterwards.

I melt in more than one way at his thoughtfulness, while he starts grinding his erection into my ass. He likes being behind me. And to my astonishment, I realize I like it, too. It's nuts. I've never trusted anyone enough not to face them while we were fucking, and when I do, they *have* to be under me, or I go frigid.

"Quit thinking," Rowan commands and gently starts peeling my jeans down until they are by my calves and he's slithered down onto his knees.

He taps my right leg.

"Lift up."

I follow his instruction, and he pulls the rest off. He repeats the same thing on the left and when I've got both feet back on the ground, he skitters his palms up the side of my legs before they land on my ass cheeks.

He kneads my buttocks lovingly for a minute, the movement tugging the muscles and pulling all the way to my clit. A whimper escapes me. He kisses the dimple at the base of my spine then rises back up.

Once he towers over my back again, he brings his left hand to my front and ghosts it over my mound, giving me another delicious shiver, before he takes my tunic by its sides and pulls it up. I lift my arms, and he gets it off me easily, throwing it the way of the jeans.

I stand before him completely naked, but he's still fully clothed and that reminds me of things I don't like reminding of. As if he had a sixth sense about what's going through my mind, he envelops me in his arms and hugs me hard, pushing the whole length of my back against his shirt-covered front.

"It's me, Raven," he says, in a normal tone, not hushed, not growled, just matter of fact, before he cups my breasts and begins massaging them.

It's the weirdest, most delicious combination of feeling held and having arrows of electricity shoot through me each time he squeezes the nipples just right. Again, there is something tethering in the way he holds me, and the unhappy thoughts get blown out of the water.

"Is that good?" he asks me.

"Yes," I pant.

"Tell me how good it is."

"I fucking love it," I whimper. "Don't stop."

I feel strange saying those things. I'm not a talker. I'm not a screamer. I take what I need, that's it.

"Who?" he asks, and for a moment I'm not sure what he wants.

He pinches my left nipple hard.

"Don't stop, *who*?"

"Don't stop, *Rowan*," I answer, and a low growl of satisfaction escapes his throat just before he lowers his lips to the slope where my neck meets my shoulder and bites down.

Like a stallion holding his mare in place.

I saw it once in real life. My mother shacked up with a cowboy for, like, five seconds when I was in elementary school. Until she realized drugs were hard to come by in Montana. Salt of the earth type. Had a ranch, bred horses.

Rowan licks over where he's just sunk his teeth into me and puts his mouth to my ear.

"I said, quit thinking, Raven. I'm gonna eat you out tonight until you forget every last one of those bad memories that haunt you. Until the only thing that matters is my tongue in your cunt and my lips on your clit. You hear me?"

He bites me again, sharper.

"I said, you hear me?"

"Yes," I press out.

He stops kneading my breasts for a second.

"Yes, who?"

I reach up to push his hands back down on my tits as I answer.

"Yes, Rowan. Don't stop."

He starts up again and suddenly his voice turns serious in my ear.

"You clean? Or am I gonna get me a dose of syphilis if I suck you up?"

The nurse in me smiles at his knowledge. Not many people know that oral can give you such delights as syph, the clap or herpes. Not to mention pretty much everything else. You just have to be unluckier for everything else. Syphilis, gonorrhea and herpes, they love a bit of tongue action.

"Yes. Hundred percent. Are you?"

"Yeah, Nurse Raven, I am. I'm fully tested. And not counting last Friday's mucking about with you, gorgeous, I haven't had sex in any form in over a year."

I hear the grin in his voice when he adds the next bit.

"Other than with myself."

That gives me pause. For a moment, I forget what we're doing here, and I want to turn around, face him and ask why. It so doesn't seem like him. He chuckles against my throat.

"Surprised?" he asks, and at the same time lets his right hand wander away from my tits, down to the apex of my thigh.

"Yes," I admit, but the impulse to have this conversation is forgotten as soon as he runs a teasing finger over the soft hair on my mound.

"Crawl on the bed, Raven," he demands, releasing me out of his tight embrace as he utters the words, and I do as he says. "Scoot up. Front down, arse up, spread your legs."

I put myself in the position he wants me in. I can sense him step back from the bed a bit, his eyes burning holes into my backside while he undresses himself. I hear him fling his shirt away, unzip his denims and step out of them. Another half a minute goes by while he does nothing but stare.

"Gyrate your arse," he demands hoarsely. "I can see your cunt. It's wet, but it isn't dripping. I want it to fucking drip, Raven. When it drips, I'll lick."

ROWAN

She starts rotating that delicious bubble butt of hers in the air as soon as I say it, and it takes every ounce of my self-control not to surge forward onto the bed, grab her by the hips and plunge balls-deep into her.

But I know it would be too much, too soon.

In a strange way, she's almost like a virgin. I can't put my finger on it, but I just know I need to take this slowly. Get her to trust me, give her time and patience if I don't want to end up just a means to an end.

And I already know I want to be more than just a hook up.

It's ludicrous. We're playing a dangerous game here. She could get fired. And even if we managed to keep it under wraps, what happens when my stint here is finished? This is her last month in Europe. When Simon, Charlie, Tristan and I leave Purbeck, so does she. She says she'll go travelling for a bit and then fly home.

To take another assignment.

She doesn't even know where her company will send her next. But still I can't help wanting to be more to her than just the guest she had an illicit affair with. So I suppress the urge to take her there and then, wrap my fist around my dick and give it a hard squeeze as I watch her.

Her legs are spread, her pussy is glistening and I can see a glimpse of her clit. I buck into my fist a couple of times just because I can't help it but then I stop, fascinated by how her movement seems to milk the juice out of her.

I fucking love this view.

I see a drop of her cream collect at the end of a hair on her bush and when it falls onto the bed, I'm on her like a parched man in the desert.

I stick my whole face in her sweet, sweet cunt, my nose right in her centre, and then I shoot my tongue out and lap at her clit. She shudders violently and makes a mewling sound to end all mewling sounds. I lose myself in the pleasure of eating her out from behind until I can feel her core starting to tighten.

But I don't want her to come. Not just yet. This time I want her to look into my eyes when she does. I want to see her face when she loses control. I want her to see *me*.

I take my face out from between her legs and leisurely slip a couple of fingers along her slit instead while I talk to her.

"Flip over," I tell her but rather than comply, she stills. "Flip over," I repeat.

She slowly shakes her head.

"I can't," she chokes out.

I run a hand gently up her spine while I crawl up the bed to lie next to her. She remains on her knees, her position unchanged.

When my hand reaches the back of her neck, I clasp my fingers around the tender flesh and force her to turn her face towards me. Though she doesn't fight me, she hides behind her hair. I let go of her neck to stroke the strands out of her face, and then, finally, those indigo eyes meet mine. She's flushed and she's aroused, but she also suddenly looks younger.

Much, much younger. And petrified.

"Hey," I whisper, and she swallows.

My heart stops for as long as she doesn't respond, but then it kick-starts again as soon as she returns my greeting.

"Hey," she says back with a wobble in her voice.

There is no smile.

I tug at her in various places until she finally gives in and lies down on her front. I grab her by the waist and nudge her until she rolls onto her side, facing me again.

I cup her cheeks and start stroking her eyebrow with my thumb.

"I won't hurt you," I say, and the whole woman freezes, scrunching her eyes shut.

Shit.

Wrong fucking words.

And then it hits me like a bullet between the eyes.

But I'm a fighter, and so is she, and there is only one way of resolving this. Head on. So I take a leap of faith on my hunch alone.

"That's what *he* said, isn't it?"

There is a delayed reaction but then the smallest of nods.

"How old were you?"

"Eleven, twelve."

"It wasn't just once," I state.

She shakes her head.

"Who was he?"

"My mom's boyfriend."

My entire body goes into anger overdrive, but adrenaline has no place in this conversation.

"How often?" I ask as levelly as I can muster.

She shrugs but finally opens her eyes, only to look right through me.

"Three, four times a week over a year and a half. You do the maths."

"And your mum didn't notice?" I ask in disbelief.

I know it's probably the entirely wrong question but, really, what the fuck?

"Oh, she knew alright," she answers coolly. "I was payment."

Raven

I hear him gasp, like I knew he would. They all do.

It's not the first time I've told someone about it.

It is, however the first time I've told someone who has given me an orgasm. Which changes the dynamics. I'm sure it's part of the reason I find it hard to keep up the gazing-at-him-but-not-seeing-him routine. Especially since he carries on stroking my eyebrow with his thumb and keeps looking at me in a way nobody has ever looked at me before. Nobody.

There is no pity.

There is no 'I want to save you'.

There is just the same thing there has been the entire fucking time.

Burning desire and an understanding in those deep brown eyes of the ugliness of life that tears my heart to shreds.

"Payment for what?" he asks.

"Coke, speed, meths."

He nods knowledgeably. That's it. No further comment.

"How did it end?"

"She ODed. In front of us. He tried to save her. Couldn't. They weren't married or anything, so the state got custody of me."

"The group home."

I nod. And smile. He pays attention.

"Best thing that ever happened to me."

"I'm glad," he says, and then he stops stroking my eyebrows, cups my neck and tugs me closer.

And for some insane reason, I let him.

I let him bring me up flush against him, still lying on our sides, until our noses almost touch. I can smell myself on him and the thought of where this face and these lips were just minutes ago makes me want to rewind the time and get back to *that*. Forget all this other shit.

He's only semi-erect now, but I can feel his length between my thighs, and it doesn't feel wrong. Not in the slightest. I wriggle against him a little.

"He's lost interest," I state, trying to hide the weird hurt that comes with the realization.

Rowan smirks.

"Only temporarily. He just doesn't get off on images of young girls getting raped."

He's so fucking blunt.

I try to wriggle away a little, but his arm comes around my waist and he pulls me into a vise. And there it is again, the tethering thing.

"Uh-uh. You're staying right here, lady. Because while he might not get off on child porn, he sure as hell gets off on naked, fully grown nurses with a penchant for retro dresses and more smarts than himself."

His cock swells at his words, juddering against my skin.

"You think I'm smarter than you?"

"Yup," he nods. "You were dealt a shitty deal, but you turned yourself into something golden. Me? I'm just a dumbass with shit for brains who destroys everything he loves and keeps making the wrong choices."

"Better not fall in love with me then," I quip.

He doesn't respond to that, but the intensity in his eyes goes up about a hundred notches, giving me a rush of pleasure. Then he kisses me. A gentle, close-mouthed brush of lips against lips.

It'd be chaste if it wasn't for my taste on his mouth.

"So the words 'I won't hurt you' are a no-go," he states dryly then kisses me again. "What else is tricky?"

I want to freeze again, but his warmth, his acceptance, the way he is holding me, that fucking tethering thing he does, makes it impossible.

"I can't do missionary."

"Okay." He kisses me again. "What else?"

I sigh.

"I don't know. Don't ever ask me to wear a gingham nightie or hold a teddy bear while we're doing it, I guess."

I see him blanch a little at that but, to his credit, he catches himself. He knows I'm not joking. But Rowan also gets that I have to say it in this brushed off way, otherwise I'll collapse.

For a long time, Tom was all about the innocence. Some kind of fucked up *Little House on the Prairie* fantasy. Until I started refusing and it became some kind of fucked up thirty-lashes-for-the-slave-girl fantasy. Not ready to share that one quite yet, though.

I take a deep breath.

"I don't know, Rowan. So far, as an adult, I've always had to be on top. Always. I've never done any of this before."

His eyes go round.

"What? Nobody ever eat you out before?"

I shake my head.

"Nobody ever finger-fucked me the way you did either," I confess.

"I wish I'd known. I'd put more effort into it," he says deadpan.

I actually laugh at that.

"Liar. No way could you have made it any better."

I get a shit-eating grin for that. It lights up his whole face and this time I'm the one who goes in for the kiss. And as soon as I do, all bets are off. There is tongue, oh so much tongue, and gentle caresses down my back and then his big hands palming my ass. Until we're both panting again, and his erection has grown back to its full glory, pressing hard against my thigh.

He withdraws for a moment and looks deep into my eyes.

"You on the pill?"

My heart stutters.

"What if?"

"Then we're going to fuck."

"Yes."

"To both?"

"To both."

ROWAN

There is a moment when we are both suspended in time and then I ask her the final question.

"Is trust a trigger word?"

"No."

"Good. You trust me?"

"Yes."

The fact she doesn't even hesitate makes the next thing I do so much more of a gamble but, then again, gambling is why I'm here.

I roll her over onto her back and insinuate myself between her thighs, until my hard length rests between her lips. She's slippery as fuck and I can't resist sliding up and down just the once while she protests.

"Rowan, I said..."

I don't let her finish because as quickly as I rolled on top of her, I hook my arm under her leg to lift it up and flip us back onto our sides. Only now, her leg is firmly positioned in the groove between my waist and my hips.

"Sorry," I say. "Had to be done. This okay?"

She glares up at me. It's a trade off. If I want my cock in the right place, her head is quite a bit lower than I would like it to be. Sometimes I really loathe being this tall.

"Yes. But you could have warned me."

I shake my head.

"Nah. You would have started over-thinking it. "

"You're fucking sure of yourself for somebody who considers himself a dumb shit."

I slap her bottom and she writhes against me.

"I said dumbass with shit for brains, not dumb shit."

"Same difference."

I cock an eyebrow.

"You need slapping again?"

She grins. Her sass is back and relief washes over me.

"Not sure. Can't tell if I like it yet. Would need more of a taste."

I half-heartedly land another one on her and she frowns, the way people do when they taste a new food.

"I can feel it in my clit when you do it, so that's nice. But I don't like the sting. I don't like pain. I don't like punishment."

There is an undertone again, and for the briefest of moments, I wonder about the scars that her tattoo covers so well. But we're not going there right now. I can't handle another revelation tonight. And neither can she.

"Hmm. Noted. Is not my scene anyway," I say softly. "I can make you feel things in your clit another way, you know," I add with a smile, and gently rub up and down against her.

Her breath hitches and it doesn't take long until a blissful expression dissolves the frown. I can see in the colour of her cheeks that she's starting to ride high again. I contort myself, so I can kiss her, relishing the way her tongue and mine just play to their own rhythm.

I've never had a woman who kissed like this before. Who'd give as good as she got. Who knows what's good and what's fucking fantastic. Who goes all in.

She is a conundrum in so many ways.

Or maybe it's just that we *work*.

Those are my last thoughts before I let myself fall completely into the feel of this woman, until my need to be in her blots out all else. I reluctantly retract and whisper against her lips.

"Touch me, guide me in."

Raven

The minute he says those words, my pulse goes into overdrive.

I've never wanted anything more in my whole fucking life than to feel him inside me. Although I'm reluctant to stop kissing him, even for the briefest of time. I love kissing him so, so much. I never thought I would ever find the attraction. But, boy, was I wrong. With him, it's easy, exhilarating, addictive. We just...fit.

He holds my gaze as I blindly reach between us and slip my hand around his cock — as far around as it will go. I run the pad of my thumb over the slick head, coated in precum and my own juices from him sliding against me. I press lightly when it glides over the slit, and Rowan's whole body shudders violently.

He groans and slips his hand under my knee to hitch my leg over his hip and give him better access. Then he puts his hand over mine and together we position his tip at my entrance.

I'm breathing so hard at this point, I feel like my lungs are stuttering.

As if by some unspoken agreement, we both look down between us at the same time and watch as our hands slowly guide his head inside me. My pussy clenches around him, cramping, and we stop, looking back into each other's eyes.

He slips his other hand around my neck and holds me fast, leaning his forehead against mine. Then he slants his head and starts kissing me again, gently inviting my tongue to play. He gives us a minute, maybe even two, and slowly my vagina relaxes. He withdraws and puts his forehead back against mine.

"You good?" he whispers, and I nod.

Our breaths mingle as we look down again.

He slides in another half an inch and suddenly I can't wait any longer. I want him. All of him. Now.

I take my hand off, and because it's the one underneath by default, I also shake off his. His head jolts back a little and he looks at me with surprise, but this time I don't give *him* time to over-think it.

I look back down and thrust my hips forward, hard, watching his whole length disappear inside of me. The visual is almost enough to spark an orgasm.

"Fuck, Raven," he groans as he holds me to him. "You could've warned me. God, you feel so fucking good. Just give me a moment. I want this to last."

So I wait.

He catches his breath, and then he starts moving, ever so slowly, while he keeps on holding me tight.

One rhythm. Deep and slow.

Surrounding me with his arms.

Filling me completely.

With his cock, his tongue that's somehow found mine again and his scent.

Forever.

Or at least, for most of the night.

He fucks me with more love and devotion than anyone has ever shown me, all the way to the small hours.

And all the while, my climax builds in deliciously slow increments, one spark at a time.

Every second of every minute of every hour, so that by the time he finally, finally lets me have it, I have tears in my eyes from anticipation.

And when he does give it to me, he does it so effortlessly it's like a miracle. He lets up from our never-ending kiss and whispers into my ear.

"You ready, Raven?"

I choke out a 'yes' before he suddenly pumps into me, hard and fast but somehow never losing the rhythm or the contact all the same, until the universe blooms around me.

I don't shatter, I don't see stars.

I see flowers blossoming in the darkness of space behind his pupils, as shudder after shudder of my climax runs through me.

He guides me all the way through mine before he allows himself his own release and when he does, he does it with all his heart and soul, with everything he has.

He explodes inside of me, his whole body trembling as he shoots his load but holding my gaze all along. Then he collapses, still holding me to him, a satisfied smile on his lips.

We don't talk, we just fall asleep. Sticky and spent.

Happy.

ROWAN

I didn't scarper this time.

Yes, she's broken. Yes, I'm a fuck up. But we made magic and, for as long as she's here and I'm here, I want to keep making magic.

We have to be careful, of course, and now it's even harder than before because I want nothing more than to grab her at every opportunity and kiss the fuck out of her in front of all and sundry and let everyone know that she is mine. I'm a possessive show off and I know it, so this whole secrecy thing doesn't exactly come naturally to me. But I'm also trying to prove, to myself, to her, that I can do something right for once. And doing it right means not losing Raven her job.

So we try to act no differently from before.

We meet at the same intersections of our day, we sit with the others whenever we have free time and we take Tristan back to the pool the next two nights.

And what happens on the top floor after lights out, stays on the top floor.

Raven

The closer it gets to Sunday, the more of a buzz lies in the air.

It is always the same. Halfway day is a milestone for the guests and everyone looks forward to their visitors.

Simon is frantic because he doesn't know if his wife and kids will even show. He's undergoing some sort of odd change this week that I've never witnessed in a guest before. He's gone from argumentative and self-obsessed to quite mellow and almost pleasant to be around, but there is something weirdly incongruent about it that I can't quite work out. Not that I'm complaining. Simon not being disgruntled about wanting to change houses any longer is a good thing. Especially now that I have a secret to keep. Disgruntled people have a habit of noticing things you don't want them to see.

Tristan seems relaxed in the knowledge that his mom is certain to turn up.

Charlie pretends that he couldn't give a fig if his folks show, but I know he does. He cares about his sister being there very much. I remember how relieved he was last time when she came. She's a few years younger than him and cute as a button with all the sass of a teen who knows her sex appeal and who never had anything bad happen to her. Though part of me will always be jealous as hell of girls like her, it gives me pleasure to see that such people exist.

Rowan seems the most subdued of all of them on the subject. I know he wants to see his adopted brother, Silas, more than anything in the world. From what I can tell, that's a proper bromance right there.

Apparently Silas, too, has a brand-new American girlfriend, called Grace, and he is bringing her along. I feel a weird kind of pressure there to get along with her. Completely self-imposed because Rowan was the first to point out that having the same nationality does not necessarily make for instant friendship.

But I want this Grace woman to like me.

Fuck knows why.

It's not like we're all gonna ride off into the sunset together. But maybe, for a little while at least, I'd like to pretend. Although chances I'll even get to spend much time with them are next to none.

On halfway day, the Halosan nursing staff very much melt into the background. We are on hand should anyone need us, but we pretty much hand over the complex to the therapists, our guests and their guests.

People would start asking questions if I suddenly became part of Rowan's crowd for the day. I wish I could. I wish I could do away with the secrecy and show the world that I, Ravenna Alexandra Vanhofd, am with the sexy-as-fuck giant.

Especially because the day is already not going to go quite the way Rowan had hoped. He's disappointed because Sheena, Silas' real mom and Rowan's adopted mother, can't get away from her job. She is head of housekeeping in a hotel in Brighton and it is the height of tourist season.

Sheena is one of the people Rowan feels he needs to make amends to the most, despite the fact she's already told him on the phone not to 'be daft, and let bygones be bygones'. Those were her exact words. I was listening in to the conversation while waiting for Rowan to get off the phone, so we could cuddle some more.

Who would have known that it would only take getting thoroughly fucked a few times by an ex-gambler and bare-knuckle fighting thug to turn me into a sappy snuggle bunny?

That phone call happened late last night, just after he'd just got me to sixty-nine him into oblivion. Another first for me. I've given plenty of blowjobs in my life, mostly to shut up the men I was getting ready to fuck, and get them on their backs, but getting eaten out while sucking him off was a whole new experience.

I was still reeling from the intimacy of it all, all relaxed and vulnerable and curled up on his chest, while he was stroking my hair, when Sheena texted him that she was free to be rung if he was still awake. It was nearly midnight and she'd only just come off her shift.

I'm fascinated by the way his family operates. I mean, John and Elena are my saviors, but they run a home for twenty kids at a time, so there are strict rules about everything, including communication.

Phone times are between 10am and 12pm and between 7:30pm and 9pm. That's it, no exceptions. I don't think either of them has ever sent me a text message. If I need to unload, I write them an email and I will get one back within 24 hours, telling me how proud they are of me.

But if I ever need to run home, I can. Old fosters are always welcome. Just don't turn up without announcing that you're coming at least a week in advance. If you do, you get the disappointed look from John and hands in the air and an eye roll from Elena, and then you are made to do the dishes for the duration of your stay as punishment for your spontaneity.

I get the impression, just from those two short conversations I witnessed last night between Rowan and his adoptive mom and then him and Silas, that Rowan could turn up on their doorstep out of the blue, covered in someone else's blood, and they wouldn't bat an eyelid.

They'd help him clean up, bury the body and never ask any questions.

But that doesn't stop Rowan from being jittery about seeing Silas today. I can tell, as soon as I wake up to him watching me, that he's full of nervous energy. It's funny, I can feel it ticking away beneath his skin, despite his pulse flowing true and calm underneath the side of my hand.

The side of my hand that just so happens to be resting on his femoral artery while the rest of my fingers are curled around the erection that lies flat against his rock-hard stomach. He smiles at me when I prop myself up onto my other elbow and look back and forth between his warm gaze and his cock twitching in my grip. I look into his eyes and lick my lips.

"What time is it?"

"Six."

"How long have you been awake?"

He grins.

"Long enough to know that sleeping Raven loves my dick as much as awake Raven."

I raise my eyebrows.

"Conceited much?"

"Gorgeous, you've been hand-jobbing me in your sleep for the last ten minutes. And you're making sucky noises while you're doing it."

He pauses for effect before he smirks.

"With your pussy."

Then he changes from crass and cocky to serious in an instant.

"How long do we have?"

"Half an hour before shower."

He shakes his head in dismay.

"Not long enough."

He sighs then clasps his hand around my neck and pulls me up on the bed, so we can be face to face, which means I have to let go of his boner. Sometimes it's a real pain in the ass that he's so tall. But although he makes a small protesting noise when his length slides out of my hand, he doesn't stop tugging me up until my lips land on his.

He gives me a long, languid kiss, rolling me onto my back to thoroughly tongue fuck my mouth — for the whole of the time we have left before my alarm goes off.

I come up for air, bedazzled and disorientated with a throbbing pussy, clenching around unfulfilled need, and a clitoris screaming she wants to be touched. He rolls to his side, and I grumble.

"That's it?"

He folds his arms behind his head and nods up at the ceiling.

"Yup."

He half crunches up, looking at his engorged cock.

"See that?"

He flops back down again.

"That's gonna stand for you all day now, lady. And if he thinks of wavering, even for a moment, it'll take exactly half a second of looking at your fishnet covered calves and at your tits falling out of one of those dresses of yours, and one glance at those fuck-me-lips of yours, and he'll be right back in a state."

He turns to me and the fire in his eyes is almost scary.

"And when I get you back here tonight, he'll be fucking *burning* for you. And that's how I want it."

His speech does all sorts of weird and wonderful things to my insides. But rain on his parade I must.

"No sexy dresses today."

His face falls and it's almost comical.

"But it's Sunday," he protests in a petulant child voice that makes me giggle.

I shake my head.

"Not professional enough for halfway day."

"Meh."

He pulls me on top of him and kisses me again, deeply. I let him rut against me, his hands palming my ass, his fingers skimming my butthole and his cock sliding over my clit, stoking the fire. I'm ready to impale myself on him when he rolls me off him again.

"Uh-uh."

He shakes his head mock disapprovingly.

"Nice try but just 'cause there are no fuck me clothes to look at doesn't mean I've changed the game. The game's the same, the rest is just window dressing."

He slides his cheek against mine, the rough stubble chafing against me and giving me another thrill I never valued before. Then he takes my earlobe between his lips and sucks sharply, once, running the tip of his tongue along the lobe as he does.

"But you could wear the suspenders and the fishnets under your jeans, couldn't you?" he whispers in my ear as soon as his lips let go. "That'd be hot as fuck. Just you and me knowing what you've got on underneath. Yeah..." his voice trails off dreamily while his fingers do the walking, and he slips two of them into my pussy.

He curls them and massages my magic spot for just a moment while his thumb draws one lazy circle on my clit. I cry out and buck up at the sensation so hard, my entire butt lifts off the bed. He grins and withdraws on a rumbling parting shot.

"Time to get showered, gorgeous."

I watch him as he brings the fingers to his lips and licks them clean like a cat that got the cream then gets up unceremoniously.

This man is going to kill me with his tantric sex bullshit.

How the fuck am I gonna slide through this day?

ROWAN

One of the best things about halfway day is not having to endure the food in The Windchimes.

Despite it being Sunday, there is no pub walk. Instead, a catering company that provides a pretty decent looking all day buffet sets up in the therapy centre, so that everyone and their guests can grab food whenever, and then go wherever they fancy.

The whole idea is that we in recovery can start facing our families with our remorse while we're still at the clinic, so we can cry about it at length to our therapists afterwards. Not that crying to Lewin will get you any sympathy but even if it did, as the day unfolds it soon becomes clear that it doesn't have the sombre atmosphere you'd expect from it.

There is genuine joy in the air as each pod of people grabs their food and goes to huddle somewhere on the lawn on Halosan provided picnic blankets or elsewhere in the complex.

Or maybe the joyfulness is just me. I know I'm supposed to be all apologetic and shit, but Silas and I are too chuffed to see each other again to spoil it by dwelling on the past. I have no idea how I lived without this guy for as long as I did.

It's amazing what being dead inside does to you.

I know I've only been here two weeks but before that, I only had him back for a couple of weeks, and a lot of that was heart-to-hearting anyway, so I kinda feel like I just wanna fuck around with him for the day. But I have to honour the program, so as soon as Grace and he rock up in Sheena's Capri and we've done the bear-hugging thing, I pull him aside and I ask him straight.

"Right. Therapy says, I have to make amends. So I have to apologise, *again*, for fucking your girlfriend when she had your ugly dick in her mouth."

Grace, who is in full earshot, grins and looks around the empty car park.

"In case anyone heard that, they're not talking about *me*," she announces to an imaginary crowd surrounding us.

Then she looks me straight in the face and starts whispering, so only Silas and I could possibly hear if there *was* anyone near.

"'Cause the cock *I* suck every night is fucking beautiful. And the only cock *I'll* have inside me is his. Now show some respect and don't talk about a guy's ex in front of his current girlfriend. It's rude."

She delivers it so deadpan that for a moment I don't know if she's seriously pissed off. But then she starts laughing and slapping her thigh.

"Your face! Priceless," she howls and carries on until she has to wipe away tears of laughter.

Silas just looks on with a bemused expression on his face before he grabs her and tugs her into his side.

"We've been through this," he says to me, seriously. "We're cool. We don't need to revisit that one ever again as far as I'm concerned."

He lifts a sarcastic brow.

"Now, we can always talk about how you nearly lost me my home or how your scaredy cat arse didn't face up to its responsibilities for years or, if you really want to go to town, maybe about how you let me think you were gonna fucking kill me. And then almost did."

I shiver at that.

It was by far the ugliest as well as the most beautiful moment of my life to date.

Choking him out in our bout to the death, whispering 'trust me' in his ear as he faded away and feeling, just as he went limp in my arms, that, actually, he still did.

Sometimes you nearly have to kill someone to get them back.

I look deep into his hazel eyes, marvelling as I so often did as a kid, at the fuckloads of colours that go on in them, and well up.

"I..." I start stuttering.

But I don't get anywhere because he gently lets go of Grace to cup my neck in the hand he just had around his woman, so he can draw me in, until we're forehead to forehead.

Like ninety percent of the people on the planet, he is shorter than me, but not by as much as most, so when he pulls me down no gap is created between us to bridge the difference.

"I'm fucking with you," he says, his breath fanning over my face.

He smells of cinnamon and I know he's been chewing Wrigley's Big Red all the way here. He draws me into another hug with his other arm until his mouth is by my ear.

"I didn't drive all the way to Purbeck to talk about the shit we just left behind," he says quietly. "I wanna know how this party is going. And I wanna meet your girl."

I draw in a sharp breath. I didn't tell anyone about Raven. Not even Silas.

"How do you know there is a girl?" I whisper and feel him smirk next to my ear.

"Because, I can feel your hard-on, sucker."

His grip on my neck goes painfully tight.

"And it better not be for Grace."

I know I should leave it be, but I just can't.

"Who says it's not for you, arsehole?" I ask.

It's the moment of truth and I can feel him coil. But then I finally, after all this time, get his forgiveness. His *real* forgiveness. Silas style.

"Oh, I *know* it's for me, Rowan. You'll always be hard for me, big bro."

I can feel his facial muscles next to my cheek as his smirk goes full-on grin.

"But I also know the difference between theory and practice. So, where is she?"

Raven

For the nurses, halfway day is the only day in a guest cycle when they all get a day off at the same time, while the therapists hold the fort. That doesn't include Christine or me, so as per usual, the two of us are the only ones left behind in The Village, since the rest have gone drinking and Sunday shopping in Swanage. Unlike the therapists, though, Christine and I are not expected to meet and greet the crowd, so while we're not exactly off duty, we're not on either.

So we have a little tradition.

As soon as we can, we raid the buffet, pile two plates sky-high with all the best foods, slip away into Christine's house and up to her room, crack open a forbidden bottle of bubbly, sit on her bed, eat and get a little tipsy, but not so much we can't act sober should the emergency we're retained for *actually* happen. It's good fun, but today my heart's not in it. Or my mind. Or any of me, really. I saw every one of my guests' people arrive, except for Rowan's. Silas and his girlfriend hadn't gotten here yet when Christine and I squirreled away our plates.

Tristan's mom had turned up first, half an hour before the official time.

Then came Charlie's parents, around the same time most other people arrived. Both his mom and dad showed up, which makes a welcome change from last time when only his dad came. And they brought Charlie's little sister Ally. Tristan's eyes went wide when he saw that little peach, and he went straight over and introduced himself. Good for him. I get the feeling our swimming lessons are really boosting his self-confidence. I can already see it in his relationship with Charlie. It's becoming less and less hero worship and more two buddies hanging out. Although now Tristan idolizes Rowan instead. Not sure if that's a good trade-off.

After watching Charlie's folks and Tristan plus Tristan's mom hook up, I even stayed around long enough to watch Simon's wife and kids arrive, tense expressions on their faces, but forcing smiles. His wife suits him. You can tell that they've been together a long time in the way they walk and talk. And I can see the longing in her eyes when she looks at him when he's not looking at her. Like she still sees the ghost of the young guy he once was. Like she hasn't completely given up on him yet and is still hoping she'll have that guy back if he manages to kick his addiction. I don't fancy her chances much, though. Not because I think he won't make it — he might, he might not, hard to tell — but because he just doesn't look at her the same way. He thinks he does but, really, he looks at her like she's an old car, one he loves dearly because of the memories but that has outlived its purpose. And in the back of his mind, he already knows he'll have to scrap it. It's sad.

Of course, I could have hung back long enough to meet Rowan's brother and the American girlfriend. But I went and hid instead. Like a coward. I don't really know what that's about. It's like their arrival is going to burst our bubble, and I don't want to help them do it with me being awkward around them.

And it would be awkward as hell.

I can't be seen to hang with a guest and his group. It would raise serious questions with the Denyers, Lewin and Rothman. It'd be different if Rowan could introduce me as his girlfriend, but he can't.

And I'm not.

The thought chokes me and I can feel tears crawling up my throat. Suddenly it hits me what this is. I feel left out. I have never felt left out before in my life. Because there was never anything I wanted to be part of badly enough. But I want to be part of this. And I can't.

Fucking stupid job.

"Right, enough of this, lass. Spill the fuckin' beans. You look like someone's died. What's the matter?"

Christine looks at me sternly, an effect spoiled thoroughly by the humor glittering behind her eyes.

We're sitting in her nicely temperate room, which she cleverly chose *not* to be on the top floor. And unlike me, Christine was wise enough to claim the *biggest* room on the second floor, what the Brits call the first. The fact that it's the biggest, plus not having to contend with slanted ceilings that your six-foot-three lover constantly knocks his head on, if he forgets to hunch while he fucks you to oblivion, means she has enough space for a bed, a wardrobe *and* a coffee table with two cozy chairs and a couple of bean bags, right by a huge window with a beautiful view.

In actual fact, she has two windows, since she has two outside walls. The window by the coffee table overlooks the back garden. But there is also a window to the side of the house and because hers is the last house in the row, through that one you can see the path coming up from the parking lot.

I may have stood at that window just before I nestled in my chair.

And I may have caught a glimpse of Rowan with a slightly shorter, slightly less wide, but infinitely more dangerous looking, guy and a redhead who'd give Jessica Rabbit a run for her money in the hourglass department.

I evade Christine's current scrutiny by letting my eyes wander around the room, but there is not much to get stuck on. Though you'd expect her larger than life personality to come with a certain degree of creative chaos, her space is always meticulously tidy and normally I love visiting with her. Just not today.

I finally meet her eyes and shrug.

"I haven't got anything to say," I respond and sip my drink.

Christine is on her second glass of Moët already, but I've barely drunk a third of mine. I lean forward and pick up a smoked salmon and cream cheese canapé from my plate. Can't answer questions while I'm chewing. Talking with your mouth full is rude. One of the many useful rules my mother instilled in me, instead of protecting me and not whoring me out.

"I call bullshit, Ravenna," Christine says and snatches the salmon bite from my hand before it gets to my lips. "I'll have that, ta. You're getting to eat nowt until you tell it all to Auntie Christine. It's to do with your fighter, right?"

The canapé disappears in her big, masculine mouth and she starts sucking it, *sucking it,* while she watches me expectantly.

I look at her like a deer caught in headlights. How the fuck did she figure it out?

"Oh, come on, gimme some credit, woman. I've known you nearly a year. You're getting laid. There's no two ways about it. I see him lookin' at ye and I see ye lookin' at him. Besides, he's the only one I'd do outta this lot."

I find my tongue.

"Shit. Is it that obvious?"

She smiles, her eyes sparkling with mischief.

"Nah. I was fishing," she admits and leans forward. "Glad it worked, though. Go on, talk. I bet he's huge, right?"

"Christine! I'm not talking about it. It's not happening. Nothing is happening. I'm not sleeping with a guest. Uh-uh. I am not getting fired. You hear me?"

"I'm officially offended. I would never!"

She pauses and grins.

"Now, back to the size question..."

I take another gulp of my champagne and feel myself loosen up. I trust her. She wouldn't rat on me. Firstly, because she's a decent fucking human being, secondly because what we're doing right here, right now is a fireable offense and lastly because she has nothing to gain from it. It's not like the bosses would pay her a bonus for snitching. And she was dead grateful when I told her about Rothman trying to run interference and that I set him straight. Forewarned is forearmed.

And aside from all of that, I wouldn't be able to help the slow smile that is spreading on my face even if I tried.

"Yeah," I say with a nod, looking coyly at the bubbles in my glass. "He's not a small boy in any department."

"Well, good for you, lass."

Christine holds up her glass and we clink.

"Here's to getting properly shagged. There is nowt better in the world."

We drink.

"But this," she says, making a circle in the air with her palm to indicate my face, "is not a shagged, happy face. This is an unhappy face. Now talk."

So I tell her.

ROWAN

I start looking for Raven as soon as I walk onto the green, but she appears to have vanished. It doesn't help that we get interrupted every so often by other people making their introductions.

I see Charlie and his folks, Tristan and his mum, Simon and his family. And everybody wants to say hello to everybody and make introductions. All of a sudden, everything's become terribly British at The Village. In between, the Denyers, Alan Allsort and, of course, Lewin all require handshaking as well. The entire time I look around for black locks and indigo eyes, but she is nowhere to be found. Just as I start to get worried, Christine, Raven's second-in-command, heads us off at the buffet in the old church.

"Rowan," she says smiling as she approaches Silas, Grace and me.

Silas looks at me with a raised eyebrow and I surreptitiously shake my head. I mean Christine is nice and all, but not my type. Bit too much testosterone for my liking. And, really, I only have one very specific type left. She's about five four, the most beautiful, complex, intelligent woman alive and fits my dick like a glove.

"Hi. I'm Christine," Christine introduces herself to my brother and his girlfriend. "How do you three fancy coming back to my house? We're holed up in my room."

As soon as she says 'we' in that conspirative tone, my heart soars at the realisation that Raven has told her about us.

I'm not a dirty secret any longer.

Still dirty, but not a total secret.

Which makes me worry.

Surely people will notice if we disappear with Christine and if Raven is nowhere to be seen at the same time, they will put two and two together. Though when I look around, I realise we might just fly under the radar since numbers in The Village have swelled considerably and there are bodies everywhere. Most people have a maximum of three or four guests, some less, but there are also a few guys in houses that I have had little to do with so far who seem to have invited about twenty people each. Amazing what the promise of a free buffet will do, even in rehab. There is well in excess of a hundred people milling around, outside on the lawn and in here, dipping into the old church on food recces.

Still, I look at Christine with a frown on my face while Silas and Grace look on puzzled.

"Are we gonna get away with that?" I ask quietly.

"Sure, pet," she grins then turns her gaze on Grace. "Your name's Grace, right?"

Grace nods, confused because she has no idea what's going on, since I didn't really get much of a chance to explain anything but the basic problem with the Raven situation to her and Silas between the car park and here, due to all the fucking interruptions.

But Grace, laidback goddess that she is, simply takes it in her stride when Christine grins at her with a thumbs up.

"Good. Just play along," Christine instructs and then suddenly her volume goes super loud, which isn't uncommon for her. "Grace! Well knock me sideways with a shovel. Gracie! Long time no see! How are ye, lass?"

Then she pulls Grace out of Silas' constant loose hip-to-hip embrace and draws her into a hug to pat her enthusiastically on the back. Without even a split second of hesitation, Grace effortlessly joins in the charade.

The two of them give such a blinding performance, making up some cock-and-bull story between them about camping in the Scottish Highlands, complete with a cast of hilarious side characters, that there is a moment when even I actually question if they *do* know each other.

As their beautiful imaginations unfold, they start walking away, arms slung around each other's shoulders as if they were truly old mates. And all Silas and I can do is trail behind them with hastily laden plates and entirely genuine gobsmacked expressions on our faces.

Raven

I get fidgety about ten minutes after Christine leaves me with the promise that she's going to retrieve my man and bring the party here. My man. Her words. They scare the shit out of me, but somewhere, deep, deep down in my fucked-up psyche, I like that sound. Way too much.

I don't get time to dwell on it for long before I hear the front door of Christine's house open and four pairs of feet trampling up the stairs accompanied by raucous laughter. Mostly Christine's.

The door to her room opens, and she falls through with her arm around Jessica Rabbit, who is much prettier and less provocatively dressed in real life than her cartoon alter ego, in jeans and a tailored lace-up pirate shirt.

In real life, she is aptly named. She has a kind of simple grace that I could never attain, but without an ounce of arrogance. I would bet my bottom dollar she has no idea how much of a jewel she is.

"And then, remember when we blindfolded Paul and fed him worms, letting him think they were spaghetti? That was hilarious," she says, laughing.

She has a weird kind of transatlantic accent that makes me feel even more American than Christine and her Yorkshire twang do. The two of them are hiccuping with laughter now, tears gathering in the corners of their eyes.

"Yeah but not as funny as," Christine can barely get the rest of the sentence out because she's pretty much wetting herself, "when we fed Peter the spaghetti, pretending they were worms."

I have no idea what's going on, but their joy is infectious.

So much so, I gotta laugh at them laughing. I don't even stop when my heart goes into triple overtime, because once they're in the room, I see Rowan and the guy who I know to be Silas appear behind them with bemused expressions on their faces. While Silas stops by the redhead's side, Rowan swerves around the group.

He makes a beeline for the table and dumps the plate he's carrying next to Christine's and mine. Then he pulls me up from my chair, brushes a reassuring kiss over my lips that nearly knocks me out of my boots with surprise, turns me to face the others and cradles me possessively from behind. Christine and the redhead stop laughing and Christine's eyes go soft at the tenderness between Rowan and me.

"Guys? This is Raven," he introduces me with an almost reverent tone in his voice but releases me from his embrace again as soon as he says it, so I can make my own way toward them.

The respect makes me smile.

I'm not a possession, I'm my own person.

I take a step forward at the same time as Silas approaches me. He doesn't offer me a hand. Instead, he scrutinizes me unashamedly for a moment.

He is good-looking in a completely different way to Rowan. He's got typical boxer's charm. Slavic cheekbones, a flattened nose, and hazel eyes that are a bit disorientating because there are so many different colors in them.

He also carries a completely different aura to Rowan. There is no doubt in my mind that he is equally as deadly, but he's also way, way more serious. And when he smiles at me, it's not a broad smile but one that tells me I'll have to prove myself to him before it will ever reach his eyes.

He scares me, I realize with a jolt.

Not in a physical way because he also comes across as old school, as somebody who would never ever raise a hand to a woman. No, I am scared to the bone because I realize that his seal of approval will make or break my relationship with the man standing behind me. Relief floods my senses when Silas puts a hand on my shoulder and gently squeezes it.

"I'm Silas," he introduces himself in a voice barely above a whisper yet immensely powerful all the same.

Out of the corner of my eye, I see Christine relieve him of the plate he is carrying in the hand that isn't weighing me down. He lets her take it without losing eye contact with me for even a split second.

"I'm that fucker's best friend and brother," he adds. "Pleased to meet you."

He nods sharply at my tunic.

"You're risking getting fired for that wanker?"

I nod slowly and suddenly a naughty smile spreads across his face, one that definitely does touch the eyes and, fuck me, remodeled nasal cartilage aside, he sure is a handsome man. Model handsome.

"You're a fucking idiot," he says. "But to each their own."

He takes his hand off my shoulder to sling it around the redhead's waist and draws her to his side.

"This is Grace."

Grace and I nod at each other and I cock my head with a smile.

"You're with this asshole?" I ask her.

She grins back at me, my accent clearly falling into place for her.

"Sure am. I'm *his* yank."

She flicks her head at Silas. I raise my eyebrows.

"To each their own," I reply dryly.

She laughs, and a second later I find myself in a full-bosomed hug, surrounded by a soft woman who smells of vanilla and cinnamon and a little of car journey sweat.

"Don't fuck this up, Roe, I like her. We're keeping her," she says over my shoulder to the man who until this morning was nothing but an illicit affair.

Then he brought his family to meet me.

ROWAN

We hole up in Christine's room pretty much all day, occasional food runs notwithstanding.

Eventually, we need to leave for the obligatory communal gathering in the therapy centre at the end, during which the therapists blow smoke up our arses in front of our families.

I hate that as soon as we leave Christine's sanctuary Raven immediately becomes untouchable again. It's been the first time that I've had her all day long, to love and hold and sit on my lap, while we've been chewing the fat with Silas, Grace and Christine, and it feels right.

She didn't say it as such, but I knew she had been nervous about meeting Grace, so it's a relief to find that they get on like a house on fire.

Christine is a marvellous host and makes us all feel totally carefree. I can see that she will be great at her job as head nurse here, once Raven is gone.

I think about it as I lie in bed that night, Raven snuggled up against my side, one leg thrown over mine, and gently snoring across my left pec. She wore the stockings underneath all day, as promised, and I can smell how turned on she was, can feel her cream against my leg.

But my girl is a lightweight, it turns out, and two glasses of champagne hours ago mean I won't be getting any tonight.

But I still get to sleep in her room and, though my dick is painfully hard, that's plenty enough.

I hug her closer when the thought hits me that this will end soon. Two weeks behind us, two weeks to go. But I already know that no way on earth am I letting this one become the one that got away. All I have to do now is to convince myself that I am worth it. And then her that we both deserve some happiness.

I get the feeling the real work for me here has only just begun.

Under the light of the bedside lamp, that she didn't manage to switch off before she conked out, I trace the feathers of her tattoo with my fingertips and feel around the multitude of straight, long scars on her back that it covers up. Like splits from being whipped. She hasn't told me what they're from and I haven't asked. She'll tell me in her own good time.

The way I will tell her my stories in my own good time. The only difference being that in mine I'm rarely the victim, and even less seldom the hero.

I swallow hard as an image of Mum flashes through my mind. Not a significant one. Just a still frame from some regular morning, getting ready for school, her face slightly frazzled but still smiling as she hands me my lunch bag, her warm brown eyes, the male version of which I look into in the mirror every day, full of love for the world. For me.

As ever, I can't really bear it, so I concentrate harder on the woman in my arms, on the details of the bird in the storm on her back. It's so much starker than my ink. So much more meaningful. I feel her skin pebble under my exploration.

Her breath hitches as she burrows deeper.

"That's nice," she murmurs, making my hard-on quiver at the prospect that she may be waking up to us.

But she drifts off again and I shuffle awkwardly, so as not to disturb her too much as I reach over to switch the light off.

She slides her hand across my chest to sit over my heart as soon as the darkness envelops us. Guess she's not gone back to sleep after all.

"You are hurting," she says, and it is not a mumble.

I think about Lewin and our last session before the weekend, when the good doctor told me to make the best of halfway day. And I was sitting there in my therapy chair wondering how I could possibly make amends to a dead woman.

'Easy,' I hear my mum whisper through the darkness as clear as if she were standing in the room with us.

"I trade you my scars for yours," Raven's voice cuts through the echo of a voice long gone, and I take a deep breath.

"What was your favourite toy as a child?" I ask her in a low murmur, half hoping she'll go back to sleep, so we don't have to go through this.

There is a pause long enough for me to think I might have got my wish before she answers.

"I dunno. I didn't get to keep anything long enough for it to become my favourite," she says soberly, but then I can feel her smile against my skin. "But I used to draw faces on my fingertips and the gang on the right would sometimes go and visit with the gang on the left. If it was a big party, my toes would get involved."

She snickers.

I let it hang while I hug her closer, in awe not just of the woman she is now but of the child she is telling me about. I don't wait until she asks me back, though. I don't think I could tell her the truth if I waited for that.

"I had a marble run," I start.

I can feel her hold her breath and I know she can sense that what's coming is big.

"Not one of those crappy plastic ones but a wooden one, old. Mum bought it at a flea market for me. Lots of pieces, lots of different ways to set it up. It was my pride and joy. Just fascinated me. I'd come home every day and as soon as I was in the door, I'd start setting it up."

I swallow.

"Our house was pretty small, two bedrooms, one living-dining room downstairs, so I had to share with both my half siblings. It was ram packed with stuff all the time, so I often set up the run on the landing. I was allowed, as long as I tidied everything away by dinner. Mum would moan about having to step around it, but she didn't mind, really. Sometimes, if I had enough time before dinner, I'd set it up, so it went all the way down the stairs. And that is exactly what I did that day. I couldn't even tell you what weekday it was. It was that ordinary. Came home from school, set up my marble run, played for a couple of hours, until Mum shouted up that dinner was in twenty. So I whizzed around, collecting my shit and throwing it in its box. Like every day. Washed my hands, went down to the living room, where my brother and sister were playing. My sister was still so little she was in her playpen. My little brother was building a tower with Duplo in front of the TV. James, their dad, had just come home from work and was still in his site clothes. He was a builder and self-employed, and he was filing invoices. When I came down, he went up to have a shower. I helped Mum lay the table and then she asked me to put Sammy and Adam in their highchairs, while she went to let James know it was time to come down. I remember her steps up the stairs and her knock on the bathroom door to tell James dinner was ready. Next thing I heard was the sound of somebody taking a tumble. There was no scream. Only a gasp just before it happened, loud enough so we could hear it downstairs. I clicked Sammy into her chair and then ran out into the hallway. And there was Mum, limbs everywhere at funny angles, eyes wide in shock but not blinking any longer."

I stop talking while Raven shuffles up higher, her hand wandering over my chest, upwards to land on the side of my neck. Her thumb caresses the soft stubble on my jaw. My instinct is to bat her hand away because I don't deserve her tenderness, but I don't want to hurt her feelings. So my voice turns rough instead.

"It's a joke, right? Leaving a marble on the stairs and somebody breaking their neck. Well, it's a joke until it isn't. My life is a fucking warning story that old wives tell little children."

She clambers on top of me fully, her knees left and right of my waist, her butt hovering over my dick and her left elbow by my ear while her right hand keeps stroking my face. My brows, my stubble, my ears, my lips.

"What colour was it?" she asks softly after a while.

"Yellow," I answer without hesitation, and feel the atoms of grief and guilt rearranging themselves inside my soul.

Such an irrelevant question and yet somehow, apparently, the one I've been waiting for all my fucking life.

There are only three people in the world who I told about the little glass ball I found at the bottom of the stairs that night before I pocketed it and pretended to the world, to myself, that I didn't know how she had fallen.

From Silas, I got understanding.

From Lewin, I got fact.

From Raven, I get the forgiveness that lies in the detail. Talk about nailing it.

I hardly get time to process before her soft lips meet mine.

Raven

I have no words of comfort for him, but I have my body, and — appropriate or not — it's awake again now and it craves him. I might not be able to heal his mind, but I can sure as fuck assuage the pain by making him forget for as long as it takes us to chase our next orgasm.

I lower my ass onto his still semi-hard cock, trapping it between me and the hard slab of his abs. The movement brings me away from his face level and he lifts his neck off the pillow, straining so he doesn't lose contact with my lips.

He parts them with his tongue, delving deep inside my mouth to devour me in that way that is uniquely Rowan. He reaches up to slip a hand under my hair and cradles the back of my head, tethering me to his kiss. I grind over him as he already goes rock-solid again, bucking against me with a subdued groan, the long ridge of his cock pressing hard against me, all the way from my butthole to my clit. I extract my tongue from the tangle it is in and draw back enough to whisper against his lips.

"Roll me over."

I feel him go very still, sense the frown forming between his brows.

"You sure?"

"Yeah, Rowan, I'm sure. Help me forget."

"What if..."

"Just make it dirty enough and there won't be a 'what if'," I answer with more confidence than I feel.

"You want kinky missionary?" he asks with a grin in his voice, and actually rolls me onto my back until he looms above me, pinning me down. "That I can do."

Despite propping his weight up and shifting it a little to the side in order not to crush me, he's still heavy. So much heavier than Tom ever was. So totally different in feel and width and *everything* that I have to laugh at myself for thinking it could ever be comparable.

"You okay there, lady?" Rowan asks through my low chuckles, while he lets a hand wander between us to position his cock's head by my entrance.

"Yeah. I'm perfect," I answer as he smoothly slides inside of me.

One stroke, gentle but true. Until he's hilt-deep. Then he takes my left leg and makes me hook it over his shoulder, so I can feel his balls resting against the underside of my ass. He runs a gentle hand around to my backside and palms my buttock while he slowly starts rocking into me.

"Good?" he growls.

"Uh-huh," I answer. Because I can't find the words for 'fucking amazing'. Nobody has ever been this deep before and it's fucking magic.

His mouth finds my ear and he nibbles the lobe.

"Anyone ever played with your arse, Raven?"

"You," I mumble back. Because it's true. He's been gently skimming and probing all week and it's been amazing. But he's been waiting for me to give him the full green light, I think. I hear him blow out a breath across my ear.

"No, I mean *really*. Anyone ever gone *in*?"

He's not breaking rhythm throughout this conversation even once, his hard length going in and out of my dripping pussy like clockwork, rubbing a semicircle over my clit each time his root meets my mound, while his balls slap gently against my perineum, and just the suggestion he's making is having me clench around his dick.

The pleasure is intense and I can't concentrate, so I just garble an answer, but he hears the 'no' in it.

"No, you don't want it. Or no, you haven't had it," he growls into my ear.

"Not had it," I manage to reply through my panting. "Want."

"You are so my woman," he grunts then withdraws and slips his hand around to gather up some of my juice with his whole palm in one lewd, scooping motion. I whimper at the sudden loss of him but spark at his fingers and palm sliding over me. I cry out as he rams home again, chuckling.

"Shhh. You're gonna wake the others. So impatient. Just getting nice and slippery for you."

He starts rubbing the juice he's gathered around my butthole with his middle finger in gentle circles, going deeper and deeper until he's suddenly all the way in. I feel *full*, nerve-endings sparking fucking everywhere, little lightning strikes of pleasure firing inside me relentlessly. And through it all, I hear him groan in my ear as he starts pumping his cock into me for real.

"Oh fuck," he presses out. "Fuck this is so hot. I can feel me inside of you. Do it for me, honey, please."

He's begging. Rowan Hadlow-Fuller-O'Brien, *The Python*, is begging me to stick my finger in his ass and fuck me if that doesn't drive me right into another dimension of turned on. So I slip a hand between us, gather some juice around his pistoning dick, and then I grabble around for my target.

His butt is so tight I don't think I could get even my pinkie in without hurting him, but then he begs again, and somehow my index finger pops right inside.

"Oh fuck, fuck, fuck, fuck," he mumbles as he finds my mouth and we fill each other in every single way possible, all at once, until we come together in one glorious explosion.

Afterwards, we lie tangled and breathless for a long, long time, clinging to each other for balance.

"Kinky enough?" he asks, laughing, when we're recalibrated.

I sigh deeply.

"Yup. I think missionary is my new favorite position."

"Good," he says earnestly and kisses the top of my head. "*Mission* accomplished."

I shake my head at the lame joke.

"You're a sex god but, really, don't give up the day job for comedy any time soon."

He hugs me tighter.

"That burns, beautiful, but, hey, I'll settle for sex god."

I slap him playfully.

"Go to sleep," I order and laugh at his instant pretend snoring.

I know full well that he's nowhere near falling asleep.

We're going to clean up, and then he'll be good to go again before long.

And this time, it'll be long and drawn out.

I know my man.

ROWAN

I wake up from a deafening alarm going off that I've never heard before.

I shoot up in bed and see Raven already standing next to it, hectically pulling her tunic over her head then climbing into her jeans without bothering with either bra or panties.

"Ring Christine. House phone. Dial zero then twelve," she orders without missing a beat. "Tell her we have an emergency and to get her ass over here right away."

I scramble to reach the landline phone on her bedside table while she's already halfway to the door.

"What do I tell her?" I shout at Raven's back. "What's the emergency?"

"I don't know," she shouts back, descending the stairs. "It's coming from Simon's room."

It's then that I see the panel of lights integrated into her phone. Five lights, five room numbers. Simon's room number is flashing while the alarm keeps bleating out of the phone's loudspeaker. I lift the receiver and in a desperate attempt to shut off the noise, I push the blinking button. It works.

I dial Christine, and she answers after a couple of rings. I relay the message. Her voice is instantly alert.

"Go help her," she bellows at me then hangs up.

I throw my cargo trousers on, not bothering with anything else, and follow Raven down the stairs. As I arrive at Simon's room, Charlie is sprinting up the stairs with a defibrillator he must have retrieved from somewhere on the ground floor, while Tristan is standing in the door of his room, pale and disorientated.

One look at an ashen Simon, laid out on his back on the floor while Raven is pumping his chest, tells me all I need to know.

Charlie pushes past me and Raven starts instructing him on the defib, until the built-in mechanical voice takes over.

"Rowan," she calls out to me just before the machine tells her it's ready. "Ring for an ambulance. Tell them we have a man in cardiac arrest. Now!"

Raven

He doesn't make it.

We all fight for him as hard as we can. Me, Christine, the paramedic, the EMTs, and later the doctors in the emergency room, but he never regains consciousness.

And I feel guilty as hell.

Simon's last act on earth was to push the red button in his room and maybe if I hadn't been fucked into oblivion and hadn't taken so long to wake up, and maybe if I hadn't been butt naked and hadn't lost precious minutes getting my clothes on, I might have got there early enough to save him.

I know the point is moot.

I know it's a futile discourse.

I've lost my fair share of patients during my time as a nurse, mostly in training when I was in ER, but some in rehab also.

Halosan has one of the best track records in the industry for not losing patients, but we are still dealing with addicts and from time to time one of them dies. But it's never happened in *my* house, on *my* watch, before and that makes it feel completely different.

The fact I'm not dealing very well doesn't change Halosan protocol, though, and Halosan protocol says that I am the liaison between Simon's family, the hospital, the police and the coroner.

The basic tox screen takes ten days to come back from the lab and in the meantime, I'm the go-between for everyone involved, while all I really want to do is hide in bed and never come out.

Alone.

ROWAN

I lose my girl the moment Simon loses his life.

She just vanishes from my grasp while still in plain view.

Raven and Christine follow the ambulance and return a few hours later with the news that Simon passed away in A&E.

The Denyers immediately call a whole Village meeting in the therapy hall, where guests are offered the choice between staying the course or going into alternative arrangements. Everybody decides to stay, because nobody is in the right frame of mind to make a decision at this point.

A couple of coppers come in the afternoon and ask us if we saw Simon use anything. It seems a bit odd, considering he was here for alcohol dependency, but I guess that's regular procedure when someone dies in rehab. They search Simon's room and seal it until the coroner's report comes back. Then they leave to speak to Rothman.

About ten minutes later, Rothman, all self-important, appears in our cottage kitchen to sniff around Raven.

I listen to him offer his support with paperwork and with packing up Simon's stuff for the family, if Raven finds it too hard to deal with on her own, and my blood boils. He's such a smarmy git. Fucking opportunist. I know people like him. Masking preying on weakness as concern.

I can't believe he's using this as an opening to get into her pants. He even makes her a cup of tea while he asks her how she is coping and all that. The joke's on him 'cause she doesn't drink tea.

And, of course, she keeps him at a distance, informing him in her prime clipped nurse's voice that she is fine, and that Simon's stuff is not to be touched until the police give it the all clear and unseal the room, but that she's sure she will be able to manage once the time comes.

He buggers off again with his tail between his legs.

Next, a shallow kind of grief descends over The Village like a lead blanket, and that thing happens that always happens when somebody dies that nobody truly liked yet nobody hated either. Everybody, even people in houses we barely have had anything to do with, suddenly knew the cunt really well and liked him lots.

I keep out of it. I am not hypocritical enough to join in that chorus. But I'm not impervious either. My mind keeps wandering to his wife and kids. To that last spark of hope between them. I feel for them. But in the grey light of morning, after yet another night alone in my bed and when there is nobody around to see the truth in my eyes, I can admit to myself that what really pisses me off about Simon's death is that it has finished whatever there was between Raven and me.

It's not that I didn't try.

I intercepted her on the landing at bedtime that first night. Just stood there and waited for her to come out of the bathroom and wordlessly opened my arms to offer her a hug. She looked at me, shook her head once and disappeared into her room.

I've never known one measly shake of the head to be so devastating, but what really haunts me is the expression in her eyes.

She blames herself.

She blames *us* somehow, though I'm stumped as to how she came to that fucking conclusion.

But there it was, in her eyes, as clear as day.

I tried again the next night.

She wouldn't even look at me.

And the next.

"Just stop," she hissed.

Then the first chance she gets, she moves down a floor.

We're over.

The sad thing is, I deserve it. I pissed all over Silas' happiness with Niamh. So why should *I* get to keep the first woman I ever fall in love with?

'Cause that's what I am. Totally, utterly, irrevocably in love with a woman who now looks at me as if I am the devil incarnate.

Well played, Karma, well played.

Raven

Charlie is the first one to fall.

He comes to me on the Thursday morning following Simon's death and tells me his parents are collecting him the next day. He makes a feeble joke about how he's spoken to the Denyers and will get a whole freebie stay next time.

I smile sadly.

"I hope there isn't a next time, Charlie," I tell him honestly.

He grins.

"Don't be silly, woman. Of course there will be a next time. I'm a fucking rock star!"

He turns away from the bottom of the stairs, where we are having this conversation, and starts bounding up. Three steps later, he turns around, comes back down, throws his arms around me in a tight hug and lifts me off my feet.

"But it won't be the same without you, Ray," he whispers into my ear.

Then he sets me down and runs back up the stairs.

"That's not my name!" I shout after him.

"You need to take that up with Elias, *Ravenna*," he hollers back and then slams the door to his room shut.

As soon as he is gone the following morning, I move down to the floor below.

I can't bear being that close to Rowan any longer. He keeps looking at me with so much love, and it hurts to deny him, but I just can't go there anymore. It's like I've snapped out of a trance. And in the stark light of day, I've finally realized that what we were doing was wrong on so many levels it makes me want to hurl.

The moment I move down onto the floor below, Tristan comes to me.

He knocks on what was Charlie's room and is now mine, just after I've plugged the master phone into the socket. I'm in the middle of staring at the emergency alarm buttons on it as if I could turn back time and somehow undo what's happened, if I just hypnotize this phone long enough, when he raps gingerly on the open door.

"Raven?" he asks tentatively, and I turn to face him.

"When is she coming to pick you up?" I ask him before he can even tell me that he's called his mom.

To be honest, I'm impressed he didn't leave first. I think he might have even stuck it out, if Charlie had stayed and if the atmosphere between Rowan and me wasn't so fucking weird.

"She's not," he says. "I'm taking the train from Poole this afternoon."

"How are you getting there?"

"Hiking part of the way. Then bus. Rowan is coming with me."

My heart stops and searing pain slices through me where relief should have set in.

He's leaving me.

I take a deep breath and try to focus on the boy in front me.

Tristan shyly takes a couple of steps into the room and holds out both his hands for me to take. I slip my palms into his clammy ones and squeeze them.

"You did well, Tristan," I tell him.

He shrugs and looks over my shoulder at the wall but doesn't let go of my hands. Tears pool in his eyes.

"I really didn't like him," he says then looks at me with a vague smile through the tears. "But I think maybe he taught me more than this entire program did."

"Did he?"

"His *death* did, yeah."

He nods and the nod pushes a tear over the edge. He takes his right hand out of mine and wipes at his cheek with the back of it. I wait for a moment, but when he doesn't elaborate, I just pull him into a hug.

"You take care of yourself, kid. There is a whole world out there. There is a whole load of life to live. Don't waste it. Save the gaming for when you're old and weak and your body won't let you do the real thing any longer."

He laughs a watery laugh at that.

"That's kind of where I'm at," he says as he withdraws from me. "Thank you, Raven, for everything."

ROWAN

"Are you certain about this, Rowan? I think we've made great progress, but I'm not sure you're ready to go back out there just yet," Lewin says, looking at me with critical eyes.

I've just told her that I'm leaving with Tristan this afternoon. She's not exactly shocked.

"You think I'm gonna go gamble Sheena's house away again?"

There is surprise on her face when I say it, and then she laughs.

"You know what? I had actually forgotten that's why you're here. So no, I don't think so. To be honest, I don't think the gambling was ever your actual problem. More like a symptom of an entirely different issue."

"Isn't that true for all addiction?"

"To a point. But you are a very different kettle of fish from most people who come through here."

"I don't know if I should be flattered or insulted."

She grins.

"Oh, always flattered. It's the unusual ones that make a counsellor's heart tick."

"I thought you were supposed to see the weird and wonderful in all your clients."

"Yeah," she utters dismissively. "That is the theory. So, are you certain about this? I understand if you don't want to stay in Ravenna's house right now with what's happened and everyone else leaving and with a room that's still sealed by the police."

She pauses to pull a face which says, 'I wouldn't want to stay there either'.

"But we could arrange something," she carries on. "I believe one of Matilda's guests left before all of this occurred, so she has a vacancy in her house. You could finish your course of therapy. I know there is only a week left, but I feel that you would be so much stronger if you finished what you started here. "

I actually pretend to think about it for a moment, although I know I could never do that.

Leaving here is one thing.

Moving into another house would be a kick in the teeth for Raven that she doesn't deserve, no matter how much her rejection hurts me right now. No, it's best that I take myself out of her sphere completely. Give her space to breathe, to come to terms.

I shake my head.

"No," I answer Lewin. "I want to go home."

Lewin sighs but nods acceptingly.

"So what are you planning on doing when you leave here? Where is home?"

"Sheena's house," I say and shrug. "No idea what I'm gonna do to make money. No more fighting, though. Venue security, maybe. There are a lot of bouncing jobs in Brighton. Or I'll ask Sheena if they need a night watchman at the hotel where she works. Personal trainer. Whatever. I'll figure something out."

"Okay," she smiles, a wide smile I haven't seen on her before, and blows one of those wisps of hair that always frame her face out of her line of sight. "I want you to think about maybe doing something with your brain, Rowan. 'Cause there is a lot of it. And you know that Tristan was one of my clients here, too, right? Without breaking confidentiality, let me say that I have a strong suspicion you really helped bring him out of his shell. I hear you are a great swim coach. A great *teacher*. Just putting that out there. Sometimes these things run in families. And I want you to think about whether you want to carry on using your body to get through life or whether maybe it's time to engage your grey matter. But you're right. All of that is just the fine print. And as much as I would have liked to help you figure out the fine print, you *are* done here."

She stands up, pulls her cardigan closer around herself, despite the fact it is still hot as hell on Purbeck and offers me a hand.

"Don't fuck it up again."

I take and shake it. Her grip is firm.

"I won't," I say.

Then I leave my last therapy session, half an hour early.

I swing by the Allsorts' house to give Barbara a squeeze goodbye and then by the gym to do the same with Alan before I go and finish packing my backpack.

Raven

I'm in the kitchen, emptying the fridge of rotten food, when Tristan and Rowan appear in full hiking gear, backpacks shouldered and ready to leave. I turn around and lean back against the counter when I hear them.

"Bye, Raven," Tristan says and waves.

"Take care," I answer, nodding sharply but not moving from my spot.

We said goodbye already, we had our hug. He understands and leaves, pushing past Rowan and out of the house. The front door shuts.

And then it's just us.

The man who healed and destroyed me anew, all in one night, and me. There is so much warmth and love and agony in his dark brown gaze and I can't deal. Again. I hold my hand up in a warding off gesture. I don't want to talk to him. I can't. The pain takes my breath away, cuts off my capacity to produce sound.

But it appears I don't need to. He doesn't say anything either, and I turn my back on him.

I hear his backpack land on the floor with a thud and before I know it, he is on me, slinging his arms around me from behind and holding me in a vise-like grip.

I start struggling, but he doesn't let go.

I stop thrashing when his lips find my ear, and against all rationale, his hot breath fanning over my cheek makes my knees go wobbly and turns my insides to mush with desire.

"I'm going now," he rumbles in my ear. "But I want you to know, I'm in love with you, Raven. I'm so deeply and utterly in love with you, it hurts knowing that you exist. It kills me that you hate me. But I get it. And I deserve it. I deserve it anyway for being an arsehole. And I deserve it specifically for making you do shit that was unprofessional. But remember this, Simon dying was not your fault, or mine, or *ours*. It just happened. Shit happens. Don't beat yourself up about it. I'll get out of your hair now and that'll make it easier for you, but if at any point in your life you want me to come and hug you, or fuck, or both, ring me. I left my number on your bed. Whenever, wherever. Even if you're on the other side of the world getting around with a Zimmer frame. I'll be there like a shot."

He slips a hand around my neck and tilts my head, making me look over my shoulder at him. Then he kisses me, forcefully yet with great care at the same time, until my already violently beating heart wants to explode in my chest, and I see stars.

He releases me, and I have to brace myself on the countertop, so my legs don't give out.

Then, just as suddenly as he was on me, he's gone.

I hear him grab his backpack and seconds later, the front door falls shut once more.

I pick up a fuzzy yogurt and pour it into the sink.

ROWAN

They've made a bedroom for me out of the old living room while I was gone.

Sheena's house in Shoreham, a small town just along the coast from Brighton, is a classic two-up two-down.

Silas and Grace share the master bedroom upstairs and there is a Polish language student called Kalina, who is currently residing in my room from yesteryear, next to theirs. Sheena sleeps on the ground floor in what was once the dining room. Before I came to The Village, I was kipping on the terrible, too-short pull-out sofa in the living room for a couple of weeks, but while I've been in rehab, they've given the room a complete make over.

They got rid of the furniture, moved the TV into Sheena's room, gave the walls a coat of paint and made me a bed out of some pallets, with the biggest mattress I've ever seen on top. In the middle of the mattress, Sol and Luna, the two resident cats, are currently curled up around each other, clearly taking the job of testing it out for me very seriously. The bed more or less fills the room now and that makes me smile.

During my time on the underground fight circuit, I got used to sleeping with my feet off a bunk or tucked into a ball. If there even was a bunk. Having a bed I can stretch out on is high on my list of favourite things in the world.

Sheena also got me a wardrobe and a desk that both look suspiciously like surplus from the Palais, the hotel where she works.

"It's not much," Sheena says when she shows me. "We were going to put some finishing touches on. But you came home early."

She doesn't ask me why.

The beauty of Sheena O'Brien, the woman who became my second mother when I was twelve, is that she always either knows the whole story already or will wait until you volunteer it. I'm not volunteering anything right now.

I haven't told Silas or Grace either, but they're not stupid, they can put two and two together. Last time they saw me, I had a girl. Now I've come home early, alone.

The two of them are in the kitchen right now, cooking dinner for us all, leaving the big reveal of my new habitat to Sheena.

Standing in the centre of the room with Sheena by my elbow, I look around and swallow hard.

"Are you sure about this?" I ask, turning to her.

"Look at me," she says.

And I do.

She looks different. When I first came back to town a few weeks ago, I was shocked to see how much she had changed. Sheena used to be a model before Silas was born, worked for some seriously famous photographers. She has the most amazing bone structure a woman can have. Yet when I first saw her again, after years away, I barely recognized her. This once glamorous woman had turned into a drab, pale shadow of her former self.

My fault.

But with the threat of repossession not hanging over her head any longer, she's obviously felt the freedom to start digging out that old self.

While I have been doing my thing at The Village, she's bleached her short grey hair, got it properly styled and has started wearing makeup again.

And she's back in the designer trouser suits she used to favour when we were kids.

"You look good," I say.

"Yeah." She smiles. "My boys are back together. I'm happy."

She comes closer, reaches up and cups my face in her hands.

"Rowan O'Brien, I might not have given birth to you and I might not have spent the first twelve years of your life with you, and I'd never dream of trying to replace your real mum, but I love you. I strongly believe that fate brought me and James together purely, so I could become *your* next mummy. And so Silas could have the brother he craved. When I signed those adoption papers, I signed them for life. Through thick and thin. Not till you turn eighteen, or till the first moment you fuck up a little."

I take a deep breath, wanting to protest the 'little', but she is one step ahead of me.

"Or a lot," she adds.

"So what you're saying is that a Rowan's for life, not just for Christmas," I quip, and that makes her laugh.

"Something like that. Now bend down here, you big hulk, and give me a hug. My neck's getting stiff."

I do as I'm told and squeeze her hard. She pats me on the back then withdraws.

"Better leave you to unpack," she says and does just that.

I don't have much. Everything I own is in my backpack, everything important I own is in my jacket pockets, so it doesn't take long before I'm done.

As soon as I've packed away the last couple of things and stowed away my rucksack, I don't quite know what to do with myself. I need to keep busy, so I don't keep thinking about Raven.

During the journey home, I was okay as long as I was sharing the train ride with Tristan. Once he starts talking, the kid's really good company, and we had a proper laugh. But when we got to London, we had to split, finding different stations for our different destinations. I left him with my number and Sheena's address, telling him to look me up if he ever comes down to Brighton, before we said our goodbyes at Waterloo.

That's when reality started kicking in for me. As long as I had the kid with me, it was almost as if we hadn't quite left The Village yet. I think there was a part of my brain that was kidding itself into thinking we were just on a little day trip and would go back tonight.

The truth hit me full force when I'd made it across London and boarded the train homeward at Victoria.

Whoever said it's better to have loved and lost was a complete and utter idiot. On the outside, I might have been this massive bloke in a seat by the window, who looked like you don't wanna mess with him, but on the inside I was curled up in the foetal position around a ball of pain.

It strikes me that, actually, that is what I want to get back to. Curling up in a corner. I *want* to think about her, *want* to feel the loss, if that's the only way I can be close to her now. But before I can shell myself out of my clothes and crawl into bed, Grace calls through the house, calling everyone to the kitchen for dinner.

So I go and have stew.

It's sitting down to eat one of Silas' thick soups, more than anything else, that makes me feel the disconnect.

Five people around a table.

A week apart.

Different setting, different faces, different voices.

I look at Kalina, Grace, Silas and Sheena and wonder if all of them are still going to be here in the morning.

I think of Raven in a now empty cottage.

I wonder if she's staying there tonight or if she's gone to sleep over at Christine's maybe. I don't want her to be alone with the ghost of Simon rattling around the house.

Suddenly I feel like a complete cunt for leaving her.

I drop my spoon and look up into the round.

"Sorry, guys, I need to go make a phone call."

I leave the table in a hurry and retreat into my new bedroom.

I don't have Raven's mobile number, but I know how to dial through to our cottage and that's what I do. She picks up on the second ring.

"Good evening, The Village, Ravenna Vanhofd speaking," she answers like the pro that she is.

"Raven? It's me."

She doesn't react immediately. I can hear her breath hitch and I wonder if she's been sitting on the bed, crying.

"Did you forget something?" she asks coolly after a second.

"No, I...I wanted to make sure you're alright."

"I'm a *nurse*, Rowan. I'm fine," she says in that clipped tone she is so fucking good at.

The one that cuts you down to nothing.

I am nothing.

"Anything else I can do for you? Because Halosan staff don't fraternize with clients before, during or *after* they've left the program, and I have things to organize here. As you may remember, I'm handing over to Christine next week, and then I'll be going home. So you can imagine there is still a lot of paperwork and packing to do."

"You're going home?" I ask bewildered. "I thought you were going to travel Europe first."

She sighs audibly at that.

"I don't feel like that's appropriate under the circumstances," she answers matter of fact, before her voice softens a little. "I'm just waiting for the coroner's report and for the police to unseal Simon's room, and then I'm gone. I rang my foster parents to ask if I can come home for a bit when I leave here. Elena cried with relief when I asked. John took a tumble coming out of church on Sunday and broke his ankle. They're struggling. They got a full house and they're not young, so I'm going home to help out for a while. I've got my month holiday and once that's over, the bosses said we can talk about compassionate leave until John is back on his feet."

There is this magical moment while she is telling me all this, when it feels like I've got her back and my heart starts beating double time.

"You want me to come with you?"

It's out before I can think about it.

There is a pause. And then she delivers the final blow.

"Absolutely not," she says, voice below freezing. "Whatever this was, it's over, Rowan. Accept it. Move on. Have a nice life."

She hangs up.

I sling my phone away and it lands somewhere on the carpet. I rip the socks off my feet, peel myself out of my trousers and t-shirt and crawl into the middle of the bed. Then I let the tears flow freely.

Through the haze of my pain, I hear the clinking of dishes as they're getting washed up and the voices of the others. There is no laughter, I note, just serious, slightly subdued conversation.

I hear the kettle being boiled. Once, twice.

About an hour after dinner, Sheena goes to her room and switches the TV on. It stays with me as a low murmur, reverberating through the wall.

A little later, the tiny Polish girl's soft footsteps pad up the stairs. Kalina does her bathroom run, and then I can hear her bed creaking above my head as she, too, settles down for the night.

Silas and Grace are still in the kitchen, but so quiet I can barely hear them through my never-ending tears.

Eventually, I half drift off to sleep, an image of Raven alone in the cottage ghosting through my mind. I send her my love through the ether, even though I know it will be ill received.

Then, I finally fall fully asleep.

I don't know how much time has passed when I wake from the door to my room being gently pushed open. The house is plunged into darkness, bar the few rays of yellow streetlight that make it around the gaps in my curtains. The road outside is deadly quiet, so I guess it's past pub closing time, because our house is opposite a pub car park.

I realise I've been crying in my sleep. I guess I never stopped.

Silas slips into the room.

"You okay?" he asks in that quiet voice of his that's always rasping just above a whisper.

It's still amazing to me how that happened. Our voices breaking. Mine literally *broke*. One minute I was a normal kid with a normal voice, the next I had these thunderclaps coming out of my throat whenever I opened my mouth. His just gently, quietly matured into this mellow rasp.

I don't answer him and turn away, towards the window.

Undeterred, he walks further into the room, negotiating the dark perfectly until he reaches the other side of the bed, so I'm facing him. He sits down on the mattress by my side and his scent invades my nostrils. He smells of Silas, and sex.

"Hoof over," he says.

I hesitate for a moment, but then I do it anyway. He clambers into the bed and slips under the duvet, pulling at it until he's freed it from beneath my bulk. He throws it over me and wraps his arm around my shoulder. A fresh flood of tears makes its way up my throat. He brings his hand up to cradle the back of my head and draws me into his shoulder, absorbing the shakes wracking my body.

When I first came to live here, it had been a year and a bit after Mum had died. The shock was only just wearing off and I'd finally started crying at night. And there was this new kid in my life, who I was suddenly sharing a room with, and he came and held me. Just like this. Every time.

And now he is doing it again.

Only this time, he's not alone.

As soon as he's wrapped me in his hug, another presence enters the room, and a second later, Grace slips in behind me and slings her arms around my waist, so her hand lands on Silas' hip.

I still barely know this woman who has made Silas so incredibly happy, but together they cocoon me for a long time, Silas rhythmically sweeping his thumb back and forth over the base of my skull.

It's intense and the need to crack a joke builds up inside of me, despite my despair.

"She's broken me," I start deadpan, through the tears. "Your woman is wearing silk and I can feel her tits on my back and you both smell like you've already fucked each other's brains out tonight, but there is nothing doing here. Raven has broken me."

It's supposed to push them away, but instead they hug me even tighter.

"She clearly hasn't broken your death wish, though," Silas responds as he pulls me closer.

"Yeah, I wouldn't mention his girlfriend's boobs if you know what's good for you," Grace chips in, withdrawing a bit and slapping me playfully on the shoulder. "You creeped me out the first time I met you, we've come a long way in a short time, don't ruin it," she adds more seriously then snuggles back up to me and reaches over to rest her hand on Silas' hip again, before she asks softly, "What happened? I liked her. She was fun."

"She wasn't just fun. She was perfect," I say.

And then I tell them about the woman who broke a heart I didn't even know was up for the breaking and about the dead guy called Simon, while they keep cuddling me all the way into the small hours.

"Hmm," Grace mutters when I'm finally done. "Poor guy and all, but I don't believe this is really about his death or her feeling guilty. Can't be the first time she lost a patient. I've met a lot of nurses in my life. Too many. They're tough cookies. Sounds to me more like she has some serious intimacy issues. I watched her watch you when we came to visit. Most of the time, when you weren't looking, she looked totally freaked. Like she had no idea what to do with all those feelings for you. I bet you got too close. I swear, if that Simon guy hadn't died, she'd have found a different reason to push you away."

They hug me again, and eventually they leave.

But I don't feel alone any longer.

Raven

The last, and first ever, time I had a house entirely to myself as an adult was a year ago, when I arrived in the UK and started setting up The Village for its first intake of clients.

It was the strangest sensation. After forever having people around me, it felt super exciting — and naughty. Back then, I'd walk around the whole cottage semi-naked at night, listening to The Atomic Aces on the speaker and singing along at the top of my lungs. I guess other people do that kind of thing when they first get their own apartment. I had to get to twenty-seven and three quarters to get a tiny taste of it.

And now?

Now the taste of sole occupant is bitter.

I don't want to be here on my own any longer. It's been six nights of wandering around an empty cottage. I could have moved in with Christine, who offered me a side of her bed as soon as she heard that all my rats had left the sinking ship. Or I could have taken the empty guest room in Matilda's house.

But it didn't feel right.

Not even after the Denyers, Rothman and even Lewin took turns to come and tell me that anyone would understand if I didn't want to sleep here for the time being. Lewin, who hides a heart of gold behind her scalpel-like mind, even offered me a room in *her* cottage.

But I said no.

It would have felt like defeat.

Like I am deserting.

I'm not deserting.

I'm standing my ground.

I'm a professional.

I will stay here until it's time to go to Heathrow and get on my flight back home.

Period.

Until then, I don't really know what to do with myself any longer. Everything is in order now. Christine could take over at the drop of a hat and it would be a breeze for her.

A year ago, there was a boatload of things on my to-do list.

Recruiting nurses, conferring with the Denyers over a blueprint for therapy schedules, checking all cottages were appropriately furnished and that everything was in working order. Writing the guest handbook, setting up the deal with The Windchimes and organizing grocery suppliers. And the gazillion other things that I've forgotten I did by now.

In a way, The Village is my baby. Even if I didn't once stray from the company concept, it's got my stamp all over it. It's my final masterpiece for Halosan, my graduation from the company. Wherever they will send me for my last few months, after John's ankle has healed, it will just be a holding pen until I leave completely.

I should leave Purbeck behind with a sense of pride but, really, all I feel is broken.

Rowan broke me.

I wish he hadn't left.

I wish he'd given me another day or two to process.

I would have come around, I think.

But I'm too proud — too scared — to call him.

After Rowan was gone, I retrieved the piece of paper he left on my bed, went to the sink in the bathroom and held a lighter to it. But I chickened out and doused the flames under the faucet before the digits could catch fire. Then I saved them to my cell. My actual, real cell, not the phone Halosan gave me for my stay.

And there they sit.

Under ROB.

Now I taunt myself by looking at his number every night. It's what I was doing when he called me Friday evening.

I'm not sure whether I think if I stare at them long enough, he'll ring me again.

It's been six nights.

I moved back into my own room, under the roof, on day three. I never washed the sheets when I fled our floor, so they still smell of him. But each night, the scent gets fainter.

I miss him so hard.

And I have no idea what to do with that feeling. I've never missed anyone like this in my life. I've never missed anyone, period. And I never startled the way I do now every time the house phone rings. Always hoping it is him again. But it hasn't been.

He called me that once and that was all.

I don't blame him.

I *did* wish him a nice life.

I'm a fucking idiot.

My thoughts are interrupted by an unfamiliar, soft knock on the cottage door and then somebody lets themselves in. My heartbeat goes through the roof in the irrational hope it may be him, returning to me. It does that every time somebody comes to visit with me now.

Usually, it's Christine. Sometimes Alan comes over to check on me. A couple of times, Rothman has suddenly appeared in the house. The asshole never knocks.

Today, however, it's Ed Denyer in his full cardiganed glory.

The only difference between him and his wife Judy is that he's got less hair, the thicker glasses and that his gray cardigans are cable knit with a shawl collar while hers are flat knit with a v-neck.

They are the strangest people to work with because they present this impenetrable unit of total blankness. It makes them great group therapists, though. They never let their own issues cloud their facilitation.

The fact that they are usually always together makes the appearance of Ed on his own in the hallway extra disconcerting.

"Ravenna," he says.

And I can't help wondering, for the millionth time in my life, why people do that. Use your name as a greeting. As if they think they need to remind you of who you are. I always want to say 'well shit, so I am' but, of course, I don't.

Instead, I remind him of who he is. Because that's the correct response.

"Ed." I pause. "Where is Judy?"

"Taking the group session on her own, so I can talk to you."

"Okay," I answer hesitantly.

I wasn't really aware the morning had progressed into therapy hours already. I've been losing track of time lately without anyone to shepherd about.

"What can I do for you?" I ask, turning my back to return to the kitchen from where I came. "Do you want a tea or a coffee?"

If in doubt, offer tea.

"A cup of tea would be nice," he answers politely. "Milk, one sugar, please."

He follows me, and while I make him his tea, we have a polite chat about the weather. We come to the conclusion that it's still hot as hell outside but maybe not inner hell any longer. And apparently never too hot for the Denyers to wear their cardigans. Sometimes I wonder whether they employed Lewin based on a shared appreciation for all things woollen.

I hand Ed his tea and take my half finished, cold coffee.

"Shall we go sit down?" I suggest and indicate the dining room. "I'm guessing you didn't leave Judy to do the group session on her own so we could discuss the weather."

"Quite," Ed responds.

And then there is silence until we have changed rooms and are sitting perpendicular to one another at the dining room table. I'm at the head, Ed at the long side. Because this is my house and he is polite enough to respect that. The same way he's polite enough to knock. I wonder, not for the first time in the last year, why a man like Ed hired a dick like Rothman.

"So, why are you here?" I ask.

"The police rang this morning. They have the coroner's report. They are satisfied that Simon died of natural causes. The tox screen came back negative."

I didn't really doubt that it would, but I still feel relieved at Ed's words. Dead is dead, and I will carry on feeling guilty about my response time that night, but if they'd found drugs in Simon's system, I don't think I'd ever have been able to forgive myself for not paying enough attention on my patch.

"That was quick," I state, and Ed nods.

"Yeah, ten days is quite a speedy turnaround, I agree. But I think there wasn't really any doubt as such. So, the police have given us permission to unseal the room now. I have spoken to Simon's wife and offered to pack up his things for her, but she insisted on coming here at the weekend and doing it herself. Says she needs to do it. That's a very healthy attitude, in my opinion. She's a wise woman. But I was wondering if you want to be here to greet her, or if you'd prefer Judy or me or Frank to do it."

I frown at that. Even if it comes from a benevolent place, the suggestion is insulting.

"No. Absolutely not. Thank you, truly, but it's still my house and that's my duty."

Ed smiles at that. A warm, fatherly smile.

"That's what I told Frank you'd say when he suggested I'd offer his help."

"So it wasn't yours or Judy's idea?"

"God, no, I didn't doubt for one second that you'd want to be here for Simon's wife yourself."

I feel mollified, knowing this didn't come from the Denyers. But the finer nuance doesn't escape me.

"So how come you were giving me a choice between Frank, Judy and yourself?"

His smile turns almost mischievous. Not a look I've ever seen on him before, and quite endearing.

"Because I know full well that you can't stand Frank. So I wanted to make sure you *actually* did not want the help and weren't just refusing it because the offer came from him."

I smile broadly at that. My first real smile in days.

"Is it that obvious?" I ask.

"Glaringly, my dear, and I can't say I blame you. Frank's not a very pleasant man."

His admission surprises me.

"Why did you give him the position if you don't like him?"

"We weren't really given a choice, Ravenna, he was sent to us by one of the other stakeholders."

I have no idea what he's talking about.

"What other stakeholders? The Village is Halosan owned," I state, confused.

"Mostly, yes. But there are certain tax advantages if a complex like this is co-owned by British registered stakeholders to some small percentage. I can't remember how much exactly. You could ask Judy. Before she retrained as a counsellor, she was a tax advisor. She can explain it in depth to you if you wish."

I make a gesture to let him know I'm not that interested in the details. I'm still intrigued by the Rothman connection, though.

"So, who are these stakeholders and what's so special about Rothman?"

"Absolutely nothing, my dear," Ed says and draws a deep, exasperated breath. "The other stakeholders are mostly Rothman & Stiles. Rothman as in Rothman's family."

"Rothman & Stiles?" I prompt because I have never heard of them.

"They are a cosmetics company. Made their name some years ago by coming up with some wonder drug to slow down cell aging. Have you ever heard of RoSt anti-wrinkle cream and supplements?"

I nod. It rings a bell. It's stuff which is so far out of the price range I am willing to pay for beauty products that I've never paid much attention to it. I don't hate my frown lines enough to squander a fortune on smoothing them out.

"Well, RoSt is short for Rothman & Stiles," Ed carries on. "Frank is the youngest son of their CEO, Celia Rothman. He's a layabout who was brought up with a silver spoon in his mouth. I'm guessing he didn't have the aptitude for chemistry and hard sciences that his mother and other siblings have, so they told him to get a humanities degree with a scientific slant instead. Unfortunately for us, he chose psychotherapy." Ed suddenly stops himself and looks at me, shocked. "Sorry, that was extremely unprofessional of me."

I shrug and clink my cup against his.

"It's fine, Ed. It's nice to see behind the Denyer facade," I reassure him with a coquettish wink. "It won't go further than these walls. So why do you think he chose counseling?"

"Ego," Ed replies without hesitation. "There are two types of therapists in the world. The ones who genuinely want to help people help themselves and the ones who want to feel important. It's about their importance in their clients' lives rather than about their clients. Rothman firmly falls into the self-important category."

He pauses for a long second and sighs.

"I feel for the boy, though. He's the youngest of four and the other three are all women. With degrees in biochemistry, bio engineering and medicine respectively. I've never been a very manly man and it's never bothered me, but I think if I had grown up in that household, I would have felt emasculated, too. No wonder he has an inferiority complex."

On that last note, he gets up from his chair, changing the subject abruptly back to the reason of his visit.

"So, I'll let Simon's wife know, you'll be expecting her call to arrange a time for Friday. Do me a favour, check how the police left the room before she comes. Make it look a little tidy if they left a mess. Lived in but not chaotic, if you catch my drift."

I get up, too, and offer him my handshake.

"Thank you, Ed," I say as he slips his papery palm into mine, and it occurs to me that maybe Ed's a lot older than I always thought he was. "In case I forget to say it in the rush of departure, it's been a pleasure working here with you and Judy. I feel like we should have had this coffee in the beginning rather than at the end."

He holds my hand a little longer and searches my eyes.

"You weren't ready for friendship a year ago, Ravenna. I don't know what's changed, but you are now. It makes me both happy to know that and sad that you are not staying, so we can get to know you better. Keep in touch. Don't be a stranger. Don't go back to the States and disappear on us. You helped build this, stay part in some small way. Christine will be happier knowing that you still have her back, even if you are thousands of miles away. For all her Northern bravado, she's terrified she's going to mess up. Maybe the two of you could have dinner with Judy and me before you leave? Think about it. I'll see myself out, I'm sure you've got things to be getting on with."

He leaves me, lost for words.

ROWAN

You've got to hand it to Diego. He plays the part of the mobster prince with so much devotion, he even wears his suit to the beach.

All around us, Brighton Beach is packed with men in nothing but shorts and women in sarongs, bikini tops and flip-flops, and next to me on the pebbles sits Diego in his full, sand-coloured, three-piece Savile

Row suit. It would be even more impressive if he hadn't taken his shoes and socks off and wasn't wriggling his toes.

But I don't think he's aware he's doing it.

He's engrossed in watching Silas and Grace horse around by the water edge, while we're waiting for them to join us, so we can have a confab about potential work for Silas and me. Legit stuff. Allegedly.

I know Diego is champing at the bit to get back to running his mini empire, but he's as reluctant as I am to break up Silas and Grace's little party. I never particularly liked Diego, but we have always been united in our love for the guy who's currently giving the pretty redhead a piggyback and running into the sea with her.

"I want that," he suddenly states.

"Me, too," I concur. "But unlike me, you are still in with a chance."

"Still no call from your nurse?" he asks.

Silas must have told him about Raven. I sure as fuck haven't. So, I'm not gonna answer that.

"Still not found the balls to ask Kalina out?" I shoot back instead.

"She's too young for me," he says dismissively.

It's a ridiculous excuse. Kalina is eighteen, Diego is the same age as Silas and me. It's hardly cradle-snatching. What he actually means is that he doesn't want to drag her into his world.

Noble.

And then there is the small fact that she's really hard to read and nobody can tell if she fancies him back or not.

To make matters worse, she'll eventually go back to Poland. There is a theme here with all three of us, I guess, women that live somewhere far, far away. Although Kalina announced two days ago that she's prolonging her stay in the UK for another few months. It occurs to me that Diego doesn't know that yet.

"Well, you better get used to blue balls then, 'cause she's staying in England till the end of the year now."

His head whips around at that, to look at my grinning profile. I always did love dropping a bombshell.

"Who says I got blue balls?" is what comes out of his mouth, though I know full well his head didn't swivel around at lightning speed with indignation at the alleged state of his crown jewels.

He is interested in the info.

But I play along. We all got faces to save.

"Rumour has it, none of the Brookes and Kellies and Juanitas at the club or in the bar have been able to get near your dick in a while. But I guess nobody knows what you keep for yourself, up at the mansion."

Diego owns a building behind us on the seafront promenade with a nightclub in the basement called TripleX, which is HQ for the illegal bare-knuckle league of the south coast, a cocktail bar above it, called The Cockatoo, and some apartments up top, most of which are rented out to escorts. It also houses the offices of Santos-Benson security, and then there is an empty penthouse, which in theory is Diego's, but it's only really used for private parties. Because he still hasn't quite managed to move out of his parents' house, the Benson Mansion, yet. Nobody knows what keeps him there.

I kind of get it, though. The Benson Mansion is a nice suburban detached house out in Woodland Drive with a huge garden, an indoor swimming pool and a decent gym room. Many of the celebrities that live in this city have their residences around there, and it's nice, quiet, almost normal. I think if I ran the kind of business Diego does, I'd like to come home to a fantasy of morality as well. Not sure how that gels with seeing his cunt of a father and his drunk of a mother for breakfast every morning, but the powers of self-delusion are endless. I can attest to that.

"Where did you hear that?" Diego asks levelly.

"What? That Kalina is staying around for a while longer, or that you've been taking a break from catching the clap?"

I can't help poking him. It's too much fun.

"You're such an arsehole," he states, but there is no venom in it.

I can sense him processing the Kalina news and leave him to it, while I watch Silas and Grace come back from the sea. Silas didn't actually drop her into the waves. He took pity on her and let her slip gently off his back, so she only got wet to about mid-thigh, while he swam out then circled back to her.

You couldn't keep Silas out of the water if you tried. He's a fish.

The thought gives me a flashback to the pool at The Village, teaching Tristan to swim.

A still frame of Raven smiling at me across the kid's back.

It cuts me up as if I'd eaten a handful of shards.

When the fuck will this pain ever end?

Raven

Simon's room is actually pretty neat, if you ignore the messed-up bed.

Nobody would know that the police had been in here. You'd just think somebody got interrupted as they were taking the sheets off the bed. It's no surprise, really, because the two cops that came were very methodical. I know, because I came to offer them tea or coffee while they were in here, and then I stood outside the door to watch them for a while.

They started in one corner and moved around the room. They looked through his clothes in the wardrobe, into the safe and at the back of shelves and drawers. Then they searched the bed, turning the mattress over. I left when one of them got on the floor to crawl around with a flashlight — after they'd already long declined my offer of a hot drink and I realized I was being a politely ignored nuisance. A little while later, I heard them flush the toilet in Simon's en suite, so I guessed they'd moved their search into the bathroom area. All in all, they took around an hour, and then they were done.

Looking around me now, a wave of sadness washes over me. The last time I was *in* here I was kneeling on the floor, fighting for a man's life.

I lost.

With a heavy heart, I walk to the bed and start taking the sheets off to go in the wash. Once I've got the linen in a heap on the floor and have straightened out the bare pillow and comforter, I proceed to the bathroom. Simon's wash bag sits open on the shelf, his razor lies on the edge of the sink, his toothbrush and toothpaste stand innocuous in a holder. I look at them for a moment and put myself in his wife's shoes.

I think this is where I would break down if I were her.

If I had someone who I would break down for.

I wouldn't falter when folding the clothes, I'd falter at the point I had to pack away these intimate personal care items.

I know they were in the middle of a divorce, but he was the father of her children. A man she'd lived with for as long as I've been alive. He told me once they'd met at school and married before they hit twenty. I can't even imagine knowing someone for as long as that. Let alone being woven into their existence.

I decide I will do this small thing for her.

I will pack up his wash bag.

So she can just grab it and run.

So she can have her tears when she unpacks it in the comfort of her own home, with her girls by her side.

It's the kind thing to do.

I grab the little leather case off the shelf and pick up the razor to put it inside.

"Ah, here you are, Raven," a voice says behind me, and I startle.

I drop the bag into the sink, its contents spilling out everywhere.

I turn around.

"Frank!" I yell at the intruder indignantly. "For heaven's sake, what are *you* doing here?"

Even while I shout out my frustration at him, I become acutely aware that I am alone in the house with somebody who makes my skin crawl, trapped in a very small bathroom.

Rothman holds up his hands.

"Whoa, sorry. I didn't mean to startle you. You must have been lost in thought. I thought you'd heard me, I've been hollering your name as I was coming up the stairs," he says, unruffled by my outburst.

I narrow my eyes at him.

I didn't hear him call me and I'm *always* alert.

He's shitting me.

The alarm bells in my head go up ten bars on the volume button.

"Right," I say, trying not to make my disbelief shine through. "And what are you doing here?"

He smiles. Insincerely.

"I thought you might want some help."

While I keep a lid on showing my fear, I don't try to hide my annoyance any longer.

"You thought wrong. I already told Ed I got this."

His eyebrows shoot up.

"Ed spoke to you?"

"Yes. And I said to him, thanks but no thanks. My house, my responsibility. And, to be honest, it's my house, my sanctuary, too. So, please, in the future obey the basic rules of courtesy. Knock. If there is no answer, don't just let yourself in the house. It's disrespectful, and rude."

If in doubt, call the British rude, and they'll crumble like a dry cookie.

Well, that's the theory.

Rothman doesn't. Instead, he looks at me with something that I'm sure is supposed to be a sheepish expression but that actually just screams 'cocky asshole'.

"I'm sorry. I've been worried about you," he says gently, and I feel bile rising up my throat.

Oblivious to just how unwelcome he is, he juts out his chin to indicate the sink behind me, craning his neck at the mess I made.

"At least let me pick up that stuff for you," he offers. "So you can get on with something else. Helping out would make me feel a little better about giving you a fright."

He comes another step towards me and raises his hand to stroke his knuckles down my cheek.

It's then that I snap.

I bat his arm away and step right up to him, going toe to toe.

I grab him by the shirt collar and pull his face down, so he doesn't miss a single measure of the venom I'm about to spit at him.

He's appropriately shocked to have me in his space, and at my unveiled aggression.

And here, we peel away the cocky asshole and unveil the wimpy, entitled Brit.

And here, we peel away the professional nurse and unveil the fury of a little girl who survived hell.

"Read my lips," I start.

In the periphery of my vision, I can see his trousers twitch. He's sicker than I thought. He's getting off on my anger. So I cool it. I still hold him, but my voice turns to ice.

"Fuck off, Frank. Drop the kind, considerate act. I ain't buying it. Leave me the fuck alone. I don't like you. I never liked you. You're a creep. Consider this your only warning. Next time you sneak up on me or touch me in *any* way, I will have your balls. I know a thing or two about scalpels and keeping stuff in jars."

I release him and give him a shove.

"Leave!"

He looks at me, stunned, and then he turns and hurries away, muttering something about a psycho bitch.

I hold my breath until I hear him pull the front door shut.

I stand for a few more minutes, concentrating on willing the bile back down, slowing my heart rate and regulating my breathing before I return my attention to the items in the sink.

A small hairbrush, a shaving brush, a small tub of shaving cream, a roll-on deodorant, dental floss, an asthma inhaler, a pair of nail clippers.

I put them all back in the wash bag and add the items from around the sink. I zip up the bag and take it with me to leave it on the nightstand, where Simon's wife will find it tomorrow.

Then I collect the dirty linen from the floor and make my way to the washing machine downstairs.

ROWAN

"You want to do what?" Silas leans across the white tablecloth at the posh fish place that Diego has taken us to for lunch and looks at him as if he's lost his marbles. Which, frankly, he has.

It turned out that I was wrong thinking Diego was champing at the bit because he needed to get back to what he calls work. Turns out the reason he was full to bursting point with energy when we were sitting on the beach was because he couldn't wait to talk to us about the grand plan he's come up with that'll turn him into a fully legitimate business mogul.

So he took us for baked oysters and lobster in The Lanes and told us about his harebrained scheme.

Apparently, the government are putting the contracts for the two brand-new young offenders institutions they have been building on the outskirts of town, up for tender soon. And Diego wants to bid on running them.

Silas shakes his head as he sits back in his seat and scrutinises Diego.

"You want to buy a prison," he states soberly.

"No, Silas, I want to run a borstal," Diego replies with a broad grin. "Two, actually. A young offenders institution and a secure training centre. Right next to one another."

"You're insane, Diego," Silas huffs.

He's addressing Diego by his town name because, well, we're in town, but in private he often calls him George. He and Sheena, and by default Grace and Kalina, are the only people I know who can do that without Diego getting arsey.

"You haven't the first clue how to run a prison," Silas adds with a deep frown.

Diego makes a weighing up gesture.

"I don't know about that," he says seriously and fixes Silas in an icy stare. "I've been running a stable of give or take thirty fighters since I turned twenty. I built the biggest fight club league on the south coast. The only *remaining* fight club league on the south coast, to be precise. I run an apartment building full of whores and a cocktail bar that actually turns a profit. Any idea how cut-throat the hospitality business is? Plus, I already have a security company with a great team that's separate from the rest, at least on paper. A security team that, I'd like to remind you, you are still part of, because I haven't seen a resignation letter from you yet, even though you appear to have been taking the longest holiday since holidays were invented. All in all, I'd say I'm supremely qualified to keep a lid on eighty unruly kids. Especially if each of these kids comes at thirty-five grand a year keeper's fee. I mean, how hard can it be?"

Silas crosses his arms in front of his chest and looks away, eyebrows raised.

"He's got a point," Grace pipes up.

She's got balls, Silas' girl, I give her that. Women at Diego's table are supposed to shut up and pretend they have a vacuum between their ears. Not that they are normally present when talk is about business. It shows how much respect she's earned in a very short time that Diego will speak so freely in front of her.

Silas turns to look at her profile, incredulity showing all over his face.

"Don't fucking encourage him," he says quietly.

She turns to stare right back at him.

"Why the fuck not?"

She's really developed that mouth of hers.

"He's right," she carries on. "He's got better credentials than most to run a youth prison. I can see it. He'll just need an educational program, some teachers and a head of housekeeping."

"It's not a prison," Diego says to Grace, exasperated, but then his grey eyes get a twinkle in them. "Housekeeping, you say?"

He turns his attention to Silas again with a mischievous smirk.

"You reckon your mum's bored of The Palais yet?"

I laugh when I see Silas' face fall completely as he looks from his girl back to his boss and oldest friend. I raise my hand.

"I think it's nuts, but it's also perfect," I say.

And I mean it. I can actually see it. I can see them all working in this stupid fantasy of Diego's and actually make it work. For everyone. Even for the poor sods they'd be rehabilitating.

I just can't see a place for me in it.

Because in my heart of hearts, I'm still going to America.

I'm still following a woman who thinks she doesn't want me any longer.

Diego looks at me.

"You in then?"

I shake my head.

Silas cocks his head and focuses solely on me.

"You don't feel it's finished, do you?"

He can still read my thoughts like no other human being on earth.

"No," I answer.

He frowns.

"Then fucking well ring her, you idiot."

Grace looks at her glass as if it were the most interesting object on earth and swivels it around by the stem.

"You want to be the pot or the kettle there, honey?" she gently ribs him under her breath.

'Cause it sure as shit wasn't Silas who came for his woman in their story, it was very much his woman coming for him.

But I have a funny feeling if I wait for Raven to come to me, the Zimmer frame I mentioned to her will be a fucking reality.

If ever.

Raven

After I put Simon's sheets in the washing machine, I'm at a loose end again. I contemplate going for a hike or for a dip in the pool, since there is nothing to stop me. But some invisible chord ties me to the house. I don't want to leave it unattended.

I don't know what I think will happen if I do, but it just doesn't feel *right*.

There is a key to the front door I could use to lock up with, but since it's mostly Rothman I don't trust not to come in to sniff my used underwear, or whatever other kinky shit he's into, it's no use. All the senior staff have a master key to all the houses. I have no idea what exactly I think I'm protecting, but I know I'm protecting *something*. Maybe it's just territory and the reason it feels so strange to me is because I never had any to protect before.

So instead of going outside, I waste the afternoon reading and watching terrible pre-millennium British made-for-TV crime dramas, until Christine comes for a visit after all her chicks, as she calls them, have been fed.

Christine is great company, as always, and doesn't once mention the dead guy, or the guy I miss, as we spend two hours chatting about terrible pre-millennium British made-for-TV crime dramas. Although her version of 'chatting' is mostly re-enacting a whole load of iconic characters I've never heard of. She does an ingenious impersonation of the actor who played Hagrid as some detective called Cracker, and when she leaves, I know what is on my to-watch list once I get home.

I feel the lack of her as soon as I shut the door behind her.

After she leaves, I make myself a hot chocolate to take to bed with me and switch off the lights downstairs. I'm halfway to the top floor when the house phone starts ringing, and my heart starts pounding in my chest.

There is only one person I can imagine who would ring the house at this time of the night.

I sprint up the rest of the steps, splashing hot chocolate all over the place and not giving a shit. When I pick up the receiver, I'm out of breath, not with exertion but near panic.

"The Village, Ravenna Vanhofd speaking," I press out between breaths.

"You okay?" The thunderclaps on the other end sound worried.

"Yeah, yeah, I'm fine. I just ran up the stairs."

He chuckles.

"Knew it was me?" he asks confidently.

He's still a jackass.

"What do you want, Rowan?" I ask him, snippily, though really what I want to do is tell him I miss him, I love him, I want him back.

I love him?

Shit.

I don't know.

Is this what this is?

Maybe.

How the fuck would *I* know?

"You," he says at the other end, and I realize he left me quite the pause to think in before he answered my question. "I want you," he clarifies, as if it needs clarification.

And then he hangs up.

What the fuck am I supposed to do with that?

I suppress the urge to phone him back to call him an asshole and choose to go to bed with murderous thoughts and without brushing my teeth instead.

ROWAN

It doesn't take me long to pack my backpack after I speak to her. I grab enough to last me till the end of the week, which should have been my original leaving date. I might be deluding myself, but I just *know* we're not over.

She's my one, I can feel it in my bones. I *know* so. I knew it when I first saw her, I knew it when I left, and I knew it every second in between.

There is, of course, the very real chance that I'm just justifying an obsession and that I'm about to turn into a fucking stalker, but time will tell. If I get back to Purbeck and she tells me to turn the fuck around, I'll turn the fuck around.

But we need some kind of actual ending first.

One that is to do with *us,* not with someone else's tragic circumstances that have nothing whatsoever to do with either of us.

It's too late to catch a train tonight, so I will leave first thing in the morning, but I want to be ready, so I can just grab my toothbrush and go.

I roll up my last pair of pants and stuff them in the backpack, and then I go to find Silas.

Silas, Grace, Diego and Kalina are all still in the kitchen, talking. Diego came over for dinner earlier, hoping to ambush Sheena with his idea for her next career, but she's on a late today and not back yet, thus has yet to be informed of the role she might play in Diego Benson's newest live-my-life-as-a-movie plan. Prison films were always his second favourite, after all things Tarantino.

I go to rejoin them and as soon as I appear in the door, Silas takes one look at me and just knows.

The women can tell by our faces that something is up and fall silent.

Diego, who's leaning on the counter by the kettle waiting for it to boil, takes a little longer but eventually he, too, shuts up.

Silas glances away from me, concentrating on stroking Luna, who is standing in his lap, milk-treading his thighs, for a good half a minute before he says anything.

"When are you leaving?" he asks into the loaded silence, not making eye contact.

"Tomorrow, early. First train I can catch."

He nods.

"Let's wait till Mum gets in, I'll ask her if we can borrow the Capri. I'll take you."

I can tell in his tone there is no arguing, and I'm grateful. At least that way if Raven does refuse me, Silas will be there by my side on the way back. To mop up my tears. As he does.

Diego looks back and forth between us, frowning.

"Where are you going?" he asks.

"Purbeck," Silas, Grace and I answer in one breath.

Kalina claps her hands, excitedly.

"To see nurse? Good idea! Bring back here, I want to see woman who fells mountain of man like you."

Behind her back, Diego rolls his eyes and I can't help but grin at him.

I sit down across from Kalina and give her a comedy wink.

"You like big men, do you?" I tease, one eye on Diego.

His grey eyes gather storm clouds.

She shrugs.

"Big is good," she says.

I swear she can feel Diego's miffed reaction in her back and it's totally hitting the spot she was aiming for. Diego is the welterweight to Silas' middleweight and my heavyweight, and he never liked that little fact, but that's just how he was put together.

"But blond is better," Kalina finishes what she started, on a big grin that Diego can't see.

Then she gets up and leaves the kitchen without turning around to him.

"That one is a minx," I say, once she's out of earshot.

Diego turns to the kettle on a grunt and adjusts himself.

I think about another blue balls comment, but I decide to leave him be.

Every man has a snapping point and I think he might be close.

I like being alive.

I'd like to stay that way.

Raven

I don't know exactly what it is that wakes me, but it's still pitch black outside when I burst back into consciousness with that particular start all emergency room nurses around the world know only too well.

It differs from the normal kind of shooting up in bed as it comes with the sure-fire knowledge that all your wits are required about you, *right fucking now*. It takes me a split second to put the feeling in context of the cottage, but then I realize what's rattled my cage.

There is someone in the house.

I can't hear them, but I can feel their presence as they silently pad around the floor below me.

I get out of bed quietly, counting my blessings that I've reverted to sleeping in PJs since the night Simon died, and reach for the hairspray on my nightstand.

In the States, I always carry mace, but the Brits are squeamish about that shit. It's classed as a weapon, and the British don't do weapons. They're illegal here. Not just a little bit, a whole fucking lot. So I go for the next best thing. A faceful of Volume Plus Hold might not incapacitate an assailant, but it'll buy you enough time to turn the tables from victim to perp.

I leave my room, treading as softly as I can, navigating the landing and the stairs in the dark. After a year here, I know this house like the back of my hand, know exactly how many steps there are, and which one creaks unless you step right on the outside.

When I get to the floor below me, there is a moment when I wonder if I'm simply just losing it.

Because everything seems totally normal.

It's calm and quiet. The doors to all the three guest rooms are firmly shut, the way I left them. I'm about to turn back upstairs and put the whole thing down to paranoia in an empty house, when I hear the faintest noise coming through the door of Simon's room.

A shudder goes through me. I don't believe in the supernatural, but the whole thing is too fucking eerie for my liking.

I think for a moment and decide that no matter if ghost or intruder, surprise is the best form of attack. Then I take a deep breath, barge through the door and switch the light on, hairspray at the ready in the other hand.

Frank Rothman drops the flashlight he is holding, and his other hand clasps around an object as he turns to me from the nightstand, cussing.

"For fuck's sake, Raven, just piss off," he snarls at me, and I can tell immediately that he's been drinking.

He's not super sloshed, but his eyes are glassy and the distinct odor of expensive Scotch comes off him as he comes toward me.

"You fucking Americans, always sticking your fucking oar in. There is nothing to see here. Go back to fucking bed."

I frown as I try to deduct what it is he's hiding in his clenched fist, but I don't get a chance to see it before it disappears in the pocket of his pants, and he's almost on me. For a moment I think he's about to attack me, but then I realize that he's just gonna try to walk past me and out of the house.

Interesting tactic.

The problem Frank has is he sure as shit ain't no Jedi master and there is plenty to see here, so I grab him by the arm as he tries to push past me.

"Nice try, Frank. What's in your pocket?"

It's only when he turns on me and slaps the hairspray can out of my hand that I realize maybe that wasn't the wisest move. I let his casual attempt at escape lull me into dropping my guard. Big fucking mistake. He leans into me and I can see the humiliation from earlier still burning behind his eyes.

He snarls.

He fucking *snarls* as his face comes close to mine and his sour breath fans over me.

"What's in my pocket?" he repeats my question, while he grabs my wrists and bends them behind my back, bringing his body right up to mine.

"I'm going to show you what's in my pocket."

He's so close, I can feel his cock stirring in his pants as he bends my right arm up so high it pins my hand between my shoulder blades, and I want to squeal in pain.

But I don't.

I don't, because this is where the voice in my head splits into the familiar duet I haven't heard in years.

There is Raven and she's screaming. She wants to fight. With everything she has.

And then there is Ravenna. Cool, calm, collected. She wants to survive. With everything *she* has.

Only for the first time ever the three of us realize that I don't have to choose between them. They can work, *together.*

So when Rothman brings my other hand back around and forces it into his pocket, not the one he's put the item in, but the empty one, the one right next to his growing erection, Ravenna strokes her fingertips along his hardening length through the fabric. Rothman quivers as his eyes bore into mine, and then a smile unfurls around his angry mouth.

"You like this, huh?" he growls.

He searches my eyes and I allow Raven through. Just a little, just enough for him to see the fire burning inside of me and to let him mistake it for lust.

"Oh, fuck, yeah," he croaks as he lowers his mouth onto my neck to bite me.

Hard. It fucking hurts.

I push down the curses that want to come up my throat and give him a whimper instead. I think it's unconvincing, but he buys it.

"I knew it," he pants and bites me again.

The fucker is gonna leave *marks* on me.

"Oh, baby, I'm gonna make you come so hard," he groans into the crook of my neck as he starts backing me up against the bed.

In my mind's eye, Ravenna is standing behind Raven, holding her back with her arms slung tightly around her shoulders, while Raven is already warming up, throwing air punches from beneath the vise.

Patience, Ravenna whispers in her ear.

The three of us slip the hand caressing his cock out of his loosening grasp and out of his pocket, only to cup his package fully from the front. His hand follows ours and pushes it down on him, making us rub him up and down.

"Take him out," he demands between more bites.

We fumble with his button and his zipper and free his skinny long penis, pushing his briefs and pants down one-handed, because he still hasn't released the hand behind my back. Raven is getting impatient, she's ready to punch him the fuck out, but Ravenna insists we push the briefs down a bit further, pretending we're gonna go down on him. Until his knees are trapped by the fabric.

Then we let Raven off the leash.

And the world turns red.

ROWAN

It's the middle of the night when my mobile rings.

Sol, who's been sleeping in the valley between my legs, jumps up with a protesting meow when I scramble around to find my phone on the floor by the bed. I peek at the number flashing up. The brightness of the screen hurts my eyes.

It's an American number and though it's probably some kind of scam call, there is a small part of me that, when it sees the country code, can't help but hope it's her. Though it makes no sense that she would call me from her private mobile and not from the cottage or her UK company mobile. I don't even know if she has a private one. Only one way to find out.

I take the call, my heart doing funny shit in my chest.

"I need your help," she says by way of introduction.

There is everything I need to know in these four words and suddenly I'm more awake than I've ever been in my life. And I realise that the amount of people I would bury a body for has just gone up from three to four.

I don't ask her the details.

I don't ask her what we are talking about.

I don't even ask her who it is we need to dig a hole for. Though I have a very strong fucking idea.

All I say is, "Do I need to bring a shovel?"

"No," she answers soberly, and I love the fact she is immediately with me. "I took his vitals. He's unconscious, but he's stable. But I don't know if he'll bleed out internally. I need to call the police, but I'm scared, Rowan. I don't know what'll happen to me. What's British jail like?"

"What did you do?" I finally ask, my stomach bottoming out at her words.

I've never been so scared in my life. For her.

"I beat the shit out of him," she answers calmly. "You ain't the only fighter around here, ya know."

I knew that already, honey.

But I don't say it. I stick to the facts. We might need them.

"Who is 'him'?"

"Rothman."

No surprise there then.

"What happened?"

"He tried to fuck me."

The anger that rises up in me is so all consuming I can't talk for a moment. The guy's dead. He might not be dead yet. But he fucking well will be. I'm gonna get my arse to Purbeck right fucking now and I'm gonna finish what she started.

"Rowan?"

I hear her voice bore through the roar in my head and realise I missed something she said.

"Sorry, say that again," I manage to respond through gritted teeth while I swing my legs out of bed.

"Don't go all Incredible Hulk on me. I can *hear* your thoughts and I'm a hundred and twenty-seven miles away."

I note that she knows exactly how far away from one another we are, and that makes me smile despite everything and everything. Somebody has been on the web to figure out the distance between us. And I'd bet my arse that was before she found herself in the current situation. She fucking missed me, too. The thought calms me a little.

"I need your help," she reiterates. "But I need you to stay cool. I need your brains, Rowan, not your muscles. I need somebody I trust to figure this out. *Before* I call the cops. There is more to this. I don't know. I think Frank's somehow responsible for Simon's death. But I can't see how. The tox screen came back negative. He broke in here to get something from Simon's room. I caught him and it started from there. I can't fucking think."

Her voice breaks off. She sounds exhausted. I'd bet my life the adrenaline she was running on is wearing off right about now, and in about twenty minutes she'll hit a complete low.

"Okay, gorgeous, we're gonna figure this out, but back up a bit. Where are you now and where is Rothman?" I ask her, as much to get a clearer picture of the situation as to keep her talking.

I pin the phone into the crook of my neck and pull on my trousers.

"In Simon's room. I tied him to Simon's bed. I'm just sitting here, watching him. Need to make sure he doesn't choke on his vomit. He was drunk. I guess he needed some liquid courage to break in here."

"Gag him," I say. "We'll be there in two hours. Three at the most if we run into road works."

"I can't gag him," she says, matter of fact. "I need to keep his airways clear. I'm a nurse, for fuck's sake. I swore the Nightingale pledge. Rowan?"

"Yeah?"

"You're not coming here to finish him off. I appreciate the sentiment and all, but *my* life is not some gangster movie. I just need some time to figure this shit out and then we're doing this the *legitimate* way."

What the fuck is this with everyone's obsession to go legit today?

"Okay. We'll talk about it when we get there," I concede.

"Who is 'we'?" she asks after a pause, puzzled.

"I'm bringing the cavalry."

She takes a deep breath, probably to reiterate the no-killing-Rothman rule, but I cut her short before she can get the first syllable out.

"Trust me, Raven, you *want* me to bring the cavalry. Silas is gonna make sure I stay on the straight and narrow."

She sighs.

"Hurry. I don't know what to do if he wakes up."

"Well if you can't gag him, knock him out again."

"Rowan!"

I chuckle.

"Chill, baby. We'll sort it out. I'm gonna hang up now, so I can recce a car and get Silas out of bed. But I'll give you a ring once we're on the road. You'll need to let us in when we get there. Can you do that without leaving him?"

"You can let yourself in. Use the keypad. I'll send you the staff code."

"Great."

"And Rowan?"

"Yeah?"

There is a long pause and I'm starting to get antsy 'cause I want to get going, but I'm glad I stop myself from hurrying her along once she's spits out what she wants to say.

"I want you, too."

I have an impulse to laugh and make a comment like, 'You didn't need to knock some slimy asshole out to let me know that, you know.'

But I don't.

I know it's probably the closest she'll ever come to say, 'I love you' and if that's all I'm gonna get, I'll take it. Without turning it into a joke.

Instead, I get back to business, though I doubt I can mask the grin in my voice.

"I'll phone you from the car. Hang on in there, beautiful."

Raven

I go into a kind of Zen zone for the next couple of hours, only interrupted by the occasional check on Frank's stats.

He's good.

After a while, I come to the conclusion that he's more passed out drunk than climbing up the coma scale, which is a big relief.

Doesn't change the fact he'll have bruises tomorrow.

But so will I.

I count my blessings that he was two sheets to the wind when he decided to pay Simon's room a visit. Halosan trains all its nurses in physical restraint and I've taken a number of self-defence classes in my life, but that doesn't change the fact Rothman is a fit enough man who's a head taller than me. So I am more than thankful for his sloppy punches and that his coordination had already fallen into the bottle.

I owe Halosan a chair, though.

The only one that was in here is in pieces. If Rothman were a vampire, I could stake him through the heart with the remnants. I keep one of the legs by my side, just in case he needs another knock over the head. It doesn't swing quite as well as a baseball bat, but it's solid enough.

The lack of chair is why I'm sitting on the floor now, with my back to the door, while I stare at the object I've placed on the carpet in front of me.

It's Simon's inhaler.

I had almost forgotten that Rothman had swiped something from the room by the time the thing fell out of his pocket.

It slipped onto the mattress when I was using his pants to tie his feet down.

I had to make do with whatever I could think of. I could have kicked myself for taking the sheets downstairs to the washing machine earlier. But, as they say, hindsight is twenty-twenty.

So, currently Rothman is spread-eagled on the bed, tied down with his pants, his belt and his shirt, which I ripped in two. It's not ideal. I'd rather have kept him in the recovery position. But securing someone down and keeping their airways free is a contradiction. I erred on the side of keeping myself safe. Sue me.

When I was finished, I threw the comforter over him.

Then I rang Rowan.

He called me back twenty minutes after the first call, from the car, like he'd promised, but I told him to hang up and just get here. I was worried any more talking would wake Rothman up.

I know I said to Rowan that I couldn't figure out what Rothman was doing in here, but the longer I look at the object he came for, the more of an idea forms in my head.

Dawn has already turned the night into early morning when I'm about to reach for it and take the canister out of the blue plastic shell to inspect it further, but I think better of it at the last moment. My fingerprints are already all over the outer. If my hunch is right, I'm contaminating evidence if I go in without gloves. I need gloves. And an evidence bag. And my laptop.

I get up, walk over to Rothman, check his vitals and flinch as he groans in his sleep.

But he doesn't wake up, so I decide I'll risk it.

ROWAN

Silas and I drive without conversation.

He's at the wheel, while the stereo of Sheena's Capri blares Dropkick Murphys all the way. It's pretty much the only intersection of his and my music taste, so we never argue what to put on.

Other than the Murphys, he is very fucking British in his music choices and I'm very fucking American. Same with literature. Same with cars. Same with bikes. I don't have a bike licence but if I had, I'd get a Harley. Don't care if it's a cliché. Big git like me belongs on one of them.

Silas does have a bike licence and he is all about Japanese sports bikes. Which, again, is the British choice 'cause there ain't a British bike industry left. He had one. A Honda. Had to sell it. Because of me and my debts. He doesn't know it yet, but as soon as I'm sorted, I'm gonna save up to buy him another one. Or whatever else he wants now. I think I saw him ogling Kawasakis the other day.

Much as I try concentrating on mundane things, such as making amends to the guy next to me, and what bike to buy him, my thoughts keep flitting to Raven and what she is doing right now.

I rang her as soon as Silas and I got on the motorway, just like I promised, but she told me to hang up and just get our asses there. She didn't want Rothman to wake up from her talking, but she didn't want to leave the room either. I had to concur. She shouldn't. She should keep a close eye on him until we get there and I can keep her safe.

Which is gonna be in around about five minutes.

I turn the volume down on the stereo as Silas turns off the main road and onto a single track that leads directly to The Village.

"We can't drive in, right?" he says.

His first words in a hundred and twenty-five miles.

"Guess not. It'd be better if we weren't seen."

We both glance at the clock. It's twenty to six. He drove with his foot to the floor. I'm relatively sure that in a few days there'll be a friendly letter from Dorset police asking for a fixed penalty fine and informing him that he's got himself a few points on his licence.

"Any early morning worshippers there?" he asks.

I shake my head.

"Only Raven, as far as I know."

"That's alright then."

He grins happily. Silas is fucking handsome as shit when he smiles and somehow looking at his profile as his lips split wide enough to show his front teeth really chills me out.

Stoic Silas is great to have on your side.

Silas enjoying himself is the most powerful weapon in the universe.

"Okay," he says and pulls into a passing place. "Showtime. Let's park up and walk from here."

We do as he says, and I want to throttle him when he starts going through the whole pathetic locking up procedure for the Capri. It's a classic with no extra security features, so Sheena insists on a steering wheel bar. It's a pain in the arse to lock in place and costs us valuable minutes, but Silas shoots me one look and I keep my mouth shut. He's right, Sheena would kill us if we got the girl but lost the car.

When he's finally finished twatting about, he emerges from the Capri and launches straight into a jog.

"Come on, then," he shouts as he scoots ahead.

I catch up with him in two seconds flat, and we fall into rhythm next to one another easily. There is something really soothing about the familiarity of this. About jogging side by side with my brother in the quiet of an early morning.

"Have we got a plan?" he asks when the entrance to The Village comes into sight.

"No."

"Alright then," he says under his breath, as we come to a halt in front of the gate and I start punching in the code Raven gave me. "Good to know."

We step into the complex and stop for a moment to look around.

As expected, there is nobody about yet.

I follow Silas' eyes as he scans the curtains of the houses, all still drawn.

"We gotta be quick," he says factually. "Whatever the plan is."

Raven

I'm so deep down the rabbit hole of internet research, I'm completely lost in a warren of info around RoSt Cosmetics and their associates by the time I hear the door open downstairs. I look up from a research paper I'm reading by one Dr. Phillip Stiles, who may or may not be related to the Stiles part of Rothmann & Stiles aka RoSt, on the potential medical usage of endorphin stimulating agents in the suppression of cravings, to listen out for the footfall on the stairs.

It's Rowan.

I would recognize the sound of him moving any day, but it's more than that. The quality of the air in the house changes with his entrance. And for the first time in hours, I feel truly safe.

There is a second set of footsteps, which must be his brother's.

As they draw nearer, coming up the stairs, I wake fully from my research trance and my heart flips out in my chest with anticipation.

I get up from my perch on the floor and open the door to meet them on the landing.

I don't even get to take a real look at him before I'm scooped up in Rowan's arms and he does that thing that I've seen mothers do to children after a fall. He runs his hands all over my back to check me over then takes a small step back to skim them over my head, my face and down my arms. I want to burst into tears at his tenderness.

At the edge of my vision, I see Silas squeeze past us into the room, while Rowan runs his palms back up my arms until his search stops on my shoulders. His eyes zoom in on something on my neck, and my breathing stops when I realize what it is he must be seeing.

I checked myself over in the mirror when I dashed to grab the gloves earlier and I know I'm sporting a healthy set of bite marks that Rothman left there. I'm lucky he didn't pierce the skin. Human bites are more susceptible to infection than animal ones. They can be lethal.

Rowan's already dark eyes turn even darker with anger.

"That him?" he asks, his jaw setting.

I nod and put myself between him and the door.

"No killing," I say, only half joking.

Because it takes me one look into his face to understand that he absolutely would. This man, my man, is a hell of a lot more dangerous than I remember half the time, and it gives me an unholy thrill along with a healthy dose of naked fear.

"Say it, Rowan," I demand.

He doesn't answer immediately, searching my eyes for heaven-knows-what first, then sighs submissively.

"No killing the cunt, got it," he answers.

There is a twitch around his mouth when he says 'got it' that reassures me enough to step aside. It seems to be just in time because we can hear Rothman groan, and a second later Silas' voice floats over to us.

"Guys, we got a live one."

ROWAN

He bit her. He fucking *bit* her.

I wanna rip the cunt to shreds and feed him to the pigeons.

"Do pigeons eat meat?" I ask Silas as I walk through the door to Simon's old room, after I've already begrudgingly pledged the no killing policy to Raven.

"I think they're vegetarians. But we could always ask the Bensons if their pitties need a snack," Silas answers, while he pushes the blade of his flick knife harder against Rothman's jugular.

I love this guy so hard it's fucking unreal. Silas is the most peaceful fucker in the universe, yet he'll beat people to a pulp for a living to protect his mum from losing her house and play the part of ruthless killer to help me avenge my woman.

"I don't think they keep pit bulls anymore," I respond. "They're all gentrified now. It's packs of hounds and flat caps these days."

Silas shrugs.

"Hounds need to eat, too."

Rothman is pissing himself on the bed. Literally pissing himself. He's covered by a duvet, but you can smell it through the feather down. It's hilarious because he doesn't know the only reason Silas carries a knife wherever he goes is because he's seriously into picnics. It's basically his travelling cutlery. Last thing he cut with it was probably an apple or some cheese.

I go over and rip the covers away to reveal Rothman's shame. The cunt whimpers. He's not said a peep since Silas has come in here, but now he takes a breath as if he wants to say something, while he looks at me with the kind of terror I want him to feel for the fucking rest of his life.

"Guys," Raven says appeasingly behind us, and I turn around to look at her.

"Yeah?"

"Can I trust you not to cut him up while I go to the bathroom? Frank just reminded me that I've needed to pee since before I caught him sneaking around."

She looks at us sharply and we both nod.

"Great, glad we have an understanding, gentlemen," she carries on. "If you want to do something positive while I'm gone, ask him what's in the inhaler."

Rothman fixes her in his stare as she approaches him with a clear plastic freezer bag, dangling from her hand. Inside is a bog-standard blue asthma inhaler.

"That's what he came to swipe from the room," she explains. "But Simon wasn't asthmatic. I looked it up, because I was second guessing myself. Although that kind of thing doesn't normally escape my attention. There is nothing referring to *any* bronchial issues in his medical records. So, Frank," she says, stepping up to Rothman on the side opposite Silas to lean right into Rothman's face. "What is the police lab going to find in the canister, huh? Because it sure as shit ain't gonna be salbutamol, is it?"

She drops the bag on Rothman's chest and turns on her heels.

"Over to you, guys. Back in a moment."

Rothman strains against his ties, watching her back as she leaves the room. Tears start running down his face when he realises she's leaving us to it. His eyes dart from Silas to me to Silas.

Silas leisurely takes the knife blade off his throat and points it at the piss that has saturated Rothman's underpants and has spread into the mattress around him.

"Is that getting cold yet?" he asks. "Horrible feeling, isn't it? I can't remember the last time I pissed myself, but I will always remember the feeling of it slowly growing cold around me."

He shakes himself in disgust.

"So here is the deal," he carries on, smiling angelically. "The sooner you fess up, the sooner we can clean you up and do what needs to be done."

He raises his eyebrows at Rothman who escapes Silas' scrutiny by turning his head towards me. Silas puts the point of the blade on the side of Rothman's chin and forces him to look back at him.

"Wouldn't do that, mate. Don't look at him. He's pissed off as hell 'cause you tried to fuck his girlfriend. Not a smart move. Not smart at all. The only thing that keeps you alive right now is the fact Raven said so. Are we clear?"

Rothman makes an acquiescing sound.

"Are we clear?" Silas repeats.

"Yes," Rothman answers, his voice like gravel.

"It speaks," Silas comments in my direction then looks down at Rothman again. "You thirsty?" he asks Rothman.

"Yeah."

"Okay, then tell us what we need to know, and we can get you a glass of water."

"Drop the knife!" a voice interrupts us, accompanied by the unmistakable sound of a shotgun being cocked and startling all three of us.

Mine and Silas' heads spin around and Rothman lifts his up from the mattress, all of us staring at the door, where Alan Allsorts has appeared, games rifle pointing right at Silas. I stop breathing and hold up my hands. I watch Silas out of the corner of my eye as he slowly puts down the knife and copies me.

"Where is Raven? What the fuck is going on here?" Alan asks, looking back and forth between all of us, bewildered.

And with the gun still very much pointing at us.

He lowered it away from Silas' head as soon as Silas let go of the knife and is aiming it more in the region of his knees now, but I still don't like it.

"Raven is fine," I reassure him, just as we hear the toilet flush. "That's her on the bog, Alan. She called us. Rothman broke in and when she caught him, he tried to rape her..."

"I did not try to rape her!" Rothman shouts at Alan. "She came on to me. They're nuts, Alan. Shoot them."

I can see the cogs turning behind Alan's eyes. He's weighing up what he knows about me against what he knows about Rothman. And then he lets the gun sink. Silas and I exhale in sync.

"What are you doing, Alan?" Rothman whines at him. "You've got to help me. These guys are thugs."

Alan nods pensively.

"I can see that," he says, and then he grins. "But you're a slimeball, Frank. And I'll take my chances on thugs telling the truth over slimeballs telling the truth any day."

Raven arrives behind him.

"Alan! Shit! It's not what it looks like..." she starts, but he shuts her off immediately.

"It's alright. I gather you had a nightly visi–" he stops abruptly mid-word when he sees her neck. "What on earth? Who did that? Did Rothman do that?"

She nods.

And up comes the gun again, this time pointed at Rothman.

"Stop!" Raven commands, sounding only mildly panicked.

I guess guns really don't freak Americans out the way they get to us.

"Put the hardware down, Alan. He didn't come here to hurt me."

Her voice relaxes when Alan lets his hands sink, though not completely.

"He came here to steal something from Simon's stuff," she carries on calmly. "An inhaler that I bet has some kind of substance in it that's supposed to help with the alcohol craving but actually freaking kills people."

Rothman sinks down back onto the bed with a groan that tells us all she's hit the nail pretty much on the head.

"But he hurt you?" Alan reiterates.

"Yes."

"Who tied him up?"

"Me."

"Good girl. Tidy job. Why did you call on those two rather than me, Raven?" he asks, and he actually sounds hurt. "That's what I'm here for. I'm here to protect you lot. And if there's a rat, I protect you from the rat."

Raven puts a hand on his arm.

"If you were in trouble, who'd be the first person you'd call?"

"My wife," he responds without thinking.

"Exactly," Raven says, with a soft smile on her face in my direction.

Alan looks back and forth between the two of us.

"You two? You're together?"

We nod, stupid grins on our faces.

"We're together," we both admit.

Alan's mouth splits into a full-on smile.

"Hah. I knew it. That makes me happy. Now that's settled, you," he says, indicating to Silas by jutting his chin out, "go make a round of teas and coffees for everyone. Raven, go to Frank's house and grab some clean clothes for him. Rowan, help me clean him up. Then we call the police. Agreed?"

We all nod at him like compliant little children, and then we get to work.

The British Police don't fuck around, that's for sure.

As I move to the front of Poole Police Station after my witness statement, I catch the tail end of a conversation that makes me believe they're already seeking warrants to search Rothman's family's homes and the RoSt labs.

And they've already started hauling in other witnesses from The Village, while I was in the statement room. When I get to reception, Gillian, the nurse who runs the house Rothman swapped clients around in, and two of her guests are sitting in the waiting area, watched by a young female police officer.

The cops also asked me for contact details for Reece Miller, the guy who we nearly lost on our walk in April. My idea. He was an alcoholic and one of Rothman's one-to-ones. It might be just coincidence, but I doubt it.

I asked the detectives who interviewed me if I'll get arrested for tying Rothman up, but apparently not. Unless Rothman decides to press charges, they explained, what I performed is what the British consider a citizen's arrest. Obviously, I should have alerted them immediately once Rothman was bound, they reiterated, rather than call on my friends, but they reckoned any judge will understand that I acted irrationally in my terror. They really didn't think Rothman *will* press charges, though. Because, to quote the older of the two, 'we've explained to him that it'll just look like sour grapes and that he's better off fully cooperating with the law without making life difficult for any of the witnesses of the Crown Prosecution Service'.

He winked when he said that.

I think they liked me.

Before I leave the station, I stop at the front desk and ask the officer behind it if he knows where Alan, Rowan and Silas are.

We were all asked to follow the police car that picked up Rothman, but once we got here, we were split up. Before we called the police, Alan told everyone to tell the full truth, minus mentioning any knives or death threats.

He took the knife off Silas and heaven knows what he's done with it, but he's reassured us it's clean and gone. He also leaned heavily on Rothman, telling him to keep his fucking mouth shut about that part, or he'd find out just how many of Alan's old SAS unit were making a living as prison guards these days. I think it was mostly bullshit, but Rothman nearly wet himself a second time, so I'm pretty sure we're good.

Alan was cool about the cops knowing about the gun. Apparently, he has a license and can't see that he's going to get arrested for pointing it at what he thought were intruders. It's such a weird country. Shit themselves at the thought of a stiletto knife or a handgun but waving an Elmer Fudd in people's faces is totally okay. Go figure.

The young officer behind the desk looks at the visitors log and tells me that all three of them left the station over half an hour ago. I frown and turn toward the exit.

The detectives told me I was free to go, after they took my email details, phone number and postal address in the States, so the court will be able to get in touch with me about trial dates.

Things I learned today: British police need to release or charge a suspect within twenty-four hours. This makes them really shift their asses as soon as they have somebody in custody. Once they have charged somebody with something as serious as manslaughter, the Brit version of murder in the second, which is what Frank is looking at, there is no chance for the suspect of being released on bail. The accused is remanded in custody, and the way the guys in the building behind me are motoring, I'm confident Rothman ain't coming out of here again if he's guilty.

Also, manslaughter has to go to Crown Court rather than Magistrates Court, no idea what the difference is, and that can take up to a year. I try to feel around the idea that I'm tied to this case, this place, for another twelve months of my life. It feels okay, *right*.

I have a sneaking suspicion everything will feel right from here on out, as long as Rowan is involved. I wonder if he meant his offer to come home to the States with me and take care of John for a while. I really hope so.

I'm allowed to go home, the cops said. Of course, I am, they can't keep me here against my will just because I am a witness. But they were very clear they'd want me to come back and make my statement in court in person. It sounded like the Crown will pay for my plane ticket back to England when they need me. Although, if Frank really is guilty of getting Simon killed, I would have been happy to pay for the ticket myself.

Fucking asshole.

Blinding anger rises in me for the millionth time in the last few hours.

I need to get out of here.

I step into the revolving tinted glass door and a couple of seconds later it spits me out onto the street in the glaring midday sun. There is a moment of total disorientation when I try to consolidate the hours that have passed since we called the police with the day before me.

I yawn.

I'm so fucking exhausted it's unreal. I haven't felt like this since my time in ER.

And I'm starving.

My stomach growls at the idea of eating itself.

I look up and down the road, but there is nothing here other than residential houses for as far as the eye can see. Diagonally opposite, on the other side of the road, a sign outside one of the houses advertises it as a Quaker Meeting House and for a moment I am tempted to knock on their door. Ask them for a bowl of oatmeal. I'm that hungry. Nausea makes my head go woozy for a moment and I shut my eyes.

Where the fuck is Rowan?

Halfway through the thought, a horn honks as a car approaches. I open my eyes again, only to see Alan's SUV pull up next to me, Silas riding shotgun. The back door opens and Rowan folds himself out of the car. He comes to my side just in time to steady me.

"Whoa, hey there, beautiful lady. Feeling a bit wobbly?"

I nod as I lean into his hug.

He smells like home and safety and Rowan.

And like burger.

He definitely smells like burger and fries.

I step back in the hug, swallowing.

"You went for food?"

He nods, his hands still firmly on my hips.

"Yeah, they said you'd be a while longer, so we went to get some food. You hungry?"

"Starving."

"Well, hop in then. I hope you like a good old-fashioned cheeseburger," he says, grinning. "'Cause that's what I got you."

I take a moment before I follow my instincts to dash into the vehicle like an alley cat in search of scraps and stare into his eyes.

"I think I love you," I tell him.

Because I do. I think. I still don't really know what that means but, actually, I don't care any longer. I do know I *want* this man. By my side. In my bed. In my heart. *Inside* of me. Not just for now but for always.

He grins.

"Yeah, yeah that's what they all say when you bring them food."

Then he turns serious, more serious than I've ever seen him. He leans down to plant a sweet, gentle kiss on my lips. Totally not a Rowan kiss, yet entirely him. I can feel his smile as he mumbles against my mouth.

"Glad you realised."

He holds me firm when I want to step back and slap him.

"I think I love you, too," he adds, seriously.

Then he laughs, steps out of our embrace, turns me in the direction of the open car door and slaps my butt.

"Go eat, woman."

DIEGO

"Drinks are on me," I say as we pile into my bar, The Cockatoo.

It's such a shite name, but I'm stuck with it. It's too successful to change anything. Cocktail drinkers like naff crap like that.

"I bloody well hope so," Rowan answers, and walks straight to the bar, plonking his butt onto *my* bar stool.

People in this town have been dropped for less.

This fucker, though, walks in a cloud of protection he isn't even aware of. Normally, I don't give a fuck about family connections, but Rowan is the brother of my best friend and that counts for shit in my head.

Said best friend, also blissfully unaware of his status in my life, trails behind, waiting for their women to return from the loo, where Raven and Grace made their first pit stop when we walked in.

Silas is like that.

Old-fashioned British gentleman through and through. Women are seated first and all that.

Mind, if I'd had Sheena as my mum, I would probably have turned out the same.

Instead, I had *my* mother.

Who never ever forgave me for eating my twin.

Yeah, no shit.

Oleandra Benson's, my beautiful but dumb as shit mother, first and only pregnancy was marred by the fact that initially there were two heartbeats, but at twelve weeks, there was only one foetus left. They call it *vanishing twin syndrome*. My mother calls it 'the devil ate his sister'. In her head, my twin would have been the girl she longed for. A little dress-up doll with angelic hair and blue eyes. I got the blond hair but grey eyes and, God forbid, a *penis*.

Bitter much?

On the plus side, my mother giving me the middle name Diego, which means supplanter in her native tongue, no less, provided me with a ready-made town moniker once I stepped up to the bar at eighteen, and took over the fledgling fight club my father had created.

It just sounds so much better than George.

My dad and his Britain First bollocks. I hate nationalists. Especially ones that marry a Spanish girl. Especially ones that get the Saint George's cross tattooed on their chest. That's Saint George as in that Roman soldier, who was born in Turkey to Syrian parents, killed in Palestine and buried in Israel, and who never set foot on the British Isles.

Fucking brain-dead idiot.

He was well pissed off when I started calling myself Diego.

Apparently, that's not respecting my English heritage.

But eventually, even his two brain cells had to admit that it's a great name.

And at the end of the day, it's all about image.

Even 'keepin' it real' is just a fucking illusion.

A hearty slap on the back wakes me from mulling shit in my head.

"You coming, boss?" Silas asks as he and the women move past me to join Rowan at the bar.

I hate that he calls me that, even in jest. He might still be on my payroll as a bouncer, but he's my *friend* for fuck's sake.

The few decent childhood memories I have, all have Silas in them. They're usually of us, sitting on the threadbare carpet in Sheena's old house on Albion Hill, watching Tarantino films, eating microwave popcorn and feeling like the shit because we were watching over 18s.

Little did I know then that I'd grow up to be *in* a fucking Tarantino film. I was still young enough then to think my father was a decent, if a little shady, guy. Oh, sweet innocent little George, where art thou?

I love that in my head I can have thoughts like that, and nobody asks me how to fucking spell that shit. Because that's another one of the major disappointments I am to my mother. I can't spell for love nor money. In either Spanish *or* English. My Spanish is atrocious anyway, but I'm majorly dyslexic in whatever language you chuck at me. Doesn't affect my brain for numbers, though. On the contrary, I'm fucking shit hot with numbers. Much to my father's delight.

But I really don't want to spoil the last evening that these guys in front of me and I are going to be together for in a long while by thinking about that cunt. So I snap out of it and follow the others to the bar, where Grace is already arguing with one of the Kellies, who is serving today.

"What the fuck do you mean, you don't know what a Blood and Sand is?" Grace growls at her then turns to me. "Your bar staff is shit, George."

I see Kelly's eyes grow wide at the fact that Grace dares to call me by what is basically my dad's name. Nobody around here would ever dream of doing that, but these guys, this small round of people, they do. It pisses me right the fuck off, but I let them anyway.

I take off my suit jacket, hang it on a hook below the bar, take the cufflinks out of my cuffs, slip them in my waistcoat pocket, and roll up my sleeves before I deign to shrug at Grace.

"You want a cocktail they don't know, you go make it yourself," I tell her.

Grace's eyes spark up. She used to work at a bar in a hotel in Washington D.C., where she is from, and she's fucking great at cocktails. I've been trying to get her to work here for weeks now, but she doesn't want to. I'll grind her down eventually.

She swans behind the bar and starts doing her thing.

"You can go, serve the other customers, Kelly," I dismiss my bartender. "Grace'll take care of us tonight."

"Damn right, I will," Grace says as Kelly huffs off.

"I'll have a..." Raven starts, but Grace cuts her short with a gesture.

"I'll decide what people are having."

"Ok," Raven says, reluctantly.

I have only known her for a few days, but she has issues handing over control, that's crystal clear.

"But I don't want to be hung over on the plane," she tells Grace.

"Ditto," Rowan says, nonchalantly, as if he flew all the fucking time.

Silas and I shoot each other a look. We know for a fact that tomorrow is the first time Rowan's ever getting on a plane. And he's shitting bricks. But we let him have his bullshit.

"You're not getting on a plane until tomorrow *evening*," Grace answers with raised eyebrows. "That's eight hours to get rat-assed, eight hours to sleep, eight hours to get over your hangover. You'll be fine."

She puts the first cocktail she's made in front of Raven.

"Try that. If you don't like it, pass it back to me. Waste not, want not, as my mum used to say."

Raven takes one sip then puts a protective arm around her drink.

"Nope, that's mine," she states, and keeps sipping as if it were a religious duty.

Grace laughs and looks at Rowan through eyes like slits.

"Now, what to make for you? Hmm. Maybe I'll create something specifically for you. Let's call it the First Time Traveller, shall we?"

Trust Grace to take the piss where Silas and I don't dare.

Those guys really lucked out with their women.

Am I envious?

Maybe a little.

But I don't really have time for all that mushy shit right now. And it's not like I can't get my dick serviced any time I like. I could go up to Kelly right this minute, snap my fingers and say, 'Upstairs, now!' And she'd follow like a good little lamb and let me fuck her any which way I'd please.

They all do.

I'm not an idiot, though, I know they have no interest in *me*. They want Diego. The danger and the purse.

What they get is a piece of meat between their legs, an orgasm or two and the cab fare home. Depending on my mood, they don't even get the orgasm. I don't really give a shit if they get off or not. I learned the hard way that if I do the gentlemanly thing and make them come before I do, they become clingy. I don't like clingy. It's a ballache.

But all of that doesn't mean I wouldn't give my eye-teeth for being looked at the way Grace looks at Silas right now or kissed the way Raven is kissing Rowan right now, with all she's got, giving him a thorough taste of her cocktail. My dick starts stirring, just because the two of them are fucking hot to look at.

Live porn to the left, true romance to the right.

None of that is on the cards for me, though. Not now, and probably not ever.

A ruckus at the door grabs my attention, just as Grace puts a suspiciously green drink in front of me.

"What's the green shit in there?" I ask her, only half paying attention because one of the bouncers at the door is waving me over.

"Absinth," she answers with a smirk. "The devil drinks Absinth."

"Cheers," I say sarcastically, before I leave them to see what's happening at the door.

"Sorry to interrupt, boss," Arlo, the doorman, says as soon as I approach. "But there is a girl outside, insists you know her and that she is allowed in, but she hasn't got any ID and she looks like she's about twelve."

I nod and put a hand on his arm. I like this guy. He lost his hearing in one ear in a league fight to Silas and now wears a fuck ugly hearing aid, but he never even thought of ratting on us and is still genuinely pleased to see Silas when they meet. I like the ones that take responsibility for their own decisions. Can't stand whiners and blamers.

"No sweat, Arlo," I tell him. "I appreciate the caution."

Then I step through the door and look at the Polish pixie on the step outside.

I don't blame Arlo for not letting Kalina in. She doesn't look twelve, but she doesn't look her age either. She's eighteen, nearly nineteen. Her birthday is in a few weeks, as I found out yesterday when Sheena told me that she's planning a trip to London for the occasion and asked if she could count me in on the theatre tickets. So now I'm going to go see a musical for the first — and hopefully last — time in my life. Shoot me now.

"Finally!" Kalina huffs when she sees me, and I have to suppress a smile.

She isn't doing the age thing any favours by wearing denim dungarees and leaving her face makeup-free below her ultra-short pixie cut.

The first time I ever saw her she looked very, very different.

She was wearing a black and green skin-tight, very short sequin dress, six-inch heels, heavy makeup and a choker.

I will never forget that image.

How could I?

I've wanked over the memory a hundred times since.

It fucks with my brain when I try to merge the vision in front of me with the girl from that day. It makes me feel dirty, and not in a good way. Especially since I like the girl in front of me almost more than the sequinned jailbait siren.

I'm a fucking pervert.

"She's cool," I say to Arlo, and I can tell he is suppressing a look of surprise when I offer Kalina my arm.

She grins triumphantly at him as we walk past. I look down at her tiny frame and I catch a glimpse of the fact that she is wearing nothing under her dungarees other than a black bra.

She's not even a B-cup, but my dick springs to attention.

There is a special hell for people like me.

I remind myself that she's *all* wrong.

Not just the age thing.

I *like* my women *with* curves. Big tits, big ass. And long hair I can wrap around my fist. Grace would fit the picture, if she were a brunette. And if she wasn't with Silas, and if she wasn't so damn *Grace*. Raven, too. If she wasn't...and so on.

But this thin, boyish thing on my arm? Not in a million years. Not even if I wasn't seven years older than her.

So why is it her nails, which are lightly scratching over my naked arm below my rolled-up shirt sleeves, are giving me shudders all the way to my toes and to the tip of my dick?

Fucking criminal.

We arrive at the bar amidst hollering greetings. Kalina slips her arm out of mine and hops onto a barstool in a practised, elegant move that totally belies her look of the day. This girl is just a bag of contradictions. She opens the tote bag she's been carrying under her other arm and takes out a mobile.

"You're famous!" she exclaims, looking at Raven. "Look!"

She scrolls until she finds the article she is looking for and shows us. It's from the online edition of one of the better newspapers and all about the scandal around RoSt Cosmetics and the illegal drug trials on humans they were running at The Village where Raven worked, though thankfully Raven isn't actually mentioned by name. Kalina reads out the whole article with enviable fluency in her sexy-as-hell Polish accent and when she finishes, Raven sighs.

"Shit, that sounds almost like Halosan were in on it. That's exactly what my bosses are trying to avoid."

Kalina shrugs as she puts the phone away then turns to Grace to receive a drink.

"Oh, Gimlet," she purrs appreciatively.

Grace and Kalina have a giggle fit that nobody else understands, before Kalina takes a sip. Then she carries on talking to Raven.

"You cannot avoid what press think, yes?"

Raven shakes her head.

"No. But it's still not good. It's why they want me to go back to the States and lie low until Rothman's trial."

Rowan slips off his bar stool and slips his arms around her from behind.

"You were going to do that anyway, remember? Only now you get to do it with *me*."

Grace laughs behind the bar.

"Yeah, how exactly did you swing that, Raven? When we came to visit you at The Village, it was all hush-hush because you're not supposed to be fucking clients, but now they're *paying* him to stay with you?"

Raven grins into her drink.

"We're not fucking. He's my security guard. I just happen to have met him as a guest."

"And they bought that?" Grace asks.

Raven shrugs.

"I think they *want* to buy it. I'm pretty sure they're going to cut me loose after the trial, so they don't really give a damn. Good thing is, that'll also be way after my tie-in expires, so I won't owe them shit either. They don't even want me back at work in between. It's basically 'shut up, lie low, make us look good in court, here have your salary paid in the meantime'."

There is a moment when she seems almost sad, but then Rowan squeezes her harder, and she shuts her eyes, leaning back against him with a blissful smile on her face.

It's a beautiful picture.

One day, I want a woman to lean on me just like that.

DIEGO

Brighton Bad Boys II

Kalina

"Happy birthday to you, happy birthday to you, happy birthday, dear Kalina, happy birthday to you."

Grace is singing at the top of her lungs as she barges into my room, carrying a tray with a cake on it. I already know it's raspberry and white chocolate, because Grace is the world's worst secret keeper when she is excited. I also know that Silas baked it late last night, since the house we live in is small and you can't really hide things like using the oven from the other occupants.

What I didn't quite expect were the nineteen little candles on top, all lit, which wobble precariously as Grace navigates the many bits and pieces of small vintage furniture that I have accumulated over the last six months of staying here.

'Here' is a two-up two-down — as the British call it — house in Shoreham, a small town on the south coast of England, just seven miles out of Brighton, owned by Sheena O'Brien. Sheena is Silas' mum. She is also landlady extraordinaire to one lucky language school student, *c'est moi*, as well as to Silas and his girlfriend, the very woman who is currently looking expectantly at me. I guess Grace wants me to hoof over on the bed, so she can sit down and let me blow the candles out.

I shuffle to make space for her, and she lowers her butt onto the mattress then shoves the tray in my face.

"Put your lips together and blow," she says, and I giggle.

A nice, girly giggle.

"It is whistle, no?"

She grins at me.

"Blow the fucking candles out, Kalina, we have shit to do today," she answers, and it occurs to me that being Silas' girlfriend really hasn't done the obscenities quota in Grace's speech any favours.

The American woman in her mid-twenties who I met a few months ago wasn't shy of the occasional cuss word, but she didn't pepper her language with continuous swearing, like she does now. Grace also sounds more British all around now. I guess it's what happens to people if they become so entangled with a British bad boy that they decide to move continents to be with him.

Not that Silas is a bad-bad boy. He's a kitten compared to his friend Diego, aka George Benson.

My heart trips when I think of George, and that annoys the hell out of me. George 'Diego' Benson is everything I don't want or need in a guy. Like the perfect do-not-shop-for-this list. Yet there is something about him that...

Argh. Don't go there, K, don't go there. Concentrate on the job.

I banish all thoughts of him. For now, anyway. Since he's coming to London with us tonight to see a musical, tickets for which Sheena organised as my birthday treat, it'll be a short-lived exercise.

Instead, I concentrate on Grace's beautiful smile and the flickering sea of candles in front of my face.

I shut my eyes and blow hard.

"What did you wish for?" Grace asks immediately after the flames go out and puts the tray down on my lap.

That I could tell you my birthday is on Christmas Day, not in August. That I could tell you there are candles missing and we're not as far apart in age as you think. That I could talk to you in my real voice. That I could let you see the real me.

I love this woman so hard. She is the first actual friend I made in such a long, long time. She is smart and kind and funny and just so totally *Grace*. I take the tray and stretch over to put it on a stool next to my bed then sidle up to her and sling my arms around her.

It's a Kalina thing to do. Kalina is exuberant and pixie-ish and hugs people all the time, provided they let her.

Kristina, the real me, is much more reserved. She is a doer, not a hugger. Unless you're family, then she's quite tactile. She's the Goth rock to Kalina's chart pop.

Grace hugs me back hard, ruffling my short hair. Like a big sister. Like me, with my little brothers.

For a moment, I wonder if Grace would still like the real me, or not so much.

"That is secret," I answer her question, muttering into her mane of long, dark red tresses, because that is exactly what people expect you to say. "Thank you, Grace."

She draws back and looks at me with a little sadness.

"Hey, least we can do. Must be tough having a birthday so far away from home."

I make a dismissive gesture.

"Pah, it's harder on my parents than it is on me," I declare.

The sadness disappears from her face and the smile comes back.

"Your English is getting so good," she comments. "That was a perfect sentence. Go you, lady!"

Ah shit.

I shrug.

"Language school costs fortune, Tata says. So I work hard."

She gets up.

"Yeah, but not today, you won't. No studying allowed on your birthday. There is a breakfast table downstairs and presents, and then there is a spa day at The Palais, and then there is London. So get your pretty little ass in gear, lady. Prepare to be spoiled rotten."

"Presents?" I ask, astonished.

I kind of knew about the spa day at The Palais, the hotel where Sheena is head of housekeeping, and I knew about going to London, but the idea of presents makes me feel extra guilty about this charade.

"Well, one," Grace holds up a finger. "I couldn't let everybody else give you something but not me."

"But I thought you chipped in on the theatre tickets already," I protest, once again forgetting that my English is not supposed to be that good yet.

It's happening more and more often around these guys because they make me feel too comfortable. I should have changed accommodation when it became clear I had to stay longer, but I didn't want to. I like it here. So I extended my stay with Sheena.

Really, I should be finished with the job by now and be back home. This is proving to be one of the toughest cases I've ever had.

To my great relief, Grace doesn't notice my slip up this time, because she is too busy explaining.

"Uh-uh. That's old news. George took care of the tickets in the end. He wouldn't let any of us pay him back a cent, I mean penny. Says since he was the one who insisted on renting a box instead of getting normal seats, it was for him to pay."

"We're getting a *box*?" I exclaim.

Grace's green eyes go round and her hand flies to her mouth.

"Oh crap," she mumbles behind her palm. "That was supposed to be a surprise."

"Yup, George is gonna have your hide," Silas says as he appears in the door. "Kalina, you'd better work on your acting skills before tonight and act really, really surprised when we get there. Now, are we having breakfast before the cats eat it, or shall we let them have first dibs on the smoked salmon anyway?"

At 'smoked salmon', I'm out of bed and sitting at the breakfast table in no time. One of the few things Kalina and Kristina do share is an enduring love for all things seafood.

Bring on the caviar.

DIEGO

I'm in that magic state between sleep and consciousness while your dick is hard and the dreams are good, when an unwelcome knock raps on my bedroom door.

"Diego?" my parents' maid Daisy — yep we have a maid these days, complete with a black and white uniform and surgically enhanced tits — calls out hesitantly from the other side.

None of the staff here at the Benson Mansion really know whether to call me George, as my father does, or Diego, as my mother and most of Brighton's lowlifes do, and Daisy is new to this stupid game that is my life.

"Come in," I respond but refuse to open my eyelids.

Under the duvet, I wrap a hand around my dick and run the pad of my thumb over the slit to spread the large bead of precum that's gathered there. The dreams were *very* good.

As Daisy steps into the room, I slowly, surreptitiously start stroking myself. I don't want to scare her off of the bat. I'm pretty sure she knows what the deal is around here, but she is so new, I haven't tried her out yet.

"Your father sent me to wake you. He would like you to join him for breakfast," Daisy informs me.

Fuck. Not a sexy thought.

The old man wanting to have breakfast with me means he wants to talk shop, and I avoid mingling my business with his business these days. Most of the time, I just don't want to fucking know.

My father is a complete cunt. His dealings hurt innocents. People. Animals. Society.

Me? I'm just half a cunt. The people — and it is always people, never other creatures — who get hurt in my line of business all know what they are letting themselves in for and are old enough to make that decision.

Plus, lately I've been trying to go properly legit. I have this fantasy that people will finally leave me the fuck alone if I do. Being a fledgling don in this city is a pain in the arse most of the time. People always want something from you. Your money, your connections, your hide.

They never just spend time with you for the sake of spending time.

There are exactly six people on the planet who I can just be me with. Two of them, Rowan and Raven, are presently in America. The other four I am taking to London to see a musical tonight. For Kalina's birthday. A fucking musical. Never thought I'd be seen dead going to one of those. But that's what she's into, so that's what she gets.

Thinking of Kalina gives me the familiar surge of lust, guilt and self-loathing that always comes when I conjure her face up in my mind's eye. Or when I see her in real life. Or if I just think her name. Half her name, even.

The language student living under my oldest and best friend's mother's roof right now is the most hauntingly beautiful, sexy creature I have ever seen, yet so, so wrong in all respects. She is too young, too scrawny, too boyish.

I like tits and an ample bottom I can bite into, long hair that I can wrap around my fist while I fuck into a woman, who jiggles a little — not too much — from the impact. There isn't a single jiggly bit on Kalina. Even her tiny tits appear to be made of the alabaster the rest of her seems to consist of. A girl like her, and at nearly seven years younger than me, Kalina is definitely a *girl*, should only ever evoke feelings of protectiveness in anyone, never ever carnal desire.

Yet even berating myself for thinking about her in that way in the first place makes my dick quiver in my fist. I can't win.

I'm fucked.

Somebody is clearing a throat, and I remember that Daisy is still in the room, waiting to be dismissed.

"Come closer," I tell her instead, smiling with my eyes still shut.

People call me handsome, reminiscent of Brad Pitt, back when he was younger and bleached his hair, and they say I have a killer smile. I've seen Daisy looking. They all do. Some look at my face, others at my purse. None of them at *me*.

But they don't need to, provided they open wide.

I listen out as she steps up to the side of the bed. They are not hesitant steps. Good. I guess my father's already put her through the drill.

"Want to earn a bit extra today?" I ask her bluntly.

I never used to pay for sex. I don't need to. But lately I've started feeling more comfortable if it's a business transaction rather than fucking with their dreams, literally, of landing me and my wallet more permanently.

I can hear her swallow before she answers.

"What would I need to do?" she asks.

I throw off the duvet to reveal my hand pumping my boner.

"Suck me off," I say.

She doesn't miss a beat.

The mattress dips when she gets on the bed, and I roll onto my back.

As soon as her lips find my cock, I put my hands behind my head and let her service me.

She's okay at this.

Not great, not bad, but a decent average.

She sucks nicely up top and pumps the base with her hand in a rhythm that works for me.

I relax into it.

Behind my shut eyelids, I see large brown, nearly black eyes, looking at me hungrily as a matt purple painted mouth runs up and down my shaft. I see high cheekbones in a heart-shaped face popping out more starkly as her cheeks are sucked in. In my fantasy, I hear her whimper with lust as she worships my cock like no other woman has before.

My orgasm comes hard and fast, the actual woman on my cock withdrawing before my load lands in her mouth.

I open my eyes and look at Daisy's blue irises and her pink, glossy lips as she scrambles from the bed with a demure smile and rights her uniform.

"Good?" she asks.

"Good enough," I say.

I know I'm being a complete arsehole, but I intend to reimburse her well enough for her not to mind too much.

Still, the comedown is huge.

Not the right woman, not the right mouth.

"Tell my father I'll be there in fifteen."

I love doing Grace's makeup.

I'm a little bit peeved because today there isn't much to do since she's chosen to dress up as the bloody obvious — and eighties singer Tiffany was not exactly known for her dramatic eye shadow. She was all about that girl next door look. Sheer lipstick and lots of blue jean shades.

Possibly the trickiest bit of transforming Grace today was finding a fringe hairpiece that matches her hair colour. No Tiffany without a fringe. Or bangs, as my American friend calls it.

I pick a raspberry pink lip gloss and start dabbing it on Grace's lips.

She is so damn pretty with her green eyes and her plump mouth that has these neat little folds at the corners, giving her a permanent cat's smile. Her lips are so, so kissable. Whenever I apply lipstick on her, I want to kiss it off immediately, just to taste what they'd feel like.

Not that that's ever been on the card between her and me, because I think Grace is very devoted to Silas. And very hetero.

I, like most self-respecting ex-boarding school girls, swing a *little* both ways, despite the fact that my school was mixed and the segregation between girls and boys was not even per house, just per floor. That's good old Germany for you. Would have been unthinkable in Poland.

But even with the boys just a flight of stairs below us, we did a bit of experimenting on the girls' floor. And I can't say I didn't like it. I *really* learned to French kiss from Lauren Watson, the girl in the room next door, and one of the disproportionately large number of British diplomat and army brats that boarded alongside me.

Lauren was something else, just thinking about her kisses still makes me wet now, years later, though I'm very sure I'd take a man over a woman any day in the long run.

A man with plump lips.

George has plump lips. I've heard people compare him to Brad Pitt in looks, but they are so, so far off. Even Brad Pitt in *Thelma and Louise* doesn't have a patch on naturally blond, grey-eyed, sultry-mouthed George Benson.

I sigh out loud, and Grace giggles.

"You alright there, lady? That's one hell of a sigh. Need some private time before the limo gets here?" she teases. "Wanna share who you were thinking about?"

I smile down at her coquettishly and shake my head then move around to the back of her.

"What do you mean, limo?" I ask evenly as I pull the headband gently over the back of her head and lift her long hair out of the loop.

"Well, it's George. I'm fully expecting a limo, don't you?"

I hadn't given it a thought, beyond the fact that I get to spend a whole evening with the man I've been lusting over for months now. A completely off-limits man. Not that my heart knows that. It trips dutifully at Grace mentioning his name. It's not interested in the prospect of a limo in the slightest, though. As far as I'm concerned, George 'Diego' Benson could pick us up on a rusty old bicycle. Though that would be a long trip to London. And I'm not sure where we'd put the others.

I'm so fucked.

I try to distract myself by combing Grace's hair with my fingers. I love doing her hair almost more than doing her makeup. I miss having long tresses to play with. Of all the things I had to give up, getting rid of my hair was the hardest. It used to be down to my butt, and I used to spend hours experimenting with it. Updos, downdos, around dos. But long hair is a hazard in my line of work. It was the day I cut it that my father finally believed I was serious about my chosen profession.

One day, when I'm too old to do this shit, I'll grow it long again.

Until then, I'll just play with my friend's hair.

DIEGO

The limo hire service is dead on time and the driver arrives to collect me from my parents' house at three in the afternoon on the dot.

I don't need to live with my folks.

I own an entire six floor building on the seafront, with a nightclub called TripleX in the basement, a cocktail bar on the ground floor and a bunch of apartments, most of which are rented out to hookers who want to work independently but who like the security I can offer them. One is also rented out to a couple of the bare-knuckle fighters from the league I run from TripleX, and another serves as the office for Santos-Benson Security, a legitimate stable of security personnel that I hire out.

Whichever way you look at it, I deal in humans — a modern-day slave trader. My ancestors would be so proud. Although so far, I have stopped short of getting involved in cleaning crews and fruit pickers. I have *some* morals.

Not that any of what I do makes enough money to buy a building like that. I didn't. I inherited it, along with some older prostitutes who are now retired. It was the last of the big seafront properties that was owned by just one person. My grandmother.

Nan hated my dad's guts, but apparently, she doted on me. Could have fooled me, but her last will and testament said otherwise.

It's funny, because everyone thinks my parents going up in the world was somehow to do with a notorious fire in one of the most contested properties in Brighton, the occurrence of which realigned the powers in this city somewhat. The implication being that Dad organised it. It's complete baloney. My father will always be a two-bit-hustler. No more, no less. I guess that's why Nan despised him so much. He just wasn't up to scratch.

But she was a shrewd woman and she didn't want a family feud on her hands. She knew it would piss off my dad royally that she wasn't going to leave him 'The Brick', as it's lovingly called in the family. So, long before she died, in order to soften the blow, as a kind of runner up prize, she gifted Dad enough money to buy a house on Woodland Drive, and to carry on playing at being a criminal on a bigger scale.

He really is shit at it, though. Mostly because he's got a vile temper. I'm forever picking up his tabs. He constantly needs watching, which is part of the reason I still haven't moved out of Woodland Drive. There is a penthouse flat at The Brick that is technically mine, but I only use it for business meetings, those that don't relate to Santos-Benson Security, and shagging.

The penthouse remains decorated pretty much exactly how Nan left it and still has most of her furniture in it. The old bat had impeccable taste, so I don't particularly want to change any of it, but it means it never really feels like my place either.

Plus, call me a pussy, but after a long night in town, I kind of like coming back to the leafy suburban neighbourhood of Woodland Drive. The nature out here balances the blood and the gore and the sweat and the stink I deal with at work.

I should look into buying my own place somewhere away from both, really. But I'll be paying back the mortgage I had to take out on The Brick in order to pay the inheritance tax till kingdom come, and I don't really want to settle myself with any kind of debt that doesn't have a business return on it.

I force myself to stop mulling my living arrangements. Today is dedicated to Kalina's birthday, to forgetting business and number crunching for a few hours. It's a rare luxury and I intend to make the most of it.

I wonder what she'll make of my outfit.

I wonder what *she* will be wearing.

I've only ever seen her out of her tomboy clobber and in full war paint once. The first time I saw her, she was dressed up to the nines, all dramatic silent film type makeup, a very short Charleston style sequin dress, heels no woman who isn't soliciting should be able to walk in and a *choker*. A fucking choker. She looked like an evil fairy queen, come to haunt my every fantasy. And she has.

Little did I know then that beneath the veneer of that one night lay a way-too-young girl who is just, well, really fucking nice. Who bakes and sings along to pop songs on the radio at the top her lungs, who works hard at improving her English every day at the language school she goes to and who spends her days off working in a charity shop. I struggle every day with having to consolidate my evil fairy queen with the girl who feeds me home-baked goods whenever I hang out at Sheena's house. What I don't struggle with is knowing that I'm not gonna go there. But that doesn't mean I can't treat her to a really fucking nice birthday, so far away from home. And if that includes dressing up in stuff I haven't worn in years, then so be it.

I sling the battered black leather jacket I had to dig up from the back of my closet over my shoulder. It's August and way too hot for leather, but it's part of the look, so it's coming with me. I learned that where it was always on the big side for me when I bought it, it's now kinda snug. I've bulked out a bit since my teens.

"Diego?" my mother's unsure voice floats down to me from halfway up stairs.

I turn to look at her, unsurprised by what I find. She's swaying slightly, clutching the banister for support. She's already plastered, or maybe she's still plastered. My mother often starts the day as she means to go on, with a double measure of brandy. My guess is, she has a permanent alcohol level of a minimum of one per mille. She starts getting wobbly around one point five. But then again, it is afternoon already, and by the fresh bruises on her neck and upper arms, her and Dad had a particularly *fun* night. For him.

When I was little, she used to wear high necks and long sleeves all the time. She gave up on hiding her war wounds the day I cottoned on. I've begged her to leave him, but she hates me too much to entertain anything I say to her.

"Yes, Mother?" I answer her.

"Where are you going? Your father wants you back in time for dinner."

She must be confused by the clothes. She actually thinks I'm sixteen. Which puts her more at two point already. That's high this early in the day, even for her. For a moment, I wonder if I can leave her. But then I think, *fuck it*. It's not like she even wants my protection.

"He can fuck off," I answer and turn away to leave the house.

The driver of the limo is waiting outside, halfway between the long, sleek black Lincoln and our front door. I notice that he's trying to hide a puzzled expression on his face.

I'm pretty certain I know what that's about.

My long-time associate Eric at Red Carpet Cars probably told the guy his pick up was of a businessman from the 'Benson Mansion'. Now the poor sod is wondering if he definitely has the right address. First, there is my outfit and then, well, the house my parents left the old neighbourhood for, back when I was still at school with Silas and I had no idea yet that I was going to be fucking minted once Nan popped her clogs, is no more than a detached five-bedroom mock Tudor family home. It's got a triple garage and a big enough garden to have a separate indoor pool structure and a summer-slash-guest house, so it's a fuck load bigger than the house I grew up in, but it's not what the average person thinks of when the word 'mansion' is mentioned.

It started as a joke. Between Silas and me. Then the joke kind of stuck. Now everyone in fucking Brighton calls it that and nobody knows why.

"Mr Benson?" the driver asks hesitantly but politely as he retreats to get the door for me.

"Diego," I answer. "Mr Benson is my father."

I see the recognition flicker in the man's eyes. He has heard of Diego. That always helps.

I'm about to lower my body into the limo when I hear my father's voice behind me.

"Where are you going, son?"

I turn to him. He's standing in the doorway, panting as if he'd run to catch me.

"Out. To London," I answer him.

"I told you, I needed you tonight," he shouts angrily.

I hold my hand up to the limo driver to signal that I will be back in a moment, and then I walk back towards the house and meet my father face to face.

"I'm not having this conversation in front of other people," I tell him quietly. "I told you this morning that I was busy. I am busy."

"Doing what?" he asks with a snarl. "What's so fucking important you need a limo? More to the point, what is so fucking important that you think you can just blow me off like that?"

For a moment I feel like I'm sixteen years old and like I'm not actually calling the shots around here. Maybe it's the clothes. Without my standard Diego attire, I feel my armour is missing.

"I am taking my friends out to the theatre," I answer truthfully and sigh. "And, technically, I could only blow you off if we'd had an appointment for tonight. Which we did not. You asked me at breakfast to come along and I declined because I had a prior engagement. That is not blowing somebody off. That is sticking to the diary."

"You really think you are something, don't you?" he snarls. "What friends?"

I debate for a moment whether to tell him, while he carries on glaring at me. But I know that he will find out anyway. Better to hear it from the horse's mouth.

"Silas. His girlfriend Grace. A girl called Kalina." I pause because I know the next bit will be like a rag to a bull. "Sheena."

"Sheena O'Brien?" he spits out, his head going a nice shade of choleric-red. "You dare take that bitch and her spawn out for a jolly?"

There is bad blood enough between my old man and Sheena O'Brien to fill all the abattoir troughs in the county. Although, really, it's more between Sheena and Dad's best friend, Cecil O'Brien. The surname is no coincidence. They are all old Brighton and they've known each other since they were primary school children. Cecil was Sheena's husband for a while, back in their twenties. She kept his name, which is how Silas ended up an O'Brien, though thankfully he's not from the same gene pool as Cecil.

Cecil is the arsehole to my dad's cunt.

I stay cool in the face of my dad having his little paddy. Fuck knows how he made it this far in life with that temper. It is a mystery to me that nobody has taken him out yet. Or that he hasn't had a coronary. It's a constant worry. I can't stand the guy, but he's my *dad*. I have some good memories of him from when I was little. Even the biggest arsehole is a hero to his son when he's carrying him on his shoulders. And if he's the only one out of your parents who doesn't outright hate you.

"Sheena's spawn is my best friend, Dad. Deal with it. Or just butt out. Whichever. I'm going now."

I'm almost facing the limo again, in my attempt to leave a second time, when he goes that little bit further. That one place I *really* can't stand.

"What kind of name is Kalina? Is that the dirty Pollack chick they've got staying there?"

My jaw clenches.

Out of the many, many things I despise about my father it's the Britain First bollocks that I hate the most. Racism runs firmly in the family. It's the one thing he and Nan agreed on. Her family's riches were built solidly on the seventeenth century slave trade, followed by a couple of hundred years of running black, brown and yellow — her words, not mine — prostitutes.

Racism in all its forms is such a load of horseshit, but it riles me even more from a woman who made her fortune from whoring out different skin colours, or from a man who married a Spanish woman.

Yup. Oleandra Benson, nee Santos, my dearly unbeloved, ninety-five-percent-of-the-time drunk mother, must have already been totally paralytic when she let a British wanker with a Saint George's cross tattooed on his chest fuck a child into her. Well, two, actually. Story goes, I ate my twin sometime in the first trimester. But that's a whole different can of worms.

I turn back to Dad and go toe to toe with him.

It's an unfortunate vantage point because I can see all the burst little veins on his face, the spittle that landed on his chin and the yellow in his eyes.

"Don't you dare disrespect my friend like that," I hiss at him. "Go take your racist bullshit and go fuck your Spanish wife. If you still can."

He takes a breath to retaliate, but before he can rip into a rant, I step out of his space and retreat backwards towards the waiting limo.

"Save it, Dad. I'm gonna go do what the fuck I like now. And you go, do what the fuck you like. As long as it doesn't cost me any money or kills any of my friends. See you in the morning." I grin to myself as I add, "As-Salaam-Alaikum."

Then I bow out.

Kalina

I've never seen George 'Diego' Benson wear anything other than a tan three-piece suit or, very occasionally — when he comes back to Sheena's house after a workout of sparring with Silas in the gym — grey sweatpants, a t-shirt and a zip-up hoody.

So it really is no wonder that I just can't keep my eyes off his butt when he walks us to the limo, dressed in skin-tight denims. It's annoying because a red and black lumberjack shirt hangs partially down over it, obscuring half the view. I appreciate that he made the effort and came as an infinitely better-looking Bryan Adams, complete with a tight white t-shirt under the flannel, battered black leather jacket thrown over his shoulder and biker boots on his feet. But he could have left the shirt behind. I would have got the gist anyway. And I would have got a better view. Though even half the view is hot as fuck.

As we all arrive at the limousine that George made to wait for us in the pub car park opposite Sheena's house, I tear my eyes away from the backside of the sexiest devil on earth and look at the others.

I was so blown away by how different George looked when Grace and I came down the stairs and he was waiting in the hallway, I never even asked, who or what Silas is meant to be.

He and his mum decided to surprise me and while Grace and I got ready in my room, they got ready in the kitchen.

One look at Sheena in her man's suit and with her newly hennaed, carrot-orange, super-short hair and it's clear she is Annie Lennox. It suits her down to the ground. Sheena was a pretty successful model in her late teens and early twenties. She is a stunningly beautiful woman, even now, approaching fifty, and she has that slightly glacial aura Lennox had in her heyday.

Silas inherited a lot of his mum's good looks, but he's been bashed up in the bare-knuckle ring a few times, mashing in his nose and giving him an edge that is way beyond pretty boy, catapulting him into the super-hot. Before Grace turned up on the scene, I eye-fucked my landlady's son every chance I got, but never once entertained the thought of actually going there.

Firstly, because I'm on a job, and secondly because there just wasn't any crackle between us.

As I examine him now, I still can't figure out who he is going as. All I'm sure about is that he is supposed to be one of the plethora of New Romantic pretty boys that were abundant in the decade the musical we are going to see revolves around.

He, too, has gone full on *outfit*, with a short, double-breasted military jacket over a white pirate shirt, buttons open to an obscene level, baggy black trousers, ending in boots — and so many studded belts hanging askew off his hips, I wonder if he's going to develop a limp by the end of the night. He's also wearing eyeliner, blusher and lip gloss. I've got to hand it to Grace's man, he doesn't do things by half.

This is a side I never used to see of him before Grace. I actually assumed Silas would refuse to do the dressing up bit. He used to be so super serious all the time. I didn't think he had it in him.

"Who are you?" I ask him over my shoulder as George opens the limo door for me and offers me his hand to help me clamber inside.

Partially because I am stalling about putting my hand into George's and partially because I really can't figure it out.

Silas looks offended.

"Simon Le Bon," he answers with a huff. *"Obviously."*

"Simon, who?"

"Simon Le Bon. You know, lead singer of Duran Duran. What kind of eighties music buff are you if you don't know who Simon Le Bon is?"

Yeah, about that, that's more a Kalina's thing. My music taste is quite a bit more modern. And darker.

"Duran Duran, sure!" I exclaim. "Sorry, did not know singer's name. You look great."

If in doubt, hand a man a compliment and it throws them right off.

I look away from Silas, and finally take George's hand. My heart is still racing from the realisation that I've made another *faux pas*, so I try to tell myself that the extra rush I feel when our palms connect is just part of that.

Can't remember what the excuse was last time this happened, but as I look into his storm-grey eyes for a moment, just before he gives me the momentum to hustle my tightly wrapped bottom into the carriage, I realise that it's not only the lies I'm telling others that are slipping.

It's also the ones that I keep telling myself.

DIEGO

She has done it again.

It's been three months since I saw her in that little Charleston number and despite the fact, I've jerked off over the memory countless times, in reality I had nearly forgotten how extreme a transformation she can pull off.

And this time, she's gone a whole lot further.

I look at her and I don't recognise the girl in those bloody dungarees she's been wearing all summer *at all*.

In her place sits a wet dream in platinum blonde.

With green-blue eyes!

I didn't even know that was possible.

Thing is, I've never gone for blondes. I've always been firmly a gentleman who prefers brunettes. But clearly, where Kalina is concerned, none of the usual rules apply.

I've been hard since the minute she descended down the stairs, bright red lips smiling at me so widely that it showed off that sexy little gap between her front teeth beautifully.

In hindsight, it was always obvious who she was going to pick for herself as soon as we found out that the brand new musical about eighties cheese pop we had our eye on for her birthday outing was getting a bit like Rocky Horror, in as much as whole audiences had started dressing up as appropriate pop idols of the era for the shows.

Kalina is tiny, has that gap between her front teeth and absolutely rocks a beauty mark painted above her lip, as I'm finding out.

Personally, I would have preferred a dark-haired version of Madonna, but who cares? The girl opposite me in the limo, sipping champagne and fishing for the strawberry slices in her glass with her tongue is fucking gorgeous, in any hair or eye colour.

I unashamedly stare at her as she lounges on the light grey leather seat, a perfect vision in silver white, from the tip of her newly bleached hair to the silver pumps on her feet. The skin-tight satin dress she is wearing gives an illusion of curves I never thought I would see on her. It's knee-length and shoulder free, showing off her creamy calves below and her delicate clavicles up top. I have a thing for nice clavicles. Girls this skinny usually have an ugly hollow just above them, but Kalina doesn't. Her clavicles curve beautifully, creating a perfectly inviting shallow dip at the bottom of her throat that I could run my tongue around all evening.

It hits me that this is the difference between a woman who was meant to be this size and a woman who hungers herself into it. Kalina was meant to be exactly the shape she is and, devoid of jiggly bits or not, that makes her sexy as hell.

"You okay, George?" she asks with a big smile, and I realise I've been staring maybe a little too long. "Are the hair and the eyes freaking you out?"

She runs her hand through it and winks, while it hits me that her English has come on in leaps and bounds lately. A few months ago, she wouldn't have used the articles 'the' in that question, and probably got 'are' and 'is' confused.

Her vocabulary has become huge, too. I mean, better than some English arseholes I know, who communicate mostly in grunt.

I'm not going to point it out to her, though.

I reckon it's an awareness thing. I think when she's relaxed it flows, but if I make her conscious of how good she's becoming, she'll start stammering and making mistakes again.

I have the same problem when I need to write something.

I'm seriously dyslexic, though my spoken English is fucking fantastic, thank you very much. But I really can't spell to save my life. At school it used to get worse whenever my English teacher would point out that I was spelling something correctly. If, for example, I had just written 'choreography' right and he'd praised me for it, then there wasn't a hope in hell I would be able to get the next word in the test down on paper with the letters in the right order. Not even if the next word was something super simple, like, say, 'the'.

So I keep my trap shut in order not to make her feel self-conscious.

Instead, I steal the bottle of Krug out of Sheena's hand and refill Kalina's glass.

"No, it's not freaking me out," I answer her question. "I'm just enjoying the view."

"You like blondes, huh?" she says lightly, but I can feel the sting she is experiencing underneath.

I'm not having that. Not on her birthday.

"I like what I see," I admit with a small smile. "But what I see is not a blonde. It's a girl who could rock any hair and eye colour under the sun."

"Way to go on the cheesy compliments, Bryan," Grace interjects cheerfully, leaning forward to hold out her glass.

Silas, who's sitting next to Kalina and Grace, rolls his eyes.

"Oh fuck. We're not gonna call each other by our fancy dress names all evening, are we?" he asks, horrified. "I didn't sign up for that shit."

Sheena, who is sitting on my side, snorts a laugh.

"Let me get that straight, baby," she says to her son. "You let me put blusher on you for this gig, but you refuse to be called Simon?"

Silas rubs his hand over his face in despair.

"Whatever," he mumbles before he looks up to make eye contact with me, realisation dawning on his face. "I look like a complete twat, don't I?"

I grin.

"Yup," I confirm then point at myself, trying to mollify him with a bit of self-deprecation. "But at least you don't still fit into the clothes you wore at sixteen."

He smirks at that.

"Thought I recognized the threads. I can't believe you still have all that."

"What can I say," I tell him, holding his gaze. "I'm bad at letting stuff go."

It almost seems like the women stop breathing for a tick, specifically to appreciate the little moment my friend and I are having here.

This is as close as I'm ever going to get to telling him that I fucking love him and that he will always be my friend, no matter who holds what position in this shit show that is our life.

It's beautiful, even if I do say so myself.

Then Silas breaks the spell by looking away, a grin on his face, and Kalina leans forward to grab my attention back.

"You used to wear clothes like that?" she asks with round eyes.

I laugh.

"Well, yeah. Suits aren't really a fashionable thing if you are a teenager in Britain. Too much like school uniform," I inform her.

Kalina leans back with a mysterious smile playing on her lips and looks to the side.

"What?" I ask her.

I see her smile unfold into a full-on flirtatious grin as she turns back to me.

"Nothing. Just that Madonna has thing for, what are they called?"

She pauses for a moment, gesticulating up and down to indicate, well, basically, *me*.

"Ah, yes," she finally carries on. "Blond bad boys in lumberjack shirts."

Then she leans back, nonchalantly sips her drink – and unashamedly eye-fucks me for the rest of the ride.

Kalina

The man is painfully hot.

He's hot in his suits, he is hot in sweatpants, and he is extra scorching in *this*.

And he's giving as good as he gets.

I don't take my eyes off him for the rest of the ride to London, and he never once wavers in looking right back at me.

By the time we get to the restaurant where we are going to have our pre-show dinner, I'm a bundle of hot, desperate, slippery need.

Just from *looking*.

I'm so lust drunk, and yeah, a little tipsy from the champagne, I barely take in the white linen on the tables and the general silver service ambience when we enter the place.

I do realise, though, that we stick out like sore thumbs. Thing is, I wouldn't have minded going somewhere much simpler but, of course, we are limited to places that have parking for stretch limos.

To my relief, the maître d' doesn't bat an eyelid as he comes over to greet us. From what he says to George, I get the idea that George explained to them ahead of time why we are not rocking up in the formal wear that all the other patrons are wearing. I guess it is that attention to detail that makes Diego so successful.

The maître d' ushers us to follow him and my whole body catches fire when George puts his hand on the small of my back to guide me to my place at the table.

I've been in the company of many men in a lot of different guises and at a lot of different functions but not one of them has ever actually done that. I always thought that was just a romance novel cliché. I guess not.

We are barely seated when Grace and Sheena excuse themselves to go to the toilet. They look at me expectantly, but I shake my head.

"I'm good," I say with a smile.

It's a lie. I need to pee. It's been a two-hour ride, of course I need to pee.

But I'm also not getting through this evening without doing something about the state I'm in.

So I will wait for them to return before I will make my own excuses.

Timing is *always* key.

DIEGO

She's so turned on, I can fucking smell it.

Her pussy is calling to my tongue like a siren.

I bet she tastes divine.

Our little game of don't-look-away in the limo has left her in that delicious state of permanent arousal, and when I put my hand on the small of her back, I can feel her shiver with lust through the cool fabric of her dress. A shiver that goes right up my arm, through my heart, into my balls and to the tip of my permanent hard-on.

She is absolutely killing me.

I make sure she is seated at the head of the table, as is befit for the guest of honour, and take my place to her left. Grace sits down opposite me and Silas next to her, so Sheena ends up opposite him, on my other elbow. We have barely ordered drinks, when Grace and Sheena excuse themselves.

Kalina stays and peruses the specials menu.

I pick mine up, and the letters immediately start swimming in front of my eyes. But it doesn't matter. I made sure I had the restaurant read out the specials to me over the phone earlier, while I was on my way to pick up the others. I've already made my choices and memorized them.

For a moment, it occurs to me that Kalina also might need help with the menu. Her everyday English may have expanded exponentially in the last three months, but these posh places with all their poncy linguistic acrobatics are maybe a bit too tricky for her grasp still.

I feel like a failure.

I look over my menu, trying to catch Silas' eyes. He's one of the very few people I am not directly related to who know how difficult reading is for me.

He wasn't looking, but the force is strong between us today, and his head comes up almost immediately. His eyebrows ask me if I need help, but I surreptitiously shake my head and then indicate to Kalina and the menu with my eyes. He blinks in understanding.

"You okay reading the menu, Kalina?" he asks, and it pains me that I can't be that person for her.

She looks at him and frowns. She seems seriously puzzled for a moment. Then understanding lights up her features.

"Pardon?" she says in a pretend French accent, which is cute as hell. "Oh. Ah. No, thank you. I'm fine. It's all here in French as well."

"You speak French?" I ask her, intrigued.

She turns to me and smiles.

"Qui. Und Deutsch, och Svenska, y un poco de Español."

"Wow," I say, genuinely impressed.

"I didn't know that," Silas says, eyebrows raised.

We are interrupted by the waiter bringing us a breadbasket with all sorts of fancy artisan bread rolls, the sommelier hot on his heels.

On one of Grace's recommendations, supported by the respectful nod of the sommelier, we have moved from champagne on to a Pinot Gris. Due to the lack of Grace's presence as he returns with the bottle now, the sommelier appears to choose me to go through the whole wine tasting spiel, but I indicate for Kalina to do it.

It's her birthday, she gets to say yay or nay.

No idea if she knows anything about wine, but she does a great impression of somebody who does, and the Pinot passes muster. Once the sommelier has retreated again, reassuring us that the waiter will come back for our food orders as soon as everyone is at the table and we're ready, Silas picks up the conversation from before.

"That's impressive, Kalina," he ponders. "And unusual. I don't want to sound like a typical English prick, but usually people in the rest of Europe learn English as a foreign language first, or not? How come you learned, like, all the other ones first?"

She looks at him blankly for a moment, while she chews on a piece of bread then she laughs and shrugs.

"There are more than two hundred languages spoken on the continent, Silas," she answers in perfect English. "So speaking three or four is hardly all of them. My family considered German and French the more important ones. We lived in Sweden for a bit. And I chose Spanish next because it sounds nice. And because I like Spanish literature. And Spanish art. The food is good, too."

I can't help it.

"What about Spanish men?" I ask, and watch Silas chuckle silently.

She smiles mysteriously and gives me another one of her sultry gazes, eyelashes at half mast. It really shouldn't work this well with her naturally dark eyes obscured by those green-blue contacts, making it hard to read what's actually going on in her mind, but fuck me if my dick isn't trying to burst through the buttons on the fly of my Levi's now.

"Ah," she says with a regretful note. "Most Spanish men are dark. I told you before, I prefer blond."

Silas laughs out loud at that.

"You two crack me up. Just so you know, you're looking at the best of both worlds there, Kalina. That bastard is half Spanish, believe it or not."

She draws back a bit and her eyes go from bedroom-heavy to round so fast, it's comical.

"For real?"

I nod.

"For real."

"So, Diego..." she starts, questioningly, waiting for me to fill in the blanks.

"Is my actual middle name," I answer.

She leans into me again, lightly putting a dainty hand on my arm and scorching me all the way into the deepest, darkest corners of my lust-addled mind.

"I'm finally finding out things about you today," she says and searches my eyes. "I like it."

There is an interesting emphasis on the word 'you' in there that makes my heart break into a tap dance routine.

Then she abruptly retracts and gets up, just as Grace and Sheena reappear at the table.

"Excuse me, people. Looks like I need the toilet after all," she announces. "If the waiter returns, I will have the grilled artichoke hearts, then the lamb cutlets."

On that note, she grabs the rest of her bread and swans off in the direction the other two women just came from.

Kalina

I'm sure there is a special kind of prison, somewhere in France or Switzerland or some other country where they are still big on etiquette, for people who walk through a swanky restaurant, munching on the free bread filler-uppers, but I'm starting to feel too woozy to care.

Tasting the Pinot Gris was the straw that broke the camel's back, or the drop that brings the bowl to overflowing as they say in my native tongue. Which seems more fitting, given the circumstances. I only had two glasses of champagne in the limo, but I haven't eaten since breakfast. If I don't count the strawberries.

And there is also still the small matter of me feeling hornier than I ever have in my life. That's not helping with clarity of mind either.

Which is why I'm about to do something about it.

As I weave through the main body of the restaurant, dutifully ignored by the other patrons, I hope and pray that this upper-class establishment has the kind of toilet cubicles that give you full privacy.

My hopes are rewarded with an expanse of 'restrooms' that truly deserve the name. The individual cubicles are generously sized and completely built up in brick and mortar, tiled to the ceiling and with solid wood doors.

There are three in total and each of these little havens for bodily functions has its own marble sink, overlooked by a gilded mirror. The obligatory hand wash and hand cream dispensers rest in a wire holder screwed to the wall. There is a wicker basket with rolled up hand towels on a plinth and a stylish laundry bag made from Hessian to put the used ones in. Next to the toilet roll holder, a small silver box is screwed to the wall, containing an array of different sanitary products along with a bunch of those paper disposal bags that have a Spanish flamenco lady printed on them. I never knew what that was about but seeing her always makes me happy. And, of course, there is a bowl of potpourri, dispersing its scent from a specifically designed alcove in the wall.

I look around me while I pee and try to work out when the last time was, I went to somewhere like this.

It's been a while.

It's nice.

I step up to the hand basin after I've finished relieving myself, and stare at the woman in the mirror while I soap my hands.

I don't know her. She might be anyone.

This green-blue-eyed platinum blonde sex goddess might well have no qualms about getting herself off in a restaurant toilet.

And I really need to get off if I want to make it through this evening.

I watch her as I hitch up my dress to my waist and spread my legs a little, and a thrill runs through me, but it's just a little *too* weird this. So I lean forward to rest one arm on the edge of the sink and my forehead on top of the arm, closing my eyes. As soon as I do, I see George's face. His luscious mouth. His stormy grey eyes, always so soft when he's at Sheena's house but so harsh when we see him in town, doing business.

I focus back on his lips as I slip two fingers past the edge of my soaked panties and dip into my creamy folds. My finger pads become his mouth, moving over my clit in teasing circles. In my head, I beg him to enter me, but he has other plans. A third finger becomes his tongue as it runs around my dripping hole, dipping in and out. At home in bed, I would try to draw this out for a while, but I need to get back to the table and I've been waiting for release all afternoon, so I move his imaginary mouth back to my nub and let him rub his tongue over it in earnest. Two fingers, long strokes, one rhythm. The way I like it. My orgasm builds in seconds and I welcome it with open arms.

But it runs through me like a pretty sparkler rather than a firework.

Everything that is supposed to happen happens.

My heart rate speeds up, my insides contract rapidly around nothing, my clit pulses under my fingertips and more cream seeps out of my pussy.

I feel mildly satisfied.

And I'm not sad.

But I'm not sated either.

Nowhere near.

I grunt in frustration and straighten up. I grab one of the hand towels, wet it through under the cold tap and wash myself between the legs. Classy, I know, but I'm not prepared to carry on running around with a mess between my legs. The cold terry cotton hits me and the sensation is both cooling yet still arousing. I can't win.

Once I'm clean, I wash out the little towel with soap and wring it out properly before I toss it in the laundry bag. I waddle over to the sanitary goodies, my panties still pulled down, select a slimline pad and put it between myself and the irrevocably damp fabric.

I straighten myself out, go to wash my hands one last time.

My heart speeds up at the idea of going back and sitting down next to George again – and I resign myself to the conclusion that while I might just have taken the edge off it, the fever just won't be doused. That the only way to douse it is to get George Diego Benson, no more quotes in my head now I know it's his real middle name, to stick his dick in me and fuck me till we're done.

I take a last glance at the woman in the mirror.

Maybe she can succeed where Kalina failed.

DIEGO

Kalina is different when she returns from her trip to the toilet.

Less flirtatious. More focused. Still sexy as hell but not every breath she takes goes straight to my dick anymore. Which is a good thing. Because I'd like to enjoy her company for a bit without constantly having thoughts of eating her out flashing before my mind's eye.

During the meal, I notice that she isn't drinking the wine. She is sticking to water and sobering up rapidly. When I offer to fill her wine glass during the main, she holds a hand over it and shakes her head.

"No, thank you. I want to stay clear in the head."

I like that. A lot.

I like a woman who can pace herself, and I suddenly realise that I've never seen her properly drunk.

She has come to The Cockatoo, my cocktail bar, with Silas and Grace a fair few times in the last couple of months, often enough for the bouncers on the door not to try to ID her any longer, and for the bar staff to know her drinks are *always* on me, if I'm there or not. I've also been around Sheena's house when alcohol was flowing in the kitchen, but I've never seen Kalina sway or slur her speech or become glassy-eyed. Not even close.

In a way, this nineteen-year-old girl has more maturity than most of the women in my life, present company excepted. Grace, too, ain't a lush. She's worked hotel bars since the day she was old enough and knows her limit. And Sheena is Sheena. She can drink for England one night, and then not touch the stuff for months. I pry my eyes away from Kalina for a second to look at the profile of the woman on my other side, who for so many years while I was growing up was the only viable mother figure in my life.

She notices me looking and grins without turning to catch my eye.

"What are you staring at George Benson?"

"You," I say, raising my glass. "Thank you."

She glances sideways at me, puts a fork of food in her mouth, chews, swallows, dabs her lips with the linen napkin, takes her glass and clinks it against mine.

"What for?" she asks with a suspicious undertone.

"Being his," I pause to indicate Silas, who is absorbed in feeding Grace a titbit from his plate, "mum and probably the only maternal influence I've ever had."

She laughs so hard at that, she never even gets to sip her drink before tears of laughter start rolling down her cheeks. Silas, Grace and Kalina all look across to us, puzzled, until Sheena's halfway composed herself again and pats my back.

"George, if I was your only maternal influence you got problems, honey. You should go see a therapist," she announces to the table at large then finally raises her glass. "To my boys, present and absent, and to the fact that I was a completely shite mother to the lot of you," she says merrily.

"I'm not sure I should drink to that," Silas says with a grin before he takes a sip.

"You should always drink to the truth, baby," Sheena retorts, and follows suit.

Kalina looks somewhat bewildered around the table and sips her water. Then she turns to me with a frown.

"What do you mean?" she asks earnestly.

"What he means," Sheena starts, before I can get a word in edgewise, "is that these two," she pauses to indicate Silas and me, "have been raiding my fridge, wearing my carpets thin and watching illegal films in my living room since they were yay high."

She indicates the height of a leprechaun.

"Oh!" Kalina exclaims. "I didn't know that. I knew you were at school together, but I did not know you were that close!"

She claps her hands with joy and then suddenly she turns serious.

"Now I understand better, why you would not allow Rowan to kill him."

A shudder goes through me at the mention of the fight I so stupidly organised, which could easily have seen Silas snuffed out by his adopted brother. If it hadn't been for the fact that his stupid brother loves him almost as much as I do. Almost.

Suddenly Kalina's hand reaches out and cups my cheek. Her touch is gentle, loving, and I want to cup her hand in mine and press it down, but, of course, that is not the relationship we have.

"Don't beat yourself up about it," she says softly and lets her hand sink away. "We all want to impress our parents. Want their, what is the word, approval. You were not to know they were going to pay Rowan to kill Silas. I mean, how could you? Who does a thing like that?"

My father and his best friend, that's who.

But I don't say it. I don't want the memory of one of the darkest moments of my life to taint this evening. Silas has forgiven me. He and Rowan are good. And after years of this stupid master-and-servant relationship Silas and I developed once I became Diego, through all of what's gone down in the last few months, I have finally, finally, got my friend back.

I look over at Silas and he shrugs.

"What she said, man. It's water under the bridge. Your father and Cecil O'Brien are the cunts in town. You're not," he says before one of his rare smiles transforms his face into the handsome bastard that he really is. "You're just a teeny tiny bit of an arsehole."

"Language," Grace says and slugs him on the arm.

He looks at her with feigned wounded pride, rubbing the spot.

"Ouw-a. She," he says accusingly, jutting his chin out at his mother, "said shite earlier, but nobody hits her."

Sheena swallows the mouthful of food she's been chewing and smiles sarcastically.

"That's 'cause I'm the matriarch around here. Keep up, child!" she retorts.

Sheena and Grace clink glasses and drink to that, while Kalina concentrates on me again.

"Tell me more about yourself," Kalina says.

"Like what?"

She shrugs.

"The usual, I guess. What music do you like? What do you do to relax? What books do you read?"

I take a deep breath.

"Classic rock. You're looking at it. I don't," I answer her questions in succession, and see Silas' head snap up on the last answer.

He knows how significant a confession that is.

Kalina has just been let in on the best kept secret in Brighton and she doesn't even know it, because she is frowning deeply at my answers in non-comprehension.

"I don't read," I clarify. "I listen to audio books."

Her face lights up with understanding.

"Ah. I get it. Busy man, no time to read. But you can listen to audio book while you are working out, yes?"

I could chicken out here if it wasn't for Silas looking at me intensely, daring me to show her the chink in my armour.

I shut my eyes.

"Yes but no." I take another big breath. "I'm really badly dyslexic. Do you know what that is?"

She stares at me for a moment and then smiles a smile that I don't quite understand, almost as if she was totally relieved about something.

"Yes," she answers my question. "I know what that is. Does it bother you?" she enquires.

As if we were talking about a blister or something.

As if it weren't important.

"Yeah," I answer. "Of course it does."

She lifts her eyebrows at me the way people do when they berate a silly child.

"It is no big thing, yes? Especially not today. You can use the dictate function on your phone. Like you say, you can listen to audio books. And it clearly does not stop you from being successful. You must be good with numbers, no?"

Yes, I am. And I'm happy that she recognizes that, but I'd be lying if I said I wasn't peeved at how easily she dismisses the bane of my life.

"I don't think you get it," I say with an edge to my voice.

But she just smiles and makes a brushing off gesture.

"No, maybe not. But at least you can see stars at night."

"Huh?"

She leans in until we are so close, I can feel her breath fanning over my face.

"I have minus three in both eyes. Without my contacts, I can't see a thing," she whispers.

Then she presses a kiss on my cheek, and all my blood goes south again.

Kalina

My accent is all over the show.

I'm messing up left right and centre here, but the strange thing is, nobody seems to notice.

It's this man. He's got me twisted in knots in ways nobody ever should be able to twist up anybody, but specifically not me and specifically not this *criminal*.

Because that's what he is, no matter which way I look at it.

But in a sense, so am I.

Right or wrong, what I'm doing in the UK is not legal.

I'm operating without a licence, under a false name and I entered the country on a fake passport. All in all, that little package carries a sentence of around ten years.

Still, we are universes apart, George Diego Benson and Kristina Kaminski.

I carry on studying him as we get back into the limo after the restaurant, but this time I try to keep the heat on a low simmer and enjoy just watching a happy, insanely attractive, guy in the company of friends, while George, Silas and Grace laugh at Sheena's stories.

The wine has loosened Sheena's tongue and she's regaling us all with anecdotes from the eighties. It was her decade, after all, she reminds us. And for a time then, she was hot property on the international model market. Which means she met quite a few of the stars the show we're going to see pays homage to, and she has great fun telling us who used to be nice, who used to be nasty and who used to be downright stupid. If she is to be believed, brains were not the forte of many eighties pop stars.

The limo crawls through the West End until we arrive outside the theatre. The driver stops and comes around to open the door for us. George climbs out ahead of the rest of us, to help first Sheena and then me out of the limo, followed by Silas who holds his hand out for Grace. A small group of foreign students stops and gawks at us for a minute before their teachers usher them on, but other than them, nobody on the busy pavement looks at us, or our ride, twice. And I wouldn't expect them to. Limousines are as common a sight around here as black cabs and buses.

I leave my hand in George's after he helps me out and take a moment to breathe in the atmosphere, while Silas and Grace are still peeling themselves out onto the street.

I've been to the West End in London a few times in my life and it's a strange place. Almost like the world's earliest theme park, but for nightlife and entertainment.

Every building is a theatre, or a club, or a bar. And it's always super busy. If you time it right, you can see many of the grand names in British acting shuffle around the district in their day clothes, as they go from work to lunch, back to work.

"Shall we?" George asks after we have all assembled, and nods at the theatre.

He looks down at our still entwined hands and then meets my eyes with the question if he has permission to keep them like this. I nod, once.

My hand feels right in his.

Electricity sings between us, but it also feels safe. I've never had that before. I've felt the chemistry with people and I've felt protected. But I've never before felt both with the same person.

He smiles a soft smile when I acquiesce, and leads me to the VIP entrance, trusting the others to follow us.

As we pass the steady stream of people that is already streaming into the building, I check out the crowd's costume efforts and rate the competition. I spot at least five other Madonnas, and one who clearly couldn't decide between Madonna, Cindy Lauper or Pat Benatar.

George follows my gaze and stops for a second to bend down and whisper into my ear.

"Not a patch," he says, his breath on my earlobe giving me goose bumps.

We are let in by a sour looking woman who leads us first into a cordoned off area and then upstairs to a VIP bar. There aren't that many people here. It's a Friday evening performance of a generally sold out London show, but I guess it's not the premiere. I'm a little disappointed because half the people up here did not make the effort to dress up and I was really enjoying people watching downstairs and grading individual effort in my head.

George asks us what we want to drink and then orders this round plus another couple of bottles of champagne and sparkling water for our box for later. Predictably, the bartender looks me up and down, because even dressed as Madonna I'm apparently not convincing as of age. Before he can say something, I rummage around my handbag and pull out a passport.

"Here," I say, with a smile, and hand it to him, already opened on the picture page.

He smiles gratefully because I spared him an awkward moment and his eyes light up when he sees the birth date.

"Oh, happy birthday," he says with genuine warmth and hands me my drink first. "Hope you enjoy the show tonight."

I thank him, tug the passport away and wait for the others to be served.

George looks over my shoulder, down my cleavage and into my handbag.

"Is it annoying that you have to carry your passport everywhere, little lady?"

I grin up at him.

"Not as annoying as people calling me little lady, no," I retort, and then laugh at his crestfallen face. "I'm playing with you. I don't mind." And because I clearly like living on a knife edge when it comes to him, I add in a lecturing tone, "It makes sense anyway. Never know when you have to leave the country suddenly, you know."

I say it with enough humour that he doesn't blink. But his eyebrows go up anyway as he nods approvingly.

"Noted. Wise woman."

"See?" I tease. "That is *so* much better than *little lady*."

Then I turn around and cock my head for him to follow.

We collectively go to stand around a high table, sip our drinks and watch the most interesting thing here, which is a backstage door opening and closing from time to time with technicians and the occasional cast member in varying degrees of makeup dashing in and out.

"We should have stayed downstairs," Grace voices what we are all thinking after a while. "There was more to see there."

"You want to go hang out with the riff raff?" George asks me, and I nod.

"Let's go, then," he decides, picking up his drink.

We all follow suit and are about to carry our beverages back to the staircase when the stage door opens again, and a photographer steps out into the bar. From the way he carries himself, it's clear he's a regular feature here. He does something with the lens of his camera, scans the room for a photo op and then looks straight at us. He lets the camera sink and zeros in on Sheena. I can practically see the cogs turning in his head, before he crosses the room like a man possessed and heads straight for her.

"Excuse me, are you...?"

"Annie Lennox?" She laughs. "Only for tonight, ducky. But I appreciate the compliment."

He stares at her a moment longer.

"Sheena Smith. You *are* Sheena Smith."

DIEGO

I can tell Sheena is taken aback.

She didn't expect that.

But she plasters on a big smile and nods.

"Yes, I am," she admits. "Though you are showing your age, young man, by recognizing me, I tell you."

The guy chuckles at 'young man'.

He's around the same age as her, aged equally well, with a bold, nicely shaped head, a beard to compensate for it, and the trim figure of someone who is naturally active but not ashamed of the aging process. I wouldn't mind that figure when I'm twice my age. My dad has got seriously thick around the middle in the last few years.

The guy also has sparkling blue eyes and full, smiling lips going on underneath the beard, which makes me instantly like him. He's kitted out in the standard aging photographer uniform of jeans, white shirt open at the collar, a *very* good quality silk waist coat that tells me he earns a decent living, and equally expensive black shoes you can run in.

I catch Silas' eye and pass on my approval. Just because. He smirks back at me. Before we can have a longer wordless conversation about how happy we are for this little interlude, because it sure as shit is good for Sheena's soul whenever something reminds her that she wasn't just forgotten fodder in a relentless industry, the photographer guy finds his tongue again.

"Sorry, I should introduce myself. I'm sure you won't remember me. Paul Green. We were only ever on set together once. I'd just got my first gig as an assistant runner. It was—"

"The Malta shoot." Sheena finishes his sentence serenely and smiles at him.

A real smile this time. Warm and friendly, like she rarely gives to anyone but her closest circle.

She holds out her hand, so he can blow a kiss on it. And he fucking well does. But it's not an affected or cheesy gesture on either part. When he straightens up, he looks at her with total adoration. He's so totally absorbed by her, he doesn't even see us.

Silas and I confer again. We like the guy.

"Of course, I remember you, Paul Green," Sheena says sweetly. "You were the only help on that shoot who would look at my face when all the other jerk-offs were looking at my frozen tits. A girl doesn't forget the boy who's there with a robe as soon as the photographer shouts 'take five'. I take it this is a regular gig for you?" she asks, indicating the theatre at large.

Paul nods.

"Yes, it is. I do all the promotional shots for this production company. There are a couple of cast changes tonight, which is why I'm here. Updated pictures for the website."

While the two of them chat, the place suddenly starts filling up around us and a glance at my watch tells me it's quarter of an hour till curtain time.

"Sorry," I say to Kalina. "I think we missed the boat on people watching, Kalina. It's time we found our box."

She makes a gesture that tells me she doesn't mind in the slightest, accompanied by a look that says, 'who cares, look, Sheena's got an admirer'.

"We will go ahead, Sheena," Kalina informs her. "See you in a moment." Then she turns to Paul Green. "Nice to meet you. We will be back here for the interval. See you then."

I have to work hard not to laugh out loud. Kalina couldn't be more obvious in her matchmaking as she practically drags me away and gives Grace and Silas a flick of the head to tell them to follow us. Out of the corner of my eye, I see Grace pulling Silas along in a similar fashion.

We have barely settled in our box, where the champagne and the mineral water I ordered are already waiting for us in coolers, when Sheena follows us.

"That was quick, Mum," Silas teases.

She sits down and sighs.

"He had to go back to catch them going on stage," she says dreamily, before she turns to me with laser sharp focus. "George?"

"Yes, mam?"

"Don't fucking calling me mam. Right, if - *if* - I was to stay in London tonight, would you make sure Kalina gets home alright?"

I frown at her for a moment, not quite catching her drift. But then I remember that Silas and Grace have booked a room in a hotel for after the show tonight, because Grace finally wanted to go sightseeing in London. Silas, who like all true Brightonians fucking despises London, still hadn't taken her until now, despite the fact she's been around since the beginning of May, give or take a couple of days when she misguidedly went back to the States. They offered for Kalina to stay, too, but she refused. She's been to London a few times and said she had work to do at home. But I think it's mostly because she didn't want to gatecrash their romantic weekend.

"Of course," I answer Sheena's question.

Sheena turns to Kalina.

"Kalina, ducky, would you mind awfully? It might not even happen but," she grins unapologetically, "it's been a long time since I got laid."

"Mum!" Silas exclaims.

Sheena turns to him with a 'what do you want, Chuck?' face.

"I promise I'll make him use a condom," she tells him dryly, before she delivers the next line. "Hopefully several. But at our age, you can never tell."

Silas looks down at the full champagne flute that I just handed him and screws his eyes shut.

"I could really murder a beer right about now," he mutters, just as the lights in the auditorium go out and the music starts.

Tough luck.

Kalina

I have no idea what the show is like.

I am too obsessed with the potential prospect of getting George alone for the whole ride back to Brighton. Two hours. A lot can happen in two hours.

And it would be kind of perfect. Madonna and Bryan fucking in the back of a limo then parting their ways, and by tomorrow he can don his suit again and I can get back into Kalina's dungarees — and nobody will be any the wiser.

But with a bit of luck, the fever will finally be gone, and I can concentrate on my job from there on out.

It's not his fault that this assignment is taking so fucking long, as far as I can see George and his associates have nothing to do with my case, but the fact I've been mooning over this bad boy hasn't exactly helped my general focus.

To finally get the chance to fuck him out of my system would be a golden opportunity.

So I spend the first half of the show hoping that Paul Green will show up in the bar for the interval.

I spend the second half grinning like a moron because he does – and then Sheena never returns from the bar because the two of them are too engrossed in catching up, show forgotten.

We go to find them after the final curtain and they are still so fully absorbed in each other's company, it takes them about a minute before they realise we're back and standing behind them. The sheepish grin on Sheena's face is all I need to see to know it's my lucky night.

A whoosh of nerves goes through me at the thought, settling in the pit of my stomach as a throb of anticipation.

"So," Silas pins Paul Green in his gaze, "is Mum staying with you tonight?"

He says it evenly but because he is Silas, the threat is always implied. Even with the remnants of Simon le Bon's makeup and in a silly New Romantic shirt, he looks nothing short of the deathly fighter that he is.

Sheena rolls her eyes at her son's bluntness but appears unflustered.

"I hadn't quite got there, darling, but thanks for brokering the deal for your old mother. I feel cherished," she tells him caustically.

Then she turns to Paul Green.

"Am I?" she asks him softly.

He smiles at her and holds out his hand to help her off the barstool.

It's all the answer she needs.

DIEGO

I have no idea what I just watched on that stage.

I was too preoccupied with the idea that I might have to sit through a two-hour journey with Kalina as my only company, *sans* chaperone.

It's going to be torture.

But I have morals.

Not many but I do where it counts.

She is too young for me. Too innocent. Too nice.

She does not belong in my world.

When I first met her, I had her down as a bit of a gold digger, but the more I got to be around her, the more I realised to my shame that that was just a preconception about Eastern bloc women, which I inherited from my father.

Dad propagates two sorts of racism. Openly cuntish, and in the form of subliminal messaging. Whereas I learned to recognize his openly cuntish ways early on, I still find myself caught up in thoughts sometimes that spring from the more surreptitiously racist shite he subjected me to during my formative years.

Kalina isn't in England because she is looking for a well-off husband. She is just a real sweetheart EFL student, who likes to flirt and who plays with fires she wouldn't be able to handle if they got out of hand.

She's also wicked smart and doesn't need to choose life as a kept woman. She could probably go to work for the United Nations with that language brain of hers.

"Where do you live, Peter?" I ask the photographer once it's clear that's where Sheena is headed tonight.

"Willesden," he answers, and I sigh inwardly.

Willesden is a very decent neighbourhood, but it's the opposite direction for us and dropping those two off will put another hour on the time I will end up spending in Kalina's company, alone. But no way am I letting Sheena go to an address we haven't checked out.

"You here by car?" I ask Green, and he shakes his head.

"No, motorbike, actually," he answers, and his face drops.

Presumably, he has just realised he hasn't got a second helmet to sling on Sheena to take her on the back of it.

"Oh, what'ya got?" Silas throws in, because he's still hankering after getting another bike after he had to sell his.

I scrub my face to hide my annoyance because I already know before Green answers that between here and when we drop Silas and Grace off, the conversation will now be solely about motorbikes. Something I have zero interest in. Not my thing. Wearing a helmet makes me feel claustrophobic. And not wearing one is a) illegal and b) fucking stupid.

"Ducati," Green answers to an approving nod from Silas. "But I can leave that in the garage here and pick it up tomorrow. We'll take a cab."

"No," I tell him resolutely. "I will drop you two off at your place in my limo," I inform him and pre-empting protest, I add bluntly, "I want to make sure we know where you live."

Silas gives me a small smile and even Sheena smirks. She is wise enough not to protest. She might be our senior and guiding star in life, but she is still a woman going home with a man she's only just re-met. She is also a woman with an appalling track record in relationships, so even if she did have objections, she'd just be outvoted by us.

There is no further discussion on the matter, and Peter excuses himself to get his kit before we leave. Silas catches my attention, while we carry on milling in the rapidly emptying bar.

"A word," he says.

We move away from the women to stand out of earshot.

"So," he starts, pinning me in his hazel gaze.

Silas' stare when he gets intense is fucking scary. Right now he's doing scary plus on me and I have no idea what I've done.

"Yes?"

"You're dropping Grace and me at the hotel, then you're making sure Mum and that guy get safely to his place. Make sure you watch them go into the building."

"You trying to teach me to suck eggs here?"

He holds up a hand and that's when I see that he's actually barely suppressing a grin. The bastard is fucking with me.

"I'll take a picture of them before you drop G and me off, so we have a record of his face, and he knows it," he carries on as if I hadn't interrupted, before he starts grinning openly. "And then, you will have a long ride home. A very long ride. With Kalina. Alone. In the privacy of a limo."

I get serious at that.

"Look, Si." I haven't called him Si since we were twelve. "You don't need to give me the big brother speech. I'm not touching her. Don't worry."

He outright laughs at that. Then he looks across to the three women until Kalina gives him a little wave, Grace blows him a kiss and his mum cocks her head at us. He turns back to me.

"Get real. If any of those three has set her sights on a man, you don't stand a chance in hell, mate. And I've been watching the way she looks at you since I took them to the track that time. And I've seen her suck an ice lolly, too. If she decides tonight's the night, you're toast, Benson."

He comes closer as if he's about to hug me, slides an arm around my waist and slips something into my back pocket.

"So have a few of these," he says merrily. "I went to the loo earlier and got some out of the dispenser for Mum, then I thought I'd better make sure you're covered and all. But," he adds, and his tone suddenly drops an octave, making it tricky to understand him without listening *very* carefully, because Silas only ever talks under his breath in the first place, "if you two do it, you treat her like the *person* she is, you hear? Don't treat her like one of Diego's whores. Treat her like George's friend who he's sleeping with, if you catch my drift."

I panic at that.

"What does that mean?" I ask him.

I manage to make it sound like a challenge but, actually, I'd really like to fucking know, because, frankly, I have no idea. My life hasn't exactly been full of male role models that show you how to treat a female with decency.

"You make sure she comes, either before or after you, doesn't matter. You don't take more than she is willing to give. And you don't drop her afterwards like a piece of meat. You take her back to our house, make sure she is snuggled up in bed and bring her a cup of tea or hot chocolate before you leave. And make it with milk not with water like it says on the packet. The packet is bollocks. Leave on a *good* note. And if per chance the two of you feel that fucking in the back of the limo is not enough and you stay the night, then you don't leave tomorrow without taking her for breakfast first. Got it?"

"Fuck off," I say good-naturedly.

And I swear to myself that I will never ever tell him how fucking grateful I am for his unsolicited advice.

Kalina

There is something about time when you are waiting for a particular moment to happen. It bends. On the one hand, it takes forever to get there and on the other, it's too soon when it arrives.

Today my moment arrives when George climbs back into the limo after standing outside to watch Sheena and Peter Green disappear into a really normal looking semi-detached house. I'm peeking through the open window and it looks like on the inside Green's house is probably as big as Sheena's, but unlike our place in Shoreham, this has a full driveway frontage. It's funny because when I think of London, I always forget that most of it doesn't really look like a big city at all. Most of the boroughs look like any other English town.

I say as much to George as soon as he slips back into the seat opposite me and tells our driver through the intercom that we are ready to roll.

It's kind of an inane comment and makes me sound like an airhead tourist, but it hides my nerves. And also, Kalina was always *supposed* to be a bit of an airhead. Just didn't pan out that way on the night, so to speak. Sometimes a role takes on a life of its own, especially if you play it for a long time, all day every day.

George smiles and nods politely at my comment before he pushes a button that operates the window and lets it slide back up, but he doesn't reply.

And then we look into each other's eyes across the distance between us.

And look.

And look.

My heart is racing.

My clit is pulsing.

My insides are clenching.

And suddenly I'm tired of the charade.

I like this guy.

I like him a lot.

Once my job here is done, I will never see him again but, no, I don't want to fuck him like this.

I once fucked a guy with mirrored sunglasses and he never took them off. It was erotic at the time but after I felt like shit.

I don't want George to feel like shit when I leave the limo and he gets taken home.

I don't want Madonna and Bryan.

I want us.

I want him to look into *my* eyes when he enters me.

I want him to see *me* when I come.

"Shut your eyes," I tell him.

They are my first words in fifteen minutes, but he doesn't flinch, just smiles and does as he is told.

I grab my handbag and take out a contact lens container and small bottle of saline solution. I fill the compartments, balancing the little double pot on my thigh. It makes a hissy sound and I hear George chuckle.

"Sounds naughty," he says. "What are you doing?"

"Shhh," I say, looking across to make sure he's still got his eyes shut.

I pop the contacts out and feel my eyeballs expand. I never wear a bra, I really don't have use for them, but I imagine the feeling is similar to what Grace feels when she releases her tits from their daily prison.

"No peeping," I mumble, while I put the lenses away.

Next, I shimmy out of my panties, fold them and stow them in my handbag.

I hitch my dress up a bit more, so that the hem sits just a hand width below my butt.

Then I take in the sight of him for a moment, while his eyes remain closed. He really is unbearably handsome. And right now, he looks nothing like the slick gangster I met a few months ago. He still looks like trouble but of a very different kind. A hot, dishevelled guy with dirty blond hair long enough to sink my hands into, but short enough not to look untidy, high cheekbones and the most luscious lips on the planet. They pull into a smile.

"Can I open them yet?"

I lean back and spread my legs just enough so he will see I'm pantiless.

My heart is about to explode with equal parts anxiety and lust, but before I can dwell on just how embarrassing it would be if he refuses me now, I take the plunge.

"Yes."

His eyelids flutter open, and he takes in a sharp breath as he stares. At my face.

"You've taken them out," he says in wonder.

Quick as a flash, he gets out of his seat, reaches across and pulls me over onto his lap, so my knees land next to his hips and my naked pussy settles right on top of the buttons of his Levi's and the sizable hard rod beneath them.

Not that he's noticed I'm bare.

He's too busy looking into my eyes, my cheeks clasped in his big palms and his thumbs sweeping over my cheekbones.

"I can see your eyes," he says on a happy sigh.

And then he kisses me.

Not gently but like he owns me.

No, wrong. Like I own him.

No, wrong again. Like we own *each other.*

Like we've *always* owned each other.

DIEGO

Kissing her is like coming home.

Or how I always imagined coming home would feel like.

It's relief and feeling safe.

It's hot and sweaty and raw.

It's warm and sloppy and comfy.

It's leaving behind all pretence.

And a whole lot of tongue.

So much tongue.

So much hunger.

This girl is on fire.

For *me*.

Not for the danger, not for the perceived status, not for the money, but for *me*.

She's not here to demurely please the boss and then cream off the top.

She's here, in my lap, because that's where she wants to be, where she *belongs*.

My hips buck on their own accord as she wriggles her pussy over the hard ridge of my dick and groans into my mouth. If she wasn't holding my tongue hostage, I'd be laughing at the next realisation that hits me.

This girl is never gonna whimper. She's gonna growl and roar as she takes her pleasure. The dainty little kitten is a lioness in disguise.

The thought alone makes me feel my orgasm gather in my spine.

I extricate my tongue from hers and pull her forehead to mine.

"Kalina, baby, slow down. I'm gonna spurt like a teenager if you don't slow down."

That gets me a pair of lips twitching into a grin against my mouth.

"I don't care," she says, and takes my hand from her cheek to slip it into her dress and hold it over her heart. "Can you feel that? Feel how fast that is beating? That's how turned on I am at the thought of you creaming your pants just because I kiss you. Go on, make a mess of yourself. I made a mess of myself all day, *looking* at you."

Have women told me I'm good looking? Sure.

Have they tried to please me with dirty talk? Sure.

Never done a damn thing for me other than remind me of cheap porn.

I've never felt a comment someone made in my fucking *balls* before, but now I have.

Before I can process, though, that my sweet, innocent, untouchable, too-young language student clearly speaks fluent vulgar, *real* fluent vulgar, she goes back to work, without any words.

Her tongue slips back into my mouth and her pussy starts rocking relentlessly against my crotch. Lucky me, she loses herself in her own pleasure so much, her hand loosens its grip on mine and I get to slip it further under her dress to find a perfect tit.

It's tiny, but oh so perky.

And it nestles into my hand like it's got a mind of its own, begging me for caresses.

I always thought I wanted that whole boob-spilling-out-of-my hand thing. Boy, was I wrong. Her pointy little tit feels amazing, like a perfect, exotic fruit made to sit whole in my palm and to be devoured whole. I flick my thumb over the hard nipple, and she presses further into me with a low growl in her throat.

Her move is aided by our driver speeding up as we hit the motorway. The velocity melts with her ferocity and she is pushed up hard against me, but her riding the buttons on my jeans is becoming painful now. Before I can say something, though, she already *knows*. She lifts her butt up and detaches her mouth from mine once more.

"Off," she says, reaching between us and popping the first button on the fly.

She keeps her arse in the air while I undo the rest and shuffle to tug my jeans and briefs down to give my junk just enough space to spring free.

She doesn't look down.

She doesn't *inspect* the goods like all the others do.

She just wraps her delicate hand around my girth, positions me and looks into my eyes as she slides her hot, wet pussy down on me.

Then she just sits there.

And smiles.

"Fuck, Kalina," I press out. "I'm gonna come and you'll be so disappointed."

"You keep saying that," she says on a laugh. "Now, shhh."

She kisses me softly to seal my lips and then draws back to keep looking into my eyes as if they were the only thing that mattered here.

I know what she means, though.

Sure, we're connected below, and I want to move so badly I think I'm gonna die if I don't, but - BUT! - up here are her eyes, deep and so dark they're nearly black, and yet so open I think I can see her *soul*.

Her face turns serious and I know she feels the same.

And she can't hack it for long.

She burrows her face into my neck.

"I can *feel* you," she whispers and rocks ever so slightly.

My dick quivers inside her and I'm two seconds from losing it when what she says clicks on a completely different level.

Shit! SHIT!

"Kalina," I whisper, and gently try to push her off me a little.

Enough so I can see her face again, but not so hurriedly I'm gonna shoot my spunk inside her from the friction.

"Kalina, condom," I manage to say. "In my back pocket."

She shakes her head and grinds back down.

"You dirty, George? You fuck without condom a lot?"

I'm not and I don't, but I'm also not hyper-vigilant like some people. I take the blow jobs I'm offered without a rubber, but I won't give head to any of the whores at the club or sink my dick into any of them without sheathing myself. I'm not fucking suicidal. And the last thing I want is one of them tagging me with a baby.

I shake my head, but I put in the caveat.

"No, but I'm no saint," I confess.

She shrugs.

"Neither am I. I'll take my chances."

I take a big breath and am about to lift her off me, when she realises what that sounds like and holds up a finger between us.

"But I will not get pregnant. I have..." her voice trails off as she frowns, clearly searching for a word that isn't in her repertoire. "Thing," she says in the end, pointing down between us and then indicating something about an inch long with her thumb and forefinger. "Spiralka."

I catch her drift and stare at her in wonder. It's the first time I've ever heard her utter a word in Polish. It's super cute, and it somehow brings her even closer. As if she just dropped the last curtain between us. I look at her with my heart exploding in my chest and my dick demanding to crawl even deeper into her, and I realise to my astonishment that I actually trust her.

I never thought I would have it in me to trust a woman on her word alone. If any woman before her had told me she had the coil, I would have wanted to see a written statement from the doctor who put it in. Or better yet, I would have wanted to watch him put it in.

"And I want to do this," she carries on, dragging me out of my head again.

She rotates her hips just a little so her clit slides over my pubic bone and spreads her cream all over me. "I want to feel you, George. I've wanted to feel you for months. Every time I see you, my first thought is what would it be like if you were inside of me."

She does that hip rotation thing again, and I make a strangled sound in my throat — before I can't help myself any longer.

I grab her by the hips and start fucking into her from below like a man possessed.

But as desperate as I am, I don't want this to end just yet.

After ten or so hard pumps, I sling one arm around her and hold her still again, tight against my body, counting my breaths. It's something Rowan, Silas' brother, waffles on about a lot. Some tantric bullshit about drawing out your release with breathing techniques. I never paid attention. Didn't see the point. I haven't got time for shit like that. You fuck, you come, you get back to business. But it's amazing what goes into your subconscious when you pretend to be too fucking important to be listening.

I breathe through the tightness in my balls that tells me I want to shoot my load, and then I move again, slower this time.

Kalina makes a sound of frustration.

"You're killing me, George. I was so close."

"Me, too, baby, me, too," I say, grinning at her. "But we've got another couple of hours to kill. And I intend to enjoy every fucking second till then."

I tug the top of her dress down to release her tits to my view.

Kalina

I nervously hold my breath when my breasts spring free from the clingy fabric of the dress.

It's stupid, really.

He's already hilt-deep inside of me. He's hardly going not to finish what we started just because my boobs are too small. And I've never in my life felt self-conscious about my lack of curves.

It's just that all of the women I see hanging around him are about three times my size in all the right places. Plus, hanging around with Grace 'Jessica Rabbit' Turner for a few months can give any smaller woman a complex in the long run.

It doesn't help that he's just staring at them and not saying a word, though the hand that was playing with the left one under my dress until a couple of minutes ago, isn't exactly stopping now he's got a visual. I take that as a good sign and relax a little.

He leans in, gives the pert nipple of that one a long lick then tweaks it. My insides clench around his length, and I unfreeze fully. It's not really possible to stay self-conscious when he leans in to the other one and sucks it into his mouth. All of it.

My whole right breast disappears into this man's mouth, and the sound of satisfaction he makes while he does it gives me the most unholy thrill of my life.

And then he sucks.

And tweaks.

And fucks into me again.

Slowly.

Minimally.

So each time he hits my cervix, he holds me down for a second and grinds his pubic bone over my clit.

Until I can't stand it any longer.

"George," I beg and grab on to his shoulders, hoping he gets what I need.

He kind of tilts his head, so he can look up at me with my tit still in his mouth, and then he blinks his permission at me.

DIEGO

I wanted to drag this out for hours, but Kalina has other plans. And frankly, by now I'm so far gone, no amount of breathing exercises will help me last.

She is so fucking gorgeous, looking down at me, her face flushed, her dark eyes heavy with lust and burning with the need to come.

I suck her tit a bit harder, enjoying my *fruit,* and she groans so loudly I wonder how soundproof the soundproof glass that divides us from the driver really is. Normally, I wouldn't care, but I don't want her to feel embarrassed afterwards.

Not that there is anything I can do about it.

I've just given her the go ahead to ride me as hard as she needs to and like an avalanche, there is no stopping her now.

She clutches at my shoulders, and then she starts moving in a way that makes her earlier hip circles fade into insignificance.

This woman can fuck.

And she is fucking me.

Hard.

Until she explodes all around me with the full-on war cry I expected of her, her tight cunt squeezing me relentlessly into submission, milking my dick of every last drop of my spunk.

When she comes down, she collapses onto me with a giggle.

Her arms wrap themselves around the back of my neck and her lips come to rest on the rapidly beating pulse in my throat.

We're panting, heart to heart, and she's still holding my quivering, slowly softening cock inside of her.

The impulse to retreat quickly — to catch and tie the condom we never used, before I drop out fully and we have a mess — is strong, but then I realise there is no need.

The mess is already there.

And it's fucking glorious.

Kalina

After I come, I wait for the sadness to descend.

I often crash hard.

I have a bit of a history of post-coital depression. It's not so bad that I don't want to have sex a lot, but sometimes it really hits me. Then I have a bit of a cry, a bar of chocolate or two and a day in bed, and eventually I'm reset.

I want to say that there is no comedown after finally - finally! - getting to ride George Benson's fine, fine dick, but it would be a lie.

I snuggle into the crook of his neck and revel in the afterglow of my orgasm as long as I can but inevitably, I can feel the tears pricking the back of my throat as he goes soft and plops out of me, the sticky mess we made quickly growing cold between us. I push my nose deeper into his skin to take a last lungful of his scent before I suppress my emotions and put on a game face. I will deal with the darkness later.

This is why I prefer to fuck them and then get the hell away.

But there is no escape here. We're going seventy miles an hour on a motorway and there is probably around an hour left of our journey.

So I plaster on a smile before I lift my face away from its hiding place and shuffle back on George's lap.

"Hey," he says softly, and then he reaches out to help me pull the bodice of my dress back up.

"Hey," I say back, looking at everywhere but him, because I have a funny feeling that if he can look into my eyes, he'll know that something isn't quite right.

He's not stupid, though.

He catches my chin in his hand and holds me still, so I have to meet his gaze.

"You okay?" he asks me with a slight frown.

I nod, still working hard to suppress the tears that want to come.

"Hungry," I answer.

"Sugar crash? Or proper meal hungry?" he asks without missing a beat, while he lets go of my chin and starts taking his shirts off.

Once the flannel lies discarded next to him, he pulls his t-shirt over his head.

Now he decides to show me his chest.

I've never seen him without at least a t-shirt on.

He's all slabs and abs, just like Silas and Rowan, only sleeker. I've heard Silas say before that George is the welterweight to Silas' middleweight and Rowan's heavyweight. I can appreciate that now and for a moment, my blues are forgotten. I reach out and run a hand over the planes of his chest.

"Proper hungry," I answer his question, and he chuckles as he catches my hand to stop its explorations.

"Give me half an hour, woman. You just totally rocked my world. Let me recalibrate."

He says it so casually. But I catch something in his eyes as I glance at him that tells me he isn't lying.

I got to him.

I don't want to think about the implications of that. I'm too busy being surprised at the fact he seems to be able to keep my sadness at bay, so I store that knowledge for later.

He pushes the t-shirt he's taken off into my hand and smiles.

"Here, you can use that to clean up, unless you have a sink in that handbag of yours."

He takes me by the hips and gently lifts me off his lap, holding me steady until I'm safely seated by his side. Then he lifts his butt and pulls his briefs and jeans back up.

While I do as he suggested and mop myself, he does up his fly then pushes the button on the intercom.

"Chris," he addresses our driver. "Can we stop at Pease Pottage, please?"

I like that he says please.

"What's Pease Pottage?" I ask, while I fold up his shirt into a small cube, so our combined gunk stays on the inside.

I look at it indecisively, because I don't quite know what to do with it.

"Service station," he answers, and takes it off me, grabs his leather jacket from the middle seat opposite us and stuffs the tee into a pocket.

I think of the pants in my handbag and grin.

Looks like George Diego Benson and Kristina Kaminski are equally classy.

He sits down again and puts his flannel shirt back on.

I say a silent goodbye to his abs as he buttons it up, leaving only the top one open.

"The pasty and the burger places will be shut now, but if we're lucky, they have caviar and blini in the all-night supermarket. That's usually what they got left."

I know him well enough to know he's not joking.

"Will there be creme fraiche, smoked salmon and mackerel, too?" I ask, seriously excited at the prospect now.

He laughs and slings an arm around me, drawing me to his side.

As if I am his woman now.

And I don't want to overthink it.

I had an orgasm and I'm not depressed. That's more than reason for celebration, and I'm not pissing all over it with thoughts of the future.

Especially if the immediate future has seafood in it.

DIEGO

We arrive at Pease Pottage a few minutes later. I step out of the limo as soon as Chris parks up in front of the entrance of the mini mall, not giving him time to come around and open the door for us. He gets out and stands in by the driver's door, looking across the roof at me.

"You want us to bring you a coffee?" I ask him.

He shakes his head.

"No, thank you, sir. That's very kind but I had some sleep while you were at the theatre. If I have coffee now, I won't be able to sleep until the afternoon once I clock off. But if you don't mind, I'd like to go to the toilet, please."

"Of course," I answer. "Go ahead."

"No, no. I'll wait until you are back, of course. Thank you, sir."

I nod, and for a moment I wonder what it must be like to have a job where you have to ask permission to go take a leak. Even at school, I often just got up and walked out, because it's a bodily function, right? I got more detentions for going to pee without asking first than Silas got for talking in class. Quite an accomplishment, because even though he is a tight-lipped fucker now, back then we called him motormouth.

Kalina's legs appear in my view as she shuffles out of the limo and I reach down to give her a hand. Once she's stood next to me, she pulls the hem of her dress down as much as possible and shivers a little. It's August, but it's two in the morning and it's cold for a skinny girl with no panties, no tights and bare shoulders.

I realise with a start that I've never considered somebody else's body temperature, or general comfort, before in my life. Yet here I am, offering the driver coffee and thinking about a woman's need for a jacket. The weeks hanging with Silas, Sheena, Grace and Kalina have turned me fucking soft.

I crawl back into the limousine, retrieve my leather jacket and try to hang it on her. Emphasis on try. The entire width of her shoulders is so narrow, it barely stays there. Even when she puts her arms through the sleeves, and I zip it up for her, it doesn't really stay on. She looks ridiculous.

She's laughing so much throughout the whole process that tears form in the corners of her eyes. When I finish pulling the zip up, she looks at me, flapping the sleeves that are about a foot too long for her arms about, before she doubles over, laughing even harder.

In the background, Chris clears his throat.

"Would you maybe like a blanket instead?" he asks.

"That would be lovely, thank you, Chris," she answers between short breaths and more subdued giggles.

I note she's memorised his name.

I like that.

Chris goes around to the boot, pops it open and hands her a soft-looking, black woollen blanket. She thanks him, folds it into a shawl and slings it around her shoulders. We start walking toward the entrance, but she stops suddenly to take a lungful of the shawl's scent.

"Hmm," she murmurs. "Smells like cashmere."

She searches around for a label.

"Knew it," she says, pleased with herself.

Then she hooks her arm into mine and lets me lead the way inside.

Somewhere between waiting for her to clean up in the toilets and plundering M&S of smoked oysters, salmon, mackerel, caviar and a tray of sushi, it hits me that Kalina really is no stranger to the good life.

And I stop for a moment to wonder how a girl with that much class ended up in Sheena's house and on my dick.

"So," he says, and I already know what is coming before he drops the next smoked oyster in my mouth. "Tell me something about you, Kalinaaa..."

His voice is stuck on the 'a' because he doesn't even know my, Kalina's, surname.

"Jasinski," I inform him, once I've swallowed the oyster.

They are delicious. Trust the English to take a fine food, smoke it and pack it into a tin. You'd think these were disgusting, but out of the buffet of snacks we bought, they are by far my favourite. Maybe because they're a new sensation. Maybe because they are just that good. Time will tell.

I open my mouth, so he can drop in another one. I'm lying with my head on his lap, huddled under the cashmere blanket and feeling totally cared for by this guy feeding me titbits. For a long moment, I marvel at how different he has been today from the guy I've known so far. I like who is beyond the three-piece suit so much, I want to preserve him in this state forever.

Whoa - forever?

He doesn't even know who you really are, Kristina, stop!

I inwardly show myself the middle finger and then I realise that George is still looking down at me, waiting for me to answer his original question.

"What do you want to know?" I ask.

"Everything," he says on a sigh, and fingers the cashmere blanket. "Like how come you can recognize cashmere by smell?"

I frown at him because that's just about the most stupid question I've ever heard.

"Because it has a special smell," I tell him, not leaving room for any doubt as to how idiotic a question I think that is.

"Yeah but, how do you know that?"

"What?" I tease him. "Because I'm Polish and not a cashmere goat?"

He avoids my eyes and bites his lip. He knows he's being a prick.

I push off the blanket, lift my head out of his lap, sit upright and turn so I'm facing him side on with one foot on the seat, leg bent at the knee and hugging it to my chest, and one dangling over the side. It means that my bare pussy is back on display, but I really don't care right now.

"I think you'd be surprised if I took you to Poland at what you'd find there," I set him straight. "But just for the record, I'm Polish, but I didn't really grow up there. My mum's a scientist. By the time I was twelve, I'd lived in Bern, Paris, Stockholm and Berlin. I've spent less time in Poland than anywhere else in the world. And I'm not some poor charity case looking for a meal ticket. My parents are not rich but, how do you say, very comfortable. And my mother always had the philosophy that you want a few quality clothes that last, and that are worthwhile packing when you move, instead of a whole lot of cheap stuff. That's how I know what cashmere smells like."

I flop back into my previous position with my head on his lap, my heart racing in my throat.

I've just told him more about the real me than I've ever told Grace. So far, I've always managed to avoid giving any personal info out by distracting from the subject or hiding behind a lack of English. I think after today, the cat is firmly out of the bag where my command of their language is concerned, but I was never going to tell any of them that much detail of my actual background. The rule by and large is, the longer the assignment, the closer to the truth you stay because, as the Germans say, lies have short legs, and there is nothing more suspicious than getting caught in contradicting yourself. But you should never reveal so much you become traceable.

He looks down at me through narrowed eyes.

"I don't believe you," he says very slowly. "You've been fucking with us all along, haven't you? There is no chance you learned to speak English like this in just a few months. No way."

He's serious, but there is no way I can fess up to the truth here. It would blow a hole the size of a crater in my cover. And as much as I want to and as certain as I am that he has nothing to do with the case, I just can't. It's too dangerous. So I shrug and grin up at him instead.

"What can I say? It's my superpower. Languages are my talent. It's mostly mimicry. And the more languages you learn, the easier it is to pick up another one. And English is super easy compared to most languages. Your objects don't even have a gender!"

- 450 -

I watch as he keeps scrutinizing me and I can tell the exact moment when doubt turns into pride. He's proud of having bedded an intelligent female. Good man.

"I've fucked a genius," he states and leans down to kiss me.

I kiss him back before I gently push him off me a little.

"Correction," I say, staring into his beautiful grey eyes. "You've been fucked by a genius."

He sighs.

"True," he says, and seeks my lips again, only to carry on muttering against them. "But I've never been good with the tenses. I'm confusing the past with the future again. What I meant to say is..."

"You're going to fuck a genius," I finish the sentence for him.

And then I let him kiss the shit out of me and leisurely finger my pussy, until we pull up outside Sheena's house.

DIEGO

She is super close to another climax, just before Chris pulls into the pub car park opposite Sheena's house. I've been kissing her and leisurely finger fucking her the whole rest of the journey, but I deliberately wouldn't let her come again. Just yet.

I decided sometime between her telling me off for my preconceptions and realising that she is about twice as smart as I am that I was going to stay the night. I want to hear her roar again.

Only this time I'll be *making* her. I'm not just gonna sit there and let her take her pleasure. I'm gonna rock her world the way she rocked mine.

It's a matter of pride.

Or so I tell myself.

Kalina

He never asks if it's okay for him to stay over.

He just thanks Chris, gives him a huge tip and tells him to get the company to bill him for the blanket — because, apparently, I'm keeping it. Then he leads me by the elbow across the street to Sheena's house and helps me with opening the door.

Not that I mind, I was maddeningly close to coming just before Chris parked up and if George wasn't going to finish what he started, I would have dug up the vibrator I can't ever use in this house because the walls are paper thin. Not that that ever deters Silas and Grace.

When we step inside, George gives a last wave to Chris as he drives out of the car park, shuts the door, hangs his leather jacket on a hook next to it and takes my handbag from me to put it on the hallstand. Then he takes off his boots and socks, all the while looking at me with fresh desire. As if it wasn't nearly dawn after a long day, as if we hadn't already had sex, as if I was fresh as a daisy.

Just that look makes me go all gooey again. Inside, and where it matters.

As soon as he's barefoot, George backs me up against the wall and picks up where he left off in the car. His hand slips into my short hair as he bends down to spear his tongue deep into my mouth. He groans and his grip tightens, when I immediately give back in equal measure. I have to stand on my tippy toes to meet him, but as soon as he realises, he bends his knees a bit more to take the strain off. Our tongues play like they've practiced their dance for a lifetime already. Like they've never needed another play partner. I've never had a man I've been so in sync with. It's amazing. I could do this forever, but I'm also still burning for the release he's been teasing out of me for the last hour, and I growl in frustration.

His hand immediately slips back between my legs and he carries on in exactly the way he caressed me in the limo, stroking my folds with two fingers, long slides, starting from my clit, down into my hole where he slips them in to massage my magic spot for a moment, before he retracts them to start from the top. Over and over. It's maddeningly good and within minutes, I am really close again.

He detaches his mouth from mine for a moment.

"You ready?" he asks, pulling the hem of my dress up, all the way past my waist and over my head when I lift my arms.

"Depends," I answer, muffled by the fabric that's being pulled past my face.

He looks at me for a moment, taking me in. I can feel my defences going up already. I've heard it all in my life. From 'you look like a boy' to 'you look like a child'. But he just smiles.

"Wow, a pixie with brains *and* a six-pack. You're the fucking hottest thing I've ever seen."

Quick as a whip, he turns me around to point me at the stairs and slaps my naked butt. Not hard. Not like a man who's into paddling and all that, but playfully.

"Upstairs," he says. "Now."

I make it to the second step before he changes his mind.

"No, actually, stop there," he demands. "Bend over. Hands on the step. Don't look."

I do as I'm told, while I hear him pop the buttons of his jeans and shimmy out of them. There is another noise of fabric rustling, signalling he's pulling his shirt off.

I can feel the air move when he steps up behind me then the tip of his cock brushing my arsehole.

It's not where he is headed, though. I know as soon as he reaches down and spreads my folds with one hand to get access. I'm guessing the other is wrapped around his cock as he lines it up. He dips in a little, just enough to hold it there, and to make my insides clench. Then he repeats his question.

"Are you ready, Kalina?"

"Yeah," I answer but before I've breathed out the word fully, he rams home.

Not so that it hurts but so that I feel it in my teeth.

He steadies me with one hand on my hip and another clasping my nape, as if I were a kitten he's about to pick up by the scruff. And then he fucks into me. Withdrawing all the way and pushing back in, over and over again, until I scream his names, both of them, begging him not to stop. *Never* to stop.

And when my orgasm hits, it's like I'm being shot up in a shower of bullets.

DIEGO

After I fuck her on the steps, I collect her up in my arms and carry her up to the shower. I make sure the spray is nice and warm before I put her under and soap first her and then me.

She remains silent throughout our shower, and a bit shaky. And though I feel like the fucking shit for making her come that hard, it's also mildly disconcerting. She seems almost sad, and I can't figure it out.

I shut off the spray and when we step out, I grab a towel and rub her down before I grab one for myself. She huddles inside the terry cotton and perches on the side of the bathtub as she watches me dry myself.

Finally, she speaks.

"Are you staying?" she asks, and I stop towelling to look at her.

I frown.

It suddenly occurs to me that I never really asked her if that was okay.

"Unless you throw me out, yes, Kalina, I'd like to stay," I say neutrally.

She gives me a small smile.

"Cool. Sheena keeps spare toothbrushes in the kitchen drawer."

"Why the..." I start but don't finish because it's Sheena and pondering Sheena's logic has driven more mentally robust men insane. "Okay, I'll be back."

I sling the towel around my waist and leave her behind to go in search of a toothbrush.

I find a few dozen single use ones in packaging that tells me they came with compliments from the Palais, the hotel where Sheena is head of housekeeping, in a drawer that also has an equal amount of partially used complimentary soaps, spare light bulbs, single shoelaces and an array of rubber bands in varying sizes.

Before I leave, the cat flap opens and shuts. Once, twice. Luna and Sol, the two cats that live here, come to trip me up and demand food. I have no idea how much, or what, they get, but I'm guessing they haven't had anything since yesterday afternoon and that they won't shut up until they're fed.

I rummage around the kitchen until I find a tin with cat biscuits and I put some in their bowls for them. I check their water and fill it back up, and then wonder if I should make Kalina a cup of tea. I turn to the door and there she is, wearing the nerdiest thick-framed glasses — and a smile.

The sadness that seemed to have taken hold of her after we christened the staircase has gone.

Good.

"You coming up?" she asks, making my heart trip with the realisation that she actually *wants* me to stay.

"Yeah," I say. "I just thought I give these guys something to eat, so they don't keep us up meowing."

She looks at the cats and then back at me and there is such a brand new, soft expression on her face that I realise that even at her most relaxed, we normally only ever see a hardened, guarded version of Kalina around.

"You're nice," she states.

And then she turns around and holds out a hand behind her back for me to grab on to.

I take it and we go to bed.

Kalina

I'm not big on hugging people, but I was born a snuggler.

I like curling up to people.

I never had issues cuddling up with Lauren after we'd make each other come either, or my first boyfriend, Arion.

But ever since I've left school and started training then actually working the field, I've found that whole sharing a bed with a man after sex thing tricky. I've heard intimacy being described as a cocoon by people, but for me it's more like a spider's web that just keeps growing each time you spend cuddle time with somebody. And before you know it, that intimacy is the background your life happens against — the web that is everywhere.

And I can't afford that, yet.

One day, sure. When I'm too old to do what I do, but still young enough to have babies, I'll grow my hair long again, get a desk job, find a man and let my life be spun in silk. But that day isn't here, and that man won't be *this* man.

I *know* this.

But it didn't stop my entire being from screaming *yes!* when he asked me if it was alright for him to stay the night.

So now I'm lying here, in my bed in Sheena's house, squished up against his hard chest as he lightly runs his fingernails over my back and makes a half-arsed attempt at suppressing a yawn.

I'm not surprised he's tired. After the shower, we kissed and explored each other some more, though we were both too lazy to actually fuck again. Now dawn is breaking, and it really is time to go to sleep.

He kisses the side of my head.

"You still awake?"

"Hmmm," I murmur.

"Can I ask you a question?"

"Hmmm."

"When you were begging me to go faster on the stairs you used both my names. Why?"

I smile against his chest. It's a damn good question. There was a moment on those stairs when he was fucking into me when fun, gentle George went out of the window and I knew I was being fucked by a guy who is also kind of ruthless and wears three-piece suits while he orders people to fuck other people up. A guy who has blood on his hands. As far as my intel says, he doesn't have hits put on people, it's just not the British way, but there *are* people out there who are missing an eye or are relearning how to speak because of what Diego's thugs did to them. Or to each other. Most of his business is purely being the ringmaster for the modern gladiator game that is bare knuckle fighting. His philosophy is very much, 'they know what they are letting themselves in for and if I don't organise it, somebody else will'. A twisted part of me can see his point. There are other parts to his mini empire that I'm not as clear about, but I know enough about him to know he doesn't hurt women, children or animals. For somebody of his status, he appears to have quite the moral code and I like that. More than that, it turns me on. Diego isn't ruthless as much as he is anarchic and fuck me if that doesn't get my own rebellious pussy all hot and bothered.

"I think because I like you both," I answer at long last.

"You know I *am* both, right?"

I can feel him hold his breath and get the significance of what he's asking me here. It is important to him that I understand who and what Diego is as much as that I understand that underneath there is also this guy, in the jeans and lumberjack shirts, who is nice to cats and listens to classic rock. I nod against his skin and he runs a hand through my hair.

"Good," he says. "Because tomorrow morning, George is going to take you for breakfast, but tomorrow evening, Diego is gonna come to your door and he's gonna want to take you to dinner."

"Is he?" I ask, smiling.

"Yes," he says almost sadly.

I shuffle around a little, so I can trail my fingers over his abs and down the happy trail to the semi he is sporting. I take him in my hand and then slide down until my mouth is level with his tip. I dart my tongue out and give him one leisurely lick all around, feeling his cock grow back to full size in my hand immediately.

"Does Diego like blowjobs?"

"Fucking loves them," he groans.

"Good," I say as I let go of him and shuffle back up until I'm propped up on my elbow, looking down at him. "Then he had better take me nowhere *too* nice."

George slides a hand into my hair and kisses me, softly. Then he pushes me off, rolls onto his side and pulls me back in, with my back to his chest. He slides a hand under my knee and lifts my leg up then slides into me from behind.

"You're killing me, Kalina," he mumbles, in between peppering my neck with kisses. "I'm too tired to fuck you again right now, but I'm going to sleep right inside you, if you don't mind."

I crawl back, pushing him in as far as possible, and hooking my leg back over his, to tell him that's fine. He wraps his arms tightly around me, and the last thing I feel as I drift off to sleep is his cock twitching inside me.

DIEGO

It's the second day in a row that I wake up to a woman sucking my dick, but this time it's the right one — and she is fucking fantastic at the job.

And it's not even down to technique, though that is good, too.

It's the fact her mouth and my dick clearly have their very own thing for each other. They fucking play with each other and all I can do is come along for the ride.

She sucks me all the way, swallowing my spunk, and when she's finished, she crawls up to sit on my face.

"My turn," she demands, and I try to oblige and give as good as I just got.

I never had a woman literally ride my face before and there is something almost intimidating about it, but oh so good. I love how Kalina will just take her pleasure and not give a fuck about propriety.

She lets me explore her with my tongue, my fingers, my mouth, my *nose,* not once shy of telling me what she wants or of grabbing my head or my hands and directing me.

By the time I succeed in making her scream both my names again, I'm good to go for a second round. So I give her some time to recalibrate and then I claim her again, the old-fashioned way. Because I need it. My fucking *ego* needs it. I flip her over on her back and bury myself in her over and over again, making her taste herself on me when I kiss her and mingling her taste and mine in our mouths when our tongues play their own game again. It's slow and it's kind of vanilla and yet utterly, utterly filthy. We play, until she comes for me again but this time much more quietly — softer and deeper somehow. I stop kissing her then to look into her eyes as she climaxes, and it sends me over the edge. I spill my second load inside her while the ripples of her orgasm still go through her, all the time holding her gaze, resisting the urge to shut my eyes as I come. And something weird shifts in my chest.

Afterwards, we clean up, separately this time, and get dressed, her in her regular tomboy clothes and me in a shirt that I borrow from Silas' wardrobe, which also yields a fresh pair of briefs and socks for me. When I ring to ask him if that's okay, he laughs his head off at the other end before he tells Grace that Kalina and I shacked up, while I'm still on the line. I hang up to the sound of a whooping American in the background.

As per Silas' instructions, I take Kalina for breakfast. I love the fact she chooses a proper old-fashioned greasy spoon and orders a full fry up. I have no idea where she puts it all, but I sure like hanging out with a woman who loves food as much as I do and doesn't moan about the calories. She's got no time to count the fat molecules anyhow. She's too busy dissecting the shitty puns in the shitty right-wing paper that the caf provides for its customers, in that specific way only foreigners ever seem to be able to, and telling me stories about the old biddies who work in the charity shop where she volunteered until recently.

She is as funny and smart as always, and exactly the same around me as she was before, which is also refreshing. Most of the women I fuck go weird the next day and suddenly I can't have a conversation with them any longer. I say that to Kalina, and she raises an eyebrow.

"But do you ever have conversations with them before?" she asks levelly, and I laugh.

That right there makes Kalina Jasinski one in a million. If you talk to any other woman about other women you've fucked after you fucked them, they go all jealous and shit, even if you didn't let them spend the night and shoved their arse in a taxi.

Kalina doesn't get jealous, she goes straight for the intellectual kill shot.

I find it extremely hard to say goodbye to her after breakfast, but from the moment I switched my phone back on to call Silas until the last bite of fried bread disappears in Kalina's mouth, my phone goes off non-stop. I have a gazillion missed messages from last night and they're still coming in hard and fast. Weekends are big business in my world and the last time I took a weekend night off was never.

I offer to walk her back home, but instead she walks me to the train station, which is just around the corner from the caf she chose. When I automatically head for the taxi rank, she stops me with a hand on my abs.

"Where are you going? Woodland Drive or The Brick?"

She surprises me with that, twice over. I had forgotten that she'd been to the Benson Mansion, on the night the big fight between Silas and Rowan went down. But what jolts me even more is her using the nickname for my nan's building that only family and the very inner circle really use. But she must have overheard me call it that to Silas at some point. And let's face it, if she wasn't inner circle before last night, she sure as fuck is now. Inner inner circle.

"The Brick," I answer.

"Then take the train," she says. "Much faster. You'll be in Brighton in ten minutes. If you take a cab, it's forty."

I do a double take between her, the rank and the tracks and I realise she's spot on. And suddenly it dawns on me what is so fucking special about this girl, other than pretty much everything about her. She doesn't just know how to do the good life, she's never forgotten how to do the *basics*.

She's fucking perfect.

Kalina

I breathe a sigh of relief when I watch his train leave the station.

That was *intense*.

I need time to, what's the word he uses all the time?

Recalibrate.

I'm adopting that. It describes the need I feel right now perfectly.

I need to recalibrate, and then I need to get my head down and do some fucking work. The charity shop was a dead end. The Jubilee library was a dead end. And I'm slowly starting to think even the language school might just have been a coincidence, though it seems improbable. But I've dug and dug and there is nothing else Piotr Schmidt-Danczyk and Zoltan Salak had in common.

Piotr was Polish-German and came from a small town called Jülich, on the German-Dutch border. He was well travelled, even at fourteen. His father is an orthopaedic surgeon who married a prosthetics developer. It's all about knees and hips in their house. I've been there. They are very nice, middle-class people who work hard for their wealth, pay their taxes and play tennis, while making jokes about how they will need to branch out into elbow replacements one day.

Though when I met them, the jokes had gone stale and their eyes had that hollow, haunted look all of my clients have.

Zoltan was Hungarian. The only son of a single mum, seventeen when he arrived in Brighton two years ago. First in his family to show academic talent. He'd never left Hungary before he came to England. The authorities here assume he stayed as an illegal, so they were never as interested in him as they were in Piotr. Piotr disappeared only three months after Zoltan — which makes all my alarm bells ring, but clearly not the ones in the heads of Sussex police — but *he* got a proper coastal search, appeals on the internet, the whole package. Zoltan got a missing poster and a stamp on his files, saying 'wanted for immigration offences'.

While I know a shit ton about Piotr, I know very little about Zoltan, because communicating with his mum is difficult. She only speaks Hungarian and that happens to be one of the many languages I don't speak. When I contacted her initially, I emailed her in English and heard nothing back for two weeks. I thought maybe she didn't get the email and was about to send her an old-fashioned actual letter, when I got an email back, written from her address but by a friend of hers who spoke English. Bad English. After some to and fro over a number of days, we realised that if I wrote to her in French that would be easier, because she had another friend who spoke fluent French. She had them compose a long letter about Zoltan and how wonderful he was, but it didn't really tell me anything about the person, other than what a proud mother sees through her rose-tinted glasses. It would probably be useful to go and see her, but technically Zoltan isn't my job. He's just a lead and I'm not sure the Schmidt-Danczyks have the finance to spring for a flight to Hungary and a hotel, on top of what they are paying me to be here. And I don't think I'd learn enough from being there to warrant the expense. And Zoltan's mother doesn't have a penny to her name.

It's probably the toughest aspect of my job, staying clear on who is bankrolling me, and who is not. Konstantin, my boss and mentor, is very strict on that: we don't do pro bono. There are too many missing children in the world to get sidetracked off the paying gigs. We'd never make a penny. Konstantin always says it's like rescuing a puppy from a shelter. You can't bring them all home, so concentrate on the ones you can. It still bugs me, though, that the Schmidt-Danczyks of this world may get closure one day whereas Zoltan's mother will forever wonder what happened to her baby.

So I secretly hope I find both their bodies.

I never delude myself into thinking the kids I am looking for are still alive. I've recovered eight since I started working for Konstantin five years ago. Three of them in my second year of training, as Konstantin's help. The other five on my own since I 'graduated'. None of them were still breathing when we found them. Actually, none of them still had flesh on their bones.

In the business, they call us the body hunters.

DIEGO

I stop myself from answering calls on the train, it's too public anyway, and I don't bother getting a cab from Brighton Station to the seafront either. Instead, I nip down into the North Laines, like any other punter. I wade through the thousands of people out today, moving beautifully incognito through the masses of hippies, punks and tosspots, before I get to North Street and head up towards the Clock Tower, then down West Street, hangar right at the seafront, until I get to The Brick. The security on the door to the side entrance that leads up to the flats does a double take when he sees me but then he nods.

"Good afternoon, boss," he says.

"Good afternoon, Ben," I reply.

I hired him not so long ago to replace Silas' arse on the rota for as long as Silas isn't coming back to work. He will, but when he does, he won't be doing door duty any longer, that's for fucking certain. I'll give him a choice, depending on whether I get the contract for running the two new youth offender institutions that are being built on the edge of town at the moment, or not. I've put in my tender and now it's a game of wait and see.

If I get it, Silas will be my head of security there. If I don't, I need to talk to Julian, who is currently running Santos-Benson Security for me, about how we can maybe branch out and give Silas his own patch.

If he wants to, that is.

I keep asking him, but he's not giving me any answers. I think secretly he likes us being back together as friends as much as I do, but he thinks that as soon as he stops having the longest holiday known to man, we'll be back in that bullshit master-and-servant dynamic, and he doesn't want that.

Neither do I.

It's a fucking headache.

I push the thought aside as I enter the foyer. We're not in America, so there is no 'doorman', no reception and once I leave Ben behind on the other side of the door, it's eerily quiet.

The Brick is always pretty silent at four o'clock in the afternoon. The whores are asleep, and my security guys are all out on jobs or still at home waiting for the nightshifts to begin. It's at this time of day that I feel torn about keeping the building or not. For about an hour a day, this is *home*. Not quite as much as any house that smells of lemongrass and is owned by Sheena O'Brien is, but home nonetheless.

I take the lift up to my nan's penthouse, select a suit, shirt and dress shoes from the closet and change, keeping on the underwear I nicked from Silas.

Then I take the lift down to the office.

As soon as I step through the door, Lila, our secretary and Julian's wife, looks up from her laptop and breathes a sigh of relief.

"Boss, good to see you, we were getting worried."

I smile at her.

"I told you I was taking the night off. Everything okay here?"

She takes a breath but before she can answer, Julian barges through his office door into reception, Isla, his German shepherd bitch, at his heel.

"Diego! About fucking time," he starts then stops himself when he sees my face.

Nobody talks to me that way in my own fucking office. I can feel all the mellow of the last twenty-four hours seep out of me in an instant. Cat away and all that. But before I can put Julian in his place, he runs a hand through his short black hair and apologises.

"Sorry, sir. I didn't mean for it to come out that way, but we've got a *situation* and I've been trying to get hold of you since last night."

The 'sir' tickles me. Julian is ex-army and when he's stressed it still slips out. I soften a bit.

"Yeah, I know, I saw the missed calls, but you didn't leave a message, so I didn't think it was that urgent."

He nods gravely.

"I would have. But you *explicitly* told me not to ever mention anything around this over the phone ever, or in any traceable way," he says, and I'm immediately on full alert.

Of course there isn't only one thing Julian and I don't talk about unless we're eye to eye, but there is only one thing I told him we *explicitly* don't talk about, unless we're in a secure room.

I jerk my head at my office.

"I'm listening."

Kalina

In Germany, where I'm registered to operate, anyone can become a private detective, no qualifications needed. But when I decided that's what I wanted to do and found Konstantin, the only P.I. in a fifty mile radius of the small town where my boarding school was located who would even entertain talking to me, he sent me straight from receiving my *Abiturzeugnis* at school, into taking courses with the *Zentralstelle für die Ausbildung im Detektivgewerbe,* ZAD for short. Sleuth uni, as we call it.

It's exactly as lame as that sounds, but being a ZAD graduate gets you better indemnity insurance rates and less scrutiny from officials. Konstantin is a good mentor, though, so he topped up my training in other areas that the ZAD doesn't cover. Like shooting, hand-to-hand combat and covering your tracks before you've even started making them.

I have no idea what Konstantin did before he became a PI, but I'm pretty sure he must have been military or secret service — or organised crime enforcer turned good. I don't really care. I know that the work we do is good work and that often you can't get the job done without crossing the lines between legal and illegal.

Something neither the ZAD not Konstantin taught me, though, is what it means to get *the feeling*.

The feeling is not the same as a hunch. A hunch is like knowing that someone is about to knock a glass over on the table, based on all the other times you've seen people gesticulate in a particular way while a glass was a similar distance away from the table edge and at a similar angle from their elbow. It's basically the more bad-arse word for an educated guess on a grander scale.

The feeling is not the same as intuition either. Intuition is just empathy and reading people and interpreting that against the background of a given set of circumstances.

The feeling is different. It happens when something shifts in the ether, when a case you are hooked into suddenly takes a turn or gathers momentum, and you can feel it on a metaphysical level. It might be down to the work you've put into your search, the butterfly effect that follows from your actions. But more often than not, it's just that something is happening outside of your influence, but you are so *connected* to the subject matter that you can feel it in your gut, or maybe through the ripples you feel by way of the six degrees of separation. Although I think, considering we've gained another two or three billion people on the planet since that theory was derived, we must be at seven or eight degrees by now.

Wherever it comes from, the trick is to have done enough groundwork to know where to look for the shift, once *the feeling* hits.

The problem with Piotr and Zoltan is that I've immersed myself in their cases for months now, but at no point did I get *the feeling*, or any feeling for that matter. Half the time I don't even feel a connection, no matter how intensely I stare at the two photographs of two very different looking boys.

Piotr was small, slight in build, much younger looking than his sixteen years, round-faced and dark-haired, with big brown puppy eyes. He could have passed for one of *my* brothers. Maybe that's why I feel an affinity with him I've never felt with any of my other cases before. Or maybe it's the Polish thing. Maybe it's both.

Zoltan was the opposite. Built for his seventeen years, with a classic v-shaped body, light brown hair, intelligent green eyes, cheekbones that remind me a little of Silas and Sheena and thick eyebrows with a distinct kink in them and with a scar running through the one above his left eye.

I've spoken to Konstantin about it and though he keeps telling me to hang in there as long as Piotr's parents are willing to pay and that something will give eventually. I'm not so sure. It's never taken me this long to crack a case. Konstantin reckons I had a lucky streak before this and that I'm only just starting to see what our work is really like. But I think that's bull. Five years of a honeymoon period seems a bit long.

No, something is fundamentally different this time, but I don't know what. Logic tells me that I need to split the two up in my head and concentrate on Piotr. But weirdly, the single only thing I am absolutely convinced about to do with this case, which feels stone-cold most days, is that the two of them somehow belong together. Even if they disappeared months apart.

It drives me nuts.

I open my laptop and push the on button, before I go down to the kitchen to make myself some fresh coffee and hunt around for some biscuits.

I feel a bit lost. Sheena rang a little while back to let me know she's spending another night in London, and to ask if I could feed the cats, since Silas and Grace are not going to be back until tomorrow either. I'm stunned. I've never known her to take more than one day off at a time since I got here. I'm pleased for her. She deserves some fun. But the house feels unnaturally empty without everyone.

So while I wait for the kettle to boil, I allow myself to acknowledge how grateful I really am that Diego is taking me out to dinner again tonight.

Though this time I'm going to make sure I'm paying. It shouldn't matter what he thinks of Kalina, but when in years to come when he looks back at the summer he had a hot affair with a language student he never saw again, I want him to remember her as an equal, not as someone who let him pay her in meals for getting laid. And I want him to remember lots of getting laid, I realise, grinning to myself. Because much as I needed the break from him earlier, it's been barely over an hour and I already kind of miss him.

I fill the cafetière with ground coffee and top it up with boiling water then select two custard creams and two chocolate bourbons from the biscuit tin and put them on the counter. I'm about to push the plunger down on the coffee grinds when it hits me full force.

After nearly six months of absolutely nothing, *the feeling* hits me in the gut like a sucker punch.

DIEGO

"So, how come we didn't know he was coming out? And what the fuck kind of sentence is nine months for running over a kid?"

I know I haven't got my voice under control when I hear Isla snarl at me. She does it really quietly and without lifting her head off her paws, while she is lying by Julian's feet, but I know if I were anyone else taking that tone with Julian, she'd be right in my face showing me her full set of teeth.

"You know the drill, Diego," Julian answers levelly. "He's served half his sentence, he's out on licence. I don't know how O'Brien rigged it, but there was no indication Callum was going to get released before the first of September. Maybe it's nothing to do with the old man. Maybe the authorities wanted to ensure the family of that boy don't go after him. They still don't know if the kid's ever going to be able to talk or walk again, you know. If you think about it, he's been in rehab for nearly two years now. That's a long-arse time."

"Do we know where Callum is now?"

"No. Apparently they chucked him out of Lewes on Thursday. We would have known sooner if my guy's daughter hadn't been getting married on Wednesday. He'd taken a couple of days off and when he got back to work, Callum had been released. But my guess is Callum will turn up at *Fight or Flight* soon enough. I've sent a couple of guys over to Cecil's house, but as far as they can tell he's not there. I can dig around and find out who his parole officer is. Maybe they put him in a halfway house or something."

I ponder that. Julian is right. Cecil O'Brien's eldest son will show up at their family gym eventually, and since almost all my guys train there, we'll know when he does. But I'm almost certain I already know where he is.

"Chances are, he's holed up with the next in line of O'Brien's bastards," I explain to Julian.

Julian cocks his head slightly and waits for me to elaborate. Julian didn't grow up with all of us. He's a Londoner originally, and didn't set foot in Brighton until about four years ago, when he decided he was going to go into the security business by the seaside.

We built Santos-Benson Security together, after a chance encounter.

He's forever filed in my brain simultaneously under 'best decision to pull a finger out of my arse I ever made' and 'worst decision to pull a finger out of my arse I ever made'.

I met him one morning, shortly after he relocated here, around half past five. I'd just shut shop on the club and the bar, and I decided to take a stroll by the sea before heading to Woodland Drive. I did that a lot back then. I was twenty-one, I was already running this massive operation, and I often felt fucking overwhelmed by it all. I went down to the beach and there was this guy playing with his puppy. All happy. Until a wave came and dragged the puppy out. Stupid guy went in after the puppy and before I knew it, I had a drowning dog *and* a drowning man on my hands. Inlanders just don't fucking understand the sea. So I did what all decent Brightonians do — I took my shoes and my socks off and ruined a perfectly good pair of suit pants saving this guy's arse and his dog's on top. It's why I get special treatment from Isla and why, despite the fact I haven't known him since year dot, I trust Julian with my life. He owes me his dog's.

That's a pretty strong bind.

But there is a difference between trusting someone with your life and trusting them with your shit.

So, just in case he ever gets any ideas, I also have enough dirt on him to get him sent away until his wife's eggs have shrivelled up and the baby they are trying for isn't even a remote possibility any longer.

Not long after we went into business together, I found out that no matter how controlled he is on a job, *civilian* Julian has a temper. Especially if someone touches up his wife. There is a guy in a vegetative state in a care home in Haywards Heath, whose attacker the police still haven't found. I have proof, and Julian's got previous, so they wouldn't go lightly. And one of the beauties of the English justice system is, you can't make deals like they can in America. He could never sell me out to save his own skin. We can just sell each other out and take the consequences.

So we just have to trust we don't.

Aside from being a liability at times, though, I *really* value his opinion.

Because Julian is a fresh pair of eyes on our murky Brighton soup. Because he's not embroiled in Brighton the way Silas and I are. But sometimes it means he needs stuff explained to him that's just common knowledge between the rest of us. So I explain.

"Callum and his bastard brother Cormac are only a couple of months apart in age and they've always had a *special* bond. I'm not sure if the mothers literally shared Cecil in bed, but it's all a bit icky. They've always been thick as thieves those two. It's quite something because *none* of the other O'Brien children get on with each other. Like, they've hospitalised each other, revenge-shagged each other's husbands and wives, the lot. It's regular EastEnders, that family. Point being, I'm pretty sure Callum is at Cormac's house as we speak. So we station a man out there. Twenty-four seven. Got to be somebody who's dead good at camo, though. It's right out in the sticks, middle of the Downs. There are only two properties up there. A working farm and Cormac's patch. Was a smallholding once, too. Cecil bought it for the land, thinking he could develop it. Turns out it's in the middle of National Trust land. Nada developing. Grazing only. So he gave the house and yard to Cormac to live there and rents the pasture out to the local sheep farmer. So tell our guy he can't just rock up there in a car and sit outside. He's gonna have to be a bit more creative. But I want to know everything Callum does. Anything he does that can get him back inside, we fucking grass him up immediately."

Julian's eyebrows shoot up at that.

"Really? The police? That's not your normal style, Diego."

"Yeah. I know."

I blow out a long breath.

"Look," Julian says slowly. "You know I'll happily go along with whatever you say, but just out of curiosity, I know you hate the O'Briens, other than Silas—"

"Silas is not an O'Brien," I interrupt him sharply, earning me another snarl from Isla. "He just carries the name. He's not Cecil's son."

Julian makes an appeasing gesture.

"Yes, I know. Sorry, my mistake. Anyway, I know you can't stand that family, but what's this thing with Callum? What makes him so extra special that you're willing to put yourself on the police's radar? 'Cause you know that's what you're doing if you drop him in, right?"

I nod heavily.

"Yup. But, trust me, we've been in their viewfinder for a long time anyway and hopefully it won't matter soon, because soon we'll be fully legit. I've practically closed the deal on the league with Collier and once that's out of the way, I'm going to talk to the ladies upstairs."

I sigh heavily when I think about clearing out the working girls. I worry about them. The Brick is one of the very few places in town where they can work safely without a pimp. They pay extra rent for the protection we offer, but they're not 'mine'. I don't lay claim on them and I don't let anyone else either. They are totally free agents, yet they have our bouncers' back up at the touch of a button. It's a sweet deal they will not find elsewhere.

While I'm tormented about their future, I have no qualms selling the fight club league to the Eastbourne crowd. At the end of the day, it's nothing but a list of contacts that is worth around a mill. And Collier, the guy I'm selling to, is not a complete cunt like some of the people who were interested. He's also come up with a watertight cover story for what I'm *officially* selling him, so that's a bonus. At the moment, he and I are still haggling over a small number of details, but I'm sure we'll iron it out eventually.

Dad and Cecil O'Brien will be livid when they find out I'm letting the league leave town, but I don't give a fuck. Dad will be all 'I gave you this thing and you're tossing it away' which is utter bollocks because he gave me a set up of semi-organised local brawls and I turned that into a proper south coast league with *big* money flying around. O'Brien will be fucked off because he has delusions that he's somehow important and needs to be consulted about these things. When all he really is is an idiot whose personal idiocy is in love with my dad's personal idiocy. And vice versa. Peas in a pod, those two.

"Diego?" Julian prompts me when I still haven't answered. "What's the deal with Callum? What did he do to deserve your wrath?"

Is that what this is?

Wrath?

I don't know.

Maybe.

All I know is that I don't want Callum fucking O'Brien roaming the streets of my town. Or any other town for that matter.

I look Julian square in the eye when I finally answer his question.

"He killed my cat."

Kalina

I completely lose myself in Piotr's and Zoltan's files for the rest of the afternoon, churning everything over again with fresh drive, riding high on the wave of *the feeling*.

But I don't really see things that I didn't see before.

Both boys liked sports. No surprise there. Most male teens do, unless they're already too busy smoking dope and fucking. Piotr played tennis, like his parents. Zoltan played football and had started dabbling in amateur boxing before he came to England. Something his mother wasn't terribly happy with.

Both boys liked to read. Actual books. Piotr was heavily into classic sci-fi. Zelazny, Asimov, Lem. The kind of stuff my brothers are into. Zoltan read a whole load of stuff I'd never heard of and haven't got the time for. *Literature.* I don't do literature. In any language. Give me a good biography or a pulpy horror and I'm happy.

Both boys volunteered to work in charity shops while they were here, which is something the language school kind of pushes on their students. It's a good way of keeping them entertained and it has its merits in terms of having to converse with the locals. But they didn't work in the same shop. I've done a bit in each of the shops they worked in, and I doubt there is a connection there. It's all mildewy clothes, slightly deranged women over fifty, socially awkward older gents and being treated like an idiot because you're a foreigner. But it's a totally malice-free environment.

By the time eight o'clock comes around and there is a knock on the door, I've made absolutely no progress and I'm starving again, for food — and for the man who's come to take me out.

Problem is, I haven't got ready. I'm still sitting on my bed in my dungarees, unchanged from earlier in the day, with no makeup and no real desire to go anywhere. I shut my laptop, run down the stairs and open the door.

Just like he predicted, the man standing outside is very much Diego, in his standard tan-coloured three-piece suit and his fancy Italian leather shoes. Although he clearly still hasn't had time to shave and the stubble gives him a new edge. I swallow hard when I look at him because he is so fucking handsome, it hurts. I look down at myself then back into his storm grey eyes and shrug apologetically as I step aside to let him through the door.

"I'm sorry, I got caught up in work, I haven't changed yet."

He doesn't say a thing as he steps over the threshold as quickly as possible, just as everyone always does, because there is no pavement in front of Sheena's house and if you're not careful, a car will take the back of your legs off. What everyone else doesn't normally do is to bend down as soon as they're inside, sling their arms around me and nuzzle my neck to inhale my scent.

His nose still pressed firmly to the soft skin below my jaw, his beard scratching me deliciously, as he kisses my pulse, he slides his hands down over my butt. He hooks in and lifts me up, so I have no choice but to cross my legs behind his back and hold on to his shoulders.

I lean back a bit to smile at him and I catch a glimpse of sadness in his eyes that reminds me he's still the guy I spent last night with, fancy clothes or not. He smiles back at me and presses a soft kiss to my lips.

"I missed you," he says, and I laugh.

"It's not even been five hours, Diego!"

He flinches slightly when I call him that but then he grins.

"You been counting?"

"Maybe a little," I admit.

"Good," he says, and then he pins me against the wall and kisses me in earnest.

My heart leaps when our tongues meet, before it simply concedes defeat and wanders straight into my panties, to pulse between my legs. I can honestly say that no other person has ever had the power to turn me on this quickly. He thoroughly tongue-fucks me for a solid five

- 472 -

minutes, pinned against the wall in Sheena's dimly lit hallway before he withdraws, panting.

He rests his forehead against mine.

"I had better let you go get dressed, otherwise we'll never make it out of here."

I jump off his hips when he takes a step back and look up at him.

"Would that be a bad thing?"

He frowns.

"What do you mean?"

I shrug.

"Can't we just stay here? I'll order some Thai. Do you like Thai?"

"I like Thai," he confirms, slightly bewildered.

"Okay. Then let's order Thai and just pig out on Rowan's bed in the living room."

He looks at me suspiciously.

"Why Rowan's bed?"

I comedy-punch him.

"Because it's the biggest in the house," I giggle. "And there is *nobody* here. We can make a complete mess, then go to sleep in my room and clean it up tomorrow."

He looks at me as if I'd proposed a trip to Narnia.

"You don't want to go out?"

I shake my head.

"Not really, no." I sling my arms around his hips and make puppy eyes at him.

"Look, you live with your parents and *staff*, I live with..." My voice trails off for a moment because what do I say here? "A whole lot of people. This is the only chance we'll ever get to have a place to ourselves again, unless you book us a hotel room somewhere." I scrunch up my face, because I really don't like that idea. "And that would make me feel cheap. Like a whore. Not that there is anything wrong with prostitution. A woman's body is hers to do with whatever she wants. But I don't want to be that woman. So let's enjoy the opportunity. Also, it's my turn to pay for dinner and I bet I couldn't afford whatever you had in mind. But I can afford a Thai from the place around the corner."

His face breaks into the biggest, most gorgeous smile I have ever seen on him.

"You want to buy me dinner?"

"Yup."

"You want to sit on the biggest bed in Sheena's house and eat Thai with me?"

"Yup."

He toes off his fancy shoes and shucks himself out of his suit jacket at the same time.

"You're on, baby girl. You are *so* on."

DIEGO

She won't let me fuck her again before dinner, but she soon lets me peel her out of the dungarees, so she's dancing around in panties and a tight t-shirt that leaves her belly button on show, while she phones the Thai place and orders for us.

We grab plates, spoons and forks from the kitchen, but when I try to grab chop sticks, she slaps my hand and lectures me on Thai food being eaten by hand traditionally. I file that information away for later with a naughty grin. And wonder once more how come I underestimated this girl quite so much. I spent so much time over the last few months telling myself that she was too young for me and a no-go zone, that through my haze of repressed lust I didn't see how worldly and clued in she actually is. I find it hard to believe she turned only nineteen yesterday. Between the girlie giggles and the carefree attitude there lies a competence that's comforting, and seriously belies her age.

We settle in what was once the front room and lounge around on Rowan's enormous bed, talking about everything and nothing, in between me grabbing her and kissing whatever part of her body happens to present itself at the time, much to her squealing delight.

While she is writhing on the bed semi-naked, I'm still in my shirt, pants and waistcoat, and have been ordered to stay decent until we've taken delivery of the food, so somebody can actually answer the door.

We haggle over who gets to tip the driver. She's already paid for the order over the phone, but after playing dirty for a bit, it looks like I'm allowed to dish out the pocket money. I blackmail her consent out of her by kissing her ankles until she screams because, apparently, that's her ticklish spot. Once I get her to agree, I let go and she crawls over to sit on my lap, her knees by my hips, the way she did in the limo last night. She hovers with her arse in the air though at first, not nestling down on my hard on. Her panties are soaked through and I know she's being mindful of leaving a visible wet patch on the expensive cloth of my trousers if she sits down on my crotch. But I really don't fucking care about the suit pants and I don't care what the delivery guy is going think. I pull her down by the hips, willing to let her smear her cream all over me. I *need* the contact on my dick or I'm gonna implode.

As soon as she sinks down, settling on the ridge, she can't help but groan. I fucking love that sound and I fucking love the weight on my dick. I palm her butt, and she starts rocking back and forth as she finds my mouth. I let her take the lead as she kisses the fuck out of me, deep-throating me with her tongue in a way no other woman has ever claimed me. I'm about ten seconds away from coming in my pants, and I think so is she, when there is a knock on the door.

She detaches from me and scoots off my lap with heavy eyes then points resolutely at the door.

"Go! Hunt! Bring food! No food, no..."

She substitutes the word by dry humping the mattress and making porno noises.

I don't think I've ever before been turned on within an inch of climax one minute and laughing to the point my belly muscles hurt the next.

This girl is going to be the end of me.

Kalina

Sex, food and fun.

- 475 -

That's George Diego Benson in a nutshell, when he's not too busy being gangsta boss.

I love it.

Once he brings the bags with the food containers in and we dish them out on a tray on the bed, I order him to take his clothes off. He obliges, so when we eat I do it with the view of a cross-legged, shit hot man, wearing nothing but briefs and a devilish smile.

We only get about halfway through our meal, before he decides it's time to finish what we started before the Thai turned up. He tells me to eat up what's in my mouth then lifts the tray and takes it over to Rowan's desk.

With his back still to me, he shimmies out of his briefs before he kind of hunches forward. His right hand disappears around his front and I know he is fisting himself when he makes his next demand.

"Get naked," he says on a grunt.

I take off my panties and t-shirt, while I watch how his bicep and back muscles swell as he squeezes his cock. He is still holding it tight when he turns around and I see the head is glistening with precum already. He runs his thumb over the slit, spreading the drops and then lets go of it. I whimper at the sight. Despite the fact we've fucked I-can't-remember-how-many-times in the last 24 hours, I hadn't really *seen* him yet. In all his beautiful, engorged glory. The sound that leaves my throat when I get the full visual comes from deep within me and takes me by complete surprise. I've never whimpered for a man in my life.

He locks on to my eyes and clears the space to the bed in two long strides. The expression on his face is so feral, it makes me scoot up the bed, despite how much I yearn for him. He gets on the mattress and prowls over to me on his hands and knees, until I'm fully backed up against the headboard, knees drawn up.

He sits back on his haunches and his hand goes to the nape of my neck, possessively, just like the night before, and he holds me there, looking deep into my eyes, not doing a thing.

He just looks.

And looks.

And looks.

Until my knees fall away to the side, and my heart wants to jump out of my chest with longing, while my clit is pulsing so hard, I think I'm going to come already. In the periphery of my vision, I can see his cock quiver in answer to my pussy's call.

They're singing their own song down there, while we sing a different one up here.

Yet it's all the same.

It's fucking insane.

A small smile turns up the corners of his mouth.

"You can feel it, too, can't you?" he asks, searching my eyes.

I nod. There is no denying this anyway.

"Good."

He grins, never breaking eye contact.

"Spread 'em wider," he demands.

And I do.

He takes a languid look down my body and back up again, and then he takes my left leg with his free hand and hooks my ankle over his shoulder before he lets himself fall forward to line himself up at my entrance.

"You're gonna come, baby girl. You're gonna come as soon as I ram home, you hear me?"

I want to laugh.

This is so not my game.

I want to cry.

Because it suddenly *is*.

Realisation hits me like the Titanic hitting the iceberg.

With this guy, *everything* could be my game.

I can feel his grip tighten in my neck and I focus on his eyes again.

"I mean it, Kalina. You're gonna come." He rams home in one swift, all consuming slam. "Now!"

And my traitorous pussy does just that. She contracts around the sudden fullness he creates, and the world explodes in a thousand colours.

My saving grace?

He's only about two seconds behind me.

DIEGO

Kalina is a snorer.

Not a terrible one but not a dainty one either. She did it last night, too. It should get on my nerves, but for some strange reason, listening to the melodic vibrations coming from her nostrils doesn't irritate me in the slightest. On the contrary, it makes me smile as I tighten my arm around her sleeping body and pull her shoulders more securely onto my midriff, so her head is resting on my abdomen and her breath fans over my belly button.

I like that she has this little flaw, otherwise I think she'd be too good to be true.

I run my hand through her short hair feeling the bleached strands in wonder. She murmurs in her sleep, making my heart beat faster and even breathing a little life into my utterly exhausted penis.

It should be impossible to stir him but stir he does.

She is like a drug.

We fucked again after we finished the second half of our meal, during which we told each other a bit about our 'previous'. She is so far removed from the innocent I painted her as all this time, it's ridiculous. Maybe it's because continental women start earlier, but she sure as shit has seen a lot of action in her short years. When she told me about her lesbian adventures, I nearly choked on the ice cream she'd found in the freezer for dessert.

Then we did it again.

We fucked and talked and ate and fucked and ate and talked.

Until about an hour ago, when she fell asleep on me.

We never even made it up to her bedroom.

She was still dragging hard from yesterday's long night and, actually, Rowan's bed really is fucking gigantic compared to her poxy twin upstairs, so I'm not complaining. It's easier for me to hold her in my arms, while I check my phone and keep on working, in the vast expanse of a queen size.

Kalina might not be used to waking nights, but this is my normal.

In my line of work, there is no nine to five. I rarely go to sleep before seven or eight in the morning and normally I don't get up before three in the afternoon.

So I lie here, with the most amazing girl I've ever met curled up on me, shagged into oblivion yet wide awake, and trawl through my messages. I listen to the voicemails through my earpiece then let the phone read my text messages to me.

Julian checked in a while back to say I was right, our guy outside Cormac's house had spotted Callum and was tailing him now. Our guy was asking what to look out for, and I come up kinda empty. It's a fucking good question. So I just whisper 'anything illegal, tell him to get evidence if he can' into the dictate to text function on my phone, and hit send. Kalina grumbles a little when she hears my voice but settles again when I stroke her cheek.

I don't know quite who I am soothing more here, her or me.

The more I think about Callum being out, the more bile rises in my throat.

It's terrible for the kid he hit, but when that happened, I was kinda glad because it finally got Callum fucking O'Brien off my streets and behind bars. I really hoped they'd lock him up for a long, long time.

I'd been waiting for him to slip up on *something* for almost a decade.

The fact that it ended up happening because of a lousy hit and run sucked for his victim — I would have preferred for the coppers to catch him with a few kilos of coke or something — but as far as I was concerned, the whole thing was a gift horse, and that scum of the earth was finally gone. Or so I thought. Until the judge handed the sentence down and I thought I'd fucking misheard. Eighteen fucking measly months for leaving a healthy boy in the road with a traumatic brain injury. I could pretend that I was righteously outraged about it, but there is a part of me that seriously questions how much higher above Callum I really sit in the bottom of the emotionally literate barrel, considering I'm still more angry about the cat than I ever was about the kid.

He wasn't even my cat, really.

He was just a stray tom that used to come to the bottom of the garden at Woodland Drive. But he was my *friend*. As much as you can be friends with a creature that will take a bloody swipe at you by way of greeting and take your finger off along with the treat you're trying to feed it.

But there was something royal about him, something that commanded respect, with his bold tiger stripes and his big balls, swaggering around the neighbourhood and fucking kittens into any female cat that hadn't been spayed yet. It's why I called him Nuts. 'Cause that's what he was, the fucking nuts.

I liked Nuts. A lot.

I like cats in general. They're cool. They do their own shit and they know no master. I also like dogs, but I don't want one. Too fucking needy. But they're cool in their own way. I never understood why people always ask you if you are a dog or a cat person, as if you can't like both. As if it were a crime to give the 'wrong' answer.

In my house, 'cat' was *definitely* the wrong answer. To my old man, they're something you sic the dogs on, and to my mother they are basically vermin, which is so twisted my brain gives up trying to get on that. But it's why nobody got why I was so upset when Callum murdered Nuts.

Dad and Cecil laughed at the carnage that little cunt left behind.

Laughed.

My blood starts boiling again and tears shoot into my eyes when I think of the torture Callum put that poor cat through, and not for the first time in the last twelve years am I seriously contemplating putting a hit out on the guy.

I have the connections, I have the means.

I'd be doing humanity a favour taking that arsehole out before he can procreate.

It's why everything to do with Callum has always been *explicitly* off the record where Julian was concerned. I wanted to keep my options open, though I've kind of blown that now that I told J to put a tail on him and lifted the coms embargo regarding Callum.

That's probably a good thing, though. Because the problem is, outside of Hollywood, crime novels and a whole other level of society that I am not — and don't ever wish to be — part of, other than as an occasional entertainment supplier, there is no such thing as the perfect murder or a loyal assassin. And I really don't fancy going to prison for any length of time, let alone for life.

Especially not now that I've found the perfect little vixen to share my bed with.

The thought doesn't even freak me out.

Somewhere between looking into her eyes when she came under me last night and fantasising out loud with her about a threesome over ice cream earlier, I decided I want to keep her.

It should be scary, but it's not. Not even remotely.

It's just a fact.

And, yes, until now it would have been irresponsible to bring a woman into my life, but I'm so close to going legit, it's not such a big deal any longer. I'll be able to keep her safe.

I put my phone away and drag her up higher, so I can press some kisses to the top of her head.

"You're nice," she mumbles sleepily into my chest.

"Hey, Kalina?" I whisper.

"Hmm?" she answers, but I'm certain she's still mostly asleep.

So I risk it.

"Wanna marry me?"

"Hmm," she answers faintly. "Ask Kristina."

"Who's Kristina?" I ask.

But she's snoring again.

I smile.

At least she didn't say no.

Z

I knew it was going to get bad again as soon as I heard the ròka's voice up above.

I cried.

He'd been gone so long that I really thought he was never coming back. The first few months after he miraculously disappeared, I kept waiting for him to return, but then I relaxed. I even dreamed that the óriás would let us go eventually.

The óriás on his own has not been so bad.

I mean, he'd still kill Guppi in the blink of an eye if I tried to escape again, but he'd make it quick and painless. The ròka would get his kicks first. He'd make Guppi suffer, make me watch the torture and when he's sufficiently riled up, he'd get me to bend over with the promise of saving Guppi.

He'd come in two pumps.

Then he'd get the óriás to explode Guppi's neck.

He *always* comes in two pumps. Then he lashes me and calls me a dirty homo.

The óriás isn't like that. He's not into us. Or pain. I'm pretty sure he's into women. Big-breasted and big-hipped. Mama-types with tits he can suckle on. He's not very bright and I'm not sure he understands pain. He'll do anything the ròka will tell him, but he generally just leaves us be, until it's time for the 'monkeys' as he calls us 'to perform'. It makes him snigger every time he says it.

It's been 760 times I've heard that phrase, take away a few for those empty days, *after* Bonsai and *before* Guppi, when there was just me, waiting to die, and the cameras on the walls.

And take away another few more days three months ago when *nobody* turned up for almost a week. The first night he didn't come down to get the dirty dinner dishes, I heard the dogs bark up top when somebody came to take them. But nobody came to get us. I didn't try to alert them. I saw the dogs two years ago when I was brought here. Anyone who comes to take them is part of the ròka's and the óriás' crowd. That doesn't mean they know we're down here, but it means that even if Guppi had climbed the ladder and banged on the hatch, I'm certain they wouldn't have helped. They'd have taken Guppi and I wouldn't have been able to keep him safe, because my chain only stretches to about two metres from the ladder. I'm not losing another little one. I need to protect him as long as I can. So we sat stumm until the noise subsided and they were gone.

After a few days, the óriás did come back, his face black and blue, split lip that had been stitched up and climbing gingerly down the ladder.

He seemed relieved to find us in place and alive.

That is the difference between the ròka and the óriás.

The ròka is a sadist and completely unpredictable.

The óriás is like a pig farmer. Sticks to his routine, cares for his animals, until it's time to kill them. He tells us what he wants done and how to make it look and as long as we are good performing monkeys, he feeds us three times a day, makes sure we're clean and that the toilet is emptied before the place starts to stink.

When Guppi got sick, he even took him above and let him sit in the sunlight for half an hour each day, until he got better. The ròka would never have done that. At the first sign of sickness, the ròka would have snuffed Guppi out and gone to get a replacement. After Guppi got better, the óriás even bought us supplements and a daylight lamp.

I miss sunlight.

When Guppi came down after his excursions, I would hold him extra tight through the night, and I could smell the sunlight on his skin.

He smelled of freedom.

Kalina

I wake up the first time around eleven, still cocooned in Diego's arms.

Diego? George? What am I going to call this man?

I prop myself up on my elbow and look at him in the faint light that falls through the gaps in the curtains. He looks relaxed, peaceful, and I lose myself in studying his features.

- 483 -

This close up, in the semi-darkness, and not blinded by his Northern European colouring, I can see the Spanish influence. In the strong jawline and those luscious, luscious lips. In his beard that has grown so much again overnight that it is now already soft to the touch, rather than bristly, as my gently exploring fingertips find out.

He smiles in his sleep and then begins chasing those fingertips with his mouth, until he catches my index and my middle finger between his lips and sucks them in, licking gently over the pads with the tip of his tongue. The sensation shoots straight to my cervix and my breath hitches.

"You're awake," I whisper, hopefully.

"Hmmm," he answers sleepily, his tongue still toying with my fingers.

I gently extract them from his mouth and run the pad of my thumb along the bridge of his nose.

"Hmm, that's nice," he mutters.

"Can I ask you a question?"

"You just did."

"Funny."

"What's your question? And can I go back to sleep if I answer correctly?"

"Which do you prefer to be called, George or Diego?"

His eyes flutter open at that and immediately scrunch up in thought.

"I dunno. George is my father's name and he's a cunt. But it's also what Silas and Sheena call me, so that makes up for it. Diego means 'supplanter'. My mum gave me that name, because my dad wouldn't let her call me Diablo."

"Your mother wanted to name you *devil*?"

He shuts his eyes on a nod.

"Yup."

"Why?!?"

He lifts his hand up and cups the back of my neck to draw me down to him, until his mouth lands just below my jugular and he starts nibbling on the skin below my pulse.

- 484 -

"Because, baby girl, before I feasted on beautiful Polish women, I ate my twin."

I push against his restraint to look back down at him with raised eyebrows.

"Well, that's kind of gross," I say, laughing, and let my eyes roam over his body with interest. "So you got like a third eye or an extra pinkie somewhere? Isn't that what normally happens when twins merge in the mother's belly?"

The expression in his eyes changes to disbelief.

"What?"

"Genetic chimerism it's called, right? Is that why you have two names? You're really two people?" I tease him. "Like in King's *The Dark Half*?"

I can tell I've lost him, and then remember too late that he doesn't read.

He frowns and I can tell he's getting angry.

Feeling insecure will do that to people.

Ooops.

I hop on top of him, cradle his head in my hands and lower my face to his.

"I'm sorry," I say, and try to kiss him, but he holds me off.

"It's not funny," he says sternly. "My mother *hates* me because there were supposed to be two of us, but she only got one. And no, I am not a chimera. I didn't eat my twin, really. That's just what she claims. According to my nan, she had a bog-standard miscarriage. Of one. But she's spent her life convincing herself it was the *wrong* one and it was *my* fault."

He searches my eyes, trying to convey how deeply that hurts, and my heart bleeds for the boy I see. The boy that wasn't good enough. Whose mother rejected him because her body couldn't hold on to two lives. I stroke his forehead and I feel his anger dissipate a little.

"Then your mother is stupid," I tell him softly. "She should have been grateful that she managed to keep at least one of you. *I'm* grateful she managed to hang on to *you*."

I try again to kiss him, and this time he lets me.

Relief washes over me as soon as his lips meet mine, and I make a mental note not to be so flippant around him anymore.

What starts as an apologetic, gentle meeting of mouths soon turns heated and after a few minutes, he rolls me onto my back. He withdraws and braces his arms beside my head.

"What do you *want* to call me?" he asks, and the return to the original question tells me we're good. I reach up to run my fingers through his beard.

"Diego," I say with conviction.

"Why?" he asks.

"Because your mother might have given you that name out of, what is the word, spite, but you made him. You built him. He's *yours*."

My words spark a fire in his eyes I haven't seen before.

He growls before his mouth crashes down on mine, and seconds later he is buried inside me again.

I've never been appreciation-fucked before but, boy, is it good.

I don't think I will ever get enough of the feel of this man.

DIEGO

The second time we wake it is afternoon and we're surrounded by a trio of amused faces. Silas, Grace and Sheena clearly all came back on the same train and are standing in a semicircle around the bed, looking at our tangled bodies.

The grins on their faces tell me that they're having an absolute field day with this.

As soon as I realise what exactly it is they are staring at, I draw the blanket up to cover Kalina's naked butt — and my junk. Kalina is lying face down across my chest, so she was mostly covered, but they got a good eyeful of my best bit.

My *very happy* best bit.

Sheena laughs.

"Too late, boy. But don't worry, ain't nothing I haven't seen before." She pauses before she delivers her punchline. "But last time, it was a lot smaller."

She turns towards the door to the tune of Silas groaning.

"Stop making it weird, Mum."

She throws him a coquettish look over her shoulder.

"Nothing weird about this, baby. Like everybody else in this house, I've been rooting for those two to shack up for *months*. If, as a side benefit, I get a glimpse of a damn fine penis on a damn fine man, that I didn't give birth to, I'm not complaining."

"Muuum!" he wails, while Grace doubles over and generally looks like she is pissing herself with silent laughter.

She pulls her phone out of her back pocket. Presumably to take a snap.

"I'm going to go make some tea if anyone wants some," Sheena says as she moves out of the room and down the hallway. "I'll be in the kitchen, burning toast."

While this exchange is going on, Kalina starts burrowing deeper into my left pec. I can feel from the sudden heat on my skin that her face is flaming.

"Guys," I plead with Grace and Silas. "Come on, give the lady some privacy."

Kalina giggles against my nipple and says something of which I only understand a muffled 'no lady'.

Silas doesn't move an inch but just looks at us, kind of critically but also pleased.

"You took her for breakfast?"

I nod.

"And I wanted to take her for dinner," I say defensively. "But she bought me Thai instead."

For some inexplicable reason, that makes him happy, and I get treated to one of Silas' rare real smiles.

"Cool," he says.

With my attention on him, I hadn't noticed that Grace wasn't taking a picture at all.

She is video calling someone.

"Hey," a woman's voice on the other side of the screen answers. "What's up?"

It's an American's voice.

"You're calling *Raven*?" I ask her indignantly.

Raven is Rowan's brand-new American girlfriend — I can't decide if I'm bucking a trend here by deviating from bagging a Yank or hopping on the bandwagon with another foreigner. Raven and Rowan are currently somewhere near Phoenix in deepest, darkest Arizona. They went there to help Raven's old foster parents out in their group home, after her foster dad broke his ankle.

Grace grins at me and shrugs unapologetically.

"Only 'cause I know Rowan doesn't pick up if you try to video chat," she says to me over the top of the phone then gazes back to Raven on her screen. "Is Rowan with you?"

"Sure thing. Is everything okay?"

I can hear the worry in Raven's voice. She only stayed with Sheena, Silas and Grace for about a week after Rowan brought himself a nurse back from rehab, but that's the Sheena and Silas effect. Those two fucking grow on you like a cancer in five seconds flat.

"Yeah, all fine," Grace reassures her. "Just need to show him something."

Before I can cotton on to what's coming next, the person on the other side has clearly changed, because Grace turns the camera on Kalina and me and I catch a glimpse of a shirtless, sweating Rowan, looking confused.

"You owe me a hundred bucks, Ro," Grace shouts as she pans over me and my increasingly giggling girl.

"Why? Who is that girl?" Rowan asks.

Kalina pulls the blanket tighter around her, so her tits are covered when she lifts herself off my chest and turns to the camera to give Rowan a little wave.

"Hi, big guy, how are you?"

- 488 -

I feel a little pinch of jealousy when she says that. Compared to Silas, I'm lean, compared to Rowan, I'm fucking scrawny. The guy is like a fucking oak tree or something. As if she can feel my hurt, Kalina turns away from the phone to kiss my chest, right above my heart.

"You bleached your hair, pixie-girl," Rowan says. "You look weird."

On the little screen, Rowan looks from her to me, and then his dark eyes scrunch up.

"Is that *my* bed, Benson? You better clean that shit up properly. I don't wanna come home to sleep on your spunk."

Before I can retort, Silas has suddenly grabbed Grace's phone, in a move so fast we are all reminded of why his fighter name is The Snake. He plonks himself down on the chair by the desk with his shoulder to us, to talk to his brother.

"You're coming home?" he asks hopefully, and in a matter of only two minutes, a second stab of jealousy goes through my gut.

"Yeah. We've been talking about it. I'm tired of deserts and cactuses, or is it cacti? Whatever too many of those fuckers are called," Rowan answers, his baritone sounding as tired as he claims to be. "I want to see some green. I want to breathe without getting a lungful of dust. I want shorter vowels. I'm homesick already. I know it's pathetic, but I am. And Raven feels like she only just got to meet you lot. I think she misses Grace's cocktails and your cooking."

We all grin at that. While Grace sits down at the bottom end of our bed to carry on listening in to what Rowan is saying, I go fishing for my briefs. I shuffle them on awkwardly under what little cover Kalina has left me with as Rowan continues.

"Her dad is much better and, actually, one of their other grown-up foster kids is coming home to help in a few days, so it's not like we'd be leaving them in the lurch. We just have to convince Halosan that it's safe for Raven to go back to England now, rather than wait for Rothman's trial. But honestly, I don't think there is any direct danger from the Rothman family or their company. I don't know if you've been following this, but it looks like they've all turned against each other in a bid to come out individually unscathed. Charming bunch they are. And Frank is their favourite sacrificial lamb. He deserves it, that fucker."

I hear in the tone of Rowan's voice that he'd still happily break Frank Rothman's neck, given half a chance. And I'm pretty sure it's more to do with the fact that the therapist tried to fuck Raven without her consent than with the fact that Rothman was personally responsible for the death of one of Rowan's rehab cohorts, because Rothman was putting clients on an unsanctioned drugs trial for his family's company. While the guy who died wasn't exactly Rowan's favourite buddy, Rowan is fiercely protective of the little black-haired rockabilly punk, who happened to be his allocated nurse at the Halosan clinic in Dorset where it all happened. He's very much a 'you touch her, you die' kind of guy.

I look at the girl next to me, and I know how he feels. I'm the least brave of the three of us. I train and I will spar with Silas, but I've never put myself in the ring. Call me a pussy, but I don't like getting hurt. They used to nickname me The Roadrunner because I'd punch and leg it out of the danger zone. But if anyone threatened Kalina, I wouldn't care how much bigger they were. I'd stand my ground and take every blow coming my way, fighting to the death for her. It's a weirdly empowering feeling and it makes me gather her to me and plant a noisy kiss on the top of her head.

"So get that arsehole out of my bed. I'll need it," Rowan says to Silas by way of ringing off, but suddenly I remember something, and I make a gesture to Silas to stop him from hanging up.

Silas frowns at me then back at the screen.

"Hang on, the arsehole wants a word, I think."

He gets up and brings me the phone. Because it's Grace's, it's got a cutesy case with glitter and shit and for a second, it hits me that this is the fucking perfect opportunity to have this chat. I doubt anyone's tapping into Grace's and Raven's phones yet.

"Hang on a sec," I tell Rowan before I look around the room.

I'm torn between sending the girls out, which would come across as massively chauvinistic and sending all of them out, which would make Silas suspicious that I'm going to get his brother into trouble. Wouldn't be the first time. Grace catches my eye, throws up her hands and gets up off the bed.

"I don't wanna know," she states. "Just don't get my man in trouble, Benson, and we're good."

Her delivery is first class threatening. She's clearly been hanging with Sheena too long.

On the upside, she leaves on her own accord, pulling Silas down for a quick, possessive kiss on her way out, to remind him to stay good. I don't blame her. She thought she'd seen him die once this year already. That was plenty enough for her. And she's a *good* girl.

"I *do* want to know," Kalina says resolutely, and sits up cross-legged, wrapping the whole of the blanket around her.

I hold her gaze for a second.

She is challenging me.

Either I let her in, completely, or we're over before we've begun.

"*Diego*," she says, and the way she stretches the word tells me everything. "I *do* want to know."

"Is there something specific I'm waiting for here?" Rowan asks, mildly irritated. "Or were you just finding it hard to say goodbye, lover?"

I look over to Silas and find the same question in his eyes, so I clear my throat and decide to trust. It's not like I'm making Kalina an accessory to a crime. Yet.

"I wanted to ask you about something. Mid-May, when you were staying with us at the mansion, Goran says he took you to a dog-fighting thing and you ended up beating the guy who ran it to within an inch of his life."

"That may or may not have occurred. Though if something like that did occur, then I'd say that is a vastly exaggerated statement. I'd say that the hypothetical cunt we're talking about could have got off worse, since last I heard, he didn't have any permanent damage. I'd also say that that's a crying shame."

He's walking while he's talking, and I realise that he's moving into a landscape of varying shades of brown, away from any other people. Away from Raven. He stops somewhere and sits down on a rock.

"Why? Friend of yours?" he asks, and I realise he still has issues making the split in his head between me and my father.

It's a recurring issue people have, and it fucks me right off.

"Don't be a cunt. You know I'm not into that shit. It's just fucking wrong."

He nods, and I can see he believes me.

- 491 -

"So why the question?"

"Well, I was thinking. Occurs to me that around the same time that incident may or may not have occurred, Cormac O'Brien spent a few days in hospital because someone beat *him* up, you see. There aren't a lot of people big enough to put Cormac in A&E, and there aren't many people who Goran is afraid enough of not to snitch on. Just saying."

On screen, I can only see Rowan's face and shoulders, covered in tattoos that are already baking in the Arizona mid-morning sun, but from the jerky movements off camera, I can tell he is angrily kicking at the dirt. We might have been fighting over the same guy's top spot for years and we might not be best mates, but when it comes to animal cruelty, Rowan and I have an accord.

He sighs and looks back into the camera.

"Okay, I didn't get to see an actual fight. Otherwise, I would have torched the fucking place. Goran took me to Cormac's house — if you wanna call it that — because, I don't know, I think he wanted to buddy up or something. I had no idea where we were going, or what for, or to whom. I mean, I'd only just got back into town after how many years? When I left Brighton, Cormac was still a kid. Just one of Cecil's thousand and one bastards, you know. I had no idea. But when we got there, Cormac was all over me. Needy, like. I think he is missing Callum. I mean, they were always together when we were kids, remember? Like Laurel and Hardy. Well, if Laurel was a creepy cunt and Hardy was a giant idiot. I think it hit him hard when Callum got sent down. And I got the feeling he doesn't get many visitors out there, you know. Like, even his father doesn't really want to touch him with a bargepole 'cause he's so fucking dumb. I got the feeling Cecil set him up out there in the sticks, so he isn't constantly reminded of the fact that that numbskull originated in his balls. Anyway, for whatever reason, Cormac was super happy to see me and then he showed me his kennels and started insisting that he wanted to show me two of his dogs fight each other. I kept trying to tell him I didn't want any part of it, but he just didn't listen. The guy seriously has only one brain cell. So in the end, I made him listen with my fists. I called a cab and left Goran there to pick up the pieces. I reported Cormac to the RSPCA as soon as somebody answered their fucking phone the next day, but they did fuck all. When I chased it up, they said they'd sent officers to the property, but there hadn't been any dogs there. I'm guessing Goran or Cecil or somebody went and cleared them out that night. I'm gonna ask you again now, why are we talking about this?"

"Callum's out," I answer, and Silas who was sitting at the desk, listening with his head down, looks up at me.

He knows how much I hate Callum.

He knows *why*.

Nuts is buried in the back garden of this very house.

Back when Cecil and Callum and Dad had got tired of laughing at me and left me behind with the body of my furry friend, I gathered up what was left of him, each piece I could find, wrapped him in my shirt and I brought him here. We weren't even that close at the time. Silas had moved from the old neighbourhood to Shoreham and got a *brother* to replace me. I had moved from the old neighbourhood to Woodland Drive and was going up in the world. But it never crossed my mind to take Nuts' body anywhere else. I didn't even think about it, just followed my homing beacon and came to the only person I trusted. Thankfully, Rowan wasn't in that day. I think he was training. But Silas was here. He helped me bury the cat, held me while I cried my eyes out, never mentioned it again, and a month later spent his entire pocket money on a hazelnut tree to plant on top. That's Silas.

"That was swift justice," Rowan says sarcastically to my statement that Callum's back in society.

Rowan might be as criminally inclined as I am, but neither of us condones the shockingly short sentence Callum got for mowing a perfectly healthy teen down and leaving him with life-changing injuries. That's legal speak for brain damaged.

"Hmm," I answer. "Bit too swift for my liking."

"Let me guess," Rowan says. "He's holing up with Cormac now."

"Yup," I nod.

"The dream team is back together."

"Yup."

"I know that tone, Diego. You want to take them out."

"I'd love to," I admit. "But I'll settle for off the streets."

"So you were wondering if I saw anything we can pin on them while I was there?"

I nod.

"Something like that," I admit.

He shakes his head, sadly.

"Nope. Other than the dogs, I saw nothing the pigs might be interested in. Sorry," he says, and then a smile spreads over his face. "But if you need help *finding* something, I can be on a plane in a matter of days."

"Cool," I say. "Get me some flight details and I'll spring a business class for you and Raven. See ya."

He nods curtly, and the screen goes blank.

Kalina starts laughing next to me.

"Well," she says. "I didn't understand a word of that, but it was hot," she proclaims, and climbs onto my lap, immediately tugging at the elastic of my briefs that I only put on ten minutes ago.

"Right," Silas clears his throat and gets up. "I'll check on that tea."

He shuts the door behind him, and then I'm alone once more with a girl who clearly thinks I'm the hottest guy ever to walk the earth.

Life could be worse.

GUPPI

Z hisses when I put ointment on his ankle.

"Sei kein Waschlappen," I mumble, and he clips me playfully around the head.

I've taught him quite a bit of German, and he's taught me some Hungarian, but I know he didn't understand that I told him not to be a wimp just now, other than by my tone.

We used to be more careful with the play fighting because we didn't know if it would trigger my collar. But as the weeks turned into months and the months turned into almost two years, we stopped thinking about it too much.

Z says that's human nature.

You become less scared the longer something doesn't happen.

If he's right, then maybe one day I'm un-scared enough to just trip the mechanism and end it all.

I kiss his leg just above where the flesh is swollen and red.

The big guy, the one Z calls Óriás, which means giant in Hungarian, came earlier and swapped the shackle from the left ankle to the right.

He swaps it over every other week, so the skin can heal, then swaps it back again.

Still, after two years, it has left scars all around Z's lower leg.

Z says when we get out, he'll get tattoos to cover them up.

He still says *when*, not *if*, and I love him all the harder for it.

Z says he'll get tattoos to cover up *all* his scars.

He'll be a walking canvass.

They never touch *me*, but the one Z calls Ròka, fox — for his red hair and his pointy face — loves whipping him until he draws blood. I think it's because Ròka is scared of Z. Because Z is big and *virile*, even at only nineteen, and Ròka is... small.

That's why Z is shackled to a chain, and I am not.

Or maybe they know the threat of my head being blown off will always be enough to keep me in line.

I fear for Z now that Ròka is back. It sounds insane, but the months when we were just being looked after by Óriás were almost *nice*. With Ròka out of the equation, there were no beatings, and we were allowed to just get on with selling what we apparently sell best.

Love.

Romance.

Gentleness.

Z's big penis in my little mouth.

According to Z, it's not what they first had in mind when they set this up. He knows because there was a boy before me. Z called him Bonsai. I'm sure that was as much his real name as Guppi is mine. Z gave me my name, too. He says he won't call me by my real name because then, when we're free, I'm still that person. I know his real name and he knows mine, but out aloud I call him only Z.

Z says Bonsai didn't survive the kind of brutal stuff Ròka thought would sell.

So when they snatched me and brought me back here as his replacement, Z insisted on doing it differently. He basically told them they could blow my head off and shoot him dead, before he'd rape me, but he'd agree to break me in gently.

Ròka whipped him until Z's entire back was dripping with blood, but he held fast.

And they went with it.

Apparently, it sold.

Big time.

Still does.

And our lives depend on it.

I kiss Z's leg again and he catches my face in his palm, tilting it, so I'm looking up at him from my position of kneeling in front of our bed. He runs a hand over the sparse fluff on my upper lip and narrows his eyes.

"We need to wax that," he says, in English, but so quietly the microphones won't pick it up — we hope.

The Ròka gets really angry if we say anything that shatters the illusion. And we're not exactly in a no camera zone right now. We're right in the middle of the shot.

I hate it when he waxes my fledgling beard. Not because it hurts like a bitch, which it does, but because there is a part of me that wants to shave like any normal guy. I've always been small for my age, been told I look effeminate, and I should be allowed to like that I'm finally starting to turn into a man. But I know that waxing makes more sense. It's more thorough, it leaves no room for telltale shadows.

And I *need* to carry on looking young.

Z can grow and be hairy all he likes. Actually, I'm starting to suspect the more *manly* he looks, the better. But if I start not looking underage any longer, they'll get rid of me.

They'll feed me to the dogs.

Literally.

Z says that's what they did with Bonsai.

Kalina

Diego leaves Sheena's at four o'clock on Sunday to go back to work, and I immediately feel a bit lost. Grace and Silas invite me to go to the beach with them, but I don't want to be the third wheel. So I decline and go back to my laptop.

I have another stab at Piotr and Zoltan's files, but I keep distracting myself with thoughts of the weekend.

I can't concentrate.

Each time my mind wanders, I can feel Diego's lips on mine, top and bottom set, can feel him moving inside me. Like he's left an indelible imprint.

But it's not just the physical memory that keeps replaying in my mind. I think about all I've learned about him in the last two days, about how complex he is. I think about the dynamics between him and Silas and Rowan, which are fucked up yet somehow *beautiful*.

I think about how much I want to keep him.

And I get curious.

I wasn't lying to him when I said I only understood a fraction of what he was talking about to Rowan on the phone. I got as much as there is some guy named Cormac who organises dog fights and a guy called Callum who's just been released from prison, and Diego wants to set them up somehow.

He clearly hates both of them, but he seems to be gunning mostly for Callum. Wonder why. Wonder what this Callum has done to incur his wrath. The other thing that clicked was the recurring theme of an O'Brien in the mix. Sometimes I wonder if they are just short of surnames in Brighton and surrounding areas. I hesitate for only about a second before I decide it's not stalking my new temporary boyfriend if I have a little dig around the net and see what I can find on this Cormac O'Brien character.

So I do.

Nothing.

Well, nothing around here.

There is an American author by that name I've never heard of.

On a hunch — and because everyone in a twenty-mile radius who isn't called Benson seems to be an O'Brien — I type in Callum O'Brien.

And get the whole story.

Callum O'Brien, also known as Callum Carter and Callum Bosworth, was arrested in September two years ago, after failing to stop at the scene of a road traffic accident. His silver BMW X5 was caught on CCTV when it mounted the pavement and mowed down 14-year-old pedestrian Daniel Mantas, a promising young footballer whose parents had recently moved to Brighton, so he could join the Albion football club's youth program, and who was out for a run.

Daniel Mantas was taken to the Royal Sussex County hospital with life-threatening injuries. Callum was arrested at the *Fight or Flight* gym, after calling the police on himself, only hours after the accident. Callum claimed he lost control of the vehicle due to a sneezing attack and then panicked. He was taken into custody, charged and released on bail within a few days. The case went to trial almost a year later and Callum was sentenced to eighteen months behind bars for causing injury by dangerous driving.

Callum's victim sustained life-changing injuries. At the time of the article going to press, it looked like he was going to be dependent on a carer and a wheelchair for the rest of his life.

I look at the pictures that accompany the story. One is Callum's mug shot. The other is of Callum arriving in court, looking smart in a dark business suit and flanked by a woman I presume to be his mother on one side and a lawyer-type on the other.

Callum's the weaselly type, slight in built, with ginger hair and brown eyes. He looks like any other guy, but on the mug shot there is a mean slant to his mouth. Or maybe I'm just imagining it because of what I've just read. How can anyone hit somebody and then just leave them to die?

There is no picture of the victim in the article, a comparatively short piece from the local newspaper website, published on the day of Callum's sentencing.

But there is a link to the CCTV footage.

I let the mouse hover over the play button for a bit before I decide to go ahead. Despite of what I do for a living, I still feel squeamish when I see reels of people getting killed or injured. The bones I recover are already dead. They bring closure to the living. Watching a life being snuffed out is a whole different kettle of fish.

In the end, though, I click.

The footage is not too grainy but quite far off, so you can't make out Daniel's features. The time stamp tells me it was very early morning, which would explain why the light is grey and there is hardly any traffic on the road. With a jolt, I realise that I recognize the front of the cafe that's partially in the shot, still shut at that time of day. I actually know that part of Brighton quite well. It's in Kemp Town, not far from the language school headquarters. I've had paninis in that cafe once.

Whoever cut the clip did it so that you are staring at an empty section of street for a good fifteen seconds before anything happens. I guess to ram home how quiet and ordinary a morning it was. Or maybe just because otherwise it's over in a blink of an eye. Because once it happens, it happens so fast you can hardly process what you see before it's over.

The smallish figure of a blond teenage boy suddenly appears from the right, running along the pavement. He's wearing a blue and white hoodie, blue jogging bottoms and white trainers, and appears to be steadily pounding the pavement at a fast run. But something about his movement doesn't sit right with me. Before I can decide what it is, though, a fat silver BMW enters the picture from behind the kid, mounts the pavement, hits him side on and catapults him out of shot.

I watch the clip five times, trying to figure out what it is that bothers me, but in the end I give up. I'm wasting my time, and I have other stuff to do.

I briefly click through some of the other links that came up in the search but don't find anything more than what the first article already told me.

There is no mention of Callum being released anywhere, but I wouldn't expect that. Not big enough a case for the press to be interested. When I do the maths, though, I get why Diego and Rowan seemed so pissed off at the system. If Callum's recently come out, he only served nine of the eighteen months.

I wonder if Daniel was somehow connected to Diego and if that is why he's going after Callum. For a moment, I consider widening my search, but then I decide I'm going to ask him next time I see him, rather than snoop around. I don't want to treat Diego like a case. It seems wrong.

So I shut the computer, grab a large bar of chocolate from my secret stash and go and run myself a bath instead.

Diego

I meet with Julian in the office at five and we discuss jobs for next week, as is our normal Sunday routine.

Our company provides some bodyguard services for celebs that live on the south coast, but mostly we hire out security staff for events, and sometimes even prisons. HRM prison service needs agency staff just as often as other industries do, which can be quite the advantage in terms of keeping tabs on the players currently inside.

Because event security is our main bread and butter, weekends are too busy for Julian to take off. So he, Isla and Lila clock off Sunday nights and come back Wednesday mornings, while I stay in The Brick's penthouse rather than go home to my parents.

Lila keeps our calendar well organised, so we're usually through with our Sunday meeting in a couple of hours.

Today is no different, despite the fact my thoughts keep wandering to a small bleach-blonde, previously brunette, pixie girl who sucks dick like no other.

"Boss?" Julian asks me, and by his tone I can tell he's been trying to get my attention for a while.

I clear my throat.

"Yes? Sorry, what was that?"

"Our guy up in the hills," he says, meaning the man he's put on Callum and Cormac. "He's wondering how long this assignment is for. He's set up camp in an empty barn, and it sounds like he is all set for the long haul, but I think he might want to have a timescale as to when he'll be relieved, or if there is a rota, or what."

I nod, thinking about it.

"Has he had anything to report?" I ask, somewhat superfluously because if there had been anything Julian would have told me about it already.

Julian shakes his head.

"Nothing. They had a supermarket delivery yesterday and that's it. No comings, no goings."

"Ok." I think about the info I got from Rowan for a moment. "Does he know if there are any dogs up there?"

Julian frowns. In his world, everybody and their dog's got a dog, so it hardly seems worth mentioning.

"I don't know." He pulls out his phone. "But I can find out."

He types a message out annoyingly fast and hits send. A couple of minutes later, his phone pings.

"Hmm, Arlo says it's practically a secure compound, so you can't see over the fence anywhere. And he hasn't found a vantage point to look down into it from, but he's working on it. He's heard dogs barking. But he can't tell for sure from which direction. It may have come from the farm next door."

I roll my eyes.

"You had to put a half deaf man on the case, didn't you?"

Julian shrugs.

"He's a good kid and he's fucking good at camo. He blends like no other. And since that fight, when Silas beat him to a pulp, he's been little use for anything other than surveillance. I put him on the door, people see his hearing aid, and they take advantage. Shit, he nearly lost his other eardrum because people think it's funny shouting directly in his *good* ear."

"Maybe we need to get him a more invisible hearing aid. Something a little less nineteen seventies than what the health service issued him with," I ponder, and Julian grins.

"What?" I ask him.

"You're a good man, Diego."

"Fuck off," I say good-naturedly.

Julian takes that as his cue to scrape back his chair and whistle for his wife and dog.

"Let's go, girls!"

Isla stands up from her place by his feet and Lila appears in the door with a big grin, holding his jacket out for him.

"You called, master?" she says sarcastically.

"I did," Julian says, and smacks her bottom on the way out.

Hard.

I hear her giggle all the way through reception, until they step out into the hallway and the office door shuts behind them.

Julian and Lila were already married when I met him and puppy Isla on the beach that day. They've been together nearly ten years, through thick and thin, through army years and civilian life. And I just know they still fuck like they've only just met.

I want that.

I want a forever girl.

I kind of want her right now.

So I ring the one who I've got in my scope for the position, as soon as I leave the office and step into the lift to go up to the penthouse.

She answers on the third ring.

"Hey," she says, and the acoustics tell me she's in the bath.

"I miss you," I say. "You want to come over to my place tonight?"

She doesn't answer straight away, but I can hear her breath hitching a few times, the telltale sound of suppressed tears.

She's crying.

Not happy tears.

I'm instantly on full alert.

"Kalina? Are you okay? What's going on?"

"I'm fine," she says. "I get like this sometimes," she adds, sniffling. "After sex."

I take a big breath but don't get a chance to speak.

"After *good* sex," she stresses, and it warms my heart that she's thinking of my ego, even while she is clearly struggling with her mood. "Like a comedown. I'll be fine. It usually happens a lot more often. I guess...I guess, we did it so often this weekend I didn't get time to crash."

She laughs at the thought, though I know full well she's still crying at the same time.

Is it weird? A woman who likes sex but who gets a kind of hangover afterwards? Maybe.

But I don't care.

I want so badly to wrap her up and hold her until the sadness goes away, it feels like a physical need. I've never known anything like it.

"I can't leave here, right now," I explain. "Because I'm on call. But I can send a car to pick you up. Bring an overnight bag and I'll cuddle you, baby girl. Or, you know, if more sex helps..."

I let my voice fizzle out and hope she sees my humour for what it is and doesn't take it as an insensitive comment.

She is silent for far too long, but I don't want to push her.

"Are your parents going to be there?" she asks.

I'm confused for a moment, but then I realise that she doesn't know about the penthouse. She's only known me as still living with my folks.

"I'm not at Woodland Drive, baby girl. I'm at The Brick. I have the penthouse here."

"You do?" she asks, surprised.

I can hear by the water splashing that she just sat up straight in the bath. I think I've got her intrigued.

"I do," I answer with a smile.

"So why do you stay with your parents all the time?"

Good question.

"It's complicated."

It's the lamest of lame answers, but it's the best I can muster right now.

"Can we get seafood?" she finally asks, and the relief I feel at the knowledge she's decided to come over is second to none.

"As much as you like."

Kalina

I'm stunned when I enter Diego's penthouse.

I've never been in the apartments part of this building before. I've only seen the club and the bar until now. Seeing the rest of it gives a whole new dimension to this guy, who waited for me downstairs to arrive and wrapped me in his arms as soon as I got out of the car he sent.

I was going to tell him that I could take the train here, but he insisted and, to be honest, as emotionally unstable as I still feel, I didn't want to be out amongst people. So I let him.

I also let him carry my bag and let him keep me by his side with his hand resting lightly against the nape of my neck. It's an immensely possessive way of guiding someone, more intimate somehow than the classic position at the small of the back. More protective. I like it. It also works better because of the height difference between us. Diego's not quite as tall as Silas is, but he's still six foot something and I'm five foot. While Grace and Silas can easily walk with their hands in each other's back pockets, that is not on the cards for Diego and me.

Having arrived in the penthouse, I immediately step away from his hold on my neck, though, and look around in awe.

The place is gorgeous.

You exit straight from the lift into an open plan living and dining area from which two doors go off. It's decorated in deep greens and blues and vintage golds and yellows. There are exquisite pieces of antique furniture wherever I look and expensive Persian rugs to boot. It's nothing like what I expected of Diego, but it's so *me*, the real me, it's ridiculous.

"This is beautiful!" I exclaim. "Can I look around?"

He laughs at that, scrubbing a hand over the back of his head.

"Of course, mi casa es su casa."

So I shake off my boots and take off, exploring every room. One of the doors that leads off the main room leads to a master bedroom with a four-poster bed and an en suite with a freestanding bathtub. There is a double French door that leads out onto a balcony, full of well-maintained pot plants. The living room's other door leads into a short hallway, from which you get to another bedroom/study, a guest bathroom and a kitchen.

All the rooms are equally as tastefully decorated as the main room and *opulent,* but not garish. I realise quickly that the furniture, the paintings and prints on the walls are all *real.* A lot of the art dotted around seems to pertain to the slave trade somehow, which I feel seriously awkward about, but I know that slavery paraphernalia has been high in the favour of buyers lately. As my father would say, the more questionable the taste, the higher the price. At a quick calculation, I see furniture and art around to the tune of about a quarter of a million euro.

Diego doesn't follow me around while I explore and by the time I bounce back into the living room, he's taken his shoes off and is waiting for me on one of the sofas, a menu of the best fish place in town spread open on the coffee table before him. It's not a takeaway menu, it's the leather bound one that they give you in their restaurant. I recognize the distinctive logo at the top of the page immediately, because he's taken us there before.

I guess if you are George Diego Benson, you can order takeout from *anywhere.*

He pats the seat beside him without looking up from the menu. He keeps his eyes trained on the letters with such intensity, he looks almost like a child who hasn't learned to read yet but is pretending hard. I know he *is* pretending because I also know he knows that menu like the back of his hand. I'm not sure why he isn't looking up at me. There is this odd shyness around him. Almost like he doesn't want to meet my eyes, now that I've seen his place.

I take him in fully for a second. He looks beautiful against this background of pure class, sitting there in his trademark tan suit pants and waistcoat over a crisp white shirt.

I gingerly sit down next to him, acutely aware that I'm parking my butt on an original Biedermeyer couch, and stare at the table in front of me.

I can't help it.

I have to run a hand over the polished surface of the wood, admiring the patina.

"This is *actually* a Chippendale, isn't it?"

I don't even pretend that it's really a question. It has the desired result, though. He stops looking at the menu as his head shoots up and his eyes bore into my profile.

"You can tell?"

I turn to him, grinning, and shuffle around to make myself comfortable on his five-grand sofa by crossing my legs.

"You been to my room?" I counter.

"Yeah," he says, and then it dawns on him.

"What? All that shit you've collected while you've been here is *real*?"

"Well," I say, making a gesture that encompasses my surroundings at large. "Define real. Ikea is real. It's not as if your coffee cup falls through one of their tables because they're imagined. My stuff is a bit *more* real, but not as real as *this*. It's gorgeous, Diego, absolutely beautiful. I want a place like this one day."

He looks around, a little shell shocked and also as if he's seeing his flat through different eyes. I suppose he is. Through mine.

"I'd get rid of the slavery paraphernalia, though," I add. "That's not for me. It worries me a bit that that seems to be your thing. But for your information, it sells for good money at the moment."

He cocks his head at me, smirking.

"I might look into that. Not that keen myself. I inherited it," he informs me then narrows his eyes. "This is not just something you dabble in, is it?"

As soon as he asks, my heart starts beating faster.

I don't want to lie to him more than I absolutely have to.

I weigh up how much the truth here can hurt me. Or him. Probably not a lot.

So I nod, with a proud smile.

"My dad's an antiques dealer. I grew up with this stuff. Well, not quite as fine as most of yours, but close. Whenever we have anything like this, it doesn't hang around for very long."

He frowns at that.

"I thought you said your mother was a scientist and you moved a lot?"

"And?"

"How do you keep a shop like that?"

"Easy. You buy and sell wherever your wife happens to be. That's the beauty of antiques. You can find them anywhere and sell them everywhere. Ever heard of an invention called the internet?"

He smiles at my teasing, and then suddenly that hand is in my neck again, pulling me towards him, until his lips are almost on mine.

"So you like my place, huh?"

"I love it," I say.

I get a gentle kiss for that, before he draws back and searches my eyes.

"How are you feeling, baby girl?" he asks me seriously, and I love that he isn't just glossing over my low from earlier.

"Better, now I'm with you," I answer without thinking.

And I realise with a start that that's true.

He makes the blues go away.

DIEGO

She stays.

We stay.

We fuck and eat and talk, then do it all over again in reverse order.

And we rearrange the penthouse a little.

I take Kalina's advice and pack up Nan's more questionable pieces of art and artefacts to have them taken into storage. I don't know what to do with them. They're highly valuable but selling them, making money off them, feels like I'm just carrying on the wrongs of my family. Maybe they can go in a museum one day. But for now, they are in boxes and out of sight, and as soon as the shackles in cabinets and pictures of slave auctions and statues of wrestling Africans are gone, the place immediately feels different.

Then, on Tuesday, while I'm in the office downstairs for a few hours, flowers arrive. Kalina's ordered a different bouquet for every room, and when I come back upstairs it's like she has purged the place of resident evil somehow.

By the time Wednesday rolls around, it doesn't even occur to me to go back to Woodland Drive.

For the first time in my life, I truly acknowledge to myself that no matter what I do, my mother will always be a drunk, and that I can't protect her from my father's temper if she doesn't want to be protected. He might beat her to death one day, he might not. But I can't carry on living my life trying to shield someone from their own choices. It hurts to admit it, but it's made better by the fact that I now have somebody to admit things like this to.

Kalina is a master at listening and in only a couple of days I've told her more about myself than anyone ever, including Silas. I wish she'd reciprocate more. I'm dying to find out more about her, but somehow, she always brings the conversation back to me, or to general subjects. I won't press her, though. And I won't betray her trust by getting someone to dig around her background. I've known her for months now and my gut tells me, what you see is what you get. She might not share a lot of detail about herself, but she is honest where it *matters*.

Like the post-coital depression thing.

It's not an easy thing to bear when you make your girlfriend come on your face and then again on your cock until she screams with ecstasy, and half an hour later you find her crying in your arms. But it doesn't happen every time, and I feel honoured that she lets me see that part of her and *lets* me hold her. She says she never really stayed with any of her bed partners before past orgasm, so we're on par there.

That's what she calls them. Bed partners.

I wonder if that's what she calls me in her head, too. I'll ask her when she gets back.

I'm standing in the penthouse kitchen, stocked with actual groceries for the first time since Nan died and am preparing some *tapas* for us — because that's as far as my cooking goes — when I hear the lift arrive. Kalina has no idea how much trust it took for me to give her her own lift key. But I wanted her to feel like she can come and go as she pleases.

As soon as I hear the lift door open, my heart does that funny little tap dance it does every time she's about to come back to me.

She is still enrolled at the language school and studies hard every day for a few hours, though I have no idea why. Her English is fucking *perfect* by now. I suspect she is now just learning the whole of the Thesaurus by heart. She sure doesn't need help with the grammar any longer. She has that down pat. I really don't know why she decided to prolong her stay, but I'm grateful she did.

I don't go to meet her in the living room. Much as I want to run to her, grab her and kiss the shit out of her, I don't want to crowd her with too much domesticity. There is a free-spiritedness about her that I feel would make her run to the hills if we started playing house in the traditional 'honey, I'm home' way.

I'm fucking amazed she's still here with me as it is.

So I stay put and wait for her to find me. She takes her sweet time, going to the toilet first and washing her hands.

I'm in the middle of cutting manchega into little squares when I hear her soft footfall behind me. Before I can put the knife down to turn around and finally kiss her, she has slung her arms around me from behind and has plastered herself against my back.

"Hmm," she murmurs. "Man."

That sound alone gets my dick to stir. But it helps, too, that she makes her intentions immediately clear by unbuckling my belt. Her dainty hands pop the button on my trousers, pull the zip down and without further ado, she shoves my briefs and trousers down to let my instant hard-on spring free. She wraps one hand around it and gently gives it a tug, making me double over and brace myself on the counter with a groan.

With her other hand, she blindly pushes the chopping board with the cheese to the side, nearly shoving the already prepared, assorted dishes of olives, artichoke hearts and chorizo over the edge. I help her in her obvious endeavour to clear the space in front of me, visions of fucking her as she sits on the counter crowding my lust-filled brain.

But that's not what she has in mind.

She pulls me around *by my dick*, and when I face her, she grins up at me.

"Hop up."

I frown, not quite understanding.

"On the counter, gorgeous man. Get your butt up there. I'm hungry."

I'm too stunned not to do as she asks.

It's an odd feeling, once I'm up there. I've had a fair few women, while they were sitting on bars and counters and tabletops, but I've never been parked somewhere like that.

I don't get much time to think about it, though, as she shoves my shirttails aside and lowers her mouth to my cock.

She licks over the head and suckles for a moment before she lets off and speaks with her mouth still full around it.

"I've wanted this all day."

And then she goes to work, licking and sucking and squeezing me in that voodoo shit way she has, until I find myself with my fingers digging into her scalp and shooting reams of come down her throat. She takes every drop and swallows then licks me clean for good measure, while I'm still hunched over her, feeling the spasms of sheer after-bliss ripple through me.

When I stop shaking, she kind of snakes up under the shelter I form for her and pulls me in for a kiss. Our tongues tangle for a bit, but then she withdraws and reaches out blindly for a couple of pieces of cheese. She pushes one between my lips and pops the other into her own mouth, grinning.

"Hmm, manchega and sperm. Good combination. What do you think?"

I smile down at her as I gently push her back to give me enough space for hopping off the counter.

"I think you are an evil fairy queen who has bewitched me and is emasculating me a little more every day," I say as I pull my briefs and trousers up, storing my junk away. "And I like it."

"Emasculating?" she asks.

I cup her chin in one hand and look at her seriously.

"Taking my manliness away," I explain.

"You're wrong," she says, reaching out for an olive and letting it hover in front of her mouth. "There is nothing manlier than a man who can take as good as he gives."

She pops the olive in between her teeth and bites down on it with a smile that tells me she knows full well there is no arguing with that.

And it's in that exact moment that I realise I'm thoroughly fucked.

There will never be another one like her.

She is *it*.

Z

The ròka has been different since his return.

I can't explain it, but it keeps me awake at night. Not that it takes much to keep me awake.

He's less confident, maybe. But also less human somehow. If that was even possible.

And he actually lives above now. He used to come here three, four times a week to check on us, and get his kicks, but now he's around all the time.

I can feel his presence above, like a heavy pressure in the air. But even if I couldn't, he comes down twice a day now. Every day. Just stands and looks at us.

At Guppi.

I don't want him to look at Guppi.

The ròka hasn't whipped or fucked me since he turned up again and that makes me nervous.

I raise my hand in the semi darkness, we always have to keep some light on, in case viewers check in, and gently stroke Guppi's hair.

He's lying with his back to me. We were spooning earlier, but then, when he fell asleep, he subconsciously shuffled away. Guppi isn't gay, he was deeply in love with a girl in his class back home before fate dealt him this shitty, shitty card, and when he's not awake, his body *knows*. It hurts every time he puts distance between us, though I don't blame him.

We are who we are. It's not like we get a conscious choice.

I've always known which way I fall, it's why the ròka picked me.

And stupidly, I've fallen for Guppi.

I tried so hard not to, but at one point, when you are pretending to be a couple twenty-four seven, a *loving* couple, fact and fiction blur.

My body loves him.

My dick fucking adores him.

And my soul wants to protect him.

My heart soars when he shuffles back against me, takes my hand out of his hair and slings it around his waist.

My brain knows he's only doing it because I've woken him and he's acute enough to slip straight back into the act, but my heart wants to believe he's seeking my love.

Kalina

I know full well that I'm playing a dangerous game.

Well, not dangerous, but stupid.

Stupid for my heart, stupid for my soul.

But I can't help it. The man is addictive.

And the food is good. Maybe a little too good.

It's Thursday morning and he's brought me waffles in bed. Waffles! Not American style with bacon and syrup, which is also good, but Austrian style with hot cherries and whipped cream. I have no idea where he got them. He asked me what I fancied for breakfast and I told him that's what I wanted, as a joke, and he found somewhere that delivers the very thing. Or maybe he knew where to source them already. He seems to have internalised the menu of just about every eatery in Brighton. And he sure knows how to use that knowledge.

I look down at my dwindling six pack when I step out of the shower and straight into the towel he is holding out for me then look at him, still as ripped as always, and groan. I've always been able to eat a lot for my size without piling on pounds, but I also tend to train a lot, which keeps my metabolism up to speed. I haven't been for a run in a week now and it already shows.

I look mock disapprovingly at his six pack and scrunch up my nose as he towels me dry. His dick, which he's only just used to my full satisfaction, is already semi-hard again, telling me he finds me as addictive as I find him. The knowledge gives me a thrill.

"What's with the face, baby girl?" he asks me, while he takes much longer than strictly necessary to rub the terry cotton over my still throbbing clit.

I already know he'll get me off again before we leave the bathroom, either finger fucking me gently or eating me out from behind as I stand over the sink. We've figured out that if he manages to wring a third, gentle orgasm out of me within half an hour of the first and the second, I hardly crash at all. Romantic that he is, he's compared it to having a joint when you're coming down from a coke high. Apparently, he used to do a lot of coke but now not so much. When I asked him why, he told me coke was good for building an empire but not so much for maintaining it.

"Kalina?" he asks me again. "What up?"

I poke his rock-hard abs with a finger.

"How do you do that? How do you stay this trim when you eat so much? You haven't been sparring with Silas for over a week, you haven't been back to your mansion to use the pool, but you look the same. Look at me!"

I pinch the skin on my belly to demonstrate.

He frowns.

"What am I looking at?"

"Fat."

He laughs at that. Outright, until tears pool in the corners of his eyes. When he quietens again, he sprawls a hand across my belly.

"You are the trimmest girl I know, Kalina. A week's not gonna make any difference," he says, caressing my skin. "What do you do to look like this?"

"While I've been here, I've been running every day. At home, I weight train a little."

I don't tell him about the hand to hand combat. This lot are obsessed with MMA. If I tell him I do combat training, he'll tell Silas and then Silas will drag me to the gym and then things are going to get even more muddled than they are already.

Diego examines me closely, while he lets his hand wander lower and slip between my folds. He caresses me lightly, gently milking the juices from me, increasing the pressure only slightly with each new coat of moisture that my pussy gives him to work with. Until he has enough to slide his fingers over my clit in leisurely circles, all the while carrying on the conversation.

"You look like a gymnast," he says.

I smile.

"I may have been in my school's gymnastics squad," I admit.

"Hah. You ever considered MMA?"

I shake my head and feel shit for outright lying to him.

He doesn't pursue it, though. He's too busy making my body feel good.

And he makes it feel very good. I come on his hand within minutes, a sweet brush of an orgasm, amplified by his lips coming down to meet mine in a soft, loving kiss.

He withdraws his hands from between my thighs then bends down to pick me up and hold me in a tight hug for a few minutes, heartbeat to heartbeat.

When he sets me back down, there is a silent exchange between us. His eyes ask if I'll be okay and mine let him know that I'm pretty sure I will be.

Then he looks down at his stomach, going straight back to our previous conversation.

"You know what? You're right. I'm not going to stay like this either if I don't do something again soon. And I really don't fancy going home for a swim. My father is out for my blood at the moment."

"Uh? Why?"

"He's found out I'm selling the league. And he's pissed off I didn't come home last night, because he wanted to tear into me about it. Anyway, enough of that. You wanna go for a run later?"

"Absolutely," I answer with a happy clap. "I've got to go and get my running shoes from Sheena's, though."

He cradles my cheek in his palm and smiles hesitantly.

"About that."

"Yeah?"

"How would you feel about us bringing *all* your stuff here?" he asks but holds up his other hand before I can answer to signal that he isn't finished. "Think about it before you say no. Because it's going to get a bit crowded at Sheena's again."

I want to ask why, but then the penny drops.

"Rowan and Raven are really coming back?"

He nods.

"They are landing Monday morning."

In typical Diego style, he leaves the bathroom to give me space to think about it. He has an acute sense for not crowding me. It's something I've already come to appreciate about him.

The idea of moving in with him for the rest of my stay is insanity, but at the same time worth considering. Before Rowan and Raven went to the States, there was a week when all of us, other than Diego, were packed into Sheena's house, and it was a nightmare. Six people. One bathroom. Not even funny. And I got far less work done than I have in the last few days here.

Also, Shoreham is out in the sticks, here I am physically much nearer to where Piotr and Zoltan disappeared, which makes me feel like I'm closer to the centre of the case itself.

I've set my laptop up in his spare bedroom and I've been working when Diego is in the office or down in the club. In actual fact, the peace and quiet up here has really helped me concentrate. I love Grace and

Silas but being on permanent vacation means they're very *present* all the time.

Konstantin suggested that if I'm still convinced that there is a connection between Piotr's and Zoltan's disappearance, I should go through all the missing persons cases from that year again, for the whole of the UK, and see if something strikes a chord. I attempted it before, but it's a *lot* of cases. Well over one hundred thousand children and teenagers go missing in the UK every year and one to two percent of them stay lost. Most of them are in Piotr's and Zoltan's age range. That's a lot of pictures and stories to go through, and after a while it becomes like scrolling through a list of varieties of the same product with different specifications — you just stop taking it in. So I could really do with the focus the penthouse affords me for a while longer.

And I really, *really* like this man.

I slip into the silk bathrobe he bought me on a whim two days ago, the reimbursement for which we are still haggling about, and follow him out.

I find him in the bedroom, already mostly dressed for work.

"Okay," I say, and watch how he tries to suppress a smile while he buttons up his waistcoat.

"Great," he answers levelly. "We'll go and grab the rest of your things this afternoon."

DIEGO

I only get to go running with her once before the weekend demands my return to my normal life-rhythm.

We've compromised for the last few days, somewhere between her early-riser-early-sleeper lifestyle and my never-go-to-bed-before-seven-in-the-morning-and-sleep-till-at-least-noon routine.

It's worked out well. At least for me.

Kalina's classes at school seem to vary widely in start time, and I suspect she's also been skipping a few, but that's none of my business. And she clearly studies really hard to make up for it. She's set herself up a proper little work corner in the spare bedroom.

It's nice to be with somebody as driven and as capable of self-occupation. There is no moaning when I need to go downstairs for work, no demands on my time when I'm busy. I've never had a proper girlfriend before, but even the casual floozies I've always had hanging off my arms were normally more needy than Kalina is.

For me, changing my working hours has meant I'm available to spend more time with Julian in the office, rather than in the club, which doesn't really need me now that the fights are moving out.

We've had Arlo up in the hills all week, but there's been nothing to report. He tails Callum whenever he leaves, but Callum never seems to go anywhere, other than to the petrol station. Cormac apparently never leaves. Julian went up there to give Arlo a few hours off at some point and to train a camera at their gate from Arlo's hideout. So we'd know if Cormac went out, while Arlo is on Callum. But nothing.

If Julian thinks the effort I'm putting into this, just to avenge an alley cat, is insane, he hasn't said so. Thing is, for me it would be enough even if it had been 'just' Nuts, but I'm pretty sure that Callum tortured other animals, too, long before he and Cormac apparently got into the dog fighting business. I *know* so.

Callum was that kid who caught flies and ripped half their legs and wings off to laugh at them as they were going around in circles, who drove a spade through earthworms to see the two halves wriggle, and who put his own hamster in the microwave to watch it explode.

One thing we know for almost sure, though, is that they aren't doing dogfights up there at present. Julian flew a drone over the grounds, while Callum was out and Cormac was inside the house, and while that confirmed that there are a couple of dogs back up there, Cormac appears to have swapped the pitties for a couple of Dobermans. Guard dogs. I wonder what they're guarding. And I wonder where the pit bulls went that Rowan spoke about.

I'm a patient man, and I'm happy to play the long game, but right now I feel the need to bury Callum forever burning like a physical need.

I tried for years, long before Callum ran over that poor boy, to find out where he was getting his money from, hoping I could get him into shit with the rozzers. I knew he wasn't getting it from his old man. Cecil O'Brien doesn't bankroll any of his kids, unless they earn every penny. I was surprised when he set Cormac up with the small holding, makes me wonder what Cormac did to deserve that. But Callum is fucking useless. Though apparently brilliant at covering his tracks.

No matter how hard I had Julian look, no matter how many favours I pulled, I couldn't turn up anything on him. Nothing. Not a bleeding morsel of incriminating info.

So I dreamed up other solutions, but I didn't have quite the resources then that I have now. Or the time. Not by a wide margin. You can't be waging a vendetta while you're still building a business. Vendettas are for pudding.

Plus those were also the years that Silas wasn't talking to me, outside of the bare necessities, and Rowan was MIA. Wars without an army you trust are doomed to fail.

I can't wait for Rowan to get back to town.

Rowan's different from the rest of us. Not just because he's a fucking giant who would kill for the people he loves without thinking about it twice, but because he left Brighton for a few years, and in that time, he saw the kind of shit on the underground of the underground circuit that I might know about, but never had access to. Nor do I want to.

If even half the stuff Rowan told me when he was holed up at Woodland Drive with me, preparing for his big fight with Silas, is true, then he even played gladiator for *the people* at some point. No-rule fights, weapons and all, that leave maimed and dead bodies in their wake, held in disused tunnels and catacombs that only *the people* have access to.

The people compared to whom I'm just a bottom feeder. A single fucking piranha, playing at being a shark.

The people, who don't go by definitions like Mafia, Bratva, Yakuza or whatever other idiotic name gets banded about. Because it's beneath them. Because they all bear an uncanny resemblance to the same faces that have run this country for the last five hundred years.

The people to whom money is simply not of interest, because it's always just been there, and whose perpetual boredom with life drives hobbies and desires that nobody, who isn't as degenerated as them, wants to even think about.

There was a point when I thought maybe they'd actually got to Rowan. I wasn't sure any longer, if the Rowan who loved Silas as much as I do was still in there, and I got seriously worried that he was *actually* going to kill his brother. But he came through. He played us all and had us fooled, which makes him a prime candidate for the job I need him to do.

Rowan's dealt with *the people* and survived, in body *and* soul, so I'm pretty sure he's got the balls to help me out here. He practically said as much.

If I can't legit find out how Callum's been financing his expensive car and clothes and the substantial coke habit he had before he went into prison, Rowan will help me create a little scenario instead.

I'm thinking of planting a substantial amount of class A's. Meths seem a good choice. It's cheap to buy and really pisses the judges off at the moment. Coke? Smack? *Ah, chucks, here is a seven-year sentence, see you in three and a half.* Meths? *Into the can you go, throw away the key we will.*

I always had Callum down as pushing product anyway, mostly because he liked to sample it a lot, but none of my contacts has ever bought from or sold to him. And there isn't anyone around here in the narcotics business worth knowing who I haven't asked.

I would have had Rowan on a plane the day after our video chat, but it turned out he and Raven had to sort out a more permanent visa solution for Raven first.

They haven't said anything, but considering Las Vegas is only four or five hours drive from Phoenix, I'm pretty sure I know what that solution was.

Roll on Monday and bring me some newlyweds.

Kalina

"Weird choice," Sheena says to me as she sits down on the spindly chair inside the cafe I have chosen for our lunch date, and looks around the shabby place. "Why *here*?"

I look at it through her eyes and understand why she would ask. It's run down and smells slightly of chlorine. The marble tops of the tables are all cracked, the cracks showing up in that deep black you only get from a patina of dirt accumulated over a long time. No wonder we are the only customers, despite it being lunchtime. There are several dozen better options, nearer to The Palais and The Brick that I could have chosen from, when I asked her if we could meet up. But this is the place outside of which Daniel Mantas was knocked down, and while I've got nowhere further with my own work, I've been distracting myself by sticking my nose into Diego's business. Or trying to, at least.

Ever since Rowan and Raven came back, the guys have been holed up in the Santos-Benson Security office plotting the downfall of Callum O'Brien. I'm not allowed into the meetings, but I hear enough on the fringes — when we're all out for drinks, when Rowan and Silas come up to the penthouse to say hi to me, or when Diego is on the phone to any one of them — to be getting more and more intrigued. And to worry. For the guys, but also that my cover may get blown by association and jeopardise my case.

So I'm doing the 'best defence is offence' thing and have asked Sheena to meet me today, in the hope I can pick her brain. Sheena is acute, though, so I have to tread carefully.

"It's close to the language school," I answer her question, because I'm not going to give away my game just yet.

I've played Texas Hold'em with Sheena too often to show my bluff too early. Although I'm not sure I haven't already, when her gaze snaps back to mine from the pitiful display of paninis and bagels behind the counter.

"Cut the crap, Kalina," she says.

The way she says it lets my heart slip into my gut. I've seen her do this to Silas. It's the tone she has when you're about to find out that she knows far, far more about your business than you could ever have dreamed of. But I'm not stupid enough to hand feed her incriminating information by reacting with anything other than the obvious.

"What do you mean?"

She cocks her head and smiles. The patented Sheena O'Brien 'there ain't nothing happening in this town I don't know about, ducky' smile.

I'm in deep shit.

"You haven't been back to your language school in *two months*, Kalina," she informs me. "I *know*, because I actually stopped by there to see if you wanted a lift home a few weeks ago, and they told me when your last day was. Kept my trap shut because I wanted to see where this is going. Had a feeling you were maybe sticking around for *other* reasons."

I'm instantly relieved, because I realise she thinks I stayed because of my crush on Diego.

Heat creeps into my face but not because I'm embarrassed.

I feel genuinely guilty about having lied to this woman, who has been my landlady for nearly seven months — well, *was* until a few days ago — and who's been like a totally non-intrusive surrogate mum all that time. It doesn't matter that she thinks I was an eighteen-year-old, somewhat shy language student who needed nurturing when I came. I know for certain she would have treated me the same if I'd come to her house as Kristina Kaminski, twenty-four-year-old private investigator, looking into the disappearance of two teenage boys a couple of years ago.

But for as long as I thought the language school was at the heart of the case, it was important not to blow my cover.

Is it important to still maintain it now, I wonder?

Yes, there is serious prison time if I get caught having entered the country on false papers. But how likely is it that this band of criminals I've got myself involved with will grass me up? Sheena might not be directly involved in anything illegal, as far as I know, but I know she knows about every friggin' thing her boys get into. And that includes Diego.

"You're awfully quiet, girl," she says to me with a grin, before she snaps her fingers at the waitress who seems to be too busy wiping the counter, to come over and take our order. "Can we get some service here, young lady?" she demands in her 'head of housekeeping' tone.

It's terrifying.

The woman behind the counter looks up.

"You order at the counter," she responds, somewhat perplexed.

Sheena's eyebrows shoot up.

"*You* might," she retorts. "We sure as hell don't. Bring yourself over here and take our order, *please.*"

It's magic to see how the waitress just hops to it without a second thought. We ask for coffees and paninis and as soon as she has left us, Sheena's laser-sharp eyes bore into me again.

"So, I'm gonna ask you again, Kalina, why *here*?"

I nod toward the window.

"Out there is where Callum O'Brien ran over that boy."

Her smile tells me she already knew exactly where we are and why we are here.

"Uh-huh," she says. "First honest answer you've given me in seven months. So what d'ya wanna know?"

"Just trying to figure out why Diego is so intent on going after this guy, but the guys won't tell me. Not even Raven or Grace know what's going on," I answer. "But they're more like..."

I stop talking to put my fingers in my ears, shut my eyes and make loud singing noises. Which happens to be the exact moment the waitress brings over our coffees.

Sheena laughs, her eyes having mellowed out, from laser-cutting to sparkling-amused. Which I've learned in our poker games means she's going in for the kill.

And then my brain catches up.

"Wait. What? What do you mean the first honest answer?" I ask.

"That, right there, ducky. And using phrases like 'intent on'. There is no way on earth you only learned to speak our language in the last seven months. And then suddenly cracked it in the last week and a half. Not a chance. I'd buy a huge improvement after all this time. But you? You suddenly speak *British* English through and through. Mannerisms and all. Like someone who grew up with it. Not as your native tongue, I do buy your accent, but around it. You spent plenty of time around English people, long before you got here. You may fool the rest of them, hell, George is so head over heels in love with you he wouldn't see the bullet coming if you cocked a gun right in his face. But I've seen your makeup case. I've seen the twenty different coloured pairs of contact lenses, the hairpieces, the way you can use makeup to change someone's fucking bone structure. I don't know who the fuck you are, but I *do* know you're not who you wanted us to believe you are."

She stops talking and lets what she said hang between us, to allow for the waitress to bring over our paninis. Sheena pries apart her mozzarella and pesto one to look critically inside, while I just stare at her, stunned.

"You didn't spit in it, did you?" she asks the retreating back of the waitress.

The young woman spins around with horror on her face.

"Of course not!"

"Good. Because I know people," Sheena says, grinning, and then bites into her panini.

She looks at me expectantly, but not with hostility. Chews. Swallows. Puts the panini back on the plate and reaches across to pat my hand.

"I don't know what to say," I tell her, honestly.

"Well, I'd prefer the full story. But I have a feeling you can't, or you are not ready, to tell it. That's okay. But I need some answers here. Depending on what they are, I will answer your questions about Callum best I can. Deal?"

I nod, helplessly.

I've never been in this situation before. I've always successfully remained a ghost. I come, I find the bones, I let the parents know I found them and where, so they know it was me who tipped off the police. Then I anonymously let the authorities know as I'm already leaving whatever country I'm in. It works. There was one time that the police clearly thought it was a hoax and needed a bit more nudging, and another when the parents suddenly refused to pay up, claiming the police had found the bones without my help. Konstantin dealt with both of those instances. I love my job for itself, but payday is important. Yet throughout it all there has never been a time when I got embroiled with the local crime element before. In hindsight, a bit of a miracle, really.

"Are you police?"

I shake my head, and she relaxes. It's kind of lovely that she just takes my word for it. I could be lying through my teeth. But I guess she trusts the truth in our relationship, despite not knowing who I really am.

"With *any* of the authorities?"

I shake my head again.

"Free agent?"

I nod.

"Which one of my boys are you after? I'm guessing George, but then I see you look at him with the same gooey eyes he makes at you, and I'm not so sure any longer..."

She lets her voice trail off and searches my eyes, while she takes another bite of her panini. There is an open threat in them. The implication is, it doesn't matter which one. If I'm here to harm any of them, I'm dead.

I've known all along that Sheena is well connected. Silas and Diego often refer to her as 'old Brighton'. She went to school with Diego's dad and with Cecil O'Brien, the father of all the O'Briens, other than Silas. She was even married to Cecil for a while, which is why her and Silas share the surname with Cecil and his brood. But because she had clearly fallen out of favour with all of them and is living in a shitty house in Shoreham, working herself to the ground in a hotel and renting out rooms at home to students, I never considered her as one of the Brighton players.

But the way she looks at me now leaves no room for speculation about the fact that she *could* be, if she wanted to be. That if I prove to be a danger to any of her boys, someone will soon have to come hunting for *my* bones.

I laugh when I'm nervous, so I laugh.

"None of them," I tell her, and she stops chewing for a moment. "I swear, Sheena. It was complete coincidence that the language school placed me with you. I'm not here for any of them. I didn't even know they existed before I came here. I'm on a completely different mission, I *promise*."

She starts eating again and remains silent until she's finished her lunch.

I still haven't touched mine.

And I still haven't asked my question.

I can't gauge if she believes me or not. I need her to believe me, and if I now ask her for help with prying into Diego's business that'll make me look suspicious all over again.

She jerks her chin at my plate.

"Eat, Kalina, if that's your name. It's not going to get any better by letting it congeal."

I do as I'm told, and she cocks her head, watching me chew through narrowed eyes.

"You know," she says after a while. "I don't believe in coincidence. Or fate. At least not the rigid kind. I don't believe in God either, though I was brought up Catholic. But I do believe in right and wrong. They might not always be the same right and wrong that the law considers as such, but they exist. George is a good man. Silas is a good man. Rowan tries to be a good man, which makes him a better man than most. I also believe that sometimes things happen for a reason. For example, I reckon that the reason I met James, Rowan's stepdad, had nothing to do with James, or me, or those two little cuties James brought with him and wanted me to play mummy for. I believe the sole purpose of that particular failed relationship of mine was to bring Rowan into our lives and keep *him*."

I have no idea where she is going with this and I don't find out, because she stops there. She takes a deep breath, and suddenly her eyes go very soft as she looks at me. It's the way she looks at Silas and Rowan and Diego. And Grace sometimes. And I realise with a start that I've truly become one of her ducklings. It doesn't last long, because then she straightens up and takes a sip of her coffee before she decides to keep her end of the bargain.

"So, Callum. I don't really know why George hates his guts quite so much. To be honest, I never question why anyone hates anything to do with Cecil. To me, that's like the natural order of things, or something. But I do know that it's got nothing to do with the poor kid Callum ran over. I strongly suspect it's to do with a dead cat that's buried in my garden."

I let my hand holding the panini in front of my mouth sink back down without taking another bite as I stare at her in disbelief.

"A cat?"

She nods.

"Callum is a little sadist, and a cat killer. And Diego loves cats. All animals, really. And according to Silas, the one buried in my garden was a favourite."

I lean back in my chair and look at her aghast.

"He's waging a war for a *cat*?" I ask again and feel my heart double in size. "I love him so much!"

Sheena laughs while she scrapes her chair back.

"Yeah, we know. I've got to go back to work. I've got this."

I watch her as she goes to the till to swipe her debit card and plonks a hefty tip in the tip jar. Then she comes back and puts a hand on my shoulder.

"I never finished what I was trying to say earlier. I don't believe in coincidence. I'm pretty sure you ended up in my house because you were *meant* to. You're meant to be exactly where you are and with whom." She smiles gently. "The question is, to what end? Is it just for the two of you, or does it serve a higher purpose? Whichever it is, though, don't break his heart, Kalina. George hasn't had a lot of love in his life and it's a bit of a miracle he turned out as well as he did. If you make him feel loved, he'll be devoted to you *for life*. And it will crush him if he finds out you played him. So whatever the reason you're keeping your secrets, make damn sure they are worth it."

Then she leaves without looking back.

Diego

"Your father is on the line again."

Julian, Silas, Rowan and I all look to Lila as she pops her head around the door of my office and rolls her eyes.

"Fuck's sake," I answer, exasperated. "Tell him I'll ring him when I get around to it."

"Yeah," she says. "You know, funny that. 'Cause that's what I said to him already. Every time he's called, in fact. Which has been every goddamn hour of the day so far. Can't you just take his call, please? I'm not getting anything done here. And I've got a four-day conference to re-rota before tomorrow morning, because you and Julian have some *private* engagement all of a sudden that requires half of our best workforce to do *something* else."

I sigh.

Lila is pissed off because she doesn't know what's going on. She doesn't like it when Julian goes all secretive on her, and I get it. She's had years of being a soldier's wife, worrying about him from afar, and civilian life was supposed to change all that. By and large it has. She knows most of what we do, on and off the books, but this is different.

"Just block his number for the time being," I tell her with a reassuring smile. "He'll get the hint."

She narrows her eyes at me.

"Is that why he can't get through to you on your mobile?"

I grin at her.

"Maybe."

She rolls her eyes again then retreats back to reception.

As soon as she is gone, they all stop looking over their shoulders at the door and Silas' eyes meet mine, with a frown above them.

"What does she mean, 'half of your best workforce'? Who else is involved in this?"

"Nobody. Just Arlo," I answer.

We have a communal laugh at that then return to the meeting.

"Who's actually been pretty great," I admit. "If we ever have another situation where we need a guy camping out in camo, he's the man for the job."

"I'm glad you found his talent," Silas says. "'Cause fighting sure as shit wasn't it. He was a godawful fighter."

Arlo wasn't that terrible, otherwise I wouldn't have let him into the league. But I know that Silas still feels crap about costing the guy half his hearing, so he's kind of obliged to say shit like that.

"So, what's camo-guy found out then?" Rowan asks, on a yawn.

It's Wednesday, early afternoon, he and Raven have been back three days, and Rowan's still struggling with the jetlag, while Raven by all accounts was fresh as a daisy this morning and has abducted Grace to go on a train ride to Chichester. They invited Kalina along, too, but she said she had to go to school today. I worry a little about that. I love having her to myself, but Kalina and Grace were becoming really good friends before Raven turned up, and now that Kalina's moved in with me, I fear that she will get pushed out of the friendship. I feel a twinge of jealousy on her behalf at the thought.

I realise I've tuned out from the discussion when I hear Rowan recap what Julian just said.

"So, basically, he's been up there a week and he's got fuck all to report. And that makes him great at the job how exactly?"

Julian bristles at that. The three of them are sitting in a semicircle in front of my desk and because I didn't tell them where to sit, when they came in, Rowan put himself in the middle, opposite me. That pissed Julian off from the get-go. Thing is, *I* know Rowan didn't do it on purpose. For Julian, though, it's an act of insolence by the new recruit. He knows and trusts Silas, because Silas has been working for me for years. He barely knows Rowan, other than as the mystery fighter that took Silas out a few months ago and is thus the reason Silas hasn't been back to work. In the last hour, Julian's had to get his head around not only Rowan's particular brand of 'don't give a shit' but also around the dynamics between Silas, Rowan and me. I'm sure books have been written on dynamics like ours, so I don't blame Julian for feeling uncomfortable and for getting shirty with Rowan right now.

"That's exactly what makes him great, numbskull," Julian tells him off. "You ever spent a whole week in a sheep barn? Pissing and shitting in a hole in the ground, not showering, eating from cans, barely sleeping, focused on the same vista with fuck all happening the entire time? Yet not once calling in to say you've had enough?"

Rowan turns to him and smiles at his anger.

"Can't say I have. Not that particular scenario, no. There are plenty of things I could tell you about that I *have* done, though. Less Mad Max, more Hunger Games. But I'm not gonna. 'Cause I ain't into pissing contests. We can have a wank off later, if you like. See who shoots their load further. But I don't think that's your scene. I get the memo, though, soldier. You like your little lookout boy. That's awesome. We're cool. Let's move on."

Silas sighs heavily and pinches the bridge of his nose between his fingers.

"Okay," he says in that subdued voice of his that somehow demands attention more than the angriest shout. "So Arlo hasn't seen anything out of the ordinary at all. If you want to call two guys in a farmhouse getting not a single visitor other than the food truck all week ordinary. What else have we got?"

Julian perks up at that.

"Site fencing," he says with a grin and waits until all eyes are on him. "When I went up there to give Arlo a break and fly my drone, it occurred to me that the reason he couldn't see shit even from a higher vantage point was because they're using construction site panels as fencing around the whole lot."

"I think you'll find I mentioned that already," Rowan growls, which is true.

He told us about it earlier, when he described his visit to Cormac's farmhouse to us.

"Fuck ugly," Julian carries on, ignoring him. "And, more to the point, not legal. You need planning permission for anything over six foot six. And those panels are more like eight, maybe higher. It's the kind of stuff you'd normally have around an industrial development. So I looked into it. Turns out, the panels were erected as a temporary site enclosure as part of a rebuild on the farmhouse. Over two years ago."

"Rebuild of what?" Rowan mutters. "It's still a shitheap."

"Thing is, those building works lasted only about a month, according to the neighbours," Julian continues. "Then they halted. Before any building inspector ever came to check on anything. But the panels have stayed up all that time. The neighbours have complained to the council a fuck load of times about it, but nothing ever gets done. The thing is, they're like a mile down the road, so I guess the council doesn't think it's a priority."

"What?" Rowan asks, sarcasm dripping from his lips. "You're saying we go after them through planning? Well, that's really gonna fuck 'em up."

"No, numbskull," Julian starts, but doesn't get any further when Silas suddenly gets up.

He pushes one hand down on Rowan's shoulder, keeping him in his chair, as he looks across the top of Rowan's head at Julian.

"Julian? You gotta stop insulting my brother. I respect you, mate. You've always been a good manager. But right now, we're not here as your little boyband, or as D's bitches. We're here as friends and brothers," he explains patiently, but when Julian still frowns at him in confusion, Silas changes tack. "Look across the table. What do you see?"

"Erm. My boss and business partner?"

"No, numbskull. What do you *see*? Visually. I give you a hint, what's he wearing today? What's fucking different?"

"A t-shirt," Julian says then ducks a little under the table to double check the rest of my attire. "Jeans. Boots."

"Exactly," Silas says. "You're not looking at the three-piece-suit twat. You're looking at George Diego Benson, The Roadrunner, my oldest fucking friend and by default Rowan's brother's oldest fucking friend. So make no mistake. You keep insulting Rowan and it's gonna get ugly. And it ain't just gonna be two of us who're gonna go for ya. We clear?"

The beauty about Silas making threats is that he does it so evenly, Isla remains completely oblivious. The dog doesn't even look up from her place by the window, where she has been sprawled out to let the sun cutting in warm her fur.

Julian looks to me as he digests this information, comprehension finally dawning. But Silas being Silas absolves me from having to back him up with anything more than a curt, affirmative nod, by turning his attention on Rowan next.

"Swapsies," he demands.

He takes his hand off Rowan's shoulder, and without a second glance at Julian, Rowan gets up and swaps seats with Silas. As soon as Silas sits between them, the atmosphere in the room changes. Silas cements the new serenity by turning his head to Julian and carrying on as if nothing had happened.

"Now, you were saying?"

I can tell that Julian is dumbfounded for a moment, but he glosses over it quickly.

"The point wasn't the fencing, though one might ask oneself why it is still up and who they are paying to keep it there. The point was that I pulled the planning application for the building works. Nothing interesting there. Standard rebuild stuff, as far as I can tell. But guess what I else I found on the site plans?"

He gets up.

"I'll show you. I'll go get it," he says and leaves my office.

Silas, Rowan and I sit in silence until Julian returns a couple of minutes later, flapping an A3 sheet of paper about. He lays it out on the table and remains standing over it. It's the printout of a site plan. He points at a separate rectangle on the plan, a structure away from the main building.

"Look, that's an old air raid shelter. And a pretty big one by the looks of things."

"What? Out there? Why would there be an air raid shelter out there? Makes no sense," I say, but the lettering on the plan verifies his words.

"Because, at one point during the war, that farmhouse was an evacuation home."

"Cool," Rowan says.

"Very," I agree as my mind starts bounding like a happy puppy.

I look at Julian and he looks right back at me. I know we're thinking the same thing. And a childish part in me wants to jump up and shout 'knew it!' but, of course, I don't.

"You don't think we need to plant any product, do you?" I ask him with a smile.

He shakes his head and sits back down, satisfied.

"Nah, I think you'll find plenty when you get there," he answers with a wide grin, and turns to Rowan. "You didn't see anything that told you they were cooking up there?"

Rowan ignores the taunting undertone and draws his eyebrows together, thinking. I see his cogs ticking before he shakes his head.

"No, I was kind of focused on Cormac and trying to get across to him that I really didn't want to see two dogs ripping each other to shreds, you know. Also, there was so much junk up there, you know what the backs of farms look like, well this one looks like it fucking everywhere, front and back and all around, I could easily have missed it, especially if it's underground. And it's not like he gave me the grand tour, you know. Oh, and here's my bedroom, and these are the kennels and by the way, over there is where we cook up the meths. But it makes perfect sense. I can see it as clearly as you can," he concedes and gets up. "Well, it's been fun but sounds like I'm not really needed here. Thanks for the flight tickets, though. Flying business is much more fun than economy. You even have somewhere to store your legs."

He tips his head at me as if he's actually about to leave.

"Sit down."

"Why? If you're sure, just tip off the cops, sit back and watch the show."

I shake my head at him.

"No, I don't just want to be sure, I want to be *certain*," I answer. "And if they've really been playing Breaking Bad up there, I want to know who their cookie is. Can you imagine Cormac or Callum making meths?"

I watch him sit down again.

"Exactly," I add. "Now, let's..."

I don't get further than that before a movement on the security feeds that stream on the screens above my office door catches my eye.

"Motherfucker," I curse as I watch my father enter the building.

Right behind my woman.

Kalina

"Good afternoon, Kalina, Mr Benson."

I feel the presence breathing down my neck a split second before Ben, the doorman, names him for me. I have no idea where he suddenly came from, but he's so close I can't exactly turn around without bumping my face into his chest. So we are already through the door and in the building by the time I manage to clear enough space between us to be able to turn around and stick my hand out.

"Hi, I'm Kalina, nice to meet you, sir," I say, trying my hardest to sound sincere.

The last and only time I saw this man, he was braying by the side of an emptied pool, rooting for Rowan to finish Silas off, for good. That alone would make me despise him, but the few things Diego has told me about his father didn't make him any more desirable to be around either. As if to proof the point that he's a prize arsehole, he doesn't take my hand but just looks at it in disgust.

"I know who you are, Polack."

"Suit yourself," I answer and turn around to walk to the lift. "Diego is in the office."

I don't expect him to follow me. The Santos-Benson Security office is on the first floor, and I assume he'll take the stairs, so he doesn't have to breathe the same air as the dirty Polish gold digger he clearly sees me as.

I assume wrong.

He stays where I left him, until the lift arrives, the door opens, and I've stepped inside. Then he suddenly clears the distance between us in long strides and slips into the metal box with me, just before the doors slide shut. The hairs on my neck stand up instantly, but there is nothing I can do about this. I've already turned the key in the keyhole that allows me to go all the way up to the penthouse, and we're beginning to ascend.

I reach out to press the first floor button, but with a swiftness I wouldn't have expected of a man of his bulk, he slaps my hand away and then puts his body between the panel and me, forcing me to retreat if I don't want to touch him.

I really, really don't.

He's not gross to look at and he doesn't smell bad. In fact, he doesn't smell that dissimilar to Diego, though his aftershave or deodorant or whatever is more assaulting. And I'd be happy if Diego looked like him by the time he's in his fifties, maybe minus a bit of the bulk. George Benson senior still has a full head of hair, blonde like Diego's but with grey in it, making it a shade lighter overall. His bone structure isn't as attractive as Diego's and his lips are thin, but he hasn't aged badly. He'd be pleasant enough to look at, if it wasn't for his eyes. The same shade of grey as Diego's but watery and without any humour or passion in them, they crawl over me with undisguised hatred, taking in my tank top and shorts. It's hot as Hades outside today, and my dungarees needed a wash. I wish I had waited another day now, because something else glitters in his eyes when he trails his gaze back up my naked legs. Something that puts me on high alert.

"So you're the reason my son won't take my calls," he says under his breath. "Can't say I see the attraction. Let me see."

He reaches out and grabs my left boob, squeezing it hard through the fabric of my tank top. I yelp, while he shakes his head.

"You've got no tits, girl."

Still holding my breast in a vice so painful it takes my breath and makes my eyes leak, he leans down to look into my face and snarls.

"You sure you *are* a girl?"

Then he grins.

"I think I might find out for myself. Wouldn't be the first time junior and I shared a whore."

And that's when I unfreeze.

Diego

I'm not quick enough.

I've barely got out of my chair by the time he's followed her into the lift. My sudden movement wakes up Isla and she starts barking, while I watch in horror as the camera inside the lift shows my father leaning towards Kalina and grabbing her breast.

I see red. Literally. Red dots start dancing in front of my eyes.

I pull out the drawer of my desk and take out the 1911 I keep there, fully loaded. All three men in front of me blanch, especially Julian.

"You keep a gun in our *office*?" he asks, as he springs to his feet. "Fuck me, Diego, we never agreed to that. What if—"

"Shut up," I cut him short. "Guys, he's going for Kalina."

Silas and Rowan are already up and looking at the screen, when I say it. Unlike Julian, they might not be comfortable with firearms in general, but as soon as they realise what's triggered me, they don't question me, and we become one unit. We scramble out of my office, past Lila, leaving behind Julian and his still barking dog. As soon as I'm out on the landing, I look at the panel above the lift door, telling me that they've already reached the top floor. Rowan gets to the lift first and starts pressing the call button, but nothing happens. Of course.

"Fuck, fuck, fuck!" I exclaim and start running up the stairs instead, Rowan and Silas hot on my heels.

We pound the steps, two or three at a time, until we get to the steel barred door that prevents people from getting up the last flight of stairs to the penthouse. When I was a kid, it still had a normal lock with a keyhole, but even then, I always wondered what would happen if there was a fire and Nan wouldn't be able to get to the key. So the first thing I did when I took over The Brick was to change the lock to a combination dial. I've never been so grateful yet so impatient at the same time. I stick the gun into the waistband of my jeans and with trembling fingers turn the dial back and forth on the combination.

Everything just takes too long.

Finally, there is a soft click and I swing the door open. The three of us start running again until we get to the fire exit door of the penthouse. It leads into the short hallway at the back of the penthouse, where Kalina's study room, the kitchen and the guest bathroom are. I storm along the corridor, Rowan and Silas still at my back, until we get to the living room.

I stop dead at the view in front of me.

The lift door is open, my father's unmoving body lying half inside, half out. Kalina has her back to us and is trying to drag him by the arms further into the penthouse. She is breathing heavily, struggling with his bulk.

"Baby, stop!" I shout, and she jumps two feet in the air as she drops my father's arms.

She turns towards my voice, and a new surge of anger rushes through my body. Her tank top is ripped, exposing a breast, a stream of blood is flowing from her nose, and one of her cheeks is starting to swell from a cut. I unfreeze and in a few steps I'm with her, catching her trembling body in my arms.

"He, he..." she starts against my chest but can't get the words out.

I wrap myself around her, kissing the top of her head, and hold her tight until I can feel her breathing relax back to normal. I watch as Rowan and Silas come around to check on the arsehole on the floor. They finish the job Kalina was doing and drag him fully into the penthouse then kneel by his shoulders, flanking him left and right as he coughs back to life.

It's a very distinctive cough.

The cough of a man who's been choked out.

I release Kalina from my embrace, keeping my hands on her shoulders, and scrutinize her face. Despite the blood, structurally the nose doesn't look too bad. I already know the doctors won't set it if we go to A&E. The cut on her cheekbone is more of a scratch, left no doubt by my father's signet ring. She looks up at me then down at herself before she glances over her shoulder at Silas and Rowan.

"I..." she starts again, but I interrupt her.

"Hang on," I tell her and then pull my bloodstained t-shirt over my head.

I bunch it up so I can pull the neckline open wide and carefully slip it over her head, avoiding any touch of her face. She smiles up at me gratefully as she slips her arms through the sleeves. I pull the hem down and smile back at her.

"Right," I say. "Better?"

She nods, tears pooling in her eyes.

I bend down to kiss them out of the corners before they can spill over.

"Don't cry, baby girl. If you cry, it's gonna hurt like a bitch when it hits that scratch and on the inside of your nose. You're safe. You're good. You did good," I say, straightening up and frowning at my own words. "How on earth did you manage to choke out a two-hundred-pound man, Kalina? You know what? Who cares?" I add immediately and gently draw her back into my chest, making sure she's angled on her good cheek and I'm not squishing her nose. "I'm glad you did. I'm sorry I wasn't here to protect you, baby. It'll not happen again."

I catch Silas' eyes. There is the question in them as to what we're going to do with my father. He is sitting upright now, still coughing intermittently and clearly dizzy.

"Okay," I say as I once again reluctantly dissolve Kalina's and my embrace. "You go, clean yourself up. We'll deal with him."

Her hands slide down my waist and one of them catches on the grip of my 1911. She doesn't freak. Not even a little bit. She just narrows her eyes at me and puts a beseeching expression in them.

"Don't kill him, Diego," she says. "He's not worth it. It's not worth going to prison for."

I laugh and tilt her chin up.

"I don't know who you think I am, baby girl, but I haven't killed anyone *yet*. We're just gonna have a little talk, my old man and me. About women and how we treat them."

A weird expression crosses her face then, but it's fleeting and ends in a grin.

"Promise?" she asks, and relief floods me when I realise she's still got her humour.

"Promise," I say. "But there may be a teeny tiny bit of castrating."

She pops an eyebrow at my caveat, and I immediately know that my girl is fully back in the room.

"Well, of course it would be a teeny tiny bit of castrating. That's all you would have to work with, no?"

I grin back at her.

"Careful what you're saying when you're talking about a man's father's dick size, baby girl."

"Hah," she huffs. "Your penis is from your mother's side," she retorts, batting her eyelids in her bashed-up face, before her eyes go wide when she realises what she just said, but then suddenly the cute funny look disappears and she gags. "I know, because I felt his. He's got a dog's dick. Pointy. Yuk."

She spits it out.

Her words add fuel to the rage still burning beneath the surface of the care I'm dishing out for her. She can sense the change in me and when I cock my head in the direction of our bedroom, she nods and makes herself scarce.

I wait with my eyes shut, listening out for her movement through the flat, until I hear the en suite door shut. Then I open my eyes and turn my attention to my father.

I walk across and kneel down in front of him. Silas and Rowan have stayed by his shoulders, still on their knees. Neither of them so much as flinches when I take out my gun, take the safety off and hold the barrel to my dad's forehead. He looks at me in disbelief and doesn't say a word. I'm not sure if he's just scared, or if he's still disorientated from the choke-out. I don't really care, other than that I want him to comprehend what's happening.

"Kalina says not to kill you. But, you see, my father raised me to ignore what the womenfolk have to say."

I let it hang, long enough for a wet patch to appear at the front of his trousers and the stench of somebody shitting themselves to permeate the room. Both Silas and Rowan, closer to his backend than me, avert their faces for a second.

"Gross," Silas says.

Rowan nods and then looks at him over my father's head.

"We learned something for the future, though," he says.

Silas frowns.

"What's that?"

"You put a knife to their throat, they just piss themselves. You break out the guns, you got shit on your hands."

They grin at each other over some private joke then turn back to me, waiting as to what happens next. It dawns on me in that moment that I could truly pull the trigger, and these two would be one hundred percent behind me. No matter if I decided to try to disappear the cunt in front of me or if I decided to call the police and claim self-defence, they'd back me up. Either by carrying the carpet roll or sticking up for me with a bogus story in the witness stand. It's the most powerful feeling I've had in my life, and I swallow hard.

As if he'd read my thoughts, which he probably has 'cause he's Silas and he can, Silas decides to put in his two pennies' worth.

"If you're going for the self-defence story, you probably wanna move back a bit and point the gun at somewhere less obvious, you know. Close-range head shot will *always* look like an execution."

I love the way he discusses this with the same calm he does everything else in life. I catch Rowan's eye, and we grin at each other. There really is a reason we love this guy so fucking much.

"Son," my father whispers, and my eyes snap back to his.

I push the barrel harder against his forehead.

"No," I tell him. "Not anymore. If, *if*, I let you live today, I will have nothing to do with you any longer. Unless I hear about you hurting another woman. In which case, I will come after you and kill you then. Are we clear? And I mean *any* other woman. That includes Mum. Leave. Her. The. Fuck. Alone."

I let the gun sink and put the safety back on.

"You want him gone?" Silas asks.

I nod.

"Just put him out in the street, let him make his way home with crap in his pants."

Rowan and Silas get up, grab my father under the armpits and heave him up. For a moment, while I'm still kneeling and they're all already upright, I look up at the man who I worshipped as a boy, loathed as a teen and have come to hate as an adult. I wait for him to threaten me, to tell me he'll come after me or some shit like that, but there is nothing. One look in his eyes and I know he knows he's lost.

"Get rid," I say, before I get up and leave the room in search of my wounded girlfriend.

Kalina

I've cleaned most of the blood from my face when Diego opens the door to the bathroom and slips in behind me. There are still two ugly shadows of blood ringing my nostrils, but when I tried to dab at them with a cotton bud it hurt too much, so I stopped. The scratch across my cheekbone is already crusted over, the flesh beneath and around it starting to colour dark. It's throbbing but it's not a kind of pain that bothers me. The nose is a different matter. It hurts like a bitch. And I look a mess.

"I look a mess," I say to Diego as our eyes meet in the mirror.

He smiles and strokes lightly over my shoulders.

"You look beautiful. Like the cutest warrior I've ever seen."

He bends down to pepper my neck with soft kisses then straightens up again.

"You want me to take you to a doctor?" he asks, and I shake my head.

"No. No point. It'll heal. Painkillers would be nice."

He reaches across my shoulder to open the bathroom cabinet.

"Help yourself. Ibuprofen, paracetamol, codeine, all there. If it's too bad, I can get you some morphine. Medical grade. No probs."

I shake my head.

"Ibuprofen will do."

He takes a packet down, pops two pills out of the foil pack for me and places them in my outstretched hand. I swallow them with a bit of water from the tap.

"Anything else?" he asks when I straighten up again and our eyes meet once more in the mirror.

"Touch me," I say. "Wipe out his hands on me."

He smiles at that and gently pulls up the t-shirt he covered me with. When he comes to my face, he takes the same great care not to touch it he took earlier, and then I'm standing there in my torn tank top. Rather than take it off the same way, he grabs it left and right of the tear and rips it completely, so he can slide it off my shoulders. Each movement he makes is slow and deliberate, but he hisses, when he sees my breast. There is a huge bruise on it from where his father had grabbed me. He looks at it and tears form in his eyes while he keeps staring at it, his lip trembling, his movements frozen.

"God, Kalina, I'm so sorry. I should never have dragged you into my world, I'm..."

I spin around to face him and reach up to grab him by the neck and pull him down to me. Forehead to forehead. It works, because it's about the only part of my face that doesn't feel tender right now.

"Shhh," I say. "Don't cry. I *chose* to be with you, okay? It's not like you picked me up in a bar and I thought you were some harmless businessman. I *knew* who you were, Diego. I've known you for months. And the first time I met *your father* he was shouting for Rowan to kill Silas. My choice to be here. You didn't make me. Now *please* will you put your hands on me?"

He nods, blind with tears, and then he hides his face in my neck and starts skimming his hands lightly all over my body. I already took my shorts off earlier and put them in the bath in cold water to soak the blood out that my nose dripped on them. So the only scrap of fabric I'm still wearing is my thong, giving him easy access to my butt cheeks.

He slides his hands over them and cups them, massaging them gently, while he starts nuzzling my neck. A moan escapes me as his kneading of my backside pulls and tugs at my clit, teasing me and making my pussy release her honey.

He pulls my bottom half in closer but makes sure he doesn't squish my hurting breast. I feel the hard ridge of his erection behind his jeans nestle against my naked stomach, and a shudder of pure sexual joy runs through me. Even battered and bruised, I can still make this man hard as rock, and that's a power rush like no other. As if to verify my thought, he lets off my neck and looks into my face before he starts kissing my brows and then moving his lips gently over my unhurt cheek to my mouth. There is something extra sexy about having somebody kiss your swollen upper lip better. He licks gently at the seam and I open up slightly. We keep the tongue play light, just the tips chasing each other around a bit, because we both know a full-on kiss would hurt my nose and lip. But it doesn't matter. In a matter of minutes, this gentle caressing has my pussy dripping and the need to be touched by him becomes unbearable.

"Touch me," I whisper against his mouth.

He chuckles.

"I thought I was," he quips.

"No," I say, and reach around to grab one of his hands off my buttocks and bring it around the front to shove it down my thong. "Here."

"Demanding," he says and laughs again, quietly, as he runs his middle finger down my slit and back up again to circle my clit.

I groan out loud, because the sensation is pure relief, like the first sip of an ice-cold drink on a hot day. I push against his hand, panting.

"More," I say. "Make me come."

He kisses me again lightly before he answers.

"That's generally the plan. On my hand, my cock or my mouth? Your choice, baby girl."

"All of them," I moan.

"At the same time? Tricky."

I grab his wrist and pull his hand away from me, shove my thong down and spin around, bracing myself on the edge of the sink as I push out my butt.

"Fuck me," I demand from his reflection.

But he's already one step ahead of me, unzipping his jeans and pushing them over his hips, along with his briefs. His cock springs free and brushes over my butt. A happy shiver of anticipation runs through me. He crouches a little to line himself up at my entrance and his right arm sneaks around me to my front. His left hand guides him in, while his right goes straight back to rubbing my clit. I make eye contact with him in the mirror and he groans when I make him watch me as I slide my tongue over two of my fingers, coating them in my saliva, before I reach down and tangle my fingers with his, massaging the base of his cock between the V they form as he keeps circling my nub. I watch our fingers dance, mesmerized, as they get slicker with my juice. I feel his movements inside me go jerky, and his legs shudder with the strain of crouching and fucking into me at the same time. It's glorious and when I look up again, the minute our eyes meet, we both lose ourselves in an explosion of spasms, as our orgasms hit us hard and fast.

Still clenching and unclenching in the aftermath, I sling my hand up to snake around his neck and make him focus on me in the mirror again.

"Thank you," I say, and he smiles, skimming his hand ever so lightly over my bruised tit.

"Any time, baby girl. Any time."

DIEGO

I don't want to leave her behind — I have visions of taking a bath together and then making her come a second time, eating her out on my bed — but the moment I detangle from her, I hear Rowan's thunderclap voice boom through the flat.

"Diego? We're back!"

I sigh and spin Kalina around.

"You gonna be okay? You sure you don't want a doctor?" I ask her.

She smiles crookedly. She's gonna smile crookedly for a few days.

"I'll be fine. They're not going to do anything. I know the procedure."

I frown at that because it catapults me straight back to the question from earlier. How did this slip of a girl get a handle on my dad and choke him out? And what does she know about broken noses?

"Hello???"

This time it's not Rowan's voice reaching me but Julian's, and it sounds a fuck load closer than Rowan's did. Like he's just on the other side of the door, in my bedroom. I open the bathroom door and see that I'm right. Julian is standing in the middle of my bedroom, holding a laptop open in his hands and is looking around.

"What the fuck, Julian? Do you mind?" I say and quickly close the bathroom door, so Kalina has her privacy.

Julian pulls a face at me, the kind of pissed off look *women* get when you're not appreciating them enough for their liking and they kind of suck their cheeks in between their teeth.

"Well, excuse me, but I thought I'd better check on you. You'll understand once you've seen this," he says with a nod at the screen in front of him. Silas appears in the bedroom door behind him and shrugs.

"Sorry, man, I told him it was a bad idea to come in here, but he insisted," he says and then throws a small object at me.

I catch it and realise it's Kalina's lift key, which explains how they all got back up here.

"That was still dangling," Silas explains then jerks his chin out at Julian. "He insisted on coming up with us. Thinks you're in danger from Kalina."

"What?"

I'm so stunned that I don't know which one of the two to focus on.

"You'll see," Silas answers, grinning. "He's got CCTV footage of Kalina and your dad in the lift. He showed us on the way up. The girl's a killer. She is fucking amazing. If you hadn't just sold the league, I'd say branch out into women fighting, you got a champ in your bed. You want me to go make some coffee? You look like you need one."

"What? Yes. Thank you, Silas."

He disappears from the door and I make a gesture to tell Julian to follow him. Once I've ushered him out successfully, I close the bedroom door behind me and point at the coffee table.

"Go on then, show me."

He puts the laptop down and sits down on the sofa, making space, so I can sit in full frontal view. Rowan and Silas have both disappeared to the kitchen, which means the first time around that he shows me the footage I get it without a soundtrack of their commentaries.

There is only one camera installed in the lift, in the corner opposite the doors, so you get a view of who's entering and of the button panel.

It starts with the bit I've already seen. Kalina is entering the lift by herself, putting the key into the keyhole that gets you to the penthouse. The doors start sliding shut and my father squeezes in between them. Kalina says something to him and then tries to reach for the first-floor button. He slaps her hand away before it touches the button and puts his body between her and the panel. She backs up and he leans down, saying something to her. Then his hand darts out and he grabs onto her breast. Red hot anger flows through me once again when I see this part for the second time today. But then I hold my breath as the section of the scene unfolds that I didn't witness, too busy running after my damsel in distress. Who is not a damsel at all, it turns out. There is a fraction of time while he's holding onto her when she is frozen but then, all of a sudden, she *moves*. She leans in, cups his balls, squeezes until his grip loosens on her tit. It's then that he lands the punch on her that breaks her nose, but that is the only other move he gets to make. She twists away, out of shot, and the next thing I see is her foot kicking his kneecap. Another spin, other foot, other kneecap. Another spin, first foot, back of the knee, repeat on the other side. He falls forward, onto his knees, and she climbs him, blood streaming from her nose but gripping his hair in both hands. Literally, *scales* the fucker until she's sitting on his shoulders and then she crosses her legs and her slender thighs start squeezing his neck while she is cupping his jaw in with one hand and holding the top of his head with the other, preventing him from biting at her or moving his head at all. You can tell in the way he is twitching that he doesn't know if he's coming or going. Kalina's entire upper and lower body have become one powerful vice, intent on choking the fucker out. And she does. The elegance of her move when he starts falling forward is second to none. She lets go and is on her feet above him, her feet securely planted left and right of his hips, the second his face hits the floor. The rest of the footage shows me how they arrive at the penthouse and how she rolls him over and starts dragging him, then it loops back to the beginning.

"See?" Julian says when we watch it the second time around, and points at my bedroom door. "She's a fucking killer, Diego. Honeytrap, I tell you."

"Don't be fucking stupid," Silas says as he and Rowan come in bearing trays with coffee and biscuits.

They put them left and right of the laptop onto the coffee table and start pouring coffees. Rowan's phone pings in his pocket and he takes it out to look at the message, leaving Silas to hand out the mugs.

"Oh, cool. Grace and Raven are back early. They're rolling into Brighton station now. Wanna know where we're at," he says, flopping down on a chair by the head end of the coffee table.

Silas and I exchange a look over the mug he's handing me. Raven's a nurse. It would do Kalina good to be looked at by a medic. I nod at him.

"Tell 'em not to get on the train to Shoreham but come straight here," Silas says, and Rowan starts tapping.

Once he's sent his message off, he snatches a packet of Hobnobs from the table and starts unravelling the plastic.

"You don't mind, do you?" he asks after he's already taken a bite out of the biscuit, so it fits into the mug Silas has put in front of him when he starts dunking. "Funny. I always had you down as a custard cream man. You've just risen in my estimate, Diego. I'm impressed."

"He *is* a custard cream man," Silas throws in. "My guess is, Kalina bought those. She likes all things oaty. Give her a flapjack and she's your friend forever."

He lasers in on Julian, who is the last to have a coffee thrust at him.

"Which is why your honeytrap theory is utter bollocks, Julian. She's lived with us for *seven* months, man."

"Look at it!" Julian exclaims exasperatedly, pointing at the screen where we've gone back to the bit when Kalina's got Dad in her full body vice. "That's a trained fucking killer. That's not some girlie who's done a few self defence classes, where she learned to hit someone with a French stick and key his eyeballs. That's a *fighter*. I tell you, she is not who she pretends to be, Diego. Be fucking careful."

"He's right," Kalina says from the bedroom doorway, where she stands, dressed in a new t-shirt and leggings, looking petrified.

Kalina

Sometimes your number is up. It's as simple as that.

Clearly, today my number is up.

I'm gonna have to trust these guys and throw my lot in with them *properly*.

It scares the living daylights out of me.

I work alone. I'm a free agent. Always. Before I came to Brighton and I got slowly absorbed in the vortex that is Sheena's house, I never even went out for fun in a group. When I hit town for a drink, I always went alone. None of the going out in tribes for me or buddying up with a wing woman. I love the freedom to make my own decisions, to call the shots on when, where, what and with whom — without the duty of babysitting someone else, or being babysat.

I anchor myself in Diego's eyes as he looks across to me, shell shocked but his gaze still full of care and passion, waiting for me to explain myself.

It's why I don't register Silas prowling over until he's standing right in front of me and gently cups my chin. He tilts my head this way and that, scrutinising the damage. I'm the oldest of my siblings at home and this is a new feeling, the feeling of a protective brother looking out for you. His hazel eyes lock onto mine.

"You iced it?"

I shake my head, and he makes a hissing sound before he looks over his shoulder at Diego.

"George, you fuckwit. You need to put an icepack on that, otherwise her eye is gonna swell shut by tomorrow. You should know better than that. What the fuck did you two do in the bathroom?"

Diego and I clear our throats at the same time and Silas rolls his eyes, blushing slightly along the jawline. Unlike the rest of the guys around here, he doesn't wear his virility on his sleeves, or as a perma-tent in his trousers. I know Grace is a very satisfied woman, thanks to the paper-thin walls in Sheena's house, but out in public Silas is, well, mostly discreet with his desire, where Rowan and Diego are definitely not. Rowan is the worst of them, and it's no surprise that he laughs out loud at Diego's and my obvious distraction-from-pain activities.

"Yeah, that works, too," he says through the laughter and makes a beeline to the kitchen. "I'll go get some ice for you, Kal."

Satisfied that his brother is on the case, Silas turns back to me.

"Did you take any pain killers?"

I nod.

"Ibuprofen."

"Oh for fuck's sake," he groans, looking back at Diego. "What is this? Amateur hour? Ibuprofen will thin her blood and make her bruise even more! You should have given her some morphine."

Diego mumbles something about offering it, but it's obvious Silas isn't listening as his eyes come back to mine. He lets go of my chin.

"So, which one of us are you after, killer-bee?" he asks, evenly.

I bark out a nervous laugh.

"Déjà vu. That's exactly what your mum asked me at lunch."

"Mum knows?" Silas exclaims but then shakes his head and throws his hands up with an eye roll to heaven. "Of course she does."

"And what was the answer?" Diego asks coolly from his perch on the sofa.

His tone makes me swallow hard. Gone is the love from his grey gaze, replaced by storm clouds of barely suppressed anger.

"You know what?" I ask, finding my sass among the soup that's coursing through my veins, a stew of physical aftershock from the fight, post-orgasmic comedown and feeling pushed right out of my comfort zone with the idea of telling them who I am and why I'm here. "You lot really are full of yourselves. I'm not after *any* of you. Shocker, I didn't even know any of you existed before I came here. It was complete coincidence that the language school placed me at Sheena's. I'm not a cop, I'm not interested in any of you, I don't give a shit what you do with your lives. I'm..."

I don't get to finish my rant because suddenly I start shivering violently and my legs give way beneath me.

The world turns black, just as I feel Silas catch me midair.

DIEGO

I see her collapse and my life stops.

Not just my heart, my entire fucking *life*.

It's the weirdest sensation.

As I jump up and clear the room in a few hasty steps to take her from Silas, who thankfully caught her as she blacked out, I realise I don't actually give a shit who or what she is. And it dawns on me that I've known for ages that something was off.

We all did.

We just didn't *want* to know. Because we like her.

I like her. I *trust* her.

I have no idea what her deal is, but I trust in what is between us. I trust in the magic we make when we're together. I trust in the way she just *fits*.

By the time I get to Silas, he's got her securely in his arms, carrying her like a groom carries his bride. I hold out my arms, my heart pounding in my throat with fear, and he wordlessly transfers her across to me.

Rowan comes back, talking as he enters the room.

"Sorry that took so long. I can't believe you don't have an actual icepack. Those points for the Hobnobs you scored? I'm taken them away again for making me...oh shit," he says when he sees Kalina's limp body.

I carry her back to the bedroom and put her on my, *our*, bed.

Silas, Rowan and Julian all follow me in. Rowan hands me a satchel of ice cubes wrapped in a kitchen towel. I gently press them against Kalina's cheek.

"You should get her to Doctor Morten," Julian says solemnly, breaking our silence.

Morten is the doc we take fighters to if shit goes *really* bad. We try to avoid him because he costs you a kidney to scan your kidney but included in that price is a state-of-the-art MRI scanner, in a private clinic that holds no records and has no witnesses.

"No doctor," Kalina mumbles as her eyes flutter open.

She smiles at me weakly and her hand comes up to cradle mine. She gently pries the ice satchel from me and presses it to her cheek herself while she shuffles into a half upright position.

"I'm okay. I just need some sugar," she mutters.

Silas silently dashes away and returns with the open roll of Hobnobs and my coffee.

"Here," he hands both to me but looks at her, critically. "I don't know, Kalina. You might have a concussion. He hit you pretty hard."

I hand her a biscuit, after I've dunked it for her, and she starts nibbling on the soggy edge.

"Don't be stupid. If you have a concussion you blackout immediately. Not half an hour and an orgasm later," she retorts. "It's just shock."

"Yeah, or a really good performance," Julian says sarcastically.

We all turn to him, but it's Rowan who speaks.

"Right, enough, soldier boy. One more word and I'll deck you just for the fun of it."

He goes toe to toe with Julian to illustrate the point. The point being that Julian might be ex-army, but Rowan is a descendant of giants on one side and a Japanese martial arts master on the other, or so the story goes, and the most lethal bare-knuckle fighter in all of the land. Rowan glares at him until Julian backs down.

Kalina meanwhile finishes her Hobnob and drinks half my coffee, all the while holding my gaze.

She's pleading with me not to hate her. She's telling me to lose the guy she doesn't know, and who doesn't trust her. I lean in and kiss the tip of her nose.

"Julian?" I call out and reluctantly take my eyes off her to look at the guy in question.

"Yes, boss?"

"Go downstairs, check on your wife. Tell her she doesn't have to take you off the conference rota after all. Callum and Cormac can wait."

I hear him take in a sharp breath. He doesn't like being dismissed, but he's too much of an order follower to argue. It's why our meeting was serendipitous for him not just on a lifesaving and dog-saving level but on a business level, too. He might have had fantasies about running his own security business, but he would never have made company director material. And he knows it, too. Which is why he is happy with how it is and why he doesn't argue now. He gives me a sharp nod and retreats out of the bedroom. Rowan stalks him part of the way, undoubtedly to watch him step into the lift. He returns a few beats later with a big grin on his face.

"He's gone," he informs us, and Kalina visibly relaxes.

"Right," I say gently, running my hand through her short hair and cradling her good cheek. "Who are you? Why are you here?"

She grins, turning her face in my palm and kissing the tip of my thumb.

"Ask me how old I am, first," she teases.

I blanch at that and lift the hand off her to run it through *my* hair.

"Oh fuck. Please tell me you're legal," I groan.

She nods, her grin widening.

"Totally. I'm actually only a year younger than you."

I see Rowan's eyebrows shoot up at that in the periphery of my vision.

"No fucking way!" he exclaims.

But she doesn't look at him, she still looks only at me.

I feel a mix of annoyance and relief. Annoyance for all that time I spent, agonising over lusting after a barely legal girl. And relief, because no nineteen-year-old should be *that* experienced between the sheets. I sure as shit wasn't at that age and only now do I realise that it was bothering me. Fragile male ego and all that. I'm a dick.

She holds her hand out for another biscuit and I give it to her.

"I'm gonna fill you guys in," she says and takes a deep breath then huffs it out in a series of rapid little puffs. "I'm not going to tell you my real name, though," she states. "Not because I don't want you to know, or because I don't trust you, but because it means that if the police ever

- 550 -

interrogate you about me, you can honestly say you knew me only as Kalina Jasinski."

I hear all the implications of 'knew me', and it slices through my heart like a dagger. She never had any intention of sticking around. But I push it aside for now. Right here, right now, she's in the palm of my hand.

"You wanted?" I ask.

She shakes her head.

"No. But I should be," she answers.

"You're a criminal?"

She shakes her head again.

"No. But not all my business practices are strictly legal, so I use a cover identity."

"And what is this business that you practise?" I ask in a slightly ribbing tone that's supposed to cover up my nervousness.

"I'm a private investigator."

Kalina

I was saved by the bell. Literally. Before Diego, Silas and Rowan could react in any way to my little revelation, the doorbell rang, followed by pings on both Silas' and Rowan's phones, announcing that Grace and Raven were downstairs.

So right now I'm alone in the bedroom with Raven, who's thrown everyone else out of the room, and I've got a torch shining directly into my left eye.

I don't really know Raven — after all, we only spent a week together in the same house before she and Rowan left for America — but I like her. She is competent, no-bullshit but also kind of darkly edgy, the same way Rowan is. They belong.

She also has the coolest tattoo on her back I've ever seen in real life, dresses like a fifties pin up, petticoats and all, and has taught me how to do victory rolls on Grace like a pro. I was half in love with her already just for that when she and Rowan left, but right now I appreciate her on a whole different level.

There is something about being checked over by a medical professional that makes you feel like a child getting a hug after a tumble.

Reassurance.

Safety in the knowledge you're in good hands.

Raven gives off all of that.

She switches the torch off then asks me to get up and runs me through a few exercises that remind me of the way American cops check out if somebody is drunk.

I have to walk in a straight line, touch my finger to my nose with my eyes closed and do a few more coordination tests. She asks me some memory questions, and then we're done. I clamber back onto the bed and Raven examines my face one more time before she shrugs.

"I think you'll be fine. You'll look like shit tomorrow, but your brain's okay so far. To be on the safe side, rest for forty-eight hours, preferably in bed. Get Diego to keep an eye on you. If you develop a headache, or your vision goes blurry, go to the hospital. Like, right that second. But it's unlikely to happen. It's rare to get a concussion or brain swelling from injuries to the face. It kinda acts like a crash zone in a car. It would be a whole different story if he'd hit you directly in the forehead or, worse, around the side or the back of the skull."

There is something in the way she says it that makes me suspect she has firsthand experience of this, not just as a nurse. But we don't know each other anywhere near enough for me to ask her about it. So I just nod gratefully. Which hurts. Every little movement of my head hurts now. The power of the ibuprofen didn't last long.

She watches me wince and nods sagely.

"You need something stronger than over the counter painkillers?" she asks.

"Diego already offered me morphine," I answer, and her eyebrows lift. "But I don't want any. I don't like opiates. They make me fuzzy in the head."

She laughs at that, which from what I already know of her is a rare occurrence.

"Respect," she says. "But, you know, we have these drugs for a reason. Don't be a martyr. If it gets too hard to cope, don't be too proud to take something stronger. I'd rather we got it the legal way, but I think where these guys are concerned, resistance is futile. Whatever you take, though, just be careful so you don't end up liking it too much."

"I hear you," I reassure her.

Raven's spent the last half a dozen or so years as a rehab nurse, so I know she's not being flippant. She holds my gaze for a second and then turns to the closed door, satisfied.

"You can come back in now!"

On her shout it immediately opens and Grace falls in first, followed by Diego, Silas and Rowan. Grace comes over to me and shunts Raven out of the way, making her shuffle along so she can lean in and give me a hug. She keeps it so light it's more like a brush of air around me and of all the things that have happened today it's that what finally makes me cry.

But not for too long.

Diego was right.

The tears hurt like a bitch on the inside of my nose.

Diego steps around the others to the other side of the bed and climbs up to stretch out next to me, offering me his arm to lean into. I snuggle into him, inhaling the scent of his skin as the shirt he threw on after the bathroom but never buttoned up falls open and allows my cheek to use his bare chest as a pillow. I feel immediately more settled. And a little turned on. Again.

Grace sits down on the edge of the bed, next to Raven. Silas clears the only chair in the room of clothes by dumping them on the floor and draws it up to the foot end. Rowan sits down on the floor, opposite Raven and Grace, with his back against the wall and one knee drawn up.

Once everyone is settled, there is a moment of silence, bursting at the seams with their curiosity.

Grace is the one who pops the bubble.

"Spill, girl!" She laughs. "Private fucking eye?"

"What?" Raven asks, unsure of what's going on.

The guys hadn't got to that part in their retelling of the afternoon, when she threw them out to examine me. I guess they filled Grace in while Raven was inspecting the damage. I decide Raven is the least betrayed person in the room, so probably safest for me to hold eye contact with for now and concentrate on her.

"I'm a private detective, I specialize in finding remains of missing children. I've been working undercover in Brighton for the last seven months, investigating the disappearance of two teenage boys two years ago, Piotr Schmidt-Danczyk and Zoltan Salak. They disappeared within three months from one another, and they both were here as students of Babeltowers International before they vanished. It was the only connection they shared, so I went in as a language student to investigate."

Raven nods, taking the new info in with a neutral expression, but in the periphery of my vision, I see Grace's eyes growing bigger with every word I speak.

Grace is an innocent in a round of shady characters. Raven's not exactly a criminal either, but she seems to take the type of life Rowan led until recently much more in her stride than your regular goodie-two-shoes. Grace may not be super prim and proper but compared to the rest of us, she lived a pretty regular existence before she came to England and met Silas. I know from some of her late-night-over-ice-cream confessions that she often still feels like she's living in a movie right now, where she's bagged the least bad of the bad boys, but a bad boy nonetheless.

"And?" asks said least bad boy from his chair right now, while my own one is absently running a hand up and down my arm.

Though I remain plastered to Diego's side, I shuffle into a more upright position before I answer Silas. I take a moment to brace myself then face up to his hazel stare. Despite my ever-growing feelings for the man by my side who's making me feel better just by holding me, I feel like I owe Silas my explanation the most. And I'm most terrified of his disappointment in me. It comes with the territory of having lived in his house for seven months, I guess. Of all the people in this room, I have known Silas the longest and shared the most food with him. Most of which, *he* cooked. That counts for something.

"And nothing." I sigh. "I'm in a, what do you call it, cul de sac."

"Dead end. You are *at* a dead end," Rowan corrects me from the floor and pulls his phone out of his pocket.

"I'm *at* a dead end," I repeat to him then concentrate on Silas again, whose face is giving nothing away. "The language school came up empty. I spoke to Piotr's host family, posing as his cousin, but they had nothing that wasn't in the police report. And they have watertight alibis. Plus they are still reeling from the incident. They're never gonna recover from having lost somebody else's child. When people go missing, it ripples so far, you can't imagine..." I let my voice trail off for a moment, remembering all the families and friends of the missing I've brought closure to over the years, before I go back to telling them about the non-event that is the most difficult case in my career so far. "On the other hand, Zoltan's host mother barely remembered him. It was more like a youth hostel run by this single woman, who is clearly just treating these kids as a business. She has eight students at a time, packing in four per room on bunk beds. Like sardines. The kids get a locker and a mattress, cereal for breakfast and a pot of gloop for dinner. The complete opposite of what your mum does. I tracked down each of the students Zoltan bunked with. Spoke to all of them on the phone, but none of them could tell me anything much. Normally, I'd go visit them, but Zoltan's mum isn't the paying party in this. Piotr's parents are bankrolling me, and other than me, nobody is convinced the two disappearances are connected. My boss thinks I'm, what's the phrase, barking up the wrong tree but lets me follow my instincts as long as I don't bill Piotr's parents with any expenses spent on Zoltan."

"Whoa, hang on," Diego says at this point. "You have a boss? What does he know about us?"

I tilt my head to look at him and roll my eyes.

"Nothing, he's not interested in you. Deal with it."

It raises a chuckle from both Silas and Rowan.

"Continue," Silas says.

"So I spoke to all of Zoltan's, what shall I call them, fellow sufferers. It sounded like they didn't have a very good time while they were here and basically tried to stay out of the house as much as they could. Having seen the house and the host, I'm not surprised. It's filthy, it's cramped, the woman is horrible, and it smells of towels that have been folded away before they were dry. The only thing they did tell me about Zoltan that she conveniently forgot was that he stayed out all night a few times. While they all stuck to the curfew, Zoltan didn't come back and claimed he'd slept at the beach."

"So he was gay then," Silas, Rowan and Diego all say in the same breath.

"What?" Grace, Raven and I respond, equally *una voce*.

"You can't sleep at the beach here. Coppers will come and move you on in two seconds flat," Diego explains, his hot breath fanning over my head, before he drops a quick kiss on the crown. "So 'sleeping at the beach' is Brighton gay slang for hook ups, usually in one of the two main gay clubs."

"Both of which are at the seafront," Silas rounds off the info.

And suddenly I sit bolt upright, because it is something I never considered.

Zoltan's mum never mentioned anything about him being gay, but he might have hidden it from her. People still do. Especially in a country like Hungary, where over half the population are Catholics. Though Zoltan's sexuality shouldn't have any bearing on the case as such, a predilection for casual hook ups very much could. Casual sex opens cans of worms for crimes of passion, date rape and accidental killings by a complete stranger. It would also mean a connection to Piotr's disappearance was highly unlikely. My mind is reeling at a thousand miles a second with a million new possibilities — all annoyingly revolving around the *non*-paying element in this gig — when Grace pipes up, brows drawn together in thought.

"Yeah, but would a foreign student know that? And how old was this kid? Do these clubs not card you?"

"He would, if those are the circles he's hanging in," Rowan points out, while I answer the other half of the question.

"Seventeen. But he could easily have passed for older. He was built."

"What about the other one?" Raven asks.

"Piotr?" I ask on a sigh and sink back down again. "He was fifteen, but he was the opposite. Like, really small for his age. Slight in built. Big, innocent eyes. Could have been one of my brothers."

"You have brothers?" Diego asks, a sharp reminder that he doesn't really know me still.

"Two," I say. "Both younger than me."

"Real or imagined?" he enquires sarcastically, and I slug him in the stomach.

"Real, you arse. And before you ask, most of what you know about me is true. I just may have left out the odd bit."

"Such as?"

"That I spent six years at an international boarding school where the common language was English and most of the other students were British army kids," I say with a shrug.

He gently slugs me back for that.

"Superpower, my arse."

I turn my head to grin up at him sweetly.

"You know what the most annoying thing about you is?" he asks, and I shake my head. "That you're fucking cute as a button even when your face looks like it's been put through a mangle."

"Does it really look that bad?" I ask seriously.

"Worse," the entire round replies.

"I want to get back to the story," Grace says. "You got any pictures?"

I nod, slowly.

Telling them why I'm here is one thing. I'm not sure if I'm ready to show them my notes, though. On the other hand, their input is already proving more valuable than I could have ever imagined. In ten minutes, they've given me more new avenues to explore than I've come up with in *months*. But I'm also really tired all of a sudden and hungry.

"Tired?" Raven asks.

She's been the quietest so far, but her nursey sense obviously just kicked in.

"A little. But more hungry."

"Hey, no problem," Rowan says and pulls out his phone. "Let's order some pizzas."

Raven shakes her head at him.

"Not a good idea. Chewing is really gonna hurt her for a few days. Soggy pasta would be better."

"No problem. I'll give Sheena a ring," Rowan deadpans.

Everyone in the room who's ever had to endure Sheena's cooking laughs. Raven is the lucky odd one out, but she's heard enough stories to get the gist. Silas gets up from his chair, picks up the clothes he dumped on the floor and puts them back on it before he turns back to look across at Diego and me on the bed. He locks eyes with me.

"Do you *want* us to know the rest?" he asks evenly. "It's your case. This is your *work*. You can always tell us to fuck off out of your business, Kalina."

Trust him to have the courtesy to ask. Trust him to just accept this new version of me so readily. I've always wanted a big brother. It dawns on me that my wish has been granted. At least for now.

"Yes," I answer, and I realise that it feels good.

Suddenly, it feels like I don't just have a new brother, I have a crew. I've never had a crew.

Silas nods.

"Okay, then I suggest you get some rest, I'll see what I can find to cook in this house and if not, Grace and I will get some groceries. I'll make you something nice and soft, but *not* soggy."

Rowan takes a breath, but Silas cuts him short.

"I know you want pizza. I can see the pizza thought bubble above your head. Order some pizza if you must. But I'm cooking something for Kalina," he says and then ushers everyone out, until only Diego and I are left on the bed.

"You know he's the real boss, right?" I say.

Diego chuckles.

"Always has been."

"You mad?"

"At him? No. At you? A little bit. But not really. I was, before you decided to drop out of the scenery. But that scared me so fucking much that now I don't care who you really are, I'm just glad you *are*."

"You actually mean that, don't you?"

He turns onto his side, slides his hand across my stomach and tugs at my hip, so I do the same to face him. He holds my gaze for a very long time, making my heart beat faster with every second that passes. Then he smiles.

"Yeah, I do. I love you, whoever you are."

Before I can say anything back, he puts a finger to my lips.

"Shhh. Don't say anything. I didn't say it to hear anything back. I said it, because I do. One day you might feel the need to say the same. But when that day comes, be sure. Don't say it with one foot out of the door. Say it when you're content to leave your passport in a drawer somewhere."

I swallow hard at that.

Some days your number is up.

And sometimes, somebody's just got your number.

DIEGO

I watch her swallow hard at my words and though it hurts that she clearly isn't as far in as I am already, there is a flicker in her eyes that tells me I stand a chance.

I'll fight for that chance. Tooth and fucking nail.

Before this afternoon, I thought I'd found an equal in bed, in food, in leisure. But now I know I've found an equal full stop. How many women are there in the world that are this badass but so fucking cute? That understand the grey nuances of right and wrong? Of legal and not so legal? Of there being more than one version of you? It all makes a lot more sense now. Why she neither balked at my business, nor painted me some ruthless criminal without a moral compass. How she can accept all the different incarnations of me. How she got me *just right*.

She watches me watch her and a faint smirk appears around her mouth.

"What are you thinking?"

"I'm wondering how you know what's in police reports of cases that I assume are still open, even if they've gone cold."

The smirk grows into a grin.

"You pay attention," she says.

I sigh.

"If you can't read properly, you kind of have to," I admit.

"I've noticed. Like I said..." she starts.

"...not all your business practices are legal," I finish.

She nods, yawns, and winces, all at the same time, because opening her jaw that wide clearly hurts.

"Right," I say. "Enough talk. You rest for a bit."

"Will you..." she starts, grabbing my hand and pulling it across to cup it gently over her bruised tit.

She never finishes the sentence because she doesn't need to. I get it. She wants protection, the healing of a gentle touch. So I keep it there, not moving, just shielding and she makes a happy sound, deep in her throat that wakes up my dick.

There is a knock on the door and Silas steps back into the room, once I've called out that it's safe to come in. He takes the two of us on the bed in with a soft smile before he clears his throat.

"Right. You have no food. Well, nothing I can work with. Grace and I are going shopping. You want anything else?"

"New face," Kalina quips, sleepily.

I shake my head and remove my hand from her breast to dig in my pocket for the lift key and throw it to him.

"Cool. We won't be long," he tells us as he catches it. "I know what we're getting, and it won't take long to cook. Rowan's still hell-bent on pizza, though. What about you, George? Salmon and baby spinach with new potatoes or a Domino's meat feast with extra pepperoni?"

"Bit of both?"

He grins.

"Thought you would say that. You got about an hour and a half, maybe two hours. Is that okay?"

"Hmmm," Kalina mumbles into my side, already half asleep. "Can you chop the spinach really fine and put in loads of cream?"

Silas frowns.

"Wasn't planning to but sure, if that's what you want."

"Hmm," she purrs happily, making my dick even harder. "Kremowy szpinak."

As soon as Silas has pulled the door shut behind him again, my hand goes back to her tit. Kalina slides her fingers lightly over my abs and unashamedly dips below my waistband. She finds my hard-on and chuckles as she wraps her fist around it.

"It's what happens if you speak foreign around me," I defend myself.

"Liar," she mumbles, giving me a loving squeeze. "It's what happens when I'm around."

I kiss the top of her head.

"You should sleep."

"I know," she mutters. "Can I hold on to this? It makes me feel safe."

"I already told you, you can hold on to it for as long as you like."

"Hmm."

She snuggles deeper into me as she gently runs a thumb over the head and begins pumping me.

"Kalina," I say threateningly.

Her only response is to let go, slip her hand out, pop the button on my jeans and pull the zip down. Then her hand goes straight back under my boxers and back to work.

Slowly, gently, leisurely.

Kalina

He groans loudly and the sound shoots straight to my core.

I really want him to finger me to sleep right now, for the pleasure to distract me from the pain in my face. I want him to stroke my pussy that's already sodden again just from the knowledge that I have this effect on this man, until I come on his hand, and then I want to drift to sleep with his fingers still inside me.

And he obliges, not a word said.

While I still leisurely fist his cock, he turns to his side and the hand that was cupping my injured breast slides down and into my leggings. He doesn't bother tugging them down but works beneath the fabric.

"Hmm, no panties," he murmurs as his fingers part me. "And so wet. Always so wet."

"Only for you," I mumble.

"Cheesy line," he says as he circles my clit.

"Truth," I reply as I spread the precum over his slit and around the head, softening my touch when my thumb slips across his banjo string.

He shudders.

Then he does something new between my legs. He crooks his fingers and starts running the knuckles over my clit, my slit, my hole in slow, rocking motions, until I press up against it as hard as I can, panting, my own fist mindlessly pumping him harder with every drag of the knuckles.

Up, down, up, down.

I can already feel the first clenches of my orgasm, when he unfurls his hand to finally shove two fingers inside me, curling onto my magic spot while his thumb takes over rubbing my clit. He pumps inside me and I mimic his motions with my fist, thrust for thrust, my thumb running across his head, my fingers tightening around his shaft with every stroke he gives my insides. He shatters with a loud growl, a split second before I do, his semen spilling all over my hand. The feeling, the power, pushes me over the edge and I come just as hard on his hand, spasming up against it as if plugged into a live wire. As soon as I still, I clamp my legs shut around his hand, so he doesn't withdraw it — and with his softening cock in my hand, I drift off to sleep.

His hand is still between my legs and my hand still on his dick when a soft rap on the door and a muffled, thunder-clap voice, telling us dinner will be ready in five, wakes us up. Our eyes open at the same time and we look at each other, while Diego responds groggily to Rowan that we'll be with them shortly.

We find it hard to detach but we do, and as soon as I'm out of the cocoon, I notice the throbbing in my face. I watch Diego get out of bed and move towards the en suite.

"Diego?"

"Yes, baby girl?"

"About that morphine..."

He turns back to me, his face immediately full of concern.

"That bad?"

"Yeah, I think so."

"I'm gonna kill that motherfucker."

I can't help but snigger.

"What?"

"Has it ever occurred to you that your own father is the only person you can correctly call a motherfucker?"

"I think I liked you better when you didn't speak English so well, and I only understood half of what you were saying," he deadpans before he goes back to the subject of painkillers. "I'll make a call. You'll have some here in about twenty minutes. Raven can probably tell you how much is appropriate for your body size. My guess is, if we give you as much as we give the fighters, you'd drop dead on the spot."

By the time he's made the phone call, and we are both cleaned up enough not to smell of stale come any longer, dinner is ready and served in the living room. There is salmon, spinach and potatoes for everyone and pizza on the side, that I wisely forego. Even chewing the delicious soft food Silas made for me has me in agony, and by the time the courier turns up with the morphine and a bunch of syringes, I have dropped all my reservations about opiates. It's good that Raven dishes out the dose, while mumbling something about totally losing her nurse's licence over administering illegally acquired prescription drugs if anyone ever finds out, otherwise I'd probably OD in my greed for relief.

The numbness is almost instant and comes with that fuzzy rush of euphoria only opium-based products will give you. Like a rocket of cotton wool hitting you right in your soul.

I kind of lied when I said I don't like it. I like it very much, for about ten seconds. Then I normally panic. Now I'm learning that I like it a lot longer, that I don't panic, provided I feel safe.

The last couple of times I had anything like this, I didn't feel remotely safe. More the exact opposite. I was hunting the bones of a junkie kid gone missing in Thailand and was partaking among a round of his associates, sitting between rats and cockroaches in a half-collapsed shanty, overlooking a river that was more plastic than water. Gaining trust by smoking heroin may have been one of the least smart moves of my career. I kept wondering if they were gonna sell me or murder me, and afterwards I felt mildly sick and dozy for days, and Konstantin nearly fired me, followed by an endless lecture about how far undercover is too far, while paranoia-me worried I'd instantly become a junkie. But I found the bones.

Now, it's completely different.

I'm fed, I'm snuggled, it's clean and I'm surrounded by people who will protect me, and I have a man by my side who will *pull a gun on his own father* to keep me safe.

"That's big," I say enthusiastically out loud, and all eyes turn to me.

We're all gathered around the coffee table, Diego and I on the sofa, Silas and Grace cross-legged on the floor and Rowan in a massive armchair that would swallow the likes of me whole but for him is just about right. Raven's gone to dispose of her gloves and the syringe she used to inject me.

"Uh-oh," says Rowan and leans over to snatch the last slice of pizza from the table. "Here we go."

"No really," I say. "You guys are wonderful and you," I add, focusing on Diego who's massaging my feet in his lap, "are the most amazing man alive. I—"

"Don't say it, Kalina!" he interrupts me sharply and scowls. "Say it when you're not whacked out on morphine, when it's just us, when I know your real name and your passports are in the drawer. *All* of them."

"Hmm. You're cute when you're angry," I hear myself reply. "I do, though."

"What did I miss?" Raven asks as she re-enters the room and makes a beeline for Rowan's lap. "She flaking out?"

"Not flaking out," I say. "Just trying to tell *people* how much I fucking love them."

"Uh-oh," Raven responds and plonks herself sideways down on top of Rowan. "She's cussing. I've never heard her cuss."

"You don't know me very well," I say with a laugh.

"No shit," Diego hisses.

"Hey," Grace interjects, getting on her knees to stack some of the dirty dishes and clear space on the table. "Keep it peaceful. Why don't we go back to Kalina's case? I wanna know more." She holds a hand up behind her to Silas, who takes a breath to interrupt.

"Save it. She already said she wanted to share *before* she was doped up."

I beam at her. I love her sooooooooooo much. She's the best.

"You're the best, Jessica Rabbit. Somebody grab my laptop?"

She lowers herself back onto her haunches, so she can flip me off, because she hates the nickname Rowan gave her. It fits her, though. She has that kind of figure, just a bit more of it, the hair, though it comes out of a bottle, and the green eyes. Her mouth is infinitely better than Jessica Rabbit's, though. She's got these big, full lips that curl up at the corners into a permanent cat smile. I focus in on them now. They look soft and pillowy and delicious.

"You know you got the best lips out of every woman I've ever seen, right?" I ask her. "I so want to kiss you one day."

Grace flashes her eyebrows at me with a coquettish smile, Diego and Rowan both groan and I can feel Diego's cock twitch in his jeans under my foot. Silas looks at me stoically with the barest hint of a grin. Oh good, that's definitely not a no-not-my-woman-lips-off. I store away that info for another time.

Grace jumps to her feet.

"Where is it?"

"Her study," Diego answers, and my heart pitter-patters at the fact he calls the guest bedroom *my* study.

Silas jumps up.

"I'll show you."

We watch them disappear.

"How long do we give them?" Rowan asks, while he unashamedly runs his hand up Raven's calf and under her dress.

Raven slaps his hand as it travels higher up her leg. Not that it stops him.

"I don't know how you people get anything done," I comment, rubbing my foot over Diego's crotch. "All you do is make out and eat."

Diego catches my foot and flashes me an amused grin.

"Says the main culprit," he says and lifts the foot up to kiss the arch. "How are you feeling?"

"Better," I respond on a sigh.

"Good."

Our eyes are on another as he moves his mouth to my toes and starts sucking on the big one, running his tongue over the pad. It should tickle, but I nearly shoot off the sofa with pleasure at the sensation. I'm vaguely aware that at the edge of my vision Rowan's hand has disappeared *very far* up Raven's petticoat and she's hiding her face in the crook of his neck now. I can't help but shoot them an actual glance. Rowan doesn't make eye contact, but I know he sees me looking and I'm almost certain he flexes his arm muscles for my benefit, so I *know* what he's doing to his lady under there. I'd bet my last cent that he has got his hands on her pussy by now, rubbing her clit through the fishnets she's wearing. She's trying hard not to show it, but she's squirming in his lap and though I can't hear it, I can see she is panting by the rapid rise and fall of her chest. I look back at Diego sucking my toe and realize he's been watching me watch them. He grins around my toe then pops it out of his mouth with a last hard suck.

"You like watching, baby girl?" he whispers hoarsely.

"Love it," I admit.

His eyes darken at that, and he runs his hand so fast up the inside of my leggings-covered leg, the friction leaves a burning sensation in its wake. He cups my sex when he gets there, squeezing hard and pushing the heel of his palm into me.

"Mine," he growls, and I shake my head despite the heat that fills my body.

"No, mine. You'd look silly with a vagina."

I hold my breath in anticipation of his reaction. But then he laughs, lets go of my pussy, grabs me by the hand instead and pulls me upright into a side-hug. His mouth finds my ear.

"You can watch, you can make out with girls, but I draw the line at another man's cock inside you," he murmurs. "Understood?"

I draw back and swap position, *my* mouth finding *his* ear. I nibble on it first, to make him more compliant.

"Why would I want another cock inside me when I can have this one?" I ask, my hand finding his raging hard-on to give it a squeeze as hard as he just gave me. "What about your cock inside me and a girl licking us both at the front?" I add, just for good measure. "But no sticking yours in *her* either."

He draws back and looks at me, so intensely, the rest of the room falls away.

"I changed my mind. I don't care about your name and you can staple your passport to your forehead for all I care, I'm fucking keeping you."

"Romantic," I snort.

"Oh for fuck's sake," Silas says from the hallway as he and Grace are about to re-enter the room. "Leave you two bastards alone for two minutes and you start a fucking orgy."

Raven unfurls out of whatever bliss she was experiencing at the hand of her man and shoots Silas an admirably composed look.

"One, there are four in this *orgy*, so don't be a sexist asshole and only call out the guys. Two, your woman's lips are twice the size and twice as smiley as before you left to 'get a laptop', because as we all know laptops are soooo heavy. So spare me the holier than thou shit."

Rowan grins at his brother and hugs his woman tighter, slowly retracting his hand out from under her skirts to envelop her in both arms.

"I love her," he declares.

Silas nods.

"Yeah, we know. It's why you married her. You told Mum yet?"

Rowan's face falls at that.

"Wow, you really know how to kill the mood."

"Good," Grace says, overtaking Silas with Kalina's laptop under her arm. "Because if everybody is finished having their orgasms or whatever, I want to get to this. I'm interested in this. I'm finally getting to know my best friend in the UK and it's fascinating. So I want you all to shut up until story time is over."

She sets the laptop down on the table where she made space earlier, opens it and fires it up for me then plops down.

At the same, Diego's phone rings and for the first time this afternoon, he doesn't ignore it. I'm not surprised because I know even before he's picked it up that it's from Julian. Diego is the only person I know who assigns an individual ringtone to each of his contacts. Another little trick not to let the dyslexia get the better of him, I guess. My heart goes mushy again at the thought of this amazing, resourceful man.

"You're fucking shitting me, Julian," he says after he's picked up and listened to the other end for about half a minute. "I'll be down in a minute."

He hangs up, angrier than I've ever seen him, gently lifts my feet off his lap and gets up.

"Sorry, guys, I need to go downstairs. Julian's lost the plot. He's really fucked off with how we treated him earlier. Says if I don't meet him right fucking now, he's gonna quit. I can't afford that. Not right now, anyway. There is too much going on. I think I need to go and eat some humble pie."

He turns to me, leans down, bracing himself with one arm on the sofa as he gives me a concerned smile.

"I won't be long, I promise. Don't start without me, I want to hear this, too. And I want to help, if I can."

Then he touches his lips gently to mine, angling his head carefully to avoid my nose.

He straightens up and starts buttoning his shirt on the way to the bedroom. Silence falls over the rest of our group. A handful of minutes later, he re-emerges with tan dress pants instead of jeans encasing his legs, Italian leather shoes on his feet, waistcoat securely fixed over the shirt and in the middle of shrugging himself into the suit jacket to go with it. He runs his hands through his hair, then waves to all of us as he passes and marches to the lift. He pushes the button, waits until the lift comes and leaves without another word.

"Shit," Silas says, as soon as the lift door shuts behind Diego.

"I feel bad," Rowan adds but then shrugs. "On the other hand, if that arsehole really quits, I'll happily run Santos-Benson Security for him. Can't be that hard and I'm kinda unemployed right now."

"Julian is a good guy," Silas rebuffs him. "Or is there an *actual* reason you don't like him?"

"Nah. Never really met the guy before."

Silas sighs.

"You're gonna have to deal with the fact that you were gone for fucking years, man," he tells Rowan bluntly. "You can't just storm into town after fuck knows how long and expect everything to be the same and to know every player in the game. Julian is important. Besides," he adds on a grin, "do you really wanna do prison security for George's youth detention centres? I sure as fuck don't. Sounds like a ball ache."

Rowan makes a 'forget it' gesture.

"Ain't gonna happen. I know he's put the tender in, but I'm also pretty sure he's gonna withdraw when he realises it's a boatload of work for a lot less return than he is used to. I've had a look at the numbers. The return is as bad as on any other regular honest investment."

"Why didn't you tell him?"

Rowan shrugs.

"I like watching him when he goes off on his tangents. And I think it sounds kinda fun, actually. Looking after a bunch of fucked up kids."

"You'd be good at it," Raven says to him gently, stroking his arm, and he smiles back at her lovingly.

But then his face falls.

"Shit!" He scrubs a hand over the back of his head, looking at Silas. "I need to go apologise, don't I?"

Silas nods.

"I knew you'd get there eventually. Go!"

DIEGO

When I step into Santos-Benson Security, Lila is not at reception.

I expect her to have gone home, but instead I find her standing with Julian by the window in his office, Isla sitting by his other side, all facing me when I enter, bathed in an orange glow by the sunset outside. It's like they're posing for a picture to hang by the fireplace and I'm the photographer.

Isla gives me one of her practically inaudible, happy greeting barks that only very close people get and pounds the ground with her tail when she sees me. It's a reminder that to her I'm part of her pack. Julian strokes her head and then crosses his arms in front of his chest, feet hip-width apart, looking me straight in the eye. We call it the stance. Lila has one hip hitched against the windowsill, with a hand resting on the other one and glowers at me.

There is a long moment of silence while I rasp my hand down my throat and back up again.

"I'm sorry, Julian," I finally say slowly. "Adrenaline was running high. I apologise for the way you were treated earlier."

He relaxes a little at that, but I can tell he's not remotely satisfied yet.

"You need to get shot of the O'Brien brothers, Diego," he responds with urgency. "They're loose cannons."

"Cormac and Callum? Yeah, I know, Jules. It's my vendetta, remember? I'm not gonna lose sight of that, don't worry. But when your girlfriend is threatened with rape by your father and he breaks her fucking nose, that takes precedence. I'm surprised you of all people can't see that. Imagine that had been Lila. We'll get to the O'Briens eventually. It can wait. Tell Arlo to go home for the weekend. It's all good. I'll take care of Kalina for a couple of days, make sure she doesn't suddenly develop a brain bleed, you know the drill, and then we'll get back on track after the weekend. Few days aren't gonna make a difference to anyone. If we're right and they're cooking meths up there, then they'll probably still be doing that next week, too. What's the rush?"

He looks at me dumbfounded for a moment and then shakes his head as if he's looking at an imbecile.

"I don't mean Cormac and Callum. I'm talking about those O'Brien brothers," he says and points at the ceiling.

"*Those* O'Brien brothers up there?" I enquire, mimicking his gesture, just to make sure I'm getting it right.

Julian nods.

I shake my head and stare silently at him for what seems like minutes before I speak. Not because I'm evaluating what he's saying but simply to keep the fury roaring inside me under wraps. How dare this arsehole make any demands on me? How dare he try and tell me what company to keep? Who the fuck does he think he is? When I finally speak, though, it's in an even tone. Matter of fact. Cold.

"Not gonna happen, Jules. I trust them more than I trust you, or you," I add, jerking my chin out at Lila. "And even her." I indicate to Isla. "And she's a dog."

Julian breaks stance and starts pacing.

"What the fuck? Really?"

"Yeah, really," I tell him. "So you can either get on board with that, or you can pack your things and I'll arrange a generous enough severance package, so the three of you can take a year off and re-orientate yourselves then invest in something else. No hard feelings."

Julian stops pacing and looks at me, aghast.

"Wow. You're serious."

"What? You thought I wouldn't call your bluff?" I ask, laughing.

"We know things," Lila throws in but stops elaborating when my gaze snaps to her.

"You're trying to blackmail me? I'd be *very* careful with that, Lila. I can prove things about your husband that will land him in the can for a very long time. I don't work without insurance," I cut her short.

She blanches and loses her pose.

"No, that's not what I meant. Not at all. I meant we know things about..."

I shut her up once more with a gesture and look back to Jules.

"You're a good guy, Julian, and I don't want to lose you. Or you for that matter," I say, looking at Lila again. "I think we make good business partners. But those guys, up there? They're my *family*. So no matter what you think you know about them, I don't care. I trust them. I *love* them."

"What? Even me?"

Rowan's voice reaches us from reception, just before he steps through Julian's open office door.

"You left the door open," he says with a shrug when he comes to a halt next to me. "Anyone could walk in, you know," he adds and turns to my profile. "We're gonna revisit that little declaration of love in a minute, but first I need to do something."

He marches towards Julian and sticks a hand out.

"Hi, I'm Rowan. I've known Diego since way back, when he was still George Junior, and I hate the fucker because he's my brother's best friend, which means he's fucking competition for my brother's affection and my brother's affection is like the best thing ever, other than my woman's affection. But back when George aka Diego aka the fucker behind me and I met, there was no woman yet, so my entire love life revolved around my brother. But, and that's a big but, I also kinda love the fucker behind me *because* he's my brother's best friend. And because he's kinda sexy and because he's a dreamer who keeps our collective lives interesting. So I would die for him. And I mean that literally. But not if I had to chose between Silas and him. Then I'd die for Silas. But so would Diego, so no points. Point being, I'm sorry I behaved like an arsehole to you. Silas reckons I'm jealous because you've been around *my* guys for all those years that I wasn't around. He's probably right. He usually is. Bottom line, I behaved like a prick and I called you a soldier boy and that's not on. I apologise. Maybe we can start over?"

He delivers his speech with the biggest, sincerest smile on his face, while Julian just looks up at him as if a tornado were going through the office. Which is kind of what's happening. At the end, Rowan's hand is still suspended between them, but Julian hasn't taken it. Lila, in the meantime, has gone soft on Rowan. I can tell by the look in her eyes. She nudges Julian with her shoulder and finally Julian unfreezes, smiles thinly and takes Rowan's hand.

They shake, and while they do, Lila focuses in on me.

"I didn't mean what you thought I meant, Diego. I meant..."

"...we have info on your girl," Julian finishes his wife's sentence.

"You have what?"

"Uh-oh," Rowan says, his head briefly falling forward before he straightens up again. "Go on then, what have ya got?"

"No!" I declare. "I don't want to know. She's already told us who she is and what she does, Julian. We know she's a P.I. and she's here investigating some missing kids cases. In actual fact, she was just going to share more information with us when you decided to pull your little 'I'm quitting if you don't come down immediately' stunt."

"She also gonna tell you that she's been looking into *your* shit?" Lila interjects triumphantly, and my blood runs cold.

"What?"

"Come, take a look at this," Lila says and marches over to Julian's desk.

She turns the computer screen around, so I can see it, and wriggles the mouse. The screen pops to life. She scrolls down and I realise I'm looking at a long list of words and phrases, interspersed with chunks of writing, before my brain does that thing it does when it's confronted with a whole load of letters and no spacing, and all I see is a jumble of ants.

"What is it?" I ask.

"I'll read for you," Rowan says and steps to my side, taking the mouse off Lila.

Julian and Lila know about my dyslexia. They have to, to do their jobs. But sometimes people forget in the heat of the moment. They are also both well aware that barely anyone in my life knows the truth and that they are dead if they ever disclose. So it probably comes as a shock to them when Rowan comes to my assistance. I think this, more than anything, rams home to them how close we really are. I can feel the air shift as Rowan rattles off individual words and phrases to me, mostly to do with missing people. Names. Places. Events. Dates. Stuff you'd type into Google. Callum and Cormac come up. Repeatedly.

"Just gimme the upshot," I tell him after a while, "'cause I'm just not following."

"It's internet searches, I think. And then there are email transcripts here..."

I don't hear the rest as it finally dawns on me what I'm looking at and my head snaps around to Julian.

"You've been spying on Kalina's computer?"

Julian glares at me. It's then that I realise he is pissed off way beyond Rowan taking the piss earlier. He's right on the cusp of losing his shit.

"Yes, we have. And before you go all boss man on me, hear me out, yeah?" he responds, and starts pacing again. "You bring this kid in, Diego, who you know fuck all about. Suddenly, she's in the building. She has a *key* to the penthouse. She knows about the club, she turns up at the fight of the decade, she's seen *the* faces. She knows about *fucking everything*. And you have no checks done on her, nothing. Just blindly let her follow you around." He takes a breath and stops pacing to go toe to toe with me. "Thing is, if she is here to bring you down, we are going down with you. And I ain't re-homing my dog and waving at my wife from behind prison bars, just because you couldn't fucking keep it in your pants."

"Stupid girl," Rowan mutters behind me.

I can tell from his voice and the clicking of the mouse that he is still engrossed in the computer.

"Does she not know how to use a password?" he adds under his breath.

"Oh she does," Julian stupidly says, leaning to the side to talk around me. "And VPN. She's quite the security fiend, actually, another reason you shouldn't trust her. But Lila went old school on her," he adds with pride. "Put a little bug on her actual machine. Doesn't even need to get into it. Tells us what she's typing as she's typing it in. We have every word she's typed into her machine in the last five days."

Julian has at least thirty pounds on me, and army training, but he's shorter than me, and that thing they say about rage appears to be true. Without thinking twice, I pick him up by the collar and shove him up against the window so hard, a crack appears on the inner pane. He's lucky the office is double glazed, otherwise his head would be sliced open now. Behind me Lila screams, Isla starts barking and suddenly there is a sharp pain in the side of my thigh as canine teeth dig in deep. But I don't let go of the fucker in front off me.

"You went into my apartment? You fucked with my girl's computer?"

I spit in his face as I shout at him. Isla's growls get more menacing and her jaw shuts down harder, piercing my skin as she tries to drag me off Julian.

"Enough!" Rowan's voice booms through the room.

"Diego, let the arsehole go. He's got a point. Julian, call off the fucking dog or I'll choke her out. I'll try not to kill her, but no guarantees."

I let go of Julian at the same time as he tells Isla to back off. Isla whimpers as she lets go of me and goes to her blanket as told. I can feel blood trickle down my leg as soon as she unclamps her mouth, but I don't pay it any attention, as I take a couple of steps back.

Julian holds up his hands in a pacifying gesture before he comes forward and rubs the back of his head where it made impact on the glass. Unlike me, he's blood free.

"I'm sorry, man. But you just wouldn't listen," he says defensively, the anger he was brewing seemingly evaporating with the pain in his skull. "I tried to tell you a couple of times to be careful, but that girl has you wrapped around her little finger. So, yeah, I took the liberty of watching our backs. You can thank me later."

"If you ever, *ever*, set foot in my place again without an invitation," I say coolly, "the two of you are dead. If you ever break into my or my girlfriend's computer again, you're dead. If you ever go behind my back..."

"Yeah, yeah," Rowan interjects. "We get it, they're dead. Personally, I'd shoot them right now and adopt the dog. Come have a look at this."

I turn around.

"I don't want to."

"Yes, you do."

The resoluteness in his voice and the concerned look on his face propels me forward.

"So, I've clicked through most of this, while you two had your little heart to heart there. Most of her notes and emails are in German, addressed to a guy called Konstantin. I'm guessing that's her boss. And then there's an email in French to some woman named Janka," Rowan explains as he clicks through some documents. "I can't see the email addresses because I guess they got autofilled and I'm guessing the thing they put on her computer literally tracks the buttons on the keyboard being pushed, right?" he asks Lila, and she nods. "There is nothing there that makes me suspicious, though," he carries on. "She doesn't once mention any of us, or you, or the club or anything. Unless we have code names, and I can't read German. But it doesn't feel like it's about us. Sounds stupid I know. Call it a gut feeling. I think the only reason those two muppets thought Kalina was snooping on you was because she typed in 'CCTV Callum O'Brien' a million times and that would have got her here each time."

He's brought up an internet browser and mimicked her search while he was talking, and now clicks on a link that takes us to the CCTV footage of Callum mowing down Daniel Mantas. I know it well, along with just about everybody in Brighton, and half the country. We saw it plenty often at the time. It was played on the news back then for days on end, for shock value.

"Okay," I say hesitantly.

"But other than that, it's all about those boys she mentioned, they come up all the time. Zoltan whatever and Piotr so-and-so. It's all about them. And the rest of her search history makes me think she was trawling through missing persons databases. I guess she was trying to see if..." His voice trails off, and a deep furrow appears between his brows before he continues, deep in thought, "...if there were any other disappearances around the same time. And maybe..."

"Maybe what?" I ask impatiently.

He goes back to run the video footage of Callum and Daniel again. Then looks up, and back and forth between me, Julian and Lila but really deep in thought.

"Maybe she wasn't looking at that footage because it's connected to you at all, but maybe because it falls into the same timeline."

A weird feeling crawls up my spine when he says it, that thing that people call 'as if someone is walking over my grave'.

"What are you saying? You think *Callum* is somehow connected to *Kalina's* case?"

He shrugs.

"I dunno. Or maybe she's just sticking her oar into your shit because she ain't getting anywhere with her own shit and that's what couples do. Nose around in each other's business. Point being, are you sure these fuckers here haven't got a tracker on *your* computer?"

Both Julian and Lila raise their hands defensively at that, and I laugh.

"I doubt it," I say to Rowan. "Using something that tracks the keys on my keyboard will tell you that I push the dictate button a million times a day but nothing else."

Rowan looks at me as if I'm stupid.

I turn back to Julian and Lila.

"You been recording me?"

"No!" they both shout, but I realise we have a problem.

"I believe you," I say slowly. "But I don't trust you anymore. You broke my trust. I'm sorry." I sigh deeply and rub over the wound on my thigh. "Wipe that shit," I say, pointing at the computer in front of me. "Wipe it clean. Do *not* keep any records of any of it, anywhere. You," I single out Lila, "will come back upstairs now and remove whatever device you put on Kalina's computer. We'll see this weekend through, and then on Monday the three of us *will* sit down and talk about that severance package."

Julian looks crestfallen.

"You're choosing some girl over us?"

"It's not about that Julian. It's about betrayal. But yes, I'd choose Kalina over you."

"Her name is not even Kalina," Julian shouts in frustration.

"I *know*," I yell back at him.

"But don't you wanna know what it *is*?" Rowan asks with a grin in his voice.

I spin back to him.

"No! Yes! But from her. Argh. How do *you* know anyway?"

"Well, she doesn't sign emails to her boss with a fake name, does she?"

"Okay, stop! Enough! Let's go."

"Shame," Rowan mutters behind me as he and Lila follow me out. "If I had a Kristina, I'd want to know."

He can't see my face.

So he doesn't know I heard.

Or that I'm smiling from ear to ear.

Kalina

I wake up the next day in an empty bed, groggy, with wool in my head, nauseous and thirsty. My face hurts again, but it's bearable.

I sit up gingerly, and steady myself on the mattress for a minute before I make my way to the en suite.

I go to the toilet, wash my hands and drink some water straight from the tap then open the medicine cupboard to pull down some paracetamol. No more morphine for me, I decide. No pain relief is worth *this* feeling. Only after I've downed two pills do I dare to take a long hard look in the mirror. Half my face is bruised, my nose is still swollen, and I won't win any beauty contests, but I'm not as puffed up as I was last night, and on the whole it's not as bad as I feared.

I very carefully brush my teeth and then walk back into the bedroom, where the curtains in front of the open French doors are billowing from the sea breeze. It's nice.

I draw them back, squint at the sunlight and step out onto the balcony to look across the sea, shielding my eyes with one hand. It's such a clear day, you can see France on the horizon. It's absolutely beautiful. I take a lungful of the salty air and a funny feeling blooms inside me. *Home.*

I sense his presence before I hear him.

"Good morning, beautiful," he says, stepping through the door behind me. "I thought I heard you were up."

He slings his arms around me and holds me lightly against him, his soft linen slacks fluttering around the back of my naked legs.

"You weren't there," I say.

"I was making coffee. I brought you some. It's on the nightstand. How are you feeling today?"

"Better. I've taken some paracetamol."

"You need Raven to give you some more morphine? They're going to be here in half an hour anyway to check on you."

"No, I feel fuzzy. I don't like it."

He bends down and kisses the side of my neck.

"Okay."

"What happened last night?" I ask. "You left to talk to Julian, but you didn't come back."

"I did. You don't remember?"

I search my memory. There is a jumble of pictures and snippets of conversation.

"No, I do. Kind of. Did you, did you come back with Lila?"

"Yeah," he answers, and I sense he's holding his breath.

"Did she, did she do something to my laptop?"

He sighs.

"She *un*did something to your computer," he says heavily, and I spin around in his arms so fast, it makes my face throb again.

"What?"

"I didn't know, Kalina, I swear. She and Julian bugged your laptop a few days ago. Not like broke into your system, but they have transcripts of what you've typed since. They thought you were after me. I've already told them we're done."

"Whoa," I say, taking a step back. "Slow down. So how much do they know about me?"

"Not a lot. Not more than you'd already told us. And..."

"And what?"

He grins.

"And I don't know if I should stick with calling you Kalina, baby girl, or Krissie."

I look him straight in the eye.

"You call me Krissie and I'll cut off your balls. If you absolutely have to, it's Kristina. Not Kris, not Krissie, not Tina. You call me Tina and you lose both, your balls *and* your dick. But, actually, I never liked any of it. It's a yearlong reminder that I was short-changed on a birthday," I say, and he frowns inquisitively at me. "My birthday is on Christmas Day," I explain. "Honestly, I like being Kalina a whole load better. I like having my birthday in the summer. I like having an *actual* birthday, full stop. Can't I just be Kalina?"

He steps up to me and cradles the good part of my face in the palm of his hands, searching my eyes, making my heart beat faster.

"You can be whoever you want to be when you're with me," he says softly then angles his face, so the gentle kiss he presses to my lips won't hurt me.

And it's that exact moment I understand why they call it 'falling' in love.

Because I fall.

All the way.

DIEGO

I take her back to the bedroom to cuddle and drink coffee, but we keep it chaste for a change because we don't have much time left before the others arrive.

They rang me at ten this morning, eager to come back, Rowan hinting that he had news.

We never finished what we'd started last night because Kalina had almost completely zoned out by the time Lila, Rowan and I came up from the office.

I got Lila to debug Kalina's laptop — by peeling off what just looked like nothing more than an innocuous black sticker — and sent her off, before I carried Kalina to bed. Raven examined and dressed my dog bite, which is mostly bruise and one small nip, went to check on Kalina's vitals one last time and then the others all left.

I'm tired today, because I held her all night, waking with a start every half hour or so to check on her breathing.

She feels good in my arms now, sipping her coffee and telling me a little more about herself. I still don't know her real surname, and I don't ask. But she tells me freely about her brothers, both of whom are much younger than her, and still living with her parents. There is a little bit of bitterness in her voice because it sounds like while she was shipped out to boarding school, they always kept her brothers with them. She tells me about the school and the people there, the girl she had a hot liaison with, and how her mother and father hated her career choice so much they practically disowned her. I can't say I blame them. She lives a dangerous life.

I feel like she's finally letting me in, and it's an amazing feeling. The way I imagine it would feel if I looked at a page of writing and it finally all fell into place.

She tells me all of this while she lets her hand wander over my abs and chest, tracing the lines and ridges with her fingers, and I'd be lying if I said she wasn't making me hard. She's making me super hard, but some of the permanent urgency has gone between us and I like it. My phone pings by our bedside and I lean across to pick it up. It's Silas telling me they're downstairs.

I shuffle up and she rolls off me to let me get up.

"The others are here," I say, and lean down to brush a careful kiss over her lips. "I want to revisit those stories later. Especially the ones around Lauren Watson."

She laughs at that and reaches over to give my cock a quick stroke through my linen slacks.

"You like the idea of me kissing girls, huh?"

I growl at her touch.

"I like the idea of you, full stop," I reply and use all my willpower to leave her.

"Cheesy line," she calls after me.

"Truth!" I shout back, and go to let our friends in.

Kalina

I get up and throw on a pair of shorts and a new skin-tight t-shirt then pad after him into the living room, arriving just in time to greet the others as they step out of the lift.

"Morning, guys."

I wave at them and then realise that Diego has laid a breakfast out on the coffee table for everyone. There's more coffee in a thermos, sugar and milk, juice, jam and butter. Silas and Grace pile out first, carrying bakery bags.

"I brought croissants," Silas says. "But if that's still too hard for you to chew, I can make some scrambled eggs for you, Kalina. We bought some eggs yesterday."

Raven comes out next, marching past them to make a beeline for me. She comes to a halt in front of me and checks out my bruising with soft fingertips.

"Hmm," she says. "Looking good. You need some more morphine?"

I shake my head.

"No, thank you. I'm good. I took some paracetamol earlier. They're doing the job."

She beams at that, her indigo eyes sparkling with joy.

"Atta girl," she says. "Good job on the not getting hooked. You know about alternating paracetamol and ibuprofen?"

I nod.

"Of course, you do," she says on a laugh. "You're the original badass."

Then she turns to the others to help Silas and Grace unpack the bakery products.

They haven't just brought croissants. They've brought pastries and pizza whirls and bagels and soft cheese and smoked salmon.

Tears well up in my eyes and I gingerly wipe them away before they can spill over. Silas catches the movement as he looks up from the table and winks at me with a smile.

He and Grace disappear to the kitchen to get rid of the bags, and that's when I notice that Diego and Rowan are still standing by the lift having an intense exchange at whisper volume. They both look a bit rough around the edges, but Rowan looks worse for wear. He's carrying a black, ratty messenger bag and pads it to emphasize something he's telling Diego.

I catch Raven's eye. She's sat down on the sofa and is patting the space next to her. I go to sit down and take a soft looking custard Danish from the plate of offerings in front of me. I frown at her inquisitively while I bite into it. She shrugs.

"He didn't sleep much last night. Don't be mad at him, but I think he got his teeth stuck into your missing boys. I don't know. He came back from apologizing to that Julian guy with the cogs in his brain ticking so loudly, it was giving *me* a migraine. And then on the way home, he was searching up stuff on his cell and then, I don't know, like I said, he's been up all night. Not because of me, if you catch my drift.

- 582 -

It's the first time since we've been together, we didn't fuck at least once, which is so not like him. I sometimes think he'd still get it up even if the house were on fire, the zombies were outside, and the apocalypse was raging. Scrap that," she says on a laugh. "He'd get extra hard if the house were on fire, the zombies were outside, and the apocalypse was raging. But last night? Something changed after he looked at his cell. Like I said, he stayed up, and then he disappeared for a good four hours, early this morning. Alone. Didn't even take Silas. Came back with that bag." She nods to indicate the messenger bag that Rowan is currently taking off his shoulder. "I don't know. The only time I've seen him like this was when we had Simon Rothman tied up on the bed at The Village, trying to get a confession outta him. I've asked him what was up, but so far I just got grunts."

She leans forward to grab a plate, cutlery, a croissant, jam and butter. Grace and Silas come back and drag the other sofa in the room closer to the table.

"We should have done that last night," Grace says with a laugh when they plonk themselves down. "Are you two going to stand there all day?" she adds in the direction of Diego and Rowan.

They split apart and come over. Only now do I realise that Rowan looks almost distressed. I've not known him long, but distress is not congruent with anything I know about him. If Silas looked equally worried, I'd think something was wrong with Sheena, but he seems as happy as Silas ever does, cutting little pieces out of all the bakery products to feed them to Grace as hors d'oeuvres.

Diego pulls over another chair from the corner of the room, and while Rowan takes up residence in the same enormous armchair he occupied last night, Diego sits down opposite him on the new chair. Silas looks from one to the other, picking up the same vibe I am.

Those two know something we don't.

And judging by their faces, it's not good.

DIEGO

Rowan and I let them eat breakfast in peace, but as soon as everyone's had their fill, I nod at Rowan. He clears his throat and addresses Kalina.

"I'm sorry, but I've got a confession to make. When we went down to the office yesterday, I saw some of the stuff you've researched since Lila bugged your laptop."

Kalina frowns at him but doesn't interrupt.

"You've been watching the clip of Daniel Mantas getting run over like a million times," he carries on. "And Julian and Lila thought you were doing it because you were sticking your nose into Diego's business. Is that really why?"

It's the first and only time I've seen Kalina blush. She throws me a 'forgive me' look before she answers.

"Well, yes. Initially, that was true. I overheard you talk about Callum and I was curious. It's kind of what I do, you know. Finding out stuff."

"But that's not why you kept looking at it over and over, right?" Rowan enquires, almost gently, like he's prising information loose that she doesn't even know she has.

He's good at this, I realise. Interrogation. In a different life he would have made a good cop. Or psychotherapist. I want to laugh at the thought, but I suppress the impulse because I don't want to break the spell between them.

"No," Kalina admits, dragging out that one syllable. "I, I don't know. Something was wrong. In the way Daniel was running. But I couldn't work it out. It bothered me."

If Rowan is surprised by her answer, he doesn't show it.

"So it wasn't just the time stamp on the video?" he asks evenly.

"What?" Kalina asks, clearly confused.

"She didn't make the connection," Silas comments at this point, and I realise the brothers have already talked about this.

Of course they have.

"I think you've been working the same case too long," Rowan says, and holds his hands up when Kalina takes a breath. "No offense. I'm sure you're shit hot at what you do. If you weren't, nobody would have pay-rolled your expenses for this long to find their son. And I've never done what you do, so I'm an amateur. *But,* when you're missing the bleeding obvious, then you've got to a point when you can't see the woods for the trees any longer. I bet what's been bothering you, without you realising, is the time stamp. I googled your missing boys. Zoltan disappeared in July, Piotr in October, Daniel got hit in the September between. Same year. But you've been looking at that year so much, you're not *seeing* it any longer. What I'm saying is, I think it's all connected."

I watch Kalina go pale, and I start to stand up. I want to sit with her, but she makes an unmistakable gesture in my direction, without breaking eye contact with Rowan, telling me to stay where I am.

Her show.

I understand.

And sit back down.

Kalina

The minute Rowan says it, I feel the rush of recognition.

He is still wrong, the time stamp wasn't what was bothering me subconsciously. He's also right, I didn't see the woods for the trees. But now I know what else I wasn't seeing, what was not right with the way Daniel was running.

He wasn't running like he was exercising. He wasn't even on a route to run for exercise around here. Why go up the streets if you can run along the seafront?

Daniel looked like he was running scared. Literally.

As I hold Rowan's dark brown gaze, everything else falls away and I can see a scenario unfold in front of my mind's eye.

Daniel running along the seafront, down by Madeira Drive, which would make sense, given where he lived. Callum cruising along, spotting him, getting ahead of him, getting out of the car, intercepting him, trying to grab him. Daniel ripping himself loose, charging away. Callum sprinting back to his waiting car, following Daniel, losing him as he runs up the steps to the upper level. Callum panicking, turning around, going back to reach the upper level, searching for Daniel on the empty streets, finally seeing him again, and hitting him *on purpose*.

To kill him.

To kill the witness to a botched kidnapping.

Rowan surreptitiously shakes his head at me. Somehow, he knows what I'm seeing.

"No, it would need two," he says into my thoughts. "There were two people in that car that day. One to grab and one to drive. Cormac would have done the grabbing. Callum the driving. Which is why Daniel got away. Cormac is big, but slow. Really fucking slow. In the head and in his movements. I bet Callum didn't even wait for Cormac to get back in the car. Just left him standing there, which is why you can only make out one shape in the car on the footage."

"I'm so lost," Grace exclaims at this point, but I can barely hear her because I'm still fully hypnotized by this weird mind-melt Rowan and I are currently in.

"It gets worse, though," Rowan carries on. "I Googled your two boys because I wanted to see pictures of them." He takes a big breath. "And I *know* them."

DIEGO

"What?" Silas asks, and I realise that Rowan only let him into the know this far until now.

I'm not surprised. If what he's told me by the lift is true, this falls firmly into the realm of entertainment for *the people,* and I know that a large chunk of Rowan doesn't want his brother to find out how low he really sank while he was away.

I get it.

After what Rowan told me when they arrived, I'm still reeling from the realisation of how few degrees of separation really stand between me and *them.* Only about two at latest count.

Rowan sighs deeply and looks around, leaving Kalina shell shocked as she processes the information.

"I don't know, guys," he says. "I'm not sure you want to know about this. It's horrific and once you've seen it, you can't unsee it." He turns to Grace. "You specifically, Grace. The rest of us, we can deal, but you are..."

"...an innocent," Kalina finishes his sentence.

I look at Grace and I see her lips quiver. Silas takes her hand, turns it palm up and presses a kiss into it. They look into each other's eyes for a long moment and he pushes a strand of hair behind her ear. It's like something from a movie, but the tenderness is broken unceremoniously by Raven, who jumps up to brush crumbs off her dress. And to give Rowan a dressing down.

"Don't be a chauvinist, Rowan O'Brien. She's American. We grow up watching people get killed and maimed live on TV every friggin' day of our lives. *Real* people. *Real* time. You ever watch somebody be shot in the head or clubbed to death in the streets? I bet she has. Now that is horrific. I'm sure she can deal with whatever you got."

Rowan looks at her with sad, tired eyes.

"Not quite sure why I'm the chauvinist if Kalina calls her an innocent but I think this is Grace's call, really. Honestly, if I could unsee what I'm about to show you, I would unsee it in a heartbeat. The other thing is, if we do this, if we do something about this, we're gonna piss off some seriously influential people. It's *dangerous*. On a whole new level."

That gives all of us pause. In the end, it's Silas who breaks the silence.

"Well, at the moment you seem to be the only one who knows what you're talking about," he starts and then focuses in on me. "Other than George, maybe."

I hold up my hands.

"Hey, I haven't seen it. I don't subscribe to those channels. *I* wouldn't even know who to pay for access to those channels. Neither would I want to. Look at Rowan."

Rowan frowns at me.

"Well, somebody put cameras up in *your* family's pool when they thought there was gonna be a snuff movie to be had there," Rowan retorts sharply. "So don't pretend you're that far removed."

"Cecil," I say. "I already told you, that sideshow was set up by Cecil. The camera, the lights, the pumping out of the pool. I was gonna have you two fight old style, in the garden, for *fun*. I thought having you two fight would be cool for the two old geezers to watch, and I thought maybe it'd finally settle shit between you. And then it all blew up when

Cecil took over. Man, there was a point when I thought you were in on it, Rowan. *You* were the one who'd come fresh from the gladiators."

The colour drains from Rowan's face and I realise I've fucked up as soon as Silas' voice echoes through the room. Not the subdued everyday version of it but the powerful, highly alarmed one.

"You fought for *the people*?" Silas exclaims, and pins his brother in a death stare.

Silence stretches out between them until suddenly Silas jumps up and clears the space between them in two steps. He clasps his hands behind Rowan's head, sinks onto his knees in front of him, and pulls Rowan down with him, until they are forehead to forehead.

"How many, Rowan?" he asks, a tear running down his face.

"I don't know," Rowan whispers, his eyes, too, glistening with tears. "Two, maybe three. They don't tell you. But the others were still breathing when I left the ring, I swear."

Silas pulls him into a hug, cradling his head before he claps him around the ear, still in the embrace.

"You could've got killed, you stupid twat."

I watch them hug hard for a minute, Rowan's shoulders shaking as he cries into Silas' shoulder. It's unbearably intense.

My eye wanders to Raven, wondering if she knew that the man she sleeps with every night has killed people. People who were prepared to kill him in return, but still.

There is an expression on her face that tells me she knows *everything* there is to know about her husband.

And doesn't care.

Kalina

I don't even know what's going on anymore. I meet Grace's eyes across from me and she shrugs, equally lost.

So we just watch as the brothers hang in each other's arms, rubbing their faces into each other's shoulders until they're done crying.

It doesn't take them long.

Eventually they detach, Silas gets up and looks around.

"Right. Recess," he says and grabs some of the dirty dishes off the table.

He looks at Grace and jerks his head in the direction of the hallway. She jumps up and grabs some more stuff off the table then follows him. We're left behind in tense silence until they come back. They sit back down on their sofa and Grace looks around.

"I'm in," she says.

Rowan nods sadly, gets up and retrieves the messenger bag from the back of his chair.

"Okay," he starts while he begins taking hardware out of the bag and laying it out on the table. "I want to make this clear before anyone gets the wrong idea about me. I had nothing to do with this side of their *entertainment* industry. I've seen this before only because I was owned by a lord for a while who was a huge fan of these two. He made us watch it sometimes, I think to see who was turned on. Or maybe it turned him on to watch us watch it. I don't fucking know. Those people, they really are different from us. Centuries of holding the power and inbreeding really do stuff to the genetic code, I guess. They're like a fucking subspecies of degenerates." He pauses while he hooks up an ancient-looking laptop to something that looks more like an ancient walkie talkie than a phone and then carries on. "There was a lot of talk about if this was real or just set up to look real. I always hoped for the latter. 'Cause those boys, they look like they actually, I don't know, love each other, I guess. But then somebody told me there'd been one before the little guy, the one I think is your Piotr, though the big guy, your Zoltan, only calls him Guppi. Guppi in return calls him Zet. So, yeah, somebody said there was a boy cast, they called it cast, before Guppi. Little Asian looking kid. Zet called him Bonsai. But then, apparently, the whole thing was a lot rougher. Rapey, s&m-y. I never saw any of those episodes. But the woman I went to get this stuff off this morning, she says they were properly cruel. Thinks the Bonsai kid probably snuffed it. Says the program disappeared for a while and then they rebranded it. New boy for Zet and rather than go for the brutality angle, they went for a kind of paedo-romance-in-captivity feel."

"What the fuck?" Silas asks what we're all thinking, and Rowan sighs.

"You'll see," he says as he fires up the computer, and looks up to home in on Diego. "This isn't running over your wi-fi, don't worry," he says, and I realise the walkie talkie thing must be a first-generation satellite phone. "They make sure nobody can be traced viewing this."

"You trust the guy you got this stuff from?" Diego asks, indicating the items on the table, and for the first time ever, I hear fear in my lover's voice.

"Woman," Rowan corrects him. "And yeah," he adds. "If I can't trust her, I can't trust anyone outside this room."

Raven flinches at that and looks back and forth between her man and the hardware.

"Who is she?" she asks sharply.

"The woman who bought me out of my bind."

"Why?"

"She loves me."

Raven inhales audibly and he looks up at her, frowning.

"Not in that way. I saved her daughter. I helped her escape an abusive relationship. It's a long story. I'll tell you another day. The lady I saw this morning is...just imagine Sheena if she had daughters not sons, was part of the upper ten thousand and had *access* to things us mere mortals will *never* have access to."

Raven relaxes at that.

"I thought they could long decode satellite phones," I throw in.

"Yeah, I'm sure they, whoever they are, can," Rowan answers. "But *they* would need to know that the satellite in question exists first."

It's around about then that I realise just how big an operation we are talking about here.

"We're all gonna die," I mumble.

Rowan shrugs as he fires up the laptop and keys in some numbers that he's written in biro on the inside of his arm into the phone he's got hooked up to it.

"This isn't recorded," he says with a warning undertone. "It's been running since Zoltan disappeared, so I'm sure somebody out there has recordings, but I can only link us into the live feed. We have access for today, that's it. That's all the money I had."

"How much?" Diego asks.

"Ten grand a day," Rowan says.

"I'm in the wrong business," Diego quips.

Rowan shoots him a death glare but is distracted by Silas.

"You still got ten grand lying around like that?" Silas asks suspiciously.

"I was saving up," Rowan mutters, not making eye contact, before he turns the screen, so all of us can see.

"What for?"

Silas' voice is sharp.

"To buy you a bike," Raven hisses at him, while Rowan gets up to move around to the sofa, making Raven and me bunch up, so he can sit next to her.

"That true?" Silas asks softly, and Rowan shrugs.

"You sold yours to pay my debts. I owe you," Rowan answers, matter of fact, then points at the screen. "Watch."

We all lean in closer as the laptop goes straight from a black screen into a live camera feed, by-passing any of the normal operating system interfaces.

And then the room around me falls away as through the skyline of our brunch, I suddenly see the boys whose bones I've been hunting for the best part of a year.

The faces I've looked at a million times.

Older, paler, but *alive*.

They are lying, naked but for a shackle around Zoltan's ankle and a thick metal collar necklace, wound around Piotr's neck like a snake, on a bed in what looks like a brick-built basement without windows.

And they are facing each other, kissing.

Z

Guppi is the best kisser I ever experienced. He gives it his heart and soul, despite the fact he's not even into me. But I wouldn't know from the way his tongue happily plays with mine, how he goes from gentle to sloppy to heated and all the way back again. I know it's so very wrong, but just the tip of his tongue touching mine gets me instantly hard, always, even after two years with nobody but him for company.

One day, when he gets out of here and he's put all of this far, far behind him, he'll make some girl very happy with that mouth of his.

There aren't many like him, and I kissed a fair few guys before we ended up here.

Most of them in the two weeks before the ròka approached me outside the gay club I kept hanging around, but that wouldn't let me in because I wasn't old enough.

Brighton was like a dream come true for me.

In my little town in Hungary, being gay is still a big problem. Or rather, a problem once more. Some of the older guys say there was a period when things were more liberal, but since Orbán's been in charge, it's been totally okay to openly hate homosexuals again. Especially in small Catholic towns like the one I'm from. So at home, any fooling around was always charged with worry that my mum might find out. She wouldn't have survived the shame.

When I first got to Brighton, I was blown away by how many men there were openly out in public, holding hands, being affectionate, making out on the beach. Normal couples living a normal life. And I wanted a piece of that.

So I hung around outside the club, like a dog waiting for scraps. And I got plenty. I'd find guys to go off with as they spilled back out pretty much every night. I'm not wired to be a manwhore, one day I want to settle down with the right guy, but two years ago I was just rampant with lust and *opportunity*.

A kid outside a candy store.

And then the candy man came and said, "Hey, I know a private candy store where they don't ask for ID if you're with me, you fancy coming along?" and like a total idiot, I got into his car.

Classic story.

I didn't fancy him, but I thought, hey, why not. And he seemed so harmless with his slight built and his ferrety face.

The devil comes in a small package.

DIEGO

We draw the line when the little one starts kissing his way down the big guy's torso and his mouth starts closing in on the big guy's hard-on. "That's enough of that for now," Rowan says as he turns the screen away, as if to give them privacy, absurd though that is, but doesn't cut the connection. "You get the gist."

He looks around at us, while I look at Kalina. She is white with shock and trembling. I exchange a look with Raven who is sitting next to her and we silently get up to swap seats. As soon as I lower myself down, I put my arm around Kalina and absorb some of the tremors running through her. She can't bury her face in my chest because I'm sitting on her bad side, but when she looks up to me, eyes filled with unshed tears, I know she wants to.

"They're alive," she whispers, and I nod.

"You know, they didn't look too bad," Grace says thoughtfully.

Raven laughs sarcastically.

"What, for a couple of kidnap victims held as sex slaves you mean?"

Grace shrugs.

"Yeah, I guess," she defends herself. "After the deal Rowan made out of how horrific this was gonna be, I expected worse. They look well looked after."

"If you ignore the shackles and the scars on the big one, yeah," Raven says.

Grace scowls at her.

"I'm not saying I wanna subscribe for more instalments, Raven. I'm just saying they don't look completely broken," she hisses.

"Do *I* look completely broken?" Raven asks sharply, and I decide it's time to intervene.

"Pack it in, people, not the issue right now," I shut them up forcefully, and look to Rowan. "This is not a Cecil set up," I inform him. "No way is Cecil involved with gay porn, not even for *the people*. Not a chance. He and Dad narrowly avoided jail for beating a gay couple half to death when they were still actively pursuing their Britain First crap. Cecil's greedy, but he's got his principles. They are despicable, racist, homophobic, sexist principles, but they are principles. And there is no way Callum set this up without his dad's connections. You're jumping to conclusions all over the show. I'm not sure you're not barking up the completely wrong tree here."

Rowan jumps up and starts pacing.

"I'm not. I know I'm not. I can feel it in my bones. Wait till you hear them speak, Diego. I saw way more of this at the time. I've heard their captors talk before. You never saw them, but I swear, they sound like Brightonians, like O'Briens. I mean, not that I thought that *then* but knowing what I know now..." He looks at me almost pleadingly. "They're keeping those boys up there. I just know it. We need to do something about this."

And suddenly I get it.

If there is even a remote chance he's right, then he was up there while those boys were already captive. And he was fighting for the right of some dogs not to kill each other, while these kids were kept like animals, fearing for their lives, *right fucking under his nose*. I exchange a glance with Silas, and he nods.

"Sit down," he says evenly to his brother, and then he focuses on me. "I hear you, George, but maybe they didn't need Cecil to set this up. Maybe there is more to Callum than we know. Or maybe Cecil did send the camera crew up there to set it up for the dog fights. I mean, makes sense. People who remote view people fight to the death probably also remote view dogs mauling each other. So what's to stop Callum going, 'Lookie here, crew, do me this solid on the side, get me in with your distributor, don't tell my dad and I'll pay you a bonus?'"

"What?" Rowan asks as he stops prowling and throws himself back onto his original chair. But then he holds a hand up as his gaze falls onto the screen that only he can see right now. "Shit, where'd the big guy go? This is never good."

He leans forward to turn up the volume button.

GUPPI

I can still taste the salt of Zet's semen in my mouth when I shuffle back up and stroke his face. His eyes are shut, and I know he hates himself right now. He always does, and my heart bleeds for him.

None of this is his fault.

I'm glad he finds me attractive. I'm glad he can get an erection and I can get him to climax. I'm glad my mouth can still override any self-loathing he feels about making me do this.

Because otherwise we'd be long dead.

I stroke his tears away and he cups my hand in his when we hear the hatch open. I stiffen at the sound of Ròka coming down the ladder.

"Nice performance, boys," he says when his feet hit the concrete floor. He leans with his back against the ladder and smiles.

A shudder runs down my spine.

I've seen him look at me since he's come back.

The way he used to look at Zet.

I guess his tastes have changed.

"Come here, little one," he says, crooking his finger.

"No!" Zet jumps up and runs towards him, the chain yanking him back and making him fall to his knees, just a couple of metres shy off reaching Ròka. As always.

Ròka grabs a whip out of the stand he keeps by the ladder and cracks it hard across Zet's back, once, twice, three times. And then he loses it completely.

"Get." Crack. "Back." Crack. "To." Crack. "The." Crack. "Bed."

With each impact, I see his erection growing in the jogging bottoms he wears below his exposed, pale torso. He used to wear suits when he'd come around, but since he's moved in above, we've come to know the slob side of him.

His penis is fully tenting the cotton fabric now.

I know what it looks like. I've watched him fuck Zet with it more times than I care to remember. I was never allowed to shut my eyes. If I shut my eyes, he would whip Zet harder or tell Óriás to hurt Zet another way. He was too afraid to fuck Zet without Óriás holding him down. He's clearly not afraid to take *me* without Óriás' help.

"Zet!" I howl. "Please!"

He hears me and retreats, shuffling back on his hands and knees, blood dripping down the side of his back, leaving a metallic smell in the air and a red trail on the floor.

I advance towards Ròka, keeping steady eye contact with him all the way. I run my hand gently over Zet's wild hair as I pass him.

"Stay," I whisper.

Ròka grins wider with each step I come closer.

"Good boy," he says, when I come to stand in front of him.

We're the same height. I've grown much taller in the last two years, which makes it easy for him to pull me in for a kiss without having to move. He curls his fingers around my collar and pulls me in, hard and fast enough for the joint in the metal to make a clacking sound. My heart stands still as I wait for my world to turn black, but nothing happens, other than Ròka's thin, hard lips crashing onto mine. He parts my lips with his tongue, and I want to vomit. One hand still on my collar, his tongue relentlessly, skill-lessly thrashes around my mouth as he runs his other hand down my naked torso and cups my limp penis. He draws back.

"Still not into men, eh?" he asks as he gives my ball a gentle squeeze. "So, how come, I've seen *him* wank you off, huh?"

I swallow.

"Always with my back to him," I whisper.

"What? You dream of girls while he's fucking you?"

I don't know what the right answer is here. I don't want to die. I don't want Zet to die. I feel a tear coming loose and running down my cheek.

Ròka laughs as he runs his hand around my backside, probing my anus with his fingers.

"You hear that, big guy?" he shouts at Zet. "You still haven't fucked the hetero out of him." He licks the tear from my cheek. "Well, maybe I can help," he says, and spins me around, so I'm facing the ladder.

"Hands on the rung," he demands.

I do as he says, and I can feel his eyes crawling over my butt. I hear him take something out of the jogging bottom's pocket and then the unmistakable sound of lube being squirted out of a tube into a hand. He touches me again, spreading the jelly all around my hole, penetrating inside with his thumb. Bile rises in my throat. But I won't give him the satisfaction.

I listen to him push his joggers down. His erection bounces against my now slimy crack.

"You got a nice arse, kid," he tells me while he spreads my cheeks and lines his tip up against my anus. "It's what the viewers like most about you. Your arse. So I can't mark you. Which pisses me off. I'd like to whip you until you scream. But let's see how much I can hurt you on the *inside*."

He chuckles at his own joke and there is a suicidal part of me that wants to laugh at him. Zet is *big* by any standards and he's never once hurt me in two years. Chances of Ròka's pathetic little penis doing any damage are slim.

I regret that thought as soon as he rams himself inside me.

And fucks me till I bleed.

Kalina

We can't see where Piotr has gone, he's off shot somewhere.

We just hear his screams as he's clearly being raped by the man whose voice we've heard taunt the boys but who we haven't seen.

The only person the cameras can pick up is Zoltan, sitting on the bed, bleeding from a number of slashes across his back and watching what's going on off camera with horror in his eyes, tears streaming unfettered down his face.

We're all cramped behind Rowan's chair, because he wouldn't turn the screen back around, even when we shouted at him. I think he was too frozen to move. So we all moved instead.

Grace at some point turned away, but didn't go to find a bucket, so kudos to her. Raven beside me feels like she's bursting with anger, as if she is about to climb through the laptop and catapult herself into the scene and take out whoever the fucker violating Piotr is with her own bare hands.

The exchange she had with Grace earlier makes me believe that this is all a lot closer to the bone for her than for any of us.

Even me. And I've lived and breathed these boys for seven months.

This is *my* case.

But I haven't caught up yet.

I still just feel kind of numb at the revelation that I have two live ones. And I realise I don't know what to do with that.

I also know this is bigger than anything I've ever been involved with.

And I'm scared.

The shit I'm seeing and hearing scares the fuck out of me.

But then I hear Piotr scream once more and Zoltan howl in anguish, and suddenly my protective chip kicks in.

I pry my eyes from the screen and look at Diego and Silas next to me, enraptured by the scene in front of them, before my eyes fall onto Rowan, still in the chair, still oblivious to us all having crowded around him.

They all stare until the sounds subside.

The faceless, bodiless voice off screen laughs again.

"Thank you, boys. I'll see you tomorrow," it says, and a second later we see Piotr limp back into the picture, bent over, holding his stomach. He makes it to the bed, sinks down on his knees in front of Zoltan and lies his head into Zoltan's lap.

We watch Zoltan, murmuring words in Hungarian as he strokes his hair and they both cry.

Rowan slams the laptop shut.

"Fuck!" he screams.

Silas and Diego hold him down in the chair with one hand each. They look across to one another then down at Rowan.

"Well, at least now we know you're right," Silas says evenly.

I tap Diego's other arm to get his attention and frown at him inquisitively. He nods.

"That was definitely Callum's voice," he explains.

"Or someone who sounds *exactly* like him," Silas muses. "And that would be rather a coincidence. I think we can safely say, Rowan was right. They're not cooking meths up there, they're abusing teenagers for the entertainment of the depraved. And the victims happen to be *your* clients' kids," he adds looking at me. "Well, welcome to Brighton. It's a *small* town, even if it pretends to be a city."

"You finished being funny yet?" Rowan growls. "We've gotta get up there, right fucking now."

I see Diego's hand push down harder.

"No, we don't," he says coolly. "We need a plan. A solid one, because if they've been doing that shit up there for *two* years, all the way through, even while Callum went to prison, then they've made a ton of money somewhere and they feel safe. As in, safe from the police. They took the smaller boy—"

"Piotr," I interrupt.

"They took Piotr," Diego carries on. "A month *after* Callum had already been charged for running down Daniel Mantas and was out on bail. I bet you Callum let the coppers bust him at his father's place deliberately, because someone on the inside tipped him off that there was CCTV, and he knew he wasn't gonna get out of that one. But by handing himself in, he gave the police no recourse to search anything anywhere. Especially not a property that is owned by his brother. He's a lot cleverer than we gave him credit for. And fucking well protected. Which means we're on our own. No authorities."

Grace peels away from the group first to go back to her seat on the sofa. She sinks down with a groan, grabs a Danish from the table and looks at it.

"I shouldn't want this," she says. "But I really need some sugar right now."

She bites into it and watches us all disperse back to our seats. She chews and when Silas sits down, she boxes him in the arm.

"I never signed up for this shit," she says good-naturedly but with tears shining in her eyes. "It was supposed to be last ever fight, and then riding off into the sunset together, remember?"

He looks at her seriously.

"I don't have to do this. I *will* not do this, if that's what you want."

She looks from him to me, to him, to Diego, to him, to Rowan, to him, to Raven, to him, back to me.

"Like hell, you will," she says through a grin, takes another bite, and searches out Diego. "We need to get those boys outta there. Go on then, George, what's the plan?"

"No," I throw in resolutely. "My case. My boys. My plan. Just give me a minute to think. And some more *practical* info. And my trunk."

DIEGO

"Shit! I'll never be able to unsee that, Kalina! What the fuck?"

I'm staring at my semi-naked girlfriend who's currently standing in front of the mirror in our bathroom, wearing a black, super tight long tube vest that comes to her navel and completely flattens out her tiny chest to nothing. I've been informed it's called a binder and is a thing in the female to male transgender market.

But that isn't what is sure to give me nightmares in the foreseeable future. I'm used to the upper half of Kalina looking like a boy.

What I'm not used to is seeing a dick hanging between her legs.

And by dick, I don't just mean some strap on sex toy. No, we're talking about a super realistic, appropriately small for her size, flaccid penis, foreskin and all, plus an equally convincing set of balls that are so artfully stuck to my woman's pubic mound, I have to do a double take to distinguish between her actual skin and the silicone flap that comes up her tummy. It's weird as hell, but she just laughs, as she bends down to put on the special briefs that apparently go with the set. She shimmies them up.

"Do we have a van?" she asks, though I've already told her it was covered.

"Better," I answer and hear her take a deep breath but get in there before she does. "Not just a van, an ex-police riot van. Blacked-out, bulletproof windows, cloned plates."

She grins to herself.

"You know, I could get used to working with you," she says, and my heart does a weird little flip. "I never knew anyone who could magic so much stuff in that short a time. Is it traceable?"

"Everything is traceable," I answer soberly. "But the guy I got it from is solid. And he has no love for the O'Briens. So in the unlikely event that he ever puts two and two together, he'll probably give us a slap on the back. He'll make it disappear after, all included in the price."

I realise how cocky I sound as soon as she goes toe to toe with me, looking up into my eyes.

"Will he keep his mouth shut even when the bodies start piling up?"

And there it is. The truth.

There are only two ways today can go. Either with all of us dead or with Callum and Cormac dead, and the kids free. There is no in between.

We can't trust the cops, we can't trust *anybody*.

And we can't let Callum and Cormac go without putting all our lives in danger. Forever.

Kalina, Silas, Rowan, Raven and I all know the deal. Raven was scarily involved in drawing up the plan. Something about the rigor with which she got her teeth stuck in tells me this is somehow part of her own redemption. Whatever drives her, her medical knowledge and love for forensics has come in extremely handy. I'm a little bit jealous, because I'm basically just the resources guy.

We decided to leave Grace mostly in the dark. She still thinks we're just going to knock Callum and Cormac out for a while, grab the kids, and go home. So she is on aftercare detail only.

The boys will need an innocent to hold them when the truth sinks in.

Kalina is still waiting for my answer, and I nod almost imperceptibly.

"Good," she states and steps away. "I can't decide what eye colour."

She indicates her makeup trunk.

A trunk that I am fast learning has a second tray full of serious transformation shit.

There are hair pieces, prescription contact lenses in all eye colours imaginable, fake lashes, fake brows, facial prosthetics and, apparently, a set of silicon crown jewels fit for a teenage boy.

I'm going out with a female version of Ethan Hunt, minus the bullshit masks.

I look at her brand-new regular boy's haircut that's brought out her naturally dark colour on the short back and sides, leaving the slightly longer top with a growing out bleach blonde look.

"Green," I say.

"Okay, we'll go for green," she acknowledges, as she begins to get into the rest of the clothes she's laid out.

She's chosen a distressed pair of children's camouflage combat trousers, tight enough around her crotch so that they subtly show off her 'packer' and just a little too short. She secures the waist with a cheap studded belt, to make it extra difficult for anyone to stick their hands down her front prematurely. Up top, she's gone for a slightly oversized, long sleeve baseball shirt with black arms that come to her fingers. She tucks the shirt into the combats and secures the belt.

"How do I look?" she asks.

"Like a wannabe baby punk, who's wearing last year's trousers and whose uncle still cuts his hair," I answer.

"Perfect," she mutters as she bends down to select a pair of contact lenses from her box of tricks.

She turns to the sink and I watch her put them in.

I'm still not happy with her plan. It's a good plan, and watching her come up with it — once I'd furnished her with the site plan we had in the office, courtesy of Julian, and once we had an extended look around the satellite view on Google Maps, so she could get a feeling for the lay of the land up there — was watching a genius at her creative best. What she's dreamed up is so utterly bonkers, it's probably gonna work, but there are elements of it I still don't like.

Like that she is going in alone to start off with.

Like that she's still black and blue in the face from what my dad did to her and that my instincts are screaming to protect her, put her in bubble wrap and never let any other harm come to her ever again.

Like that she's about to turn into a killer. If she isn't one already. I didn't ask. But I wouldn't be surprised any longer.

Like that I might lose her.

But I don't get to say any of it. When I tentatively mentioned earlier that she's still healing and shouldn't be putting herself in harm's way so soon, she just shrugged and said the bruising made her look all the more authentic for the role.

"Stop freaking out, Diego," she says into the silence between us now, as she puts the second contact lens in and blinks a couple of times.

Then she turns to me and beckons me closer.

"Cup me," she demands.

"What?"

Instead of answering, she takes my hand and presses the palm against her fake package.

"Squeeze," she says.

"You gotta be kidding me," I answer, but she just lifts her eyebrows, so I squeeze — and withdraw my hand rapidly, as if it had been scolded, a second later.

"Fuck me, that feels so real!"

She laughs.

"How do you know, big boy? Got something to tell me?" she teases, as she jiggles her butt around a bit. "That's good, it didn't come loose. Normally, I'd wear a harness, but since chances are he's gonna try and feel me up, I thought I'd better go without."

"Normally?" I ask, astonished. "How often have you done this?"

"Couple of times," she answers nonchalantly then points at the bathroom door. "Let's go, I can manage about eight hours in a binder before I get claustrophobic. Vamos."

Kalina

It's still hot as hell despite the fact it's already seven in the evening by the time I push my bicycle up the stony path towards the entrance of the O'Brien's farmhouse. I've been walking alongside the panels that shield it for a while now, and I can finally see the frontage of the brick building, breaking up the monotonous wall of weathered white panelling now.

Cormac and Callum's only neighbour's house, a working farm, lies a mile behind me. In the very far distance across the hills, I can see them still out in their combine harvester, using the last of the evening light to bring in their crops. Their business, far away from the action, is a welcome bonus in a plan full of holes and potential failings. I reckon we have about a couple of hours before the light will fade and they'll turn in. We'd best be gone by then.

Maybe the gods are with us today.

I hope so.

I'm sweating like crazy under my binder, but the pressure it exerts also gives me a sense of calm.

My characters always do. Maybe there is a weird sense that I can't be killed if I'm not me. I don't analyse it too deeply.

"Nearly there," I mumble into the mic, hidden in the earphone dangling in front of my chest.

"I love you," Diego's voice comes back through its counterpart, sitting in my left ear, and my heart does a somersault.

It's weird to not be alone.

I've never had backup before.

Hell, I've never had to recover live ones before. I can't decide if either is a blessing or a liability.

Silas, Rowan and Diego are sitting in the van that brought us out here, parked up between the neighbour's working farm and Cormac's small holding, in a turning place where a path, carved by farm vehicles, goes up by the side of a pasture with cattle in it.

When I left them there, they were sitting in the field, open lager cans that they weren't drinking from by their sides. A bunch of city boys in black jeans, t-shirts and sunglasses, out on the Downs for a beer. The way they looked together, next to the black sprayed riot van, they could easily have passed for a band, taking a break from recording, or lost between gigs. They looked hot as shit. In both senses of the word.

"Tell me that again when today is over," I answer quietly, and then I fall silent.

I've come to the door in the building. It's a typical farmhouse frontage with five wonky stone steps leading up to a dark blue painted door with a timber canopy above it, and rows of windows in desperate need of cleaning. The paint on the door and the canopy is bubbling and starting to peel off. The flowerbeds left and right of the steps are unkempt, full of knee-high grass and pretty wildflowers. Butterflies and bumblebees are dancing in the air around them.

I leave my bike lying at the bottom of the steps, ascend and knock on the door.

I expect the dogs that the guys told me about to bark, but nothing.

My heart sinking, I knock again, harder.

After a few more minutes, I hear noises from the other side of the door.

"We're on," I mutter, just in time before the door opens, and a giant of a man steps out, looking at me suspiciously.

He's almost as tall as Rowan is, but rather than muscled, he is *fleshy*, with a face that looks more Neanderthal than homo sapien. He seems to be made of a human and a spare somehow, and I wonder for a moment if this guy can really be related to the picture I know of skinny Callum O'Brien.

Cormac doesn't speak, just looks at me dumbfounded through light blue, glassy eyes that tell me the lights are on, but nobody's home.

"Hi," I start, and run the back of my hand across my sweaty brows. "I'm sorry to bother you, but I was wondering if I could maybe use your phone? I had an accident," I explain, pointing down at my bike. "And my phone got smashed."

He doesn't move, doesn't say anything, just stares at me in his food-stained shirt and jeans, and starts scratching his balls.

I wait, and then I hear shuffling behind Cormac.

"Who is it, Cor?" a voice says.

It's the same voice we heard a couple of days ago, while Piotr was screaming in pain off-camera. It's a voice we've heard multiple times since. Diego sprang us more money to extend our 'subscription', because we needed more time to set things up, but we wanted to keep an eye on the boys. It was the hardest decision I've ever had to make. Blast them out that day and risk failing and putting everyone's lives in danger or leave them at the hands of a sadistic rapist for another couple of days and come prepared.

A small smile forms around Cormac's mouth as he withdraws inside to let Callum step into his space. It's then that I realise Cormac's pleased with himself. Like a cat bringing its mate a live mouse to play with. An involuntary shudder runs through me.

"A boy," Cormac answers his brother, and moves away fully to let Callum fill out the doorframe.

Well, as much as Callum can fill out anything.

He looks nothing like he looked in the pictures I saw. Gone is the smooth, boyish face and the suit he wore for court. Instead, his bones jut out under translucent, spotty skin, and he's wearing filthy jogging bottoms, combined with a muscle shirt, that shows off absolutely nothing to write home about. He's weedy, and for a moment I wonder how come Zoltan has never taken him on, but then I take another glance at Cormac's retreating form and the answer is obvious.

My skin crawls as Callum's eyes wander from my toes, up my body, to my head and over my face. His already unnaturally dilated pupils, saucer-like despite the bright evening light, grow even wider at the bruises he sees. He looks over my shoulder.

"You're on your own, mate?"

It's clever, his use of 'mate', making the boy he sees in front of him feel grown up.

"Yeah," I answer, and turn to pretend to look where he's looking then point at my bike. "I got a flat and fell. My phone's broken. Could I maybe ring my dad from your phone? He'll go mad if I come home after dark."

I let it hang, letting him draw his own conclusions from the state of my face about my fictitious violent father. Callum's eyes scrunch up suspiciously, snapping back to mine.

"Where are you from? What's your accent?"

"Poland," I answer.

He opens the door wider.

"You been in England long?" he asks. "You speak good English."

"We always come for work in the summer."

I'm just gonna trust the fact that old preconceptions die hard and that he has no idea that Poland has its very own deficit of migrant workers these days. He doesn't look like the type to follow international politics.

"Where are you staying?"

"Poynings," I reply, naming a village about an hour's bike ride from where we are.

"That's quite a way," he says, visibly relaxing.

I shrug.

"Sometimes you need to get away."

Again, I let it hang, hoping I haven't overdone it. But then he smiles widely, and I can feel the air shift in my favour. He steps outside to stand next to me on the top step and looks down the bank at the bike.

"What happened?" he asks, eyeing it from afar.

"Tyre burst and I crashed," I reiterate. "I'm alright, but look," I answer, producing a cheap-as-shit old, dead smartphone with a smashed screen, into which my pretend earphone wire is plucked, from my front pocket.

He looks at it and then at my face again before he points at the door.

"Come in. Are you thirsty? I can get you a drink and we'll phone your parents."

"Dad," I correct him as I slip the phone back into my pocket and start going inside. "It's just Dad and me. That would be great. Thank you so much, sir."

Again, I wait to see if the 'sir' is too much, but he's lapping it up.

"What happened to your mum?"

"Tactful fucker," I hear Diego hiss in my ear, and nearly choke on my own spit.

"Dead," I answer Callum through a cough.

"I'm sorry," he says, and it's almost believable. "That's sad."

I shrug again.

"I don't remember her," I tell him as we move further into the house and from a chaotic hallway into an equally chaotic living room.

It smells of somebody vaping, popcorn and caramel flavour, mildew and stale food. But none of it can mask the distinct burnt-plastic-bathed-in-ammonia odour of meths. I understand now why Diego thought they were cooking up here, Callum is a bona fide meths head.

The furniture in the room is old but not antique old, more like nobody-with-taste-has-lived-here-for-decades old. My guess is, Cormac got the house complete with everything in it. That, or he is a vintage Laura Ashley fan.

It's dark in here. They could really do with a window cleaner.

They could really do with any kind of cleaner, full stop.

There are food wrappers, empty cans and bottles, mugs with mould growing in them, dried up food plates and just *stuff* everywhere, all covered in a thick layer of dust and grime. A bunch of flies are buzzing around the lamp shade under the ceiling. I quickly scan my surroundings for cameras but can't see any. It would be difficult to spot them, but then again, who would want to spy on *this*?

Callum indicates a sofa for me to sit down on.

"Wait there and I get you something to drink and my phone," he says, already leaving, and then shouts at Cormac who's disappeared to somewhere else in the house, as soon as he's in the hallway. "Cor, get..."

He reappears in the door to the living room, looking at me.

"What's your name, mate?"

"Jakub."

He disappears again and carries on shouting his command at Cormac as he moves further into the house.

"Get Jakub's bike inside!"

"You're in, right?" Diego asks in my ear, and I jump.

I'm *really* not used to having a team.

I cough twice for yes.

"Right, we're on the move to point two. Don't take too long, baby girl."

I don't cough this time. The 'baby girl' gets to me, and I can't allow anything to get to me right now. The next ten minutes are crucial.

I watch Cormac go past the open living room door, carrying my bicycle through the hallway. I hear a back door slam shut somewhere and extract a small silver box from my back pocket, straining my ears to catch any noise. I open the box and take out one of the syringes I brought. This one is prefilled with enough morphine to kill a horse. I take the cap off, put it in the box, slip the box back into my pocket and hide the syringe up my sleeve, acutely aware of how close the needle is to my skin. Then I shuffle along on the sofa, so if Callum sits down, he has to sit on the other side of me.

I feel eerily calm when he returns with an open can of Coke.

"Here," he says and puts the can down on the messy table in front of me. "Do you like Coke?"

"Sure," I respond but don't make any move to drink from it or touch it.

Instead, I slowly take my earphone out of my ear and hang it around my neck with the other one.

"You have a phone?" I remind him timidly.

Callum pulls a mobile out of his jogging bottom's pocket while he sits down next to me, predictably close. His knees touch mine, and I suppress a revolted shiver.

"How old are you, Jakub?" he asks while he keys in his security code and brings up the numbers keyboard on the screen.

"Fourteen," I answer.

"Great age," Callum says. "You got a girlfriend yet?" he asks by-the-by but doesn't allow time for me to answer before he fires off the next question. "What's your dad's number?"

This is so fucking cliché, I want to laugh. Instead, I hopefully manage to look crestfallen.

"Oh no! I don't know," I say. "It's in my phone, but..."

"Your phone is dead," Callum finishes for me, and then puts a hand on my knee, masking the move by leaning forward to put his phone on the table. "Don't worry, Jakub, Cormac's looking at your bike right now. He's great at fixing things. He can probably fix your tyre and get you back on the road in a bit. Relax."

I sincerely doubt Cormac is good at *anything*, but that observation doesn't belong in this charade.

- 609 -

"My dad's gonna kill me if I'm late," I mumble, and grab Callum's hand on my knee to squeeze it, while I keep my eyes downcast.

As if I'm looking for comfort in a stranger. As if I'm about to cry.

The latter is not too far off. I can feel the shiver of anticipation that goes through him as he leans back again, and out of the corner of my eye, I can see his dick stir in his jogging pants. I want to vomit. He squeezes my hand back as if to reassure me.

"Does he beat you often?" he asks quietly, and I nod.

His dick is even happier at *that* thought. I swallow my bile as I watch it twitch under the cotton and look sideways at him through tear-laced eyes.

"He doesn't like me," I say with a wobbling bottom lip.

"You know," Callum says as his hand slowly creeps higher on my thigh. "You don't have to go home. You could stay here, with Cormac and me. We'll look after you."

Too easy. Way too easy. Has he not heard of amphetamine paranoia? What the fuck is wrong with this guy?

I'm so stunned, I almost forget to make my move, but just then I hear the dogs bark in the distance. The guys are here, on the far side of the yard, if they're sticking to the plan, and I don't have time to contemplate just how fucking stupid Callum thinks Jakub is, or if his addiction has bypassed paranoia and has gone straight into megalomania territory.

"Why are the fucking dogs barking?" Callum asks, irritated, looking in the direction of the noise, and squeezes my thigh, hard. I yelp in only half-pretend pain and his eyes snap back to mine, a hunger unfurling in them that scares the shit out of me.

Time.

I throw myself at his neck.

"He whips me," I whisper into his ears. "He whips me with his belt until I bleed. And, and..."

I can feel him shudder in arousal, and then he suddenly snatches me by the hips with unexpected strength and pulls me onto his lap. He's fast, I give him that. Before I know it, he's slipped a hand in my neck and grabs hard, pinching and twisting my skin, like I'm a kitten he's taken by the scruff. I make a pained noise and his other hand slings around my waist, holding me down in a vice, his hard-on pressing against my packer. Never have I been so relieved to have a cushion of silicon between me and a pervert.

"And what?" he asks hoarsely into my ear. "You little, dirty shit. You like it, don't you? You like it when your daddy beats you, don't you?"

This is sicker than anything I've ever been involved in, and I realise with total clarity that I have no regrets about what I am about to do.

I go into a complete Zen zone when I shake the syringe out of my sleeve behind his back, while he keeps giving me burns in my neck, keeps giving me glimpses into the soul of a true sadist I never wanted to have. I yelp each time he twists, to keep him occupied, plead with him to stop, which just gets him more riled up.

It's messy and vile, and then I'm ready.

I have the element of surprise when I push up onto my knees, as if I'm trying to make a break for it, but then instead of drawing away from him, I come closer, cradling his head in the crook of my arm. In one sharp move, I twist him, so the side of his neck is exposed. I know I don't have to hit a vein for the morphine to do its thing. Intramuscular will take a bit longer, but it'll do just as well. But today, the gods are with me, and I manage to come in shallow to slam the needle right into his jugular. I empty the syringe without a second thought, while he's trying to thrash in my grasp, but he doesn't stand a chance. Between the meths already in his system and the morphine hitting his heart, he convulses, once, and then he stops breathing.

For good.

One down, one to go.

Despite all the motion, the needle is still sticking in him when Callum stills, another freebie handed to us from the universe today. It blocked any blood trickle, one of the things I was worried about.

I gently lower his head onto the back of the sofa, careful not to dislodge it now of all times. My knees are starting to burn from the position I'm in, but I can't sit back down. I'd get his last ever piss all over my trousers.

I dig in the side pocket of my combat trousers for my set of tactile gloves and pull them on quickly before I carefully separate the needle and syringe from one another. I swap the syringe with one from the box that has a small residue of morphine in it, and, just as importantly, no fingerprints on it yet. I gently slide it onto the needle still in situ. It's a complete bitch of a job, but I manage. I can finally get off the dead man, only to pick up his limp hand and manipulate it to mimic the action his fingers would have performed on the syringe.

I stand before him and contemplate my work for a moment.

Chances are it wouldn't stack up under actual scrutiny. Chances are, even with no fingerprints, I have left DNA all over the show, but Diego seemed pretty sure the police aren't gonna look too hard into the circumstances of a double overdose up here.

Against all instincts, I even give myself a moment to think on what I've just done. It seems the human thing to do.

I come to the conclusion that it's funny how far removed the idea of killing another human being is, only until you actually do it.

Then it's just another thing you can do in life.

I guess, I *hope*, it all depends on who it is, though.

Because I feel no remorse here.

So I turn to find my next victim.

Diego

"I'm back," she says into my earpiece and the relief I feel is second to none.

I catch the guy's eyes and see my feelings reflected in them.

We heard a lot of what went on, and the viler Callum got, the more problems Silas and Rowan had keeping me from scaling the fucking site fencing.

"You okay?" I ask heavily, while Silas and Rowan keep throwing sticks and conkers over the panels.

On the other side, two dogs keep barking rabidly, and Cormac keeps telling us to stop and that he's gonna come after us in a minute. He thinks we're kids, having a laugh or something. He really is a dumb shit.

"It's done," she says in our ears, and we know what that means. "R, move in, front door is open, make sure you wear all the kit. S, keep the idiot busy. I'm gonna come out and see if I can get him to call off the dogs," she commands. "D, watch the live feed and tell me when I've got all the cameras."

I don't like it. I want to be in there with her, fighting back to back. She is mine to protect. But I know Rowan is the better choice for the job. He's the most lethal weapon we have. Other than the girl I've been sleeping with, apparently.

"There may be some more cameras in the yard," I remind her. "For the dogfights."

"Maybe," she says, and I can hear the shrug in her voice. "It's a risk I've got to take."

"I doubt it," Rowan's voice enters the comms as he turns away to grab the rest of his garb from the van. "If there were any, I'm sure they went off air when the dogs left. You worry too much, D."

"Shhh," Kalina silences us. "I'm at the back door now."

She goes radio silent again. We're already all wearing gloves, but now Rowan dons a balaclava to compliment the long sleeve turtleneck he changed into after we left waiting place one. Another one of Kalina's attentions to detail, making sure none of his tattoos show in case there are more cameras. She is frighteningly good at this. She even picked out this line of trees on Google Maps that border onto the property, under which we have parked the van, and then she sent Grace up here in a hire car yesterday to make sure you could *actually* park here. At first, I wasn't sure if it was just a way of keeping her involved without putting her in harm's way. But by now I know Kalina's simply that meticulous. My woman is fucking amazing.

Under cover of the trees, Rowan moves like a shadow along the side of the site panels until he gets to the corner of the property. There he will be exposed to anyone driving past, but to our advantage you can see the traffic coming over the dirt road for miles in either direction. Rarely anyone ever drives up here. Today is no different. I watch him look out then disappear from view. I get back in the van, where we have the laptop and satellite phone set up with the stream of Piotr and Zoltan, muted. It's weird to think that they are only maybe a hundred yards from where I am right now.

I watch them, while I listen through my earphones to Kalina as she calls out to Cormac.

Kalina

"Hello?" I call out and start waving as soon as I get to the back door.

I debate for a moment whether to take the earphone out of my ear again and take the gloves off, but I decide Cormac is too dumb to notice anyway.

He and two viciously barking Dobermans are on the far side of the yard, the dogs brainlessly jumping up at the panels. Cormac is shielding his head with his hands from the stuff Silas keeps throwing over, too dim to move away. When he spots me, he looks flustered. I feel almost sorry for him. But then I remember that smile on his face when he presented me to Callum and the emotion vanishes into thin air.

"S, stop throwing stuff," I whisper into the mic-earphone, and seconds later, Silas seems to have followed my instruction.

Cormac takes his hands away from his head, and his eyes dart back and forth between me and the dogs, still barking at the panel, as if he can't decide what to do next.

I can feel Rowan approach in the darkness of the house behind me.

I lift a hand and leave it in the air, hoping he'll understand the gesture. He does and stops.

I start walking slowly towards Cormac and the dogs. One of them catches my movement, stops barking at the panel and turns to bare its teeth at me. That's when Cormac springs into action. He grabs the snarling dog's collar with one hand and the jumping one's with the other then drags them away to a kennel next to where I'm standing. They stop barking as soon as he manhandles them across the yard like big soft toys. They yelp as he throws them in the cage, one after the other, and bolts it shut.

"You shouldn't be out here, boy," he says slowly when he turns back to me, frowning. "Where is Callum?"

"Toilet," I say and then inspiration hits me. "He says there is an old air raid shelter here. Says you would show it to me, and he'd come out in a bit."

Cormac's eyes light up at that. It's almost sad, how relieved he is at an instruction he thinks he understands.

"Come with me," he says happily, and beckons me towards what looks like an old hay barn, open to the front, and full of machinery clutter.

There are old tractor wheels here, some big rusty parts that clearly come from miscellaneous farming vehicles, piles of rubble, the chassis of an old Ford transit. It's the same chaos as in their living room but in *big* particles.

I follow Cormac inside, safe in the knowledge that Rowan is somewhere not far behind me, that Diego is listening to every word, that Silas is ready to spring into action and that Raven is waiting in a hire car, about two miles in the opposite direction, all ready to move at my word.

I have to trust that Diego understands what is going on and that he'll let Rowan know to stay put, until I'm with the boys.

It's an odd feeling, this being part of a web. Adrenaline courses through my veins, and I realise this could be addictive.

Cormac and I get to an old cart, literally an old cart that you would put a horse in front, and Cormac lifts the shafts up and pushes it back a few metres. Below it, there is a hatch, secured with an iron bar through two ground anchors and one anchor on the hatch door. It looks crude but effective.

"Wow," I say for Diego's benefit. "An air raid shelter in a barn. In the *ground*. That's so cool."

Cormac smiles his satisfied little smile again as he leans down and slides the bar out then opens the hatch.

"Go on," he says and points down.

I come closer and look down. There is a fixed iron ladder, leading down at least two and a half metres. If I was really Jakub, and if I didn't know what was coming, I'd be suspicious at the fact there are lights on down there, and at the stench of a chemical toilet hitting my nostrils. But I'm not Jakub, and Cormac is an idiot. So I get on my knees and begin to descend.

"Cool," I say. "Down I go."

Cormac follows me as soon as I've cleared enough of the rungs. I hear the dogs barking again and realise that Rowan must be on the move.

My guys have impeccable timing.

"Oh. I didn't realise you were coming down with me," I say up to Cormac, as much for Diego's benefit as to distract Cormac from the barking.

But he doesn't even seem to notice them. He's too busy chuckling, pleased with himself again.

For a moment, I wonder if Callum ever gave him treats for being a good boy.

I hear the boys before I see them, because I'm concentrating on Cormac's feet above me and on not getting accidentally kicked in my already broken nose.

I hear gasps, no more, before Zoltan starts quietly keening. I know it's him, even without looking, because the chorus coming from his mouth is an endless repeat of *nem*.

Hungarian for 'no'.

I finally look across to them, just before my feet hit the concrete floor.

They're naked, Zoltan is standing in front of the bed, looking at me, shaking his head violently, and hiding Piotr behind him.

I smile at him and put a finger to my lips, but he can't see me.

He's focused completely on Cormac, coming down behind me.

It's only when Cormac prods me hard with the iron bar in his hand, to push me further into the room, that I realise he took it with him. And that I shouldn't have stopped to smile.

I stumble and fall forwards, onto the ground, rolling just in time to avoid hitting my already bruised face. I hold my arms in front of it, expecting more hits. The earpiece has come out of my ear in the fall, but I can faintly hear Diego's voice through the speaker as he shouts at the top of his lungs.

Diego

We've listened to every word Kalina has said and Rowan is closing in now.

I know he's nearly there, but it doesn't change the fact that my heart stops dead when I see Kalina being pushed into the picture. The boys were standing by the foot end of the bed, Zoltan hiding the little guy behind him, and saying something over and over again that I couldn't hear, because I muted them to listen to Kalina, when I see her drop into the picture and roll, shielding her face with her arms. This wasn't how this was supposed to go. I curse her for improvising. We can't have her show her face. All the makeup and disguise in the world won't help her if the cameras pick up her biometrics.

The people will find her and kill her.

Silas looks across from behind the steering wheel and curses. He feels as fucked off with having been relegated to the sidelines as I do.

"Cover your face!" I shout into my mic, hoping it'll reach her, despite the fact that we can see the earphone on the floor next to her.

"Fuck, fuck, fuck," I curse, shutting my eyes.

Until Silas' hand darts across and touches my arm.

"She heard you," he says, and I watch in wonder as my girlfriend gets to her knees, still hiding her face from the cameras, and pulls the balaclava she was always supposed to be wearing for this part from her pocket, to pull it over her head.

A big, fleshy hand enters the shot and picks up her earphone, but it doesn't get very far as its owner, Cormac O'Brien, suddenly stumbles into full view.

Kalina

I heard him. Not through the earphones but in my head.

Cover your face.

I was in full range of the cameras.

So I hid my face in my chest, fished the balaclava from my pocket and pulled it over my head.

As soon as it's on, I turn to look at Rowan. He's kicked Cormac further into the room and is holding him in a chokehold now. Cormac passes out without much of a fight, and Rowan nods to me. My cue to go around and kill the cameras.

We're back on track.

Well, almost.

Cormac shouldn't have been down here, but we'll deal with that in a bit.

I scan the room and clock every little black ball dotted around. I pluck one by one off the walls and bring them to Rowan to crush under his foot and then sweep up the evidence to store in my pockets.

The boys just watch us, unmoving, petrified.

When I've plucked all the side cameras off the walls, I point at the ceiling.

There are more eyes up there.

Rowan looks at me then at the unconscious Cormac.

I shake my head. I'm not administering his injection until all the cameras are killed, the boys are out of here and Cormac's back in the house.

Rowan shrugs and beckons Zoltan over.

Z

I have no idea what's happening.

At first, I thought they'd brought me another. That they were going to take Guppi and kill him or, worse, that the ròka would take him for himself. I was ready to kill the óriás when he pushed his baton into the new kid.

But then another guy came down the ladder. A huge guy. Taller than the óriás and all muscle under his tight long sleeve turtleneck, face hidden by a balaclava, carrying a set of bolt cutters. He swung them at the óriás' head then caught him as he swayed and got him in a chokehold.

And suddenly the new boy was wearing a balaclava, too.

The big guy choked the óriás until the óriás flopped down on the floor. And the new boy started going around, taking the cameras off the walls. The big guy got up, pointing the bolt cutters at the unconscious óriás' neck, while the new boy brought him camera after camera to stamp on.

He crushed them under his foot, as if they were nothing. As if we could have done that all along, squashed them like bugs.

Now the big guy is waving me over.

I don't know what to do. I don't want to leave Guppi.

But then Guppi pushes me in the back and whispers, "Go."

So I go over to the óriás and the big guy in the balaclava.

He gives me the bolt cutters and beckons me close to him, so his mouth under the fabric is by my ear.

"Cut yourself loose," he rumbles. "And watch him."

His voice is like thunder in the distance, rattling me through and through, but I'm not afraid. For the first time in a long time, I feel calm. And safe.

Then he leaves me to guard the óriás and goes over to the new kid. He crouches down and the new kid clambers onto his shoulders. They stand up and the new kid reaches out to the ceiling to pluck the rest of the cameras down. With shaking hands, I do as the big guy said and get purchase on my chain with the bolt cutters, but I'm too weak. The link holds, with a small kink in it.

I am about to try again while they're still getting the last eye, the one above the bed, when the óriás sputters to life.

I look at him as he starts to come to, and I don't think.

I toss the bolt cutters away, sink to my knees, push his head up, wrap my chain around his neck and pull.

DIEGO

I watch the cameras go out one by one.

The last one comes down from the ceiling, above the boys' bed, and the very last thing I see is a close up of a pair of fake green eyes pulling them down.

For a moment, I wonder, how many people are tuned in right now, how many degenerate bastards are watching this.

The minute all the connections are cut, I panic.

I have no visual and Kalina hasn't put her mic back on since it came off.

I wait for what seems like minutes with bated breath.

And then Rowan's voice rumbles in my ear.

"Hey, dickhead," he says. "Are we off air?"

"Completely black," I answer.

"Great," he says. "Got a slight change of plan. Bear with, stay put."

Then he goes silent.

Kalina

We don't realise what Zoltan has done until the last camera is toast.

I stare at Cormac's body, lost.

This is so far off the plan, I have no idea what to do with this. He was supposed to die upstairs, in more or less the same fashion as his brother. With a little help from Rowan to hold him down.

I shake myself and look away from the problem, to Zoltan and Piotr.

Once he'd finished killing Cormac, Zoltan fleeced Cormac's corpse for the key to his shackles, found it, undid them and then went straight back to the bed to cuddle Piotr. He is holding him tight now, looking at us as if we were aliens.

"Who are you? What do you want? Where is the ròka?" he finally asks.

"We're here to get you out," I say.

"You police?" Piotr asks.

I hear a tinny noise from somewhere, and realise that my earpiece is still on the floor and that Diego is shouting at us. Rowan prods me.

"Diego is going apeshit in my ear, go put your earpiece back in before he bursts my drum," he says, and I go to pick it up and wrestle it under my balaclava.

"I'm back," I say as soon as I've got one earphone back in my ear, holding the mic end in front of my mouth. I don't know how well they can hear me through the cloth.

"About fucking time," Diego says, and I know he can hear me well enough. "What's going on?"

"Second one is down," Rowan answers in my stead.

"Tell S to do his thing and R2 to move and pick up the boys," I take over, and turn to Piotr and Zoltan. "No. We're not police. Your parents hired me to find you," I say in Polish to Piotr, and then switch to English when I see Zoltan tense up. "We can't trust the police. We can't involve any of the authorities. The people who watched you..."

I stop there, because I don't know if they know what the cameras were for, but they both nod and I get from their eyes that they absolutely knew.

"They are very powerful," I finish.

"They pay the police?" Piotr asks, and I nod. "Will they arrest Zet?" he asks, looking at Cormac.

"Why would they arrest the boys?" Diego asks, confused.

"I'll explain later," I say to the man in my ear, and then address Piotr again.

"Not if I can help it," I answer him and look to Rowan.

"Where is the ròka?" Zoltan asks again. "The other one," he adds urgently, and I realise he means Callum.

I draw a finger across my throat to indicate Callum's fate to them.

Zoltan looks to Rowan. Rowan shakes his head and juts his chin out at me. Zoltan squints at me, as if really seeing me for the first time. I guess realising that you have murder in common will do that.

"So, what happens next?" he asks me.

"I don't know," I say honestly. "This wasn't the plan."

Rowan shrugs.

"Doesn't matter," he says. "It is what it is. Give me a hand."

The last bit is aimed at Zoltan, and together they shift Cormac onto the bed, while Piotr comes and stands with me.

Once they've got Cormac on the mattress, Rowan secures the shackle on Cormac's ankle and pockets the key.

He looks down at the body then puts a reassuring hand on my shoulder. I'm amazed at his calmness.

"It's the best we can do, K. Let's get out of here and get these kids home."

But the kids shake their heads.

"I can't," Piotr says, and points at his necklace. "If I go outside the fence, it will explode."

"A *perimeter* collar bomb?" Rowan asks with a deep frown. "Really? I doubt it. They're a Hollywood myth."

"Not to Brian Wells they weren't," I hear Diego say in my ear.

"That was on a timer," Rowan retorts as he comes over and looks at the metal snake around Piotr's neck.

He gently slips his hand under the collar and Piotr flinches.

"Chill," Rowan says.

Zoltan makes a growling sound and bolts over to us but stops dead when Rowan starts running the metal through his hands.

"The lock is cracked already," Rowan mutters.

"Don't you fucking dare, you arsehole," Silas' voice suddenly joins the mix with a panicked undertone.

I can tell by Silas' breathing that he's on the move, to do his thing, and that he's scared. He can't see us, but apparently he can hear his brother think. I've known Silas for seven months and I've never seen him scared. Not even when he was going into a fight that he knew beforehand was supposed to end in his death.

"You put K in danger, and I hunt you down, arsehole," Diego chips in. "Also, time's ticking. R2 will be outside soon."

"You two, get up the ladder," Rowan says to Zoltan and me, completely ignoring his brother and my man.

But Zoltan shakes his head.

"I'm not leaving without him," he says.

The boys exchange a look before Piotr's hand comes up and curls around Rowan's arm.

"Let's go up. I can go up, nothing happens," he says softly. "And I'd like to see the sun."

Out of all the things that have happened today, it is this image that burns itself into my retinas. The slight, stark-naked teen curling his hand around the massive black-clad arm of the balaclavaed giant of a man, against the backdrop of a dungeon, telling him he is prepared to die.

Rowan sighs, and with one last glance around goes to pick up the bolt cutters.

The muted sound of the dogs barking reaches us as we silently climb the ladder.

Then they stop.

PIOTR

I trust them.

I trust them to take care of Zet after I'm gone.

I still trust them, even when we come out of the barn and step into the orange glow of the setting sun, squinting at the light we haven't seen in so long, and I see a third man in a balaclava, kneeling in the kennel with the dogs.

Or maybe it's *because* I see him with them that I start trusting.

The pair of Dobermans haven't been here that long. They came a little after the other dogs went, and I've never seen those two relaxed, until now. They are lying on the ground, one on each side of the crouching man, being gentled by his hands. They bark again briefly when they spot us, but he shushes them, and they still. Neither óriás nor ròka ever managed to shut them up with just a word.

The big guy tells Zet and the new kid to stand with the dog guy, but while the new kid goes across without hesitation, Zet remains by my side.

"Honestly, kid," the big guy growls at Zet. "We gotta get a move on. Go!"

I turn to Zet and put a hand on his heart. Tears pool in his eyes, but then he bends down to kiss my forehead and finally moves away.

I wish I was the kind of brave that meant I was calm.

I'm not.

My heart is hammering in my chest when the big guy turns the collar, so the lock is at the back of my neck.

"I don't want to accidentally nip anything important," the big guy rumbles. "So I gotta stand behind you. You ready, kid?"

I turn my face up into the sun for a moment, before I nod.

"You gotta bow your head," he says from a little way off, the lengths of a pair of bolt cutters away.

"Okay," I whisper and press my chin to my chest.

I feel the cold metal of the cutter's mouth slide between my skin and the collar.

And then I wait.

Diego

I was supposed to stay in the van, but there is a point when stuff goes sideways where you don't give a fuck about the plan any longer.

That moment came for me as soon as I realised why Silas was getting so agitated with his brother. I spent so much time with those two arseholes in my life, I can read the subtext and all.

So I left the van and entered the house to join the party. I arrive at the back door to the yard just as Rowan turns his face away and squeezes the bolt cutters shut.

- 624 -

Nothing happens.

Literally.

There may be a break in the collar now, but it stays on the boy's neck.

Rowan lets the cutters sink and steps back up to Piotr. I see Zoltan being held in place by Kalina as he tries to move across to his...what?

Friend?

Lover?

Cellmate?

Across the yard from us, Rowan examines the gap in the collar and after a minute gently slides it around, so the opening sits at Piotr's throat.

"One more time," I hear him rumble quietly in my earpiece, and I see the kid nod.

The boy is shaking like a leaf and a thin stream of pee has started trickling down his leg.

They assume their positions again.

This time, Rowan doesn't just avert his eyes when he pushes the cutter handles together. Through the eyeholes in his mask, I can see him scrunching his eyelids shut. And then he cuts.

The collar falls away in two pieces and they clonk onto the ground.

Zoltan rips loose from Kalina and runs across to Piotr and scoops him up in his arms.

I catch Kalina's eye as we all unfreeze, and she points resolutely into the direction of the exit.

I think I might get a thorough bollocking from my girlfriend later for breaking protocol.

But as I wipe a tear from my eye while I move back through the dark hallway, I know it was worth it.

Kalina

Diego disappears from the back door porch and a minute or two later, I hear him in my ear.

"Good job, guys. Idiot check. Get out. R2 is here."

Silas is the first to move and already gone by the time I have collected my bicycle from where Cormac dumped it outside the back door. I join Rowan, Piotr and Zoltan where they are still standing. Rowan is looking at the two pieces of the collar, which he's picked up off the floor. Zoltan is still hugging Piotr, soothing him with long strokes over his naked back, while Piotr carries on shaking.

"Let's go," I say to Rowan.

Still nobody is moving.

"Come on, kids, time's ticking," Rowan says, pocketing the collar pieces. "There is a car outside for you. And *clothes*. Time for you to put some fucking clothes on."

Zoltan gently pushes Piotr off him.

Piotr just stares at Rowan, frozen.

I can't even imagine what's going on in his mind right now.

It's Zoltan who snaps him out of it.

He cups his face and tilts his head away from Rowan until he's got eye contact. Then he leans down and presses his forehead against Piotr's.

"Let's go, Guppi. We're free," he whispers against his lips.

But as I watch their naked backs, wheeling my bicycle behind them through the hallway of a dead pervert and his dead goon brother, I can't help but think that they're never really going to be free.

Diego

Those fucking dogs.

In the preparations, we had the most disagreements about what to do about those fucking dogs.

Nobody wanted to kill them, nobody wanted to leave them behind to potentially starve if the O'Brien brothers weren't found any time soon, but nobody knew quite what to do with them either.

The only one out of us who was even prepared to go near them was Silas.

Silas has always had that Riddick thing going on. He can basically communicate with animals, though he'd never be dickhead enough to say so. I have no idea how he does it, but by all accounts, it took him exactly two minutes to convince those hounds of hell to roll over. So now they're sitting with him in the van behind Rowan and me, yapping happily as he gives them treats and gushes over them.

Like we don't have enough other problems. Like we don't have a whole load of other, inanimate evidence to get shot off, we now also have a couple of, presumably micro-chipped and registered to either Cormac or Callum, *live* dogs on our hands.

I fucking hate my best friend sometimes.

But that's only the half of it.

While we waited for Raven, Kalina and the boys to clear away and put sufficient distance between them and us, we've been sitting in the van and Rowan's filled us in on everything that didn't work out like it was supposed to. Which is almost everything, other than the Callum part.

Rowan seems totally chilled about it, though.

"Stop stressing, Diego," he says, twirling one of the pieces of Piotr's collar in his hands. "With a bit of luck, they won't find these motherfuckers until they're already goo. And then they can draw their own conclusions. If they can even be bothered. One brother shackled up and strangled with his own chain in the basement, another overdosed. And what I know of *the people*, they won't want the police to dig deeper, and they won't go after us. There are thousands of Zoltans and Piotrs. Somewhere in the world, another boy is getting put in chains right about fucking now and a little girl is getting raped for the first of a thousand times." He sighs, before he grins, cynically. "And, honestly, if *the people* ever find out about your girlfriend's skills, they're more likely to recruit her to do more jobs like this. She's good."

I nod.

"She's a keeper," I admit, more reassured by his words than I will ever admit.

"Yup," Rowan and Silas say in one breath and laugh.

Rowan puts his seatbelt on and nods to indicate I should start the engine.

"Come on, last leg. They must be nearly at Sheena's now. Now where are those dogs going, Silas?"

"Arlo," Silas responds, thoughtfully. "He lives out in the sticks by Lewes somewhere, in a yurt in his nan's garden. It's his big dream, a yurt business. It's perfect. I'm sure he'll sit on them for us for a few weeks, until we tell him to take them to a rescue. He can claim he found them in the woods."

"Living in a yurt? Fuck me. Well, that explains why he was so happy camping out in a sheep barn. He was practically going up in the world," I quip, relieved that we have somewhere to dump them. "You asked him already?"

"Nah, I only just thought of it."

I groan.

"You kill me, guys!"

"Come on," Rowan nudges me. "Let's get rid of stuff and things and then go home, order some pizza. Or Chinese. Or whatever those boys fancy."

"Yeah, let's definitely make sure Mum doesn't cook for them," Silas leans in from the backseat. "Imagine surviving two years of hell, only to be poisoned by Sheena O'Brien."

It's a lame joke, but we laugh about it until our eyes leak water as we drive away, quite literally into the sunset.

Epilogue I - 9 Months Later

Diego

In hindsight, I think we had more luck than sense last summer.

Rowan's predictions were exceeded beyond our wildest hopes. Nobody missed Callum or Cormac for three months. Not even their mothers.

And *the people* truly didn't appear to care or didn't have a clue where their pervert show had been coming from.

By the time a postman finally became suspicious of the house, Callum and Cormac weren't goo, as Rowan had so delicately put it, but mostly dried up bone soup.

It wasn't possible, the coroner said, to conclusively determine cause of death, or even time of death, on either of them, though he put forward some very accurate guesses.

Due to the paraphernalia, both sexual and drug-related, that the police found on the premises, the presumption was made that the brothers had been in an incestuous relationship with one another with sadomasochistic tendencies, and that Cormac had died in a sex game gone wrong, before Callum overdosed on a lethal mix of meths and morphine. It helped that on top of a substantial amount of meths, the cops also found GHB and poppers at the house, and that there wasn't a single witness statement that didn't call their relationship 'weird'.

The case ran in the national gutter press for a couple of days, but it was mostly the local paper that ran story after salacious story on the O'Brien brothers.

The legitimate sides of Cecil O'Brien's business dealings suffered so badly in the fallout, no matter how often he publicly distanced himself from his sons, he eventually sold his gym and left Brighton, taking most of the rest of his brood with him. If he still has dealings with *the people,* nobody knows. But my city has been a better place since.

Though we will never know how deeply the corruption here truly runs.

The police must've swept the old air raid shelter for fingerprints and DNA, and part of me believes that somewhere in forensics someone must know that Piotr and Zoltan were there at some point. That the chain Cormac was strangled with had Zoltan's DNA and prints all over it. But such evidence hasn't surfaced, and the boys' names have never been mentioned in connection with the case.

I hope it stays that way.

For the boys' wellbeing.

Piotr is with his parents, slipped back into his life in Germany three days after his rescue and with the least amount of fanfare possible, as organised by the genius I was honoured to share my bed with for a while. I don't know if she ever told his parents the full extent of his suffering, but I hear he has regular counselling sessions, and is going back to school.

Zoltan refused to go home.

He prefers for his mother to think he is dead. In the two days after our rescue op, Kalina and Piotr tried their utmost to convince him otherwise, but he was adamant that his mother was better off with a dead but perfect son than an alive rapist of young boys. It's such a distorted view he has of himself, we all feared he would commit suicide, if we just let him go. Plus, we didn't know how high his recognition factor is. We have no idea how many people around here watched the boys' plight. It might be none, it might be many. So we held on to him.

He stayed in Kalina's old room in Sheena's house for months on end, going out rarely, and when he did then always in disguise. We all learned a bit or two from the woman that owns my heart.

This went on until the day Arlo rang, saying one of the dogs had a cut and he didn't know what to do with it, because we'd told him strictly no vet visits. It was way past the point Callum's and Cormac's bodies had been found, and Arlo had already told us he wasn't giving the dogs up, ever. I think he'd already put two and two together by then — he'd be blind as well as deaf not to — but he is loyal to the bone and has no love for the O'Briens either, so I'm not worried.

Especially not after what happened next.

We sent Raven out to Lewes to try her hand at vet nursing and patch up the dog, and for the first time in months, Zoltan showed an interest when he heard what she was doing. So she took him with her, and when he met Arlo something clicked. Raven says it was like somebody who'd been sleep-walking suddenly waking up.

So Zoltan also lives in a yurt in a garden in Lewes now, next door to a half-deaf guy, who may or may not one day become his lover, and with two dogs that somehow reconnect him to the most traumatic period of his young life. And apparently that's exactly what he needed. It works. I'm past the point of questioning these things.

While I'm dead sure that Arlo knows exactly by now how, *and why*, Callum and Cormac died, Julian is another story. If Julian ever did wonder how come the very people I was hoping to set up with a drugs charge ended up dead as a national horror story, he never said.

We didn't part ways in the end.

Once the dust settled that week, Silas persuaded me to rethink, and I'm glad I did.

In actual fact, Julian, Silas and Rowan are kind of running Santos-Benson security for me now, as a team. Grace has just started filling in at reception, because Lila is finally pregnant and past the miscarriage window, but half the time I find Grace downstairs in The Cockatoo instead, giving the barmaids hell for being shite.

I offered Raven a job, too, but she declined, her exact words were 'not a fucking chance'. She says keeping Rowan on the straight and narrow is enough involvement for her for now. She's still waiting for the Rothman case to kick off and is volunteering at The Martlets in the meantime. But though she'll deny it, she does unofficially keep an eye on the medics that supervise the fights in TripleX now for me.

Yeah, I sold the league — and went into white-collar boxing instead.

All legit and above board. And great fun. Who knew watching office bods trying to land hits on each other could be such a laugh.

So in the end, I withdrew my bid for the youth detention centres.

I realised the return was shit for a boatload of work, and I really didn't want to sell The Brick to babysit a bunch of delinquents for the rest of my life. And life is good for my guys right now. Why upset the apple cart.

I would have done, sold The Brick, but only for her. She refused my offer, though, because she knows that I love this building and everything in it.

And I love my penthouse.

It's my home.

And it will always be hers, too, if she decides it's safe to come back one day.

EPILOGUE II - 9.5 MONTHS LATER

Kalina

I lived in fear for months.

I didn't sleep very well most nights, and I was scared ninety percent of my waking hours.

I thought it would dissipate, once they officially closed the case, but it hasn't. Not really.

I sleep a little better now and I'm only scared half the time, but I'm still afraid.

Not so much for myself, I think I could get used to life in prison if it came to it, but for the boys.

It's why I didn't want Diego to come and visit me, no matter how often he begged.

I returned Piotr to his parents three days after we walked out of the house of horrors.

Splitting the boys up was heart-wrenching. The two nights that we hid them at Sheena's house they remained inseparable. We'd offered them a room each. Sheena was happy to stay at the penthouse with Diego and me and give one of them her room. But no matter how often Zoltan told Piotr it was alright, that he 'didn't have to do that anymore' and that he could sleep in his own bed, Piotr clung to his protector like a limpet.

I don't blame him, I wouldn't have trusted us either.

Though I think watching me transform from a boy back into a woman as soon as we got to Sheena's helped a long way. So did having Grace around. The woman is like a balm for tortured souls.

When Piotr and Zoltan said goodbye to one another, they held each other for the longest time, until Zoltan mouthed 'take care of him' at me above Piotr's head. Then he ripped away, turned and went back into Sheena's house, never once looking back at Piotr, Diego, Silas and me, as we stood in the pub car park opposite, ready to drive to the marina.

Diego had chartered a sailboat, so he and I could take Piotr to The Netherlands.

Watching my man skipper a boat was a totally new side to him that I'll never forget. I should have known he sails, being a seaside boy, but it still blew me away how happy and free he looked out on the ocean, despite our frightened cargo.

My blond, sexy pirate. I still dream of him.

There was one hairy moment, when we got to the other side and the officials looked at Piotr's stolen passport. The likeness was good, but the passport was British, and I was worried they would query his accent. But one thing I've learned in life is that if you are young, but not too young, white, or at least white enough, and look 'expensive', but not too 'expensive', nobody will look too closely. Not even the Dutch. So we passed with ease, and then the next morning we parted ways.

I kissed my sexy blond pirate goodbye, and Piotr and I got on a train to Germany.

And that's where I've stayed.

My parents are still there, for now, and I rented a flat not too far from them. I started spending time with my brothers a lot. They're out of the awkward teen phase now and you can have actual conversations with them. Every couple of weeks, I get on a train to Jülich and check in on Piotr.

Konstantin and I parted ways. He doesn't know exactly what happened in Brighton, but he understood the need for Piotr's return to be as publicity-free as possible. And he understood that the case had changed me, fundamentally. So currently, I'm jobless.

I have enough money saved to keep me going for a little while, and I'm not above taking handouts from my parents, so I'm not worried financially, but I have no idea what to do with my life now.

So I read a lot. And I've started learning Mandarin. For a while, I still tried to find out who the other boy was, the one Zoltan called Bonsai and that he says Callum and Cormac fed to the fight dogs, but I never got to the bottom of that one.

Some children just stay lost. Some aren't missed. As if they'd never been.

It breaks my heart every time, thinking about it.

So I stopped digging in the end.

I've kept in touch with the gang as much as it felt safe, and I've missed them like crazy.

Every hour of every day.

At one point, Diego offered to sell up, grab me and emigrate to wherever I fancy on the planet.

And I know he meant it.

But I also know that things are never that easy.

We have families. Mine is blood. His is love, sweat and tears.

And he's bigger than just him and me.

We all are, but he's one of those people who keep a place's lifeblood pumping and taking him out of Brighton would leave a hole in the city's heart — and in his — that mind-blowing sex and fine seafood cannot fill in the long run.

And I want the long run.

With him.

I've missed him so much.

Mind, body and soul.

Each time I hear his voice on the phone or see his beautiful face on my screen, I want to cry.

Each time we hang up, I do.

But not today.

Today, I cut the connection on our call with a smile on my face and my heart beating like crazy, knowing full well that very, *very* soon I'll be back in the arms of my man. He said he's brought a limo.

I grin at the thought when I step up to the border control officer, pulling my suitcase behind me. I only took hand luggage this time. Most of my Brighton stuff is still at The Brick. And the rest I don't care about.

The officer checks my passport and does a double take between the picture and me.

I've changed a lot. My hair is a couple of inches longer than in the photo and back to my natural brown, I have a kink in my nose now, and my face is gaunter. Not sleeping much does that to you.

"Business or pleasure?" he asks.

Love, I want to answer, but I know better than to fuck with the authorities.

"Pleasure," I answer, and he smiles at me, handing me my passport back.

"Welcome to Britain, Miss Kaminski."

∞ ∞ ∞

Afterword

That's it. The Brighton Bad Boys trilogy is complete. It's been a wild ride and I'm sad to leave these guys behind. I hope their futures will pan out for them. Having all fallen for foreigners, they will have a rocky road with immigration ahead - bar Silas, whose leading lady conveniently came with double nationality. In real life, a wedding to Rowan in Vegas would not suffice for Raven to be allowed to stay in the UK. And I shudder at the red tape Kalina/Kristina and Diego will have to endure if she wants to become a permanent resident. In my lifetime I have witnessed borders being opened and I have benefited from being allowed to blossom across them. Now I'm seeing the reverse happening. It makes me sad to think that my babies might not be allowed to love and to live with whomever they fall for because of some misguided idea of protecting 'your own'.

One earth, one ball in space, one humanity.

Thank you...

...to the usual suspects: my babies; the man who gave me those babies; my sister for dressing my guys; Cheyenne Blue for her invaluable advice and insight; Kathryn Calvert, my proof-reader and editor for being simply the best; Amber for helping me with the animal care and to Aubrey Brandon for writing the first ever review for Silas AND the first ever review for Rowan. I'm so glad I found you.

And thank you — you, who's reading this right now this minute. It means you took a chance on my books. I am very grateful and I hope I didn't disappoint. If you have a minute, please, please, please leave a review. Reviews mean everything — without them writers sit in a vacuum.

CONTACT

tillydelaneauthor@gmail.com

Printed in Great Britain
by Amazon